THE
BELOVED
EXILES

TALES OF THE NEPHILIM BROTHERHOOD

AUGUST ARREA

VII
PUBLISHING

First Printing 2023
First Edition 2023

ISBN: 978-1-7371661-7-7
Library of Congress Control Number: 2023900248

10 9 8 7 6 5 4 3 2 1

To request permissions, contact the publisher at:

VII Publishing
P. O. Box 1272
Clovis, CA 93613
www.viipublishing.com

Book Cover Design by: Diana Chituleska

To Zachary and Mikayla,
my beloved nephew and niece,
for whom Havenhid, and all its inhabitants,
came to exist

Table of Contents

CHAPTER ONE

THE THIEF

Anyone who happened to pass Hunter Wylde as he emerged from the impressive châteauesque Cromwell Court building in London would have never guessed he had just committed a most brazen, not to mention extremely dangerous burglary inside one of the luxury flats inside moments earlier. There was no sheen of sweat glistening on his brow, nor was there any visible tell-tale nervous twitching of his upper lip. Quite the contrary, for someone who had every reason at that precise moment not to have his wits about him, Hunter appeared cool as a cucumber as he calmly scoured his escape route that was the narrow street before him by looking first to the left, then to the right, and then left once more.

The young man of nineteen then pulled out a baseball cap and placed it on his head, pulling the bill down low across his forehead to the bridge of his nose, and casually stepped out onto the sidewalk just as a chatty group of pedestrians passed by and attempted to blend himself into the crowd as inconspicuously as possible. When he reached the end of the short block he veered away in the opposite direction of the group oblivious of his tailing presence and made his way north. It was then when he first heard the unmistakable sound; a loud cringing hiss of a wail as if a thousand radiators had ruptured all at once, and it was fused with a deep roar of metal grinding against metal.

Hunter's feet picked up their pace as he maneuvered his way through a growing congestion of traffic and people. He quickly found his way to Trafalgar Square. The large public square built to commemorate an 1805 British naval victory during the Napoleonic Wars was in the midst of marking a different sort of triumph as hordes of Scottish Tartan Army football fans gathered in boisterous celebration after a victorious match against England. Navy and white-colored team jerseys, kilts and hackles were the dress of the day, and from the sea of merriment came a swaying chorus of bagpipes being strangled as songs from the homeland were sung with inebriated pride.

Even in the midst of such hullabaloo suddenly surrounding him, Hunter's ears caught the distinctive and unmistakable roaring hiss as it erupted again and cut through the sounds of celebration like scissors through paper. Yet as loud and tremble-worthy as it was, it caused not one of the hundreds of merrymakers to flinch or take pause of their jamboree and look about in alarm for the source of such a frightful sound. Then again, why should it? Seeing as their wholly average and human ears were not equipped to hear such tumult, just as their eyes were blind to the shapes of shadowy things lurking and mingling and existing in plain sight amongst them. And, for a brief moment, Hunter felt a tinge of envy over the bubble of obliviousness afforded these naive souls as they sung their songs and guzzled their beer with funny feathered hats positioned atop their heads. For as terrifying and unnerving as the shrieking cry was that Hunter was desperately attempting to stay far enough ahead of, he knew firsthand it was nothing compared to what was actually causing it.

And one thing was unquestionable: it was getting closer. Of that, Hunter was absolutely certain.

~ ~ ~

Circling around the four massive bronze lions that appeared quite tame as drunken football fans climbed their massive bodies lying in repose at Nelson's column, Hunter pushed his way with growing swiftness through the smothering crowd. The crush of bodies made him grab all the more tighter the shoulder straps of the bulky backpack he was carrying as he passed a massive fountain near the center of the square that was being used as a wading pool by several men looking to cool off from the afternoon heat. Hunter could feel his heart pounding inside his chest when he finally managed to reach the Sir Henry Havelock statue where the celebratory crowd began to thin somewhat. With his eyes on constant alert as they worked to scan his surroundings from beneath the brim of his cap, he made a beeline for the wrought iron enclosure encircling a stairwell a few feet away leading beneath the street to the Charing Cross tube station.

He made a concentrated dash down the concrete steps and sailed over the ticket gate barrier with an effortless leap so swift his blatant fare evasion was mistaken as an inexplicable gust of wind to the steady stream of rail passengers patiently making their way one by one through the turnstiles. Through the station corridor he continued to race until he reached the escalators leading the way down to the loading platforms, and again Hunter found to his growing frustration his path blocked in both directions by passengers in no great hurry as they leisurely rode the slow-moving stairway. Without pause, he leapt up onto the railing dividing the ascending and descending stairways and, positioning his feet just so on the smooth metal surface, glided his way with great speed like a surfer riding an invisible wave. Several reprimands of disapproval from those he sailed past met his ears when he dismounted halfway down and landed on the floor below with the grace of an Olympic gymnast, but he paid the grumbling criticism no mind as his feet resumed their hurried sprint onward.

Not sure exactly where he was headed, he took a sharp left at one of the adjoining corridors leading to a loading platform. Slowing to a brisk walk past numerous portraits of history's most famous and not so famous faces adorning the tiled walls of the underground transit tube, he felt an instant panic well up inside himself when he saw plenty of passengers standing patiently along the platform but a track empty of rail cars for them to board.

Come on, come on...where's there a train when you need one?

Hunter paced up and down the long platform with growing anxiousness, his eyes fixed with a watchful urgency on the tunnel at the end of the tracks, hopeful for some glint of light to pierce the dark opening, or the grating squeal of the rail signaling the approach of an incoming train. When his eyes and ears failed to catch either, he was about to retreat from the tube and head to another platform in hopes of finding a train preparing to embark, knowing it was far too precarious for him to wait around a second longer. However, even before he turned around, he knew it was too late.

~ ~ ~

Whatever had given chase after him; the very thing he was so desperately attempting to outrun had finally caught up to him. He didn't need to turn around to know it; he felt it looming somewhere behind him, an intimidating and oppressive presence. Then there was the air itself. It became suddenly cold, bitingly so; so cold it made visible as wispy puffs of vapor each breath Hunter exhaled. Sure enough, when Hunter slowly turned his head to give a cautious look over his shoulder, he caught sight of the figure he hoped wasn't there, yet knew with all certainty that it was. It stood motionless at the opposite end of the platform, and still it wasn't enough distance between the two to serve Hunter any comfort.

At first glance, the figure appeared much like the other common souls patiently waiting for the scheduled train to arrive, only taller—much, MUCH taller—and with a build so exceptionally (freakishly, even) thin that it made the stranger dressed head to toe in layers of black all the more alien-looking. Not to mention ominous. No, there was nothing common about the figure, nor was it inhabited by anything resembling a soul. For even the dimmest bulb knows one needed to be human above all else in order to possess a soul. And anyone who was unlucky enough to look into the figure's face would have been greeted by the unpleasant sight of something far removed from humanity.

It was a ghostly mask of white, for starters; not a pleasing, warming white, but the kind of colorless white that comes to settle upon the carcass of a days-old dead fish left to rot and decay in the water; the ghoulish shade of white that dyes human flesh once it has been drained of the last beat of life. And peering out from behind that ghastly mask were two sinister eyes, red in color and hooded like that of a snake. In fact, all of the figure's facial features were snakelike, from the smooth scaled skin to the twin nostrils on a flat, noseless face. Then there was the mouth, lipless and shaped in a perpetual smile like that of a dolphin. Only, unlike that of a dolphin, the curving grin was neither pleasant or cheerful, but rather cold and menacing. One would almost expect to see a set of fangs revealed anytime the jaws to such a mouth unhinged themselves, or at the very least the intermittent flickering of a forked tongue.

"I believe you have in your possession something which belongs to me." Not surprisingly, the figure's voice revealed an undeniable hiss when it finally parted its mouth to speak.

Hunter's eyes darted frantically about in their sockets in an urgent search for way past the sinister figure.

"Go ahead and make a run for it," challenged the figure. "I assure you, it will be a futile attempt."

"I'm sorry, but...I think you might be mistaking me for someone else," Hunter replied when he finally found his voice.

The figure with its serpent-like red eyes turned his face upward and flared its exposed nostrils. "I think not! You may prove deceitful to the eyes, but not the nose," it said, while inhaling deeply the air around it. "You and your Nephilim kind carry an unmistakable stench; much like a sty marked by a drove of swine."

"Say again...Nephilim? What's that?" Hunter questioned in a tone more sardonic than it was of genuine naivety.

"Do not think to toy with my intelligence, Nephilim! You may have managed to swindle a couple of my fellow Pethens with your thievery, but your days of looting ended the moment you crossed my threshold," the figure hissed. "Why you would place yourself in the peril you now find yourself in the crosshairs of is most baffling. Surely you must know the object in your possession could offer nothing useful to you. Now, I ask you again to return that which you have stolen from me, burglar."

Hunter moved not a hair and remained firm where he stood which only seemed to incense the Pethen all the more.

"Give it back to me! Give it back!" it demanded with a rising fervor. "Or shall you push me to come and reclaim it by force, and eradicate some of these vile human rodents in the process?"

Hunter's attention immediately shifted to the numerous people standing about along the platform, and he was immediately met with conflicting feelings of pity and contempt. With their eyes locked slavishly on the illuminated screen of their iPhones or staring off mindlessly into space while pumping music into their heads through tiny ear buds stuck inside their ears, they had rendered themselves blind and deaf to the realities of the immediate world surrounding them, and more importantly to the walking serpent standing in their midst who saw them nothing more than vermin in need of extermination by an effective rat trap it was threatening to set. It was only by an unseen saving grace, oblivious as they were to it, that a long grinding screech signaling the approach of train suddenly made itself heard from deep within the darkness trapped inside the rail tunnel followed by a flicker of light that became brighter as the sound grew louder.

~ ~ ~

"Very well, have it your way," the Pethen hissed.

The figure made an advancing move toward Hunter who quickly held out his hand and cried out frantically in return, "Give me one minute!"

Within a few seconds, the train whooshed its way alongside the platform where it came to an abrupt stop. The red double doors to each of the cars simultaneously slid open and the tube became noisy with the cacophonous bustle of even more blind and deaf passengers leaving the train and passing ways with their counterparts looking to board. Hunter eyed them with a wide, fixed look of anxiousness while in his head a phantom clock ticked off the precious seconds he knew he had if he was going to time his move as perfectly as it demanded.

"Your time, and my patience, is up," the figure grumbled, when the last of the passengers straggled their way on board.

Tick-tock, tick-tock, tick-tock…

"Fine, you win." Hunter proceeded to shrug from his shoulders the bulky backpack he was carrying and held it out in front of him.

"I know when I'm licked," he said with a souring taste of surrender. "You want this back so badly then, here…take it."

"Well, then, maybe you're not as foolish as you appear," the Pethen remarked with an air of superiority.

Hunter watched intently out of the corner of his eye the opened red doors to the car immediately off to his left and grew more tense as he waited for the tell-tale click to greet his ear as the figure slowly came toward him. When it finally came, he looked once more to the Pethen and his eyes briefly dulled by a look of defeat ignited once more with defiance.

"There's just one catch," noted Hunter. "You'll have to retrieve it first."

With that, he drew back his arm and flung the backpack into the train car where it landed on the steel-grated floor with a weighted thud just as the red doors slid shut. The back of the Pethen's head and painfully thin upper body immediately flared out like that of a riled cobra, and, with its red eyes even more blood-colored and inflamed, it let loose a horrifying and jarring shriek of rage that rattled the very tube itself to its foundation. There was no doubt in Hunter's mind that any other time the creature before him would have attempted to annihilate him with its unchained wrath. But with the cars pulling away rapidly from the platform and picking up speed with every passing second, the Pethen let loose one more enraged scream before it dissipated in a plume of black and took after the train, and the backpack it carried, as it disappeared into the darkness of the tunnel.

With the Pethen out of sight, Hunter raced his way from the platform, back up the escalators and to the waiting sunlight outside the rail station. Blending himself with the crowd of people walking along the sidewalk, he immediately removed the telling red cap fixed upon his head and casually tossed it to a thankful vagrant sitting along the sidewalk begging passersby for spare change. He then reached inside the confines of the light windbreaker he wore as he continued on his way and pulled out something bundled inside a ratty terry cloth towel. Carefully, he peeled back the cloth to reveal a glimpse of a strangely carved container of sorts that looked to be carved from jade. And if one took an even closer look through the thick, green urn-like receptacle, there appeared to be a dark smoky shape slowly moving about inside.

Seeing the container was as good as it was when he had earlier pilfered it, Hunter quickly, yet with mindful caution, wrapped it back up and tucked it away once more out of sight. And only when his ears caught the distinctive wail of the duped Pethen in the far-off distance did his smug grin widen with untold gratification. Then, looking to his left and then his right as he waded deeper into the hubbub of the city, his eyes danced with glimmering specks of gold and in a flash he vanished into thin air.

CHAPTER TWO

Jacob stood facing the ravine known as Broken Earth, his feet positioned precariously close to the edge of a cliff where a sheer drop of breathtaking proportions unfolded itself beneath him. Aptly named, Broken Earth appeared to the naked eye as just that: a fracture cleaved into the earth by some unseen force and splitting it in two. A stone's-throw-wide many times over, the chasm greeting Jacob like a yawn coming from some rock monster served as a seemingly impregnable—and more importantly, impassable—invisible wall. It was as if a giant finger at some moment long ago had reached down from the heavens and etched a line in the earth, marking a clear and unmistakable divide between the pristine view of Eden, brought to life in all its sunlit-rich hues of color, revealed in a backdrop behind Jacob like some otherworldly vision, and the ice-and-snow-covered mountains standing jagged and threatening on the far side of the canyon to form the mysterious Northern Lands, under whose frozen tundra was said to exist the Underneath where the fires of damnation and a darkness unrivaled had long smoldered.

Yet the existence of this place, Broken Earth, served a far more crucial purpose than some purposeful divide between good and evil, light and dark. For it was here, on this high mountain peak, which overlooked the fabled Garden marking man's first appearance into the known world, where another storied myth quite literally took wing. They were fondly referred to as "Fledgling"; a doting nickname given to boys like Jacob who made the long climb to Broken Earth in great numbers like some secret pilgrimage over untold years reaching far back into the mountain's history.

There each boy would face down the harrowing drop laid out before them and, like young hatchlings peering warily over the brim of their nest to assess the breadth of the world awaiting them, they nervously struggled to find within themselves the strength needed to do what instinct and nature beckoned of them. For a leap of faith, as it was referred to, was a concept much easier contemplated than performed. It required the center of one's self to be fortified by the rarest of assurances, as if welded to the body's core by the hardiest of steel.

Yet even then, those who managed to gather up the necessary courage to confront such a challenge could not help but ponder, even for the briefest of moments, that by taking the small infantile step into the vast nothingness waiting to swallow them alive they could instead, in fact, succumb willingly to surrendering to their own graves.

But surrender they eventually did, one by one, like virgins being thrown by savage islanders into the mouth of a fiery volcano as a sacrifice to appease the unseen gods above. High-pitched cries—the result of a mixture of adrenaline and, most certainly, fear—followed each boy in their long and frightful fall, echoing off the walls of the ravine and then continuing to sound long after each had slipped from sight as they slipped into the dense blanket of clouds and mist at rest in the hollow of rock like some shroud laid out to block the view of whatever horrible demise awaited the boys at the bottom of the gorge. Yet each boy who drew the courage to will their feet into taking such a plunge managed to hold tight to the hope that a telltale belch of bluish light would reveal itself in a life-saving flash from somewhere within the gullet of the ravine and signal that the leap they'd taken had indeed been one of true faith.

It was in that moment the monstrous mouth of the mountain suddenly spat back the morsel fed it. Yet what emerged from the slumbering clouds was not the boy who had been swallowed whole, but a flesh-and-blood vision of something long-thought to be nothing more than a brief footnote of biblical lore. Rising up awkwardly, like a newborn colt struggling to find its footing upon a pair of spindly and wobbly legs, he would struggle to climb skyward from out of the pit, not with hands or feet, but wings—transparent and paper-thin they were in their state of delicate newness, but wings nonetheless. And from the stirring wind which came up to give aid to the furious flapping of the new appendages straining to make the slow and awkward ascent upward sounded a voice in a long, drawn-out breath which seemed to anoint each rebirth: "Nephilim…"

~ ~ ~

Whatever the mystery hidden away within the deep recesses of Broken Earth, it was further concealed by a migrating veil of cold mist that swept over the edge of the cliff on the opposite side of the ravine, where the Northern Lands resided, and spilled its way downward into the chasm as it always did like some vaporous waterfall to mix with the clouds and form what appeared to be the insides of a cauldron simmering over a fire. Even Jacob, who had spent more days than not staring down into the gullet of the ravine trying to unlock its secrets, seemed resigned this day to such a task. Instead, his attention was held hostage by the allure of something far less imposing in appearance than Broken Earth and yet far more mysterious: a necklace. Not just any old necklace, but the last existing remnant of the Fallen angel Gotham who had taken his last breath of life in the very spot where Jacob now stood.

Coiled in the palm of his hand like a small snake sunning itself on a rock, it gave off a strange and soothing warmth. It seemed to come from the vial-shaped pendant carved from the blackest of rock Jacob had ever seen attached to a rope of soft silver which caught the glitter of sunlight in small bursts of brilliance amongst the links of the chain. But it was the hint of light coming from within the pendant that held Jacob's gaze. While seemingly slight and dull to the naked eye, the pulse of illumination was strong and bright enough to reveal its presence through the thick, dense night-colored agate. Jacob remembered the night on Akdamar Island when he learned Gotham, before his great Fall, was not only Heaven's prized warrior but the untold eighth Angel of the Apocalypse. And inside the vial pendant, which had hung protectively around the departed angel's strong neck, was carried the last vestiges of the Begend: the blinding flare of light that erupted within the complete and infinite darkness of nothingness from which the creation of the universe was born, yet in whose last surviving breaths of luminance not only carried great untold power in its blinding white embers, but great destruction as well. Yet even now, with its overseer gone, the vial continued to burn with life like a heart without a body enclosed around it.

Jacob closed tight his fingers to form a fist around the necklace while trying to ignore the sensation of warmth pulsating through his flesh from the vial. Staring out over the great severing split that was Broken Earth with his eyes slowly beginning to fill with tears he desperately tried to pull back into their ducts, Jacob was besieged by memories of his much beloved friend whose loss continued to jab as painfully at his heart as the death of his own mother. And yet equal to the pain and sorrow, there was anger. A terrible amount of anger, a thousand times the size of his clenched fist and desperate to come out swinging.

Broken Earth.

Broken.

Broken.

Even before Gotham's blood had stained the ground beneath his feet, Jacob had come to look differently upon this sacred spot he was first introduced to long before that terrible day. It may have served as a barrier of protection for Eden and all its inhabitants who roamed its pristine lands from the corroding forces of darkness known to lurk unseen in the Northern Lands.

But for Jacob, Broken Earth also existed as an impassable obstacle standing between himself and his birthright; the same birthright he witnessed his fellow Nephilim claim one by one once they gathered the bravery—and, more importantly, the faith—needed to hurl themselves freely off the ledge of the mountain and succumb to what first appeared to be a suicidal plunge to a death concealed somewhere beyond the blanket of clouds and mist into which they were swallowed. Jacob himself had managed to gather about him such bravery and faith, both never before tested at such drastic lengths, to make that jump. Head-first he dove into what appeared to the naked eye as a bottomless pit, only the baptism of light he anxiously awaited in the gray swirling soup of clouds that brought forth wings out of the backs of Nephilim boys like flowers unfolding themselves from inside their buds to the beckoning sun never revealed itself. The only signs of wings came from a distant flapping sound as he continued on his perilous death spiral downward and a hand—Damiel's hand—grabbing hold of him like some saving grace and lifting him out of the nightmare he had momentarily been taken captive and back into the reaches of the light above.

His feet had refused to leave the safety and security of the ground ever since.

"Broken," Jacob spit with a quiet bitterness. But no matter how hard he tried to ignore it, he couldn't help but wonder if, in fact, it wasn't Broken Earth that was broken, but rather himself. After all, what proved to be the golden ticket in securing the wings he so desired was one's inner faith. And if there was one thing that felt fractured inside himself these days, if not broken in two, it was his faith.

With his back facing Eden bare as the day he was born except for the twin nubs of bone where wings promised him remained absent protruding prominently from underneath the thin cotton t-shirt he wore, Jacob stared out over Broken Earth as if he had suddenly been confronted by a trusted companion who had knowingly betrayed him; even as he began to secretly suspect that companion was himself. Yet all he could see was a parade of his friends rising up one by one out of the cover of the nesting clouds below to reveal themselves as the one thing he remained short of becoming: a whole Nephilim.

It made his fist tighten even more around the necklace it gripped until, with a sudden burst of anger he could no longer swallow down into the pit of his stomach, he drew back his arm and let fly the necklace out into the ravine as far as he could throw it. Then, with only a passing glance as it fell like a stone into the depths of the mist-filled pit, Jacob turned his wingless back to Broken

Earth and began to walk away. Only there was no way he could ever freely relinquish that which had come to be his most treasured possession—the last tangible memory of his beloved friend and mentor—and the act of throwing the necklace beyond the point of any recovery humanely possible was, in fact, a forced ultimatum put upon himself.

After all, he was no mere human boy despite his outward appearance. And so, when he had taken no more than a dozen steps away from the cliff's edge, he paused and closed his eyes. After taking a deep, calming breath, he clenched his jaw as tightly as he did his fists and, with his pupils bubbling with tiny bursts of gold, he stripped off his shirt and tossed it aside before spinning around, and charged full-speed at the fall awaiting him. With a head-first leap he lunged forth, pushing off the mountain ledge with his feet to tackle the openness of the vast abyss of Broken Earth with all the vengeance and determination he could muster.

The fall was instant and came with a harrowing swiftness, and it cast him without mercy or pause into the awaiting depths. Only this time Jacob faced it not with the fear and doubt that choked and twisted his insides the two times he previously attempted the plunge but with an outward determination that all but burst forth from his being like the high beams coming from a car navigating a dark, winding road. Down into the blinding fog of the clouds he swiftly slipped, but there was nothing he wished or cared to see, even the giver of wings whose elusive presence he felt lurking somewhere in the folds of the misty shroud hidden from sight; nothing, that is, except Gotham's necklace.

He soon caught sight of it in the distance beneath him, the glowing warmth of the light captured inside the vial casting off enough pale illumination to pierce the white smothering wisps of cold air swirling about him. Straightening his body like an arrow shot into the sky, he attempted to quicken his already rapid descent that made the air whistling loudly in his ears sound like screams of terror.

Suddenly, the fog began to thin and holes found a way to eat through the impenetrable vapors of mist allowing Jacob brief glimpses of the terrifying end unfolding itself beneath him. If wings were ever to sprout from his back, now would be a good time, he thought to himself while doing his best to beat back the twinge of panic he felt quiver in his insides. And yet, strangely enough, he wasn't quite ready to be rescued from the crushing death towards which he was fast approaching, nor did he have any intention of meeting it while the last surviving trace of Gotham's existence remained just beyond the reach of his fingers. So with all the strain and stretch he could muster from his body, Jacob made a final and desperate grab for the falling necklace and just as the tips of his fingers managed to hook themselves around the silver chain and pull it into his grasp there came a sudden burst of light. It erupted all around him in a blinding hue of blue. The gnarled fingers of what appeared to be flashes of lightning came at Jacob from behind and struck him, and as it did his body stiffened from a sharp and unpleasant pain. It felt as if the flesh of his upper back had been pierced twice by a blade made of fire. The pain, however, was gone before it was realized and from it came an unnatural, yet strangely natural, sensation of what felt to be a second pair of arms unfolding themselves from somewhere beneath the surface of his skin covering his shoulder blades. Stretching outward they seemed to grab hold of the very air through which he was falling and almost immediately Jacob felt his ever-deepening descent into the pit become noticeably slower, and eventually reverse course.

Wings…

Finally, they had found their place onto his back. They may have had a delicate and translucent look to them, like something found on a buzzing insect, but there was no mistaking they were, indeed, wings. Beating spastically and furiously at the air all around him, like a drowning man thrashing his arms about in the water, Jacob struggled to get used to his new appendages, flitting from here to there in the same clumsy, awkward movements an infant makes when it stands upon his legs for the first time. But in no time at all he quickly found himself moving through the air as easily and graceful as he could navigate the length of a pool, and the very strange feeling of doing what he had until then only witnessed from birds suddenly felt as natural as taking a breath.

Jacob could soon be heard hollering his elation in high-pitched whoops that bounced loudly off the walls of the canyon and reverberated to the deepest depths of the pit, the pit that had been denied the feeding of his carcass. The cries of excitement, however, quickly morphed themselves into an altogether unpleasant sound: cries of agony; a wailing of pain Jacob hoped and prayed would never again penetrate his ears. Then just as suddenly the bird's-eye view he enjoyed while gliding upon the gentle breeze gave way as it always managed to do to the horrific sight of Thaniel ruthlessly separating Gotham from his wings one at a time with a cruel and vicious swipe of his sword. The look on Gotham's face as he writhed in pain upon the ground while his blood, appearing clear like water as it gushed from the wounds made by the merciless amputations, formed large pools in the dirt almost too unbearable to witness. Yet it was nothing like the sight of the brutally wounded angel being dragged to the edge of the cliff and watching helplessly as Broken Earth was fed its first taste of death. In an instant, Gotham was gone, and the horrific realization that he would never again return from the place where the clouds slumbered brought forth a gut-wrenching sound from deep within the bowels of Jacob's being that had never before made itself heard.

~ ~ ~

Everything suddenly vanished, as memories, both the good and the bad, have a tendency of doing. With a swipe of a hand across the bathroom mirror fogged over from the steam of a hot, morning shower, Broken Earth and the Northern Lands beyond—all of Eden, if fact—were wiped from existence and replaced by Jacob's reflection unclothed and dripping beads of water. Stone-faced he stared at himself framed inside the glass as if catching sight of his reflection for the first time. And in some ways it was.

Placing his hands flat against the cold tile counter of the sink in front of him, he leaned in for a closer, more studied look at his reflected self. The first and most noticeable thing that caught his eye was also the most obvious. While he had always carried with him an athletic, if not lean, presence thanks to his time on the high school wrestling team, his body now displayed a more revealing and obvious strength tightly coiled just beneath the surface of his taut flesh. But as he flexed that sinewy strength ever so slightly, Jacob knew the body he was slowly eyeing on the other side of the glass had not found its shape on the sweaty rubber mats inside the high school gymnasium. Rather, it came from behind the stone walls of a place called Lions Bite in whose jaws he grappled with and competed against other boys of similar size and strength in contests of strenuous feats involving both brawn and sword. And also in the Forest that surrounded Lions Bite whose towering trees he watered daily with his hard- earned sweat as he trained in earnest to learn the lay of the land inch by inch until he had conquered the terrain and all its many seen and unseen obstacles like all the creatures who had made it their home.

Still, there was something else; a vagary beyond the striking cut of his physical stature.

While he still had the appearance of the youthful, red-blooded teenager he was before the discovery that he wasn't just any ordinary teenager made itself known to him less than a year earlier, Jacob somehow looked older. It wasn't the kind of age that came each year with a growing number of candles lit upon a birthday cake. Instead, it emerged in the form of a certain maturity, embedding itself deep within the teen's dual-colored eyes of blue and green with a subtle yet keenly fixed glimmer. How such a glimmer managed to find its way into Jacob's eyes was not as immediately obvious as the muscle that had found its way to his arms and torso. It could have been the result of seeing firsthand the beauty and mystery of Eden concealed from the rest of mankind behind an unseen and impregnable gate. Maybe it came to him when he stumbled unknowingly upon the dark secrets kept deep within the thicket of the Silent Forest. Or perhaps it was a lingering light of astonishment and wonderment stemming from the knowledge pouring forth from the endless books housed in the Library at Havenhid that had filled his head and refused him the ability to look at the world and those who dwelled in it the same way ever again. However it came to be, Gotham had warned Jacob long ago that such changes would one day settle themselves upon him.

"Will I ever be able to come back home?" Jacob recalled asking Gotham while sitting on the Stevens Bridge on the night before his pilgrimage to Eden began when he learned angels were as real as he was.

"Eventually…one day," Gotham replied before his face took on a rather serious look to match the cryptic tone suddenly heard in his voice. "But you will not do so as the same person you find yourself to be this moment."

Even as streams of tears began to streak his cheeks, the memory caused Jacob's mouth to tilt like a seesaw and form a slanted grin. If ever the phrase "That's an understatement" cried out for a new meaning, Gotham's words demanded it. Jacob straightened his stance and with the echo of Gotham's voice reverberating inside his head he continued to stare at his naked self in the mirror. His gaze shifted slowly, almost timidly, and settled itself on the area of the mirror that held the reflected image of his right shoulder. A faint rustle was heard, and then very slowly he began to raise what he could only describe as the feeling of a third arm. Only it wasn't an arm, but a wing that slowly emerged from hiding behind Jacob's back and unfolded itself like the speech-taking vision it was. It was followed by more rustling and a second equally impressive wing revealed itself from behind Jacob's other shoulder until he stood looking like a boy wearing an odd-shaped cape caught in a wind. The once delicate- looking and transparent limbs reminiscent of belonging to some make-believe fairytale being when they first miraculously attached themselves to Jacob's back on that fateful jump at Broken Earth were now colored gray by a waxy coat of plumage and looking every bit like the feathered wings one would see on a great majestic bird like an eagle commandeering the sky.

It wasn't the sort of thing one ever fully became accustomed to; the sight of wings fixed to the back of a human, that is. At least that was the case with Jacob as he studied almost warily his reflection while slowly turning one way and then the other to get a better view of his adorned back. How he had obsessed over hatching the two magnificent limbs from the unsightly hump-like cocoons protruding from his back ever since the day he learned such a metamorphosis was possible. But now it had happened, finally, and he could no longer feign blindness to what was right in front of his eyes; and as such he could no longer deny who and what he was, no matter how hard he may have wanted.

"Jacob?"

The sound of his grandmother's voice from outside his bedroom door broke through the silence and shook Jacob free of his thoughts. Immediately, Jacob's wings retreated and folded themselves from sight.

"I'm just finishing up in the bathroom," he replied loud enough for her waiting ears.

"Well, be quick will you?" she returned. "Your breakfast is about ready, and you don't want to eat it cold."

He quickly and begrudgingly wiped away the wetness of his tears with his hands. Then as he grabbed a towel and began to rub vigorously his damp, tangled hair with it there came the rapping of a knock.

"I said I'll be there," he loudly called out, while trying to conceal from his tone the rising annoyance he was beginning to feel at being rushed.

The intermittent knocking continued, until, finally, Jacob tossed aside his towel with exasperation and went to answer it. When he stepped out of the bathroom he immediately became aware the knocking wasn't coming from his bedroom door but rather the window. Craning his head as he slowly crossed the room, he could see through the half-closed slats of the lowered blinds something moving along the ledge of the window that was the source of the incessant tapping on the glass pane. Cautiously, Jacob raised the blinds and much to his surprise discovered a gray-spotted falcon perched outside staring back at him.

Jacob instantly recognized the fierce-looking bird of prey as the rarely seen Gyrfalcon; a striking species he had the privilege of witnessing unhindered in the wilds of Eden. To see the bird that was nearly extinct in the outside world, however, was quite an odd sight, indeed. Nor was it a lasting sight when the Gyrfalcon swiftly flew off when Jacob went to open the window, but not before leaving behind a sealed envelope on the ledge upon where it had perched. Whoever had addressed it had done so in Caelestian—the very unusual, and by now very familiar language of angels—and because Caelestian had been required learning in Study at Havenhid Jacob was quickly able to transcribe the strange markings scrawled in black ink and see that they spelled out his own name.

What could this be? Jacob wondered. With a sort of nervousness, he tore open the envelope to see what had been delivered to him, and in such out-of-the-ordinary fashion.

Unfolding the thick parchment-like paper inside, he came upon more of the Caelestian writing which Jacob's eyes carefully studied as they worked to decipher the strange and most unexpected message, but the more he read the more dumbfounded the expression of his face became.

"They can't be serious," he then muttered to himself with disbelief when finally he finished.

~ ~ ~

Less than ten minutes later, Jacob came bounding down the stairs from his bedroom; all signs of the Nephilim that he was had been concealed away under a teenage uniform of jeans, t-shirt and a well-worn pair of sneakers, as well as the tears he had shed for his fallen friend. Halfway to the kitchen, he was hit by a wall of scrumptious smells. Whatever his grandmother was whipping up for breakfast, it smelled more like a feast than anything else. Sure enough, when he entered the kitchen, he found her at the stove where she was overseeing several pots and pans and the boiling and sizzling happening inside them in the same way an army general works a map of his troops and the enemy inside a war room.

"Have a seat, it's just about ready," instructed Ava. "I've poured your juice."

Jacob made his way to the kitchen table where a glass of freshly squeezed orange juice was waiting for him.

"You don't need to go through so much trouble. I'm fine with just having some cereal," he said, sinking into his chair.

"Nonsense! You might be fine with just cereal, but I'm not. And a growing boy like yourself certainly can't start off the day right eating a bowl of Fruit Krispies, Cocoa Loops, and whatever these cartoon tigers and Leprechauns try to push on kids these days," came the reply. "Besides, you've been away for some time now, and who knows what you've been living off of while you've been away."

"They fed us well, trust me," answered Jacob as he reminisced over the kingly buffet that awaited him each morning, noon and night during his stay at Havenhid.

"Of that I have no doubt. You look as if you might have even put on a pound or two. Still, there is nothing better than a good home-cooked meal no matter what goodies the trough from which you've been gorging yourself held. Wouldn't you agree?"

The sound of her heels clicked their way toward the kitchen table and, before Jacob could answer, a plate arranged with a healthy helping of poached eggs, sausage links, hashed browns and toast was placed in front of him.

"Looks good," said Jacob, forcing forth a half-hearted smile. "Only…"

He grabbed his fork and proceeded to move the sausage to the furthest end of his plate. "I no longer eat anything that once had—"

"A face attached to it," answered Ava before her grandson could finish his sentence. "You needn't worry, it's vegetarian; same vegetarian sausage and bacon and hotdogs and whatever other fake meat I've been serving you since you were a little boy."

The surprised look that came over Jacob only drew a cocky rise of his grandmother's eyebrow.

"What…you think you're the first Nephilim I've ever had to feed before you came along?" she remarked with a veiled smirk.

Ava took a seat at the table next to her grandson looking every bit as lovely as she always had. Her gray hair was immaculately coifed into place and she made even the simplest of dresses look elegant. Looking more like she was ready to go to Sunday church services than spending the morning scampering about the kitchen preparing morning breakfast, even with the flower-printed apron draped across her front. But there was also an inner glow coming from her that out-shined her outward appearance; the kind of glow a mother radiates as she looked upon her newborn child for the first time.

"Is something wrong?" asked Ava as she watched Jacob pick at his food with his fork.

"What makes you think something's wrong?" inquired Jacob.

"For starters, it's the first time I've set a plate of food down in front of you where you haven't inhaled at least half of it within thirty seconds," noted Ava. "Secondly, you look tired. Did you not sleep well last night?"

"I slept fine," answered Jacob, though not at all convincingly. "Guess I'm just not all that hungry this morning."

Ava, however, wasn't buying it. She'd been the boy's grandmother long enough to know when something was troubling him, but she bit her tongue and didn't press him any further on the matter.

"I'm sure your girlfriend will be happy to hear you're back home."

The subtle changing of topic cast aside momentarily whatever heavy gloom had settled over him and drew his eyes away from their fixed stare at the food on his plate.

"Girlfriend?"

"Yes, Wray."

"She's not my girlfriend," Jacob said in a quiet, yet defensive tone.

"I'm sorry, she is your friend, is she not?" asked Ava.

"Yeah."

"Clearly, she's a girl."

It was nearly impossible arguing certain things with his grandmother, and Jacob sensed this was one of those topics. Still, he took a collective breath and made an attempt.

"The word girlfriend means something completely different nowadays," said Jacob. "I mean, you wouldn't call Ty my boyfriend would you, even though he is a boy as well as my best friend. At least I hope you wouldn't."

"Heavens, you'd think I just accused you of running away with the girl and secretly marrying her before a justice of the peace," Ava remarked under her breath. "Although I must say, now that we've touched upon the subject, that she'd be hard-pressed to find any mother who wouldn't be pleased to welcome her as a newly betrothed daughter-in-law. I know she was quite the help to me while you were away."

A bewildered look came over Jacob. "You've seen her?"

"Sweet girl, she is. Came by without fail while you were gone to check in on me once a week—twice even, some weeks—to make sure I was doing all right and offer her help doing chores around the house or run any needed errands I might have."

"Came by…here?" asked Jacob.

"Naturally, I thanked her but declined her kind gesture. I may have advanced in age, but being feeble or helpless is something I've managed to avoid thus far," said Ava.

"Duly noted," replied Jacob, as he regularly had in the past to his grandmother's adamant declarations regarding her well-being and independence.

"But it was rather nice to finally have someone to engage in conversation with over a spot of afternoon tea, again," said Ava. "Goodness knows this house at times can be an unbearably quiet and lonely place…like a morgue."

It became obvious the mention of Wray was a topic best avoided this morning; something Ava became quickly aware of when she took notice of Jacob's eyes slipping downward once more to stare glumly into his plate.

"I don't think you need me to tell you that she was quite surprised, not to mention more than a little upset, to learn you had left Cain's Corner," said Ava, instantly recapturing her grandson's attention. "And needless to say it was more than a little awkward for me when I was suddenly put on the spot to come up with a believable alibi to explain your absence."

"What did you tell her?" Jacob asked somewhat hesitantly.

"What could I tell her except that the time to remedy the condition which had focused itself on the area of your upper back had finally presented itself."

Jacob was thunderstruck. "You said what?"

"I don't make it a habit to entertain the wiles of truth-spinning; I was at the time, however, aware of your consultations with Doctor Gilkey regarding your back, about which you chose to confide with Wray. I simply implied you had decided under advisement to make the trip to a special facility a great distance away from Cain's Corner to correct your, uh… condition, and that you didn't really want anyone to make a big fuss about it which is why you kept quiet about it," explained Ava. "It didn't feel like much more than one of those pesky little fibs one is forced to deploy now and then, that is until Wray started questioning me about why I didn't go with you. Not only did I have to feign frailty as an excuse, but I told her my sister had volunteered to take you into her home and look after you in my stead during your recovery since I was not the best candidate to make the trip cross country."

Jacob sat looking on at his grandmother with a somewhat bewildered expression fixed on his face. "But your sister is no longer living."

"Which is why I had to make a special visit to the confessional box at St. Catherine's shortly after I spun that untruth," said Ava, sounding none too happy about having to concoct such a fib.

"Did she believe you…Wray, that is?" Jacob couldn't help but inquire

"I don't exactly give off an aura of untrustworthiness, do I?" answered Ava.

The question hardly required an answer from Jacob whom Ava continued to eye thoughtfully.

"The night before you left with Gotham," she wondered aloud after taking a sip of her coffee, "you were anxious about a great many things. Leaving your friends behind without a word was one of them. As I remember it, there was a school dance that night, which you rushed off to; to say goodbye to your friends, you told me."

Jacob sat quietly in his chair staring blankly ahead. He could still see the faces of the students of Harpus High gathered inside the school gymnasium the night of the dance in all their formal attire and the snickering whispers that came from them as he was led by Wray across the dance floor looking and feeling glaringly out of place in his jeans, hoodie and sneakers. Yet none of it mattered the moment Wray embraced him in the center of the crowd and guided their slow dance.

Wray Bliss.

Never in the history of the world had anyone been named so appropriately. The way she looked that night in her delicate dress with the dim lights shining down to illuminate the beauty of her face framed by the golden tresses of her hair spilling down across her smooth shoulders made Jacob's heart flutter like a butterfly emerging from its cocoon. But no feeling could ever come close to surpassing what it was like to have her at that moment in his arms. Jacob could still hear the sound of Stevie Nicks coming from the DJ boot and filling the gym with the delicate bray of her voice as the couple swayed to Wray's favorite song, "Sanctuary." The music surrounded them, like an oasis of an invisible sanctuary only the two of them at that moment were privy to see, slowly moving them ever so closely until—

"Jacob?"

The sound of his grandmother's voice abruptly snatched Jacob out of Wray's arms and out of the school gymnasium and immediately sat him back in his chair at the kitchen table looking momentarily like he had just been shaken awake after dozing off in the middle of algebra class. What had they been talking about before he drifted off? Oh, yes, the difficult task of telling his two closest friends he would be leaving Cain's Corner for a spell, or in his case the failure to do just that.

"I had every intention to, really I did," said Jacob. He explained to his grandmother how he went to the dance like he had told her he was, and how Mrs. Braukoff, the hawkish chaperone had the gym locked down like Alcatraz forcing him to text Ty, who was flailing away on the dance floor like someone in the grips of a grand mal seizure, to meet him outside the gym.

"Wray came outside a short while later after spotting me from inside. She was obviously shocked to see me there since I had been so adamant about not going and I told the both of them I had something important to tell them. But then I realized I didn't even know what to tell them. I mean, what could I tell them, when I didn't even know where I was going?" Jacob's muted frustration escaped him in a deep sigh before he muttered under his breath, "Not that I could have told them, even if I did."

"They're your friends," said Ava. "No matter what reason you might have had to concoct, they deserved a goodbye from you, not to wake up the next morning to discover you'd suddenly vanished."

"What can I say?" Jacob replied with a dismissive shrug. "I guess I just don't have the flair for twisting the truth as you have."

It wasn't so much the words spoken by her grandson that caught Ava by surprise, but rather the quiet yet noticeable accusatory tone heard in his voice as he uttered them. She could tell something was troubling the boy. There had been a deep-seated moodiness in him ever since he returned home unexpectedly three days earlier. Whatever it was that was bothering him, however, he was keeping it to himself, and she knew him well enough to know not to badger him into opening up about his problems until he was ready to share them.

"Well, then, it looks like I better pack a little extra food to take with us today, for goodness knows every man, woman and child in Cain's Corner will be in jeopardy when that stomach of yours comes roaring back to life come noontime," said Ava as she stood up to clear Jacob's untouched plate from the table.

"What do you mean?" asked Jacob as his puzzled gaze followed her to the sink. "Take with us where?"

"I thought it'd be nice to pack a lunch and spend the afternoon in the park," answered Ava as she began cleaning dishes. "I remember when I used to take you there when you were a little boy and how you loved to feed the ducks in the lake."

"I think I'm a little too old to be feeding ducks at the park," Jacob remarked dourly. "Besides, I'm really not in the mood for a picnic."

"Oh, come now, Jacob. It's a beautiful day today; much too beautiful to spend it cooped up inside," said Ava. "I thought it would allow us a chance to talk."

"What's there to talk about?" muttered Jacob, sounding ever more glum.

Turning off the kitchen faucet and grabbing a nearby towel, Ava slowly made her way around the counter while drying her hands. "Well, for starters, you've been home now for three days and you've barely said more than a few words about your time away."

"That's because there's not a whole lot to say," said Jacob. But even he knew how unbelievable he sounded. After all, he was a Nephilim who had just returned from the Garden of Eden. To say there wasn't much to share about the experience would be like describing the view standing upon the summit of Mount Everest with a dismissing shrug.

"Then...perhaps you'd like to tell me why you've returned home so soon," pressed Ava. "Don't get me wrong, the sight of you walking through the front door from out of the blue pleased me like you could never imagine. But you've been gone for nearly a year now, and I expected you'd be away for at least twice that amount of time."

Jacob didn't say anything at first and, instead, stared straight ahead with a vacant gaze as if concentrating on a chorus of unheard voices chattering inside his head.

"Were you ever going to tell me about my father?"

The question, when he finally asked it, came in a quiet tone, but it hit Ava as if she had been struck by a two-by-four.

"Your father? That's a rather abrupt turn of conversation," Ava replied casually while doing her best to camouflage the great aversion she had to the subject. But Jacob's waiting glare stayed firmly on her.

"What little there is to know about your father, I've already told you," she surrendered, hesitantly.

"Except the truth," accused Jacob. And if there was any question of what truth he was referring to, Jacob let roll from his tongue a name—Samael—and watched as the color drained from his grandmother's face.

As if sensing the telling change of her pallor, Ava turned away from her grandson and slowly, like a shadow in retreat, crossed to the other side of the kitchen where a large window offered a view of the backyard.

"Gotham told you," she said, staring out at the numerous flowers blooming in the garden on the other side of the pane.

"No. He lied to my face, just like you did," Jacob hissed bitterly before adding under his breath, "and mom."

"Lie is a rather strong word, wouldn't you agree? With a lie, there is an intent to deceive the person to whom such an untruth is told," said Ava. "It was never my intention, nor your mother's, to deceive you."

"What would you call it then?"

"Protecting you," answered Ava, without a moment's hesitation, "as any good mother, and grandmother, for that matter, would do."

With a faint smile residing upon her lips, she watched as a brown sparrow scampered tirelessly after her hungrily chirping nearby brood of fledglings to diligently feed one by one the food she had managed to forage from the ground.

"It is the solitary lot of all creatures in this life to keep those we bring into the world from harm at all costs. And, when we fail at it, it becomes a scar that marks us forever."

Her eyes shifted away from the view of the garden and the birds and found their way back to her grandson who remained silent as he sat slumped and brooding in his chair.

"Oh, Jacob, if only we were talking about a common childhood malady most parents face where, in my day, one only need reference the expertise of a Dr. Spock child-rearing book for a remedy," Ava remarked, taking a seat at the table once again and leaning in while speaking in a tone close to a whisper as if the conversation was a secret to be kept from the rest of the world.

And in more ways than not, it was.

"Your mother, may she rest in peace, had only her natural maternal instincts to guide her in raising you, and even what small bits of advice I could offer her were of little help. We may have shared a common thread where our children were concerned, but we had each been handed two completely different needles in which to sew forth their upbringing. From the moment you took your first breath, she decided you would have the most ordinary of childhoods possible. She wanted you to grow up as a normal boy doing and experiencing the normal everyday things of other normal boys, not because she was ashamed of what you were or in denial of how you came to be. But she instinctively knew the difficulties you would soon be facing in the years to come and, right or wrong, she was determined to pave for you as smooth and straight a road to walk for as long as possible before the sharp and unavoidable bend awaiting you eventually crossed your path."

Ava took a breath and straightened herself in her chair all the while cupping Jacob's hands with her own.

"Unfortunately, your mother was taken from you at far too young an age, and before the questions had been answered that you didn't even know needed asking," she continued solemnly. "When she finally passed, I found the shoes of your protector suddenly bequeathed to me, not that it was too uncomfortable a fit for my feet; like all grandmothers, I've kept a watchful eye on you as if you were my own since the first moment you were placed in my arms as a baby. Then came the day—overnight it felt—that I brought you upstairs to my room to finally reveal to you the secret that before you even pushed your way into this world had been locked away in a small wooden box and buried at the bottom of a trunk beneath the remnants of a lifetime's worth of memories."

Jacob knew immediately of what his grandmother spoke. It's not an easy task to forget something which ends up having a profound and irreversible change on the rest of one's life. Yet it wasn't so much the box that would find a way to forever ingrain itself in his memory but rather what he would discover was locked away inside it like some precious jewel: an old photograph of his grandmother as a young woman standing beside a strapping handsome man who was no man at all but an angel named Gothamel, looking just as vibrant and youthful as the day Jacob would unexpectedly be introduced to him six decades later. But it was the image of a young boy who had in equal measure his grandmother's good (some might even say pretty) looks, and Gotham's intense piercing eyes seen standing between the two that would capture Jacob's fascination even more so than the man who was untouched by time; a boy who would serve almost as a mirror reflection for Jacob as he came to hear a strange and foreign word pass through his grandmother's lips for the first time: Nephilim.

~ ~ ~

"You should have told me," Jacob murmured softly.

"Perhaps," answered Ava with a defeated sigh. "And we both could argue the point until one of us turns blue in the face. Yet I can still remember the look on your face when I opened the trunk in my bedroom to reveal to you the secret kept locked inside. I couldn't get you to believe the existence of Nephilim much less convince you that you were one of them. How well then do you think I would have fared broaching the delicate matter concerning your father?

"Still, I struggled with my willful silence and, after much hand-wringing, I could no longer ignore that your right to know the truth—the whole truth— far outweighed whatever best intentions I may have had concerning you. It was only after speaking with Gotham that I thought better about my brief change of heart."

The mention of Gotham's name made Jacob grow rigid in his seat. "Gotham? You spoke to him about it? When?"

"The night you discovered who and what he truly was on the Stevens Creek bridge was not the delusional fantasies of an old woman," answered Ava.

"You had rushed off to the school dance for one last night with your friends after telling me you would be leaving for the one place all young Nephilim eventually go to when the time comes calling. Gotham came to inform me of his own change of heart in deciding to take you to Eden."

"I don't understand," said Jacob with growing puzzlement. "You're saying he didn't even want to take me at first?"

"That is an altogether separate topic of conversation best saved for a rainy day by the fire," answered Ava. "Of course, I already knew from you that he had changed his mind, but when he came here to make sure I was agreeable to your leaving with him, suddenly it was I who was hesitant in letting you go."

"But...I thought you wanted me to go," Jacob was quick to reply. "In fact, you practically had my bags packed the moment I told you."

Smiling ever so slightly, Ava paused, as if to listen to her thoughts before she spoke them. "Some decisions have a habit of being second-guessed when you come to know firsthand the dangers that stalk young Nephilim such as yourself when they finally leave the nest," she said finally. And Jacob knew instantly what she meant; in fact, he could almost see the ghostly reflection of her long-departed son floating in the blue pools that were her eyes.

"Naturally, I finally relented. After all, if there is anyone who could protect you against such dangers it would be Gotham."

Jacob sat silent. And even Ava couldn't hide the hint of uncertainty that found her voice when making the statement.

"But I told him," Ava was quick to continue, "before you were to leave this house I thought it imperative that you be told the whole truth that had been denied you all these years, specifically the truth concerning who your father was. Firm as I was in my demand, however, Gotham argued against it. A Nephilim requires a clear and focused head if he is to rise up to the rigors of training awaiting him, he argued. To suddenly send him off with the weight of something so traumatic burdening his every step, would most certainly lead to failure, especially when it came time for him to take the most important step a Nephilim will ever make in securing his wings."

Jacob wanted to argue his grandmother's reasoning regarding the collusion that took place behind his back; truly he did, but he couldn't. If anyone knew the struggle of completing what was no doubt the most challenging task a Nephilim could face, it was him. Had he known beforehand the truth surrounding his once faceless father, would he have ever been able to find the faith necessary to stare down the stomach-turning abyss that was Broken Earth and take the plunge needed to unfurl two feathered life preservers hidden beneath a layer of flesh covering his back? the same way shoots of newly sprouted plants rise up out of the soil to the beckoning sun? Jacob found himself wondering. And yet it was only when he discovered the truth kept hidden from him that he managed to defy whatever fear his faith had until then been unable to push aside and emerge victorious from the jaws of Broken Earth.

"We argued the subject for some time, but I knew Gotham was right," Ava continued. "It was only after he promised to sit you down personally and tell you the whole story of how you came to be once you had managed to find your footing in the clouds that I relented."

"I just wish…," Jacob began, but his tongue found it difficult to catch his racing thoughts. "It just would have been an easier situation to handle had it not caught me off-guard the way it did."

A concerned look crept its way over Ava's face and she squeezed the boy's hand all the more tightly in her own.

"Is that why you're here at home now?" she asked. "Were they not accepting of you and the truth of who you are?"

"No…everyone seems to be actually okay with it," answered Jacob. "I mean, yeah, there's a couple boys there who tried to give me a hard time. But everyone for the most part treated me no differently than before. Even Eksel's been a lot friendly to me than he had been before."

"And your wings? I trust you now know what it's like to gaze down upon the world while soaring high above it."

Jacob's answer came with a slight crook of a grin.

"Will you show me?" inquired Ava.

"Maybe a little later," Jacob answered demurely.

Ava tilted her head slightly to try and get a better look at her grandson's face, particularly the eyes which were shifted downward and focused on his lap, and she could tell there was more weighing heavily on the boy.

"There's something else, isn't there?" she asked to no immediate answer. "What is it you're not telling me?"

~ ~ ~

After a long, cautious pause, Jacob pulled his hand from his grandmother's embrace and slowly reached for his pocket from which he removed a neatly folded, if not somewhat crinkled square of paper. Setting it down on the kitchen table, he very slowly slid it toward Ava.

"What's this?" she asked.

"An untold truth I think you deserve to know about," answered Jacob.

The pages revealed their age with the loud crackling that came from them as Ava unfolded them. Her eyes squinted at first to focus themselves on the handwriting within the folds and almost immediately widened when they instantly recognized the penmanship.

"This is David's handwriting," she muttered under her breath.

"They're the missing pages that were torn from the journal he was keeping while in Eden.

Not all of them, but some," explained Jacob.

Ava looked to Jacob with a puzzled urgency. "Where did you find them?"

"I didn't. Anahel gave them to me," answered Jacob. "He told me he found them hidden away in some random book in the Library at Havenhid not too long after David...you know...passed away."

"Hidden away...?"

As her eyes turned back to the pages in her hands, Jacob wanted desperately to caution her about the secret they held, but his tongue failed to find the words and instead he sat quietly in his chair. Mindlessly fingering the soothing warmth emanating from the pendant attached to the chain hanging from around his neck, he watched as his grandmother's eyes, framed by lines of time, began reading their way through the handwritten words that made up the long-lost journal entry. She had only finished the first of the half dozen pages when she stopped suddenly and, with a troubled and confused look mirrored in her eyes, she looked once more to her grandson.

"I don't understand...," she muttered in a voice that held an almost pleading tone for clarity. "What does this mean?"

Jacob shifted uncomfortably in his chair.

"I'm not sure I can explain it any better that what your son wrote in those pages," said Jacob. "If you read further, it becomes much clearer."

"You've read it, then?"

Jacob could only muster a nod with a nervous clearing of his throat.

The kitchen then became as silent as a tomb as Ava, hesitating somewhat, returned to the task of reading through her son's journal entry. Jacob watched as Ava's face grew visibly heavier with despair with every turn of the page until he wasn't sure she would find the strength to finish. When finally she did, her eyes closed themselves tightly but not before a tear escaped from each one and spilled their way down her cheeks. In the quiet moment that followed, Jacob debated silently with himself whether he had made the right decision to show his grandmother what was basically a final confession from her dearly departed boy. Coming to grips with the death of one's own flesh and blood was traumatic in its own right; Ava had mourned long and hard over the murderous act that robbed her child of the precious life she had given him. It was a mourning that remained a heavy weight on the heart which never eased no matter how many days separated her from the painful moment. To suddenly learn the snatching of her boy came not from some faceless nefarious force lurking in the shadows but, in fact, was the result of a conscious, premeditated moment of self-sacrifice made by her son was a striking and almost too painful revelation for Ava to confront, even as David tried to console her from beyond the grave through his handwritten words to see his decision for what it was: an act of love.

~ ~ ~

"He did love his father so," Ava finally remarked with a reflective whisper.

"Anahel thought seeing this might ease some of the pain you've been feeling over David's death," Jacob, searching for some workable response from his tongue that might serve to comfort his grandmother said.

"And how exactly did he think this might ease my pain, might I ask?" Ava replied somewhat sharply.

"I don't know…I suppose he thought at the very least it would clear up any misconceptions about David—" Jacob paused, biting down on his tongue for a moment before finishing his sentence, "being a traitor."

His words drew a narrow and withering glare from Ava.

"There are no misconceptions I hold which need clearing up," she scolded. "Oh, I'm well aware of the official version of events concerning David's last moments alive. But despite what many have chosen to embrace as fact, never once did I believe, even for a moment, that my son would ever collude with the Darkness."

Jacob could hear the hurt in her voice, even as anger attempted to cloak it, and Jacob's instinct was to leave well enough alone, but he couldn't.

"All I mean is that, well, if this journal entry shows anything it's how loyal and loving a person David truly was. I mean think about it, he was willing to give up his own life so Gotham could find favor in Heaven again and no longer be Fallen," offered Jacob.

"And you think this somehow would prove to be a consoling thing to me?" retorted Ava. "All these years I have had to live with the stain of an unfair and unjust epitaph marking the memory of my son as nothing but a weak example of a Nephilim who succumbed to the temptations of the dark side and betrayed his calling in the worst possible way. And now I'm supposed to wrap myself in the comforting warmth of vindication in the same way I might snuggle into the embrace of a cozy shawl on an especially chilly night at the news that a father could muster up the strength to cut down his own son over a lousy sword?"

"I think there's a lot more to it than how you're characterizing it," said Jacob.

Ava wasn't listening.

"I know what happened to my son. I looked into Gotham's face the night he told me and what I saw was a father as heartbroken over the loss of his only child as his mother, if not more so. Now you dare to sit there and ask me to question that love?"

"I'm not, but…" Jacob could feel himself becoming more flustered. This was not how he had hoped this conversation would go. The last thing he ever wanted was to bring more pain to his grandmother. But the can was open, and worms were spilling out and wriggling their way in all directions across the kitchen table. "How do you explain the journal pages you're holding? You said so yourself, it's David's own writing."

"What of it?" Ava spat while jumping to her feet. She quickly circled around to the far side of the table and positioned herself once more by the window. Staring out into garden seemed to bring her a breath of calm.

"There was no one David idolized more than his father. In his eyes, Gotham was the sun, the moon and everything in between," she remarked with soft reflection. "Naturally, when Gotham finally sat David down and explained how he was a Fallen, the news was deeply wounding to him because, to David, Gotham was nothing less than Heaven-worthy. So if you ask me whether or not I believe David from time to time entertained such thoughts as those he wrote about, my answer would be I'm not surprised. What son who held his father in such high regard wouldn't commit the highest form of love? But there is fantasy and there is reality, and David obviously came to the same conclusion. Why else would he have torn those pages out of his journal?"

Then why not destroy the pages by throwing them in one of the many fireplaces inside Havenhid? Jacob couldn't help but wonder to himself. Why hide them away in a book inside the Library? But Jacob kept his puzzlement silent inside his head.

"No, this has all been a gross misunderstanding," argued Ava more to herself than Jacob. "Even if David had seen his way to craft such a scheme, in the end its intended outcome would have rested upon Gotham to do the unimaginable. And while he might be a great many things, I know to the core of my being what he is and what he is not, and what he is not is a cold-blooded murderer. Certainly not of his own son."

Even in the soft hushed tones in which Ava spoke, there was an adamant fervor in her voice that Jacob dared not argue against. But as they sat in awkward silence, he could not help but remember one particular day in Eden when Gotham, for whatever reason, decided to lay bare his tortured soul and confessed to the heart-deadening deed that Ava, with all the muted love she still had for him, defended him from committing, with no one to bear witness to his heart-breaking penance but the Tree of Life and the stone crypt which held the remains of his beloved boy residing beneath the cover of its shade.

~ ~ ~

"What did Gotham have to say about all of this?" Ava asked suddenly. The question jolted Jacob from his thoughts.

"Gotham?"

"I can only imagine how unimaginably anguishing the prospect of such of thing must have been for him to hear," Ava remarked under her breath as she continued to stare out at the morning through the window while picking her way through her own flood of competing thoughts. It was only when Jacob's lack of a response caught her ear that she turned her gaze to him.

"Hello?"

"Yes?"

"I asked you a question. What was Gotham's reaction?" she asked again.

And again it seemed as if Jacob had suddenly been stricken a mute.

"I trust you showed him these pages," said Ava.

Jacob shook his head.

"Well…then I assume Anahel must have delivered the news to him."

Again Jacob shook his head, drawing from Ava a huffing sigh of frustration.

"For gracious sakes, Jacob, I feel as if I'm trying to squeeze water from a stone. Will you please answer me with more than a shake of your head?"

"Anahel never told him," answered Jacob, managing finally to muster some function of his tongue. "He said he had misgivings about sharing the pages he found in the Library with Gotham. He believed it might cause him more grief than anything to learn his son had basically sacrificed his own life for him."

Now that Jacob had shared the contents of the missing journal entry with his grandmother and witnessed her distress over it, he realized how wise Anahel had been in his decision.

"By the time he shared his secret with me, it was too late," said Jacob, drawing a narrowing gaze of curiosity from Ava.

"What do you mean too late?" she inquired.

Jacob could feel his tongue trying to pull back inside his mouth in a desperate attempt to retreat to safety through the opening of his throat and down into the pit of his stomach.

"Gotham was already gone," he managed to speak out.

"Gone? He left Eden?" questioned Ava.

Jacob began once again to shift uncomfortably in his seat, and it was then, in Jacob's conspicuous and ever-growing state of discomfort, that she took notice of the familiar pendant hanging around his neck that he was nervously fondling, and a look of dread suddenly swept over her face.

"Where did you get that?" she asked. "Get what?"

"That necklace," said Ava, with a cautious tremble in her voice.

Jacob saw his grandmother's gaze fixed firmly on the pendant whose radiating warmth he absent-mindedly was rolling between his thumb and fingers.

"Anahel gave it to me," he said before quickly tucking it away out of sight beneath his t-shirt.

"It seems Anahel has become quite the unique gift-giver where you're concerned," Ava coolly remarked in a tone tinged with suspicion. "That particular trinket, however, would not be a possession he would be privy to bequeath to you. I know this because it belonged to Gotham; it was his most guarded possession. Only one thing would be powerful enough to have removed it from around his—"

She stopped herself, biting down on her lip the moment she realized what words nearly escaped them.

"What is it you're trying so obviously hard not to tell me?" she asked in a most guarded manner.

"I think you should come back to your seat," said Jacob, knowing the difficult task that had been pressing itself harder and harder down upon him, like some oppressive weight since the day he returned home, was one he could no longer put off.

"I'm quite fine where I am, thank you," came Ava's brusque reply.

A look of dismay settled itself in the aged planes on her face that had grown accustomed to such dismay-filled moments over the course of her lifetime, and while wringing the fingers of her left hand with her right she seemed to brace herself for what her grandson was about to tell her.

"You already know what it is I'm going to say, don't you?" asked Jacob.

"There's a telling look in your eyes I first saw in the face of an angel on a day that became the darkest of my life," said Ava. "I'm praying my eyes are deceiving me this moment."

"Please, don't make me say it," Jacob pleaded in a whisper as he struggled to put on a brave front while feeling himself sliding closer toward the tipping point of tears.

"You must," said Ava. "I need to know this moment isn't some bad dream I'm desperately trying to awaken from."

The words, when Jacob finally summoned the strength to say them out loud—"Gotham's dead"—appeared to reach out and strike Ava with a numbing slap, even as she prepared herself to hear them. A long, anguished sigh was heard to leave her body, and feeling her knees begin to buckle beneath her she quickly stumbled forward a couple steps and collapsed into one of the chairs at the kitchen table to save herself from an embarrassing fall to the floor.

Not a single tear streaked her face.

~ ~ ~

A large round clock hanging on a nearby wall loudly ticked off the passing minutes as Jacob dutifully took up the unwanted task of recounting the details leading up to Gotham's death. He told of Thaniel's scheme to come into the possession of the Sword of Destiny by betraying Eden with the threat of opening the watery gateway in the Silent Forest and unleashing the Underneath's wrath on its lands. With great difficulty, Jacob described the horrible moments at Broken Earth when Thaniel, believing he finally had been given ownership of a prize long-coveted yet blind to the fact a cleverly disguised forgery had been passed into his hands, took his first swing with the weapon, and in a most horrific and butchering manner, severed Gotham's wings from his back before sending him over the cliff's edge into a long death spiral to his end.

Ava sat in silence as she listened with a glazed, numbing look settled heavily in her face, and even after Jacob had finished she remained stone-still in her chair for some time with her sad, mournful eyes fixed on her grandson and yet staring through him and past him as though she had been offered an invisible looking glass into the past, allowing her to see first-hand the tragic event told to her while leaving Jacob to wonder if she had even heard a word he said.

"So…," she finally muttered to herself under her breath, "the Sword of Destiny has managed once more to pierce my heart."

With nothing more to say—and wishing to know nothing more—she left the table pausing her retreat from the kitchen only when Jacob called out to her.

"You'll understand if I suddenly find myself no longer in the mood to picnic in the park," she said quietly over her shoulder. And of course he did.

"No worries," Jacob replied with a tone of regret for the sorrow he had unavoidably dumped in her lap. Then, before she could slip away from his sight, she he called out to her again. "Is there…Are you going to be okay?"

"I just need to be alone for a while," came the answer.

Then, before she lost what little strength she had left to keep her composure collected, she disappeared around the corner leaving nothing but the sound of her shoes tapping out her steps against the hardwood floor as she made her way to the stairs leading to her bedroom.

CHAPTER THREE

THE BLESSING AND THE CURSE

With Ava locked away in her bedroom to mourn the news of Gotham's passing, the house fell eerily silent. So much so that it became an unsettling noise in Jacob's ears that forced him to flee out the front door and go for a long walk to help clear the growing chorus of thoughts competing to be heard inside his head.

It was the first time he'd been out of the house since he returned home three days earlier. He sighed with great satisfaction as he basked in the warmth of the sun on his face while closing his eyes, to breathe deeply the fresh early summer air filled with the woody aroma of the tall eucalyptus trees that grew along the two-lane road outside his neighborhood. Of course, it was a far cry from the amazing flowery smells his nose had grown used to over the past many months, and the sunlight was not as brilliant, nor was its warmth as penetrating and soothing to the body as that which shone down from Eden's crystal blue-water skies.

Even the noise coming from the birds somewhere overhead in the trees was noticeably different; their chatter was less relaxed and held an air of urgency that was nonexistent in the feathered creatures he had come to know in Eden. But no matter the difference he took note of; the sunlight, the air, or the birds, he was just happy to be home once again. At least he thought he was happy to be home.

Jacob had walked about three miles when his feet suddenly veered left and continued their brisk but easy pace southward down Silverly Avenue where he passed the old McCollister place. Walled in behind a tall wrought iron fence, the imposing Victorian was once the home of Cain McCollister and, more importantly, the cutting that would later grow to become Cain's Corner. Yet despite its pristine appearance and renewed role as a museum for the town's history, there was something Jacob found eerily unsettling about the old manor. Spooky, even. He felt it the first time he ever laid eyes on the house as a young kid walking to school. Then, it looked more like a creepy residence for the lingering spirits of those long-gone souls who once lived there; spirits whose presence he could swear he felt peering out from behind the lace-curtained windows watching closely as he passed by causing an uneasy, tense feeling to run down his legs and into his feet to quicken his steps along the sidewalk.

This day was no different as Jacob hurried his way past the property without hardly sneaking a sideways glance at it.

"Some Light Bearer you're turning out to be. Spooked by an old house," he grumbled to himself once he rounded the corner at the end of the street and stopping just long enough to give himself what amounted to a verbal smack to the back of the head.

Continuing on, he returned a friendly wave to Mrs. Kirkegaard who was out watering a patch of colorful ground roses in her front yard before heading east down Brighton Street past his old elementary school and then, a little ways further down, Harpus High School, both of which had been deserted for the summer recess. He zig-zagged his way down several more streets before he finally came upon St. John's Cathedral, the church where his grandmother faithfully attended mass every Sunday, and the toll of whose bell could be heard from several blocks away heralding the morning hour. He continued walking until he reached Brighton's Food Mart where Mr. Hoffman was busily attending to the colorful vegetable and fruit display outside the store's front entrance.

"Well, well, well, look what the cat dragged in," Mr. Hoffman, whose squinty eyes seemed to be the result of being in a perpetual state of joviality, greeted cheerfully when he spotted Jacob coming up the sidewalk.

"Hey there, Mr. Hoffman," Jacob returned with a smile.

"What brings you out at such an early hour?"

"Nothing special. Just thought I'd go for a walk, you know, hang out," said Jacob.

"Well, you won't find a better day for doing exactly that," said Mr. Hoffman, giving the bright morning surrounding them an appreciative glance. "You've become quite the busy boy these days. Haven't seen your face around here for quite some time now."

"No busier than you. How's business?" asked Jacob, quickly steering the conversation away from his noted absence.

"Can't complain, can't complain," answered Mr. Hoffman. "This time of year's always been my busiest, what with the summer harvest coming in. Speaking of which—"

He grabbed a peach from the assortment he was attending to and tossed it to Jacob. "Your grandmother's been waiting for these. Sweetest, juiciest peach you'll ever taste, I can promise you that. You tell her I just received a fresh shipment this morning. My guess is she's looking to bake up a batch of her famous peach cobbler. She won't get a better turnout than with these here."

"I'll let her know," said Jacob.

He then dug into his jeans for some change to pay for the peach but Mr. Hoffman was quick to hold up his hand.

"With my compliments. Something to enjoy on your walk," said Mr. Hoffman. "If anything, you can tell your grandmother first-hand how tasty these peaches are instead of having to take my word for it."

Jacob thanked the grocer and went on his way.

"It was good to see you again, son, and you have yourself a good day," Mr. Hoffman said with a wave before returning to his produce.

Jacob resumed his stroll, walking to the end of the street where he crossed to a small grassy park dotted with shade trees on the other side. Tossing the peach Mr. Hoffman had given him up in the air and catching it repeatedly as if it were a baseball, he made his way to an empty playground and quickly scaled the large dome-shaped jungle gym which resided amid a swing set, slide and teeter-totter. Once he had perched himself on the metal bars at the top, he brought the peach to his mouth and sank his teeth into the fuzzy, fleshy fruit and was immediately greeted with an explosion of sweet juice that dribbled in copious amounts down his chin just as Mr. Hoffman promised, forcing him to turn his head and wipe his sticky mouth across the short sleeve of his t-shirt. Hunching himself forward, he did his best to steer clear of the drooling of juice that escaped the peach with every bite he took. All the while his watchful eyes darted about taking note of the passers-by whose numbers seemed to slowly be growing the more the morning aged. There was the young couple dressed in fitness attire and matching headbands out for their daily run that would no doubt end at the Juice Station a couple miles away for a shot of wheat grass to toast their shared dedication to good health.

Headed in the opposite direction was a young mother pushing a stroller while attempting to negotiate some kind of calming deal with a second child who, by a show of stomping and hollering, made it clear to anyone looking he was not happy to be dragged along for a long day of errands. Then there was Mrs. Hanson, a sweet old lady who lived a couple blocks away, out for her usual walk in the park with her two miniature Pomeranians who looked more like a pair of Tribbles than flesh and blood creatures as they bounced about like two fuzzy balls on leashes, furiously yapping their high-pitched squeaky barks at the sight of Mr. Beeman approaching from the opposite direction with his massive Great Dane in tow. It seemed almost too comical to Jacob watching the expression on the huge canine's face as it slowly made its way past the two spastic noise machines trying to determine if they were indeed other dogs, or a pair of squeak toys to be picked up and taken home for playtime.

All in all, it was just another typical day in Cain's Corner, or so it appeared. Cain's Corner wasn't the kind of town that had a habit of changing all that much, at least to the naked eye. And yet to Jacob's eyes it looked different than before he left; different in a way he couldn't quite pinpoint.

Or did it?

After all, how much could a town—even a fast-moving one many sizes bigger—change in just a year's time? Then again, if anyone was guilty of marked change it was Jacob.

Gotham had warned him he would not be the same person he was when he eventually returned home. Now Jacob found himself wondering if the promised transformation within him had been so dramatic, so striking, that it somehow found a way of removing him from everything else around him which had relatively remained untouched.

It certainly was an idyllic and peaceful place. In many ways, it was reminiscent of the town of Mayberry for the modern era minus the framing of an old RCA-type television surrounding it, and the exact sort of place one would look to escape in their search for a heaping helping of some home-spun words of wisdom at times when the world doled out life-changing challenges that could prove overwhelming. Jacob, however, had been home now for three days and, as he sat in the park chomping at his peach, the solace he had hoped would be waiting had so far eluded him.

One thing was for certain: Jacob hadn't planned on coming back to Cain's Corner when he did. True, the unbearable tragedy of Gotham's death, followed by the shocking discovery of learning who his father was, had shaken Jacob to the core of his being, and it seemed returning to the one last safe haven he knew of—home—was the only option of escape left to him. Anahel in all his wisdom, and even wiser words, however, caused Jacob to rethink his plans to pack his bag and leave Havenhid. And what doubt still clung to the boy afterward was cast off along with the last residuals of fear he had when he dove head-first into Broken Earth and emerge with the one thing able to convince him to finish what he unwittingly started the first day he swam out of the Dilmun Sea and stepped foot on the sandy beach leading to Eden. But Jacob's newfound determination would be cut short.

Sitting motionless on top of the jungle gym like some oddly placed park statuary, Jacob suddenly focused his attention in the direction of a grating drone of a diesel engine responsible for drowning out the peaceful serenity he had been enjoying, and saw that it came from an obnoxious garbage truck making its weekly rounds collecting trash. Yet while his gaze had fixed itself intently upon the truck as its steel hand took hold of a waiting dumpster rolled out to the curb of the sidewalk by one of the nearby businesses and noisily emptied its contents into a receptacle, his eyes glinted with reflected images of his last night in Eden surrounded by his fellow Nephilim and angel Guides on what should have been the happiest moment in his life, until the doors of the Hall of Light swung open with a thunderous clamor, and a figure of white entered bringing with it an ungodly chill one would never expect to accompany something so bright.

~ ~ ~

It was the night of Jacob's long-awaited Blessing ceremony where he would officially be declared the Light Bearer as had been promised in a little-known Apocrypha kept secret from the ages. Anahel had thought it best to postpone the ceremony to give the young Nephilim and, yes, even himself and his fellow Guides time to properly mourn the tragic events that had befallen Eden. For the next two weeks, it was as if all signs of life had abandoned the halls of Havenhid until the morning came when Anahel unlocked the door to his chamber and emerged from his self-imposed solitary confinement determined to mine light from the dark cloud that had settled itself over the Garden. And what better source of light than a Light Bearer.

The Blessing took place in the serene surroundings of the Chapel. In many ways it reminded Jacob of a baptism of sorts, just as Gotham said it would be. Quivering with the nervousness he fought hard to conceal from the sea of inquisitive eyes fixed on him, Jacob stood frozen at the foot of the altar while Anahel anointed the top of his head first with oil, followed by water while muttering under his breath the words to an unrecognizable prayer in an unrecognizable tongue. Finally, with Jacob's head tilted back, a single flickering flame of fire was set upon his forehead to burn until it slowly appeared to sink its way into the flesh and disappeared without so much as singeing the boy's skin while filling him with an indescribable warmth. When Jacob looked at Anahel and saw the solemn facade of the angel's face slowly crack to reveal the first smile to show itself in quite some time, he knew his coronation was complete, and he felt a strange joy he hadn't expected.

Afterward, with the sounds of jubilation once more filling the noble vast recesses of the Hall of Light, a grand celebration unfolded itself to mark the momentous occasion. Every square inch of the two long tables where the Nephilim had their daily meals was filled with a banquet of food worthy of a gathering of kings. With the day now retired, the conjoining of tree limbs that made up the construct of the Hall started to stir and the magnificent and exquisite Sistine Chapel-like painting that adorned the massive vaulted ceiling began to slowly unpiece itself, as it did every twilight, like a giant jigsaw puzzle as the branches retracted themselves to allow for the equally magnificent sight of the sky set aglow by the fiery colors of the setting sun not even Michelangelo, himself, could do justice in recreating. Heavenly sounding music danced its way in a gentle waltz amongst the guests and swirled upward to serenade the twinkling lights coming from a growing congregation of fireflies dancing in the air above the festivities as if mimicking the stars that one by one began to appear in the darkening sky.

Jacob had never been one to enjoy being the center of attention, but this night he felt a sort of ease in it. Perhaps it was because the focus of the celebration didn't feel so much about himself per se, but a new beginning for all of Havenhid. Then again, it may have had something to do with the feel of his newly acquired wings on his back. And even though he had yet to completely become used to his new appendages despite having them now for a couple weeks, he finally felt complete. He finally felt like the Nephilim he was and, though it had taken him some time, it was a good feeling. However, not everyone shared in the festive spirit that filled the Hall.

For starters, Jacob's arch nemesis Creed Maggert and his small band of loyal followers stood noticeably off to the side glowering and sneering at the other Nephilim who surrounded the newly coronated Light Bearer in a tight pack with necks craning to get a look at the Sword of Destiny, whose legend they had all heard so much about, yet mindful in their enthusiasm to keep a safe distance from the fabled blade. If there was one thing Creed couldn't stand it was denied his perceived rightful place in the spotlight. As far as he was concerned, there was no Nephilim more deserving of being fawned over, certainly no one more worthy of admiration, than himself. To see someone else, especially Jacob, become the recipient of such attention served to rankle him like nothing else.

The manner in which Damiel was found to be brooding, however, was an entirely different matter altogether, which Jacob made particular note of in his journal later that night.

I noticed Damiel standing off by himself in a far corner of the Hall. He feigned a smile at me whenever our eyes met, but a blind man could see how tortured he continues to be. It's as if he's found himself in a purgatory teetering between intense sorrow and an even greater anger brimming just below the surface. We've all had time to come to terms with what's happened, but it's as if no time has passed for Damiel. Then again, he's entitled to his pain. He's lost two brothers: one considered his closest of friends, and the other who committed an ultimate act of betrayal. Still, I can't help but wonder if he can't just shake himself free of the turmoil that has embraced him, or whether he won't.

~ ~ ~

Eventually the sound of Anahel's voice was heard to ring through the Hall.

"It's a heartening thing, young Fledglings, to witness the return of your smiles and laughter to this once joy-filled great room from which it had momentarily been robbed of in recent weeks. So much so, I found the idea of bringing a pause to tonight's jubilation-filled celebration as I call for your brief attention most disconcerting. But I ask for indulgence in allotting me this interruption to speak a few words that, alas, need to be spoken."

His voice was calm and measured, absent the usual fire and vigor when he spoke, and there was a staid—some might even say defeated—aura surrounding him that made his imposing stature in the eyes of the Nephilim strangely somewhat diminutive, as he stood looking out at the sea of young faces gathered before him.

"You have all shown a great deal of resilience and steadfastness in the face of unspeakable horror and anguish caused by a horrible scourge recently visited upon our fair Eden. And while levity surrounds us tonight, I know behind the curtain of laughter many of you are still mending your wounds. Betrayal is never an easy thing to overcome, especially when the slight comes from one you have come to trust and care for deeply. Trust when I tell you we are all smarting over the pain caused by this particular burr and the painful loss it has managed to seed into our hearts, and no doubt will for some time to come."

For a brief moment, it seemed Anahel might not be able to go on as his voice quivered noticeably at the unavoidable memory of Gotham's last moments of life. But he was quick to gather his composure and steady his voice.

"And while there's a part of me that wishes I could remove from each of your memories the lingering images of what took place at Broken Earth, I can't help but think a blessing—twisted though it may seem, but a blessing nonetheless—has been gifted you. For now you know firsthand the unbiased reach the Underneath has when its most foul and evil inhabitants get to slithering. Like ravaged termites, it eats its way into even the hardest of veneers, and what is perceived as light and that as dark is nothing more than a mirage, fooling even the most keenest of eyes found amongst us angels," said Anahel with a renewed assurance. "Behold the harvester of such fruit."

With those words, the angel settled his piercing gaze on Jacob with a look of gentle fondness. Suddenly, for the first time during his Blessing, Jacob felt the awkwardness of self-consciousness rise up inside himself as he felt the weight of all eyes in the room shift in unison and fix themselves upon him.

"This night, Eden owes its well-being and continuing existence as the last remaining one true paradise not to any one angel, but a Nephilim." Anahel's pronouncement drew a loud clearing of the throat from Ethan, who quickly began to glance about the Hall with a lip-puckering nonchalance when the angel's gaze shifted upon him.

"Er, that is to say five Fledglings," Anahel corrected himself as the sight of Jacob surrounded by Ethan and his three other closest friends—Max, Leos and Kairo—reminded the angel of what had occurred the night Eden was freed from its hostage-takers. But he then took a noticeable pause and a slight smile formed itself on his lips as if he was suddenly privy to a private joke.

"Funny thing…as I stand here looking at you gathered before me, I am suddenly very aware of certain words leaving my tongue," Anahel said before repeating the word "Fledgling" aloud and seemingly pondering its sound for a moment, as if it were the first time it had found its way inside his ears.

"I don't recall which of us used it first, but it nonetheless became a natural term of endearment for you, and those before you," said Anahel thoughtfully. "Like a newborn foal taking its first awkward steps, you came here to us to learn how to walk not as men, but Nephilim, and Eden embraced you and gave you the means to take to the earth like stallions, and navigate the skies not as timid young birds being pushed out of the nest for the first time, but as the magnificent winged beings you are, capable of sailing the winds in the same way tall ships once mastered the high seas. So it would be as the fledgling eventually becomes the eagle, the young boy becomes a young man."

Anahel was speaking to all the young boys gathered together before him when his eyes, as well as his words, narrowed their focus on Jacob standing in the forefront. "You are the embodiment of a promise long-believed to have been sealed away in a tomb holding the remains of bones and dust claimed by death," he said. "Now that promise burns with life once more; a beacon of hope for which, in days fast approaching, you will be the bearer in the world of man, who will never know that the one such light able to beat back the ever-surrounding Darkness was, for a brief moment in time, forever lost to them."

For a second or two, Jacob felt the weight of responsibility with which the angel's words came tightly wrapped suddenly upon his shoulders, though he did his best to keep as stoical and capable a front as possible. But then Anahel, as if sensing the boy's quiet insecurity over the colossal duty with which he had been involuntarily saddled, smiled in such a way that it lent Jacob a momentary sense of confidence that at least someone held a firm belief in himself.

"It is with this promise of hope realized," continued Anahel, "that we gather here tonight and celebrate in this most blessed of Blessings."

~ ~ ~

It was then the mammoth doors to the Hall swung open with a serenity-slaying clamor causing every head to turn at once to see who had caused such a rude disturbance, only to be taken aback at the sight of Creed's father, Sandel, standing in the arched entranceway. He swept into the great room, a stark vision of white, with pale skin nearly as ghostly as the long tresses of hair cascading down his back in great braids and a flowing garb of equally hueless clothing, and yet exuding none of the warmth usually found in such bright things.

Trailed by two hulking figures who did not look to have been bled dry of all color, Sandel strode briskly to the center of the Hall where he stopped and, like a parent who had just walked in on his children in the midst of mischief-making, took in the great room with his slow-searching eyes which sat in his skull like a pair of clear ice cubes.

"Sandel...what an unexpected surprise," said Anahel, sounding taken aback and tepid at the same time at the sudden appearance of the ghostly figure, who was as intimidating a sight as he was white. "I wasn't expecting you here tonight."

"No, I'm sure you weren't," Sandel replied with a cool drawl that was as icy as his visage.

He veered suddenly to the left, his mere presence forming a path ahead of him through the cluster of boys blocking his way as they quickly side-stepped out of his way in the same way the Red Sea parted for Moses, and made his way to one of the feast-lined tables. There he took a careful survey of the bounty of food with a look that fell just slightly short of disgust.

"So, I take it the period of mourning is over and regained appetites have called out to be fed," he remarked.

"The black shrouds that have hung in all corners of Havenhid the past few weeks like heavy window tapestries drawn to keep the sun out have been folded away, yes," answered Anahel. "But the lingering sorrow will be slow to ebb."

"Yes…I could sense the air of despair almost immediately from the moment I walked in," Sandel, making no attempt to hide his sarcasm, said.

Anahel started to explain the celebration taking place but Sandel was quick to wave him silent.

"There's no need to explain," interrupted Sandel who wandered slowly amongst the young Nephilim before his eyes caught sight of Jacob standing in the throng and locked themselves firmly on the boy. "I've been made well aware of the reason for tonight's festivities."

With that comment, the eyes of the other boys, as well as Anahel, knowingly shifted in unison to glare at Creed watching with smug delight from the other side of the Hall.

"Of that I have no doubt," Anahel remarked with a sigh before inquiring in a most cordial, if not suspicious manner. "On that note, is there a particular reason you've decided to humble us here tonight with your presence?"

"Curiosity, you might say," the white angel answered, all the while staring intently at Jacob. "Not to mention contempt."

"Contempt?" echoed Anahel. "What an odd response. And what, if I may inquire, might be causing you contempt?"

"It is not my contempt of which I speak," answered Sandel, "but yours."

To Jacob's great relief, the piercing gaze which felt like dry ice to the skin released its hold of him as Sandel looked away to face Anahel.

"But then again you knew of what I speak the moment you decided to officiate over this Blessing of which you have no authority to permit, much less perform," Sandel charged in a voice barely concealing the anger simmering beneath the chilled tone.

The look on Anahel's face sharpened itself on Sandel like a knife to the grindstone.

Taking a visible breath he offered calmly, "I know you too well, Sandel, to know you're not one to grace us with your presence on a whim. It's clear you have something of great weight on your mind of which you wish to relieve yourself. But perhaps it would be better if the two of us excuse ourselves to sort this matter out in private."

"There's nothing I have to say in secret that I would deny any pair of ears in this room," said Sandel.

"As you wish," replied Anahel, knowing it was pointless to further argue the matter.

An air of discomfort grew thicker inside the Hall and the Nephilim traded coy, unsure glances with one another about whether to leave or stay, and yet everyone remained planted where they stood, even when Sandel's intimidating presence began to slowly mingle its way amongst them.

"I recall a day not far removed from us when a celebration much like the one tonight took place within the confines of this great Hall," Sandel once again addressed Anahel.

"Come now, Sandel...I don't think that now is the appropriate—"

"You, in all your great wisdom," Sandel, ignoring Anahel's address, continued, "took the son of a Fallen into this long-guarded and protected Xanadu and, if that weren't enough, anointed the child as the Light Bearer whose coming has been foretold to the great consternation and protest of your fellow Guides."

"You cannot argue or rebuke that which is just because its chosen vessel is not to your liking," Anahel remarked. "In my opinion, the prophecy found a fine and principled boy in David in which to settle."

"Yes, I'm well aware of this opinion of yours," Sandel hissed with open contempt. "And yet in no more time than it takes the sun to retire in the west and rise again in the east this fine and principled boy as you so staunchly deemed him turned his head to show the side of his face he skillfully kept hidden in the shadows in an ultimate act of betrayal. So much so that his own father was forced to put him down like a disloyal dog that has bared his teeth to its master."

"If there is one thing I have found to be more true with the passing of time, it's that nothing is ever quite as it appears," said Anahel. "It is a lesson we would all be the better from learning, and I tell you here now, before all my detractors, that I stand by the decision I made regarding Gothamel's son."

"As I would expect from you," said Sandel, smiling ever so slightly in a way one might expect of a snake right before striking at its prey, if in fact snakes smiled. "Now here we are some fifty-plus years later and for reasons that boggle the mind you have once more ventured into the realm of the inconceivable to mine for a rare and elusive jewel you so adamantly believe will be unearthed from the muck that is Fallen spawn."

Much to his displeasure, Jacob found the white angel once again standing before him with his cold gaze settled intently on him and an even colder, unpleasant smirk shaping the mouth that housed a razor-sharp tongue. Only this time, Jacob didn't allow the intimidating presence to cause him to shrink into his own shadow, and met the coldness of Sandel's eyes with the flicker of flame set alight inside his own pupils from the growing tide of anger beginning to rise up inside the boy. And yet he didn't know which made him angrier: the tone of utter contempt and disgust heard loudly and plainly in Sandel's voice in referring to Jacob as "Fallen Spawn"; or the insinuation his place was in the muck.

"You've made your position on this matter quite clear to everyone present, Sandel, and now I will try to be just as forthcoming," said Anahel pointedly. "The role of overseer of Eden has been mine, and mine alone, since the day its Gates locked to the outside world. That includes the generations of Nephilim who have made their way through the halls of Havenhid, and the custodial duties with which I have been tasked to enforce are not one I take lightly. And while I am open to debate those decisions I have made during my tenure that some may view as flawed, you will understand me when I remind you bluntly there is only one power—much greater than even yourself, I assure you, Sandel—who will ever be in the position to challenge my judgments."

"Trust me when I say to you, Anahel, when it comes to your role as overseer of Eden, I would be inclined to agree with you and resign any aim to usurp your given authority," countered Sandel. "But the apocryphal prophesy regarding the Light Bearer, as well as the Nephilim in your care, have a reach that extends far beyond the boundaries of Eden. And as such, the authority to anoint a Light Bearer has never been yours to exercise; not then with Gothamel's child, and most certainly not now."

~ ~ ~

With those words, a tense and uncomfortable silence settled itself upon the Hall of Light, and the young Nephilim were left to ponder quietly amongst themselves what Anahel's response would be to such a public admonishment. But it was Zuriel who, after observing the exchange taking place between the two angelic titans, stepped forward to let his voice be heard.

"If I may, with all due respect," he offered calmly to Sandel. "Whether or not Anahel had the authority to officiate tonight's Blessing, one cannot ignore the irrefutable evidence that has revealed itself to us regarding the Apocrypha and the boy Jacob, no matter his lineage."

"Evidence," Sandel echoed with a dismissive snicker. "One can hardly call the mending of a wound to a Nephilim's leg due to a reckless swipe of a sword irrefutable. I would think you of all would be more discriminating in weighing such a claim considering what happened with the last anointed Light Bearer."

"You would be remiss to infer the White Circle as being a cabal formed from gullibility," Zuriel was quick to snap. "Which is why our first order of business the moment this matter was brought to our attention was to dispel the fog of skepticism into which we found ourselves engulfed."

"Yes, yes, yes, I know all about your seeking Azrael's aid to steer you toward the clearing, as I understand it, by way of the River."

"We called upon Azrael. The River was his choosing."

"And now I stand in a room of converts who believe they have witnessed the first miracle of a prophecy reborn." Sandel's scrutinizing gaze slowly searched out each of the Guides standing in different positions inside the Hall before quickly zeroing in on the hulking angel Eksel.

"What of you, Eksel?" he asked. "Does your participation in tonight's gathering mean you've undergone a change of heart; you who've been the most plain-spoken, to put it kindly, in your feelings regarding the boy?"

Eksel who never looked a day as if there existed somewhere in creation anyone or anything which could stand nose to nose with his own exceptional brawn suddenly revealed a subtle meekness in the chink of armored hardness in which he was encased.

"I'll be the first to admit I've shown little if any restraint in my disdain for Jacob Parrish and have voiced on more than one occasion words which were loud and pointed in their repugnance concerning him," admitted Eksel. "But it was only because what I was forced to witness was, in my eyes, nothing short of blasphemous."

His words brought a faint trace of glee to the corners of Sandel's stern lips.

"It's completely understandable. And how do you feel now standing in the midst of this unorthodox, not to mention unsanctioned ceremony?" Sandel who had on more than a few occasions lent an ear to Eksel's vicious ranting about the boy, asked. "Are you of the belief a Light Bearer walks amongst you?"

The Hall grew even more quiet, if that were possible, as Eksel felt every eye fix itself on him. Eksel in turn looked to Jacob, but the disdain which the boy saw plainly whenever the angel glanced his way in the past was nowhere to be seen. In fact, it had long dissipated in recent days, ever since the angel offered Jacob his apology, awkward as it was, in the chapel on the night before Gotham's funeral.

"If I were to be completely honest," Eksel began, "yes, I do!"

The answer deflated the salivating grin from Sandel's mouth while forming a friendly and sincere one on Eksel's. Jacob returned the gesture knowing the hate the angel had for him, justified or not, was no more.

"I see," Sandel remarked while struggling to conceal any hint of bitterness beginning to well up inside him. "A Nephilim, by some sleight of hand, reverses the permanent stillness only Azrael's hand can bring. An incredible feat, I myself will admit. But in no way does it prove beyond any shadow of doubt that one has been touched by the prophecy."

Damiel, who had remained a quiet and brooding observer since Sandel's unexpected arrival, could no longer hold his tongue and stepped forward.

"How can you stand there and say with a straight face it proves nothing?" he pressed with growing impatience. "Have you ever known a Nephilim to have the ability to resurrect miles upon miles of river rendered dead, including its inhabitants left to rot and decay on its surface? If not by the Seventh Grace, then by what means?"

"The Apocrypha, as you should very well know, is quite specific in its telling on what signs will reveal whom the prophecy of the Light Bearer has come to settle upon," said Sandel.

"We are all of us quite aware of what the Apocrypha states," Damiel growled with ever-growing annoyance.

"Then you'll know the true power of the Seventh Grace can only be revealed in the resurrection of a soul."

Damiel's mouth unlocked itself to answer back but Anahel was quick to silence him with a subtle quieting gesture of his hand before a word escaped his lips.

"I hear what you are saying, Sandel. And by your own words spoken just now, how can you of anyone call into question what occurred in the waters of the River?" Anahel calmly questioned. "After all, what constitutes the sanctity of life more than that which has acted as a womb for countless souls."

"I am not here to debate the qualifying markers in affirming the miracle of resurrection nor to rewrite the creed of the Apocrypha," Sandel replied firmly. "The fact remains the scale used to measure the possession of the Seventh

Grace has always required the weight of evidence which can only come from the act of reversing the current of a departed soul not sparking movement in stilled waters."

"But Jacob did do that," came a voice in protest.

The sudden outcry caused Sandel to spin around and cast his glare in the direction of Jacob where, to the surprise of everyone gathered inside the Hall, the usually cautious Ethan had stepped forward in defense of his friend.

"I'm sorry," Sandel said in a withering tone that all but dared the boy to keep his tongue from rolling back and retreating into the hole that was his throat like a spooked rodent.

"What you just said didn't happen, actually did," said Ethan. "The whole resurrecting a soul, that is."

"Keep quiet, Ethan," Jacob, wishing to not have further attention brought upon himself in what had already become an uncomfortable topic of debate, scolded under his breath. But it was too late.

"What *is* this child talking about?" inquired Sandel to no one in particular.

Ethan suddenly became as pale as the unnerving presence of white looming over him with his cold, yet burning glare and clammed up.

"I think he's referring to what happened in the Silent Forest on the night Thaniel…you know…" Max interjected. "On account of what happened with Mist."

"And whom, may I ask, is Mist?" asked Sandel.

"The wolf," answered Anahel, directing Sandel's attention to the creature sitting straight and alert at Jacob's side who was as snow-white as the angel himself, only pleasingly so. "For whatever reason, she took to the boy shortly after he arrived in Eden, and they've been inseparable ever since."

"She came to Jacob's rescue as he was being attacked by Thaniel and managed to knock him backward into the Through. But before he fell into the water, Thaniel swung at Mist and pierced her with his sword," explained Max. "If it weren't for Jacob she wouldn't be here now."

"They say the boy restored the animal's soul as he healed her wound," Anahel remarked quietly to Sandel.

"Is that what they say?" said Sandel, narrowing his icy stare on the wolf with a dissecting intensity. "Then one would be inclined to realize more clearly this call to faith by such a resounding chorus who witnessed such a remarkable aberration…if in fact it's true."

"Of course it's true. Why would we make something like that up?" Ethan argued heatedly. "Jacob brought Mist back to life. We all saw it with our own eyes."

Sandel shot Ethan a silencing glare before looking pointedly at Leos, Kairo and Max, who stood beside their friend like loyal soldiers with self-assured looks on their faces expressing a readiness to testify about the "remarkable aberration."

"If in fact it's true…" Sandel grumbled, his voice rising sharply in annoyance at being interrupted, "then, as I so stated, it's quite remarkable. But, remarkable as it may be, I must point out, lest it be forgotten by my brothers, that the true mark of one who holds the power of the Seventh Grace in hand has the ability to navigate the soul residing in a human vessel, not beast."

"Come now, Sandel, you know as well as I a soul is a soul. Why should we look upon a clear act of dominance over Death as anything less than just because of the physical shape it came to inhabit?" asked Zuriel.

"I am only reciting what we have all come to understand as the basic principle regarding the most sacred of gifts bestowed upon each of us and the rest of our brethren, and I think you would all agree with me that now is not the time to rewrite such dogma."

"Truth be told," continued Sandel, "it's not the question of resurrection that weighs heavy on my mind, but the undisputed loss of a soul."

The grim reminder brought a noticeable pall upon the Hall.

"Yes…what happened to Gothamel has left us all in a grief-stricken state, as you can well imagine," Anahel remarked glumly.

"It's not Gothamel of whom I'm referring," Sandel quickly made clear, "but our brother Thaniel."

"Thaniel conspired with that dark viper Lilith against Eden and in doing so slaughtered Gothamel in a cruel manner even man would be hesitant to commit. His fate is as it should be," Damiel snapped with brimming contempt.

"I wish I could be as steadfast in my judgment about the unfortunate course of events that have befallen this soiled Garden as you, Damiel. Particularly if I had stumbled upon them like a blind man tapping his way along a sidewalk with only a white walking cane to guide his steps."

Anahel was quick to speak before a single utterance in retort could make itself heard from Damiel's parting lips.

"You've always been prudent and direct in the aim of your words, Sandel," the angel noted. "What exactly is it you're attempting to infer?"

"I was not present in the Silent Forest to witness this so-called conspiracy between Thaniel and those forces we so revile, as was no one else in this room," answered Sandel. "No one, that is, except a jury, conveniently convened at the scene of the crime, made up of the son of our enemy and his band of loyal foot soldiers."

The white angel's eyes had once again leveled itself on Jacob, and again the boy refused to shrink under its icy glare.

"And from these babes' mouths the worst charge that could be leveled against a brethren of ours was spit forth, and without hesitation, or history upon which to build such a claim, it was believed and rendered as such without question by those who knew better."

The crushingly contemptuous tone in Sandel's voice would have forced most whose ears it met to their knees. But Jacob refused to allow the angel to intimidate him any further, even as his own knees quivered ever so slightly, and managed to offer back a firm, if not quiet, reply in return: "We told the truth."

"We liked Thaniel," Ethan was quick to add. "He was our favorite Guide. Why would we make up a horrible lie like this about him?"

"Why indeed?" Sandel, his laser-like attention remaining fixed on Jacob, questioned. "Then perhaps you can help make sense to the rest of us the nature of his demise. If in fact this so-called nefarious collusion between Thaniel and the dark mistress Lilith did indeed take place, how do you then explain by your own account the sudden turn about by the residents of the Underneath with whom Thaniel was scheming who overcame him and dragged him away kicking and screaming into the black swamp from which there is no return?"

"How does one explain with any thread of logic the nature of unfortunate beings who have been embalmed in a specially concocted formaldehyde of evil?" Anahel remarked before Jacob or the other boys could answer. "What has happened here is a tragedy beyond comprehension of which we are all trying to come to grips. I fail to see how your aggressive line of questioning of Jacob here will bring any of us one step closer to closure on the matter. After all, the boy is not on trial now, is he?"

Sandel stood quiet for a moment or two, his gaze not wavering from Jacob's.

"No. He isn't," he said when he finally answered before quickly adding in the same breath, "for now, at least."

"What exactly do you mean by that?" Damiel questioned brusquely.

Jacob breathed a sigh of relief when Sandel's leering eyes and looming shadow finally left him.

"The point of my visit this evening was to inform you I've moved to convene the Iudicium Tribunal before which Jacob Parrish here will be called upon to testify," the white angel announced.

The Hall momentarily erupted in a grumbling of confusion between the young Nephilim before Anahel restored silence with a simple wave of his hand.

"Testify? Concerning what, may I ask?" inquired Anahel.

"Surely, you didn't think I was going to allow this travesty of a Blessing to take place without recourse, did you?" answered Sandel whose unsettling grin fixed upon his thin lips was the only crack to the cold stern mask he wore. "Those who ignore history are doomed to repeat it. Be clear I am here to ensure your inclination to lend such a sacred act to mockery by befouling it with another Fallen offspring is one mistake I won't see you make again."

"You miserable—" Damiel seethed under his breath while taking three intimidating steps toward Sandel before Anahel stopped him from taking the fourth.

"As I told you, Sandel, the White Circle has already convened on the matter," Anahel noted coolly and calmly even as his golden eyes flickered with a simmering fire.

"And as I told you, Anahel, you do not hold the authority, nor does the White Circle, to make any declaration concerning the naming of the Light Bearer," said Sandel firmly. "Oh, by all means continue with your celebration; in fact, I insist you do. But rest assured the Blessing you performed today will hold no validity outside the walls of Havenhid, and the only Light Bearer that will be recognized this night are the orbs of light shining above us to illuminate this festive Hall."

"Your prejudice is only delaying the inevitable, you know that, Sandel," said Anahel. "Have your hearing if you insist, but even the staunchest denier of the White Circle was forced to accept the truth when confronted with evidence proving what has come to pass; and that is Jacob Parrish, son of Samael, is the Light Bearer long foretold, whether it is to your liking or not."

Sandel's only reply came with a widening of his grin.

"I'll send word when the boy is to appear before the Tribunal," he said as he quickly turned on his heel to leave sending the Nephilim boys gathered close about to scurry out of his way like mice caught in the path of a cat. "And I would advise that you counsel the lad in coming up with a more believable explanation concerning Thaniel's last moments. I have no doubt the members of the Tribunal—myself included—will be interested in learning what really occurred in the Silent Forest."

He was halfway to the entrance of the Hall where the two hulking figures who had accompanied him stood patiently waiting at attention when his son Creed made a beeline to stop his father in his steps in order to whisper something of what appeared to be of great urgency in his ear.

"Ah, yes, that reminds me," said Sandel, turning once more to face the gathering. "There is one more matter of great importance I have somehow managed to overlook."

"And what matter would that be, Sandel?" asked Anahel with a noted sigh of tediousness.

"The Sword of Destiny."

"What of it?" Damiel, suddenly stepping forward and taking a stance that without words all but demanded any further inquiry of the subject be directed his way, asked.

"As I understand it, Mr. Parrish is currently in possession of it, is he not?"

"He is. Though I don't see what concern it should be of yours either way."

The silence that followed, enveloping the Hall, was broken only by the clicking of Sandel's steps as he began to wander the open space of the great room in a slow, measured manner.

"When the Sword of Destiny was still in its first incarnation as an old Roman spearhead, Gothamel managed to claim its long-sought out power by seizing it from the Nazi forces bred into existence by the Darkness itself to bring forth a horror upon the populace unlike any the world could ever before imagine or come to know since," said Sandel. "The members of the Iudicium Tribunal, against my fervent opposition, saw fit to leave the spear in Gothamel's care feeling that if anyone was able to protect its power from ever falling again into the hands of a malefic force it would be the once-great-defender of the Light. But Gothamel's ability to oversee such a duty has ended, and—"

"And let me guess," interrupted Damiel, "you're here to relieve the boy of the responsibility of being caretaker of the Sword."

"I see it more as freeing him of what I could only imagine to be an unpleasant burden the weight of such a powerful weapon will surely bring him in time, if not already," corrected Sandel.

"Your compassion is exemplary as always," Damiel quipped sarcastically. "But whether it be a responsibility or burden of the highest order, I can attest Jacob here is well equipped for the challenge."

Hearing such words coming from Damiel, who was known aside from his name as the Angel of the Sword, warmed Jacob with a hugging sensation of confidence, even as it brought a darkening shadow to Sandel's steely face.

"May I remind you, Damiel, there remains in existence an unwritten agreement which states that should the line of ownership be severed, custodianship of the Sword of Destiny would be overseen by the Seraphim," Sandel grumbled dourly.

"I'm well aware of the agreement of which you speak," said Damiel. "But you seem to have overlooked one small but very important thing: the line of ownership concerning the Sword has yet to be severed. Gothamel made sure of that in his dying moments, which as you well know is the only way the Sword would have ever found its way into the boy's care."

The white angel was slowly growing more incensed.

"I can assure you the members of the Iudicium Tribunal will not stand idly by and permit the spearhead that turned a veil of Light into a burial shroud to be wielded by yet another instrument of Darkness, much less this…this…false prophecy," Sandel spit in Jacob's direction, his face screwed tightly inward as if he had just taken a swig from a glass of curdled milk.

"As I see it, they really have no choice in the matter," Damiel retorted coolly drawing another searing look from Sandel.

"I will be taking the Sword this night," Sandel hissed insistently.

"You will regret any attempt, I assure you," challenged Damiel.

As Damiel took another step forward toward Sandel as if to place an exclamation point on his threat, Jacob scurried forward placing himself in the line of fire.

"Whoa, whoa, whoa…this is getting way more serious than it needs to be," he said, placing a halting hand firmly on Damiel's chest flexed and puffed with strength ready to be expelled. "After all, Sandel's only expressing how he feels. And who know, maybe he's right."

"Well, then," said a somewhat surprised Sandel, "it appears you do, indeed, possess some reason."

"Maybe I am the wrong person to be entrusted with something as important and powerful as the Sword of Destiny," Jacob continued turning to Sandel once Damiel had cooled his heels. "I mean, no one was more upset than I was to discover I'm the son of one of the worst Fallen there probably ever was. If I were in your shoes, I'm not sure I would give me much more than a suspicious eye as well. And who knows, maybe I am exactly what you believe me to be: a false prophecy, and I'm sure much worse. So if you want to free me of this sword as you say you do, then go ahead."

A victorious smile formed itself like a snake slithering across Sandel's smug face while Damiel's became crestfallen.

"I don't believe you," Damiel protested under his breath at the boy's easy surrender as Jacob stretched open his left wing slightly to offer Sandel a glimpse of the hilt of the legendary weapon secured in a hidden sleeve formed amongst the feathered quills.

"Like I said, you can have the sword," Jacob repeated once more to Sandel while ignoring Damiel. "All you have to do is take it."

With those words, Sandel's smugness melted instantly like the remnants of a freak snow storm on a desert floor and instead the white angel reflected a renewed contempt, especially when he spied a flicker of mocking defiance gleaming gleefully in Jacob's eyes. For Sandel knew, as did everyone else gathered inside the Hall, that it would be an instant and most unpleasant end to anyone who foolishly chose to accept such a dare.

"If I were him, I'd take some pointers from Betreyel first before even trying that," Ethan remarked under his breath recalling the angel he witnessed make a grab for the Sword that fateful night in the Silent Forest only to be instantly incinerated before his very eyes.

"Good idea, Ethan. If anyone has a broom and a dustpan handy, I'll go fetch what's left of him in the Silent Forest," said Max, drawing amused snickers from the other boys. " 'Course, we're gonna need a whole heck of a lot of glue before he's in any condition to give a testimonial."

The growing chorus of giggles only served to incense Sandel more.

"This isn't over, mark my words. And I'll see you pay for this," he threatened pointedly at Jacob before turning briskly and storming off in a huff.

~ ~ ~

There came suddenly a loud obnoxious rumbling and with it the towering walls of the Hall of Light as well as the teenage Nephilim boys crowded around Jacob offering congratulatory pats to his back quickly began to disintegrate like a watercolor left out in the rain and disappeared into the ether.

The sound of a car engine backfiring loudly pierced the quiet of the morning like a gunshot and Jacob, looking stone-faced and grim just as he did that night he watched Sandel sweep angrily out of Havenhid, turned his eyes toward the noise to see an old, beat-up turquoise and white Volkswagen van looking every bit its forty-plus years rounding the corner off of Flora Avenue. Amazed that something had to come along that managed to drown out the garbage truck still slowly making its rounds, Jacob watched as the van rattled and wheezed its way along the street framing the western edge of the park, leaving a trail of exhaust in its wake. The look of amusement, however, slowly fell away from his face, as the van drew nearer grumbling and belching smoke and Jacob was able to get a glance at the driver of the rattling heap.

It was Ty Wrenwood.

Instead of waving down his best friend, Jacob climbed off the jungle gym and, as inconspicuously as he could, quickly walked away in the opposite direction. Leaving the park, he crossed Juniper Street before turning a corner and making his way rapidly down Forest Avenue. With the sound of the Volkswagen van still rumbling faintly in his ear somewhere in the background, he veered course down a small alleyway behind Mr. Hanker's hardware store and the moment he was certain he had slipped away without being detected he breathed a sigh of relief.

It wasn't that he didn't want to see his best friend. In fact, he had greatly missed Ty's eccentric antics more than he thought he would during his time away from Cain's Corner and struggled with himself not to wave down his friend as he drove by the park. Why he stopped himself, he wasn't quite certain. Maybe it was because he questioned whether or not Ty would be as receptive to a surprise reunion after having been ditched out of the blue for an entire year without so much as an explanation. Or perhaps, maybe, he wondered if his friend might discover him to be as different and changed as he felt on the inside.

Whatever the reason, Jacob knew he'd eventually be forced to face Ty sooner or later. Cain's Corner was much too small a place, with far too few alleyways and side streets to duck down to avoid his friend forever. What he didn't anticipate was the moment pouncing upon him immediately when the van suddenly reappeared and came to a screeching halt on the side of the street just as Jacob reached the sidewalk at the end of the alleyway. He stood frozen in his spot, fixed with the same startled, dumbfounded expression being returned his way from a surprised Ty slouched behind the steering wheel.

For the first time since his quiet, inconspicuous homecoming, Jacob wished he was back in Eden.

CHAPTER FOUR

SANCTUARY

"**S**o ..."croaked Jacob, desperate to break the tension as the two boys sat in the front seat of the parked van enveloped in an awkward silence. "This is an interesting ride. What happened to the Junior Lee?"

The Junior Lee was an old, run-down 1969 Dodge Charger Ty had bought the summer before Jacob left Cain's Corner with the dream of transforming the gray primer-painted eyesore into a flashy replica of the iconic General Lee that Bo and Luke Duke drove in the TV show "The Dukes of Hazzard."

"Got rid of it," Ty grumbled sourly.

"But why? Last I remember you were close to exchanging nuptials with it," asked Jacob.

"With the amount of money I was pouring into fixing it up, I'd probably come out ahead just buying the original car," answered Ty. "Besides, with the way things are today, driving around in something named after a Confederate probably wouldn't be the smartest thing. With my luck, I'd end up being fire-bombed by some woke moron who sees a tribute to the least hateful show ever on TV as the equivalent of walking down the street swinging a noose in public."

Jacob couldn't help but feel just a tad sorry for Ty as he literally witnessed the long-held fantasy of being a good 'ol boy out-running the law along the rural roads outside Cain's Corner in his Confederate flag-emblazoned chariot while honking the tune to "Dixie" slowly die in his eyes.

"Yeah, well, this could be nice, too...you know, once you get it fixed up a bit more," Jacob remarked in as uplifting a manner as he could muster while giving the musty smelling van they were seated inside a woeful once-over. "It's definitely free of controversy."

"You can say that again." Jacob's attempt to throw sunlight Ty's way only seemed to darken his friend's mood. "I look like Keith Partridge driving around in this thing."

"That's a bit of a self-inflated comparison. I could definitely see Danny Partridge, but Keith?" razzed Jacob, hoping his deprecative jab focusing on the ruddy, less attractive younger brother of the one-time TV idol and heartthrob to millions of teen girls might lighten the mood. But his attempt failed to even draw a twitch of a grin from the corners of Ty's mouth.

"I take it you're still p.o.'d at me, huh?" Jacob asked finally.

"Why should I be p.o.'d at you?" answered Ty, though it was clear from the tone of his voice there was some serious grudge-holding happening on his part. "I mean, just because you up and vanished like a fart in the wind without saying a word to anyone, especially your best friend, is no real big deal. In fact, there's people out there in the world who make their living performing similar tricks. Who knows, if you take your act out on the road to say Las Vegas, you might end up becoming a modern-day Harry Houdini. Just a word of advice: You might not want to leave your audience waiting around for a year until you finally decide to reappear again. I don't know of anyone who has the patience or that kind of attention span."

"Don't you want me to explain to you what happened?"

"I already know; Wray told me. You went away to undergo some kind of cloak-and-dagger medical procedure to fix whatever was going on with your back," said Ty, sinking deeper in his seat as he stewed. "Still doesn't let you off the hook for doing what you did. I mean…I thought we were best friends."

"We were…we are!" said Jacob.

"Sure didn't feel like it…not when you keep something like that a secret."

"Would it make you feel any better to know I felt lousy about it the entire time?" asked Jacob. "Not to mention the fact that I missed you guys and couldn't wait to get back here."

Ty said nothing in return, but instead turned his head to stare out the window, and Jacob could tell just in that moment of silence and the sight of the back of his friend's head that he was on the verge of cracking the stubborn egg.

"I want to mend fences; just tell me what I have to do," Jacob pleaded. "I'll do anything within reason; even suffer through listening to your latest outing hypothesis."

Ty, for as long as Jacob had known him, had a quirky, if not annoying proclivity of looking for and then exposing gay subtext in everything from television shows and movies to music lyrics and books. This peculiar hobby, to be sure, was not one Ty engaged in with any malice or judgment, but rather quite the opposite. Ty, himself, in fact, once attempted to equate his wacky pastime to a heroic social justice cause in which he was attempting to elevate the gay rights cause by opening up the door to a perceived closet many beloved fictional characters had been forced into and locked away by a repressive period in history. Yet while Ty in the past was usually champing at the bit to share with Jacob his latest revelation, it seemed this day he was not the least bit enticed by the offer that was rarely, if ever, made to willingly sit and listen to his far-fetched disclosures.

"I've kinda given up on all that," Ty grumbled sourly. "They were stupid, anyway."

"Oh come on, there was a time not too long ago the only way I could shut you up on the subject was with a roll a duct tape," Jacob teased. "I'll bet you anything you even have a theory on Keith Partridge."

"Sorry to disappoint you. Guess I've done some growing up since you took off."

Again more silence.

Jacob settled back his in seat with a heavy breath before glancing down with growing annoyance toward the floorboard where his feet continued to compete with Ty's backpack for space. He gave the stuffed bag a frustrated kick aside and as he did a book fell out onto the floor.

"Since when did you get into horror classics?" he asked when he picked up the book and to his surprise saw it was a copy of Mary Shelley's "Frankenstein."

"What of it? It was assigned to us to read in my English class," said Ty.

"Ah, gotcha…so you're not actually reading it."

"What do you mean by that? Of course I'm reading it. I just told you it was assigned to us to read in my English class," argued Ty. "Even if it wasn't, it's not a bad book. Much better than the movies."

Jacob held Ty in a blank stare of confusion. "But it's…literature."

"And what exactly do you see when you look at me; an 'Under construction' sign planted in my skull?" asked Ty with a huff of impertinence.

"I just mean I remember it wasn't that long ago when you were proudly touting your own special brand of achieving academic mediocracy," said Jacob. "What was it you called it; the Three C's?"

The Three C's—short for Creative Cognitive Crap—was Ty's specialized method of skating through school without straining a single brain cell over such time-consuming duties like reading books assigned in English class by perfecting the rare talent of talking rubbish out of one's backside, or, as he liked to call it, utilizing the golden rule of B.S. And no one had proven himself to be the master of such ventriloquism as Ty. Or so Jacob thought.

"Yeah, well, the Three C's is not an exact science," admitted Ty, before quietly muttering under his breath, "or so I learned."

It suddenly donned on Jacob. "Wait a minute. Why are you lugging around your backpack when it's still August?"

"Let's just say Mrs. Kretch gave me two choices: either I take a fail in her English class or she'd give me an incomplete and allow me to make up the class over the summer," explained Ty. "Apparently, the answers I gave on the essay portion of the final exam covering 'Frankenstein' was the last straw for her."

"What answers did you...?" Jacob started to ask when a lightbulb went off in his head. "Oh, no...tell me you didn't?"

Ty sat staring out the driver's side window with his lips sealed defiantly shut, but eventually even he couldn't abide by his willful resistance to answer.

"You really can't expect me turn a blind eye and pretend that Victor Frankenstein wasn't a total closet case when it's totally obvious he was, can you?" he finally blurted out.

"You did," Jacob muttered while burying his face his hands.

"Oh, please, Mary Shelley all but had Frankenstein and his 'friend' Henry Clerval playing house together. That's how they're referred to over and over again in the book: 'friend,' 'friend,' 'friend,'" said Ty, digging quote marks into the air to stress his point. "You know what 'friend' meant back in the days this book was written? It was code speak for two flamboyant dandies. If they existed back then, a big 'ol winking emoji would have been stamped beside each reference of 'friend.'"

Usually, Jacob would have already had a look fixed on his face that bordered between weariness and utter perplexity as he listened to his friend. This time, however, a hint of amusement curled the corners of his mouth. Truth be told, he was relieved to witness Ty shake off his sullen state and snap back to his old self with all his oddball charm intact.

"So here goes Victor Frankenstein on a mad quest to create a new human creation. Not a woman, as you might expect, but a man. And, mind you, not the hideous creature with the coffee table head and electrodes coming out of his neck you see in the horror flicks, but something he first sees as beautiful," continued Ty.

Unable to listen to the diatribe being spewed forth with a sort of strange fascination, Jacob couldn't help but interrupt. "Hold up," he said. "Are you suggesting he was trying to create his perfect…partner?"

"Uh…*DUH!*" answered Ty matter-of-factly. "It's only when he finally brings the Creature to life that he looks upon it as ugly. His repulsion of the Creature and eventual rejection of it is actually a rejection of his own sexual identity which he also views as something ugly and terrifying. This hateful reversal Frankenstein shows towards his Creature mirrors the deep-seated homophobia gripping society at the time. As a result the Creature goes on a violent, murderous rampage demonstrating the repressive social norms that kept Frankenstein from being an out and proud gay man in the first place."

When Ty finally finished, Jacob couldn't manage anything more than cast a blank look at his friend while trying to digest the heaping helping of unmitigated nonsense he had ever heard come from another human being's mouth. And yet it was spoken with such cavalier assuredness that Jacob couldn't help but wonder, if only but for the briefest of moments, if he had just unwittingly bared witness to an utterly brilliant deciphering of a written work that until now had gone unnoticed by even the shrewdest of literary experts.

"Wow!" was all he could reply at first.

"I know! And yet I'm the one who is forced to redo the class over the summer," said Ty who remained oblivious to the fact his friend had been left in a stunned state by both the "creative" and "crap" elements of his Three C's.

"So, you hungry?" asked Ty suddenly.

"I can eat," Jacob answered with an indifferent shrug.

"Great," said Ty with a smile as he ignited the loud rumbling of his van with a turn of the ignition key. "Because the first step in mending fences is buying me lunch."

~ ~ ~

The lunch crowd was already beginning to roll in at Rabble-Rousers when Jacob and Ty took a seat at a booth inside the quaint but popular restaurant. Looking over the menu, Jacob was suddenly reminded of the breakfast he picked at, more that ate, when he felt his stomach give out a hungry grumble. But as he was weighing all the delicious-looking options he had to choose from, he was quickly distracted by the feeling of being watched, and glanced up to find Ty quietly sitting across from him with a curious gaze fixed his way instead of the open menu he was holding open in front of him.

"What?" Jacob, feeling as though he had an embarrassing booger hanging from his nose, asked.

"Nothing," answered Ty. "It's just…something about you just seems, I don't know… different."

It wasn't the sort of thing a kid concealing a pair of wings under a t-shirt wanted to hear.

"It's probably just the hair. I've been meaning to get it cut," said Jacob as he fidgeted self- consciously in his seat while brushing his fingers through his shaggier than usual mop hoping that by combing some of the longer strands forward he might conceal whatever tell-tale sign was causing Ty to cast such a suspicious look his way.

Both boys returned their attentions back to their menus but, in a matter of seconds, Jacob felt the weight of Ty's eyes settle themselves on him once more. This time he found Ty with a curious look fixed on his face while his body slowly leaned in the same direction as his craning neck as though trying to sneak a peek behind Jacob.

"What is it now?" Jacob huffed in a tone that betrayed more an annoyance than uneasiness.

"Can't really make out much of a difference from here," Ty said as his eyes squinted themselves into two thin slits.

"A difference in what?"

"You know…" answered Ty by motioning over his shoulder to his own back with his thumb before straightening himself up in his seat. "So what exactly did you have done? I mean, did they have to slice you open and cut out the bone and muscle, or whatever it was that was causing those two weird humps on your back?"

"It wasn't quite that invasive," said Jacob.

"But you're all normal now?"

"As opposed to before when I was some misshapen freak?"

"You know what I mean," said Ty.

"Yeah, I'm all normal now," said Jacob after a thoughtful pause.

The half-hearted grin he forced forth slowly faded when he realized how untrue a statement it was that he spoke, and that even amongst other Nephilim he was anything but normal.

"So, can I see?" asked Ty.

"See?"

"How it looks; your back, that is."

The thought horrified Jacob. "We're in a restaurant. I'm not taking off my shirt in here."

"I don't mean now. Good god, man, I'm getting ready to eat here," crowed an equally horrified Ty. "I'm talking later. You know, for curiosity sake."

"Let's just wait and see," said Jacob who had no intention of making good on either the waiting or especially the seeing. "I'm still kind of in the recovery stage.

Ty's expression screwed itself up in look of puzzlement. "Recovery? How long of a recovery do you need? You've been gone for a year now," he said before his face suddenly lit up once more. "Are the scars really that bad?"

Jacob was never more relieved when the waitress at that moment saved him from the interrogation when she finally made her way to their table and, in a noticeably frazzled voice, asked to take their order. But the familiarity of her voice caught Jacob immediately, and when he glanced up, his face morphed into a look of utter surprise.

"Wray?"

She looked up unexpectedly from scribbling order notes in the pad in her hand, and when she saw Jacob seated in the booth before her it was as it she had been struck by a bolt gun used on the cows headed to the slaughterhouse to make the burgers she was serving by the armful to her hungry customers.

"Jacob?"

They both then turned their gaze onto Ty who shrank somewhat into the vinyl upholstery of the booth, especially when he caught sight of the unhappy glare shooting out of Jacob's eye sockets.

"Oh yeah…I guess I forgot to mention Wray was working here now," he said with apologetic sheepishness over his brain fart.

Despite wanting to give Ty a sharp slap to the side of his head, Jacob did his best to mask the obvious awkwardness suddenly thrust upon him by offering Wray a smile. "So, how are things with you?"

"Fine. They're fine," Wray was quick to answer, sounding as anxious as Jacob felt.

"You look great," said Jacob. And did she ever. Even in her uniform of dark jeans and unfortunate print top, she glowed in his eyes.

"I don't know about that," she giggled self-consciously while running a hand along the side of her golden blonde hair which was pulled back from her face in a sort of a loose pony tail. "You look great, too."

"I don't know about that," replied Jacob. He didn't mean to mimic Wray both in words and action, and when he caught himself running his fingers through the hair over his ear he shut his eyes and clenched his jaw with embarrassment.

"Cute," he heard a tickled Ty mutter under his breath and shot his friend a quieting look in return.

This was not the way he had hoped to meet up again with Wray.

"So when did you get home?" asked Wray.

"Three days ago," answered Jacob.

"Really? Three days." A sudden frigidness seemed to sweep over Wray and steal the slight crack of warmth found in her not fully formed smile. "Your grandmother must be very happy to have you back home. I know she was missing you while you were away."

Jacob observed a strange aloofness in her and as he held her in his narrowing gaze she began to fidget with a noticeable agitation.

"Look, I've got other tables I've got to get to, so I better take your order and get moving," she said.

She looked to Ty and quickly scribbled down his order of a cheeseburger with the works, fries and a large soda before turning back with an obvious display of impatience to Jacob.

"I'll have the same thing," he said almost cautiously. "Only make mine with a veggie patty, and I'll take a chocolate shake instead of soda."

Wray then snatched the menus from both boys in a gruff manner that all but left them with numerous paper cuts.

"I'll be back with your order shortly," she said with a huff before stomping away from the table.

"Since when did you start eating veggie burgers?" asked Ty.

Jacob ignored the question and asked instead, "So, what's up with her?"

"Whadda ya mean?" asked Ty, looking oblivious.

"Didn't it seem to you like Wray had a bit of an attitude? Like she was pissed off at something?"

"Maybe she's in desperate need of some gel insoles for her shoes," he replied. "Or maybe—and I'm no therapist by any stretch—just maybe she's a bit teed off at you."

"What reason would she have to be teed off at me?"

"Well, let's put our heads together and think about this for a minute. What possible reason would Wray have to be pissed off at you?" mused Ty as if searching the deep recesses of his brain. "Hmm, I wonder if it has anything to do with the fact you ditched her out of the blue and disappeared with no explanation for close to a year. You know, the same thing you did to me."

"But I'm back now," said Jacob.

"Wow," replied Ty, cocking his head and staring at his friend with a quizzical look. "You say that as though she just found a golden ticket inside a Wonka candy bar."

"Well, hopefully she'll get over it," Jacob muttered, though more to himself than Ty. "After all, you did."

"Whoa there, Bucky Bob, and pull back on those reins a bit," Ty quickly interjected. "Don't think all is forgiven and forgotten between you and me. I'm still harboring a little bit of disgruntlement myself."

"I'm buying you lunch," Jacob reminded his friend. "I thought that was the deal to let bygones be bygones."

"I said it was the start," argued Ty. "It's going to take more than a few fries to subjugate the rage I've been living with over such a personal sleight."

Oh, the drama, Jacob thought as he rolled his eyes.

"It's amazing what the 'Word a Day' app has done to boost your vocabulary while I've been gone. I remember a time not long ago when you thought subjugate was a grammar exercise involving verbs," said Jacob, drawing (not surprisingly) a blank look from Ty. "Fortunately, Wray is much more mature when it comes to grown-up issues."

"Hey, my middle name is 'Mature,' " Ty spat in return, before blowing into the end of his straw to shoot the paper wrapping into Jacob's face.

"My mistake," Jacob said with a muster of calm oftentimes seen demonstrated by parents in the presence of obnoxious five-year-olds. "All I'm saying is she'll come around after the shock of seeing me again passes. Trust me."

He quickly quieted himself when he caught sight of Wray headed back to the booth balancing a tray loaded with their orders.

"So that's two cheeseburgers with everything on them, and one soda for you, Ty," Wray said with a noticeable lilt of pleasantness in her voice as she placed the order on the table in front of the two hungry boys.

Jacob was pleased to see a smile returned to Wray's pretty face.

"Looks good," he said with a smile while shooting Ty a "I told you so" wink.

"Oh, and I almost forgot your chocolate milkshake," Wray said as her smile grew wider.

"Yes, you did," chuckled Jacob.

Only instead of setting the tall fountain glass down on the table, Wray raised it over Jacob's head. In an instant, he felt an unexpected assault of freezing unpleasantness rain down on him as the chocolatey confection was dumped on his head, whipped cream topping and all, and left to run down over his face, across his chest and back and into his lap in a slow frigid sticky ooze. The restaurant fell instantly silent as the other stupefied patrons looked on from their tables at the spectacle with several rethinking their choice of beverage.

"Enjoy your meal," Wray sang, looking most pleased before walking off. Ty remained frozen solid, looking as shocked as Jacob felt.

"Whoa, dude, you look like the poor victim of a freak and very unfortunate Porta-Potty malfunction," he finally managed to say all while trying desperately to keep his snickering suppressed.

Despite his frozen state as he sat stiff as board while dripping chocolate like some slow-melting fudgesicle bar, it wasn't enough to keep the slow burn of anger from finally erupting inside Jacob. In a flash, he was on his feet, slipping and sliding awkwardly across the floor made slippery by the drippings of the shake coming off his body as he chased after Wray.

When he finally managed to catch up to her, he grabbed her by the shoulder both to stop her in her retreat and to keep from taking an embarrassing header as his right foot came in contact with a glob of shake and slid out from under him and out to the right.

"What the hell was that—"

His angry bellow was instantly silenced when Wray spun around and delivered not a hard, stinging slap to the side of the face, but a full on, jaw-cracking punch that left Jacob in a more stunned state than the milkshake dumped over his head.

"You've got a lot of nerve, do you know that Jacob Parrish?" she barked back at him. "Who do you think you are anyway? First you disappear and leave town without so much as an explanation or a goodbye to your so-called friends. If it wasn't for your grandmother telling me when I finally went to your house to find out where you were I would have thought you just somehow fell off the planet or been abducted by aliens. Then you have the gall to waltz in here and order lunch like nothing had happened and tell me you've been back in town for three days. *Three*. Days."

A wave of embarrassment swept over Jacob, both by the dressing down he quietly admitted he deserved and the feel of eyes from the other customers firmly watching the bizarre soap opera from their tables, and it instantly nipped his anger in the bud.

"Look, I can explain—" he sputtered through the brown dripping mask streaking down his face, but he was quickly kept from going any further.

"Just do me and yourself a favor," said Wray, "and go scratch!"

With that she stomped off once again.

It took a little bit to embarrass Jacob, and standing in the middle of a restaurant covered in chocolate milkshake with a crowd witnessing his utter ruination by the one who set his heart to fluttering certainly fit the bill. This was most definitely not the way he pictured his homecoming to be with Wray. And if it wasn't for the fact the milkshake had felt like it had begun to congeal into some kind of uncomfortable, sticky shell around his upper body he might have bolted, but it was as if the chocolate remnants gumming to the soles of his sneakers had cemented him to the floor.

"Look on the bright side," said Ty who was suddenly at his side offering his friend a consoling pat on the back while mindfully doing his best to not soil his hand. "At least you were able to demonstrate to yours truly an invaluable lesson on how two mature people go about working out their grown-up issues with one another."

He then offered up a thin, flimsy napkin to Jacob. And while Jacob stared daggers at his friend, Ty brought a finger to the corner of his own mouth in a pointing motion. "You got a little something right here."

~ ~ ~

Over the course of the next few days, Jacob did everything he could think of to patch things up with Wray, yet nothing seemed to work. Text messages offering apology after apology went unanswered. Phone calls were diverted to voice mail, and on the rare occasion she answered the first few words he managed to get out of his mouth were met with an abrupt hang-up. Even a big beautiful bouquet of flowers, which Jacob was certain would do the trick at melting, at least somewhat, the ice shelf that had lodged itself between them were returned to him looking as if they had first been run through a chipping machine before being dumped into a box in their new mulch-like state.

"I think it's safe to say there won't be any wedding bells tolling in the near future," said Ty who had acted as courier. "She's even mad at me, and I don't remember doing any kind of disappearing act; although she made it pretty clear to me she wouldn't be opposed to such a favor."

Jacob wasn't the only one pining over the apparent loss of what had become a close and evolving friendship. Despite telling Jacob in her eloquent way to "go scratch," privately Wray couldn't help but mourn his sudden return to Cain's Corner. Not that she was sad to come upon him like she had from out the blue, but that she couldn't show him how much she had missed him while he was away. At least she thought she had missed him; she had been far too mad at him over his unforgivable slight to extend to her the common courtesy of a goodbye before he left, however, to really yearn over him during his absence.

Now that she had dumped some of her pent-up anger on top his head, she found herself in a constant state of mopiness. The days dragged on painfully, and work became a nightmare as she found herself fighting with increased frustration to keep her customers' orders straight. But focusing on such things proved a difficult task when Jacob's face somehow managed to crowd out all other thoughts inside her head, and the constant barrage of calls and texts that kept her phone coming to life inside the pocket of her apron only made efforts to concentrate that much more difficult.

One night, after a particularly tiring day waiting on tables, Wray couldn't have been more relieved to see the last customers finally pay their check and leave so she could finally call it a night. Putting up the "Closed" sign in the window, she then released her long, curled mane of blond hair from its ponytail and gave it a satisfying shaking out with her hand. Her feet were killing her from schlepping countless plates of food and drinks to table after table, and all she longed to do was to step out of her shoes, take a long relaxing hot bath and curl up in her soft robe. Before she could call it a night and head home, the task of closing up for the night remained ahead of her.

Wray looked around the empty restaurant and let out an exhausted groan at the handful of chores still awaiting her attention. Grabbing a grubby bus tub, she made her way with unhurried, shuffling steps to the table where her last customers ate. A pair of crumpled one-dollar bills and some change left to her as a tip in the center of the table seemed a fitting end to her long, tedious day and did little to perk up her spirits. At least, it's better than nothing, she tried to reassure herself. Then, with the music coming through the restaurant's sound system to keep her company in the quiet around her, Wray began to clear the table all while humming and singing along to Elvis Presley's "Always on My Mind."

"I hate that song," Wray eventually grumbled to herself as the song finally faded to a fitting ending.

When she had finished piling all the dirty plates, glasses and utensils into the bus tub, Wray grabbed a wash rag to wipe clean the table and condiments of greasy fingerprints. As she did, the beginning string of notes from a familiar melody rang out through the restaurant and instantly slowed her in her work. She recognized the song even before the lilting bray of Stevie Nicks' voice came like an ethereal sigh through the speakers. But before she could question how the obscure unreleased song had managed to find its way to the commercial airwaves, she suddenly felt as if she was no longer alone in the restaurant. Glancing over her shoulder, she was both caught off guard—and not—to find Jacob standing quietly in the entrance.

"We're closed," she announced brusquely.

"I know. I've been waiting," replied Jacob.

Realizing he had no intention of leaving, Wray picked up the bus tub and made her way towards him, all while biting the bottom of her lip to keep from bursting out in laughter at the sight standing before her. And what a sight it was. Curiously, Jacob looked like he was preparing to hunker down for some unannounced approaching typhoon, wearing a long raincoat, rubber boots and a rain hat that swallowed his head, all while standing under a large umbrella he held in one hand while gripping a white flag of surrender in the other.

Placing the bus tub on a nearby counter, Wray folded her arms tightly across her chest and craned her head forward to give a curious look out the front window at the night outside. "I didn't know we were due for a storm tonight," she noted. "Or, judging by the way you look, a hurricane."

"I just wanted to come prepared," said Jacob. "You know, in case there might be a milkshake or some other beverage within reaching distance."

Cute, thought Wray, all while keeping a straight and expressionless face. "You don't have to be worried. I've served my last shake for the night."

"That's a relief," said Jacob as he quickly tossed aside his umbrella and flag. "I was beginning to feel like a real dork wearing this getup."

"Well, in case you have any doubts, take it from someone standing on this end of the room: you succeeded," replied Wray.

Jacob gave a good-natured chuckle in return and proceeded to remove his hat and coat.

"Hope you don't mind that I hacked into your stereo system with my phone," he said.

"Ah, and here I thought it was by some weird coincidence of fate that it came on," Wray remarked with obvious sarcasm. "But if you don't mind, I think I'll go ahead and turn it off."

"Whoa, whoa…what do you mean turn it off?" There was a slight look of alarm in Jacob's face, as if she had hinted at the possibility of going to the roof of the restaurant and flinging herself off it and onto the pavement below. "You would actually willingly silence the voice of Stevie Nicks; you who have worshipped at her platform boots since the day I first met you?"

It was true. One would have to search far and wide to find a bigger and more devoted fan of the Fleetwood Mac songstress than Wray Bliss, despite the fact a good quarter of a century would pass between the band's explosive heyday in the seventies and her eventual arrival into the world. Then there was the striking resemblance between Wray and her idol. Between the long, wavy blond head of hair and gypsy-like aura encircling Wray, it seemed quite plausible collected flakes of gold dust shaken loose from one of Stevie's iconic shawls had been used to clone a modern-day version of the legend.

"I seem to vaguely remember when you used to play this song over and over again in your car while driving me home from school extolling just how great a song 'Sanctuary' was, and how it was an unforgivable travesty it was never officially released, and left to languish as an underground demo," said Jacob.

"A lot has changed since you've been gone," answered Wray matter-of-factly. "What can I tell you? 'Sanctuary' isn't really a favorite of mine anymore."

Jacob knew Wray wasn't being truthful with her words, no matter how frank she attempted to appear. Obviously, she was still highly ticked-off at him, and rightly so. But knowing better than to challenge her on her fib, Jacob said simply, "That's too bad. It's definitely become my favorite."

For a split second, the icy facade that Wray had encased herself in melted slightly; but only slightly, and only for a moment.

"What are you doing here, Jacob?" she asked coolly.

"Hoping for a chance to talk, that's all."

"What's there to talk about?"

"For starters, I'd like to apologize. It's kind of a hard thing to do when you won't take my calls and ignore my texts," said Jacob. "You know I wouldn't have left the way I did without telling you and at least saying goodbye."

"Then why did you?' asked Wray.

"I tried. In fact, it's the reason why I showed up the way I did at the Homecoming dance," said Jacob "But then when I saw you, looking like you did...I just couldn't. I even found myself rethinking leaving."

Wray could see he was being sincere and, as much as she wanted to hold tight to the grudge she had built up against him, she felt the anger that had languished inside her over the past year begin its slow drain.

"It's alright; I forgive you," she said finally with some reluctance.

The pardon brought a smile to Jacob's face.

"Really?"

Wray conceded with a surrendering roll of her eyes. "But if you ever try and pull a stunt like that again," she was quick to reprimand, "you better make sure you end up in some far corner of the world I can never reach you."

Jacob couldn't help but smirk at the irony of her threat. "Deal."

"Now get out of here. I've got to finish closing up," she said flashing him the first sign of a smile since coming home.

"Just one more thing," said Jacob. And when she inquired what that was, he held out his arms to her and asked simply, "Dance with me?"

"You're joking, right? Here? In the middle of the restaurant?"

"It's not like we have an audience or anything," said Jacob, gesturing to the sea of empty tables.

A rare and enduring shade of bashfulness flushed Wray's face, which only made Jacob step up his request. "They're playing our song."

Unable, or rather unwilling to refuse the pull of his inexperienced charm, Wray tossed the towel she used to wipe down the tables onto a nearby counter then ran her hands across the front of her apron. They both took an awkward step toward one another, and then an even more awkward gesture to embrace one another. But the self-conscious clumsiness they shared quickly dissipated once they had managed to embrace each other in one another's arms and, as they quickly submitted to the slow gentle rocking spawned by the lulling of the music surrounding them, it was as if the stretch of time that had momentarily separated them from each other had never happened.

"I remember the night at Homecoming when I dragged you inside the gym to dance to this song like it was yesterday," said Wray.

"Oh yeah?" a pleased Jacob crowed. "My Fred Astaire moves impressed you that much, did they?"

Wray gave Jacob a sideways glance. "I think you have your Freds mixed up. Try Flintstone."

"Ouch," replied Jacob, feigning a wounded look. He certainly couldn't argue with her; when it came to dancing he would be first to claim he was the owner of two largest left feet known to mankind.

"Don't laugh," said Wray as she rested the side of her face once more against Jacob's shoulder, "but when you were gone, I kept having this recurring dream about that night. It kept replaying itself over and over again, the two of us dancing in the center of the gym, night after night."

Jacob didn't laugh. In fact, he found himself recalling the nights back at Havenhid when he felt particularly homesick while lying awake in bed. It was during those time he used his power to step without hinderance across the barriers of time using the Grace of Roaming to leave one paradise for another: the Homecoming Dance. There he was able to experience something better than any dream could ever provide: the flesh-and-blood reality of reliving over and over the first time he and Wray embraced in a manner that stepped beyond the boundaries of their tight friendship. And he couldn't help but wonder, as Wray told him of her dream, if his ability to Roam had somehow given him the ability to steal her away from her own private dreamscape and take her momentarily away to the place where time stood still.

"It used to frustrate me so much," continued Wray. "Here I was so angry with you for leaving like you did that the last thing I wanted was to dream such happy thoughts about you. And yet I found myself looking forward to when the day came to an end and it was time to go to bed so I could get back to that moment when your arms were wrapped around me. Especially when we—"

She paused suddenly, her voice trailing off abruptly, and she looked up at him with a somewhat timid expression until she managed to part her lips to release the last heavy word residing on her tongue, "kissed."

Staring down into her eyes, Jacob felt a clammy, burning sensation slowly consume both of his ears before enveloping his entire head.

"Believe it or not," he managed to croak, "I had the same dream."

Then, as if to ensure that neither were asleep in bed reliving their confessed shared dream, they kissed gently and sweetly before hugging one another tightly. It was short-lived, however, when Jacob became very much mindful of Wray's hands moving their way around his middle toward his back in a delicate fashion and he instantly tensed up and took an instinctive step backward away from her as if he suddenly became aware he was in the presence of a pickpocket.

"Something the matter?" Wray asked.

"Uh…no, it's n-nothing…That is, I'm fine," he replied with a nervous half-smile. "It's just…I'm sure you have a lot of cleaning up still to do."

"There's really not that much left to do. Honest!" she assured him.

"Still…I don't want to be the reason you're here all night," he continued, adding an awkward chuckle. "Besides, I really should be getting home myself and give my ears another swabbing with a Q-tip. I think I can feel a little sticky residue still…you know, from the milkshake earlier."

Wray's head took on a slight tilt as she looked on slightly puzzled as Jacob clumsily gathered up the props he had earlier used to weaken her resolve before disconnecting his phone from the stereo and instantly pulling the plug on Stevie's serenading voice.

"I'll give you a call tomorrow," he promised clutching his phone all while struggling to keep a hold of the raincoat, hat and umbrella overflowing his arms as he inelegantly backed his way toward the entrance to the restaurant, jiggered open the door and hurried off in the direction of home.

CHAPTER FIVE

"**Y**OU'RE LYING!"

Jacob's cry rang forth with a loud, murderous rage at the figure standing before him. It was Thaniel, resurrected within the shapes of light, colors and shadows brought to life by a most unpleasant, and yet familiar nightmare Jacob found himself unable to escape since shortly before leaving Eden. It came each night without fail the moment he closed his eyes and surrendered to sleep, stealing him away from the warm comforts of his bed and dropping him in the midst of the Silent Forest's tenebrous presence.

"Gotham would never have kept something as important as who my father is from me," Jacob found himself yelling with angry denial at the spectral traitor he had come to loathe with every ounce of his being.

"Then take my hand," Thaniel dared with unflinching assuredness while reaching out to the boy.

As it always managed to before, the sight of the angel's outreached handmade Jacob tighten with hesitation. Yet he managed to find within himself the strength to take hold of it and face the vision suddenly unveiled before his eyes of Gotham and Anahel speaking in secret inside Anahel's room.

"I would prefer if what has been said here tonight in regards to Samael remain in this room," he heard Gotham say to Anahel.

"He doesn't know Samael's his father?" asked Anahel.

Gotham shook his head. "For some reason he hasn't inquired yet about who his father might be, but I can sense the question on the edge of his tongue."

The familiar wave of nauseousness swept over Jacob like some tossing wave as it always did when the truth revealed itself in its especially cruel way, forcing Jacob to yank himself free from Thaniel's grip and instantly obliterate the sight of Gotham and Anahel.

"I'm so sorry, Jacob," Thaniel said to the boy with a sympathy of which Jacob wanted no part.

"Keep away from me," Jacob snapped while scrambling backward to keep out of reach of Thaniel's move to console him. "JUST KEEP AWAY FROM ME!"

The nightmare twisted and shifted as it always did, and the brief moment of comfort Thaniel expressed to the boy was suddenly replaced with an image of Thaniel standing menacingly over the boy with the sole of his boot pressed firmly, and painfully, atop Jacob's chest.

"I would have thought one of the first things Gothamel would have taught you is never afford the enemy a second chance to catch you beneath their heel," Thaniel said, while staring down at the boy. The weight attempting to crack Jacob's ribs and crush his chest cavity was beyond painful.

"Then you admit you're my enemy," Jacob managed to gasp.

An explosion of fury was soon detonated deep within the Silent Forest as angel and Nephilim battled one another in a fierce contest over the one true treasure worth life and limb: The Sword of Destiny. It lied upon the dirt of the forest floor, gleaming brilliantly in the moonlight like the prize it was as Thaniel attempted to cut short Jacob's life in order win possession of the fabled talisman. Then there came the wolves, and in a flash of white and fang, and a splash of water, Thaniel's fate was sealed when he was knocked backwards and sent plunging into the unforgiving and inescapable black waters where the beautiful, yet deceptively evil Lilith looked on like a black widow waiting for an insect to become ensnared in its web. An instant horror and terror alighted Thaniel's eyes, especially when the presence of horrid, unseen creatures of the Underneath lurking below the surface, called Feeders, caused the water to boil with the frenzy of movement as they made their way toward the unfortunate angel.

"Call them off!" he called out desperately to Lilith. "You can't let them take me. We had a pact."

Instead, Lilith quietly watched with the coldest and unsympathetic of stares as Thaniel, realizing his fate, made a last desperate and fruitless attempt to save himself by frantically beating his wings to lift himself to safety, but it was too late. Jacob looked on in horror as the clawed hands of damnation took hold of him, and despite the angel's perfidious turn he could not help but feel a twinge of pity for his former teacher, and more importantly friend, as the two locked eyes during Thaniel's final moments.

"Zophiel." The final word to be uttered by Thaniel slipped quietly from his lips. Then suddenly he was gone; vanishing from sight beneath the black inky surface of the water as he was dragged to an unimaginable fate awaiting him in the depths below.

Zophiel.

~ ~ ~

Jacob awoke with a start, heaving for the breath frightful and unsettling sights are adept at stealing, and awash with the clamminess of a cold sweat often found amongst the sick and the startled. It took a moment for his wide eyes to search the darkness of the night surrounding him and realize he was in the safe confines of his bedroom and not the leaden grasp of the Silent Forest. Still, he was quick to jump out of his bed and make a dash to his closet where he frantically dug through the clutter crammed inside until he found what he was searching for leaning against a far back corner and inconspicuously wrapped in a flannel blanket.

Jacob peeled back the top portion of the blanket, and only when he spied the familiar glint of steel from the Sword of Destiny hidden safely away inside, did his body slacken and his breaths come in calmer waves. With his eyes reflecting the shine of the exposed sword's handle, Jacob timorously pulled open more of the blanket to expose the heart and, more precisely, the soul of the sword: the ancient dagger once belonging to a Roman guard forged as a spine of power between the blade and hilt. Instantly, his ears caught an indecipherable chorus of whispers that seemed to be breathed forth by the long-ago relic and swirl about him like a swarm of unseen phantoms.

Throughout its long history, the dagger had a way of widening the eyes of untold seekers who had the fortune (and for many, misfortune) to bear witness its fabled existence with self-glory and unbounded avarice. Yet it came to fill Jacob's sight with deference, and a far greater wariness; a wariness only someone who had ever been blessed (or cursed) to possess such a powerful and revered weapon could know. It was Damiel who set out to train Jacob in how to handle such a saber, for no one else but the Angel of the Sword held the knowledge needed to fully master an instrument of great divinity as the Sword of Destiny. Only when Jacob took the sword into his hand upon Damiel's instruction one afternoon, and brandished it in the manner swords are created to be brandished, did he first experience the power residing in, and hidden in the soul of the weapon. It coursed through Jacob's grip with an intolerable burning, in what he imagined taking hold of a bolt of lightning might feel like. And for the split second he was able to retain the sword in his grasp, it felt to Jacob as if the sword had become the world's most powerful magnet that attracted the living energy of every single element of nature surrounding him: the Forest, the sky, the sun, the air, even the ground beneath his feet; so much so that bits of rock and dirt slowly rose up in a levitating layer of debris where he stood.

There was a far deeper mystery to the sword; one Jacob would soon discover once he managed, with Damiel's help, to gain a controlled hold of the power in his grasp. It revealed itself in random visits of pain; a deep, stigmatic stabbing pain Jacob felt piercing his right side just below his rib cage. And with the pain came the swirl of voices and, stranger yet, visions; mysterious and unfamiliar visions that unveiled themselves to Jacob in the mirror-like clarity of the sword's blade. What they were or what they meant to convey, Jacob had no inkling. Yet the more they made their presence known to Jacob, the more drawn to the sword he found himself—to a point.

"The bite you suffer, and will continue to suffer for as long as you come to possess the sword," Damiel explained one afternoon to Jacob, "is a humble remembrance of the wound afflicted on one greater than you or I as he hung nailed to a cross; the very wound from which blood and water flowed forth and made the Spear of Destiny the legend it is.

"Alas, I wish I could offer a more perspicuous explanation regarding the visions you've come to experience," Damiel continued. "The nature of their manifestations are as shadows of the past, flickers of the future and breathing shapes residing between the two. What they mean to reveal or, more importantly, why I have no answer, as they are different to each who have come to know ownership of the sword. But just as the sword, by its very name, is wholly charted on a course to its divine destiny, so, too, I imagine is it serving as a guiding beacon to each of its masters in fulfilling their own untold destinies."

Damiel's words only made the power of the lance that much more overwhelming to the boy, and the voices and visions somehow residing within its gleaming strength all the more spellbinding. It was all he could do, as he remained kneeling in the doorway to his closet, to briefly run the tip his finger curiously along the grip before concealing the weapon once more within the blanket. Only then, when he had tucked the sword out of sight, did the mysterious voices fall silent.

Closing his closet door, Jacob returned to his bed where he plopped himself heavily upon his pillow while silently cursing the nightmares that seemed to take such relish tormenting him night after night as he slept. He'd been forced to suffer numerous reoccurring nocturnal visions in recent years, but this particular one involving Thaniel had so far proved to be the most bothersome, so much so that he wished he could find a way to bind the dream from ever penetrating his sleep again. Yet even as he stared with his eyes wide open at the ceiling above him, Jacob could still see the image of the angel submerged in the black pool residing deep inside the Silent Forest that had served as both a prison for Lilith as well as a doorway to the Underneath. No matter how hard he tried, he could not seem to scour the sight of Thaniel's desperate attempt to escape the inescapable muck into which he had fallen. Even when Jacob managed to close his eyes and greet a welcoming slate of empty blackness, Thaniel's voice still reverberated inside his head.

Zophiel.

Zophiel.

Zophiel.

~ ~ ~

It was with a sense of relief when Jacob was stirred from his eventual return to sleep to see the morning sunshine flooding its way through his window. He quickly dressed, brushed his teeth and as about to bound down the stairs with his basketball tucked under his arm when he noticed the door to his grandmother's bedroom slightly ajar, making him pause in his tracks.

It'd been a couple days since he had broken the unsettling news to her about Gotham's death. Since then, she had remained locked away in the seclusion of her room to mourn in private and, aside from the occasional times he knocked on her door to check in on her, Jacob gave her the space to be alone with her heartbreak. To see her door finally open, if only slightly, was an encouraging sign, and Jacob quietly snuck a peek inside the room.

He spied her seated behind a large wooden easel positioned next to the picture window overlooking the backyard where the morning was in full bloom. With the delicate precise strokes of the paintbrush clutched in her aged hand, she was diligently focused on shaping the emerging image of the painting coming to life on the canvas before her.

"Grandma?" croaked Jacob with an almost apologetic clearing of his throat for disturbing her.

Ava looked away from her painting and appeared somewhat surprised at the sight of her grandson lingering in her doorway. "You're up and about early this morning."

"Not any earlier than usual," Jacob replied.

Ava glanced at her wrist watch. "For heaven's sake, will you look at that. I got so caught up in my painting the time completely escaped me. Let me get you some breakfast."

Jacob was quick in motioning her to stay put. "I'm fine. I'm actually on my way out to play some ball with Ty."

"Oh, how nice! Then you've managed to mend your friendship," said Ava with a subdued smile.

"Yeah, everything's fine. With Ty and Wray," said Jacob. "I just wanted to see how you are doing."

Ava didn't answer at first, looking instead out the window and basking in the light shining through.

"The sunrise was so beautiful this morning," she said. "I just couldn't let it pass without trying to capture it on this canvas."

There was a sadness in her voice. And even if Jacob didn't hear it, which he did, he certainly saw it in her eyes, which were red and glassy from the tears she had shed in private the last couple days.

Jacob entered the room and set his basketball on the bed. Painting had always been a relaxing hobby of Ava's, and the walls of her room were decorated with several of her creations. Growing up, Jacob found them to be both beautiful and intriguing; now he recognized instantly and intimately the colorful landscapes as near perfect captures of Eden. There was the Tree of Life, and the River, not to mention several animals whose species would be foreign and unknown outside Eden's hidden gate.

"You never told me you had actually been there. To Eden, I mean," commented Jacob while perusing the paintings as he always found himself doing whenever he came into his grandmother's bedroom.

"That's because I never have," replied Ava. "You better than anyone would know a mortal like myself would be forbidden from such a visit. But Gotham had his own special way of sharing this mysteriously wonderful place with me, as you could imagine. It's the one thing I know the ravages of age will find defeat in attempting to steal from me, for I have not lost a single detail of it in all these years."

Jacob came up behind his grandmother to gander a peek over her shoulder at the painting she was in the process of working on and he was immediately struck by the sight of it. It showed with stunning detail and beauty the eagle-eye view of Eden from the cliff top of a high mountain one is greeted by after passing through the Emmaus Corridor from the Dilmun Sea. The vast Forest broken only by patches of open green fields here and there, and the great River of Life winding its way through it all was captured beneath the gorgeous lavender and gold canopy of an early morning sky exactly the way such a vision had branded itself inside Jacob memory. And standing with his impressive winged back facing forward was the figure of a mighty angel staring out at the view from the outcropping of rock jutting out from the mountainside and looking equally majestic and striking as Eden itself. Jacob's gaze immediately focused itself on the angelic figure, and even though the painting was still a work in progress and not yet finished, he knew instantly the shape whose back was turned was a memorial depiction of Gotham, and a fitting one at that.

Suddenly, as if to confirm such assumptions, a light breeze swept through the open window, billowing the drapes and tousling Jacob's hair, and as it did, the painted Gotham's wings rustled with life as if the painting itself had somehow become a window for the wind to enter and continue on in its drift. Jacob's eyes then grew wider as he watched as the angel somehow broke free of the constraints of the still life in which he was frozen, and with the breeze blowing gently through his long locks of hair he turned to look over his shoulder and offered a slight smile and nod of acknowledgement. Despite all the unimaginable and mind-blowing things he had come to accept as normal during his time in Eden, witnessing such an elementary miracle as a painting coming to life caught Jacob to the quick. His startled gaze shot to his grandmother to see her reaction, but she remained seated staring deeply into the painting without the slightest shift to the forlorn expression deep-set in her face, as if her eyes were blind to the remarkable vision taking place before her. Maybe they were, Jacob wondered to himself; and then again, maybe his imagination was getting the better of him.

"Perhaps this would all be somewhat easier to accept if somehow I could be assured he was finally in a good place," Ava remarked solemnly.

Jacob looked back to the painting and a somber look was quick in sweeping over him. Not only had the painting's brief breath of life exhausted itself and returned back to its original state, but he knew exactly of what his grandmother was speaking. After all, where do the Fallen go once Heaven has barred them from forever crossing past its gates? In life, Gotham had been left with two choices: to forever wander the earth like some cursed nomad or to follow his brethren who carried the same scar of God's disdain on their temple through the one set of gates left open to them: those leading to realm of the Underneath. In death, Jacob couldn't imagine Gotham was left with any more options, nor did he want to. In fact, it took all he could muster to keep his mind sealed from pondering over such unsettling thoughts.

"This is the way I wish to remember him, and the way I always will: surrounded by beauty," said Ava.

Staring hard at the painting, Jacob fought to sear the image inside his brain in order to keep all other troublesome thoughts concerning Gotham's fate forever at bay.

"I just hope he knew, despite everything, how much he truly meant to this old woman," said Ava, in a voice quavering ever so subtly with emotion.

Jacob couldn't help but be transported back to Eden and sitting on the ground in the presence of the Tree of Life listening to Gotham recite his time with Ava and how much love filled both his voice and his eyes as he spoke of his grandmother.

"He did, grandma," Jacob offered his reassurance. "Trust me, he did."

Ava simply nodded in return and reached up to give a squeeze of hope and love to the hand gently kneading her shoulder.

~ ~ ~

So marked the beginning days of Jacob's return to Cain's Corner where he slowly settled back into the slow and relaxed pace of small-town life. It may have lacked the mystifying excitement he had grown accustomed to in Eden, and that in of itself was strangely comforting. Here there was no such thing as a Light Bearer, and the daily pressure Jacob had come to know since being saddled with the moniker had vanished, as did the constant weight he had grown used to feeling of eyes always watching and studying him as though he were some lab rat that held the key for some unknown and indecipherable cure for all of society's ills. In Cain's Corner, he had grown up under the radar, an invisible boy of sorts who managed to exist without drawing any undue attention upon himself. It was rather a relief to return once more to the role he was rather comfortable with: that of a "Ghost." Sure, he continued to be haunted by nightmares of Thaniel and the Silent Forest, and the sadness, as well as the anger he harbored for Gotham which remained with him. But in Cain's Corner, there was no such thing as Nephilim. Or prophesies involving a Light Bearer. Or the cursed existence of a son of Samael, and that was more than okay with Jacob.

Escaping the shadow of one's self, however, was not as easy as simply stepping outside the reach of the sun's presence. And in Jacob's case, even the simplest of things, like stripping off a sweaty t-shirt during a spirited game of one-on-one with Ty with the muggy heat of the August sun blazing down upon them often times brought him to a sudden halt as he found himself standing before that large ineluctable mirror that often times appeared before him and revealed deep within its looking glass, not the image of what everyone else around him saw, but the true reflection of who he was. Yet as he would soon discover, such secrets, no matter how deep in the earth one attempts to bury them, have a way of being uncovered sooner or later, and usually by the most unexpected of excavators.

"I was thinking we might head up to Penuel Point tomorrow," Ty suggested out of the blue while continuing to dribble in place as he took a moment to catch his breath from running around the basketball court. "What do you think?"

"Sure. Why not?" answered Jacob.

It had been a tradition, albeit a short one, between the two boys to trek to the nearby mountains and celebrate a last hurrah of summer by strapping on a couple parachutes and leaping off the majestic pinnacle of Penuel Point with careless abandon into the breathtaking beauty spread out like a painting thousands of feet below. But strangely, Jacob received the invitation with a blank stare absent any hint of excitement he had met such plans in the years past.

"Gee, don't get too excited on me, now," Ty, noting his friend's blasé response to the idea. remarked.

"It's not that, it's just…." Jacob paused pensively as he lifted the front of his shirt he wished dearly he could shed but wisely kept in place to mop up the sweat trickling down his face. "It's been awhile since I've been up there."

"You know, you're right about that. Last I remember we had plans to go the day after Homecoming, but something happened to mess those plans up. Now, what was it? Oh yeah, that's right, you skipped town without saying a word to anyone," Ty recounted in his usual dramatic mockery.

"Really? We're going to cross that bridge again?"

"I just thought with you being back home—and being in the fence-building state of mind that you are—it'd be the perfect outing," pressed Ty. "Besides, school's going to be starting up in a few weeks, you know, and in case it's slipped anyone's mind some of us were scammed out of a whole summer."

Ty waited for response from Jacob who, instead, remained noticeably silent.

"You are planning on going back to school, aren't you?" questioned Ty.

"Haven't really thought about it," Jacob finally answered.

"Excusez-moi! What's there to think about? Are you actually trying to tell me, after all the effort you made over the years in trying to nerdify me, that I might soon be best friends with a high school dropout?"

"How did I suddenly become a drop out?"

"Why else would you need to think about something as basic as going to school?" wondered Ty. "Unless…"

"Unless what?" Jacob asked hesitantly.

"Maybe you're just a little embarrassed—and rightly so—of being left back a grade."

A look of utter puzzlement came over Jacob. "Who said anything about me being left back?"

"Well, not to point out the obvious, but you did miss a whole year of school."

"It's not like I was sunning myself on some deserted island," said Jacob. "Trust me, I spent more time with my nose in books studying while I was away than I ever did at Harpus High. If anything I should be allowed to skip a grade."

He wasn't lying, of course. The Library at Havenhid was the ultimate embodiment of higher education, and the time Jacob had spent there in Study with Thaniel as his all-knowing instructor had felt like an overwhelming exercise in treading an ocean of unlimited knowledge. To Jacob, the idea of going back to school at Harpus High was like attempting to squeeze himself into one of the miniature desks in his first-grade classroom. But, naturally, he couldn't begin to explain such things to Ty.

"Well, that's good news," said Ty. "I was a little worried our friendship might be in jeopardy."

"And why's that, exactly?" asked Jacob.

"Dude, you couldn't expect me to be seen hanging out with a dweeby underclassman. I have my reputation to protect, after all," Ty explained.

Jacob was not amused. "Are you going to do something here?" he asked as he waited with growing frustration for Ty to quit his yammering and put the basketball he continued to try, and fail to spin on the end of his finger, back into play.

Finally losing his patience, Jacob swiped the basketball away from Ty and, in an exacerbating moment where he forgot himself and where he was, he made a dash across the court in a demonstration of speed that all but made him a blur before taking a gravity-defying leap which made him appear as if he were racing up an invisible set of stairs leading to the basket. All of it, fortunately, happened before Ty could manage to spin around fast enough to follow his friend's lightning-swift movements and witness the perfect dunk shot that would have left the chin of Michael Jordan, himself, on the ground.

"What the heck was that?" Ty cried out with genuine bewilderment, as the look on his face reflected absolute confusion over what had just happened.

"You're getting slow in your old age," Jacob attempted to joke with his friend while silently chastising himself for demonstrating such a reckless and irresponsible lapse of judgment on his part no matter how momentary it was.

He braced himself as Ty traded befuddled glances between himself and the ten-foot span separating them from the rim of the basket before, thankfully, shrugging off the whole incident as some sort of hallucination. Just to be on the safe side, though, Jacob feigned defeat to Ty's less-than-impressive basketball skills and gifted him a layup knowing it was just the right kind of shiny object to make his friend forget all about the incident.

"One thing's for sure: whether you're held back or not, I know one person who's not going to be too jazzed seeing your face back on campus," Ty remarked, picking up the previous conversation from where it had been interrupted by Jacob's hijinks. "Yul Dane. Especially now considering you've moved in on his ex-girlfriend."

Yul Dane.

The name reverberated inside Jacob's head like an old forgotten voice from the past. He hadn't given much of a thought to his old rival since leaving Cain's Corner the year before. Then again, what reason did he have to do so? Because to think of Yul was to automatically have the unpleasant experience of revisiting the vision branded into the darkest corner of his brain of the groping jock on the dance floor in the Harpus High gymnasium at the homecoming dance with his arms—and more pointedly his hands—entwined like a pair of snakes around Wray. To now hear there was an "ex" where Wray's relationship with Yul was concerned was about the best news to greet Jacob since returning home, and while he basked in such news, Ty eyed an opportunity to suddenly dart past Jacob and dribble his way swiftly across the asphalt blacktop to deliver another effortless and unhindered layup into the basket at the other end of the court.

"Ex-girlfriend?" Jacob pondered the word aloud. "When did that happen?"

Ty gave an unsure shrug as he mindlessly continued to dribble the ball. "Maybe a week or two after you left. She didn't tell you?"

Jacob didn't answer; he was too full of glee to know Wray had washed her hands of the blond meathead jock's company while he was away.

"Apparently, it happened during a party Ronny Burkowitz threw at his house while his parents were away out of town," Ty continued while taking random shots with the basketball. "Now, mind you, I wasn't there to witness what went down because, well, I wasn't invited. But I have it from a very reliable source that it was quite the scene. In fact, it got so heated it ended up getting physical."

The subtle look of elation on Jacob's face instantly dissipated, and an explosion of gold bubbled within the sphere of his irises as a fast-rising anger moved suddenly inside him.

"You saying he put his hands on her?" Jacob inquired in the same quiet manner a volcano releases a hiss of steam before its inevitable eruption.

"Aaaaactually, it was the other way around," replied Ty, much to Jacob's surprise.

"*She* hit him?" Jacob questioned with a tone of incredulousness as a snowfall of delight came down to cool the rising lava.

"I believe the way it was reiterated to me was more like she cleaned his clock," corrected Ty.

Such a revelation shouldn't have come as a surprise to Jacob. After all, it was just a few days earlier when he himself was on the clock-cleaning end of Wray's right hook. Still, he couldn't hide the twinge of amusement that stretched wide his mouth as his brain worked to concoct a dramatization of the moment when Wray wiped that cocksure look Jacob had come to despise off Yul's face, even as he stood absentmindedly rubbing his left cheek which held the throbbing memory of such a strike.

"Naturally, I was skeptical it had actually gone down the way it was being whispered around school. You know how rumors take on a life of their own at HH?" Jacob couldn't help but roll his eyes while listening to Ty who himself could have become very profitable opening his own tabloid publication with the gossip mill he had constructed on campus. "But sure enough, come that following Monday Yul was sporting a nice big 'ole shiner."

Wow, Jacob mulled silently to himself, *not only punched Yul, but left an embarrassing mark. Nice going, Wray!*

"Yul, of course, argued to everyone who would listen that he got the black eye in some industrial accident," said Ty.

"Industrial?" asked Jacob.

"Yeah. He said he accidentally got hit by a hammer while helping his dad put up some dry wall," explained Ty, drawing a giggle from both he and Jacob. "But everyone knew he was full of it. It was literally the punch heard around the world. Well, at least Cain's Corner."

The two boys continued to chuckle over the image of the big and bad Goliath being taken down by a mere girl when the approaching sound of Stevie Nicks' voice blaring from a set of speakers made Ty's gaze shift past Jacob's shoulder to the parking lot in the distance.

"Speak of the devil," he said with a grin. "Here comes Tyson herself."

They both looked on at the unexpected sight of Wray, looking like a wind-blown vision, as she got out of her Jeep and made her way across the grass toward the vacant basketball courts wearing a smile that was as much mischievous as it was beguiling.

"I thought you were working today," said Jacob.

"I'm headed there now. I just thought after running around chasing a basketball all morning you might be a little hungry," said Wray, holding up a brown take-out bag.

"You must have heard of my stomach growling," replied Jacob.

A sour look crept over Ty, as though he had bitten into an especially tangy lemon, at the sight of Jacob and Wray exchanging a loving yet sweet peck on the lips.

"Never mind me," he grumbled. "I'll just pretend this basketball is a giant Swedish meatball. I'm sure it'll hit the spot."

Wray shot Ty an unamused glare. "Don't worry; knowing how you throw a hissy fit whenever you're not included, I made sure not to forget you."

Ty quickly dropped the basketball clutched in his hands to catch a second brown bag Wray was holding that was suddenly hurled in his direction.

"The tips you must rake in at Rabble-Rousers with that sunny, disarming disposition of yours," Ty remarked dryly, before opening the bag and sneaking a peek at the goodies inside.

Wray turned once more to Jacob and her eyes glistened brightly with the sight of him reflected in the deep emerald pools which held him in her gaze.

"Wish I didn't have to rush off," she said, "but I'll see you later tonight when I'm off."

"Sounds like a plan," Jacob all but gushed.

"Don't forget to tell her about tomorrow," Ty interrupted as he continued to dig his way through his sack.

"What about tomorrow?" inquired Wray.

"Ty was thinking about heading up to Penuel Point like we do every year," explained Jacob.

"Is that your endearing way of asking me to go along with you?" asked Wray with a teasing grin.

"I think it was his endearing way of asking if you'd be available to drive us like you usually do," Ty answered before Jacob could open his mouth.

"I know it's not that exciting for you, so if you don't want to go it's perfectly fine," said Jacob, directing Wray's attention back to him before she thought better of her kind gesture and snatched back the lunch out of Ty's grasp.

"No, I enjoy going along, and watching from the safety the ground," said Wray. "Although, since we now have to get up so early tomorrow, maybe we should cancel our plans for tonight."

Jacob didn't care for that suggestion. "I don't want to cancel our plans."

"Why, what's going on tonight?" asked Ty.

"There's a Creature Feature marathon showing on TV," said Wray. "And since we're both big fans of the old classic horror movies, we thought it'd be fun to stay up and watch them."

"You're kidding! I love those old Dracula and Wolf Man movies," said Ty, sounding like a kid antsy with excitement over the approach of Christmas.

Wray instantly bit down on her lip when she realized she had unintentionally opened up a can of worms. "Well…I'm sure Jacob wouldn't mind if you came over and watched with us," she offered tepidly. "Unless, of course, you have something better you'd rather do."

But Jacob made his disapproval to Wray's kind-hearted gesture more than evident when he began motioning fervently to Ty like a mime infected with a bad case of rabies behind Wray's back to decline the invite by running his finger repeatedly across his throat.

"You know, I would love to…" Ty began as his eyes darted between Wray and his friend's threatening hand signals, "but the thing is the old classic horror films really aren't my cup of tea."

The reply made Wray cock her head and brought a frown of puzzlement to her face. "Didn't you just say two seconds ago you love the old Dracula and Wolf Man movies?"

"Yes, yes I did," Ty agreed. "That is to mean, I want to love them, being the classics they are. But, see, then I watch them and I usually get the nightmares…afterwards, that is."

The odd and clumsy explanation only seemed to deepen Wray's frown.

"And that's why I didn't bother to invite Ty over in the first place," Jacob jumped in. "I wanted to save him from any possible night terrors not to mention the embarrassment of waking up in a urine-soaked bed like he's experienced in the past."

Ty did his best to absorb the discomfiting barb made by his friend as well as ignore the sudden look of disgust revealed by Wray.

"Yes…I definitely owe you for delivering me from a shameful Depends moment brought on by the horrific sight of a screeching rubber bat attached to two fishing wires," Ty grumbled in as good-natured a manner as he could manage.

But even he couldn't stay mad at his friend who signaled back a gesture of thanks as he walked Wray back to her Jeep. After all, there were certain unspoken loyalties in the Buddy Constitution understood amongst the best of friends since the dawn of friendships, especially when they involved the opposite sex. And, unfortunately, such loyalties demanded one willingly be thrown under the bed-wetting bus without making too much fuss over the sacrifice.

~ ~ ~

As for Jacob, if he felt any remorse in publicly shaming his friend as someone who couldn't handle sitting through a movie marathon featuring vampires and wolf men without the aid of an adult diaper, it was quickly forgotten later that night as he and Wray huddled in his bedroom laying on their stomachs atop his bed with a bowl of popcorn between them. The flickering bluish light coming from the TV screen illuminated the engrossed look they both shared as they watched "The Creature from the Black Lagoon" in riveted silence. Yet Jacob found it harder and harder to concentrate on the movie. And how could he not, as Wray wedged herself against him with a growing anxiousness, as the eerie and menacing music coming from the TV slowly built its way to a suspenseful crescendo leading up to the sight of the ghastly creature peering out from the black and white murkiness of its underwater lair. Each nudge sent a waft of the most delightful, intoxicating scent coming from Wray's hair, like the subtle aroma released from the bud of a newly bloomed flower to entice Jacob's flaring nostrils.

"This part always gives me the creeps!" Wray squealed suddenly at the sight of Julia Adams diving off the side of an anchored river boat into the black waters of the lagoon.

With half her face buried in Jacob's shoulder, she watched with growing apprehension as Julia cluelessly stroked her way through the water while beneath her, hidden in the black murkiness, the hideous gilled creature swam uncomfortably close alongside her underbelly and all about her, curiously studying her flailing limbs.

"Why is she even swimming in that gross swamp water any ways?" squawked Wray.

"Because if she didn't, you wouldn't be lying here twisting yourself into a pretzel," replied Jacob.

The Gill-man proceeded to dart about the water, his webbed hands reaching out in a curious, petting manner for the kicking legs, and again Wray shrieked as the creature stopped just short of grazing the skin as it continued to study the treading body.

"It's so creepy it makes my skin crawl every time I watch it," squealed Wray.

Jacob couldn't help but chuckle, and his belittling response to her growing angst drew a half-hearted punch to his shoulder from Wray.

"It's not funny! How can you sit there and not be creeped out by some hideous thing stalking some poor defenseless woman like that while she's swimming?"

"Don't you think if the creature wanted to kill her she'd be dead by now?" argued Jacob.

"*UGH!* You boys are all alike, though I'm not surprised," Wray remarked with disgust as she grabbed a couple kernels of popcorn from the bowl. "My brother's favorite part in 'Jaws' is when the girl skinny-dipping at the beginning of the movie gets turned into fish food."

"That is a pretty awesome scene," Jacob agreed, drawing a huff of exasperation from Wray.

"Thank you for proving my point."

"The simple fact is guys and girls just have different ways of reacting to things, even movies. You're ready to grab a harpoon gun and spear poor Gill-man for nothing more than going out and seeing who's swimming in his lagoon. I, on the other hand, can't help but feel a little sorry for him."

Wray nearly came out of her skin at such an idea. "Feel sorry for him?"

"Well, yeah…how could you not?" Jacob replied with a quiet, almost meek tone. "Imagine if you were the Gill-man: an ugly monstrous creation living all alone in some empty lagoon out in the middle of nowhere. One day you hear splashing where there shouldn't be and when you go to investigate what it might be you come across a strange figure in the water wearing a white bathing suit doing the breast stroke. You move in and take a closer look because why wouldn't you, and you're immediately mesmerized by the legs and arms that are smooth and without scales and the hands and feet that aren't webbed. After all, Julia Adams is as much a creature in the Gill-man's eyes as the Gill-man is in her eyes. It's the quintessential beauty and the beast tale. And call me weird, but it's a little bit hard not to feel sorry for the one who's somehow been dealt the unfortunate card to be the beast, especially when they're very much aware they're the beast. At least it is for me."

Wray's combative manner quickly subsided as Jacob's words lulled her into a quiet contemplativeness.

"I guess that's why I've always disliked the term 'monster movies' because really, for the most part, the so-called monster is really just some unfortunate soul who's been banished from society and forced to live a solitary existence. You have the Gill-man living in the lagoon; the Phantom of the Opera driven down into the sewers; and Quasimodo existing out of sight in the Notre Dame bell tower," said Jacob. "Love. Love ends up being the real monster. At some point they discover it in the face of some beautiful woman and its strong pull lulls them into the light only to find out it's something they can't have. That's when the real horror begins."

There was a thoughtful genuineness in the way Jacob spoke that caught Wray by surprise; as if he himself knew firsthand the painful curse of being some ostracized outcast forced to live out his days with his unrequited affections as his only companion. But when Jacob saw the attentive gaze Wray had focused on him, his face instantly deepened to three shades of red as if he were some fire-skinned chameleon.

"Listen to me. I'm spending so much time with Ty I'm starting to sound like him."

"Hardly. I think if Ty were here now he'd be making the case that the mask the Phantom of the Opera wore was meant to be symbolic of a man suffering from a gender identity crisis," argued Wray, causing both to chuckle. "Listening to you reminded me of how to this day I can't help but cry every time I watch 'Frankenstein.' You know, the scene where he comes upon the little girl with the flowers. I used to think it was because of what happens to the girl; you know, when she gets thrown into the lake. But now I realize it's the sweet way the creature responds when he first experiences the bonds of friendship and not being judged by the girl over how hideous he looks."

Jacob smiled in agreement. "Do yourself a favor, though," he quickly warned. "Don't bring up that scene when Ty's around. You do not want to sit through his interpretation of it. Trust me."

Again they laughed before settling back down into the movie. And as they watched while munching from the bowl of popcorn they shared between them, Wray couldn't keep herself from giving a furtive glance Jacob's way every now and then.

"What about you?" she finally asked. "What movie makes you cry?"

"There isn't one," Jacob was quick to answer.

"I don't believe you. There's no way someone who speaks as sympathetically as you just did about the Gill-man and all the other movie monsters has never shed a tear while watching a movie. So spill it!"

With painful reluctance, Jacob turned away once more from the TV and met Wray's piercing gaze fixed intently on him.

"Fine. But if you tell anyone what I'm about to share with you I swear I'll never speak to you again," said Jacob.

"Yeah, yeah, yeah, tell me already," Wray agreed in a brushed-off manner.

"There's two, actually. The first is..." Jacob hesitated at first before surrendering the answer after a deep breath. " 'King Kong.' "

Much to his expectation, Wray let out a loud snorting chuckle. "I'm sorry," she apologized while trying to muffle her amusement with her hand. "Here I was expecting you to say 'Field of Dreams' or 'Saving Private Ryan' like most guys, but 'King Kong?' How could you possibly cry over a big scary ape?"

"That's exactly the way Jessica Lange would have responded at the beginning of the movie, which is the version I'm talking about," explained Jacob. "But after she's abducted by Kong, she slowly comes to realize he's no ordinary ape. I'm not just talking about his size, either. She comes to see the noble and misunderstood soul that's hidden by Kong's outwardly terrifying physique, and at no time is that nobility on greater display than when he takes her to the top of the Empire State building. For all the time and effort she had spent previously trying to escape Kong, she ends up frantically and desperately trying to climb back into the palm of his hand and somehow keep him from taking on and ultimately sacrificing his life to the oncoming fighter jets.

"I personally defy anyone to find a better death scene than when Kong is lying bloodied and broken at the bottom of the Empire State building. The way he stares at Jessica Lange as she stands beside him crying, and all you hear is the beating of Kong's heart growing slower and slower. You no longer see an ape, but something that was somehow stuck in its evolution between beast and man. Laugh if you want, but for whatever reason it gets me in the soft spot every time."

But laugh, Wray didn't; not even the hint of a giggle. Instead, she grabbed Jacob by the back of the neck and pulled him toward her, and the two engaged in a sweet and heartfelt kiss.

"What was that for?" a noticeably surprised but pleased Jacob asked.

Wray ignored Jacob's question. "You know, I was actually named after the actress who starred in the first 'King Kong' movie."

"You serious? That's thinking outside the box when searching for a baby name," said Jacob.

"Yep, Fay Wray. It was one of my grandmother's favorite movies growing up. I'm guessing I got my love for monster movies from her," said Wray. "Anyways, she couldn't convince my mom to name me Fay, for which I'm forever grateful. So they ended up settling on Wray, instead."

"That's incredible! I mean, that totally explains everything," replied Jacob who looked as if he had suddenly been enlightened with all the answers revolving around the mysteries of life that had been evading mankind since the beginning of time.

"What do you mean? Explains what?" asked Wray, suddenly serious.

"Why you would ever go out with a big 'ol ape like Yul Dane, naturally," answered Jacob with an impish grin.

The remark garnered an equally playful swat from Wray in return. "Very funny. But if that's true, maybe you should ask yourself why it is I'm here with you at this very moment."

"Why are you?" Jacob asked as if he had been wondering that very thing at that very moment.

Despite the trace of a smile still on his face, Wray noted the serious and almost apprehensive tone in Jacob's voice when asking the question.

"Oh, I don't know," she began with a sigh while mulling her answer. "It could be I'm intrigued by a boy born with one green eye and one blue. Perhaps I appreciate someone who can take a milkshake dumped on top his head somewhat gracefully. And maybe, just maybe, I prefer a noble soul who isn't afraid to admit he cried over the death of an oversized simian."

For a brief second, she thought she caught a flash of gold in Jacob's dual-colored eyes.

They kissed again, and as they did Jacob couldn't help but wonder to himself if instead of a monster movie marathon he should have suggested a showing of a guaranteed tearjerker like "Old Yeller" or perhaps "Bambi."

"So what about the second?" asked Wray when they finally came up for air.

"The second what?" inquired a momentarily disoriented Jacob.

"You said there were two movies that made you cry. What's the other one?"

Jacob hesitated a moment before answering. " 'Titanic'."

The smile that came to Wray's face told Jacob she was much more agreeable with his second choice.

"But the tears are usually short-lived before the rage kicks in," Jacob was quick to add.

"Rage? Over what?" inquired Wray.

"Leo does everything he can to help Rose maneuver the sinking of the ship and you're going to tell me she couldn't make room for him on the floating door when they finally landed in the water?" answered Jacob.

The two chuckled and settled into another kiss, and for another moment or two the Gill- man and the lagoon in which he lurked was briefly forgotten.

~ ~ ~

Sometime between the back-to-back showings of two Vincent Price classics ("The House of Wax" and "The House on Haunted Hill") the two lovebirds eventually drifted off to sleep. At some point, a high-pitched shriek sounded from the television, rousing Wray from her short-lived rest. She glanced about her with sleep-heavy eyes, first to Jacob who was cuddled up beside her and sound asleep, and then to a clock sitting on the nightstand on the opposite side of the bed. When she discovered it was just after four in the morning, she instantly became flustered. She had not planned to stay the night and quickly got to her feet.

Careful not to make any noise that might stir Jacob, she quietly tip-toed her way around to the foot of the bed to gather up her shoes. Another shriek made her look to the TV. Ironically, the bellowing was coming from an enraged Jessica Lange in the grips of a giant gray hand punching and hitting the nose of the great Kong while screaming hysterically for the ape to choke on her. A small part of Wray wrestled with the urge to wake Jacob so the two of them could watch together and she could witness firsthand the blubbery state the end of the movie promised to leave him. But when she moved Jacob's backpack off a nearby chair so she could sit down and slip on her shoes, her attention was diverted to the thudding sound of a book slipping out of the pack and falling to the floor near her feet.

She reached down to pick it up and was about to slip it back inside the backpack when something about the book with its brown, soft-leathered cover that felt like velvet to the touch captured her interest. Cracking open the book, she instantly recognized the handwriting filling the pages inside as belonging to Jacob, from the countless notes the two had swapped between classes while at school together, and a marked look of befuddlement came over her when she realized she was holding a journal of some sort. Jacob, after all, wasn't the sort of guy she'd suspect would keep a journal. Not that he wasn't the sensitive enough type to chronicle his deepest, most private everyday thoughts. But he usually kept such telling things so close to the vest that she couldn't imagine he'd share them even with something as inanimate as a piece of paper. Yet here it was; pages and pages of quiet thoughts scribbled down in ink.

Dropping her shoes back onto the floor, Wray turned to the start of the journal and was about to read from the first page when she suddenly slammed shut the journal, denying her intrigue-piqued eyes the tiny peek they longed to be given.

What are you doing, Wray? she silently scolded herself. *How would you like it if someone poked around in your diary?*

Dismayed at herself for even considering otherwise, Wray realized the proper thing to do was to slip the journal back into the backpack, put on her shoes and be on her way. Then she made the mistake of looking once more at the TV and seeing the giant ape Kong looking dotingly at Jessica Lange as he held her under a waterfall to shower, and she was instantly reminded of the thoughtful manner in which Jacob had earlier spoke about the hideous creatures of the monster movies for which they both shared a love. Such ruminative offerings had only managed to endear him all the more to her. And if he could muse in such a charitable way about the Frankenstein monster and Kong, what reflective nuggets did he hold about her, she couldn't but wonder.

Just one page, she promised herself, and pushing aside the gnawing feelings she had of being a snooping cad she reopened the journal and turned to the first page.

Saturday, Oct. 23

So here goes my first entry.

I've never kept a journal before, and I guess the only reason I'm starting now is because grandma gave this to me before I left and I know its importance to her. Or maybe it's because my mind is on overload from so many thoughts that I'm hoping writing them down will help me sort through them and make sense of everything that is happening. I'm also bored out of my head, which is odd considering the fact we've arrived in Budapest of all places.

Wray's face scrunched itself into an expression of puzzlement. "Budapest?"

Her frown continued to deepened as her eyes raked their way further down the page and absorbing with growing difficulty words detailing lunch in some greasy diner in the middle of nowhere with a mysterious man who went by the odd name of Gotham. Only he wasn't a man but an angel, and he proved it so during a confrontation with a hunter outside the diner at a neighboring gas station when a deer lying dead in the bed of the hunter's truck suddenly sprang to life after the so-called angel laid his hand upon it and, in a vengeful rage, quickly proceeded to turn the truck into a pile of scrap metal on wheels with its well-aimed antlers and hooves.

"Thou shalt not kill," I heard him remark. "You will not find a footnote of exceptions etched in the stone upon which that commandment was written."

Wray quickly closed the journal in the same manner she was prone to periodically do while reading Stephen King's "Salem's Lot" a couple years earlier, as if fearful the words she read might come to life on the page and form the terrifying images they described. Yet it wasn't a look of terror that gripped Wray, but one of pronounced bewilderment as she stared blankly at the bed where Jacob remained a lifeless lump snoozing away in an oblivious deep sleep.

"Angel?" She muttered the word more than once out loud while attempting to make sense of what she had just read. But logical thought eluded her.

Eventually, just as she was apt to do after taking a breather from "Salem's Lot," she returned to the place in the journal she had hastily abandoned and resumed reading. This time, however, there were no more pauses, and in short order Wray ended up breaking the very promise she had made to herself when she cajoled herself into taking a peek inside the journal. One page became two; two pages grew to ten; and before she knew it she was eyeballs-deep in an otherworldly telling Stephen King himself would have a hard time weaving together with the ability of captivating her with the same raptness. And what was there not to be completely transfixed by, be it the church on Akdamar Island, with its ancient carvings and murals moving with life, or the existence of a mysterious "Gate" hidden from all mankind at the bottom of a massive lake on the other side of the world within a sea of impenetrable darkness; or the sinister Infectors lurking nearby who served as a terrifying barrier to all who attempted to pass through the Gate; or the enigmatic Havenhid whose stately and palatial construct unfolded itself to all who roamed its halls yet appeared as imposing as a bird's nest nestled within the boughs and branches of the trees that shaped it. Then there was Eden itself, not to mention the angels who resided there whose names—Anahel, Damiel, Thaniel, Eksel and Zuriel—were as alluring as their described duties.

Nothing, however, was as oddly perplexing to Wray than what she would come to learn about Jacob the deeper into the journal she read. The two of them had often made light about the two protrusions that formed a subtle yet noticeable disfigurement to Jacob's upper back and what might have caused it: Nuclear radiation contamination; twin gestating alien creatures preparing to hatch their way through the skin; and even a freakish isolated occurrence of estrogen run amok, only in reverse. But the idea that such a deformity was some divine stage of puberty reserved for the offspring of angels called Nephilim…well, that was absurd. Preposterous, even. So preposterous Wray eventually came to the conclusion that what she was reading was not a collection of journal entries as it appeared, but the writings of an overactive imagination. Perhaps Jacob had been secretly attempting to try his hand at fiction writing. Of course, that must be it, Wray was quick in agreeing with her own inner suggestion. After all, it made a whole lot more sense than the alternative.

~ ~ ~

ZOOOPHIELLLLL…

~ ~ ~

Wray had just started reading about a place called Lions Bite when there came a mumbling, rustling ruckus from the bed where Jacob looked to be in the grips of a bad dream. At some point she had forgotten where she was and was caught off guard to see the brightness of morning coming in through the window. How long had she been sitting there reading, she wondered to herself? Before she could see what time it was, Jacob was suddenly jolted into an upright position as he was ripped from his sleep with a jarring start. Wray sat frozen in the chair she had curled herself up in quietly watching as Jacob stared straight ahead with a wild look fixed in his eyes as he slowly tried to calm his heaving breaths.

"Bad dream?" Wray asked hesitantly once Jacob had relaxed somewhat.

"Yes," Jacob replied without hesitation before he realized who had asked him the question. Then his gaze shifted to where Wray was and he appeared almost taken back to see her sitting there in his room. "I mean, it was nothing…"

"I guess those old movies from last night are still potent enough to cause nightmares," said Wray.

Jacob appeared to ignore her. Then again, how could he begin to explain to her how the terror of make-believe movie monsters was child's play compared to the real-life monsters with whom he had come to be personally acquainted.

"What are you doing sitting there anyway? Watching me sleep?" he asked, instead.

It was then Wray realized she still had Jacob's journal open in her hands. And as he sat there on his bed trying to rub his eyes clean of the remaining sleep along with the residuals of the images of Thaniel being overtaken by the Feeders in the thrashing waters of the recurring nightmare that continued in its persistent stalking of him, she reached down and returned the journal back into the backpack from which it had slipped out of as inconspicuously as possible while grabbing her shoes from off the floor.

"Sorry, I must have fell asleep, too," answered Wray. "I was just getting my shoes and hoping to sneak out of here."

"I didn't mean that," Jacob was quick to say, recognizing his abrupt manner. "I just meant you should have awakened me."

"You looked so peaceful, I didn't want to," said Wray. "Besides, the last thing I want is for your grandmother to catch me tip-toeing out of here and think I'm one of those girls."

Jacob flashed her a knowing grin. "I don't think you have to worry about that."

"How so?"

"Well, for starters, she raised me to be a gentleman."

"I can't disagree with you on that point. You were the perfect gentleman last night," Wray replied.

"But more importantly, she knows full well you're just the kind of proper lady to make sure a gentleman like me is kept in line," said Jacob.

There came a loud humming from Jacob's phone on the nearby night table, and he quickly scampered over to grab it.

"It's Ty," said Jacob, looking at the incoming text on the screen of his phone. "He's at Rabble-Rousers wondering where we're at."

Jacob suddenly grimaced while digging his fingers into the thick nest that was his pillow-tangled hair to give his head a good scratching. "I forgot we made plans to go to Penuel Point today."

"So just text him back and make plans for another time," suggested Wray.

Jacob didn't look keen about the idea. "He was really looking forward to this. Besides, he's still harboring a bit of a grudge against me for leaving. Last thing I want to do is give him a reason to be more angry at me."

"Then I guess you're going to Penuel Point," said Wray.

"Don't you mean we?" corrected Jacob. "After all, we sort of need you there."

"Well, with an invitation like that, who could refuse," Wray remarked dryly.

"Great," said Jacob, springing from the bed to his feet. "Just give me two seconds to splash some water on my face and brush my teeth."

Wray watched as Jacob hurried about his room gathering a change of clothes, but the journal she had been engrossed in reading the last few hours that now resided in the backpack near her feet remained at the forefront of her mind. And even though she had settled on the idea that what she had read was a tapestry of fiction woven from the wildest fantasies nestled in the deepest corners of Jacob's imagination, she couldn't help but stare closely at his back before he slipped out of eyesight as he hurried his way toward the bathroom. But the t-shirt he wore offered no sign of anything out of the ordinary underneath, like a pair of wings. Then again, why should it when Wray had already dismissed the very idea of such a thing as preposterous.

"Nephilim," she muttered dismissively to herself with a roll of her eyes. And with that she finally got around to putting on her shoes.

CHAPTER SIX

W hen Jacob and Wray finally met up with Ty at Rabble-Rousers, two things completely unrelated yet equally unexpected occurred. The first presented itself while the trio was seated at a booth enjoying a hearty breakfast of scrambled eggs and pancakes. That is, both Jacob and Wray were trying to enjoy their breakfast that came with a nonstop serenade of yammering from Ty that began with a schooling over the etiquette of being on time, and quickly shifted to an encore presentation of "The Outing of Victor Frankenstein" as Jacob attempted to subtly change the conversation to the movie monster marathon shown the night before on TV when explaining their tardiness.

Perhaps it was the thick layer of glaze that had formed over Jacob's eyeballs that prevented them from rolling completely back into his skull as he sat through the drudgery of reliving a repeat performance of the thesis that landed Ty a first-class ticket to summer school. How his friend was able to maneuver forkfuls of pancake and sausage into his mouth while his tongue somehow managed its incessant blathering was, in itself, a marvel to Jacob. But as he sat quietly with a look of both torture and utter bafflement brought on by trying to figure out the gear mechanisms at work inside Ty's head that was responsible for the outlandish hypothesis he was being forced to listen to, another voice nearly ripped his ear clean off the side of his head.

With a slow turn of his head, Jacob peered cagily over his left shoulder and nearly fell out of his seat when he caught sight of the teenaged boy casually propped upon one of the stools lining the retro lunch counter. The kid's back was turned, denying Jacob a look at his face, but there was no mistaking the voice that was clearly laced with an unmistakable Australian accent as the boy attempted to explain to the middle-aged waitress listening patiently on the other side of the counter how to go about making an Australian version of a lemonade with all the charismatic charm he could muster.

"You know the old saying 'When in Rome'? How about I get you a plain old American lemonade?" was the response of the waitress, who was obviously not in the mood to craft drinks that were popular on the other side of the globe.

"Sure thing, sunshine," Jacob heard the boy reply before grumbling under his breath "you old wombat" as the waitress went to fetch his drink.

Then, as if knowing he was being eyed, the boy swiveled around on his stool and greeted Jacob's frowning stare with a smile and mischievous wink.

You've got be kidding me, Jacob exclaimed with silent shock to himself when he saw that, indeed, it was his good friend Max Kelly sitting there in plain sight as casually as someone sunning himself on the deck of a pleasure cruise. *What's he doing here in Cain's Corner?*

Jacob spun himself back around in his seat so fast, he nearly dislodged his eyeballs from their sockets in his skull and left them suspended in the air staring with disbelief at the sight of Max.

"Something the matter?" Wray asked as Jacob gulped down his orange juice. "You look like somebody who's just been told they've been condemned to a newly discovered circle of hell: spending eternity listening to Ty and his inane hypotheses."

"Ha, ha," Ty replied snidely.

No sooner had Wray made her jab at Ty that her own face morphed into an expression similar to that of Jacob's when she spied the second unexpected, and far more unwelcome sight coming through the doors of the restaurant: Yul Dane.

~ ~ ~

He was accompanied by two of his meathead jock buddies, and his gaze immediately locked itself on the table where the three friends were seated. Jacob remained caught up in the shock of Max's unforeseen presence just a hop-skip-and-a-jump-length's away to take any notice of Yul as the hulking blonde jock sauntered by with a slow, cocky sway in his step and an even cockier sneer curling his lip that made the returning glare in Wray's eyes all the more icier.

"I don't know about you, but I've lost my appetite," Wray remarked once Yul had passed out of earshot. "I'm going to go use the restroom and then I think we should get going."

"Yeah, sure…whatever you say," replied a still oblivious Jacob. "I'll go ahead and pay the check."

Never one to pass up the chance to free-load whenever such an opportunity presented itself, Ty was quick to jump to his feet before Jacob could look to him for his share of the breakfast bill.

"Thanks a lot, pal, I definitely owe you one," he said, giving his friend a grateful pat on the shoulder before swiftly following after Wray in the direction of the restrooms.

Jacob's thoughts, however, were too muddled to take issue with Ty's weaselly ways. Digging into the front pocket of his jeans, he managed to scrounge up just enough money to pay for the meal in the form of a few crumpled bills and some loose change which he deposited in a pile onto the table. Then, before either Wray or Ty had a chance to return, be bolted from the booth to where Max was sipping on the lemonade the waitress had delivered moments earlier.

"G'day, mate!" Max greeted his friend with a toothy smile.

Jacob's mouth remained unhinged, but he didn't seem to be able to make a sound.

"If you could only have seen the expression on your face when you got a gander of me chillin' on this stool," said a clearly tickled Max. "Like you caught sight of a three-headed hippopotamus, it was."

"I think I'd be less surprised to see a three-headed hippopotamus, to be honest," replied Jacob finally, looking no less staggered. "What are you doing here?"

"At the moment, having myself a celebratory drink for finally managing to find this needle in a haystack," answered Max. "You know, Cain's Corner isn't the easiest place to find. Took me a couple days just to pinpoint in which of the fifty states it was even located. Couldn't find it on any map. Google search was useless. Tell ya the truth, I was beginning to think Cain's Corner was something you made up, but here it is in all of its Mayberry reincarnated glory. Could've sworn I even saw Opie Taylor pass me on the sidewalk before coming in here."

He took another drink of his lemonade and immediately grimaced. "And not for nothing, but your American lemonade is a complete gutser. You might want to take a cue from how we serve it up back home."

The last thing on Jacob's mind was lemonade.

"You're telling me you risked going through the Gate on your own to come here? Are you insane?" Jacob didn't feel like a complete hypocrite asking the question; after all, it was not that long ago he had taken the same risk in his pursuit to find Gotham and quickly discovered halfway through the black suffocating shroud that was the Gate what an insane and stupid act it was to attempt such a feat without the guiding hand of an angel to safely lead the way. Just thinking about it made his stomach queasy.

"Luckily for me, I didn't have to test my sanity worrying about the Gate," answered Max.

Jacob gave Max a double take. "And how exactly did you manage that? Last I knew, the only way to get from Eden to the outside world was through the Gate. And vice versa."

"True enough," Max readily agreed. "If one is starting from Eden."

The look of confusion on Jacob's face deepened until Max couldn't help but let loose a chuckle of amusement.

"Now, don't go off like a frog in a sock," said Max, giving his friend a playful jab to the shoulder. "You see it's like this; we began our field runs a few days ago."

Clarity continued to further evade Jacob. "Field runs?"

"Damiel decided it was time for us to start taking our training and putting them to the test in real world situations. So he and Eksel took us outside Eden to run some exercises. It was pretty basic stuff they had us start off with, like how well we were able to spot civilians who were affected by Infectors. But also how able we were to blend into a civilian crowd and camouflage ourselves from eyes trained to scope out a Nephilim with the same ease as spotting an emu in a chicken coop," explained Max. "I must have been above board on that last one, if I do say so myself, since I managed to effortlessly slip away and head here, and while under Damiel and Eksel's hawkish gaze to boot."

Jacob, however, did not share the mirthful grin pasted on his friend's face.

"And how long do you think your truancy act went unnoticed?" inquired Jacob. "For all you know Damiel, or worse yet, Anahel, is on your tail this very minute. In fact I wouldn't be surprised if one of them were to walk through the door of this restaurant any second now."

"Doubtful," replied Max, unfazed at even the suggestion.

"And why's that?"

"I'm sorry, have we just met?" said Max. "Give me some credit for thinking through my schemes instead of flying by the seat of my britches."

Max then proceeded to explain to Jacob how he had pow-wowed with Leos, Kairo and Ethan the night before they were to make the training excursion outside Eden's borders. He had come up with a plan to cover his absence involving Ethan's Grace of mimicry. At the end of the day when the training session was finished and Damiel was conducting the roll call of the group before heading back to Eden, Ethan would simply shuffle his place in line and, as inconspicuously as possible, use his Grace to transform himself into a carbon copy of Max, and none would be the wiser when a full accounting of all the Nephilim had been taken.

"That was your brilliant plan?" Jacob remarked sounding about as impressed as one could be watching grass grow. "That's like the Skipper putting the fate of the marooned castaways of the U.S.S. Minnow in Gilligan's hands."

Max cocked his head in the same curious manner a dog does when trying to understand words coming from his master's mouth. "I don't get that."

Jacob, however, was not interested in getting into an onion-peeling game in trying to explain to Max the error of his ways. "You still haven't told me what you're doing here," he said with an impatient huff. "And I hope you don't tell me you wasted all your effort in an attempt to get me to come back to Havenhid because that ain't happening."

"Well, that's some fine how-de-do, if I ever heard one," Max replied, sounding just a bit offended at the suggestion. "You'd think the sight of your best friend who's traveled literally halfway around the world on your behalf would be cause for a warm handshake and maybe a 'G'day.' What do I get, instead? Unnecessary qualms."

Truth is, Jacob was more than happy to see the familiar sight of his old friend. And with the shock of the unexpected visit falling away, Jacob showed just how happy he was, not with a warm handshake or a 'G'day,' but an enthusiastic hug often shared between tight-knit friends.

~ ~ ~

"Well, well, well…as I live and breathe. Look what the cat coughed up."

Jacob didn't have to turn his head to recognize the voice as belonging to Yul Dane who had left his two friends at the booth where they seated themselves and was now standing a few paces away with arms folded observing Jacob and Max's chummy embrace.

"Hey there, Dane," said Jacob, with about as much enthusiasm as one greets their doctor during an annual exam.

"There've been rumors going around the past few days that you were back in town. And sure enough here you are," said Yul.

"Sorry to disappoint you," said Jacob.

"Yeah, well, it was nice while it lasted." It was hard to determine whether or not Yul was being facetious by the grin shaping his mouth that did nothing to conceal the contempt held in his eyes.

"Pretty strange how you just up and disappeared like a border jumper with a couple ICE agents on your tail and then reappear suddenly a year later. If you were a girl I would have hedged my bets you got yourself in a bit of trouble and skipped town to wait out the pregnancy," Yul theorized like some incompetent investigator. "So why don't you end the mystery already; why the year-long absence?"

Jacob grew suddenly serious. "You're right, Dane, no point in trying to keep it a secret any longer. The fact of the matter is I did get myself into a bit of trouble, and you're the first one I'm sharing this news with: It was a boy."

The wisecrack forced a chuckle from Max, but Yul appeared not the least bit amused even though the grin on his face widened itself.

"Word on the street is you went and had those two hideous humps on your back fixed so you'd appear a little more…oh what's the appropriate word I'm looking for? I guess it would be 'normal.' Can't really see much of a difference though, at least from where I'm standing."

The wisecrack forced a chuckle from Max, but Yul appeared not the least bit amused even though the grin on his face widened itself.

"Word on the street also has it that you've been moving in on my girl," said Yul.

"Can you be a little more specific?" asked Jacob, feigning ignorance.

"You know I'm talking about Wray."

"That's funny, 'cause the same word on the street has it the two of you broke up. In fact, the way I heard it Wray made her feelings about you pretty crystal clear when she…" Jacob paused a moment and placed a finger to his lips as he pondered his choice over the next words to leave his lips. "Oh, what's the appropriate phrase I'm looking for? Ah yes, nailed you right in the kisser at Ronny Burkowitz's party."

The grin on Yul's face instantly dissipated when the unexpected revelation met his ears. For if there was one thing that managed to burrow its way under the jock's skin it was traveling gossip that someone—anyone—had gotten the best of the great Yul Dane, much less someone of the opposite sex, and in such a public display with countless witnesses. And for a moment it looked as if Yul might charge at Jacob like some frothing bull suddenly transported to the inside of a china shop.

"Excuse me for butting in for a second, but Dane is it?" Max, inserting himself between the bull and the red flag, interrupted.

"Why don't you keep your nose outta this. This has nothing to do with you," Yul was quick to snap back.

"Was just going to introduce myself to you, mate. I'm a friend of Jacob, here. Name's Max Kelly."

Max extended his hand to Yul who naturally snubbed the friendly gesture.

"Mate? What'd you just get off the boat from Ireland?" Yul grumbled while giving the stranger a once-over in the disapproving way "Gets" from Harpus High had in looking down their nose at those outside their snobbish clique, especially someone as far outside as a Max Kelly.

"You came pretty close to getting it on the nose," Max replied in jest. "I'm actually from a place about ten thousand miles southeast of Ireland called Australia. You know, that land mass floating in the ocean on the opposite side of the globe known for koalas and meat pies, not to mention one of the seven wonders of the world called The Great Barrier Reef."

"Great!" Yul replied with a smile that was anything but. "Now, how about you doing me and yourself a big fat favor and hopping back across the Pacific to Europe like the good little frog you are?"

It took Jacob all he could muster to keep from cracking up at the deadpan expression that draped itself over his friend who looked like he might jam a finger into his ear to check for a blockage that could be interfering with his hearing.

"I take it school's not your best subject," said Max. "First of all it's the Atlantic that separates America from Europe. Secondly, Australia is not part of Europe but, in fact, is its own continent. And lastly, I think you have us mixed up with the French with that little frog comment. Although kangaroo would have worked nicely seeing how they, too, hop."

"Do I look like I'm interested in a geography lesson from you?" Yul shot back. "The only continent I give two figs about is the United States."

Max's gaze narrowed itself on the blond jock with a look of disbelief.

"No offense, mate, but I've seen brighter candles on an unlit birthday cake. Yul's grin faded in an instant as his eyes intensified their focus on the unflinching Max.

"Then how about you close your eyes, make a wish and blow m—"

Yul hadn't even managed to get all of his tacky comeback past his tongue when Max pursed his lips as though he were about to blow out a candle and, with flecks of gold suddenly alight in the pupils of his eyes like miniature sun flares erupting with fiery life, he released a gentle puff of air that yanked the jock off his feet and sent him sailing backward through the restaurant where he crashed with a great calamity into a cart a startled busboy had just filled with dirty dishes from a nearby table.

"Well, that was a smart move," remarked Jacob who looked both astonished and not at all surprised at the same time.

"A real no-hoper, that one is," said Max "Got my wish, at least."

"Yeah, and what was that?" Jacob huffed with exasperation.

"That he'd shut that gaping gob of his."

The loud ruckus of breaking dishes brought Wray and Ty racing out of the restrooms. "Curse my pea-sized bladder," cried Ty when he caught sight of Yul soiled from head to toe with breakfast remnants looking limp and dazed as his two buddies struggled to help the jock to his feet. "I knew the moment I left the table I was going to miss something."

"What happened?" asked Wray.

Both Jacob and Max gave a near identical look of obliviousness and shrugged.

"Looks like the lad took a bit of a spill," Max noted casually.

"Not surprising. I believe I noticed he was chewing gum when he walked in here," said Ty, before shooting Max a questioning eye. "And who exactly are you?"

"Oh, that's right. I guess some introductions are in order," said Jacob who appeared suddenly flummoxed. "This here is…is…"

"Lucky for you I'm not some cute sheila whose name's already escaped your lips or you'd likely be on the receiving end of a king hit," Max chastised Jacob before turning to Wray and Ty. "Name's Max Kelly."

Max Kelly

The name immediately reached out and gave Wray's ear a sharp yank as she recalled reading about a so-called Nephilim named Max from Queensland while buried nose-deep snooping her way through Jacob's journal

"I might be going out on a limb here, but between your noticeable accent and the fact that I've never seen your face before now, I'm guessing you're not from around these parts," Ty surmised with Inspector Clouseau flair.

"Funny how that works. From where I'm standing, you're the ones who speak with a noticeable accent," said Max. "But you're right I'm not from around these parts, as you say. I'm just visiting from out of town; way out of town, in fact. I was intrigued enough by what Jacob's told me about Cain's Corner that I decided to stop through whenever I found myself in the neighborhood. So here I am."

"Alright, alright, I wasn't looking for you to dump your entire life story on us," Ty muttered under his breath.

Never mind him," Wray said while shooting Ty a disapproving glare. "When he was younger no one told him about the side effects of what eating glue would have on the brain."

An awkward pause followed when she suddenly realized she was staring at the stranger a little too intensely. "I'm sorry, I'm—"

"Wray Bliss, I'm guessing" Max was quick to interrupt. "That's right. How did you know?"

"You kiddin' me? Jacob here's done nothing but talk about you."

"I think you might be exaggerating a bit there," said Jacob, whose face had suddenly taken on the hue of a newly picked turnip.

"In that case, I take it then you're already familiar with me," Ty said with an air of presumption while holding out his hand to Max.

Max, however, responded with a blank stare. "I don't think—"

"Ty. Ty Wrenwood." But his attempt to jog the boy's memory appeared to be for nil before he subtly shot Jacob a questioning glare of offense. "The same Ty Wrenwood who until this very second was Jacob here's best friend."

"Oh, that Ty Wrenwood," said Max, feigning a moment of sudden recognition. "Sorry, I must have suffered a brief attack of Alzheimer's."

"I knew it," Ty remarked smugly as he shook Max's hand before giving Jacob's neck a playful squeeze. "Seriously bro, you need to stop fawning about me; it's like so embarrassing."

"I'll do my best to restrain myself in the future," replied Jacob.

Wray, meanwhile, continued to glance furtively over her shoulder in the direction of Yul, who had managed with the help of his friends to get himself upright, shaky as he was on his feet. "Look, I don't mean to rush this Jacob Parrish love fest along, but it's getting late and Penuel Point is waiting."

Jacob gave a hesitant look at his friends. "Yeah, about that. I'm thinking I might need to take a rain check."

"You're joking, right?" said Ty who instantly appeared ready to burn his Jacob Parrish love fest membership card.

"It's just with Max showing up out of the blue—"

"Don't mind me. I didn't mean to break up whatever it is you all had planned," Max offered apologetically.

"It's no big deal. We were just going to go up to Penuel Point for the day," said Jacob.

"Why don't you come along with us," Wray quickly offered.

"What?" cried Jacob who looked horrified at the suggestion, followed nearly instantaneously by an even louder protest of "Why?" by Ty.

"What I meant was," Ty attempted to clarify when all eyes came to rest on him, "have you ever BASE jumped before?"

"BASE jumping. Isn't that the harebrained sport where you leap off something tall like the top of a building or mountain with nothing but a parachute strapped to your back?" asked Max.

"That's it."

"No thanks, mate, that's not for this bloke. If God wanted man to fly, he'd of gifted him with a pair wings just like he did the birds, ain't that right, Jacob?" said Max with a surreptitious wink and a flash of teeth to his friend who was looking more uncomfortable with each passing second.

"Tell you what, though, if you don't mind I'd love to tag along and watch," Max said much to Ty's slow-growing disdain. "Jacob's spoken quite a bit about this Penuel Point. I'm curious to see what all the hubbub is about."

"Jacob, Jacob, Jacob." The utterance made by Ty under his breath in his best Jan Brady impersonation didn't escape Max's precision hearing.

"Plus, it might be good to have an extra person on hand to identify the splattered bodies should, heaven forbid, the need arise," he noted pointedly in return.

Ty forced apart his lips and bared his teeth in a way that would best pass for a friendly smile than a snarl and said simply, "Funny."

Why this stranger from down under drew from him a twinge of contempt, Ty couldn't quite put his finger on it. One thing was certain: watching his best friend and Max head out of Rabble-Rousers with Wray in tow as though long-lost buddies reunited made the shades of green that suddenly began to color his vision all the more brighter.

CHAPTER SEVEN

P enuel Point existed for one purpose: to prove that, indeed, there was such a thing as a heaven. For it could be argued the most hardened of atheists who stood at its threshold and witnessed to the jaw-dropping picturesque vista unfurled before them couldn't help but second guess their steadfast denial in the existence of a divine entity needed to create such beauty. At least, that was Jacob's immediate feeling the first time he ever came to visit the spot.

The vast mountain range rolled toward the horizon and beyond like an endless ocean of gray. Groves of redwoods, spruce and pine trees appeared like patches of moss growing in scattered clumps upon the granite slabs of mountain that came up out of the earth to be meticulously sculpted by a glacier millions of years ago into enclosing cliffs and lofty domes reaching toward the brilliant blue sky. Shadows from a slow-moving band of billowing white and black marbled clouds making their way along the face of the steep jagged peaks, and tracing the sheer drops of countless cliffs downward into the waiting valley, gave the illusion that the mountains were moving like a gentle tide.

Standing at the helm of the scenic overlook were a handful of visitors cloistered together around Jacob, snapping photo after photo of one of the most beautiful, and surprisingly least known sites on the planet. Jacob felt as if he had secured a coveted spot on top of the world. He had stood at the exact same spot many times before, and every time it was as if it was the first time he had been gifted with the wondrous view before him. His mother had first introduced him to this marvel of nature as a young child, during better days. So mesmerized was he by the sight that it instantly became his favorite place, proving to be a refuge of sorts from the ugliness that seemed to be closing its grip tighter and tighter on the world.

Grasping the wooden rail erected in front of him to keep visitors corralled to enjoy the view from a safe position and discourage thrill-seekers from journeying too closely to the sheer drop off only a few feet away, Jacob leaned his body as far forward as possible. Looking out over the overhang he peered down into the valley below that appeared as a lush garden of green from out of a fairy tale book. The patches of trees that had gained a footing on the mountain sides grew more dense the further down they grew toward the base of the giant monoliths where they created a lush carpet of brilliant green along the valley floor. In the distance, a giant waterfall could be seen spilling over the lip of one of the towering mountain faces. As Jacob stood transfixed on the column of rushing water showering the lower elevations with a frigid rain fed from the last drops of snow melted from the highest peaks, he couldn't help but think of Eden and, even more so, the place that he had briefly come to call his home: Havenhid. And for a fleeting moment he found himself overcome with a profound feeling of homesickness. Not that such a reaction was all that surprising to Jacob; after all, Havenhid in many ways had served as equal a home, if not more, than Cain's Corner. But as much as he may have loved it, Jacob did not want to miss it. Not a smidge, even. Yet it was then and there that he realized as he closed his eyes and breathed in deeply the crisp air that was so clean and pure it seemed to slightly burn the inside of his nose while trying to push all thoughts of Eden out of his head that Penuel Point, his most favorite place to visit and refuge, now served as a memory of the heavenly place from which he had recently fled.

With some reluctance, he acquiesced to abandoning his post after glancing at the time on his watch. He threaded his way past the other admiring sightseers and made his way back to a small embankment on the far side of the viewpoint away from the crowds where Ty was found slumbering in a canopy of shade cast down from a towering redwood as he lay stretched out on his back on the ground upon a bed of dry pine needles.

"I don't know what's more offensive. The guy I saw a few minutes ago tossing his empty soda can over the cliff, or finding you here like this," Jacob remarked to the figure dressed in a dark blue track suit framed with bright orange piping.

"You forgot the rather large woman we had the unfortunate experience of crossing paths with who was squeezed into a tight pair of black leggings thirty sizes too small for her when we first drove in," Ty muttered, his groggy and muffled voice coming from behind the Yankees ball cap that was covering his face like a miniature pup tent.

"I don't get how you can be over here napping when one of nature's most majestically awesome spectacles is just a few yards away," said Jacob.

"It's pretty easy, actually. Start with a nice heavy breakfast, add in a long drive, the soothing warm sun and this high altitude, and you've got the makings of a most sloth-like afternoon," answered Ty.

"She call yet?" asked Jacob with a huff of exasperation. The "she" he referred to was Wray whose designated role on these outings was to drive the boys to Penuel Point and then head back down the mountain and park at a specific point on the valley floor that Jacob and Ty targeted as the landing spot of their free fall. Once they touched down, she would race to pick the boys up and make as quick a getaway as possible before any watchful park ranger managed to get there first and cite the group for engaging in activities strictly prohibited at Penuel Point.

Ty peered out from beneath his cap, a pained look of exertion in his eyes, and gave the cell phone perched upon his chest a quick glance.

"Negatory," he replied briskly before returning to the cover of his hat like the head of a tortoise retreating back inside the safe hollow of its shell.

Jacob could feel himself growing somewhat more antsier as they waited, especially knowing Wray was being kept company by Max. Not that he had any ill reservations about Max. They were, after all, friends; and not just friends, but great friends. But Max was a Nephilim, just as he himself was, and it was taxing enough for Jacob to keep his own secret concealed from those closest to him every single minute of every single day. The last thing he needed was to worry about someone else with the same secret not being equally as cagey.

"Least you could do is give your chute one last good look over and make sure everything is in working order," said Jacob as he grabbed his own pack to inspect in hopes of refocusing the jumble of concerns sounding off inside his head. "Remember what Max said on the drive here: there have been seven BASE jumping fatalities in the last year alone, and most of them were the result of careless mistakes made when packing the chute."

"Fine," Ty grumbled loudly, tossing aside his cap and irritably grabbing for his pack which was leaning against the trunk of a nearby tree. "I've been doing this for how long now? But along comes Max and suddenly I'm a novice."

"I keep thinking about the story he told about the guy who made a jump in the Swiss Alps and slammed into the side of a mountain," Jacob, oblivious to Ty's mumblings, said.

"The guy was wearing a wing suit. It's completely different from what we're doing," Ty snapped back. "Besides, who brings up fatality statistics and people smashing into the sides of mountains on the way to a BASE-jumping outing? That's like trying to lift the spirits of someone headed into surgery with news of how many people expire on the operating table. Cheers, mate, way to suck out all the fun to the day."

"What's going on with you?" Jacob asked as he finally took notice of his friend's soured disposition

"Nothing's going on with me," Ty mumbled in reply while checking his pack.

"The heck there isn't. Do you have some sort of issue with Max or something?"

"Why should I have an issue with your buddy? Just think it's funny for someone who's never jumped before to suddenly be an expert on the sport."

"I don't think he was trying to sound off like an expert. I think it was more like he was trying to make friendly conversation with two people he just met," said Jacob. "No one wants to feel like they're as popular as a rattlesnake in a lucky dip."

Ty glanced up from what he was doing with a look indicating he had just been struck on the side of his head by a rock.

"Popular as a rattle—…what does that even mean?"

"Just a saying I picked up from Max," said Jacob who realized the moment he heard the words leave his mouth that such adages had a habit of falling awkwardly flat when not in the tune of an Australian accent.

Great…now you're even starting to talk like him," Ty said with a mouth twisting with obvious distaste. "So how did the two of you meet, anyhow? An Outback Steakhouse."

Jacob did his best to conceal a small swell of panic roll through his body. It was such a simple question, and yet somehow during the drive from Rabble-Rousers to Penuel Point it had escaped him to think up a quick and believable fib that would pass as the truth.

"It was while I was away," answered Jacob with a dismissive shrug. "Would you believe we suffer from the same back condition?"

The response sort of rolled off Jacob's tongue and, while it cloaked the truth with deliberate ambiguity, he was proud of the fact that he had managed to avert telling his friend an outright lie.

"Well, I guess Mr. Walt Disney was right all along; it is a small world after all," Ty replied dryly.

"Guess it's not too surprising that the two of us would sort of hit it off from the get-go considering. You go through something as intense and bizarre as I did, you manage to form bonds with those going through the same of experience." Jacob bit down on his tongue as it was closest he'd come to sharing his reality with someone outside the Nephilim bubble.

"If you want me to be completely honest with you," he said while quickly reeling himself in, "I think the reason Max and I got on so well is that in a lot of ways he reminds me of you. By that I mean he's a pretty unique and outlandish character. Just in a more reined-in sort way."

Jacob had thought his words would have brought a smile of sorts to his friend's face, but it didn't.

"So, what is it you're trying to tell me; that he's your new best friend?" asked Ty.

A light of understanding lit up Jacob's face.

"Is that what this is about? You're jealous?" Jacob asked half chuckling.

"I'm glad you find it amusing," Ty murmured under his breath. "And, no, I am not jealous, conceited."

"I don't know about that. From where I'm sitting you're looking a tad bit green. Radioactive green, actually," Jacob chided in a way good friends sometimes have a tendency of doing when they learn the little ways in which to get under each other's skin.

"But you shouldn't," he was quick to add when he saw Ty's feathers were getting more ruffled than they usually did when poked fun of. "The role of Jacob Parrish's best friend has long been, and will always be played by one Ty Wrenwood. I would have figured after all this time it would have been a no-brainer to you."

Ty did his best to keep the grin from revealing itself in his mouth and marring his sulking expression, but in the end, after hearing the sincerity in Jacob's words, it was a battle lost. Then, as boys are prone to do when the awkwardness of a situation screams for a hugging embrace, they instead traded a couple of equally affectionate jabs to one another's shoulders.

"It's only fair, after all," said Jacob, "seeing as how I've pretty much locked down the part of your best friend for the unforeseeable future, right?"

"Um, sure…whatever you say," Ty replied with an apathetic shrug before returning his attention to his pack.

Jacob could only close his eyes and shake his head disapprovingly at his own self. After all, he had walked right into it.

~ ~ ~

The sound of Ty's cell phone pinging brought the two boys back to the task at hand. "She's there," announced Ty, reading the two-word text that popped up on his screen.

Jacob took a last swig of water and helped his sluggish friend to his feet. They then grabbed their packs and strapped them onto their backs.

"This is it; our final hurrah of the summer. Just like old times," announced Ty.

"Last one down buys dinner?" Jacob challenged.

Ty clasped Jacob's hand accepting the challenge as they both began counting off in unison.

"One."

"Two."

"Three," barked Ty, breaking the rhythmic count by two beats and taking off in a cheating sprint toward the overlook.

Most of the other park visitors turned to look at the two teens as they raced one another, zig-zagging their way through the crowd. Ty was the first to reach the wooden barrier meant to keep people from venturing out onto the tempting overhang followed close behind by Jacob. Ignoring the posted sign reading "Danger—Do Not Enter" as they had on previous visits, they leapt over the fence like a pair of pack-saddled cadets making their way through a military maneuvers course.

The mix of dirt and graveled rock crunched loudly beneath their pounding sneakers as they tore across the narrow finger of granite that jutted out from the overhang like a diving board leading to a pool of absolute nothingness. But in his dash toward it, Jacob suddenly became conscious of the thumping coming from deep inside his chest. Or rather it was the lack of thumping coming from within his chest that caught his attention. It was during this race toward the cliff's edge in time's past when his heart was prone to start pounding like a tribal drum; not from running but from the growing anticipation of the moment of no return fast approaching. This time, however, his heart was barely a flutter, and the anxiety that usually gripped him was vacant from his body and left his skin free of the nervous sweat which by now would have been trickling from his pores.

Following several paces behind Ty, he watched as his friend took the final two steps upon the rock before flinging himself into the open air with a loud cry of victory, arms extended out like a bird's wings, before instantly falling out of sight. A couple screams from the onlookers watching in horror from behind the railing breached by the boys briefly caught Jacob's ears, and then nothing.

Nothing, that is, except silence.

It was, for Ty, one of the few precious moments that made the experience known as life worth living: when a thing as simple as a leap offered a brief taste of eternity by engulfing him completely in the rapturous feeling of flight inside an abyss of beauty surrounding him from all sides of which he had thrown himself into headfirst. And then wind. A mighty roar whistling past the ears when the invisible wings are suddenly denuded of its feathers and the fast-approaching earth squeezes tight the stomach as it seeks to reclaim what belongs to it with the vengeance of a spoiled child.

Ty looked but was unable to catch Jacob in his sights. He deployed his chute and waited for the feeling of the hand of God to reach down out of the sky and grab hold of him.

It didn't come.

He jerked back his head and looked above him, and instead of seeing his canary yellow chute unfurled in a rectangular-shaped canopy he found it being strangled within his control lines only half deployed and fluttering loudly and uselessly in the wind. Panicked, he instinctively began tugging and pulling on the lines in an attempt to disentangle them and free his chute while glancing frantically toward the ground.

The chute had opened enough to create somewhat of a drag and slow his fall, but not enough to keep himself from being slammed out of existence once he hit the ground. And the ground was rising up to greet him at an uncomfortable speed.

Again he looked about for Jacob, and again he found nothing but open space. Not that there was anything his friend would have been able to do but share in his terror. He tugged harder at the lines and soon found himself caught in a tailspin. Had it been a ride at an amusement park he might have cried out and laughed with enjoyment. Only this was no amusement park ride.

Around and around he spun.

Faster and faster.

He felt his stomach lurch and turn over on itself. He would have vomited had he not been in the tight grip of sheer panic and fright. The world around him became a blur and suddenly the tapestry of this majestic setting was torn away revealing an ugly nightmare of a place from which he prayed he could awaken. The greenness of the valley below that had appeared as something out of a painting was now rearing up like some green monster to swallow him alive. If he could just reach downward he would just be able to touch the tops of the trees, the trees that were just readying to snap every bone in his body as he crashed through the barrage of branches waiting for him.

And then there was a shadow.

What exactly it was Ty couldn't make out as his chute—the small bulbous portion, that is, that had managed to catch air and inflate—shielded the shape from his sight. It moved overhead with a quick passing flicker and it was accompanied by what sounded to Ty's ears as a fluttering of wings. Not the gentle flutter of a delicate bird ruffling its feathers while frolicking in a bird bath, but the loud powerful flapping heard coming from the rustling canvas sails during a regatta race on the open sea.

Ty strained his eyes harder to see what was hovering above him but the spinning and his imminent demise coming closer in the advancing trees had taken its toll. He was ready. For death, that is. Only please, don't let it be too painful! he begged whoever might be listening to his last-minute bargaining. He squeezed shut his eyes. He may have briefly fooled himself into thinking he was ready for death, but bearing witness to it was an altogether different matter.

Then, just as he felt himself surrender to his fate, with a hard-fought reluctance, but surrender just the same, there came a jolt. One he had expected several hundred feet earlier, before being sucked into a vortex of sheer, undiluted panic. And the sensation of falling suddenly ceased, along with the roar of the wind whistling loudly in his ears and the uncontrollable spinning.

Thank goodness for the end of the spinning.

Ty twisted his head with great effort to look upward. While the physical spinning had stopped, his vision continued to capture the world around him in a dizzying kaleidoscope of blurriness. Suspended above him, his chute remained a limp malfunctioned ball of nylon still tethered in a tightly tangled ball. And yet he was hovering now. Floating. As though a giant invisible hook had been cast from Heaven and snagged his chute just in the nick of the time.

He could just barely catch a glimpse of something right behind the mangled ball above him. Dark. An obscure and mysterious black form behind the puff of nylon that was his failed chute and silhouetted against the brightness of the sun directly behind the shape. The flapping continued with a rhythmic cadence. Like a giant wing. Naturaly, his brain immediately shirked away from the ridiculousness of such a thought, even in his panicked state. Yet he could hear it; that powerful fluttering. He fought to focus, fighting to see through the blurred goggles he felt had been forced over his eyes.

Then suddenly he was on the ground within a thicket of trees, coming to a rest with a gentle roll rather than a life-extinguishing thud. Never had the feel of dirt and dry, prickly pine needles felt so welcoming. He immediately crawled out from beneath the tangle of rope and balled-up chute that came raining down on top of him and leapt to his feet only to be knocked down once more as an explosion of pain detonated itself in his right ankle. Wincing with agony, Ty focused his eyes skyward, scouring the lofty treetops that all but blotted from above the view of the blue sky. That's when he heard the crunching sound of approaching footsteps. Turning his head, he caught sight of Jacob standing over him, and his face immediately whitened.

"Jacob?" he asked as though he wasn't sure his eyesight was playing tricks on him. Jacob knelt down beside his friend, but as he did Ty attempted to scurry away.

"What the hell's going on?" Ty questioned Jacob who looked only slightly less terrified as Ty sounded. "Did I actually die?"

Jacob instantly understood the rationale for the question when he looked into his friend's wide-fixed eyes and caught the image of himself in the mirrored pools, specifically the sight of two giant wings seen half unfurled behind his back.

"But if I did die, then why are you kneeling next to me looking like some kind of an...of an...angel?" Ty muttered to himself as he tried to figured out the insanity of what he was seeing. "Unless..."

He suddenly reached over his left shoulder and frantically felt about the area of his own upper back before swiftly switching to his right side in search of similar feathered appendages attached to his body.

"Was it you who took the dirt nap and now you're appearing to me one last time before going to the great beyond?" he asked.

Jacob couldn't help but smiling slightly.

"Nobody took a dirt nap," he said. "Now, just relax for a minute."

He brushed back Ty's mussed hair and placed his hand lightly over his forehead.

"No offense, but if you did die how did you ever manage to swindle getting a pair of angel wings?" he asked in the groggy voice of someone drifting off to sleep.

The last thing Ty saw as he stared up into Jacob's face were the bursts of gold flashes suddenly alight in his friend's eyes, and then he felt a dark plume of unconsciousness slowly engulf him.

~ ~ ~

Wray's Jeep came barreling across the open green grassy field, horn blaring loudly, as it sped its way toward the far edge of the clearing where Jacob was spied half carrying a noticeably limping Ty from the thicket of trees sprouting at the base of the mountain. The Jeep had barely come to a stop when Wray jumped out of the driver's seat and raced to Jacob's side throwing her arms around him in a strangling hug.

"Oh my goodness, thank God you're alright!" she cried out.

"Everything's fine. Just a hurt ankle, that's all," said Jacob.

"I thought we'd lost you."

"It's okay. Really."

When he realized she wasn't going to let go of him any time soon, he grabbed her arms and helped to loosen her hold. That's when he noticed her face was tear-streaked.

"Why are you crying?"

"Are you kidding me?" Wray screeched. "I was sitting down here and watched the whole terrifying thing. I thought you were dead!"

She lunged at Jacob again and captured him once more in her tight embrace all while Ty looked on in growing disbelief.

"Um, I don't want to put too fine a point on it, but you do realize it was me who almost died," Ty remarked dryly.

Wray turned her attention to Ty and with a pouty look of sympathy gave him a hug that was not as tight and embracing as the one she gave Jacob, but a hug nonetheless.

"Do you think it's broken?" she asked, looking down at Ty's ankle that he kept lifted and free of his weight as he clung to Jacob for support.

"Nah, I think I just sprained it," he said.

"How did you manage that?" asked Wray, drawing a pointed look of awe from Ty.

"You know, I'm not really sure. But if I were to make a blind guess I'd have to say it probably occurred sometime between the moment when my chute didn't open and when I plunged a gazillion miles an hour toward the earth to my waiting death shrieking like a girl," Ty snarked.

Wray shot him a look of exasperation in return. "What I meant is, how is it that's the worst of your injuries?" she rephrased her words with a huff. "I mean, look at that mountain. How does someone survive that high of a fall and suffer only a sprained ankle? You should be in a million broken pieces."

All eyes shifted in unison to the mountain looming behind them like some great, gray beast which proved to be equally breath-snatching when looking up at the mystical monolith of nature as it was gazing down from its crown.

"Sorry to disappoint you," Ty replied, looking both somewhat offended and completely baffled that he was still upright and talking. And, for that matter, simply breathing.

"From what I could tell looking at the damage to his chute, he snagged a few tree branches which slowed his fall before hitting the ground," Jacob offered. "What did you guys see?"

"Not much. It all happened so fast," answered Wray.

"Whatever happened, happened after you disappeared behind that cluster of trees." Jacob glanced over in the direction of Max's voice to find his friend standing quietly nearby and listening intently.

"Truth is, I don't remember much of anything after deploying my chute and seeing it all tangled up. After that, it all goes black," Ty remarked with a deepening frown as though straining to scour the inside if his head.

Jacob and Max continued to hold the other's gaze, both of which held a subtle yet deep look of comprehension lost to Wray and Ty.

"We should really get out of here. Some park ranger will likely be here any minute. Plus, we need to get you to a doctor," suggested Wray.

"I don't need a doctor, just an ice pack," said Ty.

"We can argue about it on the way home."

It was then as Ty shifted his supporting hold from Jacob to Wray's capable hands and was about to be led off to the waiting Jeep that Wray noticed the t-shirt Jacob was wearing was in shatters. Specifically, the seams down both sides had been shredded from armpit to hem leaving nothing but long threads of tangled cotton hanging.

"What happened to you?" she asked with alarm.

When Jacob saw where her attention was fixed, he folded his arms in a useless attempt to conceal the damage.

"Must of snagged it while helping Ty here," he answered awkwardly.

Luckily for him, Wray's hands were full with Ty keeping her from taking a closer look and seeing that "snagged" was an understated way of putting it. For had she investigated further she would have noticed almost immediately the whole back side of Jacob's shirt was nonexistent. In fact, it appeared to have been blown out by a small, yet powerful explosion from within, centered somewhere in the vicinity of his upper back. All that was keeping the shirt from falling free of Jacob's torso was the small ribbon of material that formed the neck hole which was about all that had somehow remained intact.

Jacob traded a quiet glance with Max, and Max recognized instantly the nervous look of unease in his friend's eyes.

"I'll grab you an extra shirt from your backpack," Max was quick to offer before hurrying off toward the Jeep.

If there was one thing Jacob and other Nephilim learned quickly once they came into their wings, it was to always have plenty of spare shirts on hand at all times.

~ ~ ~

After making the long drive back to Cain's Corner from Penuel Point, the foursome found themselves right back where they had started out the day: in front of Rabble-Rousers. Wray gave a quick goodbye to everyone that included planting a parting peck on Jacob's cheek before rushing inside where her work shift at the restaurant was about begin.

"You want to go inside and have a bite to eat? After all, I still owe you dinner," said Jacob, reminding Ty of the bet they had made just before making their unfortunate cliff jump. "Of course, I didn't think you were so much of a cheapskate that you'd put your life on the line for the price of a free meal."

It was friendly ribbing that usually earned a caustic retort from Ty. Instead, Ty remained uncharacteristically quiet as he had the entire drive back to town with a somewhat dazed look settled in his face, much like a baseball player who had the misfortune of catching an incoming pitch to the side of the head.

"Paging Ty Wrenwood…you in?" Jacob called out while snapping his fingers several times in his friend's face until the vacant eyes blinked with life once more.

"What's that?" Ty muttered like someone awakening from a narcoleptic episode.

"Food? Do you want to go inside and get some?" Jacob repeated himself with remedial slowness while miming shoveling a plate of grub into his mouth with an imaginary fork.

"You know, I think I'm just going to head home and take it easy if it's all the same to you," answered Ty with an uncharacteristic sedateness

"You sure you're okay? Maybe we should drive you," suggested Jacob.

"Seriously, mom, for the thousandth time I'm all right. Just feel the need to chill tonight," said Ty.

Jacob watched as Ty climbed into his Volkswagen van parked nearby which started up with a loud rattling rumbling and he couldn't help but smile to himself; he really did look like Keith Partridge behind the wheel of that old relic.

"I'll catch up with you tomorrow," Jacob yelled out to his friend as the van pulled out away from the curb and headed up the street.

"Looks like a tree whose branches a mad gardener had a go at one too many times with the pruning shears," observed Max, who was standing beside Jacob.

Just like many of Max's peculiar sayings, this latest turn of a phrase drew a sideways glance from Jacob.

"You know, his noggin," Max attempted to make clear while tapping on the side of his own head with his finger. "Must have been some mind-bending job you did on him. Looks like someone clobbered him wonky."

Naturally, Max was referring to the Grace inherited by certain Nephilim that allowed them to influence the thoughts of others, and even alter their memories. When Jacob drew noticeably silent, however, it was Max's turn to level a sideways look on his friend.

"You did bind his memory, didn't you?" asked Max. "And by the looks of him, I'd say within an inch of his life."

"What makes you say that?" returned Jacob.

"Come on, who're you kiddin'? We both know you were the one who saved Wiley E. Coyote there from becoming forest fertilizer, and that's not something one's able to do on the sly," said Max. "My guess is you had to have a whole ball of twine to lock up tight the memory of witnessing you swooping down out of the sky with a pair of giant wings attached to your back and snatching him from certain death."

Jacob's brow grew more weighty with each passing second that Max spoke of the incident.

"Not really, no," he answered quietly.

"What do you mean?"

"I mean, I didn't so much bind his memory as scrub it clean," said Jacob with a huff usually reserved for criminals surrendering a confession after a long interrogation.

A look just short of appalling came over Max. "But…you can't do that."

"I know," Jacob acquiesced quietly.

"If Anahel found out, his head would blow like a train whistle," said Max. "Zuriel made it a point of drilling into our heads the things we can and cannot do with our Graces. And I remember specifically he made clear about Bending that memories cannot be excised completely from another's thoughts. It goes against the golden rule forbidding us to knowingly tamper with the course of human history."

"I said, I know!" barked Jacob, who was growing more annoyed at the lecture he was receiving. "I admit it…I messed up. But you weren't there."

Max refrained from saying anything in return and quietly watched as Jacob began to pace the sidewalk in an agitated way.

"You didn't see the look in his eyes when he saw me in the light of what I really am," said Jacob. "It was like in those old creature feature movies they show on TV…you know, when the monster is seen for the first time. That's how I felt…like some kind of hideous monster. But there was one moment when he looked at me with a sort of dazed expression, as if he wasn't quite sure if what he was seeing was real or a hallucination. At one point he actually questioned if he was dead. And in that one moment I thought maybe there was a chance he might understand this secret I've been forced to conceal and he'd be okay with it. I mean, this is the guy who once tried to convince me that Han Solo and Chewbacca were actually a couple and a foretelling of not only the gender-neutral movement but the species neutral wave he insists is on the horizon."

Amusing as Max found such a hypothesis to be, Jacob barely cracked a smile in telling it as his mood quickly darkened once more.

"But then, when I reached out to help him with his injured leg, he pulled back…actually pulled back away from me. That's when I could see in his eyes, at least at that moment, I was no longer his best friend, but something to be fearful of…an unexplainable thing that even he with all his harebrained and absurd theories and concepts couldn't make sense of, or rationalize...and it was one of the worst feelings I've ever felt before," said Jacob.

If there was one other person who knew exactly how Jacob felt, it was Max. And yet even he was stumped with what words he could offer that might lift his friend's dragging spirit, if even a little.

"Maybe you didn't give him enough of a chance to try," Max suggested as diplomatically as he could.

"Are you suggesting I panicked?"

"I'm just gently suggesting that maybe you were the one who expected the worst from your friend and in doing so jumped the gun."

If Jacob was leaning toward agreeing with Max, he didn't say so one way or the other and, instead, stood staring through the window of Rabble-Rousers watching Wray as she busily went about waiting on tables inside the restaurant. Max could tell instantly from the concentrated way Jacob's eyes followed Wray that his dour outlook wasn't focused entirely on what had occurred earlier with Ty, but the prospects of what the future held on the other side of the glass.

"If you don't mind me saying, she's a bit of alright," Max remarked as he shared in Jacob's sightline.

"Don't get any ideas," Jacob shot back in jest.

Max smiled and gave Jacob a reassuring pat on the back that said more than any words that theirs was a bond infused with the loyalty of the rare brotherhood they had come to share. He then stated in typical Max Kelly fashion, "I don't crap where I eat!"

~ ~ ~

The two started off walking along the town's main thoroughfare taking several turns down several streets before veering off in the direction of Jacob's home when Max asked Jacob an odd sort of a question.

"Do you think there's a chance Wray might be onto the fact that there's something not quite...normal about you?"

"I think we crossed that bridge when we first became friends," replied Jacob only half- joking.

"What I mean is do you think it's a possibility she might suspect that you're...you know..."

"What? That I'm a Nephilim? I think there's a higher probability she would come to the conclusion that I'm a member of the Justice League than have a hunch I'm half angel," Jacob said before casting a suspicious glance at Max. "Why do you ask?"

"Just something she asked while the two of us were in her Jeep waiting for you and Ty to make your jump. It's sort of wedged itself in the back of my head," said Max.

"Well, are you going to tell me what?" pressed Jacob.

"Akdamar."

"What about Akdamar?"

"That's it," said Max with a shrug. "She asked me if I'd ever been to Akdamar Island. But it was the way she asked me, as though she were fishing for something."

"What did you tell her?" inquired Jacob.

"That I've visited there in passing on my way to enter through the gate to get into Eden," Max replied with noticeable sarcasm. "What do you think I told her?"

Akdamar? Why would Wray be asking about Akdamar Island? Jacob wondered silently to himself. The better question would have been... how did she even know about the existence of such a place? Granted, Wray was well above average when it came to intelligence, and she could hold her own better than Jacob could in the geography portion of Trivial Pursuit. But Akdamar Island was such an oddly obscure place; it certainly wasn't a top destination to find its way into conversation about travel like other more well-known spots such as Paris, France, or even Morocco. Heck, even Jacob had never heard of Akdamar before the day he took a boat across the lake in which the island sat and stepped foot on its shores. So for someone like Wray to engage someone in conversation about Akdamar Island from out of the blue, especially a fellow Nephilim like Max, it just struck Jacob as being more than a little peculiar. And yet, at the same time, he knew there was absolutely no way in the world she could have any inkling to the true significance of Akdamar where he and Max were concerned, and that her bringing it up, however strange it may have seemed, could only have been by freakish coincidence.

"Did she ask about anything else?" Jacob prodded.

"Just the usual kinds of things: where I was from, how we came to know one another," answered Max. "You know, you could have saved yourself all this trouble if you had just stayed put in Eden and just toughed it out like the rest of us."

Jacob stopped dead in his tracks. "The rest of you?" he echoed somewhat incredulously. "No offense, but what I've been forced to deal with is maybe just a tad bit more stressful than what the rest of you face. Or have you already forgotten the night of my Blessing when Creed's father basically threatened to put me on trial for I don't even know what."

"Trial," Max spit. "Creed's father can take his threats and go to buggery, for all I care. It's a right load of codswallop, if you ask me."

Jacob didn't know exactly what a "right load of codswallop" was, but judging from the sneering tone in which Max spoke he assumed it to be equivalent to a huge steaming pile of cow dung.

"I also don't think you did yourself any favors running away from Havenhid with your tail between your legs," Max was quick to add, cutting Jacob to the quick.

"Is that what this is all about?" asked Jacob, looking slightly offended at the idea anyone would accuse him of even remotely resembling a cowering coward. "You know, you still haven't told me exactly why you're here. But if it's some attempt to convince me to go back, let me save you the trouble by telling you you're wasting your time."

"I'm here," Max replied pointedly to his friend, "because I think after everything that's happened it's quite easy for some people to sometimes forget they're not alone. Kairo, Leos, Ethan and I had your back in the Silent Forest when Thaniel went south; we'll continue to have your back in face of whatever slings and arrows Sandel and whoever else might hurl your way because the truth is we each of us think your blood's worth bottling."

Visibly touched by the sentiment, Jacob could only smile, albeit abashedly, and answer Max back with a telling fist bump.

"I'm also not gonna try and convince you into coming back to Havenhid," Max contended. "One would have to be an expert ear-basher to try and penetrate a noggin cured with concrete like yours with some good sense."

Jacob narrowed a suspicious gaze on Max. "And what kind of bet, exactly, are you looking to wager?"

"If I win, you return to Eden with me without gumming any complaints and finish what you started," answered Max.

"And if I win?" Jacob was quick to ask.

"Then we part ways and I'll head back to Havenhid to get my just desserts for going AWOL, no hard feelings," said Max.

Jacob gave his friend a closer study while quietly mulling over the wager presented to him. Max was a shrewd and perspicacious character, of that there was no doubt. But he was also uncharacteristically as upright an honest a person Jacob had come to know, so he knew the challenge put forth came with no tricks hidden up anyone's sleeve.

"Don't take this the wrong way, but back in Eden I smoked you nearly every time when it came to speed," said Jacob.

"Then you should have no worries about this little contest, aye?" said Max with a playful wink. "And just to prove I'm on the up and up, I'll even let you plot the course.

Jacob studied the hand that was stretched out to him and after a pause he took it readily.

~ ~ ~

They were certainly in the right spot for a spirited run. The narrow, tree-lined street they had been walking along was quiet and empty and unrolled itself like a perfectly conceived racetrack through the quaint, picturesque neighborhood. But when it came to contests between Nephilim, a more challenging course was called for over the more typical paths laid out in everyday marathons, and Jacob's eyes immediately searched the stretch of heavily forested area residing just beyond the cluster of houses and then miles further out beyond the range of normal vision until his gaze found what it was he was searching for.

"You see that tree stump on the other side of that lake over there?" Jacob asked Max.

Max followed the direction Jacob's finger was pointed where his penetrating Nephilim vision quickly caught sight of a sliver of lake water that revealed itself a good mile away, perhaps two, through a thick obstacle of trees and brush. Sure enough, on the far side of the lake he spied the splintered remnants of a tree that had some time ago toppled over and come to a permanent rest on the rocky shore.

"First one to make it there wins," said Jacob, before noting with a hint of cocksureness, "and to show what a good winner I can be, I'll even pack you a sandwich for your trip back to Havenhid."

"Did you say winner or whinger?" Max clapped back without skipping a beat. "Because my guess is you'll be too busy spitting the dummy while you're packing your bag to make any sandwiches after I hand you the humiliating defeat I'm about to."

With their good-natured crowing out of the way, the two boys took their marks on the invisible starting line, and when the word was given they both took off like two sudden gusts of wind. The street guided their sprint for just a short distance when, suddenly, they both veered off course and made a mad dash across separate front yards toward two neighboring houses. Then, with the darkening skies of the deepening dusk to lend cover to their fantastical movements from any nosy nellies who might happen to be peering out their windows at that particular moment, Jacob and Max bounded upward onto the eaves of the houses with effortless ease, and scampered across the rooftops with enough clamor that any children inside were sure to sit up with excitement at the thought Christmas had arrived early. What sounded like the hooves of reindeer coming in for a landing to children would more than likely bring a look of concern to parents visited with lesser-than-merry visions of giant rats congregating in the rafters.

After scaling the roofs, Jacob and Max found their footing once more on the ground following simultaneous dismounts and, with the same grace it takes a track runner to clear a hurdle, they proceeded to sail over the fences enclosing the two backyards and bolt onward into the thick of the woods waiting for them on the other side. Now came the moment where the challenge of the race unfolded itself, for this patch of forest was densely populated with hearty spruce and redwood, not to mention innumerable lesser woody plants and undergrowth. It also served as a giant cemetery of sorts for felled trees whose mammoth carcasses lay strewn about in all haphazard manners, like the bodies of soldiers fallen on a battlefield and awaiting burial, and with the speed at which the two boys were traveling through this obstacle-laden minefield, it would take less than a blink of an eye for either one to miscalculate each meticulously calculating step necessary to keep themselves upright and avoid taking a nasty, bone-breaking face plant that would ensure one would remain down for the count.

Luckily for Jacob, he was very familiar with these woods and, growing up in Cain's Corner, had often found himself working off the frustrations and rage that comes with being a teenager by racing through this barrier of trees. Yet to both his surprise and consternation, Jacob could see that Max was matching him foot, leap and breath, even with the darkness of night settling in and creating an even more cumbersome barrier than the physical ones they were attempting to avoid. Jacob hurtled on, driving from his feet as much speed as they could muster as he vaulted, bounded and sprang over the countless toppled boles attempting to impede his way like some spooked buck trying to outrun the flames of wildfire fast on his tail, while now and then scaling the trunks of trees still standing at attention and using them as a sort of springboard to hurl himself forward and clear the even more sizable obstacles lying in wait to block his path. But for each inch he nosed ahead of Max, it would somehow be lost when Max managed to edge himself slightly ahead, usually by performing some grandstanding, showboating feat that only drove Jacob to push himself all the harder as both the racehorse and the jockey lashing his crop.

They soon reached the lake, which appeared as a silver pool of liquid mercury under the light of the moon which by now had risen high enough in the sky to serve as a night light of sorts. Instead of changing their trajectory and following the shoreline leading around the lake to the other side where their target resided, the boys raced forward without so much as a pause. Their feet met the water with the same kind of splashing one gets when traipsing over a shallow puddle, but their weight did not sink into the depths the farther out they advanced. Instead, they skimmed across the open water like a pair of boats that had suddenly traded their sails for legs. If anyone had been watching the extraordinary sight from the shore, they would have wondered if Cain's Corner had experienced a freak weather phenomenon that had inexplicably caused the surface of the lake to freeze over. Only nothing of the sort had occurred; Jacob and Max were, indeed, walking on water. Or in this case, running. And they seemed to be enjoying every moment of their inconceivable exploit as they laughed and whooped aloud with delight even as they remained focused on the endgame of their competition which rested in their sights off in the distance.

Nose to nose they remained, pushing what speed remained in their legs to the absolute limit until each boy began to consider the disagreeable likelihood of a draw between them. Such thought made each strain even further to gain even a hair of an edge as they approached the finish line.

That's when it happened.

Jacob was the first to catch sight of it: the rearing up of a wave near the shore they were fast approaching. Only the wave was moving the opposite way toward them instead of rolling toward land. It was as if someone had grabbed hold of the edge of the lake as though it were a large carpet and given it a good hard whip to send a wave into motion. And the closer the wave rolled its way toward the boys, the larger it became; so big it became that Jacob and Max thought twice about turning tail and attempting to evade what had now become a wall of water in hot pursuit of them. But it was too late. Like a giant liquid hand coming up from out of the depths, the wave curled threateningly before crashing down upon the startled boys and washing them clean off their watery pedestals with a submerging force.

When they finally manage to break through the surface coughing and sputtering up water, Jacob and Max saw, to their great relief, that the wave had vanished and the surface of the lake had returned to its former flat self. What had caused the strange occurrence, however, was quickly spied almost at once standing a few feet from the shore in the shape of a mysterious and minatory silhouette. Who or what it was could not be decipherable at first in the darkness of the night, even with Nephilim eyes, but it appeared ominous enough to cause both boys to gather up their defenses. Yet only when the faceless figure gradually stepped forward into the moonlight and reveal its face did an actual chill simultaneously make its way down each boy's spine.

It was Damiel, in all of his strength-emanating presence.

And he did not appear happy.

~ ~ ~

"You have caused me more than a little bit of irritation tramping halfway across the world like some bloodhound following the scent of an artful convict," Damiel fumed in as controlled a manner as he could muster, like a seething kettle on a stove burner just before coming to a loud, whistling boil. "Now here I find you derelict of the good reason I thought resided in that head of yours by acting reckless out in the open for all who might happen along to see."

Somehow, Jacob found the courage needed to clear his throat and speak first. "You have every reason to be mad. But you see, we were just—"

Damiel curtly cut the boy off.

"I was not addressing you."

Now it was Max's turn to feel the burn of the angel's glare and it was a most uncomfortable feeling.

"How did you find out I was here?" he asked.

"That would be a question probably best suited for your doppelgänger," answered Damiel.

Max and Jacob both traded a look of perplexity with one another as they stood waist deep in the lake dripping of water before following the direction of the angel's gaze over his shoulder.

"Let's go, come forward!" ordered Damiel.

There came a rustle from within the cluster of trees and shrubs followed by the appearance of three silhouetted shapes that, when they stepped out into the reach of the moonlight, revealed themselves much to the surprise of Jacob and Max to be Kairo, Leos and, trailing somewhat behind them, Ethan, who was looking noticeably more sheepish than the other two.

"Well, well, well…if it isn't Gilligan, himself," Jacob cracked under his breath while shooting Max a smug told-you-so look.

"I should have known better. You squealed on me, didn't you no-hoper?" asked Max, though his accusation settled itself more on Ethan than the other two.

"Not exactly," answered Ethan, looking not so much a guilty party to tattling than ineptness.

"Then what, exactly?" pressed Max.

"I did exactly what you asked me to do. It's just…well, I was so darn nervous about being caught when Damiel began to take roll that…well…"

Both Max and Jacob's eyebrows raised slowly higher in unison, anticipating an explanation than seemed to catch in Ethan's craw forcing Kairo to step in with some clarity.

"He's right, he did do what you asked him to, and transformed himself into a double of Max. And I can attest he got the look down almost flawlessly," Kairo attempted to explain before he strangely found himself fighting back an onslaught of snickers. "That is, if you had been run through a washing machine on the hot cycle about a thousand times."

He barely got the words out when he became caught up in a fit of laughter and was joined instantly by Leos which only drew even more confused looks from Jacob and Max.

"It isn't funny," protested Ethan glumly.

"The heck it isn't," Leos snorted through his chuckles.

"I believe what they are trying to make intelligible is, while Ethan here did manage to shift himself, as it were, into Max's likeness, he somehow failed to account for the obvious difference in height between the two in his nervousness in attempting to hoodwink me," explained Damiel, noting Ethan's shorter stature compared to Max's. "Though I'm not sure what I'm more troubled by: the failure to complete so elementary a task under duress this late in the game of your training, or the idea the four of you thought for even a moment that I, or any of the Guides for that matter, would be so gullible as to have the wool pulled so effortlessly over our eyes by such an amateurish and, frankly, rudimentary trick."

"We weren't really trying to pull the wool over your eyes, and these guys were just going along with a plan I came up with," said Max, in an attempt to clear his friends from any punishment that was likely still being mulled about inside the angel's head. "I just thought I could sneak away, come here and persuade Jacob here to return back to Eden with me before any of you were the wiser. And truth be told, I was just about to accomplish that task by winning this race if you hadn't knocked me into the drink with that monster of a wave."

Jacob shot Max an incredulous look. "In your dreams. If the lake was made out of dirt you would have been eating my dust," he argued.

The two traded shots of bravado over the unfinished race until Damiel took a deep, exasperated breath and called for silence.

"Come up out of there," he then instructed Max. "You look like a lugubrious hound who's been tossed in the tub for its annual flea bath."

Max trudged his water-logged self to the shore where he attempted to wring what he could of the lake from his sopping clothes.

"We'll discuss how you will be reproved when we return to Havenhid," said Damiel.

"Great, can't wait," Max muttered glumly.

When Damiel turned and, with his charges in tow, began to retreat back into the woods from which he had emerged, there came a call after him from the water: "Is that it?"

Damiel stopped and looked back to find Jacob still standing half-submerged in the lake with a questionable look fixed upon his face.

"What else is there?" inquired Damiel. "I've recovered what I sought."

"I don't know…I just figured you'd at least try and talk me into coming back with you," Jacob replied awkwardly.

"Wouldn't I just be wasting my breath at this point?" asked Damiel.

Jacob's voice failed him as a strange feeling came over him. True he had fled Eden without so much as a glance back over his shoulder. Now it suddenly felt as if the gates to the one true paradise he had ever known were being closed in his face, and a part of him wanted to stick his foot across the threshold to keep it from slamming shut.

"Besides, I believe there's someone waiting for you at home with a far more pressing desire to speak with you," Damiel noted before Jacob could croak forth another word. "I suggest you not keep her waiting any longer than she already has."

With that, the angel and the boys disappeared into the darkness of the woods leaving Jacob alone in the serene silence.

CHAPTER EIGHT

THE BEACON

The last time Jacob stepped foot inside St. Michael's Cemetery, a cold and miserable rain fell steadily from a gray slate sky, and a sadness as immeasurable as it was insufferable pressed down upon him like some intolerable weight.

His mother's funeral had been a small affair, as quiet and understated as the woman for which it was held. The handful of mourners in attendance were not so much friends of Isabeth Parrish, but rather passing acquaintances she had come to know through the years from the local church where she attended mass every Sunday before sickness forced her into a convalescent existence. In Cain's Corner, where she arrived as a young, single pregnant woman, uprooted from a more socially full life and forced to flee in the dead of night for the small trappings of the little-known Pacific northwest town, she settled into a quiet, almost silent life. Not because she was unfriendly or closed off as some in the close-knit community long concluded, but for the safety of her son; safety that was reliant on an existence of near anonymity. And there are few places on Earth where one can successfully hide, especially when one is being hunted.

Dressed in a black suit, white shirt and dark tie, and his hair normally tousled and carefree groomed neatly into place, Jacob sat silently next to his grandmother, clutching her hand and staring straight ahead stone-faced at the bronze coffin positioned over the freshly prepared plot in front of him. His uniquely dual-colored eyes—one green, the other blue—were vacant of the gleam of life that usually filled them. Drained, even of sorrow. Any tears they held had long been shed.

When the service was finished, his grandmother, Ava, quickly composed herself, released her grandson's hand and rose to thank those who attended. Jacob remained in his seat and watched the small gathering file past the casket, some laying a single flower amid the large floral spray of white roses—his mother's favorite—that rested on top.

"You must be Jacob."

Jacob looked up to find the robed priest who presided over the service standing before him.

"I don't know if you remember me. I'm Father Cohen." With a hint of apprehension, Jacob reached up to shake the hand that was extended to him. The priest's hand was cold but his grip firm.

"The last time I saw you, you were just a boy when your mother used to bring you to our Sunday services," said the priest, sinking down into the white folding chair his grandmother had just vacated.

Reaching into the folds of the crimson and white robe he wore, Father Cohen retrieved an immaculately folded handkerchief that he quickly undid with a flip of his wrist while removing the wire-rimmed glasses perched on the end of his nose.

"Remarkable woman, your mother," the priest commented as he began to clean the lenses of his glasses. "I have many parishioners in my congregation and I have yet to come across one who has made as lasting an impression on me as she has. Steadfast in her faith when others would have crumbled long ago under similar conditions."

Jacob remained silent, though it took every bit of strength he had not to spew the toxic stew that had been bubbling inside him since learning of his mother's death. Faith? How could this priest dare sit next to him and pontificate about the wonders of faith? Look what faith had gotten his mother. Look where it led her. Right into a flower-adorned box ready to be buried in the rain-soaked ground beneath six feet of mud.

"I understand you are angry, Jacob. Believe me, I know," the priest continued, as if able to hear the boy's embittered thought, "and I won't attempt to try and talk you out of that anger; an anger you have every right to marinate in. Believe it or not, it's hard even for someone like myself to help guide someone like your mother on her journey and not be affected by what can only be looked upon as a great unfairness, instead of recognizing the true beautiful gift that has been bestowed upon her."

"Gift," Jacob muttered with seething disdain.

Father Cohen paused, then lifted his glasses toward the sky. As he examined his lenses through squinted eyes, he recited the following verse:

That power that marks the sparrow's fall

Must comfort and sustain us all.

When sorrow comes, as come it must,

In God man must place his trust.

Satisfied with his cleaning, he put his glasses on once again, neatly folded his handkerchief and returned it inside his cloak.

"Don't close your heart, dear boy, hard as it may be at this moment. For it's the one true compass we have to navigate us through this life," said the priest while giving Jacob an encouraging pat on the leg.

He then stood along with Jacob as Ava returned from saying goodbye one last time to her daughter. The brief interlude she had managed to bring to her grief had passed. She dabbed at the tears staining her cheeks with the dainty handkerchief she clutched in her black-gloved hand damp with her sorrow. Her hair maintained its perfect coif, but she appeared drawn, and her white complexion looked even more pale against the simple black dress she wore.

"I'm alright, really," she said forcing forth a smile of strength as Jacob hugged her. Then turning to Father Cohen, she again extended her gratitude for the lovely service. "You will come to the house, yes? I have enough food to feed every man, woman and child in Cain's Corner."

"I would be delighted," the priest replied. He took her arm and began to guide her across the lawn toward the waiting car service when she stopped and called for her grandson over her shoulder. "You coming, Jacob?"

"I'll be there in a bit," answered Jacob.

Ava nodded knowingly and continued on. He needn't explain further.

Left alone with his mother, Jacob felt an unexplained stillness and silence settle itself around him. Even the patter of the falling rain fell quiet. At first, he was hit with a welling wave of fear; a fear that made him suddenly afraid to turn around and face the reality that was stretched out behind him in the shape of a coffin. And when he finally did, it wasn't fear that greeted him, but the now familiar surge of sorrow that refused to release its grip on him.

Jacob approached the head of the casket and hesitantly placed his hand on the polished surface. It was cold, and felt as smooth as satin beneath his fingertips. As he stared down at the casket, he instantly realized that his hand was resting right above where his mother's face would be. The lid to the casket suddenly seemed to become transparent and he could see her in repose inside, dressed in her favorite lavender-colored dress, her beauty restored and hiding every trace of the illness that had ravaged her, and resting peacefully...oh, so peacefully.

His eyes began to well with tears; tears he thought he had long exhausted. And the anguish he had fought to quell was suddenly being released in a tidal surge from inside. He turned his face to the sky clenching his teeth tightly as he battled to punch down the overwhelming lament boiling upward inside his chest in its desperate bid for release and sequester it back into the black pit he had struggled to keep secured under lock and key. It took all his strength, and while one solitary tear managed to escape the corner of his eye, he slowly felt the pain recede.

Once Jacob had regained the control he so tightly clutched, he took a couple of deep breaths, reached into his jacket pocket and pulled from it an intricately carved wooden box his mother kept on the nightstand next to her bed. He carefully opened the lid. Inside lay the limp remains of a dove that had taken up a permanent residence on his mother's windowsill shortly after sickness had confined her to the four walls of her bedroom.

"I think he's frightened by the storm," his mother's voice sounded inside his head as he recalled the night before she died. He had awakened from a deep sleep to the sound of noises and, when he got up to investigate, he found her in her room, kneeling on the floor beside the open window where she often spent her days staring down into her garden. The dove was cuddled in the palm of her hand and she was gently stroking its head as the creature bobbed about looking very skittish by the loud, blustery wind being whipped up outside.

"He's fine, mom. He's used to being outside in all kinds of weather," said Jacob. "You on the other hand…you know you can't expose yourself to the cold like this. What are you looking to do: catch pneumonia?"

He sounded like a scolding parent. And she, likewise, responded like a child being disciplined.

"Pneumonia," she replied with a dismissive chuckle. "Do you really think I'm worried about pneumonia at this point?"

Jacob opened his mouth but stopped himself from responding. He knew it was no use to argue with her, even in her weakened state and, instead, lowered himself into the chair next to her where he silently watched her comfort her feathered companion. Something was wrong. He could see she was upset.

"When I was a little girl I remember we always had doves in our yard," she started. "They would come in droves to eat the seed your grandmother would put out for them every morning. I would just sit and watch them, finding it oh so amusing how these symbols of peace were really not that much different than any other creature on this planet, as they chased off and pecked one another over the scattered specks of food. But there was one dove I noticed who seemed to keep a distance from the rest. He had this unique white marking on his wing, and he would sit in the same spot on the same branch of the huge olive tree that grew in our yard, coming down only when the other doves had finished feeding to scavenge for any seed they may have left behind.

"One day I was outside helping your grandmother water when I caught sight of something moving on the ground out of the corner of my eye. I saw it was this particular dove sitting amongst the bushes trying to shake off the water that had splashed on him. I remember thinking how odd it was that he was on the ground like this, and as I looked closer I found much to my horror that his entire backside had been denuded of feathers, and he was bleeding. I suspect he had been the unfortunate victim of one of the many cats that roamed the area. He looked terrified. As I gently attempted to pick him up I could see one of his wings had been broken, as well as both legs. I began crying. This poor creature. Poor, poor creature."

A tear formed in the corner of her already reddened eyes and eventually spilled down across her cheek like a drop of dew clinging to the pedal of a flower.

"I took him inside and placed him in a box," Isabeth continued with her story. "My mother said there was no hope, that he'd never recover and that the best, most humane thing to do would be to put him out of his misery. Well, I just couldn't. Instead, I took him to my room and as he lay quiet in the box I placed on my dresser, barely alive and in pain, I grabbed my rosary and I began to pray. I prayed harder than I ever had before, all night, until I finally fell asleep. The next morning when I woke up I rushed to the box and he was gone."

Jacob was struck by a sharp twinge of sympathy as his mother told her story, imaging the pain and loss she must have experienced at that moment as a little girl.

"Not dead, mind you, but gone. Vanished," she quickly continued. "I was certain my mother had come in during the night as I slept and gathered up the courage to do the humane thing I was incapable of doing before I woke, but she swore to me that wasn't the case. Many years later, when I was a teenager, I contracted a horrible fever. I was bedridden for several days slipping in and out of consciousness. The doctor wasn't sure I'd make it. One day, right before the fever finally broke, while my mother was downstairs retrieving some fresh cold compresses she used to help keep my temperature down, I awoke to find a dove perched on my window ledge watching me. It didn't even occur to me that it could be the same dove. So many years had passed. But then I noticed the white marking on the wing. He had come back, miraculously. No longer broken and wounded. It was only later in life when I would come to learn this precious bird was my Beacon."

Beacon.

His mother had attempted to fill his head with a lot of creative nonsense over the course of growing up, mostly religious nonsense. However, believing that each soul was assigned one of these feathered Beacons who watched over it during its time on Earth until death, when it then accompanies the soul to the afterlife, as his mother tried to explain it to him, took the cake.

"You don't actually believe that baloney, do you?" asked Jacob.

His mother bowed her head to her breast, and her body slowly sank as though supporting a great cumbersome weight, and she began to weep. "Oh, Jacob, you are making this so difficult."

Jacob glanced down at the dove still cocooned in his mother's protective hands as it bobbed its head frantically in fear from the loud rumbling of thunder in the distance. As his eyes followed his mother's fingers that were gently caressing the dove, the slow hypnotic sweep of her calming touch suddenly made his attention fix itself on a strange white mark etched in the smooth feathers that he had never before noticed.

"Mom…why did you tell me that story?" he asked with a hint of caution.

When she didn't immediately answer, he gently placed his hand beneath her chin and lifted her head. Her cheeks were streaked with tears, and the cancer that had left her without eyelashes and brows much like the chilling weather that was plucking the leaves from the trees outside gave her ghostly white face the look of a beautiful porcelain mask in the fading moonlight, reminding Jacob of the weeping statues of the Virgin Mary he had heard so much about growing up.

"The treatment is not working," she said, her mouth trembling as she spoke. "Dr. Scully told me when she came to visit today that it has spread to the point where there is nothing else that can be done."

She was gone by the light of the following morning, and so, too, was the dove, whose expired carcass Jacob discovered lying lifeless on the windowsill shortly after his mother's death. And as the haunting memory slowly faded and left Jacob's company, he gently brushed a finger over the dove's delicate feathered body which appeared to be resting in its own miniature coffin. So soft, it was. Softer than the plush red velvet that lined the box. Then closing the lid, he carefully placed the box amid the spray of flowers on top of his mother's casket.

"So much for the Beacon theory," he muttered under his breath.

His grandmother was waiting for him inside the chauffeured car when he finally made his way across the cemetery lawn. She gave her grandson a comforting hug as he got inside and, despite his great effort to resist, Jacob couldn't help but glance out of the rain-spotted window one last time toward his mother's plot as the car slowly began to drive away. There, strangely enough, standing next to the casket, he spied a man dressed in long, dark overcoat, his brown shoulder-length hair pulled back and fixed in a ponytail. One of the cemetery workers, Jacob thought, who would now lower the casket into the ground; a task Jacob had no interest in witnessing. Instead, the man reached for the box Jacob had laid amid the flowers and opened it. He removed the dove from inside the box and gently cradled it in his hands. The man then appeared to close his eyes and bow his head, keeping his hands cupped around the bird's body.

Jacob was about to cry out for the driver to stop the car when the man suddenly lifted his head, raised his arms and opened his hands. When he did the dove, no longer lifeless popped up, fluttered its wings and took off into the air in a burst of white. Jacob stared in wide-eyed amazement, his mouth unhinging itself as he watched the dove fly higher and higher, in a nearly straight vertical line. Upward and onward it ascended, toward a break that was slowly seen to open within the dark murky sky to allow a slanting ribbon of light to unravel itself and reach toward the earth, and the more it unraveled, the brighter it became until it was almost too brilliant to look directly at with one's naked eyes. And just as the dove was about to reach the light, the car made a turn along the curving road winding a path through the cemetery and blocking Jacob's view. Quickly, almost frantically, he spun around in his seat and peered through the back window of the car, but it was too late. The dove had vanished, and the stream of light was receding as quickly as it had appeared back behind the closing curtain of dark sky. And when Jacob looked for the figure wearing the dark overcoat, he was nowhere to be seen.

~ ~ ~

When Jacob returned to Cain's Corner, he made a conscious effort to steer clear of the cemetery, despite his grandmother's suggestion he go and pay his respects to his mother. It wasn't until the day after Damiel made his surprise, and somewhat unexpected, appearance at the lake that Jacob relented and made the visit to his mother's grave site. Much to his surprise, he found going to be nothing like the horrible and unbearable day of her funeral; the sun was out and showering the beautifully perfect day with its radiance and, more importantly, the unendurable sadness that had had such a choke-hold on him was completely absent.

Then again, he was no longer the same boy he was on that dark day. Not solely, at least. Over the course of the past year, he had come to learn and experience a great many wondrous things; things which had gradually chipped away at the angst and bitterness overwhelming him the day his mother was laid to rest and replaced with a comforting peace. It wasn't that he didn't still mourn his mother's absence; in fact, he missed her more than ever. There was, however, something consoling and reassuring in knowing, without question, that his mother's abbreviated life hadn't ended with the closing of her casket, and that the small plot of earth beneath the immaculately manicured green grass and unassuming marble grave marker where she was buried was but a doorway (or Through, as the Guides were known to call such passageways) to a better, and more glorious existence, where such things as pain and sickness was barred. And it was this knowledge, above all else he acquired during his time away from home, that Jacob was most grateful to have received.

"I want you to know I'm not mad at you for not telling me what I am, or who my father is," Jacob said quietly as he sat on the grass the same way he kept his mother company when she became bedridden. "I mean, I was upset, at first. But grandma helped me understand why you did what you did. And while I am happy you are in a better place, a part of me wishes you were still here to help me figure out what I'm supposed to do next…because, I have to tell you, I'm pretty confused."

No sooner had he spoken those words did he feel a presence looming somewhere behind him. Glancing back over his right shoulder he caught the unexpected sight of Damiel standing quietly nearby.

"I didn't want to intrude," the angel said.

"I thought you left for Havenhid," said Jacob.

"I did. In fact, I was nearly halfway there when I was reminded of something that prevented from going any further," Damiel replied as he stepped closer and lowered himself in a squatting position beside the boy. "You see, your leaving Eden has created a rather bit of conundrum for me to depart Cain's Corner."

"I don't understand."

"Not too long before Gothamel's untimely departure, he approached me with a rather odd and unusual request. You see, he asked if I would serve as a sort of conservator—a guardian, if you will—in his place, should anything happen to him. I agreed to his wishes…not that I for one second believed in a million years a mortal blow would befall him and I would be called upon to fulfill his behest."

The mention of Gotham's name registered a flicker of unhappiness to the boy's face. However angry he may have been regarding Gotham's orchestrated attempt to keep the secret of Jacob's father hidden from the boy, he missed greatly the one father-like figure he had ever known who had also been his friend.

"So, you're saying you're basically now acting as my guardian angel?" Jacob questioned somewhat sarcastically, yet he couldn't help but be warned that Gotham was still, somehow, looking out for him, even in death.

"In a manner of speaking, yes," said Damiel. "And if recent weeks are a sign of what's to come, I don't expect this to be a pleasant arrangement for either one of us."

There was a noticeable trace of tension hovering between the two that Jacob couldn't ignore, and he knew the longer they continued to sidestep the issue, the more uncomfortable it would become.

"I suppose you want to know why I left Eden the way I did," Jacob remarked finally, in hopes of getting the discussion he knew was coming over sooner than later.

"I already know why you left," answered Damiel. "Which is why I let you go off and be by yourself for as long as I did, in hopes that the time would serve you well to think things over and get your thoughts in line."

Damiel appeared far more cordial and understanding about the recent turn of events than Jacob predicted; Jacob on the other hand was not as understanding.

"When I got home last night, my grandma was waiting up for me. She told me you had surprised her with a visit," said Jacob, before looking pointedly at the angel. "I just want you to know I think it was a pretty dirty trick telling her about the whole Light Bearer thing."

"Dirty trick?" replied Damiel with a slight cock of his head as though the phrase was foreign to his ears.

"You knew if she found out about me being the Light Bearer that she'd do everything she could to try and talk me into going back to Havenhid," accused Jacob.

"I assure you it was meant to be neither dirty or an act of trickery on my part when I broached the subject," Damiel answered back in a straight-forward, no-nonsense tone of voice. "The more obvious question, it would seem to me, is why would you have purposely kept a matter of such importance from her?"

"I just didn't want her to know," grumbled Jacob.

"Not want to know that her grandson has been marked with the highest favor of grace a Nephilim can receive?" questioned Damiel with an air of incredulousness. "You make it sound as though being Light Bearer is an embarrassing affliction on par with suffering an unfortunate case of scabies or athletes foot."

"That's not what I mean…it's just…" Jacob exhaled a deep breath of exasperation. "It was hard enough coming home and having to give her the horrible news about what had happened to Gotham, and then follow it up by showing her the missing pages to David's journal and revealing everything Gotham had told her regarding her son's death was all a lie. I just couldn't bear dropping a triple whammy on her with news I was the Light Bearer."

A confused look came over Damiel. "Again, you're losing me. You equate the blessing that is being Light Bearer as something as tragic as a death?"

"Well, yeah…in a way," said Jacob. "If it wasn't for the fact of being the original Light Bearer, David might still be alive today."

The perplexed look on Damiel face grew even more pronounced.

"David's death came about by his own design," said Damiel. "You of all people should know that; you were the one to whom Anahel revealed the truth with those missing journal pages."

"But if he wasn't the Light Bearer, Samael would never had tried to entice him to betray the Light and hand over the Sword of the Destiny," argued Jacob.

"If! We could spend a lifetime mulling over 'ifs' and never intersect a one with a single fact," said Damiel. "The truth is David's death was the result of the unreserved love a son had for his father. Being Light Bearer was only a means to a selfless, yet misguided end. And my hunch tells me you understand that whether you care to admit it or not."

Jacob sat tight-lipped for a moment or two.

"Maybe I just needed an excuse not to tell my grandmother," he finally admitted. "I guess I figured if she knew the whole truth about me she, out of anyone, would find a way to convince me to go back."

The expression on Damiel's face softened.

"Well, if we're going to be honest with one another, I guess I could own up to the fact that there was a small amount of dirty trickery on my part when I realized you had not been fully upfront with your grandmother," confessed Damiel. "You are, if nothing else, stubborn, and I knew I would likely have little influence in changing your mind to return with me to Eden. If anything was able to penetrate that thick skull of yours, I knew it would have to come from the voice of someone who witnessed firsthand, and understood intimately, the importance of a speck of light spied within a stranglehold of darkness. Who else but your grandmother could convey such a saving grace?"

Jacob couldn't argue with the angel, at first.

"But you saw what occurred at my Blessing," said Jacob.

"I recall the Hall of Light being filled with the sounds of gaiety as your fellow Nephilim gathered about you celebrating the momentous occasion," said Damiel. "And need I remind you Eksel, once your most vocal and staunchest fault-finder and denigrator, was leading the festivities."

"You know that's not what I'm talking about," Jacob remarked coolly. "Sandel has already nullified my Blessing."

"There's not much positive I can say about my brother Sandel, except that he is, well... consistently true to form," Damiel remarked with a resigned sigh. "I wouldn't let his actions upset you."

"No? Then how about this?" argued Jacob. And with that he reached into the front pocket of his jeans and pulled out the crumpled envelope delivered by the mysterious Gyrfalcon only a few days earlier and thrust it toward the angel.

A frown etched itself on Damiel's forehead as he looked over the contents of the document. "It's a summons to appear before the Iudicium Tribunal."

"Here I was hoping my ability to read Caelestian was off the mark," said Jacob.

"You are hereby commanded, Jacob D. Parrish, to make yourself present before this seated body of the Iudicium Tribunal, within fifteen days of receiving this edict, to provide testimony on your behalf regarding the unsanctioned Blessing which took place at Havenhid in your name on the seventh day of this month," Damiel read aloud the document. "Failure to comply with this order will institute a directive calling for your immediate detention."

"Now do you want to tell me not to let Sandel's actions upset me?" Jacob asked when Damiel had finished. "He wants to put me on trial."

"I wouldn't necessarily equate being summoned before the Iudicium Tribunal with being on trial," said Damiel, though the look of concern in his eyes spoke otherwise. "It is but a mere formality to prove you are indeed the Light Bearer and finally put the matter to rest."

"But I already proved it…to you, to Anahel, to everyone at Havenhid the morning after Azrael came to Eden and turned the River of Life black."

"And none of us now are questioning who it is you have shown yourself to be," Damiel attempted to assure the boy. "Unfortunately, there are others whose skepticism may never be sated."

The angels words did little to appease Jacob.

"I never asked for any of this, you know…not to be a Nephilim, not to have the gift of the Seventh Grace, certainly not to be the son of Samael," Jacob remarked quietly, as if confessing some grave sin he had committed to a priest inside a confessional box. "Now, I feel as if I've done some horrible thing…like I'm a criminal or something, all for simply being who I am; all for just existing."

Damiel couldn't help but share the heaviness he could see gripping the boy.

"There have been many men, much loftier than you, whose simple act of divine existence, history has labored to stamp out through stoning, lion mauling, burning at the stake… crucifixion." A flash of gold radiated from the angel's eyes as the last word slipped off the tip of his tongue like the point of a sword to pierce Jacob's heart, and it seemed to jolt the boy with a humble awakening of the company he kept just by his mere existence he moments earlier lamented. "There is nothing criminal in being the Light Bearer. But there are those forces who will see you as just that—a criminal—and worse; and they will stop at nothing to put out the light of the torch you were handed when you came into this world. The real crime would be if you were to save them the trouble by extinguishing your own light."

Jacob sat quiet for some time and looked off in the distance as he allowed Damiel's words to soak their way inside him, and as he did, he watched as a pair of squirrels engaged in a game of chase scamper after one another across the grass, winding their way around the grave markers and larger tombstones before finally scurrying up the trunk of a nearby oak tree.

"Does the name Zophiel mean anything to you?" Jacob suddenly asked Damiel from out of the blue.

Damiel remained silent for a moment or two, not answering right away.

"How did you come to know this name?" asked Damiel, when he finally answered.

"That night in the Silent Forest, when Thaniel fell into the Through, it was something he said just before the Feeders inundated him and pulled him underwater…Zophiel," recalled Jacob.

"Who could possibly find a semblance of reason being spewed from the mouth of someone caught up in the throes of his demise?" said Damiel. "You would do yourself a great favor to cast the details of that sordid night from your thoughts."

"Believe me, I wish I could," Jacob said with a sigh. "But ever since then I've been having these recurring dreams—nightmares, really—of that moment. And the more I try to ignore them, the more vivid and overpowering they become."

Jacob then gave a glance at the angel, who seemed particularly mute on the subject.

"Are you sure the name Zophiel means nothing to you?" he inquired once more.

"Zophiel was amongst the multitudes of angels I once called brother," Damiel reluctantly answered.

"Once? What happened to him?" asked Jacob.

"That is a question to which I have no answer," Damiel replied in a tone that made it clear the topic of conversation was one he'd rather avoid. Yet from the unwavering look of curiosity coming from the boy, it was clear to the angel he would not rest until he had exhausted all he knew on the subject.

"He was known as the Watchman of God," continued Damiel.

"Watchman," Damiel repeated the name to himself with intrigue.

"In layman's terms you could say he served as a spy for our Father," explained Damiel. "Before the Great War in Heaven, it was Zophiel who informed Gothamel of the uprising that was about to occur, and when it came, it was Zophiel who fed us the rebel's battle plan that ultimately led to their defeat and the banishment of a third of my brothers into the Dragon's pit of fire."

There was a visible flare of anger and a damper of sorrow in Damiel's eyes as he spoke, and Jacob found odd the notable contempt with which the angel spoke of his brother, even as he recited what sounded to his ears to be brave and noble actions.

"It was then, in the midst of that horrible War, that he vanished…disappeared…without word or trace…as if he'd never existed," continued Damiel. "No one knows what really happened to him, but the belief shared amongst my remaining brothers, and eventually myself, is that he succumbed to the whims of the Darkness; that the Dragon managed somehow to inveigle him and convince him of the rebel's motives, and thus became a Fallen himself. It is believed that later, he was the one responsible for attempting to set Heaven ablaze, and it was then that the Watchman of God ceased to exist, and the Herald of Hell was born in his once virtuous place."

~ ~ ~

"I'll go back to Eden with you," Jacob announced suddenly much to Damiel's surprise after the boy took a quiet moment or two to ponder the story he had just heard.

"Well, now, that's a surprising, if not encouraging turn," replied Damiel.

"But I'll only go back on one condition," Jacob was quick to qualify.

"And what condition is that?" asked the angel with a hint of wariness.

"That we first go and try to find this Zophiel."

The brief moment of elation that filled the angel's face was instantly scrubbed free.

"You cannot be serious."

"I know it sounds like a half-cocked idea, but hear me out," said Jacob.

Damiel open-mindedness instantly slammed shut. "It's half-cocked alright. Not to mention downright ludicrous," he balked. "There's no way I'm going to tramp needlessly around the world with five Nephilim in tow on some sort of blind scavenger hunt."

"Who said anything about tramping around the world?" argued Jacob. "If there's one thing I've come to learn about Fallen, is that many of them are out walking the earth instead of being confined to the Underneath. You must have some idea where Zophiel might be. You're an angel, after all."

"That's right, I am an angel," replied Damiel, "not an all-knowing deity like the one who created me."

"Please...I know what I'm asking might sound like an asinine request—"

"Might?"

"But you must know me well enough by now to realize I wouldn't be asking this of you if I didn't think it was extremely important."

The angel searched the boy's face and for the first time, and to his frustration, a return argument failed him.

"And what exactly, may I ask, do you expect you'll uncover if by some miracle we were actually successful in finding him?" asked Damiel.

The question at first seemed to stump Jacob.

"I haven't the faintest idea. Perhaps nothing," he said. "All I know is that these dreams I've been having of Thaniel repeating that name over and over again are just like the nightmares I used to have of Samael tied up in the desert. He was trying to tell me something...almost like a secret message. I just don't know what that message is."

Even as he spoke, Jacob could hear traces of Thaniel's voice reverberating somewhere in the back of his head as the haunting image of his face before he was dragged beneath the waters of the Through briefly pushed aside everything else in his vision, and it convinced him all the more that finding this elusive Zophiel was more imperative than ever.

"I'll understand if you refuse," Jacob said to Damiel, who appeared, albeit reluctantly, to be mulling over his options. "But I hope you understand I'll be forced go it alone if need be and use whatever resources I have to try and track him down."

"And likely get yourself in a mess of trouble," said Damiel.

The look in Jacob's eye remained one of unmistakable determination, and Damiel knew, amusingly enough, he had only himself to blame for helping put a fine unyielding point on such determination during all those sweat-watered days spent at Lions Bite.

"And here I thought agreeing to being a guardian angel would be a walk in the park," Damiel grumbled to himself before turning a somewhat surrendering eye onto the boy. "I may know of a place where Fallen are known to congregate."

Jacob perked up immediately. "You're kidding me. Where?"

"Some city called Lass Vee Gas."

The angel's mangled pronunciation drew a momentary puzzled look from Jacob. "You mean Las Vegas? You're joking, right?"

There was no hint of levity in the angel's face.

"There may be a chance—slim though it may be—that someone there may know of Zophiel's whereabouts," he said.

The prospect lit up Jacob's face. "That mean you'll help me?"

Damiel exhaled a rare deep breath of defeat. "What choice have you left me?" he questioned. "It's either that or be forced to call this Cain's Corner place my new home."

"You're joking, right?" Jacob asked half smiling.

"I told you, I gave my word to Gothamel I would look after you. If you wish to make it impossible for me to fulfill that duty in Eden, then I have no other option to do it here."

The thought of Damiel becoming the newest resident of Cain's Corner was more than a little entertaining to imagine, to say the least.

"I can't really picture you, how shall I put this…fitting in here," said Jacob.

"And it warms the cockles of my heart to know that is a bridge my feet will not have to cross," replied Damiel. "But hear me, for now it is my turn to enforce my own conditions regarding this ridiculous caper," the angel was quick to add. "You must give me your word this very moment that you will abide my every instruction from the moment we arrive at this…Las Vegas."

"Sounds fair enough," Jacob agreed.

"There's more," continued Damiel. "Should we, after exhausting our options, find ourselves at a dead end, you must agree right here and now to give up this nonsense and return immediately with me to Havenhid."

Jacob exhibited less enthusiasm over the second condition. After all, he was being forced to put all of his eggs in one basket by being offered only one roll of the dice. Then again, what better place to play craps than a city where gambling comes second only to breathing, and so he readily agreed to Damiel's conditions.

"Just a second," Jacob said when he was suddenly struck by something odd. "You said earlier there was no way you were going to tramp around the world with five Nephilim in tow. Who are…did you mean Max and the other guys?"

Even as he asked the question, he realized that was exactly who the angel was referring to and he instantly grew more excited about the prospects of having traveling companions to accompany him on this unusual, yet rousing adventure.

"Where are they?" asked Jacob.

"On a very short leash," Damiel replied with a glance over his shoulder.

Jacob followed the angel's gaze and spied Max standing a short distance away with Kairo, Leos and Ethan, all four with their arms folded across their chest and wearing identical frowns of discontent on their faces that come with being placed in a proverbial albeit invisible corner as punishment.

Even Damiel couldn't keep himself from sharing in the fit of chuckles that escaped from Jacob at the sight.

~ ~ ~

The moment of levity Jacob experienced when he was once again reunited with his friends, however, would soon leave him, and in its place a pall of gloom moved in which made his heart feel leaden in his chest as he stood outside Rabble-Rousers just as the last light of the setting sun was about to go dark. Staring through the window of the restaurant, he watched with a torn longing as Wray, oblivious of his presence concealed in the gathering darkness outside, busily went about her business waiting on tables and serving up plates of food to the hungry dinner crowd. He wanted with all his might the ability to move his legs toward the door and inside the restaurant, but he didn't dare. Instead, he unfolded a piece of paper he clutched in his hand and reread for the umpteenth time the words he had managed to scrawl down that he lacked the courage to say to her face to face.

Dear Wray,

There's not enough milkshakes you could dump on my head or a slap hard enough that you could land across my face that could make what I'm about to say to you any easier. I have to leave Cain's Corner again, this time for Las Vegas. I don't know how long I'll be gone, but I suspect it will be quite a while before I am able to see you again, if in fact you ever care to, which I suspect you won't. I wish I could explain more to you, but the truth is it's far too complicated a matter, and frankly I'm short of both time and paper to even attempt to begin. Please know I wouldn't be leaving unless it was absolutely necessary, and while the thought hurts me to the core I will completely understand if this seals your disdain for me. You, for what it's worth, will always be my "Sanctuary."

Jacob

P.S. Please tell Ty goodbye for me.

Folding the short note back up, Jacob exhaled a heavy, indecisive sigh and gave Wray one last pitiful look through the restaurant window. He then turned and walked a short distance to where her Jeep was parked alongside the curb, reached inside the open window and placed the note on the steering wheel. It wasn't without a passing moment of second-guessing himself that Jacob bid Cain's Corner farewell for the second time in his short life. And after he gave Rabble-Rousers a final last glance, he reluctantly turned his back on it. Then, with his packed bag slung across his shoulder he hurried himself across the street to where Damiel stood waiting with Max, Leos, Kairo and Ethan, and the beginning of the adventure that awaited them.

CHAPTER NINE

They rode the sky, under the cover of darkness, with Damiel leading the way like a mother duck guiding her brood of ducklings. Through the passing hours of night they flew until the skies they sailed began to take on the colors of the approaching dawn. It was then they came upon a glimmer of lights that appeared like a sparkling jewel floating in a sea of blackness that was the desert landscape choking it and they made for it.

They touched down just outside the city limits where Damiel sized up the adult playground known as Las Vegas with a chary eye. Patience, was the one virtue he never managed to possess in large supply, or for that matter, forbearance. Had he made the journey to this desert city on his own, he would have already without pause begun the task that brought him there in the first place. But unlike himself, or moreover, the city that never sleeps, the Nephilim in his care were visibly worn from their all-night flight and all but cried out for soft beds to sleep off their exhaustion. It was just as well, as Damiel understood those he sought lurking somewhere beyond the "Welcome to Fabulous Las Vegas" sign were of the nocturnal persuasions. They existed as vampires; and like vampires retreated with the nighttime shadows each time the sun peeked over the eastern horizon for the sanctuary of their coffins where they remained in hidden seclusion until the coming day had exhausted its last breath of radiance.

So with the new day just beginning, and nothing but time at their disposal, Damiel and the Nephilim hoofed it on foot in search of their own coffin amongst the countless hotels cluttering the heart of the Vegas Strip.

~ ~ ~

Leos was the first to awaken with the loud guttural yawn more appropriate for a bear and a strenuous stretching of his limbs that, somehow, briefly made his body appear as if it had elongated itself by a couple inches while delivering an accidental kick to Kairo in the process.

"Hey…watch it!" grumbled Kairo who looked exactly as someone would who had been jolted out of a restful slumber in such an abrupt manner.

"What's that?" Ethan chimed in groggily as he came to on the neighboring king-sized bed where he had managed to maneuver himself a spot alongside Max and Jacob. "Is it morning yet?"

"We've already done morning. Don't you remember? The sun was just coming up when we finally were able to go to bed," answered Leos, his voice still throaty with sleep.

"I meant tomorrow morning," said Ethan who sounded smothered with his face deep in his pillow. "I was so tired I could have easily slept through the next twenty-four hours."

There came a sound of someone fumbling for something on the night table between the two beds followed by a bright light sparked by a phone.

"It's just after six," reported Jacob who had had a fitful night and only managed to grab a few winks despite being as tired as the other guys. And before Ethan could ask, as he was about to, Jacob was quick to add a clarifying, "p.m."

Kairo, who was suddenly greeted with a burst of energy, got to his feet and galloped across the tangle of sheets while making sure to deliver a playful yet reciprocating kick to Leos' backside in passing before dismounting the bed and pulling open the heavy drapes that had been closed to block out the world on the other side of the window. A soft blue light flooded the room, the same kind of light that had greeted the travelers upon their arrival at the hotel, only the softness was caused by the approach of dusk and not the dawn. Yet it was bright enough to illuminate suddenly a figure residing as quietly and unobtrusively as the chair upon which it sat in a nearby, but still very dim area of the room, making Kairo jump at the unexpected sight.

"Damiel…you, you scared me!" Kairo gasped with surprise.

"That's reassuring," remarked the angel whose eyes mirrored the gold gleam of the retiring sun.

"You haven't been sitting there the whole time while we slept, have you?" Jacob asked, sitting up in bed.

"What would you have me do? Go downstairs to the casino and hit the slots?" came Damiel's dry reply. "Although, the thought of sitting like a drone on a stool feeding coins into a machine and pulling a lever mindlessly for hours on end was somewhat becoming a more enticing option than remaining here having to endure the symphony of snoring—and whatnot—for as long as I have."

The angel's burning gaze settled themselves on Ethan and the other boys knowingly followed suit.

"Why is everyone looking at me?" asked Ethan defensively. "I don't snore."

"Guys, you have to come and check this out." The request came from Kairo who had turned back to the window and became instantly captivated at the view from below of the Strip stretching far and wide coming to life in a spectacular display of dazzling-colored lights. In fact, it appeared that every light bulb of every size and color ever manufactured in the entire world had been required in order to create such a striking and impressive sight. For a boy like Kairo who had grown up in the unassuming existence of an African town as he had, it was the next best thing compared to Eden upon which he'd ever laid his eyes.

"It's like fireworks on the Fourth of July that never go out," he muttered in an almost hypnotic way as his eyes reflected the bright brilliance they fixed on in such a captivating way.

"Yes, it is beautiful," agreed Damiel who was now on his feet and standing beside the boy sharing in the magnificent view. "But such beauty usually conceals a hidden and unsightly disfigurement. I dare say, this city reminds me of another that, at one time, proved to be equally as bewitching as this one."

The comment was enough to briefly cause Kairo to abandon the sight before him and look with intrigue to the angel.

"Let me guess…New York?" Kairo offered before quickly correcting himself. "I take that back…Paris."

"Gomorrah," replied Damiel.

The angel's response, which sounded more like a judgment than an answer, wiped the look of wonderment clean off the boy's face.

"You know what would be a beautiful sight to me right about now? One of those all-you-can-eat buffets Las Vegas is famous for," said Max. "I'm so hungry my stomach's on the verge of chewing its way out of my body 'Alien'-style."

"Now that you mention it, I'm a bit starved myself," agreed Leos. "I say we go down stairs and get ourselves slopped."

"That won't be necessary," Damiel interjected. "I've already made arrangements for room service to deliver your meals here. In fact, it should be here any time."

"Why can't we go out and find a place to eat?" asked Max. "I've never been to Vegas before and was looking forward to getting out and seeing what all the hoopla's all about, not be cooped up in a stuffy old hotel room."

"Trust me, the hoopla, as you call it, is better left ignored and unexplored, especially by five inquisitive Nephilim such as yourselves," said Damiel. " 'Sin City', as this place is better known, is a well-earned moniker, and I'll feel much more at ease knowing you are staying put in the confines of this stuffy old hotel room while I'm away, than running about unsupervised with nothing but the enticing flickering lights as your guide."

"While you're away? Where are you going?" asked Jacob as he watched Damiel put on the long dark overcoat he had brought along for the trip that was reminiscent of the one Gotham wore when he first stepped into the boy's life.

"There's a buzzing in your head that has brought us to this infelicitous city," said Damiel. "With any luck, I hope to quiet it so we can soon be on our way."

"Just give me a minute to splash some water on my face and brush my teeth," said Jacob as he bounded out of the bed in which he was reclined.

Damiel was quick to still the boy's feet. "Where do you think you're going?"

"With you, of course."

"Not a chance you will," Damiel replied with a brisk, dismissive shake of his head and immediately gestured silence before the boy could part his lips to issue the retort positioned on his tongue. "Listen to me, and listen carefully. There's a reason the only light to illuminate these surroundings is as cold as it is false. We are in the wolves den. Hear me when I tell you, it will be dangerous enough for an angel of my caliber to tread willingly into the seedy underbelly of this glittering beast. Can you imagine what the reception would be to a brood of Nephilim, not to mention one discovered to be the Light Bearer?"

"But—" Jacob managed to croak out the start of a rebuttal.

"Did you or did you not give me you solemn word that you would abide to whatever it is I asked if I were to appease you and go along on this aimless hunt? If you've had a change a heart by all means speak it and we can be off on our way back to Havenhid," spoke the angel in a direct and frank manner that instantly made Jacob's mouth seal itself tightly, but not without begrudgery.

When it finally appeared clear the matter had been settled, Damiel gave Jacob a reassuring tousle of his hair and made for the door. With the angel's departure, a silence fell upon the room and Jacob dropped back onto the bed in a sulking heap.

"So…" Ethan's voice was the first to crack the unusual quiet that almost never existed whenever the five Nephilim boys were in the confines of the same space, and all eyes turned to him in hopes of something helpful to break the tension. "What kind of food do you think he ordered for us?"

Not surprisingly, Ethan found himself on the receiving end of the incoming barrage of pillows that were suddenly hurled his way from four separate directions.

~ ~ ~

Damiel had about as much use for Las Vegas as Las Vegas had for an angel in good standing with the heavens shading its very streets. Making his way along the crowded sidewalk, he couldn't help eye with both a sense of contempt as well as sympathy the hordes of tourists he passed, trying to navigate their way in a straight line while intensely focused on the illuminated screen of their cell phones.

Why anyone would come willingly to this God-forsaken mirage in the middle of the desert made about as much sense to Damiel as someone adopting an Ebola-riddled Capuchin monkey as a pet and hoping not to get infected. Yet here they were in their t-shirts, shorts and flip-flops, with fanny packs cinching their wide middle sections, gorging themselves on all-you-can-eat prime rib and shrimp buffets, and shoveling their hard-earned money into slot machines in a fruitless attempt to satiate their shared gluttony made all the more ravenous with each bite consumed and dollar gambled.

Damiel, on the other hand, looked nothing like the crowd of souls that in his eyes appeared so hapless. Should anyone have been let in on the secret of his true, divine identity, they likely would have greeted such a revelation with a scoff, if not outright laughter of disbelief, even if the existence of angels was widely and commonly embraced as something more than faceless characters plucked from a glorified fable, which was hardly the case. Truth be told, this angel, like most, appeared nothing like the beatific vision long branded into the consciousness of the civilian masses. With his long mane of hair framing a face that instantly was both beautiful and fearsome, he cut the striking and formidable presence of someone dreamed up within the pages of an apocalyptic western tale in his heavy boots and even heavier overcoat as he made his way along the Strip without so much as a pin prick of sweat caused by the oppressive heat of the setting desert sun shining his forehead or wetting his upper lip.

Whatever it was he was searching for, he soon turned direction and headed outside the glare of the radiant stretch of hotels and casinos; for light, no matter how synthetic, was a repellent for what he sought. He ventured his way down several streets and back alleyways that made up the West of The Strip area. There, hidden amongst The Orleans, Palms, Gold Coast and Rio, he came upon an unassuming building denuded of the glitz and shine that colored other Vegas landmarks. The building's only adornment came in the shape of a sign that spelled out "Purgatory" in dull green neon-lit letters that looked more like the color of a dirty emerald just unearthed from a newly discovered mine. With only his gold-inflamed eyes visible, Damiel stood patiently observing from the darkened doorway of a building across the street, his gaze intently fixed upon the lone figure of a man standing watch outside the entrance beneath the green buzzing sign. After some time passed, a couple was spotted making their way down the dimly lit, deserted street. They appeared to be the typical hip nightclub goers, dressed in a concerted effort to look casual and easy but with all the trendiest appurtenances fashion had to offer. As the couple approached the hulking sentry standing guard outside the door, Damiel focused his acute hearing to the exchange between the parties.

"Reficul," the young, good-looking man accompanying the dark-haired woman on his arm said.

A thumping, driving beat of music spilled out from within the confines of the building when the entrance door was immediately opened for the couple who proceeded their way inside.

Reficul.

Reficul.

Damiel curiously pondered the word that obviously seemed to serve as a sort of code or password when a light of clarity curled the corner of his mouth.

"Lucifer," he muttered to himself with marked disdain when the letters being mulled about in his mind reshuffled itself from its mirrored state. "Cute."

Abandoning the doorway, he crossed the street to the building entrance. The man standing guard at the door, who appeared to be nothing more than a hired bouncer of sorts, said not a word to Damiel but, instead, let his intimidating physical presence speak for himself. Damiel gave the figure, dressed all in black, a careful and close once over and it became immediately clear to the angel that the man was weak of spirit, but his soul was still his own and uninfected. Likewise, the bouncer gave the angel a suspicious search up and down with his eyes as Damiel did not fit the appearance of the clientele seeking entry into Purgatory.

"Reficul," Damiel finally uttered though it took some effort to spit free of his tongue. The name conjured up from mortal fables may have meant nothing to him, but its purpose and what it represented left an unpleasantly bitter taste in his mouth.

The bouncer hesitated at first, his distrustful gaze once again raked itself slowly over the angel's presence. At the same time, Damiel's own returning glare was just short of being lit by the burners from within to pierce the man's skull and arm wrestle his mind for entry past the closed doors that the supposed key in the form of a password appeared to at first deny him. Thankfully, the man finally acquiesced and opened the door, releasing the pounding energy of music concealed inside, and Damiel stepped inside the dark corridor awaiting him.

~ ~ ~

The driving beat guided Damiel down a wide flight of stairs and, appropriately, into a cavernous pit of a nightclub flooded with the same sickly green radiance that lit the Purgatory sign outside. A haze of smoke caused more by the noticeable ribbons of vapor rising from some unknown source from the floor, rather than the glowing cherries of countless cigarettes and vape pens, hung thick in the air all about the shadowy figures of the club-goers filling the rather large partying space as though they were in the midst of an inferno they should be swiftly fleeing. Even in the tenebrous surroundings, Damiel recognized immediately that the club was no ordinary night spot, nor were its patrons normal civilians. The angel had warned the Nephilim in his care to be leery as they were in the wolves' den. It then stood to reason, if the city served as the wolves' den, then he was now extending his hand precariously close to the wolf's mouth.

The angel proceeded vigilantly, his eagle-eyed gaze scouring his surroundings as he mindfully cruised his way through the club. The first thing he took notice of from the nebulous, green-tinted figures moving to the hypnotic beat on the dance floor, and lounging upon the numerous plush velvet sofas, or huddled in booths situated around the club, were the eyes. They were much like that of a feline or canine wandering about in the dark whose eyes serve as a reflecting mirror when a light is shined their way. Except in this case, the ominous glowing coming from the watchful gazes following the angel were noticeably dull and void of life. Such lifeless eyes were a sure sign of the presence of Infectors; grubbers of the Underneath who move amongst mortal civilians as clandestine shadows looking for faithless hosts to invade like the viral plagues they were. And by the number of glowing dead eyes Damiel spied watching him as closely as he watched them, it appeared the angel had walked into a nest of Infectors. Not that Damiel needed to witness the dozens of sets of incandescent eyes peering back at him to recognize the company surrounding him; he could have been led blindfolded into the club and been alerted instantly to what awaited him by simply taking a whiff of the air. If there was one thing that gave away the presence of an undesirable from the Underneath more so than the tell-tale eyes of an Infector peering out from the confines of the civilian shell it had come to occupy, it was the stench it left in its wake. It was a foul and unmistakable reek; one often mistaken from standing downwind from a rendering plant.

Yet past the gazes and through the stink Damiel continued until finally, he spied what it was that forced his feet to wade deeper inside this fetid sewer of a playground. He was spotted sitting in round booth in a secluded area of the club; a young, handsome man who at first sight appeared to be a suave and polished player dressed in dark shirt and blazer with a diamond-encrusted chain hanging around his neck to match the flashy rings lighting the fingers of both hands, but whose revealing scar marking his left temple just beneath the hairline of his slicked-back mane of dark hair noted otherwise.

Glowering at the Fallen who was too busy frolicking with the two scantily clad ladies on either side of him to take notice of the angel's hovering presence, Damiel forced past his lips a name he had not uttered in some time.

"Demitriel."

The man looked up and his eyes flashed recognition of the unexpected sight leering down at him.

"Well…if it isn't my long-lost brother, Damiel," said Demitriel in a tone that was neither welcoming or rebuking.

"Already, you're mistaken on two counts," Damiel was quick to correct, "as I'm neither your brother nor the one who is lost."

"Alas, I take it from your saccharine tone that a reuniting embrace to mark this poignant occasion is not in the cards," Demitriel teased with a put-on pout which drew a collective of giggles from the two slinky felines draped on either side of him.

"And to what, exactly, do I owe the great honor of this unforeseen visit?" inquired Demitriel. "It's been a month of Sundays since I've even heard an utterance of your name."

"I wish to speak with you," said Damiel.

"So, then…speak."

"Alone."

Demitriel hesitated a moment or two; whether it was because he had neither the desire or willingness to engage Damiel in any sort of conversation, or that he was hesitant in being alone with the angel who all but sent two daggers in his direction with his piercing glare it remained uncertain, though likely it was a bit of both. Eventually, however, he dismissed the two women at his side with nothing but a telling look and they obediently complied. Damiel remained stone-faced, ignoring the flirty, seductive looks the woman focused on him as they slithered their way out of the booth, as well as refrain from inhaling the pungent cloud of perfume they left behind.

"So, this is the paradise on the back side of Heaven for which you and the rest of my seditious brethren sold your birthright," Damiel remarked once he sat down in the booth and gave the nightclub and its inhabitants a long withering look of repugnance. "How…heartening."

"I wouldn't be so quick to knock it until you've sampled it," Demitriel retorted with a self-pleasing grin. "Besides, the prize we won is far greater than any of the cheap pleasures you see before you."

"Really? Do enlighten me on what prize that is?" asked Damiel.

"Liberation, for starters," answered Demitriel.

The first semblance of a smile made itself seen on Damiel's face for the first time since he arrived in this Sin City, though it was less a smile than a mocking sneer.

"Liberation? From what have you ever had cause to be liberated…besides of course the sin of vainglory that led you to betray our father?" asked Damiel.

"Don't castigate me about sin when the sin first committed was not by son against father, but rather father against son," Demitriel seethed as his slow-brewing anger became more visible.

"What fresh blasphemy do you now dare spit forth?" asked Damiel.

"Thou shalt have no gods before me," said Demitriel. "You are still mindful of the existence of such a commandment, are you not? It was at the top of the heap of the ten great laws written with the finger of God our Father, the almighty hypocrite."

Damiel labored to follow the line of thinking coming from Demitriel but the deepening look of confusion showed he was having difficulty in doing so.

"Oh, our father has proven himself to be perfection when it comes to etching into stone his rules as he sees fit, and holding the threat of his mighty wrath over anyone and everyone who dares question such edicts," continued Demitriel. "But I ask you who holds his feet to the fire and brimstone he created for those he deems sinners when he, himself, is the transgressor. Certainly not the third of us who were pitched without thought into the deepest caverns of darkness and fire when we dared to call his own trespasses into question."

"You speak a language of tongues even I cannot attempt to make sense of," Damiel responded with a trying huff. "What sin is it are you attempting to pin on our father?"

Demitriel sank back in the velvet plushness of his seat, and his eyes, which, in the green lucency of the nightclub, appeared as twin dying suns struggling to stay alight in the crushing blackness of the universe, trained themselves on the throngs of club patrons swallowed up in the hedonism found in the smoky haze in which they were immersed.

"Man…that is the sin of which I speak," said Demitriel. "Or have you already shed from your memory the day we were brought before man and instructed to subjugate ourselves at the feet of our creator's most beloved…*creation*…as if he, himself, were a god?"

"I do indeed remember that day, Demitriel. And you and the rest of my exiled brethren were not alone in your refusal to kneel before man when asked to do so," said Damiel. "But I fear it is yourself who suffers from selective memory, as it was not your disobedience that resulted in your being cast from Heaven's bosom, but the fire of mutiny with which you attempted to incinerate our father's house."

"There can be no Heaven with two gods," Demitriel's voice rose with an anger that brought some semblance of renewed life to the burn in his eyes.

"Spoken like the Dragon disguised as an angel who led you to your downfall," Damiel growled in return. "This false light in which you are illuminated is quite telling. For even now, after all this time, your insides churn with the green bile of jealousy and pride. You were never offended in the trespass against our father of having to kneel before another, much as you would have me believe; your indignation was, and will always be, that the kneeling was not done at your own feet. When one thinks of himself as worthy of the same pedestal occupied by God, it's not long before he eventually sees himself *as* God."

"That is BECAUSE WE ARE!" Demitriel bellowed in a roar of a voice that momentarily swallowed the rumbling stomping of bass coming from the music as he leaned, unnaturally so, across the table toward Damiel, and in his brief eruption of rage his face distorted itself into something quite unpleasant and inhospitable before receding back into the handsome visage. Damiel did not so much as flinch at the response.

"Certainly, you would agree brother of mine, we are more godlike than the inferior and defective creation brought to breath by the hand of our father," Demitriel continued after taking a calming breath.

"Look at them!" Demitriel instructed, directing Damiel's attention to the club's patrons. "You speak of vainglory, yet I ask you, have you ever before laid eyes upon such a self-admiring lot?"

The lot Demitriel referred to Damiel recognized even before he seated himself at the booth to engage in what was becoming an ever more acrimonious back and forth. They were the club-goers spread out throughout the club appearing much like lifeless mannequins whose eyes were clear of the influences of the lurking Infectors, yet spellbound by something equally as malevolent: their own selves. For each one appeared utterly transfixed by an unending slideshow of glorified selfies of themselves flashing before them on the walls and ceilings and even illuminating the green smoky air around them in the same way a cellphone screen had the power to transform its owners into hypnotized zombies.

"You cannot deny they make it so easy for us," Demitriel said of the immobilized victims enraptured by their own mirror images. "Their self-love for themselves is in many cases stronger than the gentle sway any Infector can conjure."

"You've never heard leave from my lips an argument that they are perfect," said Damiel.

"Yet you dare lecture me about betrayal, Damiel, when it is yourself and my fellow brothers who are guilty of disloyalty by coming to the defense of the true enemy of our father instead of standing by your own kind. So let me ask you this question: What has man brought to this realm of life that has proven itself so worthy of the unforgivable snub to be suffered by our creator's first awakening of life in the form of the heavenly hosts? Has it been the blind eye with which they've come to disregard and mock our father's rule of law?

Perhaps it's been the slow ravaging of this world he so painstakingly created. Or do you prefer the subjugation and wholesale extermination of entire populations of the creatures he so lovingly set loose to roam the earth by the cancer that would become man when he introduced the fear of the hunt? By their hands came even the death of our father's only mortal son, and what was their punishment? The keys allowing them to inherit his very kingdom. But by all means, Damiel, continue with your genuflections, only refrain from levying upon me your chastisements because I choose not to subject my knees to the same unsightly calluses."

Damiel's gaze all but burned a hole clean through Demitriel's skull.

"Now, who's being the hypocrite?" the angel hissed through clenched teeth. "You speak of a cancer created by our father's hand. And who exactly in all this time has been in the ear of man ad nauseam enticing and beguiling them with your twisted, wormlike ways to commit said atrocities with the vengeful hope of turning God's favor. You purposefully salt the ground then have the audacity to find fault with the trees when they ultimately wither and die."

"We do nothing but help man realize his full potential in being the wretched burdens imposed upon all of us," Demitriel replied with a smug smirk of warped glee.

"And what of them?" questioned Damiel, looking to the many patrons gathered inside the club who had obviously succumbed to the whims of the dark side. "An Infector masquerading inside the skin of a civilian is still an Infector.

Demitriel surveyed the crowd and he seemed quite pleased by the sight.

"An Infector is nothing more than a scavenger of sorts, a vulture set loose to pick the bones of the dead," said Demitriel. "Trust me, there's not a soul they've come to inhabit that wasn't first cast aside willingly like some old ratted coat."

Damiel, however, knew better about such things; especially those things Demitriel prefaced with the two most distrusting words in his vocabulary: "Trust me."

~ ~ ~

"What is it that you want, Damiel?" Demitriel asked pointedly, as if he had suddenly grown tiresome of the bellicose reunion taking place. "I'm quite certain the reason you have sought me out is not in the role of a missionary bent on bringing about my salvation."

Sadly, it was the first time Damiel found agreement with Demitriel, and yet he could not help but feel a tinge of sorrow in knowing there was nothing within his power he could do to turn the fate of the angel he once called brother.

"I came to ask you about Zophiel," he said instead.

The name drew a curious tilt of Demitriel's head.

"Zophiel?" He appeared to muse on the sound of the name. "Now, there's a name I haven't heard spoken since the Great War. What of him?"

"I'm attempting to seek him out. I figured if anyone knew where he might be it would be you," answered Damiel.

A sly, questioning grin unfolded itself across Demitriel's mug.

"What business would you be having with Zophiel?" he asked before quickly attempting a guess at his own question. "Don't tell me our father is still stewing over Zophiel's unforgivable defection during the war and has sent his most ruthless of warriors as an assassin to quell his nagging wrath."

"Then, it's true…Zophiel was a traitor?" There was a sadness in Damiel's voice; the same kind of sadness that comes with the tidings of a death.

"Traitor is such a dishonorable word; I would rather prefer 'collaborator'. And a wily, deceitful collaborator at that." Demitriel, feigning a pronounced expression of commiseration, studied closely Damiel's deepening sullen state. "What's this? You didn't know? How is it do you think we met each one of your so-called well-planned attacks head-on? Through the aid of a crystal ball?"

"And eventually succumbed to your demise when the sky was ripped open beneath your feet," Damiel fired back defensively.

"Such is the cycle of combat," Demitriel replied with an indifferent shrug. "Someone wins, someone loses…until the dogs of war return as they always do to the battlefield with a renewed taste for bloodshed."

Damiel did his best to shake off Demitriel's words as the meaningless threats often heard in the company of grousing Fallen. But as he shifted his attention elsewhere in an attempt to tamp down the growing tide of disgust and contempt he felt rising up inside him for the putrid figure sitting across the table from him, his gaze caught a most unexpected sight. On the far side of the club, he spied a Fallen by the name of Arrestel, who had reaped the reputation of being a particularly weaselly scoundrel, even amongst the disgraced and downfallen who bore wings. Except to Damiel, this particular Fallen served as a personal brand of vile wretchedness; so much so that it was all he could do to set eyes upon him and not come apart like a fissure ripping open the earth and releasing a devastating temblor of rage and destruction.

So much time had passed, so many years, and yet the surprising sight of Arrestel standing but a stone's throw from him cut Damiel to his very bones, as his eyes glossed over with the one memory he wish above all else to be purged from his psyche that retold, in unrelenting haunting shadows, the darkest day he would ever come to know.

It was the day his one and only child, Theron, a beautiful and brash young boy of fifteen, had finally reached the age to make the long-awaited journey to Eden. Like all angels who had come to know fatherhood, the crossing-point moment was one eagerly anticipated by Damiel, if not more so. As the Guide who trained all Nephilim in the ways of combat and, especially, the sword, Damiel had already quietly observed the natural way his boy took blade to hand, just as one would expect the child of the Angel of the Sword to do. But the great expectations Damiel seeded for Theron were instantly doused by a great wave of death just outside the hidden Gate leading to Eden.

Damiel was the first to reach Akdamar Island when the unutterable news made its way to Havenhid. There he was met by Johiel, not in the deceptive skin of the old and frail caretaker of the island, but as the redoubtable, youthful angel he was, and the disconsolate look fixed upon his brother's face like some horrid death mask spoke of the tragedy hidden within the walls of the island's ancient church before a single word of warning could be uttered. Johiel made the futile attempt to hold Damiel back, but he quickly realized the whole might of Heaven's army would have failed in keeping the angel from passing through the church doors. The inconsolable wail that made itself heard moments later and threatened to bring down the very church from which it came to its last stone was beyond anything Johiel had braced himself to bear.

Never before had Johiel witnessed anything as horrific as the scene he confronted when he finally forced his feet to carry him across the threshold of the once pristine church. There, on the floor beneath the hallmark dome with its ring of illuminated windows, Damiel sat in a crumpled, defeated heap of sorrow cradling the lifeless body of his son like some eery recreation of Michelangelo's doleful Pieta sculpture. Scattered across the floor around them in various heart-wrenching positions of finality were the bodies of a dozen more young Nephilim who, like Theron, were waiting to make the journey across the once peaceful waters of the Van Gölü. So harrowing the sight that Johiel attempted to throw a merciful shroud across the red-stained floor by blotting out the sun with a bank a clouds with an effortless motion of his hand

and dimming the slats of light (which itself appeared pale with sorrow) streaming downward through the dome.

The Darkness had come, Johiel later explained to Damiel once an untapped anger had pushed aside the desolation and returned the grieving father to his feet. The Darkness had come and brought with it the Black Death of genocide that would first rear its head against the Armenian people on the outlying shores of the Van Gölü before spreading throughout Turkey like some unstoppable plague.

"I should have known better than to leave them," Johiel lamented as he recalled the horror that followed. "But an unfamiliar raven came to me to deliver a message asking for my presence on the mainland. If I wished to spare Akdamar, and its church, from the storm of fire and fury which no barrier of water could hold back, the message said, then it would be in my best interest that I promptly accept this invitation to the mainland. So accept it I did, however reluctantly, leaving the newly arrived Fledglings in the care of the monks who have long called Akdamar their home. After all, who would make it their mission to target the young scions of angels? Generations of Nephilim had managed to live peaceful upbringings until this most unspeakable moment, even as the Darkness continued in its vocation to wreak havoc amongst civilians. How shamed I am in my naivety, for I had barely set foot on the mainland where I found Arrestel waiting for me, and the macabre, sadistic sneer which he greeted me made me realize instantly with a great sense of stupidity and terror that I had willingly stepped into the catch of a snare. But by then it was too late. I heard the screams come across the water in a way that turned the very blood in my veins to ice; screams only Furies have the ability to rip free from throats. When I returned, it had all been extinguished: the Fledglings, the monks, the very sanctity of this sanctuary."

"And who was it that was responsible for setting the snare that led to this butchery?" Damiel demanded to know as he stepped toward Johiel with the unmistakable glimmer of requital alight in his festering glare.

"I think it best we exhaust our mourning, and malice, while laying to rest these dear, lost innocents in the proper state deserving of them," replied Johiel who was more than acquainted with the well of wrath that resided within the angel.

"*WHO?*" bellowed Damiel who would not be denied the name he sought one second longer.

Johiel hesitated before his lips reluctantly parted to make heard the name that echoed against the church walls like some unspoken curse.

"Miseriel."

~ ~ ~

Miseriel

The very name had cemented itself like some eternal flame deep within Damiel's eyes where it burned steady and vigilantly like some marker to keep lit the cold, hard crypt where his vengeance had long lay in state. It was the kind of hand-reared anger not lost on Demitriel, who witnessed closeup the burn of such a flame during Damiel's brief relapse into memory.

"Something the matter?" Demitriel inquired, though it was clear from the slight upturn in the corners of his mouth that the recognition of Arrestel's presence by Damiel had not gone unnoticed by him.

"It's nothing," Damiel remarked with unusual quietness as he trained his stony stare on the table at which he was seated. "I'm just suddenly reminded how many of these so-called collaborators you mentioned have come to foul your ranks."

Demitriel wisely held his tongue and used the next moment or two of silence to choose his next words carefully.

"I'm well aware of the unfortunate taking of your son," he commented when finally he spoke, drawing Damiel's scowl. "Such a tragedy; to meet death at so young of age, and in such a barbaric manner. Not just your boy, but all those halflings who perished with him."

Damiel heard clearly the words coming from Demitriel mouth, but they were accompanied by other sentiments whispered into his ear by the exact same voice that worked to stoke his already burning ire and urge him to do the very thing he was struggling with all his might to restrain: to cross the club and slay Arrestel where he stood.

"I have no intention of conversing about my son; least of all with you," Damiel seethed as he fought to turn a deaf ear to the coaxing murmurs.

"Believe it or not, in some small ways I quite admire you and the resolve you possess that seems to almost encase you, like armor," Demitriel continued, paying no mind to Damiel. "It must be a strong test of your will to have the gift of retribution dangled in front of you and be unable to claim it."

The second phantom voice, however, bluntly goaded Damiel, *'What are you waiting for? Take your sword and drive it through the heart of the one who delivered your son to his slaughter!'*

For a moment, it appeared the resolve Demitriel had moments earlier complimented might finally dissolve. But only for a moment.

"I asked politely that you hold your tongue, or shall I cut it from your mouth and relieve you of your impediment?" Damiel threatened with a civil tone even as his eyes burned with fire.

"Now then," the angel continued in as calm a voice as he could manage, "I came here for a reason, and one reason only: To see if you could point me in the direction of where I might find Zophiel."

A rather complacent look came over Demitriel as he sank deeper into the plush pillowy backing of the booth. "I wish I could help you, but, unfortunately, many of us Fallen have not kept in contact with one another as brothers should since being delivered to this paradise of eternal expiation," he answered.

"Then I've dirtied my shoes for nothing," Damiel scoffed and moved to rise from the booth and exit the malodorous club that was making him grow more queasy with each passing second he remained when Demitriel stalled him.

"This, by chance, wouldn't have anything to do with the so-called Light Bearer suddenly being brought into all our lives once again, would it?" Demitriel inquired as lackadaisical as someone wondering what weather had accompanied the start of the day.

"Light Bearer? I'm sure I don't know what you mean," Damiel replied without offering even the slightest hint of telling beyond the poker-faced mask he was wearing.

"Come now, Damiel, we here may be banished, but we weren't struck deaf and dumb as well," said Demitriel. "News of such a far-reaching prophesy mysteriously resurrected has a way of making the rounds with the speed of a firestorm eating its way through a forest ravaged by drought."

"Resurrected prophesy? Sounds like the source of your news comes from the gossip of quite the enterprising muckraker," said Damiel. "The only prophesy I know concerning the Light Bearer ended when it was run through with a sword half a century ago."

The slight smile which sat unmoved on his face, however, said Demitriel believed otherwise, despite the angel's words as he rose to his feet to bid Damiel a good night.

"Well then…whatever your business with Zophiel, happy hunting," he said, rising from his seat.

"Let's not be strangers," were Demitriel's last words to Damiel, but the subtle glowering fixed in his eyes made it anything but a friendly salutation.

Damiel watched with visible contempt as Demitriel made his way through the smoky club past the waxworks interned in the trance of the virtual cellphone screens whose glow fashioned their prison bars to where Arrestel was congregating with other unsavory types and whispered casually into his ear. Arrestel glanced Damiel's way and seemed not surprised to see the angel's presence. The meeting of their eyes, however, was all that was needed to force his knee off the neck of the animosity he wrestled to keep down.

He was halfway to his feet, his right hand reaching inside his coat and under his left arm for the grip of his sword concealed in the confines of his wings that, at the same time, were poised to rip their way through his shirt and coat and anything that stood between them when a nearby voice somehow managed to still him.

"I wouldn't do that if I were you. It could get ugly very quickly," the voice warned quietly yet sternly.

Glancing out of the corner of his eye over his right shoulder, Damiel spied a figure dressed all in black sitting alone directly behind him in the next booth over with his back facing the angel's.

"You have no idea just how ugly, I assure you," Damiel replied with a snarl.

"I meant it as a warning, not an observation," returned the stranger whose face was concealed by the hood of cloak fashionably outdated by a good century or more that he wore. "Look about you…you're surrounded by Infectors…too many for even you, the great Angel of the Sword, to fend off all on your lonesome."

Damiel slowly sank back into his seat, though it was not caution to the warning offered him that caused his retreat.

"That diseased vermin helped bring about the murder of helpless innocents," he spit.

"A black-hearted wretch, I have no doubt," replied the stranger, "but believe me when I say you will find no sympathy for your loss in this morgue of the departed."

Damiel sat silent for a moment as he listened to the voice which, strangely enough, had a ring of familiarity to it.

"Just who are you, anyway?" inquired Damiel. "And what business is any of this of yours?"

"To answer your second question first, I couldn't help but overhear the conversation you were having concerning someone by the name of Zophiel."

"You know Zophiel?" Damiel, suddenly intrigued, questioned.

"I know you are seeking him out."

"Would it be presumptuous of me to inquire from you where I might find him?"

"Unfortunately, that is something with which I cannot offer you assistance."

"Then you are about as useful to me as the rest of this city and all its inhabitants," said Damiel as he again started to rise from his seat.

"I do, however, know of someone who would be able to steer you in the right direction," stated the figure.

"And who might this be, might I ask?"

"His son."

A curious look found Damiel's face as he once again found himself being returned to his vacated seat. "Zophiel has a son?"

Not that it was such a strange, out of the ordinary thing to discover. Many angels had mortal reflections of themselves roaming the earth; Fallen were certainly no different in that regard.

"Where can I find him?" asked Damiel.

"A few hours north of here," said the stranger.

He then, without turning his body, reached over his left shoulder with his right hand to pass along to Damiel a cocktail napkin clamped between two fingers. And as he did, a brief belch of smoke emanated from the underside of the napkin, as though it had been set aflame by a match.

"Who are you?" Damiel asked once more after taking the napkin from the stranger.

"To put it simply, a friend," came the answer.

Damiel turned his attention to the napkin which was emblazoned with the club's green-tinted moniker, but when he turned it over he saw that an address had been seared into the paper as if by a pen filled with fire rather than ink detailing a location less than a day's travel away. The angel swung himself around toward the neighboring booth to get better acquainted with who the mysterious stranger seated there was but, to his surprise, he found the booth to be empty, and when he quickly scoped out the nightclub with his keen eyes he spied not a trace of the hooded figure.

~ ~ ~

Damiel was more than ready to make his departure from the nightclub and its company he found both unpleasant and intolerable. Without wasting another moment, he tucked the napkin into his coat pocket and got up from the booth for the final time. As he made his beeline for the exit, he could not refrain from glancing one last time at the figure for whom it had taken every last bit of constraint he could muster from the core of his very being not to come undone and paint the very walls with his innards. Arrestel had by this time, migrated to a private corner booth with other shadowy shapes and, when Damiel passed by, their eyes met again for a brief moment that stretched into eternity. Instead of fear, however, of which any sound-minded individual would have instantly felt in the face of such a threatening presence, especially one responsible for the most egregious of crimes against the one known as the Angel of the Sword, Arrestel dared to respond with a waggish—perverted, even—smile.

Damiel, to his credit, kept his feet moving without detour, even as his gaze threatened to turn the club into a smoldering pile of ash and bone. For there was only one thing in existence with the power to keep in check the snarling beast tugging at the chain shackling it: the knowing that the reparation he had been denied that night would one day be paid him, come hell or high water.

For Demitriel, it was with a sense of a relief, veiled though it was, that he watched Damiel ascend the stairway leading from the nightclub to the surface street without leaving a drop of spilled blood in his wake, even though he had tried with all his pernicious powers of allurement to get the angel to unsheathe his sword.

"The boy is here," Demitriel said suddenly in a voice that didn't even attempt to pierce the pulsating bass of the music, and yet the attention of every single club-goer immediately diverted his way.

A slinky, dark-haired woman of exceptional beauty who had shared Demitriel's company with an equally stunning blonde before Damiel's visit approached the grim-faced Fallen.

"Are you certain?" she asked.

"I could smell his scent on Damiel's clothes as strongly as your own now sits in my nostrils," Demitriel answered somewhat disgruntled at being questioned. "Trust me, the Light Bearer is here amongst us."

"What would you have us do?" the woman asked.

"Find him, of course," Demitriel replied with a noted breath of impatience. "Do as you will with the others, but not a single hair on his head is to be harmed, is that understood? With Damiel keeping watch over him you will only have one chance given to you, if even that."

The woman nodded obediently when suddenly her eyes rolled upward and back inside her skull, like a pair of slow-rising window shades. Her legs then gave out from under her causing her to collapse in a heap onto the floor as if she had been greeted by a fainting spell. Demitriel made no move to come to her aid but remained where he stood looking down upon her without so much as a hint of alarm. Not that any concern was necessary when it came to civilians serving as hosts to the controlling and overpowering Infectors looking to stray outside their human shell momentarily, but with the intent of returning.

Demitriel watched the voluntary exorcism take place at his feet in the shape of a stirring shadow that seemed to separate itself from the unconscious body to which it was attached and slowly make its way across the nightclub floor like some oil slick migrating across the surface of an ocean. Then one by one the other patrons of the club began to drop to the floor in similar manners where they bled out more shadowy shapes until the floor reflected a kaleidoscope of ominous silhouettes making their way toward the stairway leading out of the club and to the streets beyond.

CHAPTER TEN

As was his nightly routine, Harry Klumfess went about the business of walking his dog Sparkle along the manicured streets of his neighborhood which resided outside the bustle and glare of the Vegas Strip. The gray and white terrier's legs appeared to go a mile a minute in a scurry of excitement and in the process extended the lead of the leash attached to its collar to the pulling point before the curious pooch would stop suddenly to investigate a random shrub or sniff a certain tree trunk or fire hydrant and allow its owner, whose legs didn't move with the same briskness due to age, to catch up.

The stop-and-go pattern would continue for a couple blocks until they reached the destination of a nearby park. There, after scouring the grass with his nose as though sweeping for nonexistent treasure, Sparkle would eventually settle upon an agreeable spot, assume a tell-tale wide-legged stance while hunching his back and go about desecrating the otherwise pristine park.

"Good girl," Harry always commended his four-legged ball of fur when the deed was completed as Sparkle proceeded to scratch at the ground with his back paws and send bits of grass and dirt into the air as if taking a bow for a performance well done.

Always the responsible dog owner, unlike many other pet walkers whose paths he crossed, Harry reached into his pocket for a small plastic bag to pick up the mess instead of leaving behind an unpleasant land mine for some unwitting person to accidentally step on, as he had misfortune of experiencing only a few evenings earlier. It was such an easy and effortless act of courtesy; easy and effortless once you got past the wrangling of getting the poop bag open, that is. How he hated those bags, almost as much as he hated the plastic bags in the produce section of the grocery store. They always proved to be a struggle for his stiff, aged fingers to maneuver in the frustrating challenge of finding the opening. Sparkle seemed to understand this and used the time out as an opportunity to wander about as far as the leash he remained tethered to allowed him and explore the hidden scents of the park.

This night, however, there was a strange and unfamiliar redolence in the air that put the terrier on alert. Shifting his focus from his nose to eyes,

Sparkle carefully scoured the nighttime surroundings of the park with his watchful eyes, particularly the myriad shadows cast by the trees. Sure enough, a tenebrous shape concealed within the canopy of shadows separated itself from the surrounding cloak of blackness and slowly crept its way across the ground in the direction of where Harry was standing heedless of the approaching black menace. But it didn't go unnoticed by Sparkle who let out an unsure squealing of whines before erupting in a cacophonous chorus of barking.

"Patience, Sparkle," Harry said in reply, eyes squinted in intense concentration as his fingers struggled to locate the invisible seam of the plastic bag he was certain was created by some sick sadist.

As the shadow crept closer, Sparkle seemed willing to obey any command other than patience. He began to tug with a spastic frenzy against the hold of the leash attached to his collar in the same manner he usually did whenever he caught sight of a squirrel or a cat. Only he wasn't scrambling and lunging to get at the approaching dark shape, but to retreat from it, and in quick order.

"A-HA!" Harry exclaimed with pronounced victory when he finally managed to peel apart the seam that was the combative opening of the bag and, with some effort, managed to take a knee on the grass to complete his clean-up task.

Sparkle's barking grew more incessant, as did his tugging as the black shape inched its way closer to his paws, but all of the dog's frantic dancing and dodging about couldn't save him from finally being engulfed by the inky blob.

"Good heavens, Sparkle, what did have to eat today? There's enough here to make a whole new dog," Harry remarked while oblivious to the sudden absence of barking, or tugging coming from the end of the leash as he went about bagging the doggy poop.

When he finally finished, he breathed a victorious sigh.

"There now…see what you can accomplish when you have a little bit of patience?" he said with a triumphant smile while holding up the bulging bag in front of him as if to admire while still kneeling on the ground. "Now, we can carry on with our walk."

He had barely uttered the last word when there came a sudden yank from the slack leash still gripped in his hand; so hard and forceful it was that it yanked Harry clean off his knees and sent him hurling through the air several feet before sending him tumbling across the grassy ground. Clearly dazed by the tossing he'd been given, he scrambled to readjust the glasses left dangling off just one ear and gave a startled look about for his dog who was nowhere to be seen.

"Sparkle…" he called out for his beloved terrier, but besides himself, the park was dark and empty.

He then reached for the leash that rested on the ground nearby and he frantically pulled in the slack hand over fist until he came to the end where Sparkle should have been attached. To his bewilderment, however, he found the thick, tough nylon tether had been severed, as if something had chewed its way through it; something with teeth much larger and sharper than Sparkle's.

A look of utter bafflement came over the old man as he slowly and cautiously searched the darkness surrounding him.

"Sparkle?" he called out once more, though with a cautious timidness as a cacophonous chorus of barking and howling coming from all directions both nearby and far began to make itself heard.

~ ~ ~

The raucous din of barking that sounded, as more black shapes entered neighboring backyards and passed through doggy door entrances, somehow evaded Jacob's keen hearing as he stood quietly by the window of the hotel room he was holed up in, staring down at the light show that was the city below. It had been well over an hour since Damiel had left, and each passing minute seemed to stretch itself longer and longer and antagonize Jacob's growing anxiousness. Meanwhile, the food Damiel had arranged to be sent up to the room had arrived and Max, Leos, Kairo and Ethan were hungrily diving into their plates.

"It's now official…Havenhid has soured my taste buds to all other food, even this Las Vegas grub," Max spat, tossing his half-eaten grilled cheese sandwich on the plate in front of him.

"I know what you mean…it's like I'm eating cheese-covered cardboard," Kairo chimed in as he studied the slice of pizza he was eating with a questioning eye.

"I don't know what you're all complaining about…I like it!" came a muffled reply from Ethan who was shoveling forkfuls of pasta into his mouth as fast as a swine trying to reach the bottom of its trough.

"Why am I not surprised?" questioned Leos whose look of disgust hovered between his own plate of food and watching Ethan beside him gorging himself.

"Yo, Jacob, you better come get yours while it's still hot," Kairo called out.

"Or before the human Hoover, here, sucks it all down," Max chided Ethan whose ballooning cheeks left available to him only an angry squint of the eyes to voice his disapproval.

"That's alright, I'm really not hungry," said Jacob.

"What's going on with you? You've been unusually quiet since we got here," said Leos. "You worried about Damiel?"

"No…not really," answered Jacob as he continued to stare out the window. "Just wondering what's taking so long."

"Not to get your hopes down, but you told us yourself Damiel said it was a long-shot to even find this Zophiel. Maybe whatever or whoever Damiel hoped to find here to help locate him ended up being a dead end," said Max.

Jacob didn't say anything in return, but the longer Damiel was away, the more he found himself silently wondering the same thing.

"Explain this to me again…who exactly is this Zophiel?" Ethan asked after managing to free his mouth of enough food to find his voice.

"For the hundredth time, Zophiel is a Fallen," Kairo answered with a tired huff.

"I got that," said Ethan, "but why exactly are we in Las Vegas trying to hunt him down?"

"Don't you remember the night in the Silent Forest after Gotham was killed, when Thaniel attempted to swipe the Sword of Destiny from Jacob, and ended up getting his sorry butt tossed in the Through to the Underneath instead? Well, apparently, the last words he managed to mutter before being pulled under was Zophiel's name, and Jacob thinks it might mean something important," explained Kairo.

"Are you sure Thaniel actually said 'Zophiel'?" Leos questioned Jacob. "There was a lot of chaos going on that night…maybe there's a chance you might of misheard him."

Even before the question was asked, the memory of Thaniel's final moments had surfaced as a reflection in the window in front of Jacob, just as it replayed itself like some maddening video clip on a continuous loop in his dreams, night after night, ending with Zophiel's name reverberating in a pointed echo inside his head.

Zophiel.

Zophiel.

ZOPHIEL.

"I'm sure," Jacob answered quietly but definitively. "He said 'Zophiel.'"

"What do you think we'll find out if we're lucky enough to locate Zophiel?" asked Max.

"I haven't a clue," Jacob answered with a weighted shrug revealing the tireless effort in recent days his mind had been spinning trying to come up with an answer to that very question. Then, before another prodding question could be lobbed his way, he quickly added, "Look, do you mind if we find something else to talk about?"

"Sure thing. What do you want to talk about?" Max, who could see plainly his friend's desperation to step outside the tunnel vision he had been sucked into, asked.

"I don't know…anything," replied Jacob. "How have things been going back at Havenhid?"

"Every day is a great day at Havenhid," said Kairo.

"It was a particularly great day for old Ethan here when he finally mastered the art of his Cloaking Grace recently and actually managed to transform himself into a full fledge tiger without any visible defects," said Leos, giving Ethan a playful poke.

"Now if we can just get him to transform himself into a human without any visible defects," cracked Max.

"Jeez…so I messed up a little bit trying to pass myself off as you to Damiel. Sue me," Ethan grumbled.

"I was actually talking about the skin you're wearing now," Max deadpanned.

Ethan swiveled his head around and aimed his eyes at the mirror on the wall across the room, and immediately got the wisecrack when all he saw was his normal reflection returning his curious stare.

"Ha ha, very funny," he crowed back to the muffled chuckles coming from Max and Leos.

"Don't ask me to deliver them, but Mist sends you a face-full of licks," said Kairo.

The mention of the white wolf who had been his beloved companion while in Eden brought a noticeable light to Jacob's face.

"How is she?"

"Great, aside from missing you. She sleeps on your bed every night staring at the door in hopes that one day you'll come walking through it again. She'll be beyond excited when she sees you with us when we get back."

"You really are going back with us, aren't you?" asked Leos.

"Of course he is," Max answered before Jacob had a chance to part his lips. "That was part of the bargain he made with Damiel in exchange for going on this side detour."

"You have to come back," Ethan chimed in as if more convincing on the matter was needed. "If you can believe it, Creed has become even more of an obnoxious wonker ever since you left."

"That's wanker, you wanker," corrected Max.

"Tomato, tomahto," Ethan replied with a dismissive roll of his eyes. "All I'm trying to say is he's been an unbearable douche, even douchier than usual, now that you're not around to slap him down to size. He even tried to get Anahel to kick Mist out of our room by threatening to bring the matter to his father saying it was beneath a Nephilim of his stature to be forced to sleep in the vicinity of a dirty mutt.

"I have to admit I would do just about anything just to see the look on his face when you come walking back into the Hall of Light just as dinner is being served," said Max.

"Plus you still have to meet Vessel," said Kairo.

"Vessel? Who's Vessel?" asked Jacob.

"He's our new Guide for Study," explained Leos. "He arrived at Havenhid a couple days after you left. Anahel brought him in as a replacement for Thaniel."

"Replacement?" The news came as both an expected and unexpected surprise to Jacob. "I guess it makes sense…it's just the thought of someone new taking over… So, what's he like?" he asked.

"He seems okay…for a Guide, I mean," said Kairo. "He's definitely smart, that's for sure. Half the time I don't even know what he's rambling about. Just…"

Jacob's brow rose slightly when Kairo's voice paused. "Just what?"

"I don't know…he's just…different," said Kairo. "When Thaniel was around it was like he and Library were one entity. He had a way of making learning and books exciting and new. Now it's about as exciting as when I went to school before coming to Havenhid."

"I know I'm opening myself for a verbal clubbing, but I can't help but miss him...Thaniel, that is," said Ethan, taking a breather from stuffing himself. "I mean, I know what he ended up doing was beyond horrible. I still can't get the image of what he did to Gotham out of head no matter how hard I try. But he was my favorite Guide...up until that point, anyways."

"We all feel the same way," said Leos, who would have happily taken the first swipe at Ethan with a club of words, but couldn't.

"What do you think's happening to him now?" Ethan asked though there was a timidness in his voice that betrayed a doubt in really wanting to know the answer to his question.

"Whatever it is, it's probably best we don't think about it," said Jacob.

And yet, the moment he spoke those words it was as if his brain turned renegade against his wishes and flashed before his eyes a horrible vision. It made his eyes close themselves tight as if in an attempt to wipe themselves clean and refocus, but when he reopened them the image came at him again and attempted to push aside the reality of his surroundings that was the hotel room and his friends. Only this time the strange flashing phantasm of snarling fangs and murderous blood-filled eyes brought with it an overpowering feeling of direness that seemed to find an entry into his very veins, and carry itself to every part of his being where it fed every last cell that made up his existence.

"Jacob...you alright?"

The question came as a faraway muffle inside his head that was instantly obliterated by an intense surge of pain that pierced its way through his right side just beneath his ribcage. So great was the pain that he lost his fight to hold firm his footing and fell back against the wall of window behind him.

"Forget what I said about Thaniel," said Ethan, sounding panicked.

"It wasn't you. I think he's having one of his episodes," said Kairo.

The group had only witnessed one such "episode" before, but once was all that was needed to recognize the stricken, dazed look that seemed to grip Jacob when and if it ever chose to resurface again in the future.

Max was the first to leap from his comfortable spot on the bed and come to Jacob's aid, but Jacob motioned for some space as he fought to catch his breath while clutching his side.

"My sword...I need my sword," he managed to gasp.

Realizing it was the one request no one else in the room could help oblige him with, Jacob quickly scurried his way across the floor to where his long blue and white duffel bag resided. His friends formed a half circle close about him with growing looks of intrigue as Jacob unzipped the bag and revealed a halting glimpse of the strange and mysterious sword hidden away inside. It was a peculiar way to store such a weapon, of that there was no doubt; Nephilim, like their angel counterparts, kept their blades concealed in a special sheath formed by nature within the hidden confines of the plumes that formed their wings, making it close within reach in the same way a gunslinger's six-shooter rested on the hip for a quick draw. Jacob, however, found just holding the sword to be an intense enough act all on its own; to have it secured to his being with all the immense power radiating from the steel hide like a thousand hearts beating in unison inside his chest was something he had not yet developed enough stamina to fully endure. Such power was evident the moment Jacob removed the sword from inside the duffel bag. Even those who were gathered close around him and knew better to keep their hands at a distance, could feel the authority that was emitted off the blade in a glint of bright light that illuminated the entranced looks of the five faces staring at it.

Jacob focused his gaze, which was less wide-eyed than those of his friends, on the polished surface of the blade that captured his reflection in the same manner as a mirror. But his reflection quickly dissipated in the same way an image resting on the reflected surface of a lake is scattered when a thrown rock punctures its clarity, and in its place, as Jacob had often witnessed in the past when his gaze was captured by the mysteries of the sword, other shapes and colors began to come together and create strange new scenes. The conjured images were usually those that first congregated inside his head. Only he was not expecting what was shown to him; it was Wray, and Ty. They were seen wandering down a street, but the street was unlike any he was familiar with in Cain's Corner. It was bright and alive, pulsating in a sea of blinking-colored lights.

"What is it? What do you see?" Max inquired when he noticed a change in Jacob's expression.

"They're here," Jacob replied.

"Who? Who's here?"

Jacob leaned in closer to the sword he held before him and his eyes narrowed themselves to get a closer look at his two friends when the lights surrounding them began to go out in large sections. He was then quickly given an unexpected jolt back when a snarling mouth lined with fanged teeth gnashed their way into view. Then came the eyes…the blood-filled cruel peepers unlike any he had ever before seen or knew to exist even amongst the most savage of animals. And in the midst of the snapping teeth and wicked eyes there came a scream. So horrible sounding it was that Jacob released his hold on the sword and let it fall with a heavy thud onto the floor, pulling the plug on the nightmarish vision.

"They're here and they're in trouble," Jacob huffed with an edge of panic.

"Slow down…*who* are you talking about and what kind of trouble?" Max asked in a cool and collected voice, which wasn't hard considering the only visions he and the others had been privy to witness coming from the sword were their own mundane reflections, hard as they tried to focus past them.

"Wray and Ty," Jacob snapped with a growing sense of impatience. "I don't know why or how, but they are here…somewhere…and something bad is about to happen to them."

Then, before anyone could respond to his baffling announcement, Jacob returned his sword to his duffel bag which he stuffed safely out of sight under one of the beds before proceeding to hastily put on his shoes.

"Where're you going?" asked Leos.

"Where do you think? I'm going to go find them," answered Jacob.

"I don't think that's such a good idea," Kairo muttered warily. "Damiel told us specifically not to leave this room."

"And you won't be, so you have nothing to worry about," said Jacob. "And with any luck, I'll make it back here before he does and he'll be none the wiser."

"You can't just go off half-cocked here on some image you saw in a sword that may not even be real," said Max in an attempt to slow Jacob down and think a bit more rationally.

"Trust me, Max, if you saw what I saw, you wouldn't be able to sleep tonight, or any night for that matter, until you at least went out and checked for sure whether it was real or not."

"I'm not so sure about that," Ethan, whose first inclination was to always side with the voice of reason when it came to dangerous places and, more importantly, dangerous things, argued under his breath.

"Why don't you at least text Wray and see if she is, in fact, really here?" Max suggested.

"Because when I returned to Cain's Corner after taking off the last time I was greeted with a milkshake dumped over my head and a punch I can still feel," Jacob explained to Max who couldn't help offer up a sympathetic wince. "So if she's not here in Vegas and what I saw was some weird, unexplainable hallucination, it's a can of worms I'd rather not open at this precise moment, if you catch what I mean."

Seeing it was fruitless to argue the matter any further, Max made a beeline across the room where he had ditched his own shoes and shuffled his feet back into them.

"What do you think you're doing?" asked Jacob.

"Goin' with," answered Max.

It was a sentiment shared by both Kairo and Leos who followed suit and quickly hunted the floor for their own shoes.

"Look, there's no point in all of us risking getting into trouble," said Jacob. "Besides, someone needs to stay behind and let Damiel know what's going on in case he comes back before I do."

It was all that was needed to be said to light a fire under Ethan's hedging behind when all eyes suddenly turned to focus themselves on him.

"Don't look at me," he said, making a dash for the last remaining pair of sneakers lying on the floor. "I still think this is a bad idea, but if I have a choice between a bad idea and having to explain any of this to Damiel, I'll risk going with the bad idea."

"I give you a hero of the highest order," Max remarked while grabbing Ethan in a friendly headlock and giving the top of his noggin a well-earned noogie as the group filed out of the room without a clue of what awaited them on the brightly lit streets of The Strip.

~ ~ ~

Walking along Fremont Street in downtown Las Vegas was like entering a carnival on steroids, where an immediate assault of lights and activity gave all comers the feeling they had somehow been sucked inside a massive interactive billboard in Times Square that blotted out all earthly reality and, instead, replaced it with a crazy kaleidoscope of pulsating brightness and excitement. Like a hoard of extras in a low-budget zombie flick, the slow-moving tide of tourists packing the pedestrian mall wandered through the endless offering of novelty stores and brightly lit casinos, where the constant sound of gamblers running the penny slots could be heard. The air was ripe with the alluring aroma of sizzling steaks and deep-fried fish and chips beckoning grumbling stomachs inside one of the many restaurants lining the way; as well, a string of pubs—all utilizing the same entertainment draw of scantily dressed bar maidens gyrating to music on bar tops—offered a challenging marathon course for as far as the eye could see for the liquor connoisseur looking to train for the next St. Patrick's Day pub crawl. Standing watch over everything like some oversized security guard was Vegas Vic, the iconic forty-foot neon cowboy marquee with his wide-brimmed hat slouched on his head and fluorescent cigarette dangling from his mouth.

Even a giant cowboy created from vibrant neon had a difficult task of competing with the real spectacle found amid all the lights and people. The street performers had always been a curiosity draw to this small resurrected pocket of the city that had once served as the archway to those attracted to the seedier side of life, with its strip clubs and prostitutes walking the streets. Only now, the strippers and hookers had been given a makeover of sorts, and found a new way to sell their wares by playing dress-up as showgirls or super heroines in revealing costumes that left nothing to the imagination, and raking in dollar bills by simply taking photos with admiring passersby.

Jacob and his posse, however, were not taken in like most teenaged boys would be by the fishhooks baited with flesh that had been cast in their eyesight as they slowly made their way through the crowd. If anything, the thoroughfare of glitz and glitter they walked appeared as nothing less than a boulevard created for lost souls. Passing by a pasty, overweight man wearing nothing but a tutu and strumming a guitar, they came across a heavily tattooed woman sporting a G-string and pasties giving a mock spanking to a middle-aged dwarf dressed in a diaper bent over a chair while an amused crowd looked on. But it was the young, naive child holding her mother's hand and looking bewildered while witnessing the scene much too inappropriate for eyes so innocent that caught the boys' attention, however, and they instantly understood why Damiel had earlier referred to the city as "Gomorrah" in a spat of disgust as he had.

As the boys maneuvered their way through the crowd pooling around a nearly naked Wonder Woman swinging her golden lasso overhead, and several male exotic dancers posing shirtless for photos with drooling fans, it was the several other less conspicuous street performers on the periphery that drew notice from Jacob. They appeared to blend in somewhat to the background and didn't attract the numbers of passing tourists in the same manner as the nearly naked, female Indiana Jones loudly cracking the air with her bull whip, most likely because they were of the fully dressed variety. One wore a sinister-looking mask and appeared at first as a department store mannequin until money was dropped into a nearby hat placed on the ground. The charitable contribution acted as a jump from a charger cable sparking life in the figure whose movements took the shape of a break dance routine which amazingly defied the physics and limitations of flexibility that constrained the limbs of most every other person walking the earth. Another neighboring performer also fully attired in an outfit of dark clothing simply stood upside down. That is, he stood upside down using only one hand, and he did so without showing even the smallest hint of sway to his inverted body or struggle to hold his balance, nor did his hand and fully outstretched arm bracing the concrete sidewalk betray any strain to accomplish such a feat, which the man performed tirelessly without pause.

"Fallen?" Jacob asked quietly to no one in particular.

"Yep," answered Max. "Spotted three myself."

"Same here," said. Leos.

Not that spotting a Fallen was so difficult a task to someone who believed in such things and knew what identifying traits to be on the lookout for such as the telltale scar which marked their fate as clearly as it marked the left corner of their foreheads. But Nephilim had a special advantage in sniffing out their fallen ancestors: an inherent instinct that all but went off like an alarm clock whenever they were in close proximity to the source of the bloodline that fed their own veins, whether it be tainted or not. And it just so happened the bells going off inside all five boys sounded like fire alarms as they continued through the mall.

There suddenly came a chorus of screams from overhead and the boys rolled their eyes upward in unison where they were greeted by the sight of three thrill-seeking tourists soaring through the air with arms outstretched as they rode zip line cables stretching the length of the mall, while a canopy-shaped digital sky surrounding them flashed with its dazzling light show.

"Try it with real wings and we might be impressed," Ethan cried out, earning him an immediate rap to the back of his head by Max.

"Hey…what was that for?" he grimaced while giving his noggin a soothing caress.

"If you have to ask, you deserve another," warned Max.

They passed another of the unearthly street performers; this one was dressed in an outfit more suitable for a character out of a Charles Dickens story than the modern-day streets of Las Vegas, and his clothing shared the same grayish tone and texture as his face and hands, giving him the appearance of a statue. In his right hand he held a cane (also gray and statue-like to the n a k e d eye) which was firmly rooted to the sidewalk. The man, however, sat cross-legged while suspended in midair as though he were perched atop some invisible chair, and yet there existed nothing but the cane in his hand to serve as support to keep the man propped up, impossible a feat as it was. Jacob eyed this one particular performer with an especially focused curiosity while a small group of baffled onlookers circled the man trying to figure out and uncover how the effective "trick" was being pulled off, and as Jacob studied from afar the illusion which he knew was no illusion in the slightest, the man's eyes suddenly opened and a familiar golden flash illuminated the gaze that focused itself on the boy with an uncomfortable intensity that made Jacob's feet move a tad quicker. Why, he wondered to himself, would a Fallen be posing as something as mundane and terrestrial as lowly street performers? It was a question he couldn't even begin to speculate an answer.

"Do you think it was wise coming here without having your sword on you?" Max asked suddenly, jostling Jacob from his drifting thoughts.

"What are you talking about? I have my sword," answered Jacob, and just to be sure he indiscreetly reached beneath his shirt and around his left side to give his hidden wing a feel and was met by the familiar presence of his concealed weapon.

"I don't mean the sword you were given by Damiel at Lions Bite along with the rest of us…I'm talking 'bout *the* sword," explained Max.

"For the time being, I feel more comfortable with this one," said Jacob. "Besides, a sword's a sword."

"Your daft if you think that," Max replied with a chuckle, though he understood what his friend meant. "Is it really that uncomfortable?"

"Like trying to hold the sun in your hand. Not so much pain-wise; just unspeakably intense," answered Jacob, yet knowing he could never even begin to explain exactly what it was like to hold in one's hands a weapon that was not only more powerful than all the military arsenals of every country in the world put together, but also served as some enchanted, all-knowing mirror that served as a looking glass to future events. "Damiel told me it would take some getting used to, and I think I'm starting to get a grip on it. It's just slow-going."

"Speaking of the sword," Ethan suddenly butted in. "Do you think you might have made a mistake with this last vision?"

"What kind of mistake?" asked Max.

"I think he means we've been walking around for some time now and we still haven't seen hide nor hair of your friends" said Kairo. "Maybe what you saw wasn't what you thought you saw."

"I know what I saw," Jacob insisted. "They're here…somewhere."

There was an unmistakable certainty in Jacob's insistence that managed to quiet any furthering arguing of the point, and they continued on with their search. They soon came upon a crowd of people gathered about a modest-sized stage where a street performer of the Fallen variety by the name of Cadel (according to a small sign advertising the act nearby) was in the midst of mesmerizing the crowd with a number of so-called illusions he dealt from a seemingly magical deck of cards.

"Take a card, but don't look at it," he instructed a young black boy wearing a red baseball cap resting at a tilt upon his head.

The boy did what was asked.

"Now fold it twice and set it back in the deck," Cadel instructed.

Again, the boy did what he was asked to do, folding the card once, then twice and setting it on top of the half deck the man held out to him. Cadel then placed the other half of the deck on top, sandwiching the folded inside. After a quick and thorough shuffling of the deck, he held out a fan of cards and again told the boy to take one, and the boy did.

Cadel focused his inviting yet intense gaze on the boy while the boy somewhat nervously rubbed his lips together while waiting for what was to come next.

"I see a six of clubs," Cadel finally said.

The boy slowly looked at the card clutched in his hand and a gratified smirk unfurled itself across his face.

"Er, wrong swami…that would be a three of diamonds," the boy brayed with relish while holding his card up for all to see.

Cadel allowed the crowd a moment to smugly revel at his expense over a sound failure to perform the most basic of card tricks before he calmly cleared his throat.

"I'm sorry, I should have been more precise," said Cadel. "I was actually referring to the card inside your hat."

"My hat?" the boy parroted.

"That's right…the one on your head. Go ahead and take a look."

The boy hesitated at first, casting a gaze of suspicion on the man.

Then with a huff of exasperation he reached for his cap and what he spied inside made his eyes grow noticeably larger. It wasn't without apprehension that the boy reached into his cap and pulled out the card inside that had been twice folded. When his fingers managed to unfold it he nearly leapt out of his skin when the six clubs revealed themselves.

"How you do that?" the boy asked when he finally managed to find his tongue.

"How, indeed," was all the reply given by Cadel before he quickly began to scout the crowd for another volunteer for his next trick.

"Let's move on," Max urged the rest of his group, uninterested in taking in any more of the legerdemain, especially from a Fallen.

They began maneuvering their way past the crowd just as Cadel selected his next guinea pig, this time of the female persuasion, and as he brought her onstage he asked her name. Jacob came to abrupt halt when a more than familiar voice responded: "Wray."

~ ~ ~

Jacob and his friends pushed their way back into the crowd of onlookers and sure enough, standing on the stage beside the fallen performer was Wray, looking somewhat self-conscious before the sea of eyes staring back at her yet smiling her sweet radiant smile while brushing back her mane of golden hair that was further tousled by the light evening breeze. Almost immediately Jacob felt his back hunch upward as he watched Cadel take Wray's hand into his own. Perhaps it was because he suddenly became acutely aware of the striking and charming presence gifted to all angels that somehow had not been diminished since Cadel's long fall from Heaven. But it was more likely Jacob viewed the sight of his girlfriend's soft, ivory-like hands being caressed by the angel's traitorous, unclean mitts as akin to watching flies crawling across a plate of food.

"Is this your first time visiting our fair city?" Cadel asked Wray who nodded nervously. "And are you here for business or pleasure?"

"Neither, I don't think," answered Wray. "I'm actually looking for someone."

"A boyfriend?" Cadel asked with a creeping smile before quickly answering his own question. "No, of course not. It would be a sin for a girl as beautiful as yourself not to already be adored by a beau."

Wray was not known to easily suffer moments of bashfulness, yet the compliment managed to redden her cheeks.

"And is this him...your beau?" Cadel then asked, motioning to someone in the crowd from where he had moments earlier plucked Wray.

Jacob rose up onto his tiptoes and craned his neck in a desperate effort to see past the horde of heads positioned in front of him and catch a glimpse of whomever it was the angel was referring to, and sure enough he quickly spotted Ty standing near the foot of the stage.

"You're joking right?" Wray replied.

Jacob couldn't help but join the gaggle of giggles that erupted from the crowd, especially when Ty was heard to squeak back a curt "Thanks" in return.

"My apologies," said Cadel. "But you do have a boyfriend, no?"

Wray appeared to take a moment to consider the question before offering a less than certain, "I guess you could say I do."

"I knew it...I can see he occupies your thoughts as easily as I can take note of the stars by just looking up at the night sky," said Cadel. "And I shall prove it to you and everyone standing around us."

Wray looked on curiously as Cadel proceeded to fetch a medium-sized black wooden box from nearby and handed it to Ty with the simple instruction not open it until instructed to do so. He then handed Wray a piece of paper and pen and directed her to write down the name of her boyfriend. When she had finished, he asked her to fold the paper and seal it with a kiss, which she obediently did.

"Now then, gently press the paper against my forehead and allow the identity of this most lucky fellow to pass into my own thoughts," said Cadel.

Jacob watched closely from his spot in the crowd as the angel posing as a trickster flexed his acting chops of feigned concentration with the closing of his eyes and the taking in of a deep breath, as Wray pressed the paper in a somewhat timid fashion against his forehead. Still he, like most in the crowd who were watching intently the performance taking place, jumped with surprise when the folded piece of paper instantly burst into flames the moment it was removed from the angel's forehead, causing Wray to let out a shriek and let go of the burning paper which fell to the ground like a smoldering snowflake of ash. Cadel then led Wray to a wooden stool upon which he took a seat and handed her a pair of clipping shears found in any corner barbershop.

"Now, take these and carefully, mind you, shave the hair from the back of my head," Wray was instructed.

Wray looked at the man, and more importantly the shoulder-length head of thick, beautiful hair most men would give their to possess, with utter astonishment.

"You're joking, right?" she asked, as if her ears had momentarily malfunctioned.

"Trust me when I tell you I'm not a comedian," replied Cadel who turned back to face the audience and repeated once more his directive.

"Alright, have it your way…it's your hair. Or was your hair," muttered Wray.

The clippers emitted a loud buzzing when she turned them on, and the look on her face was one reserved for someone forced to witness an autopsy when she finally gathered the nerve to take the first swipe through the mane. Large clumps of the thick, lush locks fell in an almost sinful manner upon the floor with each run of the shears across the back of the head, but it wasn't until the third stroke that Wray's expression changed to one of odd intrigue when she noticed a strange sight hidden in the stubble of the freshly shorn scalp: Lettering. A "C-O-B" could be seen etched above a "R-I-S-H" in what looked to be a concealed tattoo.

Suddenly, the hesitancy in Wray's barbering technique dissipated and the shears instantly began mowing its way through the hair as though it were an overgrown lawn in desperate need of a manicure. More letters came into view as larger clumps of hair fell away until Wray suddenly dropped the clippers onto the floor with a loud clammer in order to cover her mouth and muffle the squeal of disbelief that suddenly escaped her.

"There's no way!" she managed to screech as though she had caught sight of a real-life leprechaun holding a pot of gold.

"I'm sorry," Cadel feigned an apology while grabbing two hand mirrors and positioning them just so to give himself a glance at the back of his head. "Did I somehow manage to get it wrong?"

"There's absolutely no way!" Wray continued in her denial while half giggling with shock.

The crowd began to rumble with anxiousness to see what had staggered the girl so and Cadel finally satisfied their restlessness when he turned his back to them to offer an unobstructed look at the large denuded patch of scalp that revealed what appeared to be a tattoo of a name spelling out J-A-C-O-B P-A-R-R-I-S-H. The audience joined Wray in squawking with delight; even the Nephilim who were quietly watching with critical eyes couldn't keep their eyebrows from arching upward with wonderment.

"That's a corker of a trick; I'll give him that. Wonder how he managed it," Max was the first to respond, drawing a slow-shifting look of incredulousness from Jacob who remained standing with his arms folded and looking unimpressed.

"How do we know that's the real name of her boyfriend? She never said it out loud," someone from the crowd suddenly hollered.

Cadel had worked his illusions before enough malleable and dimwitted mortals to come to learn there was always at least one skeptical critic planted in every audience who thought they were smart enough to dumb down his otherworldly capabilities into nothing more than an explainable nifty bit of sleight of hand. In this instance, he simply looked over to where Ty continued to stand holding the black wooden box he had been handed earlier and gave the boy a nod. Ty then proceeded to open the lid to the box where inside he found a folded piece of paper. As he removed the paper from the box, he noticed it was marked by a faint imprint of a pair of lips in a subtle shade of pink that matched that coloring of Wray's own lips. And when he unfolded the paper a surprising look came over him when he saw the words "Jacob Parrish" written in Wray's familiar handwriting. When Ty held up the paper for all to see, the crowd applauded loudly, seemingly taken more by the slip of paper being inexplicably resurrected from ash than the even more inexplicable letters tattooed across the back of Cadel's head.

"Sorry about your hair," Wray said apologetically to Cadel as she prepared to step down from the stage.

For a moment it appeared as though Cadel had forgotten about the shorn state of his mane.

"Yes…it does look like I should be shipped off to a leper colony, doesn't it?" he remarked as he once more positioned the mirrors in his hands to survey the butchered backside of his head.

"If you'd like, I could shave off the rest. At least it would all be even, and hey…the bald look can be hot on some men," Wray offered clumsily.

"Thank you," Cadel replied politely, "but I've rather grown quite attached to the tresses I once had."

Then, in a show more shocking than any "trick" he had performed before the naive masses still gathered about, he bent over at the waist and gave what was left of his shorn locks a vigorous shaking out, and when he straightened himself back up there came a pronounced collective gasp when Cadel no longer sported a bald backside but a rejuvenated head of hair.

"My father sure was right when it came to Fallen," remarked Max as the crowd applauded once again while trading theories amongst themselves about how the trick was done. "Just a bunch of bloody peacocks!"

~ ~ ~

Despite the effort made in searching for them, Jacob refrained from running up to Wray and Ty as the crowd began to disperse. It was only when neither of his friends failed to notice him standing a short distance away from them and started off on their own search that Jacob called out to Wray. When she turned to the sound of the familiar voice, the look on her face was one of neither surprise or consolation at the sight of Jacob.

At least she isn't holding a milkshake, or any other beverage for that matter, Jacob consoled himself as he was reminded almost immediately, at the sight of her walking over to him, of their last coming together moment after he had skipped out of Cain's Corner unexpectedly. But there did, however, remain the hands; hands he could attest to quite knowledgeably that could ball themselves into fists and deliver a pretty potent and nasty right cross. It was that memory that served Jacob to brace himself when she suddenly lunged at him when he was within reach. Only, instead of the repeat sting of a well-deserved clobbering, he was taken aback by the pair of arms that wrapped themselves tight around his neck to deliver a warming and oh-so-good-feeling embrace. What's more, she was suddenly softly sobbing.

"Wh-why are you crying?" asked Jacob. "I thought you'd be mad at me."

"I am mad…can't you tell?" said Wray.

Jacob looked down into her face and he couldn't help but smile at the puppy-like expression staring back as he ran his thumb across her soft cheek to wipe away a stray tear. Even crying, there was a light in her eyes which captivated him, and it danced more brightly than any of the shimmer dressing the nearby casinos.

"So…that was a pretty interesting show, huh?" said Jacob, motioning with his head to the now deserted stage.

"Wasn't that wild? Did you see what he did?" sniffled Wray. "I still can't wrap my head around how he was able to read my thoughts, much less have your name written on his scalp."

"Yeah…pretty remarkable," Jacob all but rolled his eyes in reply. If only she knew how unremarkable a trick it really was to perform for someone who held the power of the Light in his hands, or in Cadel's case Darkness. "I'm just glad it was my name under all that hair and not someone else's."

"What other name would it be?" asked Wray.

"I don't know… the name Yul Dane does come to mind."

For an abbreviated moment, everything and everyone around them ceased to exist as they engaged in a playful round of slap and tickle, when Wray suddenly became acutely aware that they were being observed like a pair of zoo animals.

"Max…hi," she said to the one familiar face out of the four staring her way.

"G'day," Max answered with a charming wink and smile.

"I guess it really is a small world after all, isn't it?" she said shifting her gaze onto Jacob who looked like someone who had momentarily completely forgotten about his friends.

"I'm sorry, bad manners. This here is Kairo, Leos and Ethan…and of course you've already met Max here," Jacob hurried his way somewhat clumsily through the necessary introductions.

Wray's stare lingered pensively on each boy as she did her best not to appear like a deer caught in headlights. Yet it was the exact same feeling she had when she was first introduced to Max in Cain's Corner. Only now she felt like a deer standing in the glaring light of a semi-truck. Kairo, Leos and Ethan…the names reverberated inside her head like a pounding migraine. And why shouldn't they, seeing as she had already been introduced to these previously faceless boys in a roundabout, if not nefarious way, through Jacob's journal? Only the Kairo, Leos and Ethan mentioned in the journal weren't any ordinary boys, not by a long-shot, but in fact something called Nephilim. Jacob had deemed them as such through his own handwriting, not to mention his own self. It was only one of a number of fantastical things she had read about, and also dismissed as any rational-thinking person would as the imaginative scribblings of a bored teenager. Only now, such brush-offs were becoming harder and harder as what began as the scrawling of ink on paper was now becoming full-on flesh and blood characters standing right before her eyes.

"You certainly have a lot of mystery friends coming out of the woodwork lately," Wray managed to remark in a reserved polite manner that was the opposite of what was swirling about inside her head.

"Funny," Leos said. "Jacob's told us so much about you I feel as if I already know you."

"And what he hasn't shared we often times hear him mumbling about in his sleep," Ethan affirmed with a giggle, causing Jacob to reach over and give him a mindful smack to the back of his head.

"What'd I say?" Ethan whined while giving his noggin a comforting rub.

"Don't mind him," Jacob said to Wray, "He sometimes has trouble whenever he opens his mouth on account of his foot falling into it now and then.

There came a loud and noticeable sound of someone sucking their teeth with displeasure that caught Jacob's ear and drew his attention to Ty, whose presence he had surprisingly forgotten about.

"Speaking of people who have a habit of lodging their foot inside their mouth, the person you see right over there who, for some strange and untold reason, is being unusually quiet is my best friend Ty," said Jacob.

Ty, however, continued to stare off in the distance and ignored the friendly greeting Leos, Kairo and Ethan extended to him, and it was immediately clear by the way his arms were folded tightly across his chest that he had not embarked on his and Wray's trip to the gambling capital of the world without packing his petulant pout and righteous anger.

"Yo, Ty, come on over…I want you to meet some friends of mine?" Jacob called out in a slightly louder fashion.

Again there was no response except the visible tightening of Ty's impeccable snubbing skills as he turned his head just slightly more away from Jacob.

"Hello…is there anybody home?" Jacob crooned.

Finally, there came a sign of recognition as Jacob's voice managed to pierce the cone of silence and twist Ty's head back around.

"I'm sorry, were you speaking to me?" Ty asked snidely.

God, he's so dramatic, Jacob thought as he braced himself for something far more painful than the punch he expected from Wray.

"Of course I'm speaking to you…why wouldn't I?" asked Jacob.

"Oh I don't know…it's just lately I've gotten used to getting the brush off from you. I guess I was caught off guard."

"Brush off? When have I ever brushed you off?"

It was the cue Ty was waiting for as he instantly reached into his back pocket and produced the note Jacob had left for Wray in her Jeep the night he left Cain's Corner for the second time.

" 'P.S. Please tell Ty goodbye for me'," he read from the note before leveling his offended gaze back on Jacob.

"Look, I can explain," Jacob attempted to chime in but to no avail.

"Princess Di over here gets basically a love-dripping soliloquy explaining how hard it will be for you to leave her and how she will always be your sanctuary—which by the way…" Ty stuck his finger in the direction of his throat in a clear gesture of vomiting before quickly shooting a "no offense" in Wray's direction out of the side of his mouth. "But your friend of five years—best friend, I might add—you relegate to a P.S."

"If you let me explain…"

"Then again, I guess it's a step up for 'ol Ty here," Ty continued on with his tirade, squashing any attempt by Jacob to get a word in. "After all, the last time you left Cain's Corner I wasn't even worthy of P.S."

"So what you're saying is I could have avoided all of this had I the foresight to address the love-dripping soliloquy to you?" asked Jacob, but his attempt to force Ty to crack a smile failed.

"That's so funny I forgot to laugh," said Ty. "Look, the only reason I came here in the first place is because Wray talked me into helping her find you. Now that she has I have my own P.S. for you: See ya, I wouldn't want to be ya!"

As somewhat amusing as Ty's temper tantrum was, Jacob could see his friend's nose was genuinely out of joint and he quickly rushed ahead and blocked Ty's retreat in an effort to straighten it out.

"I'm sorry," he said.

"Don't waste another thought over it," Ty replied indifferently and attempted to step around Jacob only to have the five-foot-ten barrier shadow his efforts.

"No, really, I'm sorry," Jacob declared once more, forcing Ty's heel to momentarily cool themselves.

"I know I've always been the brains when it comes to our friendship," Jacob started to explain, drawing an oddly perplexing look from Ty.

"There better be a big 'ol but coming up soon," warned Ty.

"BUT…my brain obviously was replaced with rocks when I left that note. And frankly when I left Cain's Corner last year," said Jacob. "Thing is, saying goodbye to the people you care about the most was more difficult than I ever thought possible. Which is probably why I didn't."

For all his teasing and joking when it came to Ty, it was a one hundred percent sincere attempt at an apology on Jacob's part, and while Ty did his darnedest not to let it show, it had managed to crack the deep freeze that encased him.

"So how 'bout it? Can you forgive your best friend?" asked Jacob.

Never one to give up easily a well-earned grudge, Ty swayed undecidedly in his shoes. "I don't know…I'm going have to think about it," he replied.

"Fair enough—"

Jacob had barely gotten the words out of his mouth when Ty suddenly lunged forward and grabbed him up in a tight bear hug worthy of two siblings who oftentimes surface in front page feel-good stories in newspapers detailing a decades-long separation from one another. And Jacob was all too happy to return the embrace.

CHAPTER ELEVEN

"**D**o you trust me?" Wray asked Jacob once they had a moment alone while strolling down a fairly quiet stretch of sidewalk in the direction of The Strip, and leaving the brightness and excitement of Fremont Street behind them.

"Of course I do…more than anyone else I know," answered Jacob. "Why do you ask?"

"Then why won't you tell me what's going on with you?"

"What makes you think anything's going on with me?"

"Oh, I don't know. This is the second time you've suddenly upped and disappeared from Cain's Corner without saying anything to anyone," said Wray. "Now here we are walking down some street in Las Vegas accompanied by four boys you call your friends whom I've never seen or heard about before now. It's all a little bit mysterious and out of the ordinary, wouldn't you say?"

"You make it sound as if I'm living some sort of double life or something."

"Are you?" Wray pressed without missing a beat.

Caught off kilter, Jacob looked harder into Wray's face and realized she wasn't being flippant.

"You got me, Wray. It's obvious I can't keep my secret from you any long," Jacob said with sigh of defeat, drawing in Wray's attention even more so. "The truth is when I'm not Jacob Parrish, the everyday boy next door from Cain's Corner, I'm Bond. Jacob Bond. America's version of the 007."

Wray, who looked as if she was finally going to get the much-needed answers she was probing for, was not amused.

"Now I know you're keeping something from me. You have an irritating habit of making jokes when you want to change the subject," she said matter-of-factly. "Would you mind taking your shirt off for me?"

The question grabbed Jacob around the throat.

"I'm sorry, what?"

"Your shirt…I want you to remove it for me," repeated Wray.

Now it was Jacob's turn to feel like a deer caught in headlights, a look Wray had easily come to recognize.

"I was the only person, besides Ty, who you trusted to show the back condition you suffered from, and I just think it's more than a little strange that you haven't shown me how much its improved from whatever treatment you underwent when you left Cain's Corner last year," Wray explained before Jacob could question her motives.

"Well…that's because I'm still a bit self-conscious. I'm still in the healing phase, after all," said Jacob.

He was growing nervous. Actually, he was more than nervous; he was sweating bullets. Wray could see as much, even as they continued their stroll through the dark. Whatever secret he was keeping locked away, she had located the scab under which it was hidden and was slowly picking away at it. Only now, she found herself wondering if she truly wished to know what the dark side of the moon actually looked like in the sunlight. Perhaps, she considered, there is value in the old adage "Ignorance is bliss." Her tongue, however, thought better of such pacifying sentiments.

"I read your journal," she found herself suddenly blurting out, ripping off the scab with one swift tear.

~ ~ ~

If the request for Jacob to strip off his shirt and expose his bare back came from out of left field, then Wray's blunt confession concerning his journal was an entirely unpredicted matter that came hurling straight for him from the other side of the planet. Jacob gave a furtive glance over his shoulder where Ty, trailing out of earshot, seemed to be getting along swimmingly with Max, Kairo, Leos and Ethan, by regaling them with the absurd conspiracy theories concerning fictional movie, TV and literary characters that he himself had been tortured with since the two became friends.

"What do you mean you read my journal?" Jacob, doing his best to remain cool and even-keeled, inquired.

"First of all, I want you to know it wasn't like I was snooping," Wray attempted first to explain. "It was the night we stayed up to watch the classic monster movies. I woke up sometime after we both fell asleep and tried to sneak out without waking you, and when I moved your backpack from the chair so I could sit down and put on my shoes, it sort of slipped out onto the floor. I only glanced at it at first to see what it was, and I was immediately drawn into it."

"How much did you read?" Jacob could hear the pounding in his chest growing louder and faster. It wasn't just the queasy realization his dark secret had been exposed that quickened his heart, but the discomfiting feeling that arrives when one's most guarded private thoughts are trespassed upon.

"Enough," answered Wray, somewhat warily. "I read about a so-called fallen angel named Gotham who was the supposed reason you left Cain's Corner last year. I read about how he made a dead deer come back to life which turned around and destroyed the truck of the hunter that had killed it. I read about some church on some island in Turkey named Akdamar."

Jacob shot Wray an enlightened look. *Of course…now it was finally beginning to make sense why she had casually peppered Max the day they went to Penuel Point about whether he had ever been to Akdamar,* Jacob thought to himself. It was because she had found his journal.

"I read about another angel named Johiel, and a swarm of demons called Infectors who attacked you and Gotham before you traveled underwater through some pitch-black passage called The Gate leading to Eden…the Garden of Eden, that is," Wray noted, as if clarification was necessary, as she continued with the casualness of someone reading through a grocery list. "I read about the wolf who befriended you whom you named Mist. I read about some huge palace hidden in the trees and made by the trees called Havenhid, as well as even more angels who live there; if I can remember correctly they're names were Zuriel, Eksel, Thaniel and Damiel, and then there was Anahel who was the top angel in charge. I read about the Crescent Scar and the Seven Graces, and also about the library with its gazillion books stretching-as far as the eye can see. But funny enough, the strangest thing I think I read was regarding the four boys who were your roommates at Havenhid named Max, Ethan, Leos and Kairo…and as if things couldn't get any weirder, here we are taking a walk-through downtown Las Vegas with four of your friends following behind us who just happened to be named Max, Ethan, Leos and Kairo."

You're definitely right…that was about as strange as it could get, Jacob agreed silently to himself. So strange, he couldn't even begin to come up with even the beginning semblance of a lie believable enough to attempt to explain it all away.

"Is that all?" he croaked meekly.

"Unfortunately, you woke up just as I was about to find out what Lions Bite was," answered Wray.

Lions Bite. Whatever relief Jacob was afforded, it was in knowing she hadn't gotten far enough in perusing his journal to uncover things about himself he'd rather she never find out.

"My first thought was that you were attempting your hand at writing some kind of fictional story," said Wray.

A light of salvation immediately illuminated itself inside Jacob's head and it took all his self-control not to throw his arms around Wray and thank her for unknowingly providing him with the knife he needed to cut his way out of the trawlers net he had suddenly and inadvertently found himself caught in, like some floundering fish scooped out of the ocean.

"What do you mean by 'attempting'?" asked Jacob. "Is this your gentle way of saying I suck as a creative writer?"

The question at first seemed to catch Wray off guard.

"Creative writer?"

"Believe me, I get I'm not positioned in line to be the next Stephen King or J. K. Rowling," Jacob rambled, "but I didn't think anything I wrote was too terrible or cringe- worthy. Sure, the idea's a bit far out and fantastical to ever be taken seriously, but Mrs. Kretch seemed to like it enough to give me a B."

"Mrs. Kretch?" muttered Wray.

"Yeah…when I was in her class. She assigned us a short creative writing project and I came up with the idea of a boy who finds out he's half angel," explained Jacob. "For some reason, the story popped into my head when I first started seeing a doctor about my back troubles. Then when I went away for this latest treatment, I was so bored that I found myself revisiting the short story I had turned in for English class and began expounding on what I had already written, just in order to make the days pass more quickly. Guess I got a little carried away, huh?'

The lie poured off his tongue like a drizzle of maple syrup onto a stack of pancakes. So smoothly and effortlessly it came, Jacob worried momentarily that the star-studded night sky might aim a bolt of lightning straight in his direction as punishment.

"So...the whole thing is made up?" questioned Wray, looking like someone long overdue in coming to the realization that Santa Claus was nothing more than a holiday myth contrived by hope and greed.

"As made up as when Ty tried to peddle the idea that Han Solo and Chewbacca were the first inner-species gay couple," said Jacob. "What...you didn't really think my journal was actually a...*journal*, did you?"

He burst into chuckles, even before Wray opened her mouth to answer, as the look on her face brought him an enlightened sense of relief that he had her on the ropes.

"Well, how was I supposed to know?" Wray snapped back, though more out of embarrassment than anger. "It just sounded so...so real to me when I read it."

"Hmm...maybe I am the next Stephen King or J. K. Rowling," Jacob mused aloud to himself, provoking a smack to the shoulder from Wray.

"It's not funny." Yet no sooner had she voiced her admonishment did she surrender to a fit a giggles herself. "Okay, maybe it's a little funny. I mean, the idea of you being a nephol... nephil—"

"Nephilim," Jacob cut in with the term that had once twisted his own tongue as it now did Wray's. "And what exactly is so funny about the idea of me being one? A Nephilim?"

Wray paused a moment to take notice of the fact that Jacob was no longer laughing, but her facade quickly cracked as she broke out into hysterics once again.

"I'm sorry...the image of you as half-angel with wings sprouting out of your back just flashed in front of me and, well...it's pretty hilarious." She could barely get the words out.

The furrows in Jacob's forehead deepened as his frown drew inward toward the bridge of his nose, and he slowly gave himself a once over.

"I don't think it's all that funny," he grumbled. "For your information, I think I'd make a first-rate Nephilim. You might even say heavenly."

Jacob's pronouncement only incited Wray's laughter, and for a fleeting moment, Jacob wrestled to restrain himself from acquiescing to the earlier request made that he remove his shirt in order to silence the cackling by flexing the wings he had moments earlier managed to convince Wray was an absurd figment of her whimsical imagination, and dare her to snicker at the reality. Luckily for both of them, however, their brief levity was interrupted when Ty suddenly rushed toward them, eyes bugged and exclaiming, "Oh. My. God. Are either of you seeing what I'm seeing?"

At first Jacob felt his heart kickstart itself as he was certain by the look frozen on Ty's face that the unsettling vision he'd been given a glimpse of in the mirrored skin of the blade of his sword, had finally revealed itself. Though, instead of snapping teeth and red-lit demonic eyes he turned to find a huge billboard outside one of the countless hotels with the name "Glory Dey" radiating in a shimmering field of flashing twinkling lights had caught his friend's attention.

"Yeah, so?" said Jacob with a shrug.

"Yeah, so? Have you been living under a rock?" asked Ty. "Do you even know who Glory Dey is?"

"From the looks of it, I'm guessing someone with the ability to turn you into a full-on, drooling dweeb," answered Jacob, attracting a slow-burning look of contempt from Ty.

"It's moments like this that make me question why I'm even friends with you," Ty hissed coolly. "For your information, Gloria Dey is only the biggest, and dare I say, spookiest, medium on TV today."

"Medium?" echoed Wray.

"Yeah, you know, a person who speaks to dead people."

"I know what a medium is," Wray said with an irritated squint. "What I meant was, I can't believe you're getting your underwear in a bunch over something as hokey as a reality TV star."

"Have you ever seen her show 'Walking on the Other Side with Glory Dey'? No, I didn't think so," Ty both questioned and answered himself before Wray could get a word in edgewise. "If you did you wouldn't use the word 'hokey' to describe someone who I'm pretty confident could read you like the telephone book."

Wray, like Jacob, had learned long ago to be wise and selective when picking which battles to fight where Ty was concerned, and raging over the validity of mediums wasn't even worthy of a skirmish. Not that Ty was planning to stick around for such a debate as he suddenly made a beeline toward the hotel.

"Where do you think you're going?" asked Jacob.

"What does it look like? I'm going to check out the show. Come on."

Jacob stayed rooted to his heels.

"I don't think that's such a good idea."

"Not a good idea? This is exactly the sort thing you're supposed to do when you're in Vegas," argued Ty, but he could see his words were having no sway over his friend. "But if you really don't want to go, I guess there's nothing I can do to force you. Just thought it was the least you could do seeing how I chased you all the way out here, even after you ditched on me again like you did. But what the hay."

Perfect, Jacob thought to himself; now he was going to get saddled with a guilt trip Ty-style which were fairly difficult, at best, to brush off and even harder to ignore.

"Why don't you guys head back to the hotel? I'll be along as soon as I can," Jacob said, turning to Max.

"Are you outta your tree? You-know-who is already going to have a royal conniption fit when he discovers you defied his order to stay put," Max conversed quietly in Jacob's ear, but to no avail.

"I can't just let them go off by themselves," said Jacob. "Not after my sword revealed to me what it did."

He was careful to keep his voice low and out of earshot of Ty who was trying with little success to get Wray as worked up as he was overseeing the psychic medium live and in the flesh.

"I thought I'd never live to see the day when I would say this, but maybe Ethan was right," said Max, which made Ethan beam instantly and stand an inch taller in his shoes. "Maybe you had a faulty vision. I mean, nothing out of the ordinary has happened."

"Or hasn't happened yet," Jacob was quick to counter. "Either way, I can't take the risk."

It wasn't what Max had hoped to hear, but he also didn't pretend to be anything other than a novice when it came to all-powerful swords and the means in which they attempted to communicate with their owners through strange, mysterious visions reflected in their blades.

"I guess we'll come with, then," he said with a huff of surrender. "If we're going to get the bull's horns, might as well earn the goring."

~ ~ ~

Surprisingly—or perhaps not—the large, spacious theater, with its red velvet seats and gold accented pillars, was nearly filled to capacity when they made their way inside, sparking a smug "What did I tell you?" from Ty. Jacob, however, was in no mood for any I-told-you-sos, and even the surprisingly plush seat he settled himself into failed to erase the noticeable look of discomfort that had settled itself on his face from the moment he agreed to take part in the ill-advised detour through the theater doors. There was only one thought occupying his mind, and it had nothing whatsoever to do with psychic mumbo jumbo, and everything to do with the very real and unnerving vision that had led him to Fremont Street in the first place.

Why had the nightmarish images reflected in his sword failed to materialize (not that he was dismayed in the least that they hadn't)? And if the terrifying vision wasn't meant to sound the alarm to an imminent happening he felt sure was approaching, then what in the world was his sword attempting to communicate to him?

One thing was certain: Max, who was seated to his right, didn't seem to be pondering, much less be concerned about such puzzling matters. Neither did Kairo, Ethan or Leos who were seated next to Max and caught up in some trivial conversation. Then again, why would they be? Luckily for them, they didn't experience what Jacob had, as their eyes were blind to such sights, unpleasant or not, that now and again revealed themselves to their friend. When they gazed upon the Sword of Destiny they saw only the glorious weapon whose mythic existence was curated by the lineage of hands from which its power had passed, and not the shadow of things that sometimes manifested in the reflection of its blade like the clouded images surfacing from within a fortune teller's crystal ball. Still, at the very least, Jacob thought he'd spy some hint in his friends' demeanors that they too shared the same nagging sense of foreboding which tugged at him, warning of the six-foot-five wall of displeasure by the name of Damiel that likely would be waiting for them when the boys finally returned to the hotel room they were specifically and emphatically instructed not to leave. So bothersome was the thought, Jacob began to debate with himself which he'd rather confront if forced to do so: the teeth-baring monsters occupying his visions, or the angel whose imposing presence could be just as equally disquieting?

It was only when the theater house lights dimmed that his mind quieted itself somewhat over such worries as he focused his attention to the stage so he could finally observe what all the hubbub was about that had Ty looking as if he were perched upon a giant spring while craning forward in his seat, wide-eyed in anticipation. And spring to his feet Ty did with the rest of the audience when Glory Dey finally revealed herself to a roar of applause. It was the deafening kind of welcome usually reserved for rock stars and pop music royalty, and while Glory Dey may have existed as a giant in the world of reality TV, the woman herself was anything but. In fact, she was quite the diminutive presence. Her huge personality which preceded her like some elongated shadow, and the towering heels her feet managed to maneuver as she walked the stage, however, more than made up what she lacked in stature.

Appearance-wise, Glory Dey didn't send forth the impression of being a conduit to the dead, if, indeed, mediums had ever really managed to adopt a standardized look. If anything, she looked like she might be a stand-in for the cartoon character Pepe Le Pew, as her jet-black hair, teased and hair-sprayed to within an inch of its life to achieve the impressive height and width not seen since the poodle-dos of the eighties, came with a shocking streak of white running down the middle from the forehead to the back of the head that was very skunk-like. Then there were the nails: long feline-like talons of pressed-on tackiness adorning each finger that complemented her by-gone era hairstyle in the same way a full-bodied white wine serves as the perfect accompaniment to a salmon entree.

Her voice, when she finally spoke, carried an unmistakable accent better suited for a character on the "Sopranos" than a clairvoyant, and as she paced about the large, empty stage while teetering on those impossibly stilt-like heels, Glory began by revealing to the audience how she'd never experienced anything remotely close to true silence.

"Does anyone here suffer from tinnitus?" she asked the crowd. "When people ask me what it is like to have what I like to call 'the gift' I tell them it's like a bad case of tinnitus, only instead of a constant buzzing in your ears, it's voices, and that's what it's been like for me for…well, I won't tell you how long I've been dealing with this, otherwise I'd be revealing my age and I'm much too vain for that."

She had a charming way about her that went with her quirky, compact exterior and it instantly placed the audience in her hip pocket.

"I grew up frightened that my future was destined for a padded cell inside the local nut house because the only people I knew about who heard voices from people who weren't there were—let's face it and call a spade a spade—not playing with a full deck. And here I was a little girl living with an incessant buzz of chatter ringing inside my ears coming from people I could not see who I refer to as 'Visitors'."

She paused suddenly, both her mouth and her feet, and it was immediately clear that even as she spoke of the yatter filling her ears, there was a voice from one of these unseen "Visitors" engaging in a game of tug and war with her attention.

"Forgive me, but every now and then, there's an exceptionally loud and pushy Visitor who has no tolerance or patience to wait while I explain my process, and one such pushy Visitor has been in my ear since the moment I walked out here."

With a distracted look still clouding her eyes, Glory turned her attention to the right half side of the theater.

"Who's the young man standing in front of an American flag who's recently departed?" she asked to no particular person seated in the audience. "A young man would mean anyone who has departed the physical world before his time, and the American flag usually symbolizes someone who's served either in the military or law enforcement."

A low hum of chatter accompanied the swiveling of heads as the audience began to look all around for who would be the first in line for a message from the other side. It didn't take long for a young woman who looked to be more than a little apprehensive to raise her hand and slowly rise from her seat.

"He was a police officer," the woman said in a soft voice.

"Now there's a right spine-tingling trick for you," Max leaned over and whispered into Jacob's ear. "Throw your hook into the water by asking half of the two thousand people filling this theater if someone they lost was in the military or law enforcement and see if anyone bites. I tell ya, the hairs on my arms are standing up, they are."

Jacob did his best to stifle the chuckle he felt fighting to make itself heard as Glory appeared to quietly converse with the so-called Visitor in her ear.

"I see him clutching his chest which usually means the person has suffered from some upper body trauma like a gunshot wound," said Glory.

"He was involved in a fatal car crash during a high-speed chase," answered the woman. Glory nodded as if it was the answer she had expected.

"And he was your husband? Brother?"

"Brother."

"Because I keep hearing 'Brother, brother' in my ear," Glory said with a loud cackling laugh.

"You sure did…from his sister," Max snarked under his breath in his continuing commentary.

This time, Jacob couldn't hold back the snicker that snorted its way out of his nose.

"He wants me to tell you not to mourn his loss," Glory said to the woman whose eyes were already beginning to brim with tears she fought hard not to spill. "He tells me becoming a police officer was the happiest moment in his life and that even though his time with you and his family was short, he was blessed with the ability to spend it doing the one thing that proved to be truly the most fulfilling to him, and that was helping other people and making the world a safer place for you and your children."

The woman, unable to keep her emotions in check any longer, had tears streaming down her face much to Glory's delight, and Max's growing distaste.

"What a load of bulldust!" he grumbled, sourly. "How is it these Visitors always come in like static radio when it comes to their names, and who they are and how they died then suddenly wax poetic like they're a chatty William Shakespeare resurrected?"

"Maybe it's all just a theatrical buildup…you know, to keep everyone hanging on her every word," Ethan suggested.

"And maybe a winged wombat will come flying out of her arse before the night's over," said Max, drawing an irked hush from the man seated in the row ahead who was growing clearly annoyed by the persistent whispering.

It wasn't all too surprising a matter to find Max and the rest of the boys slouching lower in their seats from the weight of boredom that came from having to endure the insipidness of listening in on conversations with supposed "Visitors." Being exposed to heavenly lands like Eden and hidden palace-like structures cradled in the boughs of trees, or Graces that gave one the power to change his physical form, or wield the forces of nature, has a way of jading the bearers of such things. Nephilim may have lacked the ability to communicate with souls who had passed from o n e life into the next, but they knew enough from possessing the knack to communicate with each other without parting their lips and having their own thoughts and memories perused by true otherworldly beings like Damiel, and the other Guides who watched over them at Havenhid, to be able to spot a charlatan claiming to be blessed with the same faculties. Even Ty, who had led the group into the theater with the promise Glory Dey was the next best thing to sliced bread, looked as if he'd just been handed proof Middle Earth was a made-up place, which he had long argued wasn't the case.

"I don't get this," he said while looking on almost painfully as Glory attempted to read a tall middle-aged man wearing a large cowboy hat and failed miserably to hit the head of the nail with even the vaguest of messages she claimed was being whispered into her ear. "When I watch her on TV my mouth literally hangs open over things she tells people that she couldn't possibly be able to know."

"It's called editing," Leos offered with a bored grunt.

By the time Glory had set her sights on a ten-year-old girl who had recently lost her cat Molly to the tires of a speeding car, Jacob's eyes had begun to glaze over and he was ready to make a dash for the exit in an effort to save himself from the embarrassment of falling asleep in his seat when a rather peculiar sight caught his attention. Just as he leaned his head back to release a pent-up yawn, he noticed a strange, yet familiar orb of luminous green light darting about the numerous crystal chandeliers above like some aroused, radioactive moth fluttering around the bright reach of a burning lightbulb on a dark night. It wasn't the first such green light he'd seen; he'd first noticed similar dancing lights while looking out across the waters of the Van Gölü toward the mainland the night he spent at the Holy Cross church on Akdamar Island. They looked to be falling stars whose time perched in the heavens had finally come to an end, that is until he saw some of the lights moving in reverse order from the earth and disappearing from sight into the blackness of the night. He was revisited by the same curious traffic of green lights streaking down from the sky and up from the earth the night Damiel led the way to Las Vegas. This time, however, the passing lights were more dazzling to behold from the vantage point of flying high above the earth, and they only seemed to appear when the angel and the Nephilim in tow soared over the effulgence of the cities and towns they passed.

"What are those lights?" Jacob had asked Damiel while passing through a particularly busy causeway of green radiance falling and rising from a vast reaching ocean of city lights.

"They are more than just lights…they are embers from The Light," said Damiel whose answer only seemed to deepen Jacob's confusion. "Your Nephilim eyes are but observing what those of us with the ability to see such things call Dawning. The souls of the just- conceived are descending to the wombs which will deliver them to their mortal lives, while those rising are the souls of the recently departed journeying to a life everlasting which awaits them."

It was one of the most beautiful sights Jacob had ever taken in, and it became all the more arresting once Damiel explained what the glorious shower of green radiance surrounding him was. And yet he found the sight of the stray green orb bouncing about the ceiling above like a bird separated from its flock to be quite odd. He wasn't the only one to take notice of it either.

"Are you seeing what I'm seeing?" Leos leaned over to whisper, only to find Kairo, Ethan and Max with their eyes reflecting the same green dancing light.

"What do you think it is?"

"You know what it is," answered Max. "The question is what is he...or she...doing here?"

The boys' eyes moved in unison as they watched the gleaming orb sail about in circles over their heads. It was then Wray, who was also slowly losing interest in Glory Dey's psychic hit and miss show, turned to Jacob and saw his attention was intensely fixed to the ceiling.

"What is it?" she asked following his line of sight and, of course, seeing nothing but the crystal chandeliers that looked like inverted flowers made of glass.

"Uh...nothing...just got a kink in my neck," Jacob replied while feigning to rub out the nonexistent soreness at the base of his head.

His eyes, however, never lost sight of the mysterious light, and it was then that something quite peculiar occurred. The bouncing light came to an abrupt standstill, then slowly began to descend until it was positioned just above Glory Dey like some hovering green-glowing aurora. Just what exactly, Jacob wondered to himself, was this curious errant soul up to?

Naturally, the members of the audience were oblivious to the storm cloud of green positioned over Glory Dey, as their civilian eyes, unlike those of Nephilim, were blind to such things as wandering souls. They did, however, take immediate note when Glory suddenly went silent in the middle of relaying to the young girl a message from her dearly departed cat. At first, it appeared as if another voice had burrowed its way into her other ear canal, but the look that quickly surfaced upon her face was one of alarm; as if she had finally been given an unexpected glimpse of the unseen Visitors whose voices had filled her head all these years. Only it was her ears she quickly covered with both her hands, not her eyes, even as the look of what resembled panic made itself more pronounced in them. A hum of restless concern rose from the audience when Glory suddenly dropped to one knee, all while pressing her hands tighter against her ears. It appeared to everyone watching as though she were reacting to a high-pitched screeching of an alarm that had been set off, only the theater was silent beyond the rumble of whispers rolling its way through the audience.

It was a moment or two before whatever untold episode that visited itself upon Glory appeared to have passed. With some reluctance, her hands released their hold over her ears, and she slowly raised her head and gazed out into the audience with an almost disinclined look fixed in her wide eyes.

"Jacob Parrish…" she managed to mutter in a whisper that didn't make it beyond the first few rows of the theater. She then nervously cleared her throat and summoned the strength of her brash 'Sopranos'-like voice and spoke louder. "Is there a Jacob Parrish here?"

Jacob could feel his blood nearly freeze instantly inside his veins at the mention of his name. How? How did she know he was there seated inside the theater? he wondered. At first he didn't move, not even a twitch of his thumbs, until Max gave him a sharp poke to his side.

"That's you. She's calling you, mate."

Even then Jacob found it difficult to control his bodily function. Only when Wray joined with Max and poked his other side did Jacob finally raise his hand and slowly manage to rise up out of his seat and stand on his feet.

"You're Jacob Parrish?" inquired Glory Dey who looked more put off at the sight of the teenaged boy standing in the midst of the puzzled crowd.

"That's me," Jacob managed to spit out with a nervous awkwardness.

However, and for whatever reason, Glory Dey had come to call out his name, Jacob was denied the answer as she suddenly found her legs and briskly exited the stage and disappeared into the wings. The house lights were turned up soon after and an announcer's voice attempted to explain over the din of the audience in a somewhat clumsy fashion that Glory Dey had unexpectedly taken ill and the show was concluded.

"What in the world was that all about?" Wray asked aloud the question that was obviously ringing inside everyone's heads.

"Your guess is as good as mine," Jacob replied, though the only thing he cared to do at that precise moment was make a speedy return back to their hotel room instead of engaging in a game of interpreting what led to the psychic's supposed meltdown.

The group managed to maneuver its way through the crush of the crowd and out into the lobby of the theater fairly easily when it was confronted by a hulking man sporting a marine-style crewcut, a white ear piece plugged into his ear, and a boxy dark suit waiting at the exit doors of the theater.

"You're Jacob Parrish?" the man inquired, stepping in their pathway, though it sounded more like a statement of fact.

"What if I am?" Jacob asked, sounding almost as if he had been tapped by security for some illegal transgression he knew he was innocent of committing.

"Glory Dey wishes to have a word with you, if you wouldn't mind," the man answered.

"What does she want to talk to me about?" asked Jacob.

"That's something you're going to have to ask her. I was just sent to fetch you."

It sounded very hole-and-corner and not the sort of summons Jacob was at all interested in accepting. Ty, on the other hand, looked as if he had just been handed an invitation to attend the next royal nuptials at Westminster Abbey.

"Oh my god…we're actually going to meet Glory Dey," he sang while dancing on the balls of his feet like someone in desperate need of a trip to the restroom.

Just as he bounced forward to secure a next-in-line place after Jacob, an arm reached out and blocked his way like some mechanical guardrail at a toll booth.

"The request was for Jacob Parrish, and Jacob Parrish alone," the man said with a tone of finality that instantly dashed Ty's fleeting moment of giddiness.

Jacob may not have shared in Ty's brief excitement, but he couldn't deny the tingle of intrigue he had in wondering why TV's premiere psychic had sent a Secret Service clone to collect him, not to mention the more curious matter of what had caused his name to slip from Glory Dey's mouth in the first place. And so he relented in satisfying his inquisitiveness by asking his friends to wait for him before going off alone with the intimidating stranger for whatever clandestine meeting awaited him.

~ ~ ~

The man led Jacob back through the theater from which he had moments earlier left, and then through a short maze of hallways backstage leading to a nondescript corner dressing room. He rapped the door with his knuckle, waited a moment to no answer, then swung the door open and silently gestured to Jacob to enter the room.

Once Jacob stepped inside, the door was closed quietly behind him by the man who remained outside in the hallway. The room was noticeably quiet, and the only light came from a simple solitary lamp on a nearby table. Jacob found Glory Dey seated at dressing table, staring blankly at her reflection captured in a large mirror framed with extinguished lights on the wall in front of her. The only thing Jacob took notice of, however, was the aura of green of light which remained floating above Glory's head, just as it had in the theater before she fled the stage.

Jacob stood quietly waiting for some sort of acknowledgement from Glory, but when it didn't come he thought maybe she didn't realize he was there in the room and announced is presence by clearing his throat.

"Hello?" he then said in a quiet voice to which there came no answer. "Um...my name is Jacob Parrish...some man caught me as I was leaving the theater and said you wanted to speak with me."

A part of Jacob wanted to give the woman a polite nudge to make sure she was still among the breathing and had not become, as her quiet stillness began to suggest, the newest addition to the Visitors from whom she claimed to relay messages.

"My best friend Ty is a huge fan of yours. In fact, he's the one who dragged me and my other friends here tonight. He almost turned green with envy when you said my name out loud before ending your show," Jacob said while forcing forth a chuckle in an attempt to make light of the increasingly awkward moment. But the brief effort at levity disappeared from his face as quickly as it appeared. "Is that what this is about; the reason you said my name?"

Still, Glory remained silent while continuing to stare at the reflection peering back at her through the glass, and Jacob, who was becoming increasingly more frustrated and uncomfortable, looked again to the green churning cloud of light floating ominously above her.

"When I was a little girl, my favorite movie was 'The Wizard of Oz'," Glory was finally heard to say, catching Jacob off guard, both by the sudden sign of life coming from her as well as the odd, random turn in conversation she took. "Mind you, this was back in the day before you could just pop a movie into the video player and watch it anytime you wished. 'The Wizard of Oz' came on TV once a year, and it was a huge event...almost like

Christmas. And each time it came on, my two best friends would come over and we would watch it together. My friend Katie's favorite part of the movie was when Dorothy first lands in Oz and the movie goes from dreary black and white to the beautiful technicolor when she opens the door and steps out of her house into Munchkin land. My other friend Carol, however, loved the first glimpse of the ruby slippers on Dorothy's feet, and how they shined and sparkled in the sunlight."

Jacob took a seat on a nearby sofa looking like someone suffering from an uncomfortable case of constipation as he tried to make sense of what Dorothy Gale and her magic ruby slippers had to do with anything.

"My favorite part was always towards the end of the movie; when Dorothy returns to Emerald City with the Wicked Witch of West's broomstick, and Toto ends up pulling back the curtain to reveal the Wizard is really a humbug. Yet despite being revealed to be the fraud he was, he still managed in his own special way to give the Scarecrow, and the Tin Man, and the Cowardly Lion exactly the things the great and powerful Oz had promised them," Glory continued. "And by doing so he filled a hole in each of their lives."

She looked away from the mirror suddenly, as if she could no longer stand the sight of her reflection staring back at her.

"So far, I've been pretty lucky," she said with a sigh of ignominy. "There's been no Toto to pull back the curtain on the great Glory Dey."

Jacob cocked his head and fixed a questioning look on the psychic and her skunk-like hairdo. "I don't think I understand," he said. And, indeed, he didn't.

"I'm a humbug," Glory offered with as much dignity as she could muster in a blunt reply that cleared away any lingering clouds.

"You're saying you're a fraud…that you can't actually speak with dead people?" asked Jacob, though he was hardly blindsided by the admission.

"The only gift I have ever really possessed is an innate ability to read people…and the pain they carry inside themselves," said Glory.

She then proceeded to share with Jacob when the seeds of her "clairvoyance" were first planted; when her friend Carol—the lover of Dorothy's ruby slippers—was devastated by the loss of her grandmother. She revealed how she attempted to soothe her friend's pain with a good old-fashioned hug, and when that only seemed to make the tears flow more copiously she traded the hug for a message from some unseen and unnamed angel; a message of good tidings and cheer from Carol's grandmother who wished her granddaughter to know she was safe and happy up in Heaven. Naturally it was a lie, as Glory didn't even believe in such things as angels, or even Heaven, for that matter. But it was a lie that instantly dried her friend's tears, and even though her grandmother was still dead, the message, made-up as it may have been, had returned a smile of joy to Carol's face.

"When I became Glory Dey the Medium, it wasn't for money or the fame I received from being on TV. It was to act as a sort of tissue to dry the countless tears that death causes to fall," said Glory. "I learned quickly that I could be a modern-day Professor Marvel. Only instead of handing out hearts to those who came to me with hollow chests, I was validating the hope so many hold inside themselves after they lose a loved one."

It sounded noble enough, but not to keep Glory from hanging her head and mumbling quietly, "But a humbug is still a humbug."

Jacob had already harbored suspicions that Glory was a fake, but he could see her con came from a good place. But why, he couldn't help but wonder, would she feel the need to make such a confession to him, a total stranger? And then there was the matter of the mysterious cloud of green light which continued to hover above Glory that Jacob couldn't help but eye curiously every now and then.

"Are you saying, then, it was just some strange coincidence when you called out my name during the show?" asked Jacob.

Glory grew quiet, and a subtle look of discomfort rolled visibly through her as she pondered the question before, with some reluctance, she eventually shook her head and answered with a simple, "No."

"It was whispered into my ear by some...Visitor," she explained, causing Jacob to give her a confused double take.

"But you just told me you didn't hear voices. That the whole Visitors thing was made up," said Jacob.

"It's true; I never before heard voices...until tonight, that is," said Glory. "Tonight, I was suddenly surrounded by a chorus of voices. But there was one voice in particular...the voice of a woman."

She paused, as if hesitant to go any further, before adding, "She told me she was your mother."

~ ~ ~

The revelation appeared to turn Jacob to stone as he sat staring at Glory with a look of disbelief. Or perhaps, rather, it was unexpected belief.

"How do you know it was my mother?" asked Jacob.

"She told me her name was Isabeth...Isabeth Parrish. She passed away sometime last summer after battling a longtime illness, didn't she?" Glory's eyes shifted to the left, and she sat quietly transfixed for a moment or two as though her ears were fixed on some sound unheard by anyone but her, before her attention reverted back to Jacob. "She wants you to know the flowers you left for her before you left Cain's Corner were beautiful, but more importantly, she wants you to know she appreciates the time you spent speaking to her."

Again Glory's gaze shifted, and after another quiet pause, a grin of amusement curled the corners of her mouth.

"She also says, 'it was about time.' "

Jacob felt a series of tingling twinges move through his spine as though it had been turned into a harp whose strings were being plucked by invisible fingers, and he knew instantly what he was hearing was no put-on by Glory, just as surely as he was certain she was faking similar conversations with unseen Visitors during her show earlier. His gaze once more focused itself on the mysterious orb radiating above Glory and he eyed it suspiciously. He knew the green light to be a wayward soul; of that he was not questioning. Could it, though, he wondered, actually be that of his beloved departed mother?

"She's here in this room, if that's what you're wondering," said Glory, as if she had somehow been gifted the ability to read minds.

"What is she doing here?" Jacob asked in quiet voice.

"She told me she's been looking for an opportunity to communicate with you, and tonight presented it to her. Only..."

"Only what?" asked Jacob somewhat impatiently when Glory paused.

"If I relay whatever message she has for you, she tells me there is a large number of others like her hovering nearby who will likely see me as the doorway to the life left behind, and come knocking upon it to deliver messages to their own loved ones," said Glory.

For a moment, it looked like the thought of such a prospect unnerved Glory so much that Jacob would be left to forever wonder what it was his mother wished to tell him. Then suddenly the look on Glory's face brightened somewhat.

"I guess I could be faced with worse fates than hearing the voices of Visitors in my head. After all, I am Glory Dey, the great psychic of the modern era," she said with a sardonic chuckle. "It would be nice to see a day where I no longer need to reach inside a black bag like the wizard and hope what I pull out is the very thing they've been searching for."

"Then you'll share with me what she wants?" Jacob inquired eagerly. Glory hesitated only briefly before smiling assuredly.

"She asks that you take hold of my hands," she said holding out both for Jacob to grasp.

Jacob immediately thought back to separate occasions when he was offered the hands of Gotham and Thaniel to take hold of and instantly witnessed the scenery surrounding him fall away only to be instantly replaced by a completely different hem of reality and time. But he quickly laughed off such contemplations that caused him a moment's pause when he reminded himself that Glory Dey wasn't close to being in the same league as an angel, and therefore lacked such transmutative powers. And for the most part he was right when he reached out and placed his hands in Glory's; the dressing room, and the floor beneath his feet and ceiling above his head, failed to vanish. Glory Dey, however, did; or rather she faded away, but before Jacob's mind could attempt to make sense of what his eyes saw, he was greeted with a most unexpected and unforeseen sight that far overawed him more than Gotham and Thaniel's trick of time travel: the vision of his mother.

~ ~ ~

Jacob couldn't believe his eyes, despite all the unbelievable things he had come to observe since learning he was a Nephilim. There was his mother seated in front of him, looking like any other flesh and blood being, yet emanating an ethereal glow and revealing a noticeable transparency that made it clear she was anything but. She looked youthful and tranquil and, more importantly, the beauty which had been stolen from her in such a cruel manner had been returned, concealing even the slightest blemish of the illness that had consumed her.

"Is this really you?" Jacob finally asked once he managed to untie his tongue.

"My precious angel," Isabeth cooed with delight, evoking the nickname her only child had always detested that now played out like a pleasing symphony in his ears. "How much you've grown in the short amount of time since the two of us have been separated."

Jacob wanted desperately to throw his arms around his mother and hug her tightly, but he resisted the gnawing urge fearing she'd vanish from sight the second he released his hold of Glory's hands, which he grasped even tighter to ensure such a thing didn't happen.

"I…I don't even know what to say right now," Jacob stammered awkwardly. "Where are you?"

"I'm home," Isabeth replied.

"Home as in…Heaven?" Jacob pressed with a hint of hesitation.

"Where else would I choose to make my home?"

Jacob released a visible sigh of relief when he heard his mother's reply.

"You look surprised by my answer," said Isabeth.

"No…," denied Jacob. "I was just worried, that's all."

"I know. It's one of the reasons I was allowed this brief visit with you," said Isabeth as she looked upon her son with the look of motherly love Jacob had grown to miss. "It's an onerous undertaking that's been placed upon your shoulders; one that cannot be successfully accomplished when the mind is tangled in doubt. Gotham did much to alleviate some of those doubts regarding the reasons I kept the truth of what you are a secret from you, and for that I shall always be beholden to him. But there remains a lingering sense of dubiety deeply imbedded inside you that must be removed like the splinter it is, or continue to fester it shall and throw unseen twists and turns in the path before you."

"I'm not sure I know what you mean," Jacob said in return. And, indeed, his obvious cluelessness was genuine.

"You must know you're coming to be was out of an act of love on behalf of your mother, and not the fruit of deceit seeded by the Darkness," Isabeth began to explain. "The angel who fathered you did so in the most crafty and calculating of ways, appearing to me in a dream, camouflaged as something he was not. I could have easily terminated his contemptible scheme, but I chose, instead, to deliver you into the world swaddled in light than the dark shroud of a blanket he had laid out for your arrival. And now I sit here so very humbled in knowing I did the right thing as I look upon you and witness the Light Bearer I'm so proud to have mothered, and not a bringer of Dark."

More so than the harboring resentment he had held onto at having the truth of who and what he was deliberately kept from him for so long, Jacob had been saddled with a troubling torment of how he came to be that haunted him to his core. Since learning he was the son of Samael, it proved a difficult, if not impossible thing to reconcile that he could embody anything outside the realm of Darkness that inhabited the angel who helped create him, especially the moniker of Light Bearer that had been involuntarily thrust upon him. Even more so than that, he had spent more than a few restless nights tossing and turning over the fate of his mother. How could a woman who accepted the hand of someone like Samael, through trickery or not, avoid suffering the ultimate punishment for such an unfortunate transgression? Such musings had on more than one occasion manifested itself in troubling nightmares that revealed his mother languishing in an insufferable state in the deepest of depths where misery springs eternal in the form of fire and brimstone, unsightly creatures and, even worst, unfathomable loneliness. Seeing her now before him radiating the unmistakable light of salvation and not wrapped in some oppressive shroud of repentance instantly released such deep-seated fears inside him in the same way a pail of water puts out a smoldering fire, and Jacob felt the sizable weight he had been carrying roll off his shoulders. Perhaps, he surmised as he stared into his mother's illuminated face, he was no more doomed for reaping the hapless fate of being the son of Samael as his mother was for bearing his child. It was a realization that had been slow in coming, but when it finally did, Jacob let escape from his lungs a most relieved sigh. Yet no sooner had he breathed such a sigh that his mother replaced her words of love with those of a dire warning.

"Still, you are his son, much as I wish I could say differently, and he will not be reticent in allowing you to be anything other than his son," said Isabeth.

"You don't have to worry. I won't be having anything to do with him," said Jacob.

His steadfast defiance warmed Isabeth's heart, but it did little to part the clouds of gloom that had suddenly seemed to gather about her.

"I wish mutiny was a strong enough weapon to keep him at bay, but I fear his overwhelming shadow is one you will forever be forced to run away from yet never escape," said Isabeth. "There's a reason he made you, and it was not to serve as bearer of the one thing he wishes to permanently extinguish."

"I won't be running from anyone. I'm not afraid of him!" declared Jacob, and he meant it. "Perhaps it would better serve your well-being if you were," said Isabeth.

The look of concern in his mother's eyes was one Jacob couldn't ignore, but he did his best to wipe it away by giving her hands a reassuring squeeze.

"There's nothing to worry about," he said. "Samael's basically an old warship that's been decommissioned. Gotham saw to that when he bound Samael like a turkey and left him to rot in a desert prison."

Such reminders did little to comfort Isabeth.

"Strong as the shackles of the Herrinsu vine may be, Samael still found a way to pick the lock of the cell door of that very prison and cross the threshold into my consciousness, or you would not be here today. I fail to see what would prevent him from seeking out his own son in the same manner."

Isabeth's words served as a discomforting reminder to Jacob of the nightmares he used suffer night after night of the ominous imprisoned figure he would come to learn was his father languishing away in the dead, insufferable Infernal Desert while consumed in a festering and terrible rage; nightmares that ended suddenly once he destroyed the Through in the Silent Forest with his sword. As he listened to his mother, he couldn't help but wonder if and when those nightmares might find a way to resurface.

"That is why," Isabeth continued, "it is imperative you keep the one effective weapon given to you—the Sword of Destiny—secured in the sheath of your wing from this day forward. Allow it to be your fifth limb as it has attempted to become, and don't ever let it exist out of your sight or reach, as it is this moment.

"It is equally crucial," Isabeth was quick to add before Jacob could even offer a nod of promise to concede to her appeal, "that you finish the journey which brought you here and find the one they call Zophiel, no matter how evasive he may be."

Jacob was taken aback hearing the name pass through his mother's lips. "You know about Zophiel?"

"I only know the echo of the name that reverberates within your dreams, and the favor you do yourself to follow it," said Isabeth.

"I'm trying," said Jacob. "Damiel is out somewhere right now trying to find out where this Zophiel is."

"Damiel is faithful and stouthearted in his angel ways. It is where you are concerned that he has unwittingly been fitted with blinders," said Isabeth.

"I don't follow…what do mean by blinders?" asked Jacob, looking visibly confused.

"Don't misunderstand me. Damiel's devotion and allegiance to you is as steadfast as my own. But, like Gotham, he suffers a wound of guilt over the death of his son that has never fully healed, and it manifests itself in overprotective ways that at times can be smothering, especially now that the responsibility of your well-being has been placed squarely on his shoulders," said Isabeth. "Eden is the one place he knows where you will be truly safe and he will do everything he can to persuade your return there, both for your sake as well as his own peace of mind. But the walls of Havenhid were not built to serve as a cage for the Light Bearer, neither will they silence the obscure message Thaniel sowed into your fertile dreams. Nor should they."

So what you're saying, then, is that I really need to find this Zophiel character, no matter what," said Jacob. "The question is where? Damiel even said the chances we'd be able to find him are slim to none."

"The Floating City," said Isabeth. "That's where you'll find the key to what it is that awaits you there."

"But a key to what?" Jacob asked while growing ever more curious.

"Answers. For both yourself and Damiel," replied Isabeth, proving to be as cryptic as Thaniel's final words.

"And perhaps your friends, as well," Isabeth was quick to add. "It might be wise to ensure they're at your side on this trip,"

"I doubt that'll be a problem," said Jacob. "I don't think I could keep Max and my other fellow Shrikes from coming along even if I wanted to."

"It's Ty and Wray of whom I speak."

The response caught Jacob so completely off guard that the next question he was poised to ask concerning what exactly the "Floating City" was, and where was it located, dissipated from his thoughts.

"I can't have the two of them tagging along with me and the rest of the guys while we go and search for this Zophiel," protested Jacob.

"And why not?" questioned Isabeth.

Thinking the answer was as obvious as the nose on his face, Jacob gave his mother a long, hard stare.

"For starters, we're five Nephilim traveling with someone known as The Angel of the Sword in search of another angel who many believe betrayed

Heaven during the Great War," explained Jacob. "As it is, I've already had to lie through my teeth once tonight to explain away the journal I kept while I was in Eden that Wray confessed she found and partially read."

"Why lie to them at all?" asked Isabeth. "Why not just tell them the truth?"

The truth? Was she actually suggesting he go ahead and tell Ty and Wray the secret that made up his entire existence?

"I know you didn't like it much when I used to watch the classic monster films on TV growing up," said Jacob. "But whenever the truth was revealed about Dracula, or Frankenstein, or the Wolfman, or any of the others who were not like everyone else, it was usually followed by the formation of an angry mob armed with burning torches."

"You can't honestly tell me you think of yourself as one of those unsightly creatures," said Isabeth, looking disturbed at even the mere consideration of such a thing.

Jacob said nothing in return. He knew he wasn't an unsightly creature, as his mother put it; any mirror told him as much. His pleasant reflection, however, didn't stop him from feeling any less creaturely on a day in, day out basis. And while he had come to terms with who he was, and even embraced it, there was never a minute of any single day where he wasn't conscious of the fact that he no longer was a member of the human race as he once assumed himself to be, but rather a mutant. Sure, he didn't have a flat head or electrical bolts secured to his neck, nor fish gills or webbed hands and feet. But he knew even something as seemingly innocuous as a pair wings—angel wings, at that—would be enough to send anyone who saw such a sight running for the hills. And the last thing he wished was the image of himself and his wings fully unfurled reflected back in the mirror that was someone's eyes opened wide in terror at such a sight, especially if those eyes belonged to either Ty or Wray.

"Need I remind you one of the many roles called upon you in your role as Light Bearer is to serve as a bridge between man and angel," Isabeth reminded her son. "What better two people to form the crux of such an important and loyal alliance than your best friend and the girl you've fallen in love with?"

"Who said I was in love with Wray?" balked Jacob whose face instantly took on a red glow of embarrassment in response to his mother's unexpected assumption.

"Please…I may be departed, but I am still your mother. And I can spot the tell-tale sparkle in my son's eyes, even from my new vantage point," said Isabeth. "Don't sell Wray short, nor your friend Ty for that matter. They've each come to know who Jacob Parrish is and what resides within him. A pair of wings is not enough to change such bonds. Dare I say, they might even make them that much stronger."

Isabeth's gaze suddenly for the first time shifted away from her son and turned skyward as though she were alerted to some distant voice calling out to her that fell deaf on Jacob's own ears.

"Unfortunately, I must leave you now," she said with a noted sadness.

She began to rise slowly and Jacob squeezed at the pair of hands he held in his grasp in a desperate attempt to stall her ascension.

"Don't go…not yet," he cried.

"Don't worry, I'm not leaving you. Always know I am watching over you," his mother replied with a smile.

Such assurances did little to quiet Jacob. He had so many things he wanted to ask her, and suddenly, in that moment, they were an incomprehensible jumble inside his mind.

"Wait…" he called out again as she rose further out of his reach.

"What's it like?" he finally managed to blurt out. "Heaven, that is?"

If there was one thing he needed to know above anything else, it was that his mother was in a good place. And from the look that swept over her face in response he knew she was.

"Paradise," came her reply.

She was suddenly gone, vanishing into the green glowing vaporous cloud from which she first appeared, and then disappearing into the ether like a plume of smoke. Jacob stared up at the ceiling for some time, but he did so not with a long face of sadness but rather a crook of a smile. Surprisingly, for the first time since his mother's death, the anguish he had long felt over her demise was replaced, instead, with a comforting peace which took hold of him in a heartening hug.

CHAPTER TWELVE

The smile that found Jacob remained pasted on his face when he finally met up with his friends who were loitering about the entrance to the casino anxiously awaiting his return. When they spotted him, they instantly descended upon him like a swarm of mosquitos, buzzing him with questions about what had happened.

"What did she want?"

"Why did she leave the stage so abruptly?"

"Did she read you?"

"What did she smell like?"

The last question was asked by Ty, and it drew an immediate and abrupt silence from everyone.

"What did she smell like?" echoed Jacob, looking at Ty as though he were witnessing the marbles filling the inside of his friend's head spilling out through his ears.

"What's so strange about that?" Ty inquired as he took note of the puzzled looks all aimed his way. "Haven't you ever wondered what certain people smelled like?"

"She smelled like a gardenia flower left in a room filled with cigarette smoke," said Jacob who learned long ago it was a much easier go to simply answer his friend's queries, no matter how odd or random they might be, or risk being taken for an unwilling ride on one of Ty's more often than not bizarre tangents.

Thankfully, this time Jacob managed to avert such a detour when Ty sucked his teeth while shaking his head in disapproval before saying simply, "A smoker…that's too bad."

Jacob, however, was purposefully nebulous when it came to revealing what exactly transpired in his meeting with Glory Dey in the privacy of her dressing room. He shared with his friends how Glory delivered to him a message from his mother, but he declined to divulge how Glory had served as a window of sorts, to allow his mother to appear before him in a vision that could only be summed up in one word: heavenly. It wasn't that Jacob questioned whether or not his friends would believe him; in fact, he was certain they would, if not Ty and Wray, then most certainly his friends of the Nephilim persuasion who were more learned about such things. Instead, Jacob felt like the special visitation he received was something of a private nature; a sort of sacred thing, in a sense, that took place between a mother and her son, and not some supernatural spectacle to be put on display under the bright lights of Fremont Street. And so he kept the special moment close to his chest, in the same way he wore the pendant once belonging to Gotham around his neck and tucked out of sight.

"Do you believe it?" Wray asked as she walked alone with Jacob away from the others.

"Believe what?" asked Jacob.

"That your mother was really speaking to you through Glory Dey."

Jacob didn't need to think twice about his answer as the vision of his mother had remained seared in the forefront of his thoughts since leaving the casino. "I'm certain of it."

"I'm glad for you," Wray, with her eyes filled with genuine sincerity, said. "And I'm glad you got to hear whatever it is she told you. I don't think I've seen you smile—really smile—since before she passed away like you are now."

It wasn't exactly a true statement. The smile had found its way to Jacob's face briefly the night of the Harpus High homecoming dance when he shared his first kiss with Wray as they slow-danced to their song in the school gymnasium. Now, here he was wearing that same smile, though prompted by an entirely different stimuli, even as his mind mulled over a part of the conversation he had with his mother that should have traded his smile for a pensive frown betraying the internal debate he currently was having with himself.

"Wray…there's something I need to talk to you about," he suddenly found himself blurting out.

"What is it?"

She waited, but he appeared to be struggling to make his tongue function, and in many ways he was.

"It's okay," she attempted to soothe his more than obvious discomfort. "You know you can tell me anything."

I'm not so sure about that, Jacob grumbled to himself. After all, how does one go about revealing to anyone, even someone as open-minded and unprejudiced as Wray, that he was in fact a Nephilim and not expect her to go screaming for the hills? But the more he wrestled with the invisible obstacle separating himself and Wray, the more he realized his mother was right in her suggestion that he remove it. And the longer he waited, the more larger and burdensome an obstacle it was sure to become.

"I'm not really sure how to go about saying it," Jacob finally managed to say.

"You're not about to do something really cheesy and suggest we get married in a Las Vegas chapel by an Elvis impersonator, are you?" Wray said jokingly in hopes to ease the obvious tension that had coiled itself around Jacob.

The idea nearly drove Jacob from out of his own skin.

"Of course not. That would be stupid," he replied defensively before becoming even more defensive at hearing his own words. "Not that I think wanting to marry you would be stupid by any means. I only mean...well, we're just kids. I don't think it would even be legal for us to get married." He managed to close his eyes and take a calming breath. "God, now I'm starting to sound like Ty."

"I get it," said Wray, smiling. "Now, what is it you have to tell me?"

Jacob looked into Wray's eyes; the same eyes he stared into when he summoned the courage to share with her his secret trips to the doctor two years earlier, and the misdiagnosis of an affliction called winging scapula he received from his doctor concerning his misshapen back before he knew the true nature of his secret condition. There was a trusting and welcoming allure to those eyes that made him feel as though he could tell her anything, and he felt it at that moment.

"It has to do with my journal...the one you told me you found and partly read," he managed to muster the courage to get the ball rolling.

Now it was Wray's turn to look nervous.

"What about it?" she asked with a quiet apprehensiveness.

It so happened, at that very moment, both with a sense of great annoyance and great relief to Jacob, that Ethan interrupted him from speaking further when he was heard to call out suddenly, "Did anyone else hear that?"

~ ~ ~

Everyone became quietly still and listened for whatever it was that had caused Ethan to stop dead in his tracks and stand with his head cocked noticeably to the left.

"I don't hear anything," said Leos, before being quickly hushed by Ethan.

"There it is again."

This time, what sounded like a beating of wings whipping the air caught more than just Ethan's ears.

"Is that what's got your knickers in a twist?" asked Max. "Just some bird, that's all."

Yet even as he spoke, Max searched the darkness of the night sky with a marked leeriness while attempting to spy the source of the fluttering, as it not only darted about obscured in movements far too swift for his eyes to track, but sounded to his ears to be multiplying in numbers.

"I don't think that's any bird," Jacob commented as he, too, studied the sky with a noticeable suspicion.

If there was one thing a Nephilim was intimately well-versed in, it was wings and the creatures of the earth who were adorned with such appendages. Whatever was circling about them from above, it was guided by a pair of wings whose movements Jacob and Max had never before heard.

"Is anyone else here feeling like they just participated in a polar bear plunge?" Ty inquired while crossing his arms tightly across his chest in an effort to stem the sudden frigidness that abruptly took hold of the air and caused his body to tremble from the uncomfortable chill. "Or did I somehow contract some kind of Asian flu?"

Leos and Kairo took instant notice of the cloud of vapor escaping Ty's mouth with each syllable he spoke, and traded a shared look of alarm with Jacob, Max and Ethan when they, too, felt the tell-tale chill sweep over them; a chill which each boy knew immediately was caused by only one thing.

"Um…what is that?"

The sound of Wray's voice made Jacob's head swivel around and he found her staring off in the distance with a noticeably frightful look fixed on her face.

"What's what?" asked Jacob when nothing obviously untoward managed to catch his eyes.

"Over there," said Wray, pointing to a dark alleyway between two buildings on the opposite side of the deserted street where a cluster of nighttime shadows congregated just outside the reach of the street lights. "I think something's watching us."

Jacob took a closer look and he soon spied what it was Wray was motioning to: a pair of eyes, burning red in color, could be seen peering out from the dark confines of the alley like two miniature blood moons. It was obvious they belonged to an animal of some kind, but what kind of creature, exactly, Jacob couldn't quite make out, as the veil of night in which it was concealed was too dense to peer past, even with his keen Nephilim vision. Yet where his eyes failed him, his ears caught the low rumblings of a deep and hostile growl emanating in a way most unnerving from the same spot where the eyes were positioned in their ominous stare.

"Jacob Parrish...the one they call Light Bearer," a gravelly hiss of a voice made itself heard from the growling. "Surrender yourself, or an incident will present itself which will prove very unfortunate for those you call 'friend'."

"Did you hear that?" Ethan, his eyes widening with alarm, gasped.

"If you're referring to that unfriendly growl then, yes, I heard it clear it as a bell," Ty whispered in reply, making it more than obvious that the sinister voice was only decipherable by those with Nephilim hearing.

Whatever eyeball-bearing thing was lurking within the darkness of the alley, it was immediately evident (at least to Jacob and his Nephilim companions) that it was not the normal sort of earthly creature known to frequent such alleyways. Nor was it alone, as was quickly apparent when a second pair of red-colored peepers made themselves visible besides the first.

"I think we best get back to the hotel asap," Jacob suggested to the others in as calm a manner as he could.

"You'll get no arguments from me," Ethan was quick to agree.

They continued along in unison past the alley where the eyes remained watchful, moving with the same caution a hiker takes when attempting to back away from a bear accidentally stumbled upon during a walk through the woods. Down one street they retreated before turning abruptly onto another, all the while moving with ever-quickening steps which were incited by the sound of the unseen flock of wings flapping about in a stalking formation somewhere overhead and, to those who had Nephilim ears, the distinct patter of paws holding close to their trail. It, therefore, came with a notable sense of relief when the unmistakable glow radiating off The Strip made itself visible further ahead. There remained, however, a considerable distance of deserted street to clear before they would reach it; distance that would take but a blink of eye with the aid of Nephilim wings. Jacob knew, much to his chagrin, that such a mode of transportation was not an available option; not with Ty and Wray in tow. He may have moments earlier been just a parting of the lips to disclose to Wray the long-held secret he had been keeping about himself locked away; there was no way he was going to unleash such a surprise by suddenly revealing his wings and having her faint dead away right there on the street.

"There's a truck up ahead," Max yelled out, pointing to the large pickup truck which was mounted high upon four oversized wheels better suited for a tractor, and parked in front of an ATM machine. "Let's see if we can't hitch a ride from them."

They raced toward the cartoonish truck, but as they approached the ATM, they each quickly realized the two darkly dressed men huddled in the bank vestibule and fidgeting suspiciously with the cash dispensary machine were not the good Samaritans they had hoped they had stumbled upon.

~ ~ ~

The harsh, unflattering ring of fluorescent lighting inside the ATM vestibule made the two young men with their face and neck tattoos and various piercings appear all the more unsavory, as they each eyed the approaching group of teenagers with a nearly identical shifty glare. They said not a word and calmly went about their business, but one thing was certain: they were not in the midst of making a late-night cash withdrawal from the bank; not a legal one, anyway. That much was made crystal clear by the sight of a heavy-duty rope of chain that was attached at one end to a chrome hitch at the back of the truck parked at an angle alongside the curb and snaked across the sidewalk where the burglars-to-be were hastily attempting to secure the other end to the ATM machine.

"Don't say anything, and let's just keep walking," Jacob suggested calmly under his breath to his friends who obediently followed suit.

They were just about past the pickup, strolling as nonchalantly as they could down the middle of the street, when a third man suddenly appeared out of nowhere as he rounded the front of the truck to block their path. He looked to be in his early twenties and not nearly as menacing as his two associates, nor did he need to be; the gun in his hand was more than threatening enough, and it was aimed straight at Jacob and his companions.

"Kinda dangerous for kids your age to be roaming around the streets unsupervised, ain't it?" asked the man.

"Is this a trick question?" answered Ethan whose eyes were as wide as saucers, and rightly so as they were glued to the barrel of the assault rifle pointed at him and the rest of the group.

"Bit of an extreme gesture, don't you think?" Max, motioning to the AR-15 cradled in the thief's hands, asked.

"It has a way of succeeding where the mouth fails in ensuring no one thinks about doing anything foolish," the man replied.

His gaze then made a knowing and deliberate shift to Ty who was attempting a discreet reach into the front pocket of his jeans.

"Like say someone thinking about making a sneaky, not to mention stupid, move by dialing 911 on his cell phone," he was quick to add.

Ty smartly reversed course and held up his hand to reveal a small plastic container that rattled loudly when he shook it.

"No 911 call here…just a Tic Tac," Ty noted nervously before holding his hand out in a courteous gesture. "Have one?"

Jacob then quickly took a step forward and explained to the man in as calm a manner as he could that he and his friends weren't looking for any trouble and were just on their way back to their hotel. The man, in return, spelled out in as equally cool a way that there would be no trouble to be had—so long as Jacob, or anyone else in his posse, didn't have an itch to become a hero.

"Just relax your heels," advised the man, "and when we're through with what we're doing here, you're free to go along on your way."

"And what exactly is it you're trying to do anyway?" asked Ethan who had his neck craned like a pelican in order to peer around the front of the truck and observe the man's two companions busily at work trying to finish affixing the chain to the ATM machine.

"They're in the middle of setting up their Christmas account, Einstein," Leos scoffed in reply. "What else does it look like they're doing other than giving the bank a quick and dirty makeover by replacing the ATM with a drive-up window?"

"Any idiot can see what they're doing, Sarcasmo," Ethan shot back. "I guess what I meant to ask is why? If I'm not mistaken, the average sentence for someone caught stealing money from an ATM is something like twenty years."

"And what are you, a lawyer in training?" inquired the man.

"Just something I saw on TV once," answered Ethan. "I also seem to recall hearing somewhere that almost all ATM machines have less than ten thousand dollars stored inside them, and most of those have only a few thousand dollars at any one time.

"What's your point, Einstein?" asked the gun-toting thief who looked to be growing quickly bored with the conversation.

"No point," said Ethan. "Just seems like a lot of risk, not to mention unnecessary damage to the bank, for such an unimpressive reward."

The man stood quiet for a moment, as if he was taking serious consideration of the boy's words.

"That's quite a profound observation you had there, Friar Tuck," remarked the man when he finally spoke, bringing an elated glow to Ethan. "I'm almost tempted to take a moment and ponder your words...except...'

"Except, what?" asked Ethan.

"Except," repeated the thief, "I'll be a little too tied up counting all the money coming my way from the big withdrawal we're going to be makin' from that there machine once we manage to rip it out of the wall."

The thief hooted loudly with laughter, but his weak attempt at humor garnered only looks of disgruntlement from the group he continued to hold captive, especially Wray whose eyes came to resemble the sharpened points of two ice picks aimed directly at the chuckling man as she took in a deep calming breath, and muttered almost inaudibly and with great disdain, "God, I hate thieves."

Her words didn't completely escape the man's ears, and his chuckling quickly sputtered to a stop.

"I'm sorry, I didn't quite catch that," he said. "Is there something you wished to say, sweetheart?"

Never one to be easily intimidated, particularly by a perceived bully who managed to garner an extra strike against himself by referring to her as "sweetheart", Wray appeared to grow emboldened in the sights of the man's stare that was suddenly locked on her.

"I said I find thieves to be among the most loathsome and detestable walks of life there is, after wife beaters and child molesters, that is," she said in as clear and unambiguous a manner as she could. And she didn't stop there.

"God forbid you go out in the world and try and make a decent living like most people. No, you'd rather sit back and freeload off the rest of us who are actually productive and offer up something worthwhile in life."

"Uh…in case you forgot, he's holding a gun," Ethan was quick to remind Wray, as he grew visibly more nervous with every syllable of her scathing rant that passed her lips.

"Of course he's holding a gun," said Wray. "You know what they say about men who have an unnatural attraction to guns; they're usually compensating for a host of other inadequacies. Basic psychology 101."

The man, looking visibly less amused by the dressing-down he was receiving, took a step toward Wray.

"You know, for such a fine-looking gal you've got a real ugly mouth on you," he said.

Ironically, the real ugliness was revealed when the thief himself smiled a sort of perverted and revolting smile which made Wray's skin ride up on her bones. Jacob felt his body coil like a spring as he watched the grinning thief step closer toward Wray, and he was about to pounce forward when the man attempted to reach out and run his grimy fingers through her clean blond tresses. Max, however, beat him to it, placing himself squarely between Wray and the dirty feelers quicker than it took an eye to blink.

"If you think her mouth is ugly, you're gonna find mine to be simply hideous, sweet cakes," Max sneered.

What do you think you're doing? Jacob questioned Max in the way Nephilim were gifted in communicating with one another without use of their tongue.

Don't worry, mate, I've got this handled, Max replied while drilling his gaze into the thief whose grip grew all the more tighter on his gun. *This joker's wasted enough of our time. I can end this with two shakes of a wing.*

No way…not with Wray and Ty in the line of fire, argued Jacob.

Max didn't appear to be listening as Jacob caught sight of a subtle crawl of movement beneath the t-shirt covering his friend's back, and he braced himself for what was about to unleash itself when the surrounding streetlights began to flicker noticeably, before suddenly and inexplicably extinguishing themselves, one by one from one end of the street to the other. It wasn't just the streetlights that mysteriously went out, either, but the lights lending security to the surrounding businesses, too.

Then, when every last visible light on the block had been doused, including the bright buzzing fluorescent beacon shining down on the ATM machine and the two thieves it helped aid in their burglary, the familiar and unpleasant chill which had made itself felt to Jacob and his companions several blocks away once again mingled its way in a slow, frigid creep amongst them. Jacob and his Nephilim cronies each felt a simultaneous bitterly uneasy sensation travel up their spines, though it was not brought about by the sudden plummet in temperature, but rather the instant of knowing that the only thing capable of causing such a biting nip was somewhere in their midst.

"Guys…I'm not sure now's the appropriate time to be bringing this up," Ty suddenly spoke up, sending a cloud of his breath into the chilled air. "But you know whatever it was that was watching us earlier? Well, it's back…and it looks like it's brought friends with it. Many, many friends."

Everyone followed the line of his gaze to the empty vacant lot located on the opposite side of the street. There to their surprise (or perhaps not), a sea of glimmering eyes, like a multitude of stars one would find glittering in the sky above, only alight with a halting ominousness rather than inviting twinkles, peered through the dark cloak of night behind which they were concealed.

"There's so many," muttered Wray, finally sounding somewhat unnerved. "What are they?"

"Infectors."

The word seemed to subconsciously leave Jacob's mouth, and only when he realized he had uttered it aloud did the color leave his face, especially when Wray, who instantly recognized the name from the laundry list of mysterious and unusual names she had inadvertently been introduced to from what she read of Jacob's journal, turned to him with a look of alarm far more than the legion on eyes fixed on her had managed to ignite, and asked pointedly, "What did you just say?"

Jacob was only forced to suffer through a few awkward speechless seconds that followed when suddenly there came the *RAT-TAT-TAT* of gunfire as the thief pointed the barrel of the rifle he had been cradling in his arms at the sky and fired off several rounds. The leering eyes dotting the darkness of the empty lot instantly scrambled.

"What's wrong with you, Punk? You a moron or something?" one of the men focused on the felonious work of tethering the chains to the ATM barked irritably. "Why not just fire off a flare to alert the cops what we're doing here?"

"Relax…just scaring away a pack of nosy mongrels," the thief whose name drew a noticeable snickering from the teens shot back.

"Did your parents really name you Punk?" Ethan couldn't help but ask the man as he rested the rifle on his shoulder and proudly surveyed the black patch of empty space that was now free of the spying critters.

"It's a nickname. Any of youse got a problem with it?"

"Not me. I think it's quite fitting," Max replied

It wasn't long, however, before whatever creatures had scurried away reassembled and their gleaming eyes, now revealed in even larger numbers, once more pierced the cloak of night. The blinking of so many eyes—like those of a massive pride of lions watching keenly from the tall grass of the African bush—seemed to incense the thief who had briefly chased them away, and again he took aim with his assault rifle and fired. This time he sent a spray of bullets straight into the lot and directly at the glowing eyes, but no sooner had he initiated his assault than some dark flapping shape swooped down unexpectedly from the sky and struck the man's head with a glancing blow before slipping back into the folds of the night sky as quickly as it appeared.

"What the...?"

The armed thief looked about wildly for what had attacked him when a second dark shape dive-bombed him. This time he managed to catch sight of a whipping of wings and the split-second gleam reflecting off the smooth curve of what looked to be a talon, before he let loose a shriek of pain when he was greeted with what felt like a swipe of a knife's blade to the left side of his face by the unknown assailant. Reaching for his cheek, he felt the unmistakable warm sap of blood drawn from the smarting laceration sliced deep into his skin, and a look of rage washed its way over him. Jacob honed in on that vengeful look and a pang of uneasiness took hold of him.

"EVERYBODY...GET DOWN!" he barely managed to cry out to his friends when the man seized hold of his rifle in both hands and began firing haphazardly in all directions in an incensed attempt to put down whatever had attacked him.

Grabbing hold of Wray with one hand and Ty in the other, Jacob dived to the ground, where they hunkered down upon the asphalt on their knees, forming a tight defensive pod with their arms wrapped protectively around one another as the manic shooting continued. Not unexpectedly, Jacob felt Wray's body go rigid with fright, and when he looked to her he found her eyes wide as twin saucers.

"It's going to be okay," Jacob attempted to reassure her in as calm a voice as he could muster.

Her gaze then slowly shifted to where his arm was outstretched and wrapped around her and, if it were possible, her eyes grew even wider. It didn't take long for Jacob to realize her frozen state of shock stemmed not from the wild man firing off his assault rifle, or the unseen winged things buzzing past him in their continued attacks against him. Only when Jacob followed her gaze with his own did his face become a reflection of horror when he realized what had made Wray's eyes mimic two dinner plates.

~ ~ ~

Not only was his arm wrapped protectively around her, so was his wing. Both of his wings, in fact, had been unwittingly unleashed, slicing their way free through the sides of his t-shirt in an instinctive reaction by Jacob to form a protective shield around his vulnerable friends against the one or two errant bullets that were stopped dead in their destructive paths by the impenetrable plumage.

"Oh my God!" Wray gasped when she finally managed to unhitch her power of speech that had caught itself in her throat.

What followed next felt to Jacob like an eternal sentence in purgatory as he braced himself for the expected dagger of rejection he had feared would pierce him the moment his long-kept secret was revealed; when she would pull herself free of his embrace, almost desperately, as though she suddenly found herself staring at some hideous ghoul and instantly extinguish the adoring look that lit up her eyes every time she looked his way and warmed the cockles of his heart. But the moment never arrived; not the pulling away from his embrace, or the dimming of the light in her eyes, even as wide and stunned as they were, as she stared deeply into his for some semblance of clarity.

"The journal. Every…everything I read," she stammered. "It's true."

Ty, on the other hand, looked as if he had seen a ghost.

"I've been shot, haven't I? I've been hit and now I'm slowly bleeding out in the middle of the street…" he wailed in a breathless panic.

"Relax…you haven't been shot." Jacob tried to assure his friend to no avail.

"It's okay…you don't have to sugarcoat it for me. I always had a feeling tragedy would find me in my youth," said Ty while attempting to put forth a brave face. "At least I don't feel any pain, just cold…and yet I know my young unfulfilled life is slipping away from me because I'm already starting to hallucinate."

"Listen to me, Camille," Jacob said, "you haven't been shot, and you're not dying."

Ty gave himself a quick once over for evidence of the bullet holes he was convinced had riddled his body, and yet not a hint of relief greeted him when he found not a one. In fact, it was quite the opposite.

"If I'm not dying…then why do you look like you're some kind of…of…?" he wondered aloud, unable to spit out the word "angel" while eying suspiciously the large stretch of wing folded protectively around his side.

It was déjà vu all over again for Jacob, as he found himself back at Penuel Point when Ty got his first gander at the wings he was forced to reveal following his parachute mishap. Then, Jacob offered his friend some calming words to ease the bug-eyed stare fixed on the unnerving vision before him before wiping clean any trace of the incident from his memory. This time, however, he sought no remedy but the unvarnished truth. They were, after all, in the gambling capital of the world, and what better place to allow the chips to fall where they may than right there.

In a moment of relief, the assault rifle finally spit out its last bullet, abruptly ending the gunfire. As the rattled thief cursed and screamed in his desperate attempt to reload and get the bullets flying once more, his two other partners in crime rushed from the secured spot along the side of the truck where they had both dived to protect themselves from the ricocheting artillery to investigate what had set their friend off like some malfunctioning firework. An argument quickly ignited, and before long, a three-way struggle over the rifle ensured.

Seeing an opportunity for him and his friends to escape being taken hostage by the inept thieves, and escape the glowering eyes watching their every move, Jacob motioned to the others.

"Now's our chance to get out of here. Let's be quick."

They had barely managed a few steps, however, when one of the winged creatures that had set about attacking Punk in a series of fast-moving dive-bombs and flybys suddenly dropped from the sky above shrieking a horrible shrill of a scream at the group of jolted teens as it hovered in the air, blocking their path. And what a hideous and ghastly creature it was. It looked to be a bird of some kind (a relative of the crow family, perhaps), but the kind of bird one would expect to be created, or hatched, in an area set aglow by a massive nuclear contamination accident involving lethal and disfiguring levels of radioactive materials. Or, at some point, been fed the kind of transforming potion concocted by Dr. Jekyll that allowed him to mutate himself into the monstrous Mr. Hyde.

For starters, the bird-like creature was five times the size of even the most well-fed of crows. It's eyes were the color of blood, and its beak, unusually long and lined with razor-sharp teeth, made a threatening slicing sound similar to a pair of brandished scissors. Worse than the snapping beak and the rows of teeth it bared, the sight of the talons that, even in the dark, gleamed like sharpened knives were poised ready to slash to ribbons whatever, and whomever, attempted to cross its path.

Hideous as the creature was as it flapped its big black wings and held its defensive stance against any possible safe passage past it that the hapless group of teens might be contemplating, Jacob couldn't shirk the uneasy feeling he had as he glanced furtively at the empty lot on the other side of the street that something even more terrifying resided behind the cloak of night where the gathering of eyes stared back his way.

"What do we do, now?" asked Kairo.

"I say we serve this oversized Cornish hen on toast," answered Max with an itching smirk. "There's five of us, after all."

"Don't you mean seven of us?" corrected Ty.

Glancing over his shoulder, however, he was instantly gobsmacked by the unexpected sight of Max, Kairo, Leos and Ethan who, like Jacob, had set free from the hidden confines of their shirts their wings at the first sound of gunfire.

"Then again, math was never really my forte," he muttered under his breath before returning his gaze to something less challenging to his struggle to maintain some semblance of a calm composure like the carnivorous crow hybrid.

There was suddenly a low grumble of a growl from the lot teeming with eyes, and from that growl there came the familiar sinister voice that only Jacob and his Nephilim companions were privy to hear.

"We ask you one last time to come with us, Light Bearer," it said. "We shall not voice our request again."

~ ~ ~

"Perhaps it would be best if I go," Jacob said finally.

"What are you talking about? Go where?" Wray, looking more and more confused with each passing minute, inquired. There was no such confusion in Max's face.

"Are you out of your tree?" he balked in protest.

Jacob, however, saw nothing crazy in wanting to ensure the safety of his closest friends from the grotesque flying predators whose large unseen numbers could be heard circling about above by the rustling of wings, not to mention the growling faceless creatures that continued to lie in wait in the dark. But Max was having none of it.

"I won't let you do it," he said, clasping his friend tightly at the shoulder.

Thankfully, no further show of force was necessary from keeping Jacob from taking that first step he still wrestled with taking, for suddenly in the distance there was heard the familiar piecing squawk of a battle cry which Jacob hadn't heard since the day he left Eden. Jacob turned an expectant eye to the blackened heights of the night sky, and sure enough, a snake eagle he instantly recognized as his Beacon came suddenly into sight like a feathered lightning bolt unleashed from the heavens. Talons wielded and at the ready, it struck the unsuspecting crow-like mutant with a fierce full-frontal assault that sent feathers flying.

Jacob stood with his mouth agape at the fierce raptorial clash taking place mid-air amid a chorus of ear-deafening screeches and caws and the furious beating of wings. Ethan shared the same look, but for different reasons.

"Um, guys…I don't want to cause any unnecessary panic," he said, "but I have a bad feeling we're in the crosshairs of round two."

His troubled gaze directed everyone to the sight of Punk who had succeeded in wresting his gun away from his associates' failed attempt to relieve him of it and was preparing to resume firing it. But the rattled thief's attention quickly turned from the snake eagle and hideous crow hybrid still locked in their ferocious battle and settled on a far more unsettling sight: that of Jacob and his Nephilim companions with their t-shirts noticeably split down the sides and revealing the inescapable marvel that were the wings adorning their backs.

"What the…" Punk muttered as his brain struggled to make sense of the vision captured by his own eyes.

Slowly, he shifted the aim of his rifle from the two dueling raptors and leveled it at the five Nephilim who reflexively positioned their wings to form a protective shield around the vulnerable Wray and Ty. Catching sight of the move, the snake eagle sounded an enraged shriek, and with a violent swing of its body it released its ruthless and paralyzing hold on the mutant terror and sent it hurling out of sight into the dark reaches of night. It then turned the focus of its fierce yellow eyes on the gun-toting thief and made for him with great speed and aim, and only then did Punk redirect the barrel of his weapon back on the bird of prey and press his finger against the trigger.

The threatening move caused the eagle not a moment's hesitation; if anything the speed of its charge became even swifter. Max moved quicker. Plucking a feather from the insides of his wings with each hand, he finally found the appropriate moment he had long-waited for: to put to use a nifty move Jacob had taught him from his lessons with Gotham while the two were up late one night in one of the common rooms at Havenhid, and with two quick successive throws, he sent them flying through the air like a couple of darts aimed at the bullseye of a target. Punk yelped with pain when the first feather pierced the back of his left hand followed two beats later by the second feather which embedded itself in his right shoulder, causing him to stumble backward and fire off the round intended for the snake eagle into the dark sky. Luckily for him, he remained quick enough on his feet to throw himself clear of the eagle's path just as it was about to set upon him with its merciless talons positioned to do far more damage than Max's quills.

Punk dove face down upon the hard rough asphalt and, in his desperate lunge, he lost his grip on his weapon which and was now lying on the other side of the street. So frantic was he to have the security of the cold steel gripped by his hands before he suffered the stinging prick of another feather stabbing his skin, or another attempt was made to leave more hash marks on his already bleeding face by whatever winged creatures were stalking him from above, that he was oblivious to the fact he was inching his way forward toward an even greater danger; a danger far more lethal than any feather turned shank or bird- like monstrosities with teeth. And so when Punk managed to secure his weapon once more in his hands, an overwhelming sense of relief and protection swept over him, but it was a feeling short-lived when he suddenly became aware of a halting and unpleasant growl coming from right in front of him.

Only then was Punk quick to realize, in a rather unsettling way, that he was kneeling less than a foot away from the perimeter of the vacant lot, and he took immediate notice not only of the sea of eyes turned his way, but the silhouetted shapes of the four-legged variety to which the glowering peepers belonged. Beads of sweat instantly began to form on his forehead and above his trembling lip, and when more growls and snarling joined the first to form a menacing chorus, no amount of squeezing and wringing the rifle in the grips of his sweaty palms managed to slow the pounding of fear thumping against the walls of his chest.

"Nice pooch…good doggies," he cooed nervously.

Punk was quick to discover otherwise when one of the shadowy shapes suddenly lunged forth and pinned him flat on his back. All he saw was teeth— many, many teeth—and those horrible blood-soaked eyes leering down at him. In a flash, he was gone; dragged off like a rag doll into the dark recesses of the lot where the other dark shapes quickly converged on him, and his screams, more of terror than pain, were abruptly snuffed.

The two other thieves who looked on in horror at the fate of their friend took not a step to attempt and help their comrade in crime. In fact, they did quite the opposite by high-tailing it as fast as their feet could carry them to their truck, with one jumping behind the steering wheel and the other leaping into the bed. The engine had barely been turned over when the back wheels of the truck let out a loud piercing scream. But as their own fate would have it, the thieves, in their panicked desperation to flee, had forgotten one small hitch: namely the twenty-odd feet of stubborn, heavy-duty chain they had tethered to the back of the truck and secured to the ATM machine in their get-rich-quick bank heist scheme, which earlier in the evening had been prematurely crowed about for its simple brilliance.

"Go, go, go…GUN IT!" the thief in the bed of the truck screamed with growing urgency while banging on the roof of the cab.

His voice instantly went silent when a swarming cloud of teeth-baring birds suddenly broke from their vulture-like circling pattern and descended upon the truck. In a flash, they converged upon the terror-stricken man and flew off with him kicking and screaming.

This only sent a heightened wave of fright through the thief attempting to break the truck free of the shackles holding it in place as he all but punched the gas pedal through the floorboard of the cab. The back of the truck was smoking like a rubber inferno as the tires continued their mad spin. Yet no matter how furiously the truck lurched and jerked and reeled in its attempt to grab the road and speed away, the links of the chain preventing such an escape were showing no signs of give.

The bank building, however, was a different story. Cracks from the stress eventually began to form in the corners of the cement wall where the ATM machine and the building were fused together; cracks that quickly splintered and grew to form large fissures threatening to not only separate the ATM machine from the building, but cause the entire side of the building to crumble and send an explosion of concrete projectiles through the air in the process. Spying the threat, and the vulnerable position he and the rest of his group were in from the incoming projectiles, Leos quickly leapt into action. With lightning speed, he was at the back of the truck and, barely visible through the cloud of noxious tire fumes in which he was immersed, he flexed his right wing and with it swung at the chain as though it were a well-aimed ax. There sounded a loud *CLANK* as the serrated ends of the deceptive plumes which formed his wing cut through the steel links like scissors snipping a strand of hair, and the truck peeled off like a shot. Almost immediately, it began to fishtail in its escape as it barreled out of control down the street, swerving this way and that before coming to an abrupt and metal- crunching stop when it plowed into the trunk of an unyielding tree.

Somewhat dazed, the thief stumbled out from inside the smoldering heap, but he quickly shook the glitter of mini stars exploding before his eyes when he heard a loud blood-curdling shriek and looked to the sky to see a flock of the terrifying winged creatures coming his way. Screaming, he ran as fast as his feet could carry him into the darkness of the night, and the mutant birds made chase after him.

~ ~ ~

"Thank goodness that's over," Ethan breathed with a sigh of relief when the horrible screeching gave way to silence.

"Maybe you better have another look," advised Kairo.

The horrid prehistoric-looking flying creatures may have flown off, but to Ethan and everyone else's chagrin, something far worse remained blocking their way. The unseen things with the stalking eyes leering from within the vacant lot had quietly emerged from behind the veil of night where they had patiently been lying in wait, and arranged themselves four deep to form a threatening barrier blocking the young teens from any route of escape.

"Those don't look like any kind of dogs I've ever seen," Wray was quick to observe, and rightly so.

Like the monstrous, terrorizing birds before them, the four-legged beasts, who held unsightly resemblances to the more familiar collies and shepherds, pit bulls and terriers, and even poodles and chihuahuas, looked like a lab experiment gone horribly wrong. To begin with, they were of considerable size, at least three or four times that of the garden variety canine found in households the world over. Nor was there anything even remotely friendly or cuddly about them, as they stood with their backs severely hunched as if ready to pounce and tear apart anything in their path limb from limb with the noticeable knife-like claws protruding from their paws. Their menacing eyes reflected a deep-seated enmity, but it was nothing compared to the oversized fangs protruding from the snarling muzzles, from which could be heard a steady grumbling of growls. If dogs were man's best friend, then there was no questioning these creatures were its worst enemy.

"Are you sure I haven't been shot?" Ty, appearing as discombobulated and fearful as Jacob thought was humanely feasible, asked. "I mean…what's happening where the birds don't look like birds anymore and the dogs look like…like…that?"

"It's what happens when Infectors get inside of you," Max replied as casually as if he were commenting on the day's outfit he had decided to wear.

"And what the hell exactly is an Infector?" Ty asked in a voice that continued to climb in undiscovered octaves.

Jacob's response was one of surprise when he opened his mouth (though not quite sure what would come out) only to hear Wray offer up a reply in his stead that was word-for-word the exact reply he received when the chilling topic of the Infectors was first explained to him by Gotham.

"They're all the bad things that have made their way into this world," she spoke slowly and deliberately, as if reciting something etched in the bone on the back of her skull. "They're the seeds from which all sorrow and all pain is grown. They're every act of wickedness and evil, every immoral transgression. They're the embodiment of every sin committed."

"And how do you know anything about it?" Ty, who looked none the more enlightened on the subject, inquired.

Wray hesitated a moment while continuing to stare deep into Jacob's sheepish eyes before answering softly, "I remembering reading something about them somewhere not too long ago."

"You read about them…Infectors. And where exactly did you come across this disturbing and twisted nugget of information…in 'Modern-Day Monsters for Dummies'?" Ty replied with unabashed facetiousness.

Jacob, of course, knew precisely of what Wray was referring, and the unsettled look of enlightenment pooled within her eyes with which she held his gaze captive was almost too much for him to withstand.

"I wanted to tell you," Jacob bewailed in a whisper. "I just didn't know how."

Kairo was quick to remind the pair that the time for such a long-due and involved conversation would best be put off just a while longer for everyone's sake, when he abruptly shifted everyone's attention back to the hideous mongrels, which were now slowly closing their ranks on the group of teens.

"So, what do we do now?" Kairo inquired with a heightened sense of urgency.

"What we've trained to do," said Jacob, without a moment's hesitation, drawing an even more bewildered look from Wray, if that were possible.

"Trained? You're telling me there's some sort of training that exists for a situation like this?" she asked.

"I guess you were telling the truth when you said you only read the first quarter of my journal," Jacob remarked good-naturedly while at the same time feeling a small sense of relief that he would at least be allowed to sit her down and explain to her in his own way the more delicate matters expressed within the pages of his journal that he was still working to come to terms with himself.

His smile, however, quickly disintegrated when Max, Leos, Kairo and Ethan, in a collective display of the training questioned by Wray, drew their swords from the hidden sheaths within the insides of their wings as the infected mongrels advanced their way closer. Following suit, Jacob instantly lamented his gross error in judgment when he grasped the familiar grip of his weapon and realized instantly it was the sword given to him the day all Nephilim received their swords at Lion's Bite, and not the all-powerful Sword of Destiny he had stupidly left behind in their hotel room.

"There's too many of them for us to try and take down alone," Leos observed, as he struggled to keep his eye on the horde of dogs creeping up on the group from all sides.

"Pig's arse!" Jacob replied, utilizing one of Max's favorite curses that had become his own the moment he first heard it. "One of the first things Damiel taught us was that being outnumbered doesn't determine the outcome of a victory; it's the skill by which you face down your enemy, and we all know we were among his best students."

"No offense to your rah-rah-Yankee-Doodle-pick-me-up," Max piped in, "but I'm inclined to agree with Leos, as I don't recall Damiel ever referring to the enemy as anything other than the two-legged variety. Certainly not an army or oversized flea-infested mutts with giant fangs…or birds."

Jacob was caught off guard by the less than swaggering fearlessness and bravado he had grown used to (and, in fact, envied) in the face of danger suddenly coming from his friend, until he followed Max's gaze skyward where he caught sight of a dark cloud in swift approach. It was the mutant birds; they had returned from their chase and resumed their circling pattern overhead in a chorus of loud shrilling caws and squawks like a flock of hungry vultures.

"But I'll tell you this much…I'll be painting the street red with as many as I can fillet before they're able to sink their fangs into me," Max was quick to vow with the fiery confidence that had momentarily gone mute.

"Light Bearer…"

Jacob quickly turned his attention to the sound of the growling voice coming from the largest of the hideous beasts, which looked like a dysmorphic version of a pit bull.

"You had your chance," the warped pooch snarled as it leveled its threatening gaze on the boy. "Now, watch your friends be torn apart."

As the animal stepped closer with the gnarly claws protruding from its oversized paws scraping against the asphalt, like knives being sharpened on a whetstone, Jacob gripped tighter his sword in preparation to strike at the approaching menace. It was then he suddenly became acutely aware of a noticeable and distinct sensation of heat focused on the center of his chest, and when he allowed his eyes to leave the threatening beasts for a moment to see the cause, he observed the vial-shaped pendant which hung around his neck was alight with a whiteness much brighter than the usual faint glow perpetually burning inside it. And in that warmth, Jacob felt a most comforting feeling of protection and security slowly spread through his body, and replace the fear and nervous uncertainty that had begun to take hold of him in the face of such hostile creatures.

Instinctively, he removed the pendant for the first time since Anahel bequeathed it to him from around his neck. And when he did the pit bull-looking monster yelped as if it had been struck by some unseen thing when it caught sight of the radiant object.

"The Breath of the Begend…" the creature snarled with rage. "How did such a thing come into your possession?"

The pack of unsightly mutts then watched with utter astonishment as Jacob discarded the necklace onto the ground where it came to rest in all of its pulsating aura of mystery at his feet.

"Stupid boy…," the head mongrel growled, "you just let the last bit of saving grace for your friends literally slip through your hands."

Yet what appeared to be a grin framing the doggish fanged muzzle, hideous as it was, faded fast when Jacob instinctively took tight hold of his sword with both hands and raised it high over his head.

"What're you doing?" Ethan questioned, nervously.

The band of beasts already knew, and with a rabid chorus of teeth-gnashing howls, the canine pack set upon the group of teens with a bloodthirsty glint in their eyes, as did the circling flock of birds that let loose a shrill cry of rage—and terror—and descended from the sky like a furious funnel cloud to join the charge with savage speed. Jacob's sword, however, was swifter in its movement as it came down like a mighty spike. No sooner had the razor-edged tip of the blade caused but a hairline fracture to the hard rock-like shell of the pendant, than there came an immense explosion of blinding light. It rushed upward to the highest reaches of the sky in the form of a massive pillar of churning whiteness. Then, just as abruptly, it collapsed upon itself before erupting outward like some detonated cosmic atomic bomb. Both dogs and birds let out a collective scream as they were immediately and wholly consumed in the tsunami of light, and in a flash, the horrible, terrifying figures appeared to the eye as transparent, radiograph-like images revealing the even more horrible and terrifying dark figures of the army of Infectors seen squirming with rage and pain inside the cavities of the unwitting hosts they occupied. These malignant and cruel entities made a desperate, if not fruitless, attempt to escape the hulls of the creatures they had wrangled to possess, but it was too late. In their fleeing, the Begend Light incinerated the lot of the screaming demons, like gasoline-soaked rags dangled in reach of the flame from a blowtorch.

When it was over and the brilliant Begend Light had extinguished itself as quickly as it was ignited, all that remained was a rabble of dogs and birds scampering and darting about in a dazed and bewildered state. No longer were they the grotesque, mutilated incarnations brought about by the invading Infectors; the Begend Light, by indiscriminately annihilating every last one of the demons without so much as singeing a hair or feather of the defenseless animals whose hides the evil presences stealthily used as sheep's clothing, had proven itself to be a powerful antidote for the Jekyll-like serum secreted from the shadowy creep of the Underneath.

"Now that's definitely something you don't see every day," Ty, who was looking rather pallid and faint, managed to remark as he and the others watched the birds and the dogs, including Sparkle, the miniature ball of fur whose owner was still scouring the park for his vanished pooch, disburse to all corners of the night once they had regained their bearings, barking and tweeting in their race to return to their homes.

Jacob, who was momentarily paralyzed by an overwhelming sense of awe from the display of energy he had just witnessed, was further stupefied to find the pendant he had thrown to the ground and obliterated with a driving thrust of his sword to release the unexpected power residing inside, was found to be impossibly, in one piece. Not only did it look as pristine and unblemished as the day Jacob first hung it around his neck, he noticed as he lowered himself to one knee to collect the necklace, the familiar glow of light that managed to faintly pierce the thick wall of black rock from which the vial had been carved, and an even more familiar warmth emanating from the pendant as he held it in his palm. He understood then that the necklace was not just a keepsake of the angel whose neck it first adorned, but a most potent weapon; perhaps one whose power rivaled the Sword of Destiny.

~ ~ ~

Jacob suddenly became acutely aware of an incessant buzzing coming from above him, and he saw it was caused by the street lamps which had begun to flicker back to life the moment the last Infector was reduced to a cloud of fiery embers, and he felt an overwhelming sense of vulnerability creep up upon him. It was as if all his clothes had magically disappeared leaving him exposed for all the world to see in the middle of the street in an unfamiliar neighborhood. He soon realized the strange awkwardness he felt came not from the glare of the light shining down on him, but the sense of two pairs of eyes boring their way into the middle of his upper back.

Taking a deep steadying breath, Jacob rose to his feet and slowly turned around to find Wray and Ty both staring at him with identical looks of befuddlement, as if they had crossed the path of some strange and undiscovered species of animal, the likes of which no living person had yet set eyes upon before; and in some ways they had. Jacob certainly couldn't fault his friends for staring like they were; it was the core of human nature to gape at things that were strikingly out of the ordinary, and Jacob knew there were far and few things between that would prove to be more out of the ordinary than a teenaged boy with giant wings sprouting out of his back. And so he did what any seasoned sideshow attraction worth his weight in gold would do: he stood unflinching in the ring of light encircling him with his wings slightly flared so that the eyes could get a good unhindered look at that which they ogled, even when every fiber of his being wanted desperately to conceal them from sight.

What reaction he expected from either Wray or Ty, he couldn't anticipate. But he braced himself for the worse when Wray walked slowly towards him. She said nothing to him, and he in return didn't pull away when she reached for one of his wings.

"Pretty," was all she said when her fingers gently ran themselves across the hard yet waxy smooth plumes and realized at that first touch the vision before her was not a figment of her imagination. And in that very moment, nothing felt more reassuring and accepting to Jacob than the unconditional love he saw reflected back to him in Wray's eyes.

"Well, at least now we know what's been going on with your back all this time," Ty suddenly chimed in with a nervous and awkward chuckle. "You could have hit me with the rock of Gibraltar, though, before I would have ever guessed it was caused by a giant pair of wings."

If Jacob had hoped for the same favorable reception from his best friend as he had gotten from Wray, he quickly realized it might be a tad late-coming, as Ty looked to be in desperate need of some time to come to terms with all that had been unveiled to him in quick order, before he was ready to appreciate the prettiness of the wings his gaze was fixed upon with bugged-eyed disbelief.

"It's alright...I got this," Ty attempted to assure everyone, if not mostly himself, when Wray made a gesture to soothe his agitated state.

"If you think about it, it's not all that freakish a deal," Ty reasoned aloud. "I mean nowadays what's even normal? You have men becoming girls; girls becoming men; those who call themselves 'non-binary.' I've even read there's people on the brink of figuring out how to transfer the consciousness of their brain into a robot so they can live forever. I think I can certainly deal with my best friend being half human and half...bird."

The more Ty tried to rationalize things with himself, the more stuporous he appeared to become.

"Actually, I'm not half bird," Jacob explained in a gingerly manner. "I'm a descendant of angels."

"Angels…well then…" Ty replied while forcing forth a light-hearted smile, "that makes things all the more clearer."

His eyes, however, betrayed his sentiment when suddenly they slowly rolled back into the hollow of his skull, and what Jacob had feared would happen to Wray when she got a gander at what he was hiding about himself was fully demonstrated instead by his best friend: Ty Wrenwood met the pavement face first as he fainted dead to the world.

CHAPTER THIRTEEN

T he glow of yellow light illuminating the bank of large bay windows on the fourth floor of the old McCleese & Co. paper mill was the only sign that life still existed within the walls of the dilapidated brick-and-mortar building shuttered a decade and a half earlier. Inside, Hunter Wylde could be found sitting still as a statue before a large wooden table in a pose resembling a modern-day version of Rodin's "The Thinker." Except for the hum of traffic from the nearby freeway filtering its way through the windows which were slanted open to allow for the cooling evening breeze to push its way inside, and the steady purr coming from a black and white tabby named Jinx who was reclining leisurely nearby, a pronounced quietude more commonly observed inside a church embraced the confines of the large, open- aired industrial loft Hunter had called home for the last several months; the kind of quiet that follows a long, settled-in vacancy when walls begin to shed its paint, and time dutifully knits curtains of cobwebs to mark its passing.

Still, the now dusty and tumbledown machinery hibernating on the ground floor of the uninhabited mill could have suddenly awakened and roared back to life as they once had in their heyday, and the noticeable shudder their powerful working gears would have brought to the very foundation of the building, as they at one time were prone to do, would have likely gone unnoticed by Hunter. He was far too engrossed by the presence of a mysterious object resting in the center of the table before him; the same object he managed to successfully filch from the menacing Pethen in an outwitting sleight of hand deep in a crowded London tube station so many weeks earlier.

And what a peculiar object it was.

About the size of a softball, the strange piece, heavy in weight and dark green in color, looked to have been born from a hunk of jade; or perhaps, emerald. Its shape, at first glance, was reminiscent of a Matryoshka nesting doll; only instead of a smiling Russian woman painted on the surface, the top potion had been carved into a bust of some unsightly creature. And while Hunter knew it to be a container of sorts, he was certain an ever-shrinking family of even more nesting dolls did not reside inside. If anything, the object had an urn-like quality to it. The only problem was that urns, as far as Hunter knew, held the remains of people and animals no longer living, and there was definitely something moving about inside the unusual artifact that was very much alive. For through the object's dense, murky green shell, Hunter could see a dark, undefined blob of sorts swooshing slowly about, looking similar to the amoebic-like, shape-shifting innards of a lava lamp.

Mesmerizing, however, as Hunter found the unusual object and its curious contents, he found himself stumped by an even greater puzzler: How, in fact, to destroy it.

~ ~ ~

His earlier and obvious failed efforts to do just that could be seen scattered across the table in front of him in broken and twisted bits of metal and wood surrounding the seemingly indestructible object: a baseball bat, splintered and broken in two; a crowbar that had somehow been bent into a shape resembling a pretzel; several broken hammers and an axe with a bit that had been cleaved cleanly in half; even a power saw whose blade had been rendered a mangled and unusable mess. No matter what he used or what he did to bludgeon, smash, hack, and all-out obliterate the object which looked to be so easily fracturable, his strained attempts left nary a scratch on it, nor chip, or blemish of any kind.

Every failed stab Hunter made at crushing through the impregnable shell proved increasingly vexing and irksome, leaving him to pace the floors of his loft like some infuriated animal until, in his exhaustion, he surrendered to the chair in which he now sat and stared with a look of hatred and obsession fixed in his eyes at the hideous beast crowning the top of the object which seemed to be silently laughing in his face at his defeat.

Finally, in a renewed breath to his mounting frustration to destroy that which proved to be indestructible, he jumped suddenly to his feet and sent the chair upon which he sat hurling across the floor with a swift kick of his foot before grabbing the subject of his almost irrational obsession in one hand and the one last tool at his disposal that had not yet been damaged—a sledgehammer leaning against the table—with the other.

Jinx, who had made the vacant building his home long before Hunter came around and bonded with the feline, followed Hunter with his large, green watchful eyes as he made his way briskly to the center of the loft and set the object of his detestation squarely on the floor. Then taking the sledgehammer in a tight and determined two-fisted grip, he swung with every ounce of strength he could muster from his bunched and sizable muscles and brought the heavy weight down upon the head of the hideous green effigy with one crushing blow. A loud shattering sound followed, but it came not from the targeted object on the floor but the sledgehammer itself as the solid steel head shattered in a million little pieces the second it made contact with the monstrous carved bust fixed to the top of the object that Hunter was intent of turning into a pile of green dust. Immediately, a yelp of pain escaped Hunter when his focused blow was stopped dead and returned a sharp reverberation that felt like a high- powered jolt of electricity to his hands.

An eruption of gold flared briefly, yet brightly in his eyes when, with a feral cry of exasperation, he bitterly flung the wooden handle of the now annihilated sledgehammer aside when he saw the object was still in one unmarred piece. Snatching it up from off the floor, Hunter eyed with a seething anger the container, particularly the black shape that continued to shift about lazily inside it and, with the last bit of infuriation he felt rise up inside himself, he hurled the maddening object with all his might at the wall of concrete on the opposite side of the loft in a last ditch bid to obliterate it once and for all. Only it was the wall that buckled and broke and caved in on itself in ever-deepening rings of damage when the green object struck it with all the power of a wrecking ball making introductions to the side of a condemned building.

Looking drawn and depleted, Hunter surrendered his brief burst of rage to an equally encompassing sense of resignation as he made his way with lagging steps toward the now damaged wall. He took hold of the still pristine object embedded in the broken and crushed remains of cement and with a forceable yank managed to pry it free. For the first time since he swiped the object, there was now a timorous look in his eye as he studied the inexplicable piece as if it were for the first time.

"What the hell are you?" he wondered aloud.

~ ~ ~

An unexpected knock at the door was the only thing at that moment that could tear Hunter's rapt attention from the object. For as long as he had lived in the vacant loft, Hunter had not been bothered by a single visitor. Then again, there was little reason anyone would have to pay a visit to the ramshackle, deserted building, which is what made the place so appealing to Hunter in the first place. Unless, of course, the unannounced caller was a certain Pithen who had managed to pick up his scent and track it to the door of his humble abode.

It was this unsettling thought that pushed its way to the forefront of Hunter's thoughts and caused a swell of alarm to rise up inside him.

In as quick and quiet a manner as he could manage, Hunter hurried the few short feet to the corner of the loft that served as his bedroom and knelt down at the foot of an unmade bed whose iron frame was dull and rusted in places by both time and neglect. In two quick shakes, Hunter pried up a couple loose floorboards and retrieved a dingy cloth sack secreted away in the dark confines. Opening the sack, Hunter quickly shoved the stolen object he still grasped tightly in his hand inside where he also had two other similar artifacts stashed. Another knock sounded at the door, this time louder and more urgent, as Hunter returned the sack to its hiding place and then quickly covered over its existence by returning the floorboards to their proper place.

His heart was pounding inside his chest.

"Who's there?" he finally called out with an uninviting gruffness.

"Yes, uh, hello…we're looking for a Hunter Wylde," came the muffled reply on the other side of the door.

"Who's looking for Hunter Wylde?"

"It's a bit difficult to try and explain through a door, but I'm, uh…well, frankly I'm a Nephilim just like you, and I'm here with a group of my Nephilim friends, as well as Damiel."

A puzzled look came over Hunter.

"And who exactly is Damiel?"

"He's an angel," came the reply after a moment's pause. "The Angel of the Sword, to be exact."

Angel of the Sword? Nephilim?

It wasn't exactly the garden variety Jehovah's Witnesses on a door-to-door converting mission, or even the vengeful Pithen Hunter had half-expected to be lying in wait for him. Still, his guard remained up, and for good reason.

"Prove it," he challenged.

"What would you have me do to put your obvious suspicions to rest?" came a completely different voice in response directly behind Hunter, which caused him such a fright he very nearly took a tripping stumble onto the floor when his upper body spun around faster than his feet were able to reposition themselves.

In a panicked flash, Hunter instinctively grabbed for a large kitchen knife residing amongst the mangled and broken tools and utensils scattered across the table that he had used in his fruitless efforts to destroy the indestructible object he had moments before stowed away in the sack beneath the floor boards.

"Stay back!" Hunter warned while brandishing the knife on the unnerving vision of Damiel standing feet from him wings outstretched and looking like some mythical being come to life with eyes alight like two suns, and a blinding sword gripped in his right hand. "I won't hesitate to use this."

"Yes, I can see that," Damiel remarked as he eyed with some curiosity the knife whose blade was bent noticeably backwards to form a most nonthreatening U shape. "Though quite unsuccessfully, from the looks of it."

Realizing, with some redness of embarrassment, the ineffective state of his weapon, Hunter tossed it back amongst the collection of other useless tools cluttering the table.

"I'm guessing you're Damiel," he grumbled while looking the angel over with a suspicious eye.

"And you, I take it, are Hunter," said Damiel, giving the young man a studious once over. "And a rather ironic choice of names given you considering."

Hunter didn't seem to pay much mind to the subtle dig as he, too, sized up the formidable angel standing in his presence.

"So, what exactly would the Angel of the Sword want with me?" he finally asked once Damiel had returned his torch-like sword to the sheath residing within the confines of his wings which then folded themselves out of sight behind his back.

"That, you'll have to ask the halflings with whom I'm accompanying," explained Damiel. "It's they who require a moment of your time; a moment you could hasten with my eternal gratitude just as soon as you allow them inside."

~ ~ ~

With the turning and unfastening of numerous deadbolts, latches and chains, Hunter finally succeeded in opening the door of his loft to find the group of teens huddled together in the doorway, anxiously waiting to be let inside.

"Crikey, you'd think we'd be trying to get an audience with the pope," Max grumbled sourly as he and the rest of the group filed through the doorway.

Once everyone was inside, Hunter was quick to shut the door and what followed next was an encore of a series of clicks and clacks as he went about the complex routine of securing once more each and every deadbolt, latch and chain. When he had finished, he turned to find a collective stare of intrigue greeting him from his unexpected guests.

"Something wrong?" he asked.

"You in the witness protection program or something?" Ethan wondered aloud. The look of puzzlement etched in Hunter's brow deepened.

"What do you mean?"

"I think he's referring to that barrier you call a door," explained Max. "I doubt the queen of England herself has as many locks to secure the royal jewels."

Hunter gave the impressive, albeit excessive, collection of security hardware installed on his door from top to bottom in a fashion that resembled a strange coat of armor a fleeting glance but thought nothing unusual of it.

"What can I say? You can never be too careful these days," he answered in a manner that was just shy of unfriendly.

"And, uh, is this your backup security system for whoever might happen to get past that barricade you call a front door?" inquired Leos whose attention was riveted to the ceiling above him.

The others followed his gaze and they were immediately unnerved by what they saw. Hanging from the rafters were a half a dozen or so large and extremely heavy objects: an old broken-down washing machine; a rusted-out engine block to a truck, a couple of nets holding large jagged pieces of concrete; and even a conked-out refrigerator. Each were secured to a rope and suspended in a strategic cluster over the area just inside the entrance to the loft and ready to be dropped with unexpected swiftness and obliterating weight upon any uninvited guest who happened to trigger any of the numerous trip wires the group of teens suddenly took ample notice of crisscrossing their way across the floor in close proximity of where they were standing.

"I don't know if you are aware of this or not, but there's actual home security systems available that people have installed inside their homes these days that do what you are trying to accomplish with this jerry-rigged setup," offered Kairo.

Ethan, however, had a more pressing concern.

"What exactly are you afraid of getting in here?" he asked as he continued to eye with a growing sense of discomfort the hulking refrigerator poised directly above his head that promised to reduce a man of considerable size, much less himself, into an insignificant and unidentifiable stain on the floor with just one unfortunate step in the vicinity of the nearby trip wires.

"Like I said, you can't be too careful these days," Hunter repeated with an undisguised aloofness.

They had only been invited inside for a few minutes and already Jacob could sense they were on the cusp of having overstayed their welcome.

"I'm Jacob," he said, offering his hand to the young man in an attempt to put him more at ease.

When Hunter returned the handshake, begrudgingly as it may have appeared, Jacob quickly proceeded to go around the room and continue with the introductions, beginning with Max and ending with Wray.

"And of course you've already met Damiel," Jacob noted with a nod to the angel who had all but faded into the background as he explored the loft with a slow measured casualness.

Unfortunately for the youngsters, their venturing out the night before into the foul streets of Las Vegas after being strictly forbidden from straying outside their hotel room did not go undiscovered. Despite their hopeful efforts to beat the angel back to their hotel room and pretend all was as it should be, the young boys were dismayed to find a clearly infuriated Damiel calmly awaiting their return, leaving them to ponder if mutant dogs and birds were only the second worse things they'd end up facing that night.

Jacob made the attempt to assuage the crossness that had been directed at him and the other boys with laser focus by revealing the vision reflected in the blade of his sword, and then proving the prophecy by finally introducing Ty and Wray to the intimidating yet captivating figure standing before them. While Jacob was successful in dialing down the angel's anger from boiling to a low simmer, it was evident, even with Las Vegas and its frightful residents several hundred miles behind them, that Damiel, in all his noticeable silence, was still visibly stewing over the Nephilim's transgression.

Hunter, however, gave Damiel not even a second glance; he was far too taken with the sight that was Wray, as most young men were prone to be, even surly nineteen-year-olds such as himself.

"And all this time I had no idea that female Nephilim even existed. And a beautiful one at that," Hunter, his surliness momentarily evaporated, commented.

Wray who was not apt to blushing did so at such a suggestion.

"Oh, no…I'm not…," she giggled, causing her face to glow all the more red. "That is, I'm not a Nephilim. Just a normal average girl."

The glimmer in Hunter's eye argued against the idea she was anything remotely average.

"While we're doing a head count, I should probably clarify I'm not a Nephilim either," Ty piped in. "Just in case you might be wondering…which clearly you're not."

"So how exactly did you find me?" Hunter, his attention remaining firmly fixed on Wray, asked.

"It's a long story," Jacob was quick to answer, as he mindfully stepped between Wray and the young man like any protective boyfriend would. "It wasn't easy though, I can tell you."

"But you made the effort," said Hunter as his brooding manner slowly returned now that his sightline to Wray had been severed. "Why?"

"We're trying to locate your father," explained Jacob.

A startled look came over Hunter, as if Jacob had suddenly pulled back and struck him. "My father?"

"Yes…Zophiel. That is who your father is, isn't it?" Jacob said to no reply. "We're hoping you might be able to tell us where we might be able to find him."

Hunter did quite the opposite by turning his back to the group and instead taking a moment of silence, leaving Jacob and his companions to trade perplexed glances with one another.

"What business would an angel and a band of Nephilim possibly have with someone of the likes of my father?" said Hunter finally. "Better yet, what makes you think I would have any clue to where he might be?"

"Uh, perhaps the fact that he's your father," Leos replied with marked sarcasm.

"Look, I know our showing up here was unexpected and possibly a bit odd," Jacob interjected, "but it's kind of important that we talk to him. And we've come such a long way."

Hunter's stare suddenly shifted direction to the section of the loft that served as his sleeping quarters where he found Damiel continuing in his slow wandering about, and he felt a slow rise of his heart into his throat as the angel's booted feet inched their way closer to the spot of floor where his pilfered stash was secretly hidden. And when the angel took that final step, it was more than the squeak squeezed from the loosened floorboard by his weight that brought a marked look of curiosity to Damiel's face as his attention was instantly drawn downward.

A bead or two of sweat formed on Hunter's forehead and, in a quiet desperate bid, he looked to Jinx, and his eyes briefly burned forth a flicker of gold. Jinx, who had remained quietly in repose intently watching all that was going on suddenly jumped to his feet and, with a loud mew, leapt onto the nearby bed, stealing Damiel's attention from the floor as he was meant to do.

"I haven't spoken or seen my father since I was fifteen years old," Hunter, who now breathed easier once he saw Damiel step clear from his hiding place in order to scoop up the feline for a friendly scratch, explained to Jacob. "And if I have anything to do with it, I don't ever expect to, not today, tomorrow, or anytime after."

"I don't understand. How come?" asked Jacob.

It quickly became clear from the darkened look on his face that this was not the topic of conversation Hunter wished to pursue.

"It's complicated," he mumbled in reply instead.

"Does it have anything to do with you being a Weed?" Max asked, drawing a collective glare of condemnation from the other Nephilim.

"Well, that is the term we're all familiar with when it comes to Nephilim whose fathers are Fallen," Max argued in defense of his poor, and offensive, choice of words. "It's not like I was going out of my way to be some insensitive knocker."

The other boys were quick to realize, naturally, that Max's intention was not to be callous when broaching such a sensitive and contentious topic, and they turned back to Hunter to hear his reply now that their curiosity had been piqued. Hunter, however, offered up none. He didn't have to; the sullen expression on his face was clearer than any words coming from his mouth could express.

~ ~ ~

"Come now, boys. I think we've intruded on this young man's time far longer than what's deserving of us," Damiel's voice cut through the momentary awkward silence.

The angel set Jinx down onto the floor as he approached the growing collective of those in his charge and was about to usher them out of the loft, but Jacob wasn't having it.

"We can't go yet. We still haven't a clue on where to find Zophiel," he protested.

"Hunter just got through telling you he hasn't had communication with his father in many years," Damiel attempted to reason with the boy. "I told you before we began this futile search that the chances of finding him were slim if not nil. When an angel goes dark, the chances of unearthing him are naught, and as of now we have exhausted every avenue at our disposal in our quest to locate him."

"But—"

"If I thought there was any glimmer of hope in this quest of yours, I promise you I would indulge in going forth, but we can't look under every stone in every corner of the world," argued Damiel. "Now we each made a pact with one another at your mother's gravesite before we set out on this search. I've kept my end of our bargain; I believe it's time you now kept yours."

Much as Jacob may have wanted to push back against any move to call it quits he didn't, as it was beginning to feel beyond useless at this point. As hard as they had tried, and the further they traveled, the more distant they seemed to be in tracking down this elusive phantom-like figure named Zophiel; and frankly, the past couple days had left Jacob too fatigued to care about trying to solve the mystery surrounding the last gasps of a doomed angel that continued to echo like a distant church bell in the hallows of his dreams when he slept. At least for the time being.

And so he amenably turned to Hunter and raised the white flag in the form of a handshake.

"It was nice to meet you," he said with a cordial half-smile.

"Same here," replied Hunter. "I'm sorry I couldn't have been any help."

Then realizing a rather obvious barrier prevented the group from leaving, Hunter hurriedly repeated the tedious and complex process to disengage the armory of locks and deadbolts in order for the door to be opened. But as he watched the angel and his odd troop of Nephilim and two civilians file their out of his loft, Hunter was suddenly struck by something.

"You said your name is Jacob, didn't you? Jacob what?" he posed his question to Jacob.

"Parrish."

"The same Jacob Parrish rumored to be the Light Bearer?" The question caught Jacob by surprise.

"How'd you hear about that?"

"News like that's kinda hard not to catch wind of, especially with these," Hunter answered while giving his Nephilim ears a tap with his finger. "So…is it true? The rumors, that is?"

"It's true," Leos jumped in with an emphatic answer.

"I was told you'd be paying me a visit one day soon," Hunter remarked.

"You were told I would be coming here?" asked Jacob. "By who?"

"Couldn't really say. He never told me his name except to say he was a friend."

The remark drew a questioning glance from Damiel.

"I guess you're asking me about my father caught me so off guard that it slipped my mind," said Hunter.

"And did this mysterious friend say why exactly Jacob would be paying you this visit?" questioned Damiel.

Hunter shook his head and said, "Just that it was important that I lent you whatever help I could; both for you, as well as for me."

The young man stood quiet for a moment or two biting down on his lip while staring at Jacob as if for the first time.

"Look…," he began in what was almost a tentative whisper when finally he spoke, "what I said earlier about not having contact with my father over the last four years is true and all, but—"

He paused, looking like someone having a quiet internal debate about whether to continue.

"But what?" pressed Jacob.

"If it's really that important to you that you find my father, I might be able to help you," said Hunter.

Jacob's mood perked up immediately.

"Understand I can't guarantee you anything, but I have a good feeling he'd still be at the place he called home when we parted ways," said Hunter. "If you're up for it, I might be able to force myself to take you there."

"Where's there?" inquired Kairo.

"Venice."

The boys exchanged dithering glances with one another.

"Venice Beach, California…it's not that far out of our way from where we are now," Max remarked with a shrug.

"Actually, the Venice I was speaking of is the one in Italy," corrected Hunter.

"Now that would be a bit further out of our way," said Ethan.

All eyes then turned to Jacob for a reaction as he quietly chewed upon the logistics of such a proposed journey.

"What have we got to lose at this point?" he said finally. "I'd say we go for it."

With everyone agreed, Max was quick to point out they'd first have to backtrack to Cain's Corner.

"What for?" asked Ethan who was showing signs of needing a nap.

"To drop these two home, of course," explained Max, motioning to Wray and Ty.

"What do you mean home?" asked Wray. "Why can't we go with you?"

In reply, Max leaned slightly forward while stretching the loose collar of his t-shirt away from his neck to offer a peek of the curve of his wing he made rise up just behind his right shoulder.

"Remember these? They're called wings. It's what we're going to use to get from Point A to Point B, and unless you have a secret bag of pixie dust stashed away, I'm not seeing you getting off the ground" explained Max. "Now, personally, I'd be the first to offer to carry you all the way. But it's got to be near six thousand miles to Venice and—don't take this personally—that's an awful long way to be hauling what would quickly feel to my arms as a sack of potatoes."

The unflattering analogy brought a frosty look to Wray's face.

"Why can't we just take a plane?" she asked coolly.

"Because we can make it there in half the time with these," Max replied, motioning to his backside once again with his thumb.

Just when it seemed like the argument had been settled, Hunter was quick to interject with his own two cents.

"I have to agree with Wray, in regards to mode of transportation," he said. "Whether they go or stay behind, I would have pushed that we take the normal person route. If you wish for me come along, that is."

"But it'll take twice as long to get there," argued Max.

"Yes, but it'll be safer," said Hunter. "Europe has long been a hotbed of malignant forces; Italy in particular. Trust me when I tell you it'll be in our best interest to arrive in Venice as inconspicuously as possible."

Hunter's explanation made perfect sense to Jacob.

"When Gotham brought me to Eden we went by car, plane and train for exactly the same reason," said Jacob as he recalled with some semblance of longing the seemingly endless train ride they took from Istanbul to Tatvan. "Besides, I'm not comfortable leaving Wray and Ty behind; not after what happened in Vegas. Which is why I vote they come along."

With those words, Wray's face defrosted with a glow of appreciation.

"I also want to make one thing clear," said Hunter. "I'm only agreeing to escort you there. Once I show you where I believe you might find my father, I'm gone. I'm not interested in any kind of reunion with him."

Jacob could see the combination of angst and anger in Hunter's eyes at the prospect of such a face-to-face meeting between father and son, and he dared not argue the subject for fear of spooking him into changing his mind.

"Then it's settled?" Leos, who was visibly antsy to move things along, asked.

Seeing a look of agreement in everyone's face, Jacob nodded. "It's settled."

He quickly realized quite the opposite, however, when he turned on his heel and instantly came face to face with Damiel's presence looming in the doorway and looking none too pleased by the conversation he had been quietly eavesdropping upon. And when he opened his mouth to speak, it was with a grumbling finality.

"No one is going anywhere!"

~ ~ ~

It wasn't very often that a Nephilim challenged the directive of an angel, and certainly not one of Damiel's stature and mettle. Rarer still did such occasional infantile uprisings on the part of the Fledglings suffering from ruffled feathers prove victorious. And yet, after a vigorous row that lasted for the good part of an hour, Damiel found himself out-squabbled by the five persistent and headstrong Shrikes and their two civilian companions.

Not that the angel couldn't have ended the debate and restored order with one bellow of his booming voice that, when needed, had the ability to rival a clap of thunder. But he didn't. Maybe it was in heed of Jacob's threat to go it alone to Venice, if forced to, and seek out Zophiel on his own that caused Damiel's iron fist to loosen its grip on the situation at hand. Or, possibly, it had something to do with the foul, dour state of being Jacob had grown increasingly mindful of that seemed to have enveloped the angel like some unseen dark shroud ever since their short stay in Sin City.

Whatever the reason, the group eventually found itself on board a plane soaring across the blackness of the Atlantic Ocean in the dead of night for the Old World, and the hope it held the key to the mystery they sought to solve.

CHAPTER FOURTEEN

THE FLOATING CITY

"You know, your friend Max was right," Hunter said over the soft lulling drone of the plane inside the quiet cabin. The airliner had no sooner taken off and settled into its long flight when exhaustion began to methodically pick off the others and rock them to sleep, beginning with Ethan and Kairo, who were curled underneath a shared blanket and using the other's body as some sort of makeshift pillow. They were quickly followed by Max and Leos comfortably reclined in the seats one row back, where the sounds of their synchronized snoring intertwined to create a slumbrous serenade. Jacob and Hunter, however, tired as they were, resisted giving in to their fatigue and spent the time getting to know one another better and trading Nephilim tales as they sat across the aisle from their sleeping travel companions. And the more they talked, the more at ease and less guarded Jacob found Hunter to be; and the more open Hunter became, as slow a process as it was, the more Jacob took a liking to the young man.

"Right about what?" asked Jacob as he continued to stare thoughtfully ahead at the row of seats diagonally across from where he was seated, where Wray and Ty, undoubtedly enervated by the overwhelming string of unbelievable things they had been ambushed with in such a short amount of time, were also fast asleep.

"The reason I severed ties with my father," said Hunter. "I'm sure you've heard everything there is to know about the once-great Zophiel."

The tone of unmistakable shame that was heavy in his voice did not go unnoticed by Jacob.

"I don't think anyone really knows for sure what happened with him," Jacob answered as diplomatically as he could. "What I know I heard from Damiel—that your father became a Fallen after he betrayed the Light during the Great War; but even he isn't one hundred percent sure it's true."

"Well, let me clear up the mystery once and for all by revealing that it is, in fact, true. He is a Fallen, and he became so because he was traitor. And by default I became the loathsome Weed you now have the privilege of being seated next to."

The odium in Hunter's voice, even as soft-spoken as it was, did not go unnoticed by Jacob. It carried the same familiar echo of animus that not so long ago could have been expelled from his own lungs; the same echo of self-hatred that, every now and then, still rung in his ears.

"The world today likes to point its fingers, usually with disdain, at those they consider privileged, whether they be rich or white or whatever. But the Nephilim are the truly privileged. They are the fortunate and the favored just by the blessed luck of being sons of angels," said Hunter. "When I was growing up I used to think of myself as some kind of warrior; a modern-day version of a comic book caped crusader, and I can't tell you how proud I was to wear such an emblem on my chest marking me as a member of this small and exclusive club called Nephilim. Not because I believed myself to be superior above anyone else, but because I knew I was given a gift and a duty to act as a sort of a liberator for this harsh and sometimes unbearable world and those living in it.

"Imagine my surprise, then," he continued as the brief levity that came with his childhood reflection was quickly doused by a returning surge of solemn bitterness, "when I discovered I was never going to be the superhero I had fantasized about becoming, but the villain. Oh, I'm still of privileged stock, never you fear. But the exclusive club I now have a life-time membership to is one of which I would never have chosen to become a member, and yet I had no choice of whether or not to join."

While the ignominy Hunter felt remained present on his tongue as he spoke, it became less pronounced as a spark of a deep-seated resentfulness held in the pit of his innards was slowly stoked into a flame.

"I hate my father for the thing he turned himself into. But I hate him more for what his sin has made me," Hunter hissed through clenched teeth. "That's why ever since I learned the truth I've spent every waking day trying to find a way to erase this permanent mark he's scarred me with."

Jacob cocked his head with curiosity. "How do you mean?"

"I may be a Weed, but it's in name only," Hunter replied.

He went on to explain while Jacob listened intently how, in his refusal to embrace becoming the very thing he detested, he became a hybrid of what he once believed himself to be. In his own telling of how he went from being a Nephilim in good graces to a Weed surviving on the streets, alone with only his wits and smarts, Hunter revealed how he purposefully turned his fate on itself and became a vigilante against all things dark.

"Sounds like a dangerous career path," remarked Jacob.

Hunter answered with an indifferent shrug of his shoulders. "Personally, I tend to find a majority of the minions of the Darkness to be pretty cowardly. That's why their targets of choice for the most egregious of their crimes against God are almost always the most defenseless: children and animals."

To prove his point, he then proceeded to regale Jacob with a few accounts of some of the victories he managed to collect under his belt in the self-proclaimed war he decided to wage against the Darkness. One such tale which made Jacob sit up a little straighter in his seat took place in a secluded cove off the coast of Japan. As Hunter told it, he had for a short while taken up with a radical group of animal rights activists shortly after leaving home. Every year, the group made the pilgrimage to the haunting spot in hopes of somehow stopping the horrific slaughter that unfolded in the crystal blue, picturesque waters. And every year the members of the group could only look on in despair and outrage at the annual horror that took place before their eyes, as well as the lens of their cameras documenting the atrocity for all the world to see, as a small army of men armed with high-powered rifles and positioned along the cliffs high above, served as the ultimate prevention of any outside interference. All that changed the year Hunter accompanied the expedition.

With the armed men at their posts and another couple dozen men gripping long machetes as they stood knee deep in the calm waters of the tranquil cove, the annual nightmare was about to commence. It began, Hunter recollected, with the faint roar of engines coming from a line of boats approaching the entrance to the cove. As they drew closer, Hunter noticed the water in front of the boats beginning to seethe with the presence of a large pod of dolphins being purposefully corralled into the cove like a herd of wild stallions and steered toward the men with their machetes at the ready.

"I could see the presence of the Darkness in the men on the boats and those in the water, and I knew instantly what was about to transpire," Hunter told Jacob, "and without a moment's hesitation I took action."

Despite warnings from others in his group that interfering was in violation of international law, not to mention posed the very real threat of being shot, Hunter turned a deaf ear and rushed across the short narrow beach and into the water. As he explained to Jacob, he had always had a unique and inexplicable gift of communicating with animals, and his aim was to somehow reach the ears of the dolphins and convince them to turn back to the open sea. Before he could sound the first syllable of alarm to the frenzied pod desperately trying to outrun its pursuers, Hunter recalled how he himself barely managed to escape his own crushing end when he was forced to dive deep into the waters to narrowly escape the hull of one of the boats that intentionally swerved to run him over when the driver spotted him treading along surface.

When he finally managed to surface, he saw his chance to intervene had passed him by, along with the boats, and soon the first horrific cries of the ensuing slaughter made its echo heard within the seclusion of the cove. It was a sound unlike any Hunter had ever before heard. But instead of allowing the tears of defeat dribble their way down his cheeks as he felt them begin to collect in his eyes, he made them instantly evaporate from the heat of the sudden surge of rage that roiled its way through him. And in that moment, he sounded the alarm; not the alarm meant as a warning to the assailed dolphins, but a wholly different kind of convoking.

In an instant, the waters grew restless once more as a large dark fin sliced its way along the surface like a knife cutting its way through a tomato. As it sailed closely past Hunter, another fin emerged from beneath the surface, followed by another, and then another. Soon, a school of fins, looking like so many thorns on the stem of a rose, converged on the cove where they descended out of sight and once more into the depths as they approached the idling boats. The cries of the dolphins were quickly replaced by the screams of men who suddenly found the blood-stained waters surrounding them teeming not only with the helpless mammals they were in the process of butchering, but a shiver of sharks; sharks with jaws lined with razor-sharp teeth that were no match for the bloodied machetes the doomed men attempted to use to defend themselves to no avail.

When Hunter had finished, Jacob could almost see the image of the grateful surviving dolphins racing back to the safety of the open sea reflected in the young man's eyes which carried a gleam of satisfaction.

"I still say it's a dangerous way to prove a point," said Jacob.

An image instantly flashed inside Hunter's head of the vicious Pethen he had the unpleasant fortune of coming face to face with just weeks earlier in a London tube station.

"Maybe…I guess sometimes it has it's dicey moments," Hunter muttered, though he dared not share his Pethen experience with Jacob, and did his best to push aside the memory that still managed to send a noticeable tremble through him. "It was either that or the alternative."

"What's the alternative?" asked Jacob.

"Let's just say being forced to go through life being something you're not is not an option I could ever live with," said Hunter.

He didn't need to expand on his answer; Jacob knew exactly to what he was referring, and the matter-of-fact way Hunter conveyed his feelings on the subject more than rubbed Jacob the wrong way.

"You know," he grumbled in a slightly annoyed tone, "there's a lot worse things in this world than being a Weed. Just sayin'.

"Look, kid," Hunter said after giving the boy a dismissive glare, "no offense or anything, but what would you know about it?"

"Probably more than you think," Jacob shot back.

"You mean to tell me that you...?" Hunter began, but as he quietly searched Jacob's eyes the glint of flummox alight in his own was quick to recede. "I had always assumed the rumors about the Light Bearer being the son of a Fallen were made up...that it was the Darkness' underhanded way of delegitimatizing the prophecy."

"It's not a rumor; I am a Weed...just like you," said Jacob. "And I was angry about it just as you were when I found out. But I realized being angry about something completely out of my hands wasn't going to change anything. I just have to move forward living my life as the person I always believed myself to be."

Hunter appeared to accept the sentiment well enough, uplifting as it was, but something still left him visibly puzzled.

"When we were back at my place, Damiel was arguing against going to Venice and insisting you return to Havenhid," he said. "The only Havenhid I've ever heard about was the one Nephilim go to when they turn of age to begin training."

"That's right," answered Jacob. "It's a long and complicated story to try and explain, but basically, in a nutshell, I left Havenhid. Actually, ran away is more like it. I just became overwhelmed by the pressure of this whole Light Bearer business, not to mention dealing with the whole discovery of being a..."

If there was one thing Jacob hated worse than the very sound of the word "Weed," it was allowing it to pass through his own lips, and so he caught his tongue between his teeth and after a thoughtful pause continued on instead with, "well, you know."

"What I'm trying to make sense of is how is it possible, exactly...you're going to Havenhid," pressed Hunter. "I was always under the impression the entrance through Eden's gate for someone like myself—for any Weed—was strictly forbidden."

"You're right about that, and I'm certain I wouldn't have been allowed in as well if it weren't for Gotham."

"Who's Gotham?"

"He was the angel who first told me I was Nephilim and brought me to Eden. If it wasn't for him, I doubt I would have even been let inside much less allowed to stay. But somehow he managed to convince Anahel and the other Guides, including Damiel."

Jacob grew suddenly quiet and refrained from saying anything further about Gotham as the joyful memories he retained of his beloved friend that paid him a brief visit as he spoke gave way to shards of unpleasant images seared into his soul of the angel's demise.

"And they're okay with you being what you are?" Hunter, motioning to Jacob's fellow Shrikes who were now dead to the world, asked. "Unless there's been a cultural shift I missed, Nephilim aren't exactly buddy-buddy with Weeds, and yet here you are palling around with a group of them.

"Luckily for me they had as much clue that I was of Fallen blood as I did," said Jacob. "And, when they eventually found out, they didn't turn their back on me as I feared they might. In fact, they became even more loyal to me, if that was even possible. I guess that's why I consider them to be more like brothers to me than friends."

The deep bonds of friendship Jacob spoke of seemed to be a foreign notion to Hunter, yet one he seemed to hold a desperate desire to experience. Even so, he was quick to shake off such sentiments like a dog ridding its coat of bathwater.

"What about him?" Hunter asked, peering suddenly around the headrest of his seat toward the back of the plane where Damiel was spied sitting with a dour look set deep in his face while staring blankly out the window. "Is he as cheerful as he looks?"

"I promised Damiel I would return to Havenhid to finish my studies once and if we were able to find your father," answered Jacob. "I think he's just a little unhappy it's taking more time than he expected."

Jacob, however, knew there was something much deeper going on with the angel; he had felt so ever since leaving Las Vegas. Yet in many ways, Damiel was a lot like Gotham: labyrinthine in nature with the ability to erect an impenetrable wall around himself whenever a capricious mood settled down upon him.

In other words, he was a hard nut to crack.

~ ~ ~

"Looks like we have a little less than seven hours before we get there," Hunter announced as he checked the plane's progress on the computerized map being displayed on the monitor inset in the headrest of the seat in front of him. "I suppose we should try and get a little sleep before we land."

As Hunter settled into his seat to join the rest of his travel companions for a bit of shuteye, Jacob turned his attention back to Wray. What unspoken thoughts had rocked her to sleep, and what might she be dreaming of now, he wondered? So much had happened in such a short amount of time; so much had changed. He had hoped the plane ride would have offered him the much-needed time to have a heart-to-heart talk with both Wray and Ty, but especially Wray, and allow him the opportunity to explain so much that was in need of explanation. It wasn't every day, after all, that one stumbled face-first into the reality guarding the existence of angels and their winged-enhanced offspring. Even as Jacob sat staring at the cascades of blond curls spilling over the edge of the pillow upon which Wray's head rested, all he could see was the staggered expression fixed in her eyes when she caught sight of the giant wing wrapped protectively around her and realized it was attached to him.

"I always knew there was something unusually special about you, Jacob Parrish," she had told him earlier in a brief moment they managed to find themselves alone to speak about it. "I'm just glad now to know exactly how special."

The indescribable sparkle in her eye that Jacob craved as much as the air he breathed wherever she looked at him he discovered was still there. The vision of him as he really was had not managed to put it out; if anything, it somehow made it all the more brighter. But, Jacob couldn't help but speculate, would that sparkle retain its twinkle? Or would some unforeseen happening lying in wait in the future cause it to go out?

Not wishing to allow such preoccupations to rule his thoughts, Jacob got up to take a short stroll up the aisle in order to give his legs a stretch while his mind searched for a distraction. He quickly found it in the seat left vacant besides Damiel where he promptly planted himself.

"So…a penny for your thoughts," he said to the angel who replied with silence.

Instead, Damiel continued to stare out of the small portal serving as a window and into the blank black canvas that was the night.

"Not to give you a complex or anything, but from the outside looking in, you look remarkably like a death row inmate being transported to the execution chamber," said Jacob, again to silence.

"Are you planning on staying angry the entire trip?"

"Angry? What's there for me to angry about?" the angel grumbled, finally. "I find myself playing chaperone to a field trip that grows larger with every stop we make. I fear we may resemble a migrant caravan by the time we reach the Old World."

"I know something's been bothering you, and I don't think it has anything to do with where we're going or who's coming along," said Jacob. "Why don't you tell me what's got you upset. Maybe there's something I could do to help."

The boy's words drew a chuckle from Damiel, as if he had been tickled on the underside of his arm with a feather.

"You help me? What possible aide could a doe-eyed Fledgling possibly offer an angel as I?"

The chiding rebuke was felt by Jacob as a particularly cruel sting.

"You're right," he replied surly. "Forget I ever brought it up."

He was about to return to his own seat and leave Damiel to his sulking when he felt a hand clasp the upper part of his arm to prevent his retreat.

"I didn't mean that. My churlish disposition is getting the better of me,"

Damiel lamented apologetically. "Your concern was certainly not deserving of such a retort."

Jacob sank back into his seat, as did Damiel who exhaled a deep burdensome sigh as he did.

"What's going on?" the boy asked.

Damiel at first was resistant to the question, but eventually the tightness of his jaw eased.

"Last night, when I left you at the hotel room, I told you I was going in search of someone who might point us in the direction of Zophiel's whereabouts," he said.

"Were you able to? Find whoever it was you were looking for?" asked Jacob.

Damiel had been so incensed at discovering the group of Nephilim had disobeyed his directive to stay put in the hotel room, and had wandered naively into the reach of a horde of Infectors disguised as a vicious pack of dogs and flock of hostile birds, that what had occurred at the Purgatory nightclub went largely unspoken.

"Cities like the one we left behind us may serve as playgrounds of sin to civilians, but they are also alive with nests of Fallen in the same way an unclean house becomes overrun by an infestation of cockroaches," said Damiel. "When you are gifted with eyes free of the murk that clouds so many eyes, they are easy to spot, like sharks sharing the same water in an aquarium filled with minnows."

Jacob knew exactly of what Damiel was speaking as he was instantly reminded of the conspicuous figures posing as civilian street performers he and his fellow Shrikes instinctively took notice of as they walked along Fremont Street in Las Vegas.

"What I did not expect to find were ghosts," said Damiel. The statement was quick to catch Jacob off kilter.

"Ghosts? You mean like…ghost ghosts?"

As soon as Jacob heard the question leave his mouth with his own ears he was filled with a feeling of juvenile foolishness for asking it. Then again, he could not shirk how just recently he himself had a face-to-face conversation with his own departed mother.

"The ghosts I speak of are the ones I buried along with my slain son," said Damiel. "Or at least labored to bury, but I see now quite unsuccessfully."

Still not quite sure of what exactly Damiel was speaking, Jacob listened closely as the angel recounted his visit to the Purgatory and his meeting with the Fallen angel Demitriel, for if there was anyone who could point out the trail leading to Zophiel it would be he, Damiel surmised. And when Damiel, his golden eyes suddenly aglow with a distinct and unmistakable burn of fire, told of how he quite by chance spied through the wicked throng of infected club goers, the angel Arrestel, who had been responsible for luring Johiel from Akdamar Island to allow a small and stealth army of vicious Furies to enter unimpeded the Holy Cross church, where a group of young Fledglings were awaiting with unbridled excitement their long-anticipated journey through The Gate to Eden, Jacob finally understood the reason the angel's mood had taken such a foul turn.

"What did you do?" Jacob was almost reluctant to ask. Damiel's glowering gaze shifted to Jacob.

"You mean did I seize from him the same eye he conspired to steal from my son?"

It seemed the logical question, and one that would preface an even more expectant reply. For at that moment, Jacob's memory dialed its way back to a day spent in training at Lions Bite, when Damiel first shared the shocking revelation of the tragedy that had befallen not only his beloved son but an entire group of Nephilim boys waiting to be escorted through Eden's gate. Jacob recalled vividly the bitterness and venom in Damiel's voice as he recounted the horror that took place inside the church on Akdamar, but more pointedly the unflinching promise of blood some coming day when retribution would be his.

Instead, Damiel's head bowed slightly, as if from the weighted pull of regret when he confessed that such a day had yet to show its face.

"Perhaps if I had, I wouldn't be suffering the maddening haunt by these cursed ghosts I now find myself to be surrounded by," he said with a slight, though rueful grin.

"I don't know what to say," Jacob began with notable awkwardness. "One thing I remember from my mom growing up when some of the other kids began taunting me for what was going on with my back was sometimes it takes more courage to just walk away with your head held up, than to stoop down and get in the mud pit occupied by your tormentors."

Such small-town lessons met a swift rebuke from Damiel.

"Courage? Are you suggesting what I demonstrated by walking away with my sword snug in its sheath to be an act of courage?" questioned Damiel with a scowl. "Courage would have been walking out of the Purgatory with Arrestel's separated head clutched in my hand. Instead, what I revealed for all to see was weakness. And worst of all, fear."

At that exact moment, Damiel could have attempted to persuade Jacob, and quite successfully as well, of wanting to trade in his sword for the mic on one of those mindless talent competition shows plaguing television, than convince the boy of the words that left his lips. Weakness, and especially fear, were terms no one who ever set eyes upon him would ever use to describe the angel named Damiel.

" 'Eye for an eye' is a soothing lullaby for one left to marinate in ungiving vengeance. But it's also wrought with peril, especially for those of us who tread on high," said Damiel. "The moment I spied Arrestel, I was overrun by an almost enfeebling air of requital, and in that instant it seemed the only cure rested in the need for me to experience the unmistakable give of his flesh, when a head is separated from the body upon which it sits, by the swing of my sword in order to quell the raw hatred that had taken hold of me lest I never know another moment's peace."

"So, why didn't you?" Jacob asked, sounding, at first, as if he was somewhat let down by the angel's admitted self-control.

"Not to say you should have ended him," he quickly rephrased his sentiments, "but I'm sure no one would have blamed you if you had, considering. I certainly wouldn't have."

Damiel gave the boy a faint smile; the same kind of smile usually reserved for young Fledglings when they first visit Lions Bite with a naivety that often hinders their ability to see the vast forest from the trees.

"Had I done so, the Damiel as you've come to know him would have ceased to exist," he said.

What exactly Damiel meant by his words was not immediately understood by Jacob.

"The law governing retribution is a fine and inflexible line, separating just and unjust means," Damiel continued, in an effort to part the clouds of confusion that had gathered about the boy. "Some share in the belief that revenge is a dish best served cold; I tell you satisfying one's cravings brought about by malice over an entree prepared in such a premeditated way will place you on a spit over the flames that burn eternal.

"Demitriel knew this all too well. He whispered as much in my ear with egging taunts in an attempt to stoke the flames of my wrath without so much as moving his lips, and I could feel the tremors of arousal course through him in the growing anticipation that he might witness the fatal misstep that would bring about my downfall. And fall I surely would have had I drawn my sword, and fed the hunger pangs that have gnawed away at my insides over this tormenting course of time since the taking of my son's life. Arrestel breathes this night not because I turned away in an act of compliance to any precept set in stone by my father's hand, but defiance; defiance that my flesh remains unmarred by the same shameful mark that scars my Fallen brethren."

"You should be proud of yourself, then," Jacob said in hopes of lifting the angel's mood. "I doubt there's many people, including myself, who would be able to exhibit the same kind of restraint if they were in your shoes, threat of the Fallen scar or not."

"There is nothing impressive about my prudence; it is certainly not one to be lauded," Damiel grumbled in return. "I know Arrestel's complicity in what occurred at Akdamar was to serve as a diversion meant to draw Johiel and his protection away from the church. Whatever rancid ill will I hold, and will forever hold toward him, will never cloud the clarity of my hatred saved for one who actually struck the blow that ended the life of my son along with fifteen other young Nephilim boys."

"You're talking about the Furies," Jacob remarked quietly, uncomfortable to even say aloud the name of the malevolent and monstrous progeny of the damned who had filled his thoughts with so many nightmarish visions since he learned of their existence.

"Yes, the Furies," Damiel answered with a loathsome-filled breath while his eyes once more relit with the detestation coursing through him with equal burning. "But more pointedly I speak of a certain one of my Fallen brethren."

"Who?" Jacob inquired delicately when the angel refrained from any further introduction.

"I'd prefer to keep the taste of his name out of my mouth, and say rather he is a Fallen of particular ill repute, most notably for serving as Samael's unfailing henchman," said Damiel. "He is the wind that spreads the destructive spores shed by the Darkness, and it was he who brought an especially cruel campaign of death to the church on Akdamar Island.

"He is the seed of the bramble that has ensnarled my heart with its thorny vines, and he is the foulness that has settled over me and curdled my disposition these recent days. And, I am chastened to say, I fear him."

The admission brought the bloom of a smile to Jacob, as though he suddenly recognized he was the butt of a practical joke.

"You? Fear him?" he all but guffawed. "You're the Angel of the Sword. You fear nothing."

"*I fear him,*" Damiel repeated with an inarguable sternness, "because I know the same show of defiance I displayed at the Purgatory by walking away from Arrestel is one I will readily fail in repeating when the murderer of my son and I finally come to face to face, and trust me, that day will soon arrive. I fear him because he holds my downfall in his hands and he needs nary a sword to bring forth it.

"It is for that reason why I have been so unrelenting and stubborn about returning to Eden as I have been," Damiel confessed with a reluctant sigh. "I argued it was for your best interest as well as your safety but, shamefully, I'm beginning to realize it was for my own."

It was a rare thing to see even a glimmer of sheepishness in someone as indomitable a figure as Damiel, and yet even he could not hide it behind his steely front, nor, Jacob suspected, did he appear to attempt such cover.

"May I ask...why was your son, and the others for that matter, killed?" Jacob asked after a brief pause.

From the look on Damiel's face, it was a question he himself had long anguished over but all he could offer was a shrug void of understanding.

"I wish I knew. I think that's been the worst part in all of this," said Damiel when he finally answered. "But it is believed it was to prevent an unpreventable arrival."

"Arrival of who?"

Damiel looked deep into Jacob eyes and, for a moment, seemed hesitant to say anything further. But again he spoke.

"You."

Jacob didn't know what to say in return, or how to react. In fact, he was completely confounded by what Damiel even meant.

"You've heard, I've no doubt, about the Slaughter of the Innocents?" asked Damiel.

"Of course. It's when Herod the Great had all the newborns in Bethlehem killed in order to prevent the prophecy of the coming Messiah from being fulfilled," said Jacob. "It's part of the mural painted on the walls of the church on Akdamar."

"Yes...and quite fittingly," said Damiel with a sigh.

"The Apocrypha mentioning the coming of the Light Bearer is one we've struggled to keep concealed since it was first made known to us. But, alas, nothing secret ever remains so," continued Damiel. "Eventually, the Darkness came know of this hidden writing and, as you can imagine, it was met with immense displeasure and vexation."

"Are you saying what happened on Akdamar was another Slaughter of the Innocents to prevent..."

Jacob's voice trailed off at the thought of something so horrific taking place once, much less twice.

"It wouldn't be the first time the blood of babes has soaked the ground in so heinous and pointless a manner," said Damiel.

"Maybe we should," Jacob said after a thoughtful moment. "Go back to Eden, that is." Damiel responded to the kind gesture with an equally kind smile.

"If I begin this day retreating to the rabbit hole like some spooked hare at the inkling of some nearby predator then the Damiel seated beside you surely will cease to exist, and I will not stand still for such a snuffing out," said the angel. "Zophiel or no Zophiel, we will continue forward and exhaust this trail we have started upon and, with any luck, quiet the last words of a spurious angel who haunts your sleep."

With that, the angel and the young Nephilim settled quietly into their own thoughts, not to mention expectations about what awaited them on the approaching next leg of their search until, eventually, Jacob's tired eyes closed for a final time. And as he drifted off to sleep, the familiar dream that visited him nightly unfolded itself as it always did and, with it, the whispery utterance from Thaniel's lips that continued to lead the way across the globe like a trail of bread crumbs:

Zophiel...

~ ~ ~

The Venice that greeted the travelers when their plane finally touched ground was gray and vacant from the falling rain, and not the vibrant city whose streets and bridges were usually swarming with a slow crawl of tourists. From the Ponte di Rialto, the view overlooking the Grand Canal had been scoured by a heavy veil of mist hanging overhead, and turned the famous sight of the isle of palatial and stately palaces and fleet of sleek black gondolas afloat on the water from what usually appeared to onlookers as a rich and colorful oil painting come to life into a rather drab charcoal drawing. Yet even in its washed-out, colorless state of gray and gloom, Venice still managed to capture the awe-filled gazes of Jacob and his traveling companions as they stood upon the famed ornate stone bridge and took in the view like so many countless visitors before them who, over the centuries, had been drawn to the enchanted Venetian city from all corners of the world by its seductive old-world beauty and mystique.

The respite they enjoyed to play tourist was short at best when Hunter proceeded to lead the remainder of the way across the bridge and down to the banks of the water. There they boarded a waiting vaporetto that provided a water taxi along the Grand Canal's leisurely waterway. The light breeze coming off the Adriatic was cold, and carried with it a pungent mix of seawater and rain, but none in the group seemed to take notice as they were too taken by the row of grand historic structures they drifted past, like the Ca' Foscari with its late Gothic architecture colored in a pale yellow, where King Henry III of France once called home, or the Palazzo Grassi with its Classical and Baroque features.

Go to the Floating City...

As the vaporetto made its way past the Palazzo Corner Della Ca' Grande with its impressive Ionic and Corinthian columns, Jacob was suddenly revisited by the familiar voice of his mother echoing inside his head.

And as he marveled at the immense and magnificent structures that seemed to have been set adrift on the open sea like some mythical Atlantis, he finally understood his mother's directive when she briefly took ownership of Glory Dey's body. Venice was the Floating City. This was the place to where she was pointing him; the place that held hidden somewhere within its narrow streets and secreted niches whatever answers he was desperate to find. It was here, he finally felt convinced, that he would find the elusive angel whose name continued to live on as a final gasp trapped inside his dreams.

Just before reaching the mouth of the Grand Canal, the vaporetto came to a stop at the steps of a structure that was both imposing and monumental in size.

"Well, this is it...this is where I live," Hunter announced as he got to his feet and prepared to disembark the ferry. "Or rather used to, I should say."

As Max stepped onto the canal bank, his eyes like everyone else's, blossomed with wonderment at the Istrian stone and Marmorino behemoth before him and the army of statues depicting various saints and other religious figures decorating the facade.

"This? This is where you used to live?" Max asked with an air of incredulity while eyeing a statue of the Virgin Mary fixed upon the top of a colossal dome that sat upon the edifice like a crown perched upon the head of a king.

"Don't be ridiculous. I meant this is the neighborhood where I grew up. This is the Santa Maria Della Salute church I used to attend on Sundays," Hunter replied. "The house where I grew up is just a short walk from here."

As the rest of the group looked to him to lead the way onward, Hunter seemed overcome by a pronounced look of reluctance.

"Something wrong?" asked Jacob.

"Just remember what we agreed on before we started," said Hunter. "I'll take you the rest of the way and then I'm out of here. You'll have to make your own introductions."

Jacob nodded his agreement, though he secretly had hoped Hunter would have had a change of heart. Over the course of the long plane ride they had shared, Jacob had come to develop a genuine liking for the young man. No doubt due to the fact that they both shared the unique, if not unenviable bond of being descendants of Fallen blood, Jacob felt an undeniable kinship with Hunter that was different from his other close friendships. Yet it was also through this newly formed bond that Jacob understood Hunter's cagey nature rearing itself the closer he inched homeward and the desire to retreat back into the solitary world he had created for himself, despite the hope he had entertained that his new-found friend might return the comradely embrace he had received and possibly accept a place amongst the group as an honorary Shrike.

~ ~ ~

A light drizzle of rain fell as they began their walk into the quaint, bohemian neighborhood of Dorsoduro which had long been called home by the artistic and literary types seeking refuge from the crush of tourists that plagued the better-known and well- traveled parts of Venice. The metronomic echo of their footsteps accompanied the group along a quiet, narrow and wet stone-paved street formed by a row of facing houses and buildings painted in a warm pallet of rust reds, burnt oranges and mustard yellows. The leafy tendrils of lush, colorful flowering plants and vines dripped from wrought iron balconies, and charming squares and walled gardens offered a spot to sit and enjoy the congenial atmosphere.

When they came upon one of the many small canals crisscrossing their way across the Sestierre, they turned right and continued on along the quay of an even narrower alleyway where the dark green waterway flowed peacefully between another line of houses. They hadn't gone far when Hunter stopped suddenly in his tracks.

"What is it?" Jacob asked, though he suspected Hunter's feet to be growing colder with each step he took along the path leading to the place he once called home.

"It's gone!" Hunter replied with an incredulous gasp.

No one needed to ask to what it was he was referring; all they had to do was follow the disbelieving look in his eyes which were firmly fixed upon a very noticeable and very large vacant open space amid the wall of houses that had stood for centuries along the canal banks.

"This is where my house used to be," Hunter said as he made his way toward the void with slow, uneasy steps to get a closer look at the gaping hole that mimicked a missing piece to a completed jigsaw puzzle. "The front door used to be right here."

However, there was no door. Neither were there any windows, nor walls required for the vanished sills to hold the panes of glass in order to peer outside.

"Are you sure we're at the right place?" asked Ethan. "Maybe you accidentally turned down a wrong street."

"I've lived here my whole life until I ran away at fifteen. I could find my way blindfolded if I had to," Hunter grumbled in return.

"Well, there has to be a logical explanation. Houses don't just up and vanish," said Jacob.

"They do under certain kinds of accidents...like perhaps a fire," suggested Wray, though she was reticent in planting such a seed in Hunter's head.

"Or maybe even an earthquake," Ty chimed in.

Max found such a notion completely and utterly ridiculous.

"What kind of freakish earthquake demolishes only one house in a neighborhood of hundreds and leaves the others without so much as a crack in the stucco?"

"Do you have a more logical explanation that doesn't involve a cyclone and a girl with pigtails clutching a dog named Toto?" countered Ty.

It was clear from the stumped expression on his face that Max was just as much at a loss over the mystery of the missing house as were the others. So, too, appeared Damiel who had quietly approached the spot where the house once stood. He studied closely the gaping maw with his percipient eyes as he ran his hand along the wall of one of the neighboring structures of which the disappeared house had once shared, and a look of utmost worry made itself visible in his face. However, it was a strange and unfamiliar voice that echoed aloud the concerning thoughts suddenly brewing inside the angel's head.

"Earthquake…It was no earthquake that took that house."

The group shifted its collective gaze to the adjacent bank directly across the canal where they found a frail-looking elderly man with thinning white hair, and wearing an oversized sweater to protect him from the damp weather, sitting in an old rickety wooden chair staring back in an almost absent-minded sort of way.

"Who's that?" asked Leos.

"Mr. d'Artusio. He's been our neighbor for as long as I can remember," answered Hunter before quickly rushing to the edge of the canal.

"Mr. d'Artusio, it's me…Hunter Wylde," he called out in Italian.

The name brought a gradual relaxation to the severe expression fixed upon the old man's face.

"Hunter Wylde? Is it really you?" the man returned in a thin but heavily accented voice that was full of surprise. "The last time I saw you, you were just yea-high."

"Yes, sir," Hunter, who was too restive to trade familiarities at that precise moment, spouted quickly in reply. "Do you know what happened to my house?"

The question immediately washed away the glimmer of levity that had emerged in the old man's face, and returned the stark cloud of consternation that had briefly parted ways.

"Sí," answered Mr. d'Artusio, though he said nothing more.

"Well…will you tell me?" Hunter pressed.

The old man appeared pensive and tight-lipped at first as he stared ahead with his blank eyes while his stiff, weather fingers nervously toyed with one of the buttons to his sweater.

"Mr. d'Artusio?"

When finally the old man spoke, it was in his native tongue, yet despite the calm and measured tenor of his voice, it was clear to anyone listening that the words poured forth from a place of angst. Fear, even.

"I wish I knew what he saying," Wray, who along with Ty were the only ones amongst the group not equipped with the ears to translate what was being said, remarked aloud.

"He's telling of a night several months past when he was sitting just as he is now, enjoying his nightly cigar as he always does after dinner," Damiel stepped in to interpret as he slowly emerged from the background where he had lingered inconspicuously with his gaze fixed on the old man with a fiery raptness. "From out of nowhere, a man was suddenly standing in front of the house. A tall man; taller than any man he had ever seen or conceived of God having the power to stretch. Not only tall, but thin, exceptionally thin, like a rail, and covered in a long black overcoat. For a long time he did nothing, just stood with his back to the canal staring at the house.

"Suddenly, this tall man raised his hand in front of him and there came a loud and horrifying cracking sound," Damiel continued in his translation while his, along with everyone else's attention, remained transfixed on the old man as he told his story. "It sounded as if all the surrounding buildings were getting ready to crumble down upon me. And there came from deep within the earth a paralyzing rumbling so violent I was certain the ground beneath my feet was preparing to split apart and swallow me whole. That's when I saw the house—your family's house—slowly begin being crushed and twisted as if it were a sheet of paper being crumpled into a ball by some invisible giant hand."

The old man stopped abruptly to take a breath, and gather what remained of his wits that seemed to be ebbing at an ever faster rate the more he spoke. But eventually he managed to continue.

"The house was almost pulverized when I became so overtaken by fear that I screamed out for this sinister demon to cease with his evil, destructive deed," Damiel's voice resumed when the old man's finally did. "Whatever pittance of courage allowed me to set free the quivering cry perched upon my stiffened tongue I immediately cursed myself when he suddenly turned to face me and, to my horror, I saw this tall man dressed in a dark coat was truly indeed a demon. I saw him for only a moment, but his was a face one cannot erase from one's memory after witnessing it, even in the dark of night; it was like that of a snake, and his eyes lit up like two burning red coals when they caught sight of me, and the only thing I was certain of in that moment is that I was in the unfortunate company of some wicked creature that had somehow managed to claw its way through the gates of Hell.

"I wish I could say I stood brave in the face of such a sight, then again I doubt an army of brave men would have fared any better than I when the demon opened his mouth and released a terrifying cry, and with that merciless siren of a wail that made me all but want to tear my ears from my head all that remained of the house exploded and was sent my way in a hail of concrete, wood and shards of glass carried inside a searing ball of fire which hit me like a herd of angry bulls charging a red flag waved by a matador."

Mr. d'Artusio took a deep breath, and when he resumed speaking it was in his broken English that didn't require Damiel's accompanying interpretation. "It was only by some miracle from God that I somehow survived. I wish I could say the same about my sight."

"You're…you're blind?" Wray asked with quiet hesitation, though having it now pointed out it was sadly apparent, even with a canal separating them, that the milky gray pupils staring back with a glassy vacancy had been robbed of all function.

"Unfortunately, not completely," replied the old man. "The vision of what I witnessed that night is something even the blackness of blindness cannot obliterate."

"My parents…" Hunter suddenly muttered with an unmistakable sound of dread in his voice that matched the growing expression of horror etching itself more severely into his face as he listened to the old man speak. "Do you know what happened to my parents?"

Mr. d'Artusio's demeanor wilted suddenly with sorrow.

"My dear boy…do you mean to tell me all this time you haven't heard?"

"Heard what?" asked Hunter, yet the welling of tears in his eyes indicated he had a fair sense of what he was about to be told.

"Your mother…she was home at the time," Mr. d'Artusio began with all the care he could summon. "They found her a short distance from where they found me, buried in all the rubble. I'm sorry but she…she…"

Hunter didn't need to hear anymore and succumbed to a brief wrenching of sobs.

"And my father?" he attempted to ask in as unaffected a manner as he could manage while struggling to choke down the grief bubbling inside himself.

"No one has seen or heard from him since that horrible incident…even at your mother's funeral," answered Mr. d'Artusio. "I wish I could offer you solace, but, sadly, after all this time, I can only surmise his fate was the same as your mother's.

No one said anything more and all became unusually quiet except for the light splash of raindrops falling into the canal and the occasional creak from a small boat moored quayside nearby as it rocked gently upon the water. Jacob, who knew first-hand the inconsolable heartache of losing a parent, was the first to offer his silent condolence by placing a comforting hand on his newfound-friend's shoulder. And as Wray watched through her own teary eyes as the other boys, including Ty, followed suit forming a tight ring around Hunter, she asked aloud to no one in particular, "Who could do such a thing?"

The one other person at that precise moment who was clearly mulling the same question was Damiel, who remained standing just off Wray's right shoulder. And, as she repeated the question, he glanced back at the empty hole amid an otherwise perfectly intact row of houses in such a serene and benign neighborhood with a most unsettling look fixed in his eyes.

CHAPTER FIFTEEN

"**I** should have never left," Hunter muttered softly as he stared blankly at the view of the numerous boats making their way along the Grand Canal from the window of a hotel room in San Marco, where the group had retreated to decide on their next course of action.

You can't keep beating yourself up for what happened," argued Jacob.

"Why not? It's true," Hunter shot back angrily. "If I hadn't been so damn pious over learning that my father was a Fallen and run away like I did, then maybe I could have been there to protect my mother and she'd still be alive. They'd both be alive."

"Or maybe you'd be dead as well. Did you ever consider that very real and likely outcome?" Max chimed in.

"Besides, it's not for certain your father is even dead," Kairo was quick to point out. "All Mr. d'Artusio said was he hadn't been seen since the, uh, you know…accident."

"Of course he's dead," Hunter grumbled surlily. "My father may have been a Fallen, but he was fiercely protective, of both me and my mother. What happened to my mother could have only occurred if death got to him first. And if by some chance it didn't, he certainly wouldn't have left her to be buried alone."

In the silence that followed, Ty looked to Damiel and, with timid gingerly steps, he approached the angel in the same way a sightseer visiting a national park would a grazing stag in hopes of snapping a prized photograph.

"Excuse me, your grace…sir," he began with a bumbling awkwardness as he continued to find himself quite muddled at the reality of finding himself in the presence of a real-life angel. "But seeing as how you're like this all-knowing being, isn't there some sort of, I don't know…empyrean crystal ball you could consult on this whole matter?"

Damiel turned a curious gaze to the boy upon hearing such an anomalous address making Ty smile all the more nervously when he found himself in the sights of the angel's piercing golden eyes.

"Crystal ball?" Damiel repeated with puzzling intrigue.

"Forget the crystal ball part and how about we all just take a minute and consider the fact that the word 'empyrean' was just used in a sentence, and by Ty Wrenwood no less," mocked Jacob who could remember a time not long ago when Ty was called upon in class to explain the significance of the Horn of Plenty, only to detail with dead seriousness how it was blown by the Pilgrims to call the neighboring natives to the first Thanksgiving dinner, and was the forerunner to the triangle used in western days as a dinner bell.

Ty, ignoring the teasing jab, continued: "What I'm getting at is that it seems the mystery over what happened to Hunter's father can be put to rest by you just scooching on up to Heaven and asking the big guy upstairs what happened," he said, making a whistling gesture with his hand upward like a parent mimicking an airplane with a spoonful of food in hopes of coaxing a fussy infant into eating.

"I can only assume by 'the big guy upstairs' you are referring to my father," Damiel remarked, "though I can assure you the realm in which his house resides is a much far greater journey than a…'scooch.'"

The angel hadn't raised so much as an eyebrow, but the anticipation of his response—any response—was enough to cause the already anxious boy to drop fast to his knees before the last word left Damiel's mouth.

"I didn't mean to stir your wrath, most high power," Ty apologized with his head bowed low. "Please retract whatever lightning bolt you have aimed at me."

Damiel looked cluelessly to Jacob for some reasoning to explain the cowering demonstration taking place at his feet, but when all he received in return was an equally clueless shrug of the shoulders, the angel simply released a sigh of exasperation and turned to the others in the room to direct his thoughts.

"It is true angels such as myself are gifted with an extraordinary sense of perception and intuition, but all-knowing we are not. There is only one who possesses such insight, and that is the one who rules over all of us. But I can offer you this," said Damiel said, settling his focus squarely on Hunter. "Max, here, was quite right when he attempted to direct your sullenly sights to a brighter realization. Just as your blinded neighbor was blessed to see another day, it was by God's design and favor that he removed you from this place when he did, no matter the turmoil that caused the separation. The evil that paid a visit to your family home was one of particular malevolence and hostility I have not had the misfortune of crossing paths with in some time. Who it was, or why it came seeking out your family I cannot shed any light upon, except to say I could still feel its baleful energy seeping from the neighboring walls where your house once stood when I ran my hand across the sheered-off concrete. Take comfort when I say you would have fared no better than your mother, or the house that is no more, had you been there, and do not squander the grace my father has shown you with hate."

Hunter appeared to take Damiel's words to heart but it did little to bring any light to his demeanor, not that anyone in the room benefitted from any sort of lift from the shared gloom after hearing what they did.

"I guess there's nothing to keep me here any longer, so I should probably look at getting back home," Hunter said before turning to Jacob. "Sorry I wasn't able to help you find whatever it is you're looking for."

"Don't even sweat it," Jacob replied somewhat chagrined over Hunter's concern for his feelings considering his own much greater loss. "You sure you have go right this minute?"

"Don't see much reason for hanging around," answered Hunter. "They say you can never really go home again. Today, I found out how true that is. I think it best if I just push on."

Jacob didn't argue the matter any further. He may have known the pain of losing one's mother unexpectedly, but even he couldn't imagine returning to Cain's Corner and discovering everything he knew, and the house he lived in, had vanished into thin air.

"What about the rest of us?" asked Leos. "Where do we go from here?"

Max, Kairo and Ethan followed Leos' inquisitive gaze with their own to Damiel for direction.

"That decision rests entirely on Jacob's shoulders," answered Damiel, shifting the boys' attention to Jacob who looked caught off guard by the response.

"I haven't really given much thought to it," Jacob said after a moment. "It looks as though we've come a long way just to reach a dead end. Whatever the significance or meaning behind Thaniel's final words, I don't think we have much chance in finding out now, and maybe we never were meant to. So now I'm thinking the best thing to do at this point…is to head back to Havenhid."

He had no sooner spoken when he suddenly realized such a decision would shrink the group of travelers by yet another two persons and, filled with an instant coupling of guilt and dread, he immediately looked apologetically to Wray and found the same shared recognition reflected in her own eyes.

"It's alright…really," she managed to mutter through a forced smile. "I'm not quite sure the duties of a Nephilim, but I can imagine it's a jam-packed schedule. At least Ty and I can keep Hunter company on the flight back home."

She then quickly turned away and retreated to the far side of the room before Jacob could say anything further and before the tears welling in her eyes had a chance to spill down her cheek. The past few days had allowed her to see Jacob in an entirely whole new light; a light that offered a peek behind the sheer curtain of reality invisible to most people where angels tread, as well as demons, and where seemingly normal, average and everyday boys outfitted with wings and swords had enlisted to join in the battle between good and evil. Yet with such a glimpse also came the jarring realization that the curtain dividing the dual realities also served as a barrier denying her the freedom to follow. And much as she may have loved Jacob, the last thing she wanted to do was to force him to remain on her side of the curtain or distract him from what was undoubtedly his calling by twisting his heart, even it meant the breaking of her own.

It was while she was lightly dabbing her eyes in as inconspicuous a manner as possible to conceal any sign of sorrow of her and Jacob's imminent parting while listening to travel plans being made, that she happened to take notice of a shadow lurking just outside the room; a shadow whose suspicious movements were revealed by the light shining through the crack at the bottom of the door. Catching Wray further by surprise was the sight of an envelope being suddenly slid through the crack. Wray was rather apprehensive at first to pick up the rather large envelope, and even more so to open the door to the room to see who might have left it once she did. However, there was not a soul to be seen when she curiously, yet cautiously, poked her head out into the hotel's long hallway.

"Something wrong?" inquired Damiel at the sound of the door closing and then being bolted shut.

"Someone just slid this underneath the door," answered Wray, holding up the sealed envelope for everyone to see,

"Who's it for?" asked Jacob.

"It's not addressed to anyone. Should I open it?"

"Either that or you can try out your Carnac the Magnificent impression for us," Ty remarked dryly, drawing an unamused look from Wray in return.

"It looks like an invitation of some kind," said Wray, once she managed to unseal the envelope.

"Invitation? What sort of invitation?" asked Damiel.

"That I can't say. It's written in Italian."

"Lemme have a look," Max said as he stepped forward to offer up one of the many handy skills at his disposal as a Nephilim to decipher all written words no matter their origin in the same way his ears had the ability to instantly translate—and his tongue was able to speak—the hundreds of dialects from all around the world as though they were one common language.

At first glance of the invitation, Max was drawn to an image of a Bauta-style Venetian mask gilded in gold with its haunting black empty holes for eyes peering back from behind its expressionless face.

"Devoted Vavasours, you are hereby cordially invited to attend the Wurmtern Masquerade Ball," he began to read aloud as his eyes scanned the green embossed typography that seemed to radiate with a strange neon brightness from the thick black expensive parchment paper on which it was printed. "This masked affair will take place tonight in the elegant surroundings of the Chamber of the Great Council at the Palazzo Ducale."

"Devoted Vavasours? What's Vavasours mean?" asked Ty.

"It's a medieval French term used during the times of the feudal hierarchy. Specifically, it referred to a vassal whose allegiance was held by a powerful lord or baron," explained Damiel.

Kairo was the first to voice the obvious question that sprang to everyone's mind: "Who in their right mind would refer to their guests as vassals?"

"My guess would be someone with enough pull, like a lord or baron, to host a party at a place like the Palazzo Ducale," surmised Hunter.

"What's so special about the Palazzo Ducale?" asked Leos.

"The Doge's Palace, as it's more commonly known, is one of the premiere landmarks, if not thee premiere landmark of all Venice. The only party I've ever seen allowed within its walls in all my time living here are the countless parties of tourists who file through the entrance on any given day to look at the priceless works of art housed inside."

"A party in a stale old museum," Max mused indifferently. "Thanks all the same, but I don't think my faint heart could take the excitement."

His blasé comment drew a ringing of supportive chuckles from Ethan and Leos, and a glare of disapproval from Wray who reached out and snatched back the invitation from out of Max's hand.

"Typical boys!" she groused before her face softened as she looked over the invite once again with greater clarity now that she understood what it said. "I think the idea of going to a masquerade ball while in Venice sounds completely and wonderfully intriguing and romantic."

"Oh, I'm intrigued alright; intrigued anyone could find anything remotely romantic about an affair saddled with a name like Wurmtern." argued Max.

Wray paid little mind to his criticism, but as she continued to study the invitation, Jacob took notice of the familiar look of longing reflected in her eyes.

"You don't really want to go to this masquerade ball do you, Wray?" he asked her.

"Who me? Don't be ridiculous," she attempted to laugh off the question. "I mean, at another time I wouldn't necessarily be opposed to going. We are in Venice, after all. Who wouldn't be interested in experiencing the very thing that made this city so famous? It would kinda be like going to Pamplona and refusing to run with the bulls. But I also realize Ty and I have to start back home just as you have to leave with your friends."

As much as she tried to appear apathetic about the matter, she couldn't keep a glimmer of enthusiastic hope from surfacing within her doleful eyes when she pleaded suddenly, "Oh, please say we can go!"

Never one to stand in the way of Wray and her heart's desire, Jacob gave a sheepish glance over his shoulder to the rest of his traveling companions.

"We're so going to this masquerade ball, aren't we?" Ty asked, though it was more a statement of confirmation.

"Wray's got a point, wouldn't you say?" Jacob replied. "It would be kind of silly to have traveled all this way just to leave without at least taking a moment to enjoy the sights, don't you think?"

"And what about the decision we just came to regarding Havenhid?" Damiel quietly inquired.

"The day's already half shot. We can all leave first thing in the morning.

That will allow us to get a good night's rest and a chance to give each other a proper goodbye."

Looks were exchanged as a consensus on the proposal was silently debated.

"I'd be willing to stick around another night," Hunter was the first to voice agreement. "As a fellow Venetian, I guess I'm obligated to go to at least one of these balls in my lifetime."

"Sure, why not?" Max succumbed with easing reluctance. "How bad can a Wurmtern Masquerade Ball be, anyway?"

Even Damiel couldn't seem to summon the stony facade needed to resist Wray's pleading gaze, and quietly yielded his consent with a simple, if not begrudging, nod of his head much to her delight.

"Now that that's settled, we have to get a move on," Wray squealed with excitement as she quickly grabbed her coat. "We don't have much time."

"Time for what?" asked Jacob.

"To get our costumes, of course," she replied.

The expressions on the boy's faces dropped in unison as they slowly exchanged a look of marked dread with one another.

Costumes?

~ ~ ~

Following a frenetic, not to mention tooth-pulling excursion, with Wray leading a reluctant charge into a number of quaint street shops specializing in an array of Venetian masks and complimentary costumes, the group returned to their hotel with their arms loaded with the bundles from their shopping spree, only to reemerge not long after looking like a band of fugitive characters who had managed to crawl out of the very rabbit hole a golden- haired girl named Alice had once fallen into.

Hunter, cutting a rather mysterious yet dashing figure of a high seas buccaneer dressed all in black with brightly contrasting purple accents, and fitted with an ornamental mask of gold that looked to have been made from a couple handfuls of melted-down doubloons skimmed from a treasure chest, led the way to the water's edge of the Grand Canal to retain two gondolas for the night's transportation.

"Sembri incantevole," the gondolier stationed at the first boat offered his compliments to Wray who had transformed herself into a primped, powered and wigged Marie Antoinette, complete with a towering and elaborate coiffure of white curls and ostrich plumes.

Smiling, she took the gondolier's hand and stepped carefully onto the gently rocking boat, which threatened to be wholly consumed by the voluminous silver and white dress bedazzled with precious pearls and light-catching crystals that she wore. Taking a seat beside her, Jacob appeared anything but happy as he fidgeted and tugged at the breeches and, more specifically, the white tights underneath that became more binding the longer he wore his matching Louis XVI getup.

"I've been more comfortable in my stiff Sunday church clothes," he whined while shifting about in his seat.

"Look on the bright side," Ty's voice came from behind the creepy grinning white mask worn by the red-and-black-attired court jester who hopped into the boat alongside them. "You have the pleasure of sending her off to the guillotine as payback."

Wray shot him a grinning glare. "If it weren't for the fact that jesters are usually considered to be funny, I'd say your costume fits you to a T."

Jacob was hardly alone in his discomfort. Standing on the canal bank looking like some towering blue djinn in an elaborate Arabian sheik costume that was solidly periwinkle in color from the top of his turban-covered head to the upwardly curved points of his suede slippers, and adorned with numerous strands of pearls and other baubles, Damiel couldn't conceal the dissatisfaction of his own situation, even with the aid of the expressionless porcelain-white mask covering his face.

"I've witnessed every age of glad rags man has managed to stitch, knit and sew, from the shendyt skirts and headdresses worn by Egyptian pharaohs and tailcoats and starched ruffs from the Elizabethan era, to the more modern-day spats, bowling hats and tie-dyed shirts. This is by far the most ridiculous," the angel complained.

"What are you talking about? You look fantastic," Wray crowed in an attempt to assuage Damiel's conscientious mood.

"I look like a Persian version of a Smurf," Damiel grumbled with disgruntled defeat.

Unhappy as he may have been with his appearance, he nonetheless gathered together enough of himself to begrudgingly guide the curled genie slippers he wore on his feet to climb aboard the second gondola where Leos, Kairo and Ethan, huddled together like a trio of plague survivors with their matching long-beaked medico della peste masks, and Max, looking quite the elite gentleman of Venetian masquerade balls held centuries earlier in his embroidered waistcoat, ruffled cravat and powdered wig, but whose identity was concealed behind a mysterious bronze-colored wolf mask, were patiently waiting.

~ ~ ~

The two gondoliers, with their long rowing oars in hand, maneuvered their way a short distance along the calm waters of Venice's main waterway before guiding their twin vessels single file in a slow, leisurely glide down a narrow offshoot of canal named the Rio di Palazzo. The setting sun had bathed everything in brilliant golden hues cast forth in its final breaths, from the water and sky and all that resided in-between making this city of magic and mystery appear even more of a dreamscape than usual.

Beneath the several footbridges the gondolas drifted past, only one caught the attention of the passengers aboard the twin gondolas.

"The Ponte dei sospiri," Hunter said loudly enough so the parties on both boats could hear as they approached the exquisitely ornamental footbridge made of white limestone with two square windows fitted with lattice screens. "Or as it's more commonly known, the Bridge of Sighs."

"Bridge of Sighs?" echoed Wray, her eyes instantly alight with intrigue from behind the delicate lace mask that framed them.

"It was the name given the bridge by Lord Byron," explained Hunter. He then offered a short recitation by the fashionable British poet:

I stood in Venice, on the Bridge of Sighs;

a palace and prison on each hand:

I saw from out the wave her structures rise

As from the stroke of the enchanter's wand.

"Bridge of Sighs," echoed Wray once more. "I like that."

"Yeah, well, you likely wouldn't if you were the one making the walk across the bridge," said Hunter. "You see, the bridge connects the Doge's Palace with the Prigioni."

"What's the Prigioni?" asked Jacob.

"It's a prison, and those who were sent there almost certainly never left," Hunter explained. "Legend has it that prisoners being lead across the bridge to their waiting cells were known to sigh in despair as they caught their last glimpse of the beauty that was Venice, and freedom, from those two tiny windows."

Recognizing his bit of historic trivia had proven to be a bit of downer, Hunter quickly attempted to keep the mood afloat.

"There's also another legend associated with the bridge," he said.

"What's that?" asked Wray eagerly.

"It is widely believed any couple who passes beneath the bridge at sunset and shares a kiss while the bells of St. Mark's Campanile toll will be blessed with eternal love and happiness."

Wray looked to Jacob and beamed broadly at the idea, and her enchanted smile grew all the more when, as if by some strange turn of magic, a distant bonging of bells suddenly made itself heard.

"So do you think the legend is actually true or just a bogus myth made up for the sake of gullible tourists?" she asked Jacob.

"Only one way to find out," Jacob replied, and the two leaned in toward one another at the mythos' beckoning just as the shadow of the storied bridge cast itself upon the couple lovingly embracing as the gondola passed slowly beneath it.

"I'd be sighing, too, if I were a prisoner walking across the bridge, and the last thing I saw were the two of you playing tonsil hockey, only it would have been from the discomfort of trying to hold down my lunch," Ty commented with an air of nausea drawing a chuckle from both Wray and Jacob.

"Now that is a joke worthy of a court jester," Jacob lauded, while giving his friend a supportive slap on the back.

~ ~ ~

Soon after, the gondolas reached the end of the narrow canal and entered a large lagoon where the island of San Giorgio Maggiore could be seen residing upon the waters in the distance and came to a rest at the waiting quay. There, the gondoliers helped their costumed passengers out of the gently rocking boats and onto a large paved promenade, where the presence of the impressively colossal Doge's Palace greeted the group like the grand landmark it was.

The hordes of tourists that usually swarmed the popular area like bees to honey had vanished with the setting sun, and in their place other masked partygoers donning an array of whimsical costumes crafted from untold yards of rich, expensive fabrics, shiny, eye-catching baubles and wild imaginations were seen disembarking a growing number of various arriving water crafts crowded along the quay.

"I can't believe I'm actually in Venice and about to step foot inside a real masquerade ball," Wray squealed to Jacob with delight, as she eyed the arriving guests as they passed by in all of their over-the-top finery. "Have you ever seen such a stunning display of costumes?"

"I'm still too busy suffering the chaffing of a lifetime to notice," Jacob grumbled, as he continued to shift about uncomfortably and pull at his pants here and there.

Hunter, meanwhile, sidled up beside Max who was quietly taking in the first impression of the impressive palace.

"Not exactly the stale old museum you pictured it to be, eh?" he asked. Max answered with an indifferent shrug.

"Nothing to carry on about like a pork chop." he answered in reply.

The odd and completely unfamiliar phrase brought a curious frown to form on Hunter's brow. "Pork chop?"

"Just an old expression from back home. Means nothing to make a big fuss over," Max explained.

"I see."

"I have to say, I do quite fancy that lion up there," Max remarked, pointing to a large bronze statue of a winged lion perched high upon a nearby pillar.

"The Lion of Venice…he's come to serve as the very symbol of the city; a sort of mascot," said Hunter. "You'll see a few versions of him positioned around the palace."

"What's the big significance of the lion?" Kairo, who had been listening in along with others, asked.

"Legend has it, a group of Venetian merchants in 828 decided to steal the remains of St. Mark the Evangelist, one of the four apostles of the gospels who was interred in a church in Alexandria bearing his name, and bring them to Venice," said Hunter. "The merchants managed to successfully smuggle the bones back home by hiding the parts in barrels under layers of pig flesh, thereby easily bypassing Muslim inspectors horrified by even the sight of pork, as you could imagine, and immediately after, the city of Venice proceeded to build a proper burial site to house the holy remains. The result is St. Mark's Basilica which stands next to the palace, and the lion became the emblem of power symbolizing the city's patron saint."

"You sure know an awful lot about all the weird legends surrounding this city," said Ethan.

"My father was big on storytelling when I was growing up, and these legends, among others, were the stories he told me. Guess it all sort of remained stuck inside my head."

The mention of his father was quick to sully Hunter's mood which he attempted to cover by securing his mask back in place over his deflated face.

"If it's all the same to you, would you mind if we moved this conversation of pork barrels and stolen bones inside?" Damiel was quick to break up the awkward silence that followed, having taken notice of the dark cloud that once more settled itself over the young man. "It's bad enough being the risible sight I find myself to be at this moment; I don't care to voluntarily parade it in a public square."

The group joined the steady stream of other costumed guests making their way along the wide and spacious piazzetta serving as a gateway to the Doge's Palace. The open square was illuminated in the gathering darkness by several tall and ornate three-armed lamp posts sprouting at various points from the paver-stoned ground, and stretched along the entire length of the palace's immense fortress-like structure with its elaborate Gothic arches and herringbone-patterned outer wall. At the entrance to the palace, they paused in awe at the foot of a grand stone and marble staircase within the confines of a courtyard of almost lace-like arches, and the even more impressive sight of two colossal statues posed like guards opposite one another at the top of the landing.

"They're a little intimidating," Wray sighed with wonderment as she eyed the two imposing figures.

"That's pretty much the point of their being placed there, and why it was given the name Giants Staircase," said Hunter. "That would be Mars, the god of war on the left, and Neptune, the god of sea on the right; they were meant to represent Venice's dominion and power on both land and water. But more importantly their size was meant to diminish the figure of the doge during his coronation which took place inside this courtyard and serve as a stern reminder of Marino Falier."

"Who was Marino Falier?" Leos inquired, naturally. "Better yet, who or what is a Doge?"

"The Doge was basically the chief of state, and Marino Falier was the one disgraced Doge who was beheaded in this very courtyard for crimes of high treason. Those two," said Hunter, motioning to the statues that, even in marble form, looked fierce enough not to be toyed with, "made it clear to all future Doges that at the end of the day, despite what power they had, were just men, and like all men, subject to punishment for their actions."

Hunter suddenly became quite conscious of the eyes fixed attentively—perhaps too attentively—on him as he spoke.

"There I go again impersonating my father," he said blushing somewhat. "Sorry if I'm boring you all by rambling on."

"You're not boring at all. In fact, I find it all quite interesting," said Wray which only seemed to make Hunter redden all the more.

They proceeded onward with the rest of the guests into the palace where they came upon two more mythological statues perched upon twin pillars of marble—one of Atlas holding up the heavens, and the other of Hercules slaying the hydra—and a marble arched entryway leading to the steps of an equally, if not grander staircase than the one they had just gawked at moments earlier. Walking the steps of the sumptuous staircase, one could not help but find their feet slowing, as their eyes became transfixed by the numerous frescoes decorating the white stucco and gold gilded vault ceiling hovering above like an elaborate canopy.

The procession train eventually guided them through a pair of doors leading the way inside a room of stunning magnificence that stopped the company dead in its tracks. To begin with, the room wasn't so much a room as it was an immense stretch of space. Had the floor been made of artificial turf marked with large numbers painted in white, and twin goal posts been erected at either end of the mammoth room, it would have served quite adequately as an indoor field for a spirited game of football in lieu of a stadium.

Then there were the paintings.

Many, many paintings, almost too numerous to count, adorned every corner of the room and covered every inch of space of both the walls and ceiling. In fact, it appeared, at first glance, that the room itself was the construct of one ginormous painting broken up into various panels of different sizes by a complex gilded frame that wound and melded its way lei-like in a most decorative and elaborate fashion of scrolls, swirls and festoons.

Music throbbed and pulsated loudly in the air around them like a mechanical heartbeat courtesy of a costumed DJ hunched over his lit up computerized setup, and bobbing along to the recipe of rhythmic vibrations he was concocting. The group waded its way through the mingling crowd while attempting to take in the myriad scenes looming overhead of a Venice surrounded by gods and crowned by acts of heroism, valor and wartime victories eternally glorified by such famous artists as Veronese, Palma il Giovane, Francesco Bassano and Palma the Younger. Immediately below the ceiling, portraits stretching along a wall told the lineage of the numerous doges who once occupied the palace. Included in a rather strange and morbid way was Marino Falier, the ill-fated doge Hunter had earlier mentioned as having been beheaded, who was represented by a simple black cloth the palace had put in place of a portrait in a deliberate and effective attempt at the total eradication of his memory and name.

Yet fantastic as the works of art that enveloped the tremendous stretch of space in all their gilded decorative flourishes were, nothing could prepare them for the grand masterpiece that awaited them at the opposite end of the vast room when they eventually reached it. "Il Paradiso," the magnum opus of its creator, Jacopo Tintoretto, was overwhelming to behold both in size (it stretched the entire length of wall from end to end) and composition. Detailing the Annunciation of the Virgin Mary before a celestial audience of innumerable angels and other seraphic and heavenly dwellers, the ambitious painting was almost claustrophobic to behold in the roaring sea of divinity it unveiled, yet beautifully so. Even Max, whose initial impression of the palace had been lackluster to say the least, found himself standing before the massive painting with his mouth agape.

"Now that's the cat's pajamas," he conceded to himself as he stared with awe through the holes of his wolf mask and attempted to survey the painting that he quickly discovered was far too detailed for the eyes to take in all at once.

"They say it's the largest painting in the world," Hunter offered up from the nuggets of trivia he seemed to carry around in his pocket like so many coins.

The painting would likely have kept the troupe captive in their gawking for some time to come had it not been for the plentiful spread of food which had been laid out on a series of long tables nearby. Yet mesmerizing as the painting was, the mouthwatering mix of aromas coming from the buffet proved a stronger pull at the hungry, grumbling stomachs than the larger-than-life beatific vision was to the eyes. Everyone, that is, except Damiel who remained quietly transfixed where he stood like some odd blue statue.

"Something wrong?" asked Jacob who noticed a strange look in the angel's eyes as they peered out from behind the mask he wore, and yet seemed to be fixed on something far beyond the heavenly scene unfolded before him.

"There's something not quite right here," Damiel murmured in response. Jacob turned his attention back to the painting and gave a shrug.

"I mean…I'm sure it falls short in capturing what Heaven is really like in person but, to be fair to the artist, it's not like he was able to paint this from firsthand knowledge like, say, a sunset at the beach or a bowl of fruit. Still, you have to admit it's pretty spectacular."

"I'm not talking about the painting." A glint of gold revealed itself from behind Damiel's mask as he swiveled his head around and gazed out at the crowd. "Do you not sense it? There is something untowardly about this gathering."

Cool and calm as his voice was when he spoke, there was nonetheless a muted uneasiness in the angels' demeanor that didn't go unnoticed by Jacob.

"I don't sense anything out of ordinary. Just a bunch of people in silly costumes having a good time.

The boy's reply did little to relax Damiel's rigid posture, and before he could inquire exactly what got his angel's senses tingling, Wray had grabbed hold of his arm with two hands and attempted to drag him away.

"Come dance with me," she summoned with an enticing smile while pulling him toward the crowded dance floor.

Never one to enjoy putting his limited moves and two left feet on public display, Jacob was fast to plant his heels against the floor as though he were a cat being led to a tub of water for a bath.

"I was hoping to have a bite to eat first. I'm starving," Jacob protested honestly as he felt his stomach continue its grumbling symphony from inside his costume.

"One dance, please?" Wray pleaded adamantly. "You can eat afterwards."

Knowing resistance was futile, Jacob turned to Damiel one final time with a look of surrender.

"Stay vigilant," Damiel said before the two were pulled out of earshot from another and drawing a questioning look of concern from Jacob.

~ ~ ~

It didn't take long, however, for concerns of any kind to dissolve once Jacob found himself in the embrace of Wray's arms. While the other partygoers surrounding them on the dance floor gyrated and spun about to the energetic rhythm of the music being played and driving their movements, Jacob and Wray settled into a slow and easy sway with one another.

"If you would have told me a week ago that you and I would be dressed as we are now dancing at a masquerade ball in Venice, I would have thought you were crazy," Wray remarked as she glanced around at all the other couples near them before hugging Jacob just a little tighter to her. "I can honestly say this ranks in the top three most romantic moments in my life so far."

A delighted if not quizzical look came over Jacob.

"May I ask what the other two contenders were?" he couldn't help but inquire. Wray flashed Jacob a coy grin that only heightened his intrigue.

"The first would be when we slow danced together at the home-coming dance," she answered much to his surprise, and relief. "The other was when we danced in the middle of Rabble-Rousers after you returned to Cain's Corner from your secret sabbatical and begged my forgiveness."

Jacob flashed her a questioning look. "I would argue against your use of the word 'begged.'"

"You definitely begged," Wray said with a gleeful smile. "In fact, if I remember correctly, you were even waving a pitiful white flag."

"Don't remind me," Jacob, wincing painfully at the memory, groaned. "It's the one time I can look back and honestly say I looked more ridiculous than I do right at this moment."

Wray giggled briefly at the image still seared in her memory of Jacob standing at the entrance to the restaurant looking like a goofy if not lovable clown in a raincoat and matching hat, goulashes, swimming goggles, and holding an umbrella in a light-hearted attempt to make amends to her for abandoning her and Cain's Corner.

"I thought it was sweet," she assured him in a way that only her smile had the power to warm him. "All that's missing now is our song playing and this would be kismet."

"Not for me; it's playing inside my head at this very moment," said Jacob, drawing a sentimental look from Wray.

"Really?"

"What do you think my feet have been keeping time with?"

Jacob almost wished there was a way to remove the top of his skull like the lid of a pot to allow Wray to hear the throaty serenade of Stevie Nicks echoing inside his head. But, since he couldn't, he did the next best thing by positioning his mouth near her ear and humming along, much to Wray's delight, several bars of the chorus as best he could while they continued their slow sway on the dance floor. It wasn't long before he became aware of Wray's hands sliding their way unknowingly from his shoulders to the area of his upper back where the fold of his hidden wings began and his body grew suddenly tense and his humming stopped. Only this time he didn't pull himself free of her embrace as though he had been grazed with a hot poker as instinct had forced him to do in the past.

"Look," he began awkwardly, "we, uh, haven't really had much of a chance to be alone and talk about, uh, you know…things."

"What did you want to talk about?" Wray cooed with delirious happiness. The casual reply brought a puzzled frown to Jacob.

"Oh, I don't know…the growing threat of climate change; the creep factor of artificial intelligence; or my favorite: the fact that I can do a pretty spot-on impersonation of a Canadian goose just by taking off my shirt," Jacob ran through a list of topics with a sarcastic lightheartedness. "Take your pick."

"Personally, I don't find the idea of artificial intelligence all that creepy…as long as robots stay looking like robots and not made to look like wax figures come to life," Wray said, drawing an annoyed look from Jacob.

"I'm a Nephilim, Wray," he stated with a quiet seriousness. "I have a pair of wings hidden away under this getup, and it's not some costume I can just take off. You have to feel some kind of way about that."

A sobering, unsmiling look came over Wray and cast her bliss to the wind.

"You're right, I do feel a certain kind of way about all this, if you really wish to know," she replied staring deep into Jacob's eyes, and for a moment Jacob recoiled at ever having brought up the subject.

"The truth of the matter is I wasn't all that shocked to finally learn what it was you've been hiding from me all this time; who you really are."

"Who are you trying to fool?" Jacob questioned disbelievingly. "I saw the look in your eyes when I was forced to reveal my wings in Vegas."

"I also believed wholeheartedly in Santa Claus, growing up. That didn't stop my eyes from growing large with astonishment whenever I spotted him at Christmas time when my parents took me to the mall to visit him," argued Wray.

Jacob, however, wasn't easily convinced in Wray's acceptance, but Wray was quick to silence the skeptical sucking of teeth sound that escaped his mouth by pressing her finger firmly to his lips and still the shaking of his head with the simple instruction that he allow her the courtesy of hearing her through. When he reluctantly agreed, she reminded him of the night not too long back when they huddled together in his bedroom for a marathon viewing of horror classics on TV, and more specifically, the moment she discovered and read his journal.

"I can't explain the why or how exactly, but there was a ring of truth I tried but couldn't ignore as I sat reading page after page of your journal, even though what you wrote involved the most fantastic and unbelievable things: like churches with moving murals, and underwater passages leading to biblical gardens," said Wray. "I've always suspected you were a uniquely special person, Jacob Parrish; I think that's why I've always found myself so drawn to you. Only now I know just how uniquely special you actually are, and that your gift has a name: Nephilim."

"How do you do that?" asked Jacob.

"Do what?"

"Make everything so easy…as if what I've revealed to you is the most natural everyday occurrence; like that I suffer from athlete's foot?"

Wray's eyes searched the decorated ceiling above as if for an answer. "I don't know," she said finally with a shrug. "I guess that's what happens when one is a believer in stardust."

Jacob had long ago discovered the loving gaze staring back at him had the extraordinary ability to wrap itself around him like a pair of phantom arms, and he found himself once more entwined in the pleasing embrace. But this time he noticed an undertow of sadness slowly begin to surface within the emerald pools.

"What? What is it?" he asked.

She answered with a dismissive wave of her hand while attempting to shield what the delicate mask framing her eyes failed to with the other.

"I'm happy for you, please understand that," she said finally when Jacob made it clear with his insistent stare that he wasn't about to accept her nonresponse response. "It's just unfortunate it all has to end after tonight. Between you and me, that is."

"End? You mean like end end? Where'd you get that idea? Why does anything have to end?" Jacob, looking to be taken quite off guard by the remark, asked.

"For starters, I'll be heading back to Cain's Corner tomorrow. And you'll be going somewhere where I can't follow, even if I wanted to."

"That doesn't mean it's goodbye forever."

"And I hope it's not," Wray said with a buoyant if not half-hearted smile. "But the last time you left you were gone for nearly a year. God only knows how long you'll be away this time around."

Whether Jacob had not been aware of such likelihoods before this moment, or had consciously chosen to cast such unpleasant thoughts from occupying his head, hearing Wray address the elephant in the room stuck a pin in Jacob's mood.

"Don't get me wrong. The last thing I want to be is a Yoko Ono who drives a wedge between you and, well, Heaven, I guess," Wray was quick to argue when she noticed Jacob's eyes peering out from behind the peepholes of the mask he wore go blank with a sort of doleful glaze. "You obviously were put on this earth for a purpose of great importance, and I would never want to be responsible for standing in the way of you fulfilling that purpose. But that doesn't mean I wouldn't miss you; more than I think possible, even at this moment."

"And who says I have to make a choice…between you and my so-called purpose, that is?" Jacob posed the question to Wray as well as to himself. "I'm the product of an angel as are all my new-found friends, not to mention the countless others like us that are spread throughout the world. My guess is an angel's duties are a far bit more on the demanding side than us Nephilim, and if they're able to squeeze in a private life that includes a family of their own then there's no reason we can't either. I'm at least willing try if you are."

Wray said nothing in return except to stare deeply into Jacob's eyes with a glimmer of optimism glistening within her own, guarded as it was.

"Besides," Jacob was quick to add while flashing his own positive grin, "not to be a bragger or anything, but I am kind of a modern-day Superman."

The statement caused Wray's eyebrows to rise with dubious intrigue.

"You know…more powerful than a locomotive. Able to leap tall buildings in a single bound," Jacob explained in earnest. "With these wings I have, I'll never really be that far away. I promise!"

He managed to squeeze a giggle from Wray as he kissed her cheek and hugged her to him, but as soon as his face was shielded by her own profile of beauty, his cheerful smile instantly gave way to a look of intense seriousness as he found himself questioning his own assurances. Was there an air of finality surrounding the two teens that he couldn't see, even with his highly perceptive Nephilim eyes? Was this, in fact, the last dance the two would ever share together?

While pondering such troubling questions as he and Wray continued with their dance, Jacob happened to spy through the crush of other couples on the dance floor a man making his way through the crowd on the far side of the room. That is, Jacob assumed it to be a man, judging from the above average height and broad physique outlined by the floor-length cloak made of dense velvet, replicating the inky color of an even denser night, that was drawn close about him. The large hood pulled over the figure's head overshadowing the face, however, made it impossible to confirm any such presumptions.

Man or woman aside, there was nothing oddly peculiar about the figure that would serve to snag Jacob's attention, or anyone else's for that matter, especially considering that the ballroom was full of far more colorful and extravagantly costumed partygoers. Yet Jacob's gaze remained inexplicably glued to the faceless shape as it made its way casually through the crowd when, suddenly, as if sensing he was being watched, the cloaked figure turned and met the boy's inquisitive stare. Jacob instinctively narrowed his gaze in a strained attempt to catch a glimpse of the person wrapped within the cloak's drapes, and while the blackness residing inside the hood shrouded the face inside, it failed to conceal one telling clue: a gleam of golden brilliance reflected in the stare that fixed itself briefly on the boy.

~ ~ ~

The music abruptly cut to silence, drawing a collective grumble from the crowd.

"What is it?" asked Wray when quite suddenly there came a noticeable commotion near the entrance of the ballroom.

"I have no idea," Jacob mumbled in return before realizing she was not referring to his preoccupation with the mysterious cloaked figure with the tell-tale golden eyes he was craning his neck to keep in his sights as it quickly vanished into the crowd like a retreating shadow at day's end.

Suddenly, the room was overtaken by a small army clad in dark gray and ornate bronze-and-white-colored masks in the shape of goat heads with long, pointed, golden spiral horns covering their faces. They marched single-file, forcing the startled and confused crowd to part, much like the Red Sea did with the wave of Moses' staff, before spitting into two-line formations and quickly coming to attention before the presence of a most enigmatic late arrival who was revealed standing at the end of the procession.

The mysterious masquerader instantly wrangled the intense fascination and allurement of everyone in the room. He loomed large, wrapped in a magnificent cape with a dramatic high upturned collar made from the black feather quills plucked from no less than a thousand ravens. In fact, with his face concealed behind a resin-and-feather mask depicting most realistically that of raven, the caped figure at first glance appeared to be an oversized version of one of the ominous black birds. And for a split second, both Jacob and Wray were instantly revisited by the unpleasant memory they shared of the flocks of ravens and other birds which were transformed into hideous monstrosities by Infectors who had set out to attack them in Las Vegas.

The grand room quickly returned to life with the buzz of whispers, and curious eyes ogled the mysterious masquerader when finally he proceeded to make his way along the pathway cleared by the goat-headed troop now facing one another in stony silence. His striking cape with its waxy feathers catching the surrounding light like thousands of dull sequins became all the more eye-catching with every step he took as its lengthy train slowly unfurled itself and bled across the floor for a good ten feet in his wake, making him appear as if he was an oil freighter run aground and hemorrhaging its cargo into the open sea.

"Now, that's what I call an entrance!" Jacob glanced over his shoulder at the sound of Kairo's voice coming from behind the familiar long-beaked plague mask and saw his traveling companions had regrouped just behind him straining to get a gander through the eyeholes of their disguises at the curious spectacle that had entered the hall with such unabashed flair.

"It's like something you'd expect if David Bowie and Skeletor ever had a child," came Ethan's muffled comment from behind an identical hook-nosed mask both Kairo and Leos wore before his gaze shifted to Hunter who was standing beside him. "So, is he one of those…what did you call them? Doges?"

"You're a real drongo sometimes, you know that? There aren't any more Doges," Max was quick to chastise Ethan while giving him a stinging flick to the ear with his finger before also looking to Hunter with an equally uncertain gaze and asking, "There aren't any, right?"

"Not for more than 200 years now," answered Hunter.

"Like I said," Max grumbled at Ethan self-assuredly.

"Then who do you suppose it is?" asked Ethan.

"My guess…the host of this shindig," Hunter replied.

Following closely behind the hem of the long trailing feathered cape as it swept the floor of its owners footprints was a rather inconspicuous character who, for one reason or other, didn't seem to attract much notice from anyone in the room, though he most deservedly should have. To begin with, he was exceptionally tall which, by itself, wouldn't have been all that eye-catching if it weren't coupled with the fact that he was also exceptionally thin. He was dressed in a silver robe and a matching headdress traditionally worn by wealthy Arabian men while a plain expressionless mask which was also silver in color covered his face. Like the cape he followed, he seemed to glide across the floor rather than walk with any sort of decipherable gait, and he appeared to be holding something quite guarded in both his hands, which were oddly grayish in color and positioned one on top the other. Whatever it was nobody could see, if, in fact, anyone was looking, which no one was. But even if every eye in the room conspired for a peek, they would have failed, for both of the hands cradling the shielded object were quite large, only to be outdone by the unnaturally long and spindly fingers they possessed.

~ ~ ~

As he reached the front of the great hall, the party's host's feet slowed, as most visitors' feet were prone to do, while approaching the massive marvel of the painting that had earlier held Jacob and his friends transfixed. He stood with his black skull eyes focused specifically and solely on the image of the Virgin Mary being glorified by the son of God, captured against a sunburst of divine light, and he said not a word for a moment or two.

"It is a widely accepted belief that when God made man he did so in his image," he said when finally he spoke. "I am here to tell you such axiom is fallacy. Man bears no more resemblance to God than a fly to an eagle. What he created was a new breed of species—the Worthy and the Unworthy—and arranged them in such a way on this checkered board of life he concocted like so many chess pieces, then sat back to enjoy the ensuing follies like some Roman seeking amusement at his own private coliseum games. But all that is about to change, as I am here to let each of you know this night that a quite unexpected move is about to be played that will turn the tables on this one-sided game.

He turned his upper body suddenly to peer out at his crowd of guests from behind the black plumes of the flared collar of his trailing cape, appearing like some strange hybrid from a lab experiment that successfully saw the fusing together of a cobra's body with the head of a raven.

"The tradition of masquerade began in this very city more than eight hundred years ago as an opportunity for the populace to vent their pent-up tensions and discontentment. Flamboyant costumes provided the ability to completely hide one's identity for a night in a world where identity is proven to be either an advantage, or barrier. These masks, in particular, as you all have so cleverly demonstrated, have proven a most useful gift of concealment, allowing the Unworthy to roam amongst the Worthy undeterred," the host continued while running the tips of his fingers gently along the side of his own disguise. "Ours, however, is a masquerade hinged to desires that far exceed the pedestrian malfeasance and libertines that so easily gratify the blinkered, and I tell you a new dawn is creeping upon the horizon; a dawn of reconciliation, when the masks finally fall away, and the Unworthy are suddenly the Worthy."

With those words, the host turned once again to the ecclesiastical painting as a burst of applause roused itself from the gathered guests, and there came from the hollowed black- filled eye sockets of the raven mask, a wink of gold-tinged light. And with that glare of light the upper portion of the painting began to smolder and smoke, and the image of the Blessed Virgin and her son was slowly eaten away and turned to scattered flecks of ash as if by some unseen flame.

"Did you see that? Did you see what just happened to that painting?" Ethan gasped while staring with appalling disbelief at the black stain that now scarred the painting.

All eyes of the group shifted instinctively to Damiel whose sudden disconcertion couldn't be hidden even behind the cloak of his costume, but he was quick to hold up a hand in a hushing gesture before a single syllable could to be lobbed his way. *Who was this masked desecrator?* he found himself asking quietly inside his head as his own gaze attempted to bore its way into the figure wrapped in the oversized cape of feathers. *And just what kind of gathering had he and his young charges found themselves standing in the midst of?*

Suddenly, the host turned his head halfway to his shoulder as if some strange sound had found its way inside his ear and, for a moment, Damiel wondered if his unsettling thoughts had somehow echoed loudly enough inside his head to make themselves heard.

"I detect a note of reservation within these walls," said the host. "Perhaps you'd care to make your concerns known to the rest of us, Artur."

The clamor of applause quickly faded as heads swiveled and focused immediately on the one amongst them dressed like an embellished character from a Dickens novel wearing a snow-white lions mask beneath a decorated top hat whose hands had remained at his sides.

"Concerns, sir?" the taken aback guest managed to croak with noticeable nervousness when he found all eyes in the room to be suddenly fixed upon him.

"My ears couldn't help but notice your refrain of favor to my address." The host followed Artur's furtive glances at the insulting modification done to the painting. "Perhaps you find my artistic whims to be a bit on the objectionable side for your taste."

"Not at all," Artur was quick to contest, almost desperately. His voice held a noticeable Russia accent that all but betrayed the anonymity he sought behind the mask he wore. "It's just...it's a bit disconcerting to watch a beautiful painting be altered in such a way; especially when that painting has stood as one of Europe's greatest masterpieces."

The host, however, appeared to pay no mind to the dismay heard in his voice. "How fortunate it is for you, then, that you were not alive to witness the complete destruction of this very room and everything in it down to the last painting by a horrific blaze in the sixteenth century which caused far more revisions than my small, playful touchup."

Artur gave a subordinate nod in reply and had planned to say nothing further, but his tongue waggled unexpectedly before his teeth had a chance to clamp down on it.

"May I speak freely?"

The host didn't answer which only seemed to make the strip of skin above the man's upper lip glisten all the more with nervous beads of sweat.

"We have all of us used the positions given us in this life to do your bidding as best we can," said Artur. "Tonight you spoke of a dawn of reconciliation. But many here present, myself included, suspect a mutiny rather is at hand."

"Can you think of a swifter, more precise method of reaching reconciliation than through an act of insurrection?" queried the host.

A stark quietness uncommon amongst such a large gathering descended upon the hall in the moments that followed except for the rustling coming from the host's long flowing cape being dragged across the floor as he strolled about with slow pensive steps.

"A kingdom without a king is as functional as a ship afloat a stagnant ocean absent the wind to fill its sails," said the host after a thoughtful while. "You have all been passengers aboard such a stalled vessel, and I have languished for far too long as a king in search of an empty throne. But together we are about to create a stirring in the water, and the guiding force of the returning currents will soon hug the keel."

Jacob and the others in his group could not make heads or tails of the cryptic conversation taking place before them. Still, they listened on intently hoping that from the continuing flow of words being spoken, a nuance of comprehension would eventually allow itself to be grasped. Yet the more was spoken about kingdoms, and ships, and motionless oceans, the more marked became their confusion.

"There's just one small problem," a voice rang out, shifting the attention of the room from Artur to someone who looked as though he were about to take to the stage of a Shakespearean play. "The throne you eye is not vacant. Why should any of us risk willfully to expose our necks like a rafter of turkeys right before Thanksgiving by aiding in your ambitions?"

The host's eyes peering out from behind the raven mask fixed themselves uncomfortably on the gutsy man who dared to step forward and question him in such a manner.

"Why, indeed?" he mused quietly. Then, with both hands, he reached up to grasp the mask he wore and slowly removed it to reveal the true face hidden behind; a face of distinguished youth and beauty. Yet it was a beauty that was greatly disfigured by a cold and forbidding unseen presence emanating from the otherwise pleasant features, much like the bejeweled skull mask that had previously concealed it.

"Miseriel!"

Jacob heard the name being spit from Damiel's lips, and when he looked to the angel he saw behind the mask covering Damiel's face a pair of burning eyes.

"You know him?" Jacob whispered.

"I should say so," Damiel replied as he struggled to keep both his phlegm and feet in check. "He's the one responsible for the death of my son."

~ ~ ~

While Damiel and the rest of the room stood transfixed by the visage of the unmasked host, albeit for different reasons, an altogether different sight was the cause for Hunter's eyes to grow unexpectedly wide. It was that of the host's sheik-attired escort who had so far gone virtually unnoticed amid the revels of the night, which most likely would have continued, had Hunter not glanced his way by mere chance and caught sight of that whcih had been kept so guarded in the man's tight, long-fingered clutches.

To his utter astonishment, Hunter saw it was another of those strange and mysterious containers he had stealthily snaffled from its equally strange and mysterious owner in London; the same kind of peculiar object he had spent day after day locked away inside his loft trying like some kind of mad scientist to come up with some manner or method in which to destroy the seemingly unbreakable whatsit and failing at every attempt. It also made Hunter quick to recognize something he found to be quite unnerving: that the person behind the silver mask and flowing headdress wasn't just some merrymaker invited to the party, or even a particularly reserved companion relegated to bringing up the train of the host's overly long cape like some dutiful bridesmaid. Indubitably, it was one of those horrifying Pethens he had experienced the great misfortune, and even greater displeasure, of coming face to face with firsthand. It was with that knowledge, pulsating like a heartbeat at the front of his brain, that Hunter watched with an intent curiosity as the masquerading Pethen quite oddly—and with noticeable apprehension— relaxed its tight grip of the object he clutched so possessively in his hands and, for whatever the reason, set it down on a nearby table. And as Hunter watched the Pethen do the unthinkable and step away from the puzzling relic so, too, did Hunter take quiet leave of his friends and slink away as inconspicuously as possible into the cover of the crowd.

"If there is one thing I have found more vexing about mortals than their inconstancy and unearned entitlement, it's when a vavasour is remedial in recognizing that he, or she, is indeed a vavasour,"

Miseriel was heard to speak again after a long thought-filled pause that followed the removal of his mask.

No one present seemed to know who exactly their host was referring to as a "vavasour," nor did they need to, as it was made imminently clear by the chorus of screams and squeals that erupted from the crowd in a clamorous burst when, suddenly, out of nowhere, the Pethen set upon the partygoer who had dared question the host in the same manner a cat is prone to pounce upon an unsuspecting rodent. The man's eyes all but bugged out through the peepholes of his mask when the Pethen grabbed him with one hand by the throat and slowly lifted him from off the floor.

"I must say, your fixation on the delicate region of the body that connects head and body is intriguing in nature, yet not all that surprising," Miseriel, appearing quite unbothered and, in fact, rather amused at the sight of his guest gasping for air while dangling from the Pithen's crushing grip, said. "If memory serves, you've sliced and diced your way through your fair share of throats in your time, haven't you? Three former wives, and all quite wealthy to boot as well, if I recall correctly."

"What's that you say?" the host whispered while leaning in with an exaggerated look of concern as the gasping man flailed about in an attempt to form a comprehensive word. "But of course you'd have never dared to entertain the sheer idea of committing such heinous and unspeakable crimes. Finding a jury, however, who wouldn't send you straight to the gallows was an entirely different matter altogether now. And it was why, for the safety of your own highly regarded neck, you sought out my assistance in that very matter, wasn't it? But more on that in a moment."

Miseriel left the man to continue fighting for his breath and redirected his focus back onto Artur.

"Back to the subject of mutiny," Miseriel began with his thin slanted mouth offering the hint of a grin while his cold intimidating eyes reflected quite the opposite. "You are quite versed on the topic, aren't you Artur? After all, it wasn't that long ago I discovered you cowering quite pitifully in the dark confines of a safe house, wasn't it? Then again, when a man of great power as you one day discovers his position on the food change has suddenly shifted and becomes the target of an assassin's bullet, it's hard to live life much beyond that of a nervous squirrel poking its head out of its burrow for a peak of sunlight and hoping to avoid the claws of a waiting hawk. But now, thanks to me, you've been given the gift to once more journey out of your hole without the need for eyes in the back of your head, wouldn't you agree?"

The words Miseriel spoke were true; in his day, Artur Volkov was a man who had earned quite a commanding, if not questionable reputation in his Russian homeland. It was the kind of enviable repute that would eventually lead him to know firsthand an unforeseen act of betrayal carried out by the ambitions of those closest to him. Now, suddenly, this night, he recognized the unmistakable sight of such ambitions deep-set in Miseriel's handsome yet callous face staring back at him, and so desiring nothing more than to be free of the glare of the golden eyes boring its way through his flesh and to his very bones, Artur very quickly and with uncharacteristic obedience nodded agreement.

Satisfied with the subservient response, Miseriel moved on and randomly turned his attentions to other invited guests who rather hoped such luck would pass them by. First, there was a portly gray-haired fellow dressed like a glitter-coated Friar Tuck.

"You I saved from a humiliating, if not justifiable, defrocking by the holy church itself," said Miseriel. "It was by my hand that you came to trade your bishop's hat for the scarlet mozzetta of a Cardinal and enjoy the pomp surroundings of the Vatican."

"And I bless you for your benevolence," the grinning priest replied while raising an oversized golden goblet filled with wine of which he had obviously been imbibing.

The gesture, and more pointedly, the salute, drew a scowl from Miseriel who turned his grazing look elsewhere before falling upon an elegantly gowned petite woman with a pair of twisting horns more suitable for a mountain goat fixed to the top of her head.

"And you, Montserrat, speaking of kingdoms sought," he said to her, "secured with my aid the presidential throne of a country engulfed in the chaos that comes with the deposing of a regime."

The woman of South American descent bowed her head in response and batted appreciatively the dark fringe of lashes of her large almond eyes peering demurely through the delicate web of lace that was her mask.

"You have all—each and every one of you standing within the four walls of this unduly prettified room—been beneficiaries of my discretionary magnanimity," Miseriel gestured with an exaggerated sweeping motion of his hands to the crowd before him, the tenor of his voice booming from one end of the room to the other. "I wish I could say my generosity was an expression of the purest form of altruism but, alas, such displays are just not in my nature."

A grumbling of alarm was heard to escape from the crowd when, suddenly, a half dozen or so billowing contrails of blackness resembling smoke appeared to penetrate the ceiling at various points. The sight of the dark anomalies crisscrossing their way overhead like small war planes streaking across the sky after being dealt a fatal blow by enemy fire, caused wide-eyed looks of fear in the partygoers that even the masks they wore failed to conceal.

"Tell me those aren't what I think they are?" Ethan pleaded under his breath as he stood frozen with fear, cautiously following the smoking plumes dart about overhead with his rolling eyes.

"They're not what you think they are," Leos answered to placate his friend before quickly adding, "if what you think they are is anything other than Infectors."

"By Infectors, you're not suggesting they are the same kinds of Infectors we had the displeasure of crossing paths with in Las Vegas in the form of those hideous dogs and birds' are you?" Ty asked suddenly concerned.

"I'm not suggesting any such thing; I'm stating it as out-and-out fact," Kairo replied, offering zilch in the enlightenment department.

"What do we do now?" Max voiced aloud the foremost question on the tip of everyone's tongue.

"Remain calm; that's what you do," Damiel answered coolly. "And have your swords at the ready."

"And, uh…" Ty was quick to chime in, "what about for those of us who don't necessarily have that last option available to us?"

His nervous inquiry went unanswered as Miseriel's voice made itself heard once more.

"To be clear, I am not here hat in hand in hopes of earning the continued advocacy and backing I require from all of you at this particular juncture," he said. "You have all signed over ownership of your souls, and I am the sole title keeper of each and every one. That I made sure of when we sealed our compact."

For a brief moment, the presence of the circling Infectors were forgotten as the host's words brought a collective look of dire grimness from those being addressed.

"Now, I understand all about second thoughts, shifts in viewpoint, regrets even, trust me I do," Miseriel said in a soft, almost comforting voice. "Being bound in shackles can be an unjust, nay, even cruel inconvenience, but the chains of my thrall come with a generous amount of slack. You are free to question my motives as you wish; you may even find yourself resistant to what I demand of you. But do not think for one moment your mortal penchant for free will is to be exercised here."

As Jacob listened to the host's unfolding speech with the rest of the guests and trying to understand what exactly he was hearing all while keeping an attentive eye on the unsettling presence of the Infectors looming overhead, he inadvertently took notice of something quite unexpected that made his eyes widen. That unexpected something was Hunter who had snuck his way through the crowd to the other side of the room.

"What's he think he's doing?" Jacob murmured aloud to no one in particular.

"What's who doing?" Wray whispered in response.

Jacob gave a subtle nod in the direction where his gaze was firmly fixed, and both Wray and Max, who stood beside them within listening distance, quickly shared in their friend's staggered expression at seeing Hunter who was now creeping his way discreetly toward the table where the Pethen had set down the object he had carried with him so possessively.

"I thought we had all come to understand the terms of this arrangement of ours," Miseriel continued as he once again turned his focus on the guest who had all but gone limp in the Pethen's chocking grasp. "Of course, there are methods at our disposal to bring any lingering insubordinates in line that are quite effective.

At that, the guest's bulging eyes went from being filled with the discomfort of the painful crush of the Pethen's hand clamped around his throat, to mirroring abject fear when one of the smoking phantoms flying overhead was motioned to by Miseriel and descended suddenly. The sight of any Infector was unnerving enough at a distance; to look closely at the ghoulish and merciless features that formed the wicked face hidden inside the hood of the black shroud in which it was wrapped as it hovered just inches above was beyond terrifying.

"Please...no!" the man, trembling visibly with fear, pleaded. "I'll do anything you ask of me."

The pathetic capitulation caused a smile of upmost gratification to slowly unfold itself beneath Miseriel's nose. "Yes...I know you will."

The Infector, however, didn't show any signs of retreating. On the contrary, it moved in all the more closer, and as it did, its unsightly face twisted itself into an even more depraved and execrable vision, if that were possible. The man squeezed his eyes shut tightly and reluctantly surrendered to the inevitable. Yet just before the Infector could carry out the fouling undertaking the nefarious entities were set upon mankind to commit, the Pethen's attention turned abruptly and quite defensively to the table where he had left the artifact he had guarded so in his hands, and his hidden eyes instantly flared with rage at the sight of Hunter who had snuck his way through the crowd to the other side of the room and was about to swipe the precious object like the good burglar he had proven himself to be in the past.

And from behind the silver mask covering his face there came a horrifying bellow that shook the ballroom.

CHAPTER SIXTEEN

"**W**hat have we here?"

One could have heard a pin drop on the ballroom floor when Miseriel spun around to see what had so enraged the Pethen and caught sight of the figure dressed in an elegant pirate costume frozen in place with his hands inches away from taking possession of the precious object where it had been left unattended on the table.

"It looks as if our den has attracted an unexpected thief," the host noted in an unusually calm and collected manner that was polar opposite of the seething Pethen.

Hunter felt his blood run cold for a moment or two, though he wasn't quite certain whether the icy chill of unexpected dread that had momentarily turned him to stone was the result of the incensed Pethen who appeared on the verge of charging forth like a bull set loose from its corral and ripping him limb from limb, or that of the unruffled host whose calm and collected demeanor strangely threatened to do far worse.

Ultimately, his wits told him the man in the black feathered cape was the one to keep a cautious watch over; for in all the entanglements Hunter had in the past with the numerous Pethens he purposefully crossed paths with, he never witnessed anything or anyone powerful enough to make the volatile beings heel like a circus animal. And yet, with a simple, barely noticeable flick of his wrist, Miseriel stopped cold the onslaught on fury focused on the young man, drawing a disagreeable grumble from the Pethen as he rerooted himself to the floor where he stood. But not before he let loose another wall-shaking bawl and hurled the guest who had gone limp in his grasp across the room the same way one discards the core of an apple.

"He's some kind of dill, he is," Max charged exasperatingly under his breath as he and the rest of the group looked on with alarm at the unexpected predicament their new-found friend had suddenly thrust himself into. "I'm talking a Grade-A lunatic."

"We just watched a man get thrown across the room like a rag doll," Wray replied in a huff. "I'd say that puts him in the psychotic category."

"I was talking about our friend Hunter," Max made clear.

"Hunter?" Why would you say that?"

"Why would I say that?" Max echoed incredulously. "Here we are like a bunch of sitting ducks while Infectors are circling above us like a flock of vultures and Mr. Sticky Fingers decides now's the perfect time to commit larceny, and in a room full of witnesses no less."

"Mr. Sticky Fingers? How can you accuse him of such of thing?" Wray balked under her breath.

"What would you call it then, if I may inquire?"

"Yeah…what would you call it, Wray?" echoed Jacob who felt a tinge of jealousy stir inside him at hearing Wray come to Hunter's defense in such an adamant way.

"I can't believe either one of you," scolded Wray in the harshest way her whispery voice would lend while eyeballing each boy standing on either side of her with a disapproving scowl. "Hunter's been nothing but nice and obliging to all of us, even traveling half way around the world just to help you sort through your reoccurring dreams. And how do you pay him back? By assuming the worst about him when I bet all he's really guilty of is plain old curiosity."

The contrite look that briefly found Max quickly morphed into one of puzzlement.

"Curiosity?" he bleated. "We're in a museum filled with priceless artifacts. What's to be curious about that little old doodad he's nearly got his fingers stuck to?"

"Then by your own argument, if that little old doodad as you call it isn't even worth a moment's attention, it certainly isn't worth stealing, now is it?" countered Wray with a judgy glare.

Wray's riposte left Max momentarily dumbstruck, but it was the return of Miseriel's voice that stuck a pin in their squabble.

"I once heard a saying that clothes don't make the man; the man makes the clothes. Looking at you, I find myself debating whether your disguise is a true reflection of the person hidden inside, or is it the other way around? My guess is such a maxim could swing either way where you're concerned," the host commented while giving Hunter's choice of costume a slow looking over. "That said, I've yet to come across an intrepid marauder daring enough to even contemplate stealing an item of personal importance as your itchy little fingers were about to appropriate and abscond from my companion, much less attempt such a feat; which has me wondering quite curiously if you are a uniquely brave thief, or a remarkably stupid one."

Hunter stood quiet for a moment or two, uncomfortably captured in the burning inquisitive glare of both the host and the Pethen, when a nervous chuckle escaped from behind the expressionless mask he wore.

"Thief? You think I was trying to steal this…this…whatever it is?" he feigned cluelessness while gesturing to the strange canister-like object that remained on the table.

"Weren't you?"

"I wouldn't be much of a marauder, as you called me, if I chose this moment in time to commit larceny, now would I? And in a room full of witnesses no less," said Hunter, causing Wray, Jacob and Max to exchange staggered looks with one another at the familiarity of the words used in his defense.

"Truth of the matter is I couldn't help but notice earlier how protective your, uh, companion was with this, er, thing. It looked to me like the atmosphere in here was tilting towards getting a little out of hand," Hunter motioned first to the area of the room where the guest who had suffered a slow strangling in the Pethen's squeezing clutches was tossed, "and then with the a…," he rolled his gaze upward where the Infectors were holding court. "All I was intending on doing was being a good Samaritan and moving it out of the way of possibly suffering any accidental breakage."

"Besides," Hunter was quick to add, "have you forgotten where we are? No offense or anything, but if I really was a thief as you think I am, why would I trouble my so-called sticky fingers with that little old doodad when we're in a museum filled with priceless artifacts?"

Jacob, Wray and Max took the same breath of surprise when they spied Hunter's eyes peering out from behind his mask glance their way and shoot them a naughty wink, making it quite clear that his Nephilim hearing had caught every word of their whispered back and forth.

"You're a shrewd one; I'll give you that," Miseriel said in response.

Stepping slowly closer, he became squinty-eyed with ever-growing intrigue at the undeniable, if not unexpected charm emanating from behind the gold expressionless mask.

"I've never been one to forget a voice that's addressed me, yet yours I find to be distinctly unfamiliar. And since this gala is an invitation-only affair for guests I personally hand-picked, I find that to be more than a little odd," said Miseriel. "Remove your mask so that my eyes might find the recognition lost to my ears."

Hunter felt the uncomfortable icy sensation that had earlier invaded his veins return upon hearing the request, though he did his best not to show it.

"I'd rather not, if it's all the same," he demurred politely. "Like you said, the whole point of a mask at a masquerade ball is to offer a means to conceal one's identity. You know... where the Unworthy are given free reign to mingle with the Worthy."

He had barely gotten the last word of his sentence off his tongue when his mask was inexplicably peeled away from his face by some unseen force and sent sailing through the air and into the waiting grasp of Miseriel's outstretched hand, as though it were a piece of metal caught in the pull of a strong magnet. And, when Hunter's face was brought into the light for all to see, the Pethen reacted with an incensed wail, but it was nothing like the united high- pitched yowl from the Infectors that was almost too horrible for anyone with two ears to bear.

NEEEPHILIIIIIIMMMMM!!!

"Well, well, well...you are nothing if not full of surprises," Hunter heard Miseriel mutter from behind a grin better suited for a cat licking its paws while lying amid the scattered fluff of feathers from its latest kill.

Then, after motioning to both the Pethen and the Infectors for abrupt silence, he addressed his guests with a grand gesture of his arms and announced in a loud commanding voice, "It's not often that a member of the Worthy class purposefully chooses to dirty his shoes for a night of slumming with us miscreants, yet tonight we've been graced with such an honor."

It was bad enough to have the menacing gazes of the Pethen and Infectors bearing down upon him, but to suddenly have hundreds of eyes glowering at him from behind a sea of masks made Hunter feel like some kind of cornered animal.

"Please, do not take offense that your presence has failed to receive a more welcoming reception," Miseriel apologized. "But, you see, here the Worthy are seen as the truly Unworthy. Unfortunately, I hate to tell you how Nephilim like yourself are looked upon, but I think the Infectors have given you an adequate idea."

With that, the lurking Infectors shook the room with their baleful chorus.

NEEEEEEEEEPHILIIIIIIMMMMMMMM!!!

~ ~ ~

"This whole situation keeps going from bad to worse with every passing second," Kairo whispered, as Wray held her hands over her ears to muffle the grating screams of the Infectors.

"You can say that again," Ethan agreed.

"I feel like we ought to do something," Leos chimed in.

"I agree…like sneak out of here while no one is paying any attention to us," suggested Ethan.

"What? And leave Hunter behind to fend for himself?" Leos balked.

"You just saw the reaction Hunter got when it was revealed to everyone that he's a Nephilim. Can you imagine the response when they discover a whole gang of us has crashed their party?"

"Leos is right," Jacob argued quietly. "Hunter's our friend, and as I learned in the Silent Forest one night not too long ago, friends don't leave friends in a lurch."

Max gave his friend a sideways glance from behind the holes of his mask. "And what exactly do you suggest we do? A reenactment of the Charge of the Light Brigade?"

"I don't know," Jacob answered as he turned his brain over several times inside his head while looking to the rafters where the Infectors were gathered like a pack of strays with their attention fixed on Hunter, and waiting for their moment to strike. "But we've got to do something before this gets out of hand."

"Before?" Ethan squealed. "You mean to say this doesn't meet your threshold for out of hand right now?"

"It's going to get far worse, and I fear far quicker if you keep on with your incessant yammering back and forth," grumbled Damiel, who had patiently been listening to the whispered powwow taking place beside him.

"Now mind my words. You will do nothing but stay put and cool your heels where you stand," he ordered in a tone that offered no room for disagreement. "And clear your thoughts, if you know what's good for you," he was quick to add. "Infectors can hear more than that which spills from loose lips."

They knowingly obeyed and quickly scrubbed clean the insides of their heads as one would wipe down a blackboard in school, and they watched Damiel proceed to make his way as discreetly as he could through the crowd of guests, not knowing what the angel had hidden up his sleeve, before the sound of Miseriel's voice took hold of their attention once again.

"I sense an unusual weight of pluck within you," Miseriel observed as he continued to study Hunter with even more intrigue, now that the young man had been unmasked. "Shame to waste it feeding the Infectors, hungry as they might be."

Hunter gave the frightful menaces positioned threateningly above an unavoidable glance and, indeed, they appeared quite ravenous to have their way with him and did his best not to shrink an inch from the sight. Such attempts to keep hidden his unease didn't go unnoticed by Miseriel who made a beckoning gesture in the air with his hand. In quickstep, two of the goat-headed sentries were at his side and he proceeded to take from them their swords.

"Choose one," Miseriel then instructed Hunter as he held both weapons out for the young man's perusal.

"Any particular reason?"

"To use in a contest of skill against the one whose sword you don't choose," explained the host.

"I wouldn't know a good sword from a bad one," said Hunter. "Nor would I have the slightest ability in wielding one if I did, having never handled one before."

"A Nephilim not adept at delivering the bite of the lance? Have you been sequestered to the dwellings of some remote cave during your short stretch of life?" Miseriel, looking somewhat perplexed, inquired. "And how, exactly, have you managed to fend off the dangers lurking in this somewhat perilous world?"

Like most other men; with these," Hunter, raising his clenched fists into Miseriel's sightline, replied. "And with this," he added, giving the side of his forehead a tap with his forefinger. "Both have served me just as well as I'm sure any sword would."

"Well, then," Miseriel, looking rather intrigued, said, "choosing between these two fine swords should be as easy as eeny, meeny, miny, moe."

"And if I refuse?"

"Why, you get cast to the Infectors, of course. Which I'm sure will make them quite pleased."

That was one outcome Hunter was hoping above all others to avoid.

"And what do I get if I win this little contest of yours?" he asked.

The question brought a crooked grin to the host's face.

" 'What do I get?' the thief curiously queries," Miseriel muttered to himself. "Would the promise of being allowed to leave our elite soirée without so much as a hair on your head harmed be a suitable parting gift?"

"It's a trap...I know it is," Wray, who was listening intently with the others, gasped in a panicky whisper.

Any such thoughts entertained by Hunter were quickly shrugged off as he nodded his agreement to the terms after quietly weighing the options.

"Only, I'll pass on the sword," he said when Miseriel presented him once more with the two blades.

Only when Miseriel noticed Hunter limbering up his fingers while opening and closing his fists did he realize what the young man was planning.

"I'm growing more fascinated to see which is your greater Achilles heel: your pluck or what could only be deemed to be your stupidity," said the host whose grin grew all the more wider as he eyed Hunter with far greater curiosity than before the mask was removed from his face.

~ ~ ~

The ring of floor was cleared except for Hunter and one of the two sentries who had stepped forward at Miseriel's beckoning and tapped to take part in the impromptu bout. Hunter casually sized up his opponent who was standing just a few short feet away, and aside from looking like some weird Egyptian hieroglyphic come to life, what with the goat head mask with its long golden horns still covering his face, there was nothing outwardly threatening about the sentry that caused any pause as they both looked to be of similar height and stalwart build. His self-assured composure tilted somewhat, however, once the sword gripped tightly in the sentry's hand moved into motion.

The sentry impressively maneuvered his weapon between his two hands, in the same effortless and flawless manner a majorette twirls a baton, until the light-catching saber resembled the spinning blades of an airplane's propeller. Hunter quickly found himself as transfixed by the masterful show as the guests and momentarily forgot his place in the two-man demonstration of which he was a participant. That is, until the sword broke from its hypnotic rhythm, and with lighting speed, took a swipe in Hunter's direction.

Hunter managed to step clear of the incoming lance as it sliced its way through the air with a loud *SWOOSH* that was far too close for comfort. An onslaught of swings, thrusts and swipes followed in quick succession as the sentry unleashed a furious attack in Hunter's direction. Each focused blow appeared to the naked eye as a blur as they came at Hunter with lightning speed. As fast-moving as the sentry was with his sword, Hunter proved equally as swift, and evaded the razor-sharp blade aimed at his flesh with an impressive feat of dodges, vaulting, leaps and acrobats worthy of a circus showman.

"Oh...I can't watch!" Wray, whose hands had moved from covering her ears to now shielding her eyes, squealed with a tense anxiousness.

Her companions surrounding her, however, looked as if they had suffered a dizzying blow to the head with a mallet. Ty stood open-mouthed while peering wide-eyed through the peepholes of his jester's mask at the skillful battle taking place that appeared to be more of an aggressive form of dance than a deadly tussle. Even Jacob and his tight-knit Nephilim band who themselves had mastered equally skillful moves after long hours of training at Lions Bite found Hunter's unique, if not crude brand of gesticulating to be quite a sight to behold.

For some time, Hunter performed a wild array of back-bending, somersaulting and gravity defying gymnastics to steer clear of the sword without appearing to even so much as break a sweat. He retreated not once and always managed to keep a harrowing hair's width between himself and the cutting blade despite the best efforts of the sentry whose growing frustration and outright anger showed itself in the increased wild manner in which he swung and jabbed at Hunter with his weapon.

Finally, spying with his acute vision a split-second opening between the blurred sword and himself, Hunter set free his right fist which had stayed clenched and positioned in front of his chest, and met his attacker square in the center of the goat-faced mask he wore with a halting hook. The blow shattered the mask and sent it scattered upon the floor in a million little jagged pieces, but it was the reveal of the face hidden within that stilled Hunter for a brief moment.

"What 'bout that? Why he's just a kid like us," Max remarked with surprise when he and the others got a glimpse of the sentry's unexpectedly youthful face.

Ruddy and dripping with sweat, the sentry looked to be of an age that tilted more toward the younger group of Nephilim than Hunter. Yet there was a dark hardness deep-set in his eyes that blemished the youthfulness with age, and they became even more steely and hate-filled as the two stared into each other's gazes before the young sentry caught his breath and came at Hunter once more. With an unmerciful determination focused in the dark pools that were his eyes, the sentry shredded the air with his sword like a cat's claw in a ruthless attempt to get at his target. The other Nephilim, holding their breaths in huddled suspense as they watched from the sidelines the nerve-racking way their friend managed to steer clear of the swooshing blows, gasped in unison when an exceptionally close and unforgiving swing of the sentry's weapon forced Hunter's upper body to bend its way backward until it was perpendicular to the floor, and barely deny the incoming blade the taste of his throat. When he returned upright just as quickly, he did so with a fed-up look fixed to his face, and before the sentry could resume his attack, he delivered another immobilizing punch to the boy's face followed by two swift and pointed kicks: one which knocked the sword from the hand gripping it and sent it flying toward one direction of the room, and another to his attacker's chest sending him skidding across the floor in an unconscious heap in another direction.

The incredulity that followed filled the ballroom with a marked silence. There was no applause that usually followed such victories, even from Hunter's friends who quietly cheered his triumphant trouncing of the sentry, but smartly knew better than to draw attention to their presence. Still, Hunter stood before the hushed costumed crowd with a rather pleased look on his face as though he were awash in an ovation.

"Well done, young thief, That was quite an engrossing exhibition," Miseriel commented finally, though looking in many ways as though he had been on the receiving end of the final blow that left his sentry in a motionless pile on the floor. "It would appear in this instance that your pluck is mightier than the sword."

Seeing Miseriel looking so disconsolate only broadened Hunter's contentment. His glee, however, was short-lived when a horrible, and unfortunately unmistakable howl suddenly reverberated throughout the hall. Hunter knew of only one thing that could make such a noise and he intuitively looked to the Pethen who charged at him with an unbridled fury. The lightning-quick reflexes which had served Hunter so well against the defeated sentry inexplicably failed him, and before he knew what had happened, he found himself dangling several feet off the floor in the Pethen's bone-crushing grip.

"You promised I would be free to go unharmed if I won," Hunter strained to find his voice while taking cautious note of the twin flames of incensed rage peering out from behind the silver mask covering the Pethen's face.

"That I did," Miseriel, appearing unaffected or unsurprised by the Pethen's assailing move, agreed. "But you'll forgive me for failing to take into account my loyal companion's proclivity to being what you might deem to be a sore loser."

Hunter was quick to realize by the host's unpleasantly callous grin that any hope of an order calling for the Pethen to release his hold and set him back on the floor would not be given, and he suddenly found himself in a desperate struggle to wretch himself free of the spindly fingers wrapped firmly around his throat as they slowly began to tighten their hold. His esophagus soon felt as though it were being crushed in some unforgiving vice, making him fight all the harder. In a last-ditch effort, he took aim at the Pethen's head with his feet and managed a couple forceful blows, but he was quick to regret the move when he kicked away the silver mask and gave light to the ugly serpent-like face hidden behind it. The Pethen let loose a furious wail.

"Now, you will die!" the creature snarled as the nostrils of his flat nonexistent nose flared with anger.

His cry of doom was drowned out by an even more forceful voice that reverberated through the ballroom like a clap of thunder.

"You will release the boy!"

~ ~ ~

Anyone looking at Miseriel would have thought the voice issuing the demand had somehow managed to manifest itself into a physical form and deliver a stinging cuff across his face. And, indeed, in many ways it had. For as he himself had made mention earlier in the evening, he was not one to forget a voice once it had addressed him.

Slowly, and rather cautiously, he turned his attention to where the voice had sounded directly behind him and found a column of blue standing at the front of the crowd. His brow crinkled at first with perplexity at the unexpected sight of a blue djinn standing mere feet from him. Perplexity quickly gave way to unforgettable recognition when Miseriel spied the sword in the Arabian mythological figure's hand, as it was no ordinary sword, but one with a blade that gleamed with a brightness that was almost too blinding for any pair of eyes to directly behold.

"There is only one I know who possesses a sword that looks as if it were hammered from a ray harvested from none other than the sun itself; someone whose very name that, when spoken, often puts the fear of Heaven in those who hear it," said Miseriel. "I should know; I've witnessed such terror when the name took drift on the wind like some war cry...the name..."

Before Miseriel could cluck the first consonant of the name he touted, Damiel brought a hand to the top of his head and with a swift motion he had been itching to make all evening, freed himself of the cumbersome turban and mask in whose confines he had been trapped.

"Damiel..." Miseriel finally gasped with some sense of incredulity when he finally saw the angel's face uncovered, even though he was quite certain who resided behind the disguise.

Damiel's attention, however, remained fiercely fixed on Hunter and, more importantly, the Pethen in whose strangling hold he continued to dangle.

"I'm not apt to repeating myself. But in fairness to the mentally trammeled, I shall advise yet again that you set the boy down," he stated in a tone that made it clear he was not one to be trifled with. "Or shall I assist in your disinclined cooperation by cutting him free from your inflexible fingers?"

The Pethen appeared to validate the mental handicap he had been accused of suffering by looking to Miseriel for guidance, and Miseriel, knowing full well such threats lobbed by the Angel of the Sword were not empty words to be snubbed if one cherished the simple act of breathing, much less the connected use of his hand, simply gave the Pethen a sideways glance and nodded. With a grumble of disgruntlement, the Pethen reluctantly gave Hunter a vindictive toss aside that left him grunting painfully as he was sent rolling across the hard floor like a lopsided bowling ball.

"You're quite a ways from the Elysian fields of your fair Eden," Miseriel said when finally he severed his rancorous glare from the young man sprawled upon the floor and turned his attention back to Damiel. "You'll forgive the inferior accommodations, but had I known you'd be in attendance tonight, I would have made sure to have the floor replaced with a fresh carpet of clouds so as to not have you worry about soiling the bottoms of your feet."

Damiel stood quietly glaring, choosing not to respond to such puerile quips. Not that Miseriel would have given him the opportunity.

"My patient guests," his voice suddenly rang out like a town crier to those standing idly by with shared looks of puzzlement and curiosity fixed on the man dressed all in blue who had emerged from their midst holding a most unusual sword with a blade of light, "it appears as though we have found ourselves in the esteemed presence of true greatness and illustriousness. I can tell you without invention that never has there existed a more perfect effigy of righteous strength nor dutiful courier of virtuous requital when the storm clouds gather and are lit within by Heaven's unmistakable ire. Then again, I cannot help but be somewhat bias in my introduction, for he is my brother. Not to mention my banisher."

It was quite confusing for anyone listening to gage whether or not Miseriel was being sincere in what began as praiseful accolades in commending Damiel, or a screen of scorn far too sheer to veil the spitting of venom that came with the utterance of "banisher." Damiel, however, had known Miseriel for far too long to be addled by the greeting extended to him and not know in no uncertain terms that behind the cold exterior marked by an even colder smile as Miseriel stepped closer toward him that there resided two sharp fangs yet to be unhinged.

"Please don't take this as any sort of personal affront, dear brother," said Miseriel, in a lowered voice, "but this is quite an elite and selective gathering of which your name would have as much a chance of finding a place on the guest list as I am certain a portrait of myself would ever come to grace the immaculate halls of Havenhid. So, naturally, I find myself curious as to how exactly an invitation to our little reception manage to find its way into your hands in your small, secluded pocket of the world."

"Trust me when I tell you it is by happenstance that we find ourselves in the unfortunate position of occupying the same space at the same moment. Nothing more," answered Damiel.

Miseriel's grin elongated itself like one would imagine finding on a demented joker.

"What do you take me for, exactly?"

"I take you for a great many things, Miseriel," Damiel replied without missing a beat. "And, frankly, none of them are suitable for words."

The pupils of Miseriel's eyes that until that moment had floated in the whites of his eyes like two frigid icebergs despite their warm gold color, suddenly ignited with the flame of rage.

"DON'T EVER AGAIN REFER TO ME BY THAT NAME!" he screamed as his face twisted itself in an unnatural fashion with an anger frothing at the mouth.

"I cast away the name Miseriel the day Heaven cast me from my rightful place," he seethed through clenched teeth. "It is a name that came seared with my father's own, just like this unsightly mark that he branded upon my temple. And it is a name as dead to me as he is."

It was not the first time Damiel had witnessed such an outburst coming from a Fallen and appeared unfazed by the fit of temper.

"And what name, may I ask, have you settled on to be a more worthy fit than the one our father bestowed upon you?"

"Miseri," came the prideful reply. "It's a name that sings with teeth and dominion, don't you think? Like Damiel...Angel of the Sword."

Miseri...

The name had a not-so-surprising ring to it, no doubt about it. Especially when one stared into the face of its bearer with its eyes brimming with malice and the cruel crooked mouth in which resided an even crueler tongue.

"You couldn't have made a more fitting choice for your rechristening," Damiel quietly agreed.

As agreeable as he may have pretended to be, quietly or otherwise, it didn't require a man with a keen sense of sight to recognize the raw contempt simmering just beneath the surface of the angel's skin, and again Miseri's gaze shifted downward to the weapon that remained at Damiel's side.

"Your Nephilim thief is unharmed, and I hear no claps of thunder from above summoning your service. I think you're safe to retire your sword to its sheath," he suggested.

"If it's all the same to you, I feel much more at ease right where it is," Damiel replied with a dismissive sneer. "One's sword can never be too close within reach when in the company of Infectors, Pethens...or even the cold-blooded murderer of innocents."

"Cold-blooded..." The idea of such a person existing seemed to leave Miseri horrified. "Certainly you're not insinuating such a monster is lurking amongst my guests."

Damiel's revulsion became all the more focused.

"If I had a mirror at my disposal, I'd place it in your hands so you could see up close the specific monster of which I speak," he said.

An awkward smile found its way to Miseri's mouth.

"Me?...A murderer of innocents?" Miseri replied with a shaky chuckle as though the very idea was beyond preposterous.

"What else would you call someone who engages in the wholesale slaughter of a group of young boys, and inside the sanctum of a church no less?"

Miseri stood quiet for a moment until what appeared to be a light of clarity flicked on in the depths of his eyes.

"Of course. You're speaking about the Island of Akdamar, aren't you?" he asked finally.

Damiel didn't know what caused him to become even more incensed than he already was: the fact Miseri was somehow able to let fade from his consciousness the horror that had taken place on the small island inside the Armenian church, or that when his memory was sufficiently jogged the atrocity he committed didn't garner much more than a shrug.

"That was some time ago," said Miseri indifferently.

"More than a century now," Damiel made clear. "But it continues to remain yesterday for me."

"What happened occurred because of war. Sadly, war is the cause of many unfortunate and unavoidable things."

"War," Damiel growled with disgust. "There was no war."

"Oh, but there indeed was a war," argued Miseri. "The same war you believed to have ended the moment I and my Fallen brethren were cast to the merciless damnation of the Underneath, yet one which has raged on every day ever since, and will continue to until we've savored the taste of reprisal long due to us."

"Is that how you justify such an unspeakable atrocity; an atrocity you and your henchmen of Furies breathed life into and used as sheepskin to disguise your own planned bloodletting of innocents."

"Nephilim by their very nature are hardly innocents," Miseri scoffed in return. "Or at least those who come into the world baptized by the Light. By aligning themselves with our enemy, they willing and readily become the enemy."

"You killed my son, you fiendish butcher," Damiel seethed with a hate-filled hiss. "I only wish that in slaying him you somehow found success in also slaying me. Instead, you managed to do something far worse; you left me maimed with an almost paralyzing sense of fearfulness I never before experienced; fear of your name, fear of your voice, fear of your very presence."

If Damiel's ire had caused Miseri any concern or pause, he was stellar at hiding it; but this unexpected confession left him positively glowing.

"You...the intrepid and stouthearted Angel of the Sword...you profess fear of me?" Miseri asked with a gleefulness that fell just shy of giddy.

"'Tis true...but not in the way you are most likely fantasizing. The overwhelming fear I suffered, and continue at this moment to suffer, is that which rears its head when one realizes his very spirit is in peril," said Damiel, but it was clear his words were lost on someone like Miseri, so he attempted to further explain. "The moment you stepped foot on Akdamar and drew your sword against my son, you stoked within me an enmity beyond all imagining. And it is because of that enmity coursing through my veins like life-giving blood that I've existed these years since in great fear of you; fearful in knowing you and I would one day cross paths; and even more fearful of the unrestrained calamity I would deliver upon you when that time finally presented itself. Self-preservation: it's the reason I all but shackled myself to my small, secluded pocket of the world as you so called it, and why you still blight the world at large. Hardly a just trade-off."

Listening, Miseri cautiously eyed Damiel while pacing slowly in a circle on the floor.

"Now, here you and I stand, paths crossed, and I see not a trace of fear in your eyes," he commented before holding outward his arms as though he were some sort of sacrificial lamb destined for the altar. "Then have at this cold dish of vengeance you've had such a hankering to taste. Heaven knows you've waited long enough."

"Careful, oh miserable one, as your gesture of valor rings as hollow as your cowardice runs deep. For you know with full confidence I cannot embrace such temptation, much as it pains me," said Damiel. "Your sin is your sin, and as much as I detest that it's gone so far unpunished, I would tread the razor's edge of my own trespass should I take up the duty of vigilante without sanction. And you know just as well as I, that I hold at hand the proper reserve of vanity to ever desecrate the flawlessness you see standing before you with the unsightly disgrace in which you and all my fallen brethren have been so duly marked. Now, you'll understand when I convey to you that every minute I find myself in your objectionable presence, the more I feel my temperance erode," Damiel remarked in as cordial a manner as he could muster, after the two held one another in dueling glares of shared contemptuousness. "So, if you'll allow me a moment to collect the rest of my scattered flock we shall leave you to the revels of your shadowy coven."

~ ~ ~

Miseri's attention suddenly perked up.

"Scattered flock? And just how many in your masked cortège are you?"

Damiel immediately realized his blunder when Miseri, without waiting for an answer, began combing the gathering of guests before him with his searching gaze and promptly zeroed in on the huddled group of Nephilim and their two civilian accomplices. The Infectors, meanwhile, had already sprang into action and let their rage over their own failure to detect sooner the uninvited guests be heard in a united and deafening chorus. They proceeded to form an ominous revolving halo above the alarmed group like a flock of carrion birds circling a condemned calf that had strayed dangerously far from its herd when, suddenly, one of the sinister specters hastily broke from the ranks of the other phantoms. It swooped down on the startled group like all nightmares do, with a rancorous roaring howl, drawing a high-pitched shriek of fright from Wray that was drowned out only by Ty's cry of terror.

In a flash, Damiel drew back his sword and was about to cleave the approaching threat, but another blade beat him to the punch. The sword belonged to Max, and he had it at the ready, concealed within the folds of his costume, just as Damiel had advised, and at just the right moment he brought it out of hiding, and with one determined swing reduced the Infector to a defeated cloud of pulverized cinders.

"You and your Infectors might think twice about going nose to nose with this batch of innocents. They've already cut their teeth at Lions Bite," Damiel relayed over his shoulder to Miseri, with the kind of proud grin one usually finds on a father beaming over his child's first steps.

Miseri, however, showed no sign of the contemptible smirk he had displayed during most of his confrontation with Damiel, nor did he lift a finger to try and stop the company of teenagers cautiously eyeing the even more cautious Infectors still circling overhead, when Damiel motioned for them to make for the doors of the ballroom.

Damiel then called to Hunter, who continued to eye longingly the object he had earlier attempted to swipe, while the nearby Pethen busily returned the mask to his face, and motioned to him to follow along as well before he turned to do the same. Neither had taken no more than a few steps when

Miseri's voice took aim at him once more like a well-focused dagger.

"If it's any consolation to you, one could well argue I did you a favor in severing your bloodline."

The words brought Damiel to abrupt standstill.

"Not to put too fine a point on it, but that son of yours was hardly worthy of occupying the role of heir to the Angel of the Sword. Truth be told, I've seen flowers destined for a vase put up more of a fight against the clipping shears than he managed against my sword."

One could almost hear the crack of a whip in the way Miseri's tongue lashed out at Damiel with it's parting words.

"Oh, yes, it was I and not the Furies that sent your son to his eternal sleep," Miseri said with a gleeful lint in his voice, when Damiel glanced back over his shoulder with a look of wrath few, if any, had ever before witnessed and lived to describe.

"You would have done well to take a lesson from Gothamel. At least, he had the clear foresight to put down his disappointing brood," Miseri continued with his verbal clout. "Instead of holding grievance toward me, perhaps backpay in gratitude is in order for carrying out such a task for you."

Damiel stood like a smoldering pyre. It was not so much Miseri's words that brought about his slow burn (such was to be expected as Miseriel had handily earned the competitive honor amongst his Fallen brothers as being the most vile), but the sadistic cat and mouse game he appeared to be playing by feigning forgetfulness of the atrocity he unleashed on Akdamar Island when it was obvious he held to memory—and with considerable relish— every moment of that dark day.

And before he even knew it had happened, he was upon Miseri with eyes ablaze like twin cauldrons bubbling with his molten ire.

"Was it something I said?" Miseri asked with a slight chortle, while eyeing cautiously the sharp point of the brandished sword that had come fast for his throat and, in an equally swift move on his part to avoid the meeting of his flesh and the cold incoming steel, left him leaning desperately backwards while balanced impossibly on the heels of his feet, and frozen in a suspended diagonal slant resembling a domino frozen in mid-fall.

"You unimaginable creation..." Damiel spit with hatred. "I can instantly turn this party of yours into a wake to celebrate your miserable end. Is that what you want?"

"Your overwhelming desire to run me through is not lost on me,"

Miseri replied in a calm, almost serene manner. "I can see clearly how it is eating away at your insides. And it will go on eating away at your insides because as much as you would like nothing more than to see the very light in my eyes go out for the last time, you yourself admitted not a breath ago that you cannot bring yourself to extinguish the flame."

No sooner had he uttered such words with taunting assuredness, than he winced at the feel of the cold blade of Damiel's sword pressing itself even more painfully against his neck.

"Why my son?" Damiel growled forth the question that had sat inside his throat like a closed fist. "What could he possibly have done to draw the approach of your menacing shadow?"

Miseri's gaze shifted from the threat of the sword poised at his throat and settled on the visible anguish that had taken hold of the mighty angel hovering above him, and a slow look of gratification moved over him.

"Exist," Miseri said in a most casual and apathetic manner when finally he answered.

There suddenly came from the far side of the ballroom a loud echoey cry. It was soon joined by a second similar wailing emanating from the opposite end of the room. They were not the familiar caterwauling that stemmed from Infectors or even Pethens; they were in fact the cries of young boys. And the wailing coming from these unseen striplings continued to multiply until the ballroom was consumed in the cacophony of their siren. Then, in the midst of the unbearable din, Damiel's ear was turned by a familiar and unexpected voice.

"Father! Can you hear me, father?"

A stricken look came over the angel, but it was nothing compared to the expression that found him when the voice calling out to him drew his attention back to Miseri, only much to his shock, and bittersweet gladness, he found the face of his beloved son looking back at him in all his cherished wholesomeness.

"Theron...?"

"Where are you, father?"

The fire that lit the gold-colored wrath alight Damiel's eyes receded with the rare welling of tears.

"I'm here, son."

"We need your help, father. The Furies...they're coming. Oh, please help us!"

"I'm here..." Damiel cried out to no recognition within his son's terror-filled eyes.

"Father...FATHER!"

With a final high-pitched scream, the boy's face, along with the cries that filled the room, vanished like the ghostly apparition it was, and Miseri's countenance once more surfaced.

"I would think it would lend you needed comfort knowing your son's last breaths were spent screaming out for you," said Miseri who appeared more than pleased at the turmoil in which Damiel suddenly found himself consumed. "And, oh, how he screamed!"

Damiel suddenly found himself in the grips of an all-consuming seizure of tremors, and his entire body began to shake and shudder like an awakening volcano seconds before it erupts, as the last vestiges of restraint he had so desperately clung to incinerated inside his very hands. No longer did he pay any mind to the welfare of his spirit he had so struggled to safeguard. Any and all aversion he had over his name finding its way to the membership rolls of the Fallen evaporated, as did concern for the shameful accompanying mark of disgrace he so confidently swore would never mar his unblemished profile. The one and only thing the blinders suddenly fitted over his eyes allowed him to see was the justifiable cleaving of the unspeakable monster staring unrepentantly back at him. And, so, consumed by the inferno of his stoked wrath, Damiel raised his hands clutching his blinding sword and took the swing he had long-denied himself.

Just as the fatal blow was to be delivered, Miseri smiled like the cunning serpent he was, and the gravity that had held him in slanted suspension as though he were laying upon a sturdy board unseen to any eye, suddenly gave way and he fell just out of reach of Damiel's swift sword. And upon hitting the floor he shattered like a fragile vase and became a frenzied flock of hundreds of squawking black ravens.

CHAPTER SEVENTEEN

C aos ensued.

Screams erupted from the frenzied crowd scrambling to escape the cawing black squall of thrashing wings and razored claws in which they found themselves engulfed. The melee, however, proved to be just the kind of diversion Hunter couldn't ignore, and with the Pethen momentarily distracted by the swarming storm of birds and panicked guests running about like headless chickens in a desperate bid to flee them, he promptly jumped into action and made a grab for the object that remained still unguarded on the nearby table.

Just as he was about to take possession of the green jade-like whatsit, he was swiftly stopped in his tracks when an unknown pair of arms grabbed hold of him tightly from behind preventing him from seeing through his caper and tackled him to the floor.

"If you know what's good for you, you'll stay down," Hunter heard a voice warn him.

Quick to rearrange his mask which had been knocked askew, Hunter looked to see who had attacked him, and found a similarly masked figure kneeling down beside him dressed in an all-black costume that could only be described as a reimagined version of a sword-wielding Zorro.

"What is it you think you're doing?" Hunter demanded with an unfriendly scowl.

"From the looks of it, saving you the displeasure of being split in two like a piece of cord wood destined to become kindling, " came a grumbling voice from behind a black mask.

It was then that the Pethen who had spied Hunter's second failed attempt to once again take that which did not belong to him, screamed with rage and made a charge for the object it held with obsessive regard. Once the Pethen had in its protective grasp its precious possession, it let loose a bellow that caused bits of plaster to rain down from the elaborate ceiling of the great room. Leveling a hate-filled glare at the sight of Hunter sprawled upon the floor, it then swiftly tore through the surrounding chaos and disappearing from sight.

"How obtuse does one have to be to antagonize a Pethen, of all things?" the stranger scolded Hunter, once the menacing creature was gone.

"I had it under control," Hunter replied sourly. "That is, until you came along and fouled everything up, whoever you are."

"You always were persistent in learning life's lessons the hard way." There was a distinct familiarity in the man's reprimand, so much so that it all but seized Hunter like some invisible hand taking hold of the collar of his shirt inside its fist.

"Come on, and get up!" the stranger suddenly instructed. "Get to your friends, and hurry your way out of the palace if you know what's best for you."

Hunter didn't move; not at first, anyway. He was far too distracted focusing on the distinct gold-colored pupils peering out from behind the cover of the mask worn by the stranger. Recognizable as he found this mysterious figure's voice, there was something inarguable about the eyes, and when he finally found his tongue and opened his mouth to say so, the stranger was gone, disappearing into the pandemonium of swarming birds and screaming guests just as Wray came rushing to his side.

~ ~ ~

"Are you alright?" Wray asked frantically, while giving Hunter a comforting hug as Jacob, Kairo and a visibly unsettled Ty huddled around him.

"Good as can be expected I guess…considering I nearly got my neck crushed by a giant praying mantis," Hunter reassured her.

"I've got a better question. Like, are you insane?" Ty screeched as the growing stress of what was taking place around him between threatening Infectors and a spiteful Fallen exploding into a clutch of ravens continued to make his voice climb like a rollercoaster grinding its way to the top of a terrifying drop.

"To tell you the truth, I'm not all that sure," Hunter replied half-jokingly before dropping an unexpected bomb. "I think I may have just seen my father."

"You're joking! You mean Zophiel? Here?" Jacob asked incredulously.

"Either that or I've just experienced my first face to face with a ghost."

"Really? After all that's happened here tonight, you're going to bring up ghosts? Not funny!" Ty squawked.

"Neither is what's headed straight toward us," Kairo announced to the rest of the group.

They had but a moment to look and see what had brought a glimmer of panic in Kairo's otherwise cool and collected demeanor, and not a one liked what they saw. The storm of birds had suddenly changed direction and was now headed directly at the wide-eyed group like a swelling tide of rage moving along the surface of a black sea. Jacob yelled for everybody to hit the deck and, with not a moment to spare, they managed barely to escape the unpleasant blur of sharp beaks and claws pecking and swiping in a furious manner at them as the cawing maelstrom swept past.

The angry chorus coming from the ravens was deafening and almost as unbearable as the din made by the Infectors, yet somehow, impossibly, an even more frightening clamor startled the young group. It sounded at first like an explosion had gone off inside the ballroom, and when it seemed safe to lift their heads from beneath the cover of their arms, they saw the flock of birds had flown straight into the wall directly behind them and punched a rather sizable hole in the side of the building as effectively as a cannonball fired from a ship harbored in the nearby lagoon, and escaped into the darkness of the night on the other side.

"Is anyone else besides me getting to really despise birds since we started this trip?" Ty remarked snidely as he joined the others in getting to his feet.

He and the rest of the group, however, were quickly made to realize there were far more pressing matters than the fleeting nuisance of a bunch of vicious birds when they looked to the center of the now empty ballroom and saw Damiel, sword in hand, beating back a far worse plague: the Infectors.

And he was not alone.

Fighting along beside him was the mysterious masked stranger who had appeared out of nowhere to save Hunter from being turned into pulp by the bloodthirsty Pethen, and together they were reducing the screeching insidious vermin into terminated plumes of ash one by one.

"Who is that fighting alongside Damiel?" wondered Kairo.

"Haven't a clue," answered Jacob. "And I don't think now's the time for introductions."

"Do you think we should go help them?"

Damiel, at that exact moment, glanced their way as though he had overheard the question, and his face tensed up even more than the struggle of the fight had rendered it.

"What are you waiting for? Go on...get out of here!" he instructed in no uncertain terms before dealing another death blow to the dwindling Infectors.

"I guess that answers that question," said Jacob. "We better do what he says."

However, when they turned to leave the ballroom, they found their exit blocked by a half a dozen of the goat-headed sentries that remained behind despite Miseri's spectacular if not unorthodox departure. They turned to look for another avenue of escape behind them and discovered much to their chagrin more sentries.

"This is great...what are we going to do now?" Ty said in a renewed huff, as the two companies of guards slowly began to close ranks on the surrounded youngsters, with their swords drawn.

The only means of escape left to them that Jacob could see was to follow the path paved by the ravens through the crumbled makeshift breach in the palace's wall. There was only one slight hiccup with such a plan, Jacob discovered, when he craned his head through the opening for a quick peek outside: they were several floors up from the ground below with no sign of a ladder to climb down anywhere to be found. It wouldn't have posed much of a hurdle had it just been Kairo, Hunter and himself, but with two amongst them as wingless as pigs they soon found themselves in a whole new pickle.

"Do me a favor will you Hunter, and get Wray to a safe place down there," said Jacob, nodding to the ground floor straight below them outside.

"Excuse me...but don't you mean Wray and Ty?" Ty interjected.

"Don't worry...he'll get you next. But he can't carry you both down at the same time."

Jacob looked again to Hunter who remained unresponsive as he stared down at the ground below looking like someone who had a profound issue with heights.

"Hunter?"

The sound of Jacob's voice broke through whatever trance-like state had briefly taken hold of the young man.

"If it's all the same to you, I'd rather stay where I'm at and help you fend off these turkeys," he said. "Have Kairo here do it, instead."

Kairo looked to Jacob for the go-ahead, but Jacob motioned to him to remain where he stood.

"No offense, Hunter...I saw how you handled yourself tonight and you were quite impressive, but trust me this is a situation that calls for someone skilled with a sword, not just fists," Jacob explained as calmly as he could while eyeing the sentries moving ever closer to them. "Now, please, this isn't the time to argue over this. I need you to get Wray out of the line of fire, and I need you to do it now."

"Wray *and* Ty…Wray *and* Ty," Ty muttered with growing angst under his breath.

Hunter didn't appear to be listening as he once again stared down into the gulf space that separated himself and the sidewalk below.

"What's going on with you?" Jacob barked again, this time with a jostling jab to Hunter's shoulder. "Why are you acting like you have two lead anchors attached to your back instead of wings?"

"I'm sorry," Hunter replied apologetically, "but I can't do it."

Whatever it was that had left Hunter looking like he had seen a ghost, Jacob hadn't the time to try and unpack, as the twin flanks of sentries were nearly upon them.

Jacob's first impulse was to grab Wray himself and speed her away to safety. But he couldn't bring himself to leave his friends, if even for a moment, to fend for themselves in a fight in which they were greatly outnumbered. He also hesitated in bringing his own sword into the light from the hidden confines of its sheath as he still remained fraught and far from being at ease with handling something which radiated such immense power. And it was with that discomfort twisting its way through him that he peered again through the gaping hole in the building's side. His eyes first searched the promenade that ran along the edge of lagoon where they first arrived at the palace by gondolas, and then to the black waters of the lagoon itself shimmering beneath the silvery light of the moon peering out from behind the thin fingers of slow-moving clouds passing leisurely across an otherwise clear night sky.

"Alright, then…I've got another plan…I think," he said with a detectable wavering in his voice.

"I haven't even heard it yet, and already I'm not liking it," Ty noted with equal apprehension.

"Just listen to me. You're going to wait until I give the signal—"

"Wait a minute…what kind of signal?" Ty promptly interrupted.

"What difference does it make?" Jacob asked with notable irritation.

"Well, when one person tells another—or in this case four other people—

they're going to give a signal, it's usually a good idea to indicate what that signal will be. Otherwise who's to know when said signal is given, see?"

Jacob took a calming breath. "Will it work for you if I just say the word 'now'?"

"Noted," Ty replied agreeably. "Proceed."

"When I say the word 'now,' " repeated Jacob and getting an a-okay sign from his friend in the process, "we will all make a mad dash to the left of this hole."

It seemed like a pretty simple plan with even simpler instructions to follow, and yet Jacob felt a need to repeat them.

"Whatever happens just make sure you are nowhere near this opening."

"Why? What are you expecting to be coming through there…another flock of deranged birds?" asked Wray. Then, thinking better of it, she nearly held up her hands in front of Jacob's mouth. "Never mind. I think I would be better off not knowing."

The sentries by now had formed an intimidating front line before the group resembling a firing squad, but with swords instead of rifles.

"Do you intend to draw your weapon and at least face your death with some show of courage, or do you prefer to die as a cringing coward?" a voice from behind one of the dozen or so goat-headed masks asked Jacob.

"There's an old saying that recommends you should fight fire with fire," Jacob said in reply. "Personally, I never saw any problem with the old-fashion way of putting out a pesky flame in need of extinguishing."

His gaze once more shifted to the view of the lagoon framed by the crumbling hole in the wall, and the gift of the Graces residing within him instantly revealed themselves in a shimmering of gold that surfaced in his eyes. And, in that moment, the waters of the lagoon began to heave as if a giant unseen stick had been inserted from the heavens and begun to slowly stir its depths. The line of gondolas moored along the promenade were soon rocking violently and knocked against one another when, quite suddenly, a section of water receded rapidly from the concrete banks. It reared up as it ebbed, and anyone who might have been walking along the promenade at that moment might have thought fantastically the water was actually some unknown behemoth rising up from the depths as it awakened from a long slumber.

The golden flares illuminating Jacob's sight continued to dance and the massive column of water spitting and drooling in the middle of the lagoon suddenly started an assailing roll toward the shore. The incoming tidal wave cleared the concrete banks tossing out of its path the gondolas that had momentarily been dry-docked, except one, which it picked up in its watery grasp as it proceeded to career across the promenade toward the palace.

"NOW!" Jacob hollered when the golden brilliance left his eyes, and he and his friends threw themselves clear of the breach in front of which they stood.

The sentries were momentarily addled at what was happening, until a thunderous rumbling made them focus their attention on the gaping opening, and the terrifying sight of a massive wave carrying a gondola beneath its curved crest like a surfer heading straight for them. But by then it was too late; the wave and the gondola crashed its way through the breach and slammed into the helpless goat-headed troops like the giant tsunami it was, and deposited them at the far end of the ballroom like clumps of wilted seaweed on a beach.

"Everyone okay?" Jacob asked once the water had begun to subside.

They had not taken a direct hit from the wave like the sentries, but they didn't escape getting a decent soaking either.

"Aces!" Ty sputtered before mumbling under his breath, "considering my other option was drowning.

They each lent the other a hand to get to their feet as quickly as possible and flee the waterlogged ballroom before the dazed sentries were able to collect their senses floating about them. However, the group didn't get very far when Wray's dress, already a challenge to maneuver due to its voluminous size, made moving nearly impossible now that it was soaking wet with twenty pounds of water. She resolved the matter posthaste by snatching from Kairo his sword and, with a few swift hacks of the blade that her companions found unexpectedly impressive, severed her way through the once beautiful fabric and wire form like a seamstress gone mad. In a flash, the bottom half of the gown separated from her waist and fell to the floor like a curtain, and in the process revealed the surprising sight of a frilly and ballooning pair of lily-white bloomers Wray was wearing underneath.

Without pause, she then swung the sword in her hand like some odd baton and leveled its pointed end squarely at Ty's neck.

"Before you even breathe a word, no, these are not what I regularly wear; they are—or rather I should say were—part of the costume. But if you feel like you cannot contain yourself, just remember I can easily perform the same alteration to your tongue," she said in a no-nonsense tone.

Ty attempted as pleasant a smile as he could force and replied simply, "Very becoming."

Wray's gaze narrowed as she studied him questioningly, waiting for one of his trademark snarky quips to squeeze its way through his thin little lips, then returned to Kairo his sword when none made themselves heard before turning her nose up dismissively and stomping off as confidently as she could in her newly modified attire.

"Yep, very becoming...for Little Red Riding Hood's grandmother," Ty sniggered under his breath when he was sure she had moved out of earshot to Jacob, Kairo and Hunter who were having trouble suppressing their own chuckles of amusement for the very same reason.

They were quick, however, to regain their composure and slogged after Wray through the ankle-deep seawater to the entrance of the ballroom where Damiel was found wringing the water from the lower half of his costume and looking none to please doing it.

"Countless hours of training, the most powerful sword known to man, and this is the weapon you pull from your quiver?" the angel remarked to Jacob while giving the watery floor a light-hearted kick with the toe of his boot.

Jacob bowed his head slightly in the knowing that however impressive and effective it may have looked and felt to take out a dozen or so of his enemies by the power of the sea that he could make rise up and dance to his whim, he only did so because of the hesitancy he felt toward the powerful weapon sheathed out of sight within his wing, though he dare not say so to Damiel.

But the golden eyes belonging to the angel that casually shifted to take the boy into their sights revealed he was already well aware.

"Please tell me you got rid of all of those horrid and hideous...what do you call them?" Wray, attempting to break up the weighted silence, asked.

"Infectors," Damiel replied quietly. "Yes, they're gone. But there will be plenty more to take their place if we don't get out of here in quick order."

"Who was it who was helping you fight the Infectors?" asked Hunter.

The question drew Damiel's focused gaze away from Jacob to settle on the young man.

"Have a look for yourself."

Hunter followed the angel's nod to the hallway just outside the entrance to the ballroom where he spied a figure wearing a familiar costume standing just outside the direct reach of light.

"It's been a long time, boy," came the voice with the familiar ring.

The man, who stepped slowly from the pocket of shadows that concealed his face, was no longer wearing his mask, which prompted a slight gasp of surprise to escape Hunter.

"I guess my mind wasn't playing tricks on me like I thought," said Hunter.

It was impossible to tell by anyone who attempted to read his deadpan expression whether the mind tricks Hunter referred to were a welcome thing or not.

"This isn't by chance..." Jacob began while studying the stranger who stood tall and sturdy and returned the boy's inquisitive stare with a pair of eyes of an unmistakable golden hue deep-set in a face that was handsome and glowing with both youth as well as age.

"It sure is," answered Hunter in a restrained tone that made his next words all the more unexpected. "The angel you traveled halfway around the world to meet, not to mention my father...Zophiel."

~ ~ ~

Outside the palace, meanwhile, Max, Ethan and Leos could be found loitering at the top of the Giants' Staircase and keeping company with the twin towering statues of Mars and Neptune who stood on either side of them frozen in their intimidating poses like the supreme deities they were.

"What do you think's taking them so long?" Ethan queried impatiently after a quiet stretch.

"Well, let's break down what we've witnessed in the short time we've been here: A Fallen who transforms himself into a tornado of ravens, a swarm of rabid Infectors and a tall, skinny head case wearing a silver mask demonstrating the ability to snap anyone in two who dares to lay a finger on whatever the heck that green thingamajig was he was obsessing over. Take your pick," answered Leos.

"Maybe we should go back," Ethan suggested, albeit warily. "I mean, maybe they're in trouble; maybe they need our help."

Max appeared to already be pondering the idea, but shook his head, instead.

"No...I think it's best we do what Damiel ordered us to do, and that was to clear out of the ballroom. There's nothing we saw Jacob and Kairo can't defend themselves against," said Max. "Besides, they're most likely on their way here right now to meet up with us. Best we be here."

Leos noted his agreement and proceeded to step over the chain hurdle blocking access to the marble steps leading the way down to the courtyard below.

"What're you doing?" asked Ethan.

"What does it look like? Damiel told us to wait for them in the courtyard," Leos replied. "Yeah, but…the staircase is blocked off to keep people from walking on it. We saw the sign posted at the bottom of the stairs when we first arrived tonight. We have to go around this way," Ethan said, pointing in the direction behind them.

"Don't be such a soft touch, Ethan. People have been walking up and down these steps for hundreds of years. I doubt my size elevens are going to cause any lasting damage," Leos said with a sneer. "But be my guest and take the long way around. I'll be waiting for you, resting with my feet up."

Down the cordoned-off path of stairs he proceeded without a second thought, though he likely would have reconsidered his purposeful act of rule-breaking had he any awareness of Mars' head turning slightly, and his marble eyes, suddenly blinking with life, shifting their focus onto the disobedient Nephilim. Only when Mars took a rigid step off the pedestal upon which his feet had long been planted did Leos come to an abrupt pause when he felt a noticeable tremor reverberate beneath his shoes. He immediately sensed something not quite right. When he slowly turned his head to see what had caused such a rumbling, he was not prepared for the sight of the towering statue looking no more than the sculpted hunk of marble that he was, but moving about freely as if he had suddenly become something made of flesh and bone.

Mars' white vacant stone eyes somehow managed to emit an unmistakable glare of fury; enough so that it prodded Leos to reach for his sword and point it threateningly at the statue. The God of War smiled in an unmistakably unfriendly way as he appeared to welcome the boy's gutsy, if not nervous challenge. In return, he produced his own quite large sword from where his shield remained on his pedestal. He then proceeded to stomp his way down the staircase, and every powerful step felt mighty enough to Leos to crush the steps beneath the statue's feet into a fine dust.

Leos remained unflinching where he stood, even as his feet argued with the rest of his body to flee in the face of the menacing herculean sculpture descending upon him. Mars wasted no time in taking a swing at the boy with his sword, and Leos instinctively raised his to block the slicing blade. The blow, however, was so forceful it knocked Leo's sword free from his grip, but not before sending what felt like a burning jolt of electricity into his palm and up the length of his arm. Luckily for Leos, he retained his lightning quick reflexes, and when Mars immediately swung again, Leos' wings had already punched their way through the back of his costume and put him airborne out of harm's way.

"You're gonna have to be a little quicker than that, blockhead," taunted Leos, as he buzzed teasingly about Mars' head.

With his sword out of reach, Leos attempted to fight back with another weapon at his disposal that was equally as effective, and his eyes lit up with the Grace inborn in him that allowed him to sway minds. However, he discovered almost immediately a block of rock has about as much mindfulness to massage as a turnip holds blood, no matter how humanlike a sculptor's chisel is successful in transforming it. And so Leos was left to the flighty maneuverings of his wings as he darted about the air struggling to steer clear of the fury of swipes Mars directed his way with his sword.

The ruckus eventually brought Max and Ethan who had both chosen to take the long and correct way around running into the courtyard and the sight of their friend under attack by the colossal Mars left them with their mouths agape.

"Flamin' hell, what's this?" Max gasped with disbelief.

"You mean it isn't obvious this ten-foot slab of marble has somehow managed to come to life and, for some reason, is trying desperately to turn me into a shish kebob?" cried Leos who looked like an oversized insect trying to steer clear of being squashed.

Shaking themselves free of the fantastical sight, Max and Ethan jumped into action. As they unsheathed their swords, however, they failed, like their friend before them, to notice Mars' companion, Neptune, slowly turn his head and fix his white empty eyes on the two of them. He leapt off his pedestal, shaking the ground soundly when his feet planted themselves on the courtyard floor, and more than startled the two boys rushing to the base of the staircase to aid in their friend's rescue at the sudden sight of the god of the sea now blocking their way. Max and Ethan had only a moment, if that, to gather their unnerved senses, when Neptune swung his mighty arm in the direction of the two. Instead of a threatening sword coming at them, Max and Ethan found themselves dodging a fish the size of a porpoise that Neptune gripped by the tail in his left hand.

The hulking statue repeatedly swung the fish at the two boys like a sack filled with cannonballs. Each time, he narrowly missed the fleet-footed Nephilim and, instead, clobbered the decorated cobblestone ground which exploded in pulverized bits of concrete. The exhaustive game of whack-a-mole went on for some time when, much to the relief of Max and Ethan who became too drained to escape any further attempts at being clubbed, there suddenly was heard what sounded distinctly like the roar of a lion coming from somewhere in the distance that instantly froze Neptune's arm in mid-swing as the marbled god turned his attention to the night sky. Mars, too, came to an abrupt standstill when, again, the roar made itself heard, only now it sounded closer.

~ ~ ~

There suddenly appeared from the veil of the nighttime sky a lion to match the ferocious roar. Guided by a pair of large wings sprouted from its back, it swooped down and landed with a regal pounce on the courtyard floor. Like Mars and Neptune, it was not of flesh and blood but the creation of a long-ago artist; neither was it made of marble but the much more durable and precious medium of bronze as revealed by its tarnished, green-tinged hide. Max, Leos and Ethan instantly recognized the bronze creature as the Lion of Venice that Hunter had pointed out upon their arrival perched upon a tall column located in the piazza just beyond the walls of the palace. Seeing it up close pacing slowly in front of them with a stalking gait, proved far more impressive.

The boys breathed thanks for the respite they were given when their presence seemed to be instantly forgotten by Mars and Neptune, and as the two giants turned to face the pair of ferocious eyes fixed on them, it appeared that a new battle was about to ignite between gods and beast. Instead, the lion unhinged his mouth once more and released from the hollows of his bronze core, a reverberating roar that sent the two statues into a slow retreat back to the twin vacant pedestals at the top of the stairs. Only when they resumed their frozen position of standing sentinel over the staircase did the lion flap his wings and, with a victorious growl, fly off into the night.

A quiet fell over the courtyard, but it wasn't long before it was interrupted by the scuttle of footsteps belonging to Damiel and the rest of his company rounding the opposite side of the stairway with Zophiel in tow.

"Well, now, I can breathe a little easier knowing everyone's been accounted for," said Damiel.

Max, Ethan and Leos, who remained somewhat dazed by the spectacle they had just witnessed, didn't look as if they heard him.

"What's going on?" asked Jacob, as he and the others followed the trio's riveted gazes up the staircase where the two Herculean statues stood.

"Trust me…," Leos said, "you wouldn't believe us if we told you."

"Who's this?" inquired Max, who took notice of Zophiel's presence within the group almost immediately.

"You're not going to believe it, but we found him," said Kairo.

"Found who?" pressed Leos.

"Who do you think? Hunter's father," said Jacob. "This is Zophiel."

The name instantly erased from Max's face any sign of the head-scratching encounter that had occurred with the statues and replaced it with a leery frown.

"No kidding. He was here the whole time," he remarked as he studied the stranger with a scrutinizing stare. "Wasn't that convenient."

Jacob attempted to initiate introductions but Zophiel wasn't eager to exchange greetings just yet.

"If it's all the same to you, I don't think this is the safest place to start making acquaintances," he said while eyeing suspiciously the courtyard's dark surroundings. "Infectors are not known to scare off so easily, even by one so skilled with a sword like Damiel here. I anticipate their return in short-order, especially knowing there are Nephilim about. And I would be surprised if their ranks aren't reinforced by a far worse threat.

"In any regard, it would be of vital prudence on my part, if you'll forgive my saying so, not to be witnessed fraternizing with you here, and most certainly not on this particular night," Zophiel added, as the golden glare that resided within his eyes scouted anxiously the shadowy recesses of the numerous arched walkways surrounding the courtyard before quickly concealing his face once more behind the guise of his mask.

"Wait a minute…you can't just leave," Hunter implored almost desperately, before gently retreating when he took notice of his hand clasping hold of his father's shoulder. "That is, my friends here…they've come a long ways in order to speak with you."

"Yes, I know," replied Zophiel, though he could see his son was not just referring to the group surrounding him, no matter how tried he hide it. "I've been expecting you for some time, now."

"You have?" Jacob asked with surprise.

"Was it you who left the invitation to this party tonight at our hotel?" inquired Wray.

"Invitation? That, I know nothing about," answered Zophiel. "Nor would I have felt comfortable luring you to such a hornets' nest, especially knowing my son was in your company."

He looked again to Hunter whose face he had not seen for many years, and he was gladdened for the mask he wore to shield the abundance of emotions he felt come over him.

"No doubt you all have questions that have been left to marinate for some time," he said. "Come…let us go where we can speak freely outside the reach of unseen ears."

Just as they were about to turn and exit the courtyard, there was heard a noticeable rumbling that sounded as though it were coming from deep within the ground upon which they stood. Nearby, two ornate and imposing wellheads, sprouting from the center of the courtyard, began to groan. Suddenly, the wellhead closest to the group erupted not with the rainwater for which it had been designed to capture, but a column of fire. The air, however, became instantly and bitterly cold.

Max appeared, at first, to be following the trail of his ghostly, frosty breath, but, in fact, it was his ears that were leading him with slow and cautious steps away from the group across the courtyard floor. He barely took notice of the column of fire that erupted from the second wellhead as he approached it, as he was too focused on a strange and yet familiar noise. It sounded almost like the scurrying of feet coming from high and low places, as well as everywhere in between, yet when he searched closely the palace walls surrounding the courtyard, he saw nothing to which the phantom feet belonged.

Max's ears then honed in on a noise that stopped him in his tracks; it was the sound of heavy, labored breathing; mucous-filled and strained. Max had only heard it once before and he had imagined then the noise coming from someone whose throat had suffered a fatal slashing. He also knew firsthand there was only thing capable of making such a sound, and he didn't need the freezing temperature to chill him to the core to realize it.

"What is it, Max?" Jacob asked when he spied the rare sight of fear in is friend's eyes.

"Hunter's father's right…we gotta get out here. Now!"

~ ~ ~

They raced from the courtyard and out into the deserted piazza as fast as their feet could carry them, but they couldn't escape the unpleasant cold chill that settled down upon them as though there had been an abrupt shift in seasons. Yet while the cold failed to slow them, and in fact spurned them on, the sight of three silhouetted figures suddenly spotted standing ominously in the path leading to the lagoon, and their waiting boats, just beyond at the end of the piazza most certainly did.

Who they were was impossible, at first, to tell; they seemed to gather the night around them and wear it like a cloak. As the group stepped cautiously closer toward them, however, even the favor of the darkness couldn't blot out fully the youthful faces of the three boys hidden within, at least from those with Nephilim and angel eyes.

"They're just kids," Leos breathed with relief.

"No...they are not," Damiel argued in a firm yet quiet voice.

Kairo squinted his eyes to get a harder fix on the three figures. "They sure look like kids to me."

"That's the problem; you're looking, yet failing to see," Damiel replied reprovingly. "They're Furies."

"Do I even want to ask what a Fury is?" Wray whispered to Jacob with marked unease.

"No," Jacob replied bluntly, "you don't."

The name had always been one that Nephilim took fright of, no matter how brave or fearless they might be. Then again, the chilling mythos surrounding the Furies passed down from generation to generation of young Fledglings by their wary fathers, was all they knew about the terrifying inhabitants from the Underneath. For it was the rare and lucky Nephilim who came face to face with a Fury and lived to give credence to the petrifying stories they all carried in the back of their minds. Now, here they found themselves witnesses to three such fiendish entities and even Ethan—far and away the most cautious and trepidatious of the bunch—was unmoved to take flight to safety.

"These are the so-called monsters that made me need a night light when I went to sleep growing up?" Ethan said mockingly.

"I hate to burst your bubble," he then called out to the shadowy trio, "but even I look scarier than you, which is saying a lot."

"I wouldn't antagonize them, dill," Max warned under his breath, and with good reason.

Ethan, however, didn't appear the least bit worried. Not at first, that is.

Then one of the innocuous-looking Furies walked forward, and the instant it stepped beyond the periphery of the shadows within which it had been concealed, and came in contact with the silvery light of the moon hanging overhead, the image of the young boy peeled itself away to reveal an unsightly nightmare of which no amount of whispered rumors or tales could have prepared Ethan, or his less skittery companions.

The Fury, at first sight, looked like a walking corpse that had been charred beyond recognition in a ghastly inferno. Its hide was as black as coal, and from the pitch-colored face were two vacant slants of white that served as eyes which were absent pupils, or any signs of life. Its limbs were long and knobby, its ears were turned out and pointed like horns, and a pair of oversized incisors similar to tusks found on a wart hog jutted from the bottom of its jaw of its overly large mouth.

"That would be a Fury, no doubt," muttered Max, while unknowingly fingering the telling scar set in place just beneath his left eye, as he recounted a rare tangle he had with a similar curse not long before his arrival at Havenhid, and managed to live to tell about it.

The Fury attempted what appeared to be a grotesque and sinister smile at Ethan, and as it did the brief unintimidated grin Ethan held before the hideous creature came to light fell away. Suddenly, the Fury made a quick dart to the right that was so swift it looked as if it had disappeared into thin air.

"Stay alert!" Damiel barked, as he and the rest of the group turned in unison, attempting to keep all surrounding directions in their sights for the vanished black entity.

No one was more desperate to regain sight of the Fury than Ethan, while clutching his drawn sword with a death grip. But just as he slowly turned from completing a full, if not jumpy revolution, he found himself, much to his horror, face-to-face with the hideous Fury. Ethan's eyes nearly bugged themselves free from his skull when the Fury opened its mouth wider than it was conceived possible and revealed the orange glow of fire smoldering deep in the innards of the creature. And when the Fury set forth a beastly cry, its entire being emitted the fiery glow as though it was the creation of molten rock.

Ethan hadn't a chance to scream when something wrapped itself suddenly around his middle that at first felt to be the coils of a rather large snake. His sword slipped from his hand and fell to the ground with a loud clang when, with a violent tug, he was yanked off his feet. He quickly saw it was not a snake that had entwined itself around him but rather a massive tail belonging to the Fury, and at the end of the slinking tail was a large pincher like that of giant scorpion. It snipped threateningly in the direction of his terrified face like the snapping jaws of a ravenous piranha, forcing from him a high-pitched cry for help, when he realized the Fury had sprouted a pair of leathery, bat-like wings and was rising up into the night sky with him in tow like a fish attached to end of a fisherman's hook.

"What do we do?" Kairo cried out over his friend's desperate shrieks as the Fury began to whip Ethan violently about.

"I've handled plenty of Furies in my day," Damiel said with the unfurling of his wings. "It'll be my pleasure to put this one out of its misery."

Before he gained lift from his wings, the Fury let out a blood-curdling scream, and Ethan dropped from the sky and onto the hard concrete ground like a sack of potatoes along with the Fury's bloodied, severed tail that loosened its stranglehold on the boy as it thrashed wildly about like an enraged serpent. Hunter and Leos quickly pulled Ethan free of the coils and out of reach of the pincher's crushing hold which made one last mad attempt to sever him into two or more pieces, before Max jumped and stilled the chomping tail with a focused swing of his sword.

"Are you all right?" Wray asked Ethan while kneeling beside him after rushing to his side to lend him comfort.

"I think so," Ethan, looking visibly dazed as he sat on the ground trying to regain his bearings, said.

"Looks like the Force was really with you this time around to help save your bacon," Leos remarked jokingly to his "Star Wars" obsessed friend.

"Not to mention this," Ethan was quick to add.

He held up his hand still slimy and dripping with blood that was as black as the Fury from which it came, and in his grip he clutched a long gray feather he had struggled with and succeeded in plucking from one of his wings while in the Fury's grip and used the razor-sharp edge of the deceptively soft plume like a knife to cut himself free of the strangling tail.

"Why you sly dog, you," Leos cooed with a smile of approval. "You might just have the makings of ruthless demon slayer yet."

"Well done, Fledgling," commended Damiel, as well. "It's good to see the fruits of my teachings at Lions Bite finally being put to the use for which it was intended: the shedding of enemy blood, and not that of your fellow Nephilim."

Ethan felt his face go flush with a hot glow as his brief heroic moment was clouded over by the memory of the unfortunate day when he suffered an embarrassment he had yet to live down of playing Jedi with his sword at Lions Bite and, in his enthusiasm, nearly amputating the leg of one of his fellow Shrikes. But neither his moment of mettle or embarrassment was to last for more than a moment when the wounded Fury reminded anyone within earshot of its presence with a loud shrieking cry.

"Um, guys...I don't think we're quite out of the woods here yet," said Jacob.

The Fury whose tail had been docked by Ethan howled as it stomped about in pain and rage, and it was soon joined by the other two. The trio of black monstrosities, glowing with the fires of the Underneath with every screeching howl they made, looked like shapes of horror created from a fresh lava flow, as they advanced menacingly upon the anxious group. Damiel and Zophiel both positioned themselves protectively before the younglings, with their swords drawn and ready to cut down anything that dared attempt to cross their path.

~ ~ ~

Suddenly, there was heard a loud whistle from somewhere in the distance. It made the Furies stop and spin around to see what had made it, and standing at the far end of the piazza before the tall pillar upon which stood the winged Lion of Venice that had earlier somehow, miraculously, come to life and left its perch to drive the statues of Mars and Neptune back to their own abandoned perches, was yet another shadowy figure dressed in a long black hooded cloak; the same cloaked figure Jacob recalled seeing weaving its way inconspicuously through the crowd at the party inside the ballroom.

"Daemonium pariunt, vade!" came a deep and commanding voice from within the dark cloak that echoed its way through the piazza.

The order made the Furies incensed, and they screamed a response of rage in return.

"I SAID LEAVE THIS PLACE!" the voice boomed with equal fury before offering a quieter, yet no less hostile threat. "Or shall I send you?"

The Furies made their unwise choice when they stormed the dark stranger with an unleashed ferociousness and were met by a flash of silver reflected off the blade of sword brought into view from the hidden folds of the figure's cloak. There was no fight, no struggle; just three purposeful and targeted swings of the sword too swift for anyone with eyes to follow fully, and the Furies were no more.

All who witnessed the brief clash looked on with awe at the mysterious stranger who quietly and calmly returned his sword to the innards of his cloak, especially Jacob who had never before seen a sword used with such skill outside Damiel's hands; never, that is, except once above the waters of the Van Gölü against a swarm of Infectors just before being accompanied through the Gate leading to Eden.

"Who might you be?" Damiel called out to the stranger the question of which everyone in the company wished to know the answer.

The stranger remained silent for a moment or two.

"I am many things to many people," the answer came when finally he spoke. "To you, Damiel, I will simply state myself as friend."

Friend?

A startled look crept over Damiel, as he was instantly reminded of a similar introduction extended to him by another faceless and mysterious individual at the wretched Purgatory nightclub.

"We know each other then?" Damiel asked with a look of growing puzzlement.

"Oh, yes...quite well."

The stranger slowly began his approach toward the bewildered group, and Damiel found himself grasping tighter the sword in his hand.

"I am one amongst the chosen circle of nine who has returned warmth to a seat long-left cold and vacant," said the stranger whose face remained hidden in the darkness of the hood draped over his head except for his mouth, from which a voice ringing with growing familiarity came.

"I am the sheep returned to his flock after being left to wander a world overrun by wolves. I am the vintner of a sweet wine pressed from a particularly bitter fruit, and the keeper of sorrowful vigils from whose shoulders the weight of unimaginable grief and despair has been lifted; I am the giver of a single chance and the humble recipient of two. I am the forger of forged destinies, and the Lazarus arisen from the mountain chasm that spits wings and swallows bones."

"The Lazarus arisen from the mountain chasm that spits wi—" Damiel cocked his head as he repeated the stranger's words in a cautious whisper as if they were part of a witch's spell too dangerous to utter out loud.

"Can it be possible?" he posed the question more to himself than to the cloaked figure upon whom his wide eyes were fixed with a stunned, nay, disbelieving look. The angel's lips then did the unthinkable: they trembled slightly, and through them came an unexpected whisper.

"Gothamel?"

The stranger replied by reaching up and drawing back the hood from off his head, and when the moonlight presented the familiar face of the angel long-believed lost to a cruel and abrupt end at Broken Earth, all who gazed upon the slightly crooked smile and eyes dancing with a golden light framed by wisps of long brown hair were left to stand speechless.

"Stone! The! Crows!" gasped Max who was the first to recover use of his tongue.

"It can't be!" Kairo was next to exclaim with equal disbelief. "Y-y-you fell without wings. We were all there-we watched it happen."

"Aye," said Gotham. "And it was only by such a harrowing fall that took me that the lofty heights which had once served as the stone upon which my feet were grounded came to still my plummet.

"And Gothamel the Fallen became Gothamel the Redeemed!"

The declaration rang forth from the angel's mouth like a trumpet delivering a royal proclamation, and with it, Gotham flung off from him the dark cloak in which he was wrapped to unveil something equally as unbelievable as his revealed redemption: a pair of majestic wings in place of the ones that had been savagely cleaved from his back. Only they were not gray in color like the pair lost, but a brilliant white. Dazzling, actually; they appeared to radiate an inner light much like the moon above when Gotham slowly unfurled the impressive feathered appendages.

~ ~ ~

"I was beginning to wonder if he'd ever come around to showing his face," Hunter remarked, as he watched the cheerful reunion between angel and Nephilim, drawing a curious look from Damiel.

"You know Gothamel?"

"Well, all except his name, which now I understand why he kept it a secret from me.

Remember? I told you back at my loft," said Hunter.

Damiel didn't have to exude much effort to jog his memory.

"This is the one whom you were referring to as the 'friend' who forewarned you we would be paying you a visit?"

"One and the same," answered Hunter, which only etched a more curiouser look in the expression fixed upon Damiel's face.

Gotham, meanwhile, continued to bask in the warm reception from those in the group who were glad to have him once again in their company. One particular reunion he was most anxious to share in, however, was noticeably absent from amongst the welcoming committee. He glanced about until he spied Jacob standing off to the side looking quite subdued while quietly observing the merriment, and Gotham realized his sudden reappearance was likely as traumatic for the boy as watching him plunge from Broken Earth to the certain death waiting beyond the blanket of mist.

Gotham pursed his lips and smiled at the boy. "Did a cat catch your tongue, boy?"

Since Gotham's apparent death at Broken Earth, Jacob had wrestled with every consuming emotion imaginable:

Grief.

Rage.

Regret.

Now, suddenly, seeing the angel standing mere feet from him, it was if every emotion he ever felt before had been stripped away; every emotion, that is, except one. With great restraint he approached Gotham and, feeling as awkward as he undoubtedly knew he looked, he gave the angel a gingerly poke to his arm, most likely to put to rest that the figure before him was indeed real and not the sadistic creation of one of his inexplicable dreams from which he was about to awaken from and find himself upright in his bed.

"No...you're not dreaming," Gotham said with a reassuring smile, showing he had not lost his penchant for the occasional glimpse into one's thoughts.

With that, Jacob, unable to contain his overwhelming joy any longer, threw his arms around Gotham in a tight embrace that was surprising even to the angel. It was happily and equally reciprocated.

CHAPTER EIGHTEEN

"I still can't believe you're actually alive and, well, here in the flesh," Jacob remarked to Gotham, shortly after Zophiel led the group to the banks of the lagoon where they boarded two gondolas and set adrift across the calm, moonlit waters.

"You, a doubting Thomas? My, my, will wonders ever cease to exist?" Gotham replied in jest. "Would it help lay your skepticism to rest to have another poke at my arm?"

"I'm sorry. I don't mean to sound cynical. It's just…what happened at Broken Earth, what Thaniel did to you…it was just so violent and hateful I would never imagine—"

"That someone could ever hope to breathe with life after such a final end," Gotham completed the boy's thought. "Well, as you can well see, someone did, and I am here with you now and in finer form than I was before my brief absence."

"If it serves you any satisfaction, you'll be happy to know that Thaniel got his just desserts for what he did to you, and better," Max commented from the neighboring boat skimming slowly across the water alongside the one in which Jacob and Gotham were seated.

Whether or not Gotham found any glee in the news, he didn't show it and, instead, grew noticeably quiet and bowed his head.

"What happened at Broken Earth occurred months ago. What's kept you away for long?" asked Jacob.

"Reconciling my place with my father, I'm happy to say," said Gotham.

"And were you able to…" Jacob paused briefly as though second guessing the appositeness of his inquiry before hesitantly sputtering, "see your son?"

"Oh, yes!" Gotham sighed in return, as his eyes shined golden and welled up with tears that were not hinged in any manner to sadness, but gladness, "and the sight of him filled my heart more than the breath of life ever could when it returned to my lungs."

Whatever more could be mentioned on the matter—and by the serene look afloat in his eyes there was—he chose to keep it to himself and speak no further.

"Well, I for one can say the sight of you this night has filled my heart in a way you cannot imagine, as I'm certain it will fill all of Eden with similar rejoice upon your return. No matter the burden I fear will likely come with it," said Damiel cheerily.

"And what burden, exactly, is it you find me suspect of inflicting upon Eden before I have set even a toe inside her gates?" Gotham grumbled in return.

"I meant you no disparagement, truly. But looking upon you, I'm just suddenly reminded of the high regard you hold for your own reflection. I can only imagine now the insufferable sight we'll all be forced to endure while watching you preen daily in the full light of the sun, now that your arguable good looks are no longer spoiled by that hideous scar."

"Oh, that," Gotham said with a subtle smile, when he realized Damiel was playfully goading him with some good-natured ribbing over the noticeable absence of the shameful Fallen mark that had once been seared into the temple above his left eye.

"I guess I'm still getting used to it not being there," said Gotham, while gently touching the now unblemished area with his fingertips.

Hunter, who had quietly been observing the stranger Gotham, looked to his own father sitting opposite him.

"Looks like you weren't as lucky," he said.

"Lucky? How do you mean?" Zophiel replied.

"Just that it appears this is a night of unexpected resurrections, and after spending the day thinking you had been killed along with mom, you end up appearing from out of nowhere. Only unlike Gotham, I see you're still branded as a traitor," Hunter explained, while eyeing with contempt the unlovely mark that scarred his father's forehead.

"Then you know what happened," Zophiel, caught off guard by the remark, said. "How?"

"Mr. d'Artusio told me. We stopped by the house—or at least where there used to be a house—when we first arrived."

Zophiel closed his eyes and let go a deep sigh of anguish.

"I'm sorry you had to find out that way," he told his son. "I wanted to be the one who gave you the news but, when you left Venice, you did a remarkably good job of covering your tracks."

"Then…you weren't killed?" Zophiel shook his head sadly.

"I know it pains you to hear that," he said with a heavy voice, "but believe me when I say I would have taken your mother's place if I could have for both her sake as well as your own."

"How could you ever think that?" Hunter, whose hardened expression finally gave way to one of solicitude, asked. "I was just as heartbroken when I thought I had lost you as well."

"It's true," Wray, who sat nearby listening, quietly interjected, bringing a visible embrace of solace to Zophiel.

"We've much to discuss, you and I," Zophiel said, taking his son's hands into his own, and much to his delight he felt Hunter return his squeezing embrace.

~ ~ ~

The gondolas continued their way on their own accord, without the aid of a gondolier positioned at the tail of each boat to steer their passage through the night, until eventually they reached a small islet—one of the many scattered about the lagoon—the entirety of which was enclosed like some fortress behind an apricot-orange brick wall decorated intermittently with arches made of white stone.

It was through one of these arches the party passed through once they stepped off their boats, and they found themselves in what at first sight appeared to be the beginning of a large sprawling garden whose beauty was accentuated by the illumination of the waxing moon.

"Forgive my cloak and dagger tactics, but this is one of the last safe havens in Venice where one can speak freely without fear of being eavesdropped upon," Zophiel explained, as he led Damiel and Gotham down one of various gravel walkways lined with towering cypress trees, while the rest of the group followed close at their heels.

"And about what, exactly, do you foresee us conversing that would require such clandestine efforts?" asked Damiel.

"I would have thought it obvious after the transpiring of events you witnessed tonight at the palace," said Zophiel. "The Dark forces are on the move."

The ominous statement, strangely, drew a dismissive grin from Damiel rather than a stiffening of alarm.

"You'll excuse me, Zophiel, if I don't immediately sound the trumpet of warning and ready my battle armor, but news that the Dark forces are on the move is hardly news," he said. "They are like sharks in the open sea: they either maintain a state of perpetual motion or they drown."

"I am well-versed in the comportment of shadows; the same shadows that have been left to linger and meander these long years since Samuel was sequestered in his virtual prison by Gothamel here," said Zophiel. "And, still, I tell you they have, under furtive guidance, become emboldened in ways I have not seen since the days of the Great War."

Damiel became stony-faced as he shot Zophiel a sideways glance no longer absent the heedlessness he had so casually ignored.

"And by 'furtive guidance,' I take it you hold a specific name pinned beneath your tongue; and that name would be Miseriel, would it not? Or Miseri, as he so poignantly baptized himself this night."

"In the blink of an eye, you suddenly, and most fittingly, look the part of a nervous ocean wader who's just had the unfortunate sighting of a shark's fin breaking the surface of the water," answered Zophiel somberly.

As they passed their way through several sectioned areas of the garden, Ty took notice of a growing sea of fresh cut flowers and potted plants, They were placed around an equally large number of stone crosses and other large slabs of marble that obviously served as grave markers. Even in the darkness of the night, Ty could see attached to nearly every headstone was a photo of the deceased staring back, along with evidence of a recent visit by loved ones, such as handwritten notes, glass ornaments, and other sentimental mementos.

"It's late, and after tonight I'm not entirely sure when my eyes are playing tricks on me or not, but…are we actually taking a stroll through a cemetery in the middle of the night?" he asked with a note of trepidation in his voice.

"It's actually quite a beautiful place to come visit, not to mention it's also the final resting spot of several notable people like Stravinsky, the Russian composer, and ballet impresario Sergei Diaghilev," said Hunter.

"Comforting," Ty huffed, with a tight-lipped smile conveying his utter and complete disinterest (and frankly annoyance) in Hunter's mental rolodex of endless trivia concerning all things Venice. "Then the answer to my question is that we are, indeed, and for whatever puzzling reason, taking a stroll through a creepy cemetery…in the middle of the night."

~ ~ ~

Zophiel led the way through an entry arcade to yet another sectioned-off area of the cemetery resembling more of a quaint luxuriant park than a place for the dead. As the group made its way along the pathway beneath more cypress trees, they passed many mausoleums. Each was more grand and stately than the previous, appearing like miniature estates amid a landscape of flowering plants, topiary and large shade trees.

None was as imposing and impressive than the one they came upon near the center of the park setting. To begin with, it consisted of sixteen towering Corinthian pillars arranged to form a half circle around a raised slab of concrete inlaid with colorful tiles upon which resided a large ornate crypt. It was the sort of extravagant monument one would expect to be built for a deceased Roman emperor like Caesar Augustus to lie in state after passing, or at the very least one of his wealthy notable contemporaries. Two bronze angels with bowed heads kept vigil on either side of the six steps leading the way to the crypt, and a decorated relief of Michelangelo's Pieta affixed upon the two center columns overlooked the memorial, while small Grecian urns adorned the tops of the remaining pillars.

"There's something Miseriel said tonight that I can't seem to stop turning over in my mind. Something about a new dawn approaching the horizon…a dawn of reconciliation," Damiel said reflectively, while walking about in front of the ancient Rome-inspired shrine. " 'When the masks finally fall away, and the Unworthy suddenly are the Worthy,' he said. But what exactly did he mean?"

"To put it plainly and succinctly, he is speaking of a coup," said Zophiel.

"A coup?"

"That is the term used when one speaks about the overthrow of power, is it not?"

"And who exactly is he seeking to dethrone?" Damiel inquired.

"Why, Samael, of course."

Zophiel's reply drew a look of incredulousness, if not confusion, from Damiel.

"Miseriel's been quietly plotting such a move beginning the day he learned of Samael's defeat at Gothamel's hands in the Infernal Desert," continued Zophiel. Yet he could see Damiel was still skeptical with what he was hearing.

"You know intimately who and what Miseriel is as well as I, Damiel. He is a particularly stony-hearted and sadistic fiend whose cruelty knows no bounds." On that point, Damiel could not argue with Zophiel. "If Samael hadn't gained such favor in the Dragon's eyes, Miseriel most certainly would have. Is it really all that surprising to learn he is scheming to do just that while the position sits vacant?"

"Why not just slither into it like the serpent he is, then? Why all the drama of a coup?" asked Damiel.

"I'm afraid it's not as easy as it would appear for Miseriel," said Gothamel who had been sitting quietly nearby listening. "I may have significantly tethered Samael's power when I bound him and left him to rot in that sweltering hellhole where I abandoned him, but I did not render him impotent. He still holds sway over a great many Underneath dwellers who continue to remain wholly devoted to him, including the Dragon himself."

"Which is why Miseriel has been quietly growing himself a vast and potent army," said Zophiel. "The attendees you mingled with at tonight's masquerade ball are his recruiters: world leaders, magnates, criminals of particular ruthlessness, school teachers, even high-ranked members of the clergy. Miseriel's tentacles are far-reaching."

Damiel stood quiet for some time as things began to slowly become clearer as he replayed the events from the party inside his head.

"So be it," he said suddenly and without care or worry. "Let him have his army, and let them take up arms against each other. Why should we care? The more they warmonger amongst themselves, then thinner the ranks we will come to face when they refocus their aggressions on us, and the inevitable battle we've long prepared for is dropped at our feet."

"That's just it," said Gotham. "The purpose of Miseriel's army is not in preparation to do battle with the Light. If anything, it's the opposite."

A clear look of confusion swept over Damiel, and Zophiel stepped in once again to offer clarity.

"Much can be said about Miseriel, but one would be remiss to dismiss his shrewd and percipient nature," he said. "Where the Dragon and his dark minions are consumed by hate and revenge, Miseriel is a clear thinker whose ultimate objective in life rests on one thing and one thing only: self-preservation.

"Becoming a Fallen is as terminal a curse with which one can find themselves afflicted," continued Zophiel, "but not in Miseriel's eyes. To him, becoming a Fallen is a blessing. He wears with great comfort the shoes in which he's been made to walk in, and he proudly basks in any light that gives prominent display of the shameful mark scarring his face, if for no other reason than the freedom being a Fallen has gifted him; the freedom from virtue; freedom from benevolence; freedom from rectitude. It is a desolate perdition the Fallen are cast to, but for a Fallen like Miseriel, it has proven to be a state of nirvana, if for no other reason than he is a ruler in the realm of his own damnation. He is also well aware of the one solitary threat facing his kingdom."

"What threat is that?" Jacob asked, with eyes wide with curiosity, as he listened intently along with his friends.

Zophiel fixed his gaze on the boy and answered simple, "You."

"And you," he quickly added, looking again to Damiel and Gotham. "All of you, really. For you see, there is one thing of which Miseriel fears: the long-foretold battle between the Light and the Dark. He is constantly looking over his shoulder and keeping his ears peeled for the first beat to sound from the impending war drums. And while the Dragon and Samuel hold every confidence the Darkness will emerge victorious in this war to end all wars, despite numerous prophecy and revelations foretelling otherwise, Miseriel is unwilling to risk losing the free rein he has come to love, and so he has put into motion his first line of defense.

"By securing a large enough army, he knows the Dragon—despite his loyalty to Samuel—will be unable to deny Miseriel's aggressive and premeditated grab for power. He will prove successful in his mission and even Samael's most loyal supporters will be unable to keep Miseriel from assuming Samael's position. Then, with his army and the Underneath at his command, he will have secured his continuing existence for an indeterminate period, not by emerging victorious in any future battle with the Light, but by ensuring any such war never sees a single sword drawn."

Zophiel's words proved halting to all who listened to them, but none more than Damiel.

"Am I missing something?" Leos asked after a quiet moment. "How exactly does Miseriel set himself up to be king of the world with an army that lays down its weapons in the face of war?"

"By the same method that has kept me from exacting my vengeance upon him since the taking of my son," Damiel answered aggrievedly. "The promised war can only be sparked by one of their swords, not ours; no matter how justified we might be to draw first. Zophiel is correct: many of us have misjudged Miseriel's cunningness; none more so than myself. By his unexpected scheme of peace, he has found a foolproof way to keep his end at bay and ensure that the Light and the Darkness be forced to coexist in perpetuity."

"There is another significant weave of the thread to this intricate web we cannot overlook," Zophiel was quick to point out. "By setting himself up to be king of the world, as young Leos astutely mentioned, Miseriel will undoubtedly usher in a winter's darkness to engulf fully the Civilian world in a way an army of Light Bearers would find hopeless to blunt, much less one."

While Jacob found the statement to be uncomfortably dismaying, it was not nearly as dismaying as the pair of golden eyes he found suddenly fixed on him and gave him a slow looking over with nary a glimmer of confidence.

"Now you understand the purpose for which your presence was called upon at the palace earlier tonight," said Gotham.

"So, then, it was you who sent us the invitation?" asked Wray who seemed determined to uncover the identity of the unseen messenger.

"I thought it important Miseriel's plans be witnessed firsthand and not conveyed in a message delivered by a homing pigeon."

"There's just one thing I find more than a little odd in all of this," Damiel said, leveling his piercing gaze on Zophiel, after quietly chewing on all that had been told to him. "Why are you telling us all of this?"

The question caught Zophiel off guard, and Damiel was quick to pose it once more.

"For what purpose would a Fallen have to tell tales out of turn that would most definitely betray the interests of their own kind?"

"A fair enough question, Damiel," Zophiel replied, "and one I would indeed struggle to answer with any ring of truth if, in fact, I was actually one of the accursed.

"What are you implying, Zophiel?" asked Damiel.

"Only the truth, of which all of you will be the first to learn," answered Zophiel. "And that is the rumors of my great tumble from on high have been greatly exaggerated."

For those who continued to stare ahead with a look of bafflement, the marked angel stepped out from the rustling shadows of the outstretched branches of the surrounding trees and into the unobscured glow of the moon bathing the cemetery with its silvery light, and to everyone's amazement a n d most notably, Hunter's, the skeletal mark seared into his temple vanished instantly from sight.

~ ~ ~

"It's impossible!" Damiel stated with hushed disbelief when he overcame the shock of what he had just witnessed. "No Fallen has the power to manipulate or conceal the mark of the exiled."

"You're quite right. But as I just revealed, I am not a Fallen," said Zophiel, which only exacerbated Damiel's befuddlement.

"Then you've been redeemed like Gothamel."

Zophiel shook his head. "I've never been in need of redemption, as I've never incurred Heaven's wrath nor been cast from grace."

"What is it you're saying then, brother?" Damiel pleaded with Zophiel for some semblance of clarity. "If not Fallen, what would spur one from on high to even entertain such a despicable masquerade all these thousands of years?"

Before Zophiel could answer, a rustling movement of what sounded like the approach of some unseen person caught Damiel's ear, as it did Gotham's. In a flash, both angels drew their swords and took their battle stance when six strapping shadowy figures with identical Fallen marks branded into their temples stepped forward from the folds of the night and encircled the group.

"You can retire your swords; there's no enemy here," Zophiel said, before the startled Nephilim could follow suit.

He then approached one of the marked strangers who stood silent with eyes gleaming gold behind an expressionless face, and Damiel watched with intense curiosity as the two exchanged a brief conversation conveyed in unheard whispers. When they had finished, the Fallen and the others in his company adjourned themselves to nearby corners of the cemetery where they appeared to quietly wait for further instructions, and except for a gentle breeze stirring the trees, there descended a deathly quiet that was most fitting for a grave yard.

"As I stated, I am not a Fallen, except in name only," Zophiel said, when he returned his attention once again to Damiel.

"My exile, as it were, came about in the midst of The Great War in Heaven when a third of my foolish and mutinous brethren were purged from the skies in a lightning storm driven by rage and despair. I was summoned by our father and was asked a most thorny of requests. 'My constant son,' he said to me, 'it pains me to even ask this of you, especially on this most wretched of days. But, alas, it is because of your proven faithfulness that I summon you.' He then expressed his great dismay at the treachery that caused our Fallen brothers to turn on him and Heaven itself, but he was far more unsettled over the gullible and easily malleable Civilians on earth who were oblivious to what had just transpired. For he understood immediately what the aftermath of the War and the mass expulsion would mean for them, and that they would become the pawns in the chess game of vengeance that would ensue.

"And so he called upon me, albeit with great hesitation, to be party to a most unusual and unorthodox task; a task I readily admit agreeing to perform after equal hesitancy."

"And what task was that?" Jacob asked anxiously.

"To willingly surrender myself to the same fate as my outcast brothers," Zophiel replied. "And so I joined them in their long, harrowing fall with a false mark of disrepute emblazoned on my forehead. I lived as a Fallen, I looked like a Fallen and I behaved as a Fallen, and yet unlike a Fallen, I remained in the protective embrace of my father. I became his eyes and ears to all the untidy dealings and deceptive schemes hatched and plotted in the dark reaches of the rank rat hole known as the Underneath and, in return, Heaven succeeded to keep the Darkness firmly beneath its heel."

Damiel stood with a staggered look fixed on his face as he listened.

"You mean to tell me after all this time spent believing you were a traitor you were actually nothing more than a spy?" he asked.

"You were of your right mind to consider me a traitor and, in many instances, what many would consider a saboteur. Now, you know it was not against Heaven, and certainly not against our father," said Zophiel.

For a moment, Damiel was overwhelmed by a burdensome weight of shame and remorse as he recalled the feelings of contempt he had held towards Zophiel over his believed betrayal.

"What of them?" he grumbled with suspicion, when his gaze shifted past Zophiel to where his six other brethren long written off as mutineers lurked in the nearby distance.

"Exiles…the same as me, and no less beloved; sent from above to aid me in stemming the tide of the Darkness' power as it grew in strength and numbers. And to be the first to lend themselves to the ranks of what will one day soon be your army," Zophiel said, turning his gaze suddenly onto Jacob.

"My...my army?" the stupefied boy echoed.

"As powerful a Light Bearer as you may be, you will no doubt need a soldiery of unmatched might to see your mission to completion. These loyal fighters are here tonight to be the first to pledge their loyalty to you young Light Bearer."

The still befuddled Jacob had no reply when the six Exiles standing quietly at attention dropped to one knee with their heads bowed.

"Only when our commission is complete will we retreat from this fetid swamp to our rightful place where our winsomeness will no longer be marred by this fictive blemish of disgrace we are forced to bear with pride," Zophiel continued before his demeanor darkened with an abrupt grimness.

"But, alas," he said, "it would appear that the mission of this beloved exile has somehow unexpectedly been exposed for the ruse it is."

"You're talking about the attack that happened upon your home," said Max who like the others had been listening to Zophiel with great intrigue. "You think it happened because you were discovered to be a mole?"

"What other explanation could it be?" answered Zophiel, looking somewhat at a loss as he pondered Max's question. "What baffles me is how, after all these countless years, when I had so masterfully embedded myself like a tick in a soft patch beneath the Dragon's leathery wing."

"It doesn't make any sense," Damiel, looking as flummoxed as Zophiel, said. "Even if it was true that your subterfuge was discovered, why would a Pethen be sent to root out your duplicity? Pethens were created solely to perform the duty of guardian, not assassin."

Troubled as the two angels may have been by the elusiveness of the answer for which they struggled, Zophiel's expression softened noticeably when the vision of his son standing quiet and looking noticeably vacant suddenly came into his sights.

"My dear child, I am so sorry I was unable to protect your mother from the claws of the evil scourge I struggled ceaselessly to protect the rest of the world's mothers and their children from. She was a good and pure woman whose loss will forever be a splinter of regret left to fester in my skin," he said. "But if there exists some glimmer of buoyancy, it is that I find myself this night unexpectedly reunited with my son after such a long estrangement, and that I might now be able to look upon him without fear of facing the reflection of shame and disapproval in his eyes all these years, but a newfound sparkle only the clarity of truth long-denied him regarding his father can bring."

Zophiel went to take Hunter into his embrace, but Hunter, his face twisting itself into an unmistakable expression of offense, abruptly took several steps backwards to ensure the gulf of space between the two remained.

"I don't believe this!" Hunter hissed. "You're standing here telling me my entire life up until now has been nothing more than a big made-up farce...like these stupid costumes we're wearing?"

"Whoa, hold on there, mate! Were your ears too full of gum to hear what he just finished explaining to all of us?" said Max. "He just said he's not a Fallen."

"Yeah, I heard him," Hunter said unaffectedly.

"I have no doubt this all comes as a bit of a shock to you," Zophiel attempted to calmly soothe his son. "Once you've spent your anger, I can only hope you will come to understand as a clear-thinking young man that the reasons I did what I did were for the safety and protection of your own well-being."

"Understand?" Hunter bellowed in a tone that assured any semblance of comprehension would be a long time in arriving, if ever. "Do you know what it's like to grow up thinking you're the son of a Fallen?"

"Trust me, Hunter, when I tell you I lament those years lost when I had hoped to share with you the truth when you had reached a certain maturity. But now, finally, I have that opportunity, late-coming as it might be, and you can now take solace in knowing you are not the sire of a Fallen."

"And you think that serves as any consolation to me now?" Hunter cried.

Zophiel was at a sudden loss of words, as he watched quite flummoxed as his son began to pace about in a most agitated of states.

"All this time, since the day I ran away from home, I've spent waging my own private war against the dark-doers of the world in hopes of proving myself to whoever might be watching that I was not the turncoat my father was; that I should not be made guilty by association. Now I'm supposed to suddenly be elated to learn that my, 'unworthiness as a Nephilim', was all a huge concocted lie?" Hunter raged to no one in particular. "Why do you think I suffered through so many black eyes and bloody noses while learning how to become the fighter I am with my fists? It was because I knew I would never have the chance to learn how to use a sword like all the other Nephilim who would eventually get the chance to go to Havenhid."

Then, turning suddenly to Jacob, he continued with his rant, "You want to know why earlier I refused to fly your friends to a safe spot outside of the palace? It was because I couldn't."

Before Jacob could understand exactly what Hunter meant by "couldn't," Hunter proceeded to tear himself out of the upper portion of his costume and present his naked back to the numerous gazes focused his way, and it instantly became clear: he was missing the one defining thing all Nephilim possessed that made them Nephilim. Instead of wings folded discreetly against his back as expected, there was bare skin, beneath which twin bulging knobs could be seen protruding prominently in the area of the shoulder blades. The reveal instantly took Jacob back to the days not so long ago when he was struggling to sprout his own feathered appendages and spent many an hour staring at his wingless back in the bathroom mirror with a growing sense of hopelessness and despair. In gazing upon Hunter's nude back, however, he recognized something oddly different. For starters, the skin surrounding the protruding shoulder blades was blotchy and discolored, like bruised fruit, and the knobs were quite large and looked like they might pierce through the skin at any moment, and not in the favorable way any Nephilim would be excitedly expecting.

"I've tried everything....I even broke several ribs and an ankle jumping off the roof of a three-story building in some desperate hope it might force them to push their way out," said Hunter, and Zophiel quietly bowed his head to hide the anguish he suddenly felt when he recognized his own unintended culpability of his son's distress.

"May I?" came Gotham's voice, as the angel approached Hunter with his hands raised in front of him.

Before Hunter could acquiesce, the angel placed his hands on the young man's back and with a look of quiet concentration gently examined each of the protruding humps.

"What age are you? Nineteen?" asked Gotham.

"I'll be twenty in a few months," answered Hunter.

He winced slightly, and only briefly, when Gotham's fingers gently kneaded a particularly sensitive area of his wing-deprived back, and when the poking and prodding was finally finished Hunter looked to the angel with the subtle nervousness evident in most patients awaiting a prognosis from their physician during a visit to the doctor's office.

"Wings are like seedlings sprouting from the soil. Without the sun, they end up withering and dying," said Gotham. "Yours are craving desperately the sunlight, hence the bruising and tenderness, but they have not yet completely shriveled."

Hunter's posture immediately straighten itself at hearing Gotham's unexpected words of optimism.

"You're saying there's still a chance for me to get them?"

Gotham gave a subtle if not hopeful nod and replied, "You've still time…not much, but time nonetheless. I would advise you accompany Damiel upon his return to Havenhid. You'd be about the oldest Fledgling to grace its halls, but from my impression of you this evening, you've more than enough heart to stare down into the mouth of Broken Earth and take possession of your wings at long last."

"Broken Earth…what's that?" Hunter wondered aloud.

"Every terrifying rollercoaster you could ever imagine rolled into one. And then some," Ethan replied without a hint of sally.

~ ~ ~

The mood became noticeably lighter for a moment or two as Gotham's encouraging words brought the first genuine smile to Hunter's usually brooding face in quite some time; a smile that only broadened itself when father and son turned to face the other and finally surrendered to the embrace their years apart had denied them.

"Well, this has certainly been an action-packed evening, hasn't it?" noted Leos. "We've managed to uncover a shady plot to wrestle control of the dark forces by a Fallen who's willingly chosen to give himself a new name associated with suffering, survive an attack by a couple of giant statues come to life, escape not one but three nasty Furies without a mark on any of us, and reunite a traitorous angel, who we learned was never traitorous, with his wingless son who likely won't be wingless for long, and the night is only half over."

"And yet we're still no closer to solving the matter that brought us here in the first place," Max was quick to remind everyone present.

Hearing that, Zophiel relaxed the embrace he had on his son and looked to Jacob who exuded a notable eagerness simmering just beneath the surface of his quiet demeanor.

"There's much I've come to hear about the one rumored to be the Light Bearer reborn that has greeted me with glad tidings not to mention unsettled angst. But tonight I've nothing but sincere gratitude for you," Zophiel said to Jacob who was momentarily taken aback.

"Me? What did I do?"

"You returned my boy to me and allowed me the chance to finally clear the cobwebs of untruth concerning his father that had marred his vision for far too long."

"I think you're giving me a little too much credit," said Jacob who was never one to be comfortable accepting even the most offhanded of compliments. "Truth is it was Hunter who brought us here to see you."

"But had it not been for you he would have never had been presented with a reason to retrace the path leading the way back home," Zophiel argued. "And for that I am eternally in your debt."

Rather than debate the issue any further, Jacob realized he had finally been presented the moment to address far more pressing matters for which he and his friends had traveled two continents and across an ocean in search of answers.

"Zophiel—it's all right if I call you that, isn't it?" Jacob asked with mindful politeness.

"It is my name," came the answer.

Jacob felt his cheeks flush slightly at the angel's obvious reply, genial as it was.

"Back at the palace courtyard when Hunter said we had come a long way to speak with you, you replied that you had been expecting us," said Jacob. "What did you mean by that? That is, do you know why we're here?"

Zophiel stood quiet for a moment staring at the boy with his kind yet penetrating eyes before succumbing to a smile.

"Come," he instructed while placing his hand on the boy's shoulder.

"Where are we going?"

"Somewhere, I think, where matters of confession are best exercised," came the reply.

Taking leave of his fellow band of exiles who stared intently from behind the moonlit shadows like motionless statuary keeping watch over the dearly departed souls at rest, Zophiel led the way deeper through the cemetery grounds with the rest of the group and its growing curiosities in tow. Their steps led the way to a large swath of lawn studded with rows upon rows of gravestones adorned with photographs of the deceased and decorated with colorful bouquets of flowers and glass ornaments they first passed. They then walked through a maze of walls forming the ossuary where bones once buried in the ground were eventually retired after a dozen years due to the island's limited space, a nugget of trivia Hunter made sure to share during the walk.

Eventually, they reached the end of the crypts and markers giving name to the island's many deceased residents and came to the steps of a large imposing edifice residing along the water's edge at the opposite side of the islet at which they had earlier arrived. Its once salt- white facade of Istrian marble had been weathered to a pale gray by the passage of time, yet the ghostly beauty of its baroque architecture, which included a massive dome and a statue of Michael the Archangel looming above the entrance, gleamed brightly like a luminous pearl freshly shucked from an oyster in the presence of the moon dangling large from the black sky.

Zophiel ushered the way through a heavy door, and it was immediately clear to everyone that they had entered into a church when they found themselves standing inside a small chapel housed beneath the large dome. The only light made available was that from the moon which streamed its way through several large oval windows circling the wall beneath the dome, coupled with the flickering glow coming from numerous lit candles. The air was cold, and it held the pungent scent of damp stone and a lingering of incense.

"I just love these old churches," Wray was the first to comment in a hushed whisper as her gaze traveled slowly and adoringly along the towering walls made of stone and marble.

"They're so beautiful."

The remark drew a snicker from Max.

"Something funny?" Wray asked while shooting him a cool sideways look.

"You've sure a weird sense of what's beautiful, I'll give you that," Max answered with a smirk.

"And what exactly is that supposed to mean?"

"Not trying to goad you into a fight. Just not sure exactly what you find so attractive about this creepy old place."

"Creepy?"

"With a capital C!"

Wray took a beat in order to retain hold of her calm demeanor and keep from being goading into an argument Max insisted he wasn't looking to start.

"First you pooh-poohed the palace, now this church. Obviously you lack the ability to appreciate the beauty of period architecture," she said with an air of haughtiness while turning her nose up to the air in a dismissive gesture.

"Oh, I appreciate the beauty of period architecture just fine, thank you very much," said Max. "I also appreciate ruins, like the Colosseum in Rome, and this place has clearly been ruined ten times over."

Jacob saw Wray's mouth begin to unhinge itself and quickly piped in before she could launch the first syllable of her response. "You've got to admit, Wray, this place is a bit on the creepy side. Granted it's a church but, I mean, all that's really missing here is Vincent Price to offer us ten thousand dollars to spend the night."

Wray looked at the two boys as though they were blind, and for a moment it appeared as if she might burst with frustration when Zophiel stepped in and said in his deep calming voice, "I think I see where the disconnect lies in what is obvious a curious difference of opinion."

Turning then to Wray, he asked her to describe aloud the chapel. It seemed a rather peculiar request for anyone with a working pair of eyeballs could see firsthand the beauty of the serene hexagonal room she so obviously held in high regard, but with Zophiel patiently awaiting her response her eyes proceeded to make a slow and careful survey of her surroundings. First, she commented on the exquisite ring of arches framing the large oval windows beneath the hollow of the massive dome, and then of the multiple pairings of towering Ionic pillars which rose up to meet the beginning and end of each arch. She then pointed out with a lilt of delight the decorative marble accenting the pale grey stone walls before her gaze shifted downward to the marble floor and described the mosaic assortment of dusty rose-colored triangles, squares and diamonds amid numerous blueish-gray circles as a piece of abstract art one might find hanging in a museum. But it was the three delicate bas-reliefs situated opposite one another that she reserved for most of her gushing. They decorated the sides of the chapel like sculpted paintings freezing scenes of religious imagery, and each was set within a large and elaborate shrine-like carving of stone protruding from the wall. And before each relief was a small stone altar fixed with a kneeler, and draped over the top of each altar was a pristine white cloth trimmed with delicate lace.

When she had finished with her oohing and aahing, she found much to her surprise Jacob and Max staring at her with a shared look of perplexity as if she, in fact, was the one who had been rendered blind and had just described a chapel filled with unicorns and leprechauns. And it was not just Jacob and Max; Leos, Kairo and even Ethan were fixated on her as though she were some odd curiosity. Before she could ask the reason for their dumbfounded expressions, Zophiel proceeded to ask Max the same thing he had of Wray and describe the chapel.

"Would it be okay if I borrow whatever magical pair of rose-colored glasses Wray here is obviously wearing?" Max inquired facetiously, prompting Wray to shoot him an icy glare.

"Never mind any of that," said Zophiel. "Just say out loud what you are able to see with your eyes, and only your eyes."

Clearly bored with what he saw as a pointless exercise, Max let out an impatient huff, but retained enough good spirit to indulge Zophiel and rolled his gaze upward to the same spot Wray had started at: the dome.

"I'll concede this place was probably quite the looker at one time, but anyone can see the dome is severely cracked and covered with cobwebs, the windows beneath it are all busted out as if they've been serving as target practice for a bunch of rock-chucking dills, most of the pillars are in various states of crumbling, and the supposed glowing white stone walls and museum-worthy floor are almost completely covered by some nasty, gross-looking black gunk…like mold, or something.

"And as for these so-call sculptures," he continued with a gesture to one of the wall reliefs and altars Wray had found so arresting. "I'm more than a little puzzled as to what you could possibly find so beautiful about something that looks to have been on the receiving end of a sledgehammer. I mean, look at it. It's so busted up I'm not sure how one would even know it was a sculpture to begin with."

When he had finished, he turned to Wray and offered her a shrug of his shoulders as though it were an exclamation point to his presentation.

"Like I said…Creepy!"

Leos, Kairo and Ethan nodded in agreement, leaving Wray standing quiet for a moment and staring with befuddlement at the shrine Max attempted to convince everyone was anything other than the obvious picturesque vision right before her very eyes.

"Oh, I get it," she finally said to Max with a slow-coming smile. "This is all some kind of joke to mess with my head, isn't it? Well, nice try; I'm not that gullible."

"Seriously, Wray, no one's fooling with you," Jacob interjected without a hint of toying.

Having already sided with Max with his Vincent Price crack, however, he was quickly ignored and Wray instead looked to Ty for support.

"You've been unusually quiet through all this," she said in a somewhat terse manner. "Would you care to weigh in on this, or does your Y chromosome automatically prevent you from straying away from the rest of this boy tribe?"

"Oh, I'd really rather not get involved if it's all the same to you," Ty demurred. "I mean, I see everything in this room the way you described it, including this shrine thingy which, to be frank about it, I doubt the world as a whole would miss all that much if someone did take a sledgehammer to it. But on the other hand, church or no church, I've always found old stone buildings like this to have a high creep factor…especially when you're still very much aware of the field of dead people residing just a hop, skip and a jump from where we're standing. Which I am. *Very aware of.* The dead people, that is.'"

"How is that possible?" Ethan wondered aloud. "How can the chapel look one way to Ty and Wray and completely different to the rest of us?"

"I would think the answer would be rather obvious," said Zophiel.

The blank looks fixed on the faces of the boys staring back at him argued differently.

"This is their first time stretching their wings this far outside Eden's border—a quite premature and unexpected excursion at that—and they are still quite green," Damiel explained.

Zophiel nodded his understanding.

"The eyes of a Nephilim are quite powerful, as I'm sure you've already come accustomed to," he began to explain. "They can seize on things from a great distance, just like a telescope, and they can pierce the gloom of night as easily as the harshest glare of daylight.

"But there is a far greater gift provided you through your sight that quite obviously you are not even aware of; one which only belonged to the angels until your fathers passed it down to you, and that is the gift of perception, particularly when it comes to the dark forces."

"Are you saying what we're seeing now is some sort of shared illusion?" Max asked inquisitively.

"Quite the opposite, in fact," answered Zophiel. "The church has been under assault by the Darkness since the very first stone was set upon the foundation that would give rise to the first holy sanctuary, and century after century the church has managed to withstand the maelstrom set into motion against it. But even the most protected of houses cannot escape the eventual infestation of vermin, and so it came to be that the Darkness discovered a most opportune crack in the stone walls it had been hellbent to crumble, and made its way through like a worm through the flesh of an apple. They say beware the wolf dressed in sheep's clothing, but this cunning pack came in the guise of shepherds. And now we have a poisoned and scattered flock who can no longer tell the difference between the shepherd and the wolf."

He then settled his penetrating gaze on Wray and Ty who had been listening most intently to him.

"What you see is a church as it has stood on this island for some time now," Zophiel said, before looking to the young Nephilim who were listening just as earnestly. "But what you see is the state of the church as it truly exists in its ongoing desecration by the Darkness."

The explanation left an unsettling grimness to settle itself in the boys' faces.

"No offense…but I don't think I'd like very much to have the gift to be able to see anything like that," Wray said after a long moment of silence had passed. Then to Jacob, and in particularly Max, she offered up a begrudging, "I'm sorry for accusing you of lacking the ability to appreciate the beauty of period architecture."

"No foul," said Max. "I'm sorry for saying you were bratty."

"You never called me bratty," argued Wray.

"I know…but I was most certainly thinking it."

"In some ways it's almost like a modern-day version of 'The Picture of Dorian Gray,' " said Jacob.

"Wow…that's kinda harsh," Ty replied.

"How so?"

"It's bad enough having to face the world, much less your peers, with a severely botched-up nose job that earns you the highly inappropriate yet admittedly sadly accurate nickname of 'Miss Piggy,' and right before yearbook pictures are taken, but to compare such a horrible misfortune to evil forces defiling the sanctity of the church is going a bit far."

Once Ty had finished with his admonishment, Jacob stood quiet with a look of utter befuddlement for a moment or two.

"You idiot, that was Doreen O'Day from our fifth period history class," Jacob cried when he finally realized of whom his friend was speaking. "I was talking about 'The Picture of Dorian Gray.'"

Ty's eyes rolled upward in a futile attempt to search the inside of his skull while pondering aloud the name. "Dorian Gray…Dorian Gray…nope, that doesn't seem to ring a bell with me."

"Why am I not surprised," Wray muttered with a sigh.

" 'The Picture of Dorian Gray' is a book by Oscar Wilde about a man who sells his soul in order to hold onto his youthful beauty and have a portrait he has painted of himself age instead. He gets what he asks for and with each passing day that he lives a more corrupt and immoral life, the uglier the painting becomes," Jacob explained, all while watching Ty's eyes begin their slow glazing over as most literary discussions were apt to do.

"Sounds…enthralling," Ty remarked with utter disinterest, though Jacob couldn't help but imagine the manifesto his friend would indubitably concoct about the hidden themes only he could decipher between the pages of the book if he ever got the inking to read it.

"Does it work with people as well…you know, this perception thing?" asked Kairo.

"Alas, man has developed the uncanny ability to keep the true portrait of himself concealed from the perceptive gazes that might fall upon him in the same way a chameleon learns to camouflage itself on the branch of tree," Zophiel replied, much to Kairo's chagrin.

"That's too bad. If we were able to see people how they really were, like what we see with this chapel or what Jacob described in 'The Picture of Dorian Gray,' then maybe it would have saved us all from recent troubles."

"Perhaps. But it would not have prevented what transpired that fateful day with Gothamel at Broken Earth," said Zophiel.

The response caught Jacob quite by surprise. "You know what happened at Broken Earth?"

"Aye, as well as the happenings that occurred later in the Silent Forest. I may come from a clan of siblings whose vast numbers are far too dizzying for you to comprehend, but we are all well attuned to one another's trajectories, virtuous and otherwise. When one of us stumbles headlong into a fatal fall from which there is no recovering our footing, it is like hearing a pin drop."

"I didn't hear any kind of pin drop, but I did hear Thaniel say your name," said Jacob. "Right before he disappeared into the Through to the

Underneath."

"Are you quite sure it was my name that passed through his lips and not some unintelligible last gasp of a condemned soul?" Zophiel, who showed no reaction one way or the other to Jacob's revelation, asked.

"It was I who had to make sense to the boy what Thaniel had, said as he had no idea who or what a 'Zophiel' was," Damiel answered instead.

Zophiel's eyes remained downturned and fixed on his finger which was mindlessly tracing the lines carved in the marble that gave shape to one of the shrines.

"It must have left quite an impression for you to have come such a long distance to seek me out, hearing something as mundane as a name, that is," he said finally.

"Not really…I mean, not at first," said Jacob. "But when I got home to Cain's Corner I began having these recurring dreams about that moment until your name was like a constant echo inside my head. I know Thaniel was trying to tell me something, I just have no idea what. It's either that or I'm slowly going insane."

Zophiel's finger came to an abrupt stop on the stone and without saying anything further he slowly crossed the chapel to a set of black double doors.

"Well…are you coming?" he asked once he opened the doors and peered back over his shoulder at the group.

"Where to?" asked Jacob.

"To silence the nagging echo ringing inside your head."

~ ~ ~

The group followed Zophiel through the doorway that led into the deathly quiet confines of the main church which was illuminated by the warm glow of several banks of candles spread throughout. The only sound to be heard came from the collective footsteps that accompanied the group as it made its way down a white and rose diamond-patterned marble aisle situated between two long rows of wooden pews. At the end of the aisle, beneath another great dome, was an altar of impressive size with immaculate white linen draped over the top of it. To the left of the altar, was a gold candleholder which held a white candle of considerable height, and to the right was an equally sizable crucifix. Behind the altar, were three towering arched windows, and in front of each window was positioned an imposing statue; the largest of which depicted St. Michael the Archangel for whom the church had been named.

Like the chapel, the church presented itself to everyone as a dilapidated, ruinous and creepy shell of its former self; everyone, that is, except Wray and Ty. The only thing that had clearly escaped the squalid conditions was the statue of St. Michael. The warrior archangel held firm an unflinching and defiant stance as it looked out across the church with a fierce gaze while standing guard over the Sanctuary, as if silently daring whatever evil force that had defiled the place of worship to make the blunder of trying to corrode the glowing white skin of his pristine marble depiction.

When they had reached the steps leading to the Sanctuary, Zophiel came to a stop and turned to face the group, but for some time he remained quiet.

"Well?" Jacob asked finally, with an edge of impatience when the quiet stretched on longer than he could stand.

Still, Zophiel said not a word but, instead, looked past the gathered group, and with a nod of his head directed the others to turn their attention to the right side of the nave. At first, no one was quite sure what Zophiel had motioned to as there was nothing to see except row after row of empty pews. Upon closer look, however, they discovered the church was not completely empty, for seated at the end of one of the pews near the back of the church cloaked amongst the shadows where the light from the candles fell just short of reaching, sat a faceless silhouette.

"Who's that?" whispered Leos.

"After everything that's happened already tonight, I'd really be okay in not knowing," Ty whispered nervously, as his thoughts quickly returned to the other residents of the island who were tucked away in their crypts and coffins lost to their eternal slumber, or so he hoped. Despite Ty's wishes, however, the faceless stranger rose from the pew and all eyes followed with guarded intrigue as it began a slow walk along the darkened periphery of the church toward where the group was standing. There was something about the casual gracefulness in which the figure moved that Jacob at once found familiar, and it made his heart quicken inside his chest. Yet nothing could have prepared him for the moment the stranger stepped into the glow of the candlelight, causing the shroud of anonymity to fall away like a black veil, and the visibly startled group responded with a collective gasp.

"Thaniel!" Damiel exclaimed with a growl of disdain rather than shock, when confronted by the sight of the traitorous angel.

"Damiel." Thaniel's voice, quiet and meek as it sounded, was nothing compared to his downtrodden demeanor. He looked rundown and defeated, like someone who had been dropped in the middle of an oppressive desert without food or water before being plucked out just before the vultures descend. "It's good to see you."

"I wish I could say the same," Damiel, his face curdled with contempt, said in return.

Wray noticed Jacob begin to tremble as he stood beside her, and when she glanced over at him she saw clearly it wasn't from any sense of fear, but an intense anger she had never before witnessed take hold of him. At first she didn't know what had triggered it until she saw it was focused like a laser beam at Thaniel.

"This isn't the same Thaniel who tried to kill you, is it?" she whispered pensively into Jacob's ear.

Jacob refused to answer one way or the other, and his trembling only increased when Thaniel proceeded to bid Max, Kairo, Leos and Ethan a friendly hello before settling his sights on him.

The two stared at one another for an excruciatingly awkward moment before Thaniel attempted a brittle, if not friendly smile and said, "Hello, Jacob."

The salutation was all that was need to trigger the spring tightly coiled inside Jacob. With a wail of rage, he sprang forward in a lightning-quick flash of movement, drew back a fist and delivered a right cross firmly to Thaniel's jaw that sent the stunned angel hurling backward through the air and against the far wall of the church with an echoing thud. The one blow, however, wasn't nearly enough to satiate Jacob's blinding anger, and he was about to rush the stunned angel again when Max, Leos, Kairo and Ethan quickly rushed forward to restrain him.

"LET ME AT THAT LYING, TRAITOROUS WEASEL!" Jacob screamed as he struggled to free himself from the four pairs of hands that kept him from charging forward. And, in that moment, it appeared as if his broiling anger might just lend him the needed strength to shake his friends off him as easily as one would shoo away some annoying flies.

It was only when Gotham stepped forward, positioning himself firmly between Jacob and Thaniel and bellowed "ENOUGH!" in a voice that made itself heard like a crack of thunder inside the church, that a semblance of calm was restored.

Jacob slowly, if not begrudgingly, regained his composure, but still his eyes reflected the deep-seated scorn smoldering inside him like a smoking fire pit as he continued to glower at Thaniel. Fine, he thought to himself, this was more Gotham's grievance than his to settle anyway. In fact, were he not brimming with overwhelming contempt as he was, he might have actually taken pity on Thaniel at that moment knowing Gotham's method of exacting revenge would be far more punishing than anything he could muster.

Thaniel himself appeared quite taken aback—shaken even—at the sight of Gotham suddenly before him, and rightly so, Jacob thought, as he watched with some semblance of unforgiving glee as Thaniel's eyes began to well with tears.

"Gothamel…as I live and breathe," Thaniel muttered in a quiet voice. "You're alive."

What happened next, however, proved so inconceivable to Jacob—not to mention everyone else watching—that he questioned whether his eyes were playing some absurd joke on him: Gotham approached the one who had viciously and deliberately amputated both his wings with the savage aid of his sword, then buried the same blade deep into his side before sending him on a long fall to his end from the cliffs of Broken Earth, and instead of repaying such a brutal act with the drawing of his own sword, the angel reached out and took Thaniel into a warm and loving embrace and delivered a kiss to his left cheek.

CHAPTER NINETEEN

"What exactly are we watching here…some kind of reverse Judas kiss?" Max asked as he and the others looked on incredulously at the sight of Cotham and Thaniel embracing. No one, however, was more stupefied than Jacob, and he watched with a completely staggered expression as Gotham removed the costumed cloak he still wore in order to allow the emotionally overwhelmed Thaniel a glimpse of one of his magnificent rejuvenated wings.

"White…" Thaniel muttered at the sight of the radiant plumage. He then looked quickly for the mark of shame that had once scarred Gotham's forehead, and when he saw it had been miraculously scrubbed clean, he closed his eyes and released a heavy sob weighted with relief.

"Where does one begin to search for the words of acknowledgment that can adequately express the immense indebtedness one finds he owes another?" Gotham wondered aloud.

Damiel stood quietly watching the inexplicable exchange with a growing sense of bewilderment until, finally, he could no longer stomach the confounding sight.

"What is this?" he stepped forward and demanded with an accusatory growl.

"I'm afraid a shamefully unprepared and inadequate attempt on my part at offering my humble thanks," answered Gotham. "Not to mention my everlasting gratitude."

"Gratitude?"

Damiel reacted to the word as though Gotham had picked up a pile of horse dung and flung it straight into his face.

"In what warped reality does one give thanks to the headsman for carrying out their execution?" he asked.

"Oh, Damiel," said Gotham, "do you stand there filled with so much animus that your eyes are clouded from seeing clearly?"

"And just what, pray tell, have I been rendered unable to see past these so-called blinders?"

"The truth."

"The truth you say?" Damiel burst forth with a mocking guffaw. "The truth in all its hideous deceptiveness revealed itself quite plainly to me in a way I shan't ever forget, trust me."

"NO...IT HAS NOT!" Gotham's voice rumbled throughout the church, before quickly resuming its calm in the same way an ocean wave gently retreats back into the sea after crashing upon a sandy shore. "Trust *me*."

"Well, my eyesight is just fine; as fine as that day on Broken Earth," Jacob quickly jumped in when Gotham's words rendered Damiel suddenly silent. "I watched as this so-called friend of mine, and your own brother, cut your wings off your back like he was filleting a fish. We were all there and saw it happen. When I close my eyes at night to sleep I still see it. I don't want to, but I do. And now...you're acting as if bygones should be bygones."

"Hear me, Fledgling, when I tell you they are...and much more," said Gotham, much to Jacob's vexation.

"Well, maybe you're okay with pretending that your wings just up and fell off your back without cause, but I never will," said Jacob, before adding emphatically, "Ever!"

"My dear boy," Gotham said with both an understanding sigh and smile. "Have the walls of this sacred church taught you nothing? Has it already made leave of your mind that the disrepair in which you see this church appears quite the opposite to your two friends, and the rest of the world, for that matter? Don't let a skewed perception of what happened at Broken Earth prevent you from seeing what really is."

"Gothamel's quite right," came Zophiel's voice. "But I think we've gotten a little too far ahead of ourselves with all this pointless squabbling. The only way I see ourselves making any headway here in these lingering hours we have left to us is to allow Thaniel the opportunity to tell you what he shared with me on a night similar to this not so long ago."

"And by what sane reason would I have any interest in listening to one word this proven liar, amongst other things, has to say?" asked Damiel.

"You've come an awful long way to find yourself at this spot," Zophiel said with an air of appeasement. "I would think you would want to learn the reason behind the cryptic summons which brought you here."

"And because even our father gave the most wretched amongst men the bestowal of confession before rendering his judgment," Gotham added gruffly.

~ ~ ~

Standing at the foot of the steps leading to the sanctuary where the statue of St. Michael loomed large and cast its shadow over him, Thaniel found himself void of the captivating demeanor he usually commanded over his impressionable students during Study inside the Library at Havenhid. Zophiel attempted to ease the noticeable tension by offering everyone a chance to relax their feet by having a seat in the pews, but Damiel and the Nephilim in his company refused, choosing, instead, to remain standing with their arms folded in front of their chests, like a jury assembled inside a courtroom staring down a defendant and defying him to try and change the verdict it's already reached before the first argument has even been made.

"Usually, I'm not one to struggle with words," Thaniel said finally after a long stretch of silence. "Now I find myself not quite sure where to start."

"I've always found the best place to start is at the beginning," Zophiel suggested.

"The beginning," Thaniel muttered to himself as if he were not completely familiar with the concept.

"I guess that would be the morning of the Welcoming Dinner that is held each year in the Hall of Light to celebrate the newly arrived Fledglings at Havenhid," he eventually continued. "I was in the Library preparing my lesson plans for the new course of Study when I was visited by a brown and white finch with a fiery red head. A raucous little thing, as I remember, and fully intent on not allowing me a moment's peace to focus on my work as it had an important message from Johiel which demanded my full and undivided attention. The message was most welcoming and unexpected; Gothamel was returning to Eden after his decades-long retreat into seclusion, only he would not be arriving alone, but with a young boy by the name of Jacob Parrish. Needless to say, I was quite delighted by the news. Gothamel, I surmised, had finally overcome the tragedy that had befallen his beloved David and had begun life anew by having another son, and I, therefore, was only too happy to oblige the request Johiel made through that chattering finch to lend my support when Gothamel made his request to the Watchers that Jacob be given special allowance to train with the rest of the newly arrived Nephilim at Havenhid. I need not tell you, Damiel, how thoroughly wrong I realized my assumption to be when I first laid eyes on the boy Gothamel had brought before us that night in the Hall of Light."

Damiel said nothing, as he was recalling his own surprise at meeting Jacob on the beach located at the most southern edge of Eden.

"Later that night, when Gothamel requested to speak with me and the rest of the Watchers in private on the matter in Anahel's chamber, I silently wrangled with myself over agreeing to Johiel's request. This was, after all, no ordinary son of a Fallen. Yet I have always found Johiel to be quite wise and thoughtful, both in words and deeds, and I came to reason if he who had guarded the Gate to our hidden paradise with his very life since man's exile saw fit to grant this sire of a Fallen passage into Eden, then out of regard for him, I should yield to his judgment. And I must say I'm glad I did, for much to my surprise, I found in Jacob a bright and perspicacious individual, not to mention a moral and upright soul, and I must say I came to grow quite fond of him."

Jacob, however, had no use for the angel's endearing words and even less tolerance in hearing them.

"What does any of this have to do with what happened at Broken Earth?" the boy grumbled impatiently.

"I'm sure this is somewhat tedious for you to hear but, please, indulge him," Zophiel implored before nodding to Thaniel to continue.

Thaniel gave a weak smile in reply. He did not expect to be taken into the warm forgiving embrace of Jacob or any of the others if and when they ever found themselves face to face, but neither did he anticipate the level of vitriol focused on him by their collective deathly glares would be so intense and unyielding. Still, he continued:

"Undoubtedly, it was the fondness I came to develop for Jacob that I found myself suddenly fearful for him. It came at a late hour one night after Havenhid had drifted off to sleep. I was standing on the terrace of my chamber looking out across Eden's moon-drenched landscape while thinking about the day that had just taken leave of us and the new one which would soon arrive, and I suddenly found my attention being pulled to the dark shadowy woods that resides just beyond Lions Bite which we all know to be the forbidden Silent Forest."

Jacob, Max, Kairo, Leos and Ethan together swallowed nervously at the mention of the cursed forest. It had not been that long ago that the five of them had witnessed firsthand the untold dark presence residing deep within the tenebrous congregation of towering trees where light and the sounds of life had long been banished. Just hearing the name of the forest spoken aloud was enough to send a tremor of unease through the boys, which did not go unnoticed by Thaniel.

"You are not alone in your trepidation of the Forest," he said. "I myself have always found it to be not only a most unfortunate blight to spoil Eden's flawless beauty in much the same way our father chose to brand Heaven's defectors, but a frightful reminder of the close proximity in which Havenhid resides to the passageway where all the dark carnivorous things of the world can be found constantly clawing away at the door in hopes of breaking through its delicate lock."

"You didn't seem too frightened of the Forest when Jacob and I caught you paying a visit to it late one night," said Max. "In fact, you looked quite chummy conspiring with that deceptively beautiful demon woman in the water."

Lilithhhhh...

The name reverberated in a whispery gasp inside Jacob's head at Max's mention of the mysterious creature they discovered deep inside the Forest confined to a dark pool of water, and it was all he could do to cast from his thoughts any memory of her undeniable beauty as well as the unsightly horror it camouflaged.

"One does not reveal fear when approaching a coiled snake and hope not to be greeted by the sting of its venomous fangs. And your accusatory assertion makes the case as to why I was caught, to use your word, in the Silent Forest in the first place,"

Thaniel didn't expect the boys to understand his reply, which they clearly didn't, and so he explained himself further.

"There isn't much that occurs inside Eden's borders—Havenhid, in particular—that doesn't eventually make itself known to the Silent Forest, and I knew it was only a matter of time before the sinister serpent known as Lilith who resided deep within the thicket would learn of Gothamel's return," he said.

"And this was the fear of which you spoke?" inquired Damiel.

Thaniel gave a nod of his head. "I know I'm not alone when I say that at the time, and even now, the memory of what occurred the last time Gothamel stepped foot in Eden still festered inside me, and I found myself wringing my hands over the unpleasant notion of how the Darkness would respond to the return of the angel it most loathed, especially if it ever learned the boy in Gothamel's company was Samael's son. So I made the unorthodox decision to ward off such a chain of events by stepping willingly into the Silent Forest to pay a surprising and most unexpected visit to Lilith and appealing to her insatiable zeal to lead the most faithful at heart into the fires of doom by presenting to her an unmarked angel teetering on his pedestal."

"If you had such concerns regarding any preconceived dangers surrounding Jacob, you should have brought them to myself and the rest of The Watchers to be immediately addressed," Damiel scolded Thaniel.

"Arguably, you are correct, but I don't need remind you of the contentious divide that existed between all of us at the time concerning the boy," Thaniel reminded Damiel. "It was my view at the time, whether you choose to agree with it or not, that I could run interference between the Silent Forest and Jacob by dangling before her black eyes the prospect of grasping possession of the one thing she longed for most in the world, even ahead of her freedom, now that Gothamel was back in Eden's midst, and that was the Sword of Destiny. And for quite some time, I successfully managed to keep her focused on that shiny object, until…"

His voice trailed off and Damiel's brow lifted with intrigue. "Until what?"

"Until the day after Azrael was summoned to Eden and we all watched in disbelief as Jacob proved he possessed the Seventh Grace by resurrecting the River of Life, choked dead by a black death, with a simple touch of his hand," answered Thaniel. "I understood then the grave position Jacob had now placed himself without even realizing it; for there was nothing now I could hope to do that would keep Lilith from setting her sights and her most searing of hate on the boy; not even the gleam of the sword. And I knew right at that moment there was only one thing I could do in order to prevent another calamity from paying a visit to Havenhid…"

He paused again and looked with sheepish eyes to where Gotham stood and said, "and that was to kill you."

~ ~ ~

"Ahhh, now we're getting to the crux of things," Damiel exclaimed, following Thaniel's grim confession, "and alas I am no closer to understanding how one transgresses from protecting a Fledgling to murdering his own brother."

"I didn't look upon it as an act of murder," said Thaniel quietly.

"Not see spilling Gothamel's blood and throwing him wingless to a spiraling death as murder? Then what, oh knowledgeable one?"

"I'm doubtful even you, brother, could see your way to understanding my truth."

"Try me!" Damiel quickly challenged in retort.

Thaniel stood quiet and apprehensive a moment or two as he silently questioned whether to continue with his obviously pointless explanation of his actions while his gaze looked wearingly to the numerous pairs of eyes fixed on him with unwavering judgment. But then a strand of strength tightened itself inside him and he settled his sights once more on Damiel and answered his challenge.

"What you deem to be murder was, in my eyes and in my heart, an act of oblation." Damiel's jaw tightened and he narrowed the fire in his eyes on Thaniel.

"You dare to stand in the center of this sacred place and aim mockery my way with your blaspheming mouth?" Damiel fumed.

His intimidating presence stepped threateningly toward Thaniel, and had he been left to take another, Thaniel would have found himself unable to say anything at all, blasphemous or not, with his throat caught in the strangling clutches of Damiel's vice-like hands. Just before Damiel snatched hold of poor Thaniel, however, Gotham commanded the enraged angel to cool his heels.

"Your rancor is getting the better of you, Damiel," Gotham said both sternly and with understandable sympathy. "If you'll just allow Thaniel to finish what it is he has to say, you will see he holds no impiety in his words. If, however, you continue to find him to be a blaspheming lout when he is through, then you are free to tear him limb from limb without interference from me."

Damiel could not believe or comprehend how it came to be he was witnessing Gotham defending his killer, and so lightheartedly to bat, but he acquiesced to the request, though begrudgingly so, and retreated with frustration to a spot further away from where he originally stood as to put more distance between himself and any further temptation he might experience to pummel Thaniel.

Then, when a semblance of calm had returned to the church, Gotham nodded to a reticent Thaniel to continue.

"You could say the trail leading to that fateful day at Broken Earth began in the late hours on the night before Illumination," Thaniel, when he finally found his voice again, said. "It was then that I discovered Jacob and Max on a searching quest in the Library, with their wolf companion Mist watching curiously at their heels. For what exactly were they searching they wouldn't say, but I noticed quite interestingly that Jacob had in his possession a book on the Sword of Destiny he had stumbled across, and as I led them both down the spiral staircase to usher them back to their room where they should have been fast asleep, they began to pepper me with questions about the Silent Forest. I knew then at that moment the luring enchantments of that dreaded place had already begun to slither its way across Havenhid's threshold. What I didn't expect, however, is that Jacob here would be the Sower of the seed for all that would come at my hand."

"Me?" Jacob, recoiling in offense at the mention of his name, bawled.

"You told Thaniel to kill Gotham?" Ethan asked with a look of shock.

"Of course not."

"What have we warned you about before? Think before you speak!" Max said to Ethan, before delivering a thunk to the back of his head.

"Do you not remember the discussion we had that night in the Library?" Thaniel asked Jacob.

"I remember you telling me and Max about the Through in the Silent Forest, and that it led the way to another Heaven, just like the Gate into Eden," answered Jacob.

Thaniel pondered the response and smiled.

"Ah, yes…that is something we will have to come back and address at some point, won't we?" he said. "What I was referring to was the discussion that came later, after you sent Max and Mist on ahead back to your room so that you could have a private word with me. Do you remember what you asked me?"

One could almost see Jacob doing a quick internal audit of his memories before a light of clarity relaxed the crease of concentration that had formed at the bridge of his nose.

"I asked you if an angel who's Fallen could ever have the mark on their forehead removed."

Thaniel nodded in reply.

"REDEMPTION!" his voice suddenly echoed through the church, like a passionate exultation from a minister ringing out from the pulpit to jolt members of a congregation nodding off during the sermon.

"Redemption," he then repeated in a much quieter refrain.

"You wished to know if there existed a path to redemption in the same way man has been given the favor to atone for his untold sins. How I was taken by your thoughtful query as it reminded me of a nearly identical conversation I had with Gothamel's son, David," Thaniel explained solemnly. "You see he, too, came to me late one night and asked me the same thing in exactly the same compassionate manner as you did. And I realized as we spoke how extremely fortunate Gothamel was, for to have two such caring souls consciously contemplating a means for his possible salvation meant he was truly loved by both."

Then, just as quickly, the lightness in Thaniel's face was doused by a noticeable gloom.

"Yet beautiful an expression as it was," he said softly, "I found myself suddenly revisited by the despair of utter helplessness over how such pure love could have evolved into the tragedy it did for a father and son before my very eyes."

"You could not have known what would come to pass," said Gotham.

"I'm not so sure," Thaniel argued. "We as Guides are just that. We are the eyes, the ears and the very path the Nephilim rely on during the impressionable transition they undergo when they come to Havenhid. Perhaps if I were more cognizant of my due diligence I would have been more perceptive of the thoughts David was mulling. And perhaps it was due to being reminded of my perceived failings that the conversation Jacob and I had that night would stay with me long after I sent him off to bed, and never more so was that the case than when Anahel called a meeting of the White Circle to discuss the very real possibility that Jacob here could be the Light Bearer."

Damiel, who was standing in a sullen state away from the rest of the group but listening intently, remarked, "Now that you brought it up, I do recall you being unusually...suppressed during the meeting."

"I was concerned with far more dire issues than the 'what if' prospect that had been laid before the Council," said Thaniel. "If Jacob was indeed the Light Bearer foretold to come then he would immediately find himself in the crosshairs of the Darkness, and nothing would stop it from reclaiming him once it discovered who he truly was. I also knew Gothamel's shaken trust would never allow him to relinquish the Sword of the Destiny to Jacob after what had occurred with his own son, thus putting in danger the very real possibility of the Apocrypha concerning the Light Bearer never being fulfilled. These were but just a few of the dilemmas I came to ponder, and I found myself besieged by a cacophony of voices inside my head attempting to lend me sway at how to possibly clear the insurmountable hurdles suddenly before us until only a single voice remained, and that voice was Jacob and his echoing sympathy concerning the path to redemption. Suddenly, at that table where my brothers continued to argue the possibility of a Light Bearer springing forth from the loins of the Darkness, I had devised a plan which would not only safeguard the Apocrypha's second attempt at life, but also right an unjust wrong with the same swing of the sword.

"All I needed to get the pendulum swinging was do what I had so far been successful at preventing," he continued, "and that was to find a way to lure Jacob into the Silent Forest."

~ ~ ~

"Then you finally admit you lied when you told me and Max about the truth of the Through," said Jacob.

"I admit nothing of the sort," argued Thaniel. "That night in the Library when you two boys peppered me with your inquiries about the Silent Forest, I told you the unequivocal truth regarding the Through to the Underneath which resides in it. It was only later, when I realized my plan, that the truth I shared was a misstep I would have to remedy."

Thaniel was not surprised to see the confused looks staring back at him deepen in appearance and did his best lessen the bewilderment.

"To put it simply, I used the Grace of Drifting of which you should well be acquainted with by now," he said, motioning to Kairo who had learned long ago at the Crescent Scar that he, aside from Jacob who by default of being the Light Bearer possessed all the Graces, was the lone member of the group to bear this particular gift. "I revisited that night in the Library as we were making our descent down the spiral staircase, and told you the fabricated truth you now remember."

"B-b-but Max's recollection of that night is the lie. You bound his memory," Jacob, clearly flustered, asserted.

"That is correct; I did bind his memory, but in a way which made him retain the truth about the Through as I originally told it to both of you, and not that which I later orchestrated," explained Thaniel. "Afterwards, I went to Lilith and told her of the surprising revelation that had revealed itself to Havenhid. Then I patiently waited until late one night, when Lilith finally stirred Jacob from his sleep, and I watched him head off in the direction of the Silent Forest to ease his restless curiosity."

"For what purpose could you possibly have had to send a naive Fledgling unprotected into the reaches of the evil creepers of that Forest?" Damiel demanded to know.

"Believe me, the boy was no more unprotected than a turtle tucked away inside its shell, as I made sure well beforehand to alert Gothamel of my suspicion that certain Fledglings were engaging in such forbidden activities."

Gotham nodded in agreement to the shifting of glances his way seeking to corroborate what Thaniel was saying was true, but Damiel remained very much befuddled.

"The only way my plan had a chance of working hinged on the brimming well of mistrust that resided inside Gothamel," Thaniel further explained. "Having already effectively planted the seed of distrust inside his head concerning Jacob, I watched with bated breath as he tracked after the boy into the Forest like the dutiful bloodhound he was, and I knew by dawn's arrival, between witnessing the son of Samael colluding with the dark mistress of the Through, and Max's memory holding the truth I bound inside it, that I would have sufficiently stirred up the sediments of his suspicions, and Gothamel would come to me unaware that the final act to shake what was left of his faith to its very foundation would be delivered by my own tongue. And deliver it I did."

"I'll say you did," Jacob said with a hateful glare, catching not only Thaniel by surprise but Gotham as well by his response.

"Don't forget, I have the Grace of Drifting just as you do, and so one night after Gotham's funeral I decided to use it after everyone had gone to bed. I needed to see for myself what occurred when Gotham went to see you in the Library. Because despite all the horrible things I've witnessed about you, I couldn't believe you would ever say the things he told me you said. But you did say it; you said it all, including threatening to open the Through to allow the Darkness into Eden and destroy every last one us."

A pained look revealed itself in Thaniel's eyes.

"Oh, my dear boy, it cuts me to my very being to see you look upon me as the despicable monster you now do, but yes, you are correct…that horrible threat did indeed pass through my lips, and much worse," the disgraced angel admitted solemnly.

"What could be worse than threatening to destroy Eden…and us in the process?" Ethan wondered aloud.

"When aligning oneself to words and deeds of a dark bend, no matter how falsely they are intended, such words and deeds have a tendency to try and make themselves realized," answered Thaniel. "I needed a believable enough reason to convince Gothamel of my sudden mutiny, and the only thing I could come up with that was both persuasive and plausible was reaching back to a time long ago when I experienced a smidgin of disgruntlement toward Anahel for being named to the position of overseeing the realm of Eden where Havenhid resides, of which I felt I was the more deserving. After all, it was I who oversaw the building of Havenhid, and more importantly, the creation of the Library. To be clear, such disgruntlement had long- evaporated never to be considered by me again, or so I thought, until I began arguing my slight to Gothamel. Much to my surprise, what began as an expression of false indignation quickly became a real festering of resentment, and to my utter horror I found myself pondering, albeit a fleeting moment too brief to measure, that if indeed I was able to lay my hands on the Sword of Destiny I could easily correct the snub I suffered.

"Looking back, I believe it was that moment when I found myself taken in by a very real darkness that Gothamel became caught in the web of my scheme. Had he not heard a ring of truth in the indignation I later was surprised to discover I possessed, he never would have believed I could ever intend, or would have allowed, any harm to come to you. And he would have been right. How could I? Havenhid is far too precious to me and, while I have never experienced fatherhood, I have come to look upon the Nephilim who come to Eden as my children; some more than others," said Thaniel.

"Why should we believe you when we watched you butcher your own brother in cold blood?" Leos said coldly.

Thaniel hung heavily his head and Zophiel, casting a sympathetic look his way, said to him, "It's time you get to the heart of it and tell them the truth."

"I question now whether it is worth the effort?" asked Thaniel. "I doubt even the truth will ever allow them to see beyond the monstrosity of my sin."

"You owe it them, and yourself, solely because it is the truth," Gotham stressed emphatically.

Thaniel pondered the angel's words for a moment and eventually nodded his head before turning back to Leos.

"You're right, Leos, I did kill Gothamel," he said in a passive voice that still held the taut pluck of a harp string, "but not in the cold-blooded way you still see play out before your eyes, especially now as we speak of it, but rather with a warm and merciful heart."

~ ~ ~

If it was possible, the church became even more silent in the moments following Thaniel's pronouncement. No one uttered a word, much less breathed, even though the insides of everyone's head was abuzz with a flurry of confusion over what their ears had just heard.

"I remember a bilious churning twisting my insides when the time finally presented itself where I found myself face to face with Gothamel at Broken Earth," Thaniel said, after what seemed like an endless pacing back and forth of the church floor while the statue of St. Michael looked down upon him. "When he placed in my possession that thing of which I demanded—the Sword of Destiny—the retching feeling became all the more intense. The plan I had so methodically crafted down to the most minute of details had so far gone off without a hitch, and yet suddenly, much to my distress, I found myself questioning whether I had within me the fortitude to bring it to its fateful finish. Neither did I know if Gothamel had indeed supplied me with the instrument vital to my scheme. It looked to the eye to be the Sword of Destiny, but as we all know looks can be deceiving. And knowing Gothamel as I did, I refused to believe the very thing for which he sacrificed his one and only son in order to protect he would now hand over to the likes of me without nary a squabble. I, however, had crossed too far over the line to suddenly turn back, and there was only one option left for me."

Thaniel then turned to face Gotham, and the tears visible in his eyes chocked silent his ability to continue with his confession.

"There is nothing concealed that will not be revealed, or hidden that will not be brought to light," Gotham offered with a voice of comfort.

"The pained cry that left you in the moment I finally gathered the courage needed to swing my arm and separate your precious wing from your back held not a candle to the pain that pierced my very heart," Thaniel, finding his voice once again, continued. "I was instantly reminded of that darkest of days to ever visit Eden when you were on the swinging end of the sword and forced to make a most unbearable decision one should never be impelled to make, and I suddenly knew intimately that which I could never fathom: the unspeakable anguish of silencing the life of someone you truly love. And yet it was the company of that memory— that unimaginable torment—in which I managed to muster the commitment needed to deprive you of your other wing, and finally, much to my desolation, to watch the light go out in your eyes, just as you had been forced to watch it leave David's."

Seeing the tears finally spill freely from the wells of Thaniel's eyes, Gotham's, too, filled with emotion.

"You cried for me that day, just as you are now," Gotham remarked.

"How could I not?" Thaniel, trying to stem the flow, replied. "Do you remember what I told you then?"

The angel stared intently at Thaniel for a moment and nodded.

" 'Believe it or not, it is not hate that has brought us to this parting,' you said. 'Who knows, maybe one day you will thank me for this moment. If nothing else, see it as a last act of mercy from me to free you from…your cursed existence.' " Gotham struggled at the end of his recollection as his voice quivered with overwhelming feeling which he wrestled mightily to steady.

"How is it I was blind to your mission?" he asked.

"What mission?' Max asked aloud the sole question to which everyone was grappling to find as answer.

Before Gotham or Thaniel could answer, however, Damiel suddenly stepped forward.

"I think I understand. So help me…I think I finally understand," Damiel said, as he circled slowly around Thaniel with his eyes fixed on him as if face-to-face with some mysterious apparition. "This scheme of yours was never about possessing the Sword of Destiny, or Eden for that matter, was it? You didn't cut off Gothamel's wings so much as amputate your own…isn't that true?"

Thaniel said nothing at first in reply, but his silence was more than an adequate answer, and in that silence that followed, a sobering look swept over Damiel as the clarity of the overpowering realization which finally visited him that very moment settled its way inside him.

"Oh, Thaniel…" the angel sighed with a heavy heart, "now I see what it is you meant when earlier you told us the plan you had devised would also right an unjust wrong with the same swing of the sword."

Thaniel was greeted by a moment of unease when he felt the awkward weight of all the eyes in the room staring his way. Suddenly, the hate-filled glowering that had been fixed on him had given way to stunned sympathy.

"Is it true?" asked Ethan, looking like he might dissolve at any moment by the threat of tears he was fighting to hold back.

"Since the day of David's unfortunate death I have been haunted by the bonds of love a son could have for his father: both David for Gothamel as well as Gothamel for his own," said Thaniel. "I myself hold a love for my father that extends beyond every known word of affection and devotion. Yet I must confess that when it came to Gothamel, I found his sense of justice to be in many ways unjust. And at no time did I find there to be a greater display of injustice than when David sacrificed his life so that his father might be granted a redeemed one. But in truth, it was Gothamel—an embittered son who had been denounced and cast out his own father's house—who offered up the greater gift by sacrificing the one thing he held dearest to his heart. And what would be his reward for such a moving act of love and loyalty? Ineffable grief.

"For days, and weeks, and months after that dark day, I struggled to make sense of the nonsensical. David and Gothamel had both committed selfless acts of undeniable sacrifice, and I refused to believe our father could be so merciless, especially to a son he had once looked upon with such favor. Yet Gothamel still retained that horrid scar marking the Fallen, and I was determined to find out why," continued Thaniel. "When Jacob approached me on the matter of redemption, just as David once had, I explained one of the reasons why I thought Gothamel remained Fallen was because God held some to different standards when it came to sin and absolution. Where a wicked man can find forgiveness with a simple act of genuine atonement, a more righteous soul brings greater disappointment and sorrow to the heavens when he stumbles and, therefore, the journey up the ladder of penance is a far greater and challenging climb. I still believe that to be true, and when Gothamel issued his rebuke to our father that would lead to his Fall, it sowed forth an upward journey that even this mighty angel would find insurmountable in attempting to clear the rungs.

"I also, however, came to realize a much more simple explanation which I did not share with Jacob."

"Which was?" pressed Damiel.

"As great a sacrifice as the one Gothamel made, it was not a completely selfless one. His action was carried out not so much out of love for his father, but his hatred for Samael and determination he never lay a finger on the Sword of Destiny," answered Thaniel, "But far worse, he did so while in the commission of a grave sin: he killed his son."

"You're joking, right?" Max balked. "That's like some kind of impossible Catch-22 or something: he's either damned if he does or stays damned if he doesn't."

"I do not argue the perceived unfairness of it all. The waters of righteousness may appear calm at the surface, but they are churned by dangerous undercurrents that end up swallowing the many who attempt to navigate them," said Thaniel. "It's why I came to do what I did at Broken Earth: to throw a lifeline to Gothamel who had been caught in the grips of a particularly unrelenting undertow. When I ultimately drove the point of the sword into his side and sent him into free fall from the top of the cliff, it was not to further the descent of the Fall to what he had long before been condemned, but to hopefully raise him up and restore his footing on the pedestal of Grace as I believed he deserved; and I did so knowing the mark I was attempting to desperately scrub free from his forehead would be transferred onto mine. And so it was."

~ ~ ~

Damiel stood silently staring at Thaniel with a crestfallen look fixed on his face mirroring a million and one responses to what he had just heard; none of which he could muster the words to convey. Instead, he grabbed up Thaniel in his arms and delivered a smothering hug that more than expressed the remorseful sentiments brimming inside him. So, too, were the Nephilim overcome by what they had learned. Even Wray and Ty, who knew nothing of Thaniel and what had taken place at Broken Earth before this night, found themselves choked up over what they had witnessed The only one who appeared to be not as completely stirred by Thaniel's confession was Jacob.

When his friends moved to join Damiel in sharing their own sympathies as well as contrition for thinking the worse of the Guide for which they had come to care a great deal, Jacob held them in their place by initiating his own interrogation.

"Let's assume everything you've just told us is true," he said. "It still doesn't explain away what happened afterwards."

Thaniel peered at the boy from over Damiel's shoulder where he remained in the squeezing grip of the angel's arms.

"Afterwards?"

"Yes, afterwards…you remember, when we found you in the Silent Forest looking as though you were some kind of king after having the White Circle place a crown on your head."

Stirring up the memory of such an image seemed to tickle Thaniel, at first.

"Yes, that was a bit over the top, if I do say so myself," he said with a light chuckle. Jacob, however, saw nothing amusing about it.

"You can argue whether or not it's a good quality to possess, but one thing I learned from the performance I gave Gothamel in the Library on the morning he came to confront me is that I am quite proficient and believable in the department of spinning falsehoods," said Thaniel. "You can also have at the debate over whether or not I fall into the category of 'coward,' but I soon realized after my oblation at Broken Earth that Gothamel was not the only one for whom I would need to gather up all the wiliness I had up my sleeves."

"I don't understand," said Jacob, who was trying hard to follow.

"There is such an unspeakable and indescribable feeling of forsakenness that descends upon one the moment he becomes a Fallen that I pray none of you are ever privy to experience firsthand," Thaniel explained. "The moment the lightning leaves its scorched mark, you instantly feel the warmth of Heaven's secure embrace give way to cold abandonment, and you suddenly realize the terror of being thrown like a piece of meat to the feral appetites of the dark things that roam the earth. We angels who resisted the first rebellion that brought to life the Darkness and stood in solidarity with our father against it are viewed by the Underneath as especially abhorrent, and we face a particular unpleasantness should we ever become so unfortunate in our choices and come within reach of its clawing grasp. Say what you shall of me, but I did what I needed to do to hopefully blunt such unpleasantness I was imminently facing by appealing to the sinful cravings of the vermin watching from the Through."

"But you tricked them, instead," charged Ethan. "You went back on your deal to give Lilith the Sword of Destiny."

"That I did," Thaniel agreed. "You see, young one, there is only one pathway to reach the black heart of someone like Lilith. True I openly deceived her, and pay for it I did. In the end, however, nothing earns the forgiveness— for lack of better word—of an Underneath dweller, especially the deceptively beautiful Lilith, than an appeal to their one true weakness above all else: pure and unadulterated trespass. In my case, it was a hearty demonstration of avarice. It's how I came to be here tonight, by taking advantage of the limited freedom I've been granted."

"And how many points did you earn yourself for trying to kill me?" asked Jacob.

"Kill you?" Thaniel, looking genuinely shocked at such an idea, echoed.

"That is what you call it, isn't it, when you aim the end of a sword at someone's chest?"

"It pains me," Thaniel noted solemnly, "that after everything I've revealed here tonight you would still be left to think I would ever intend any harm to come to you…especially by my own hand."

"But it was your hand that was aiming the sword at me," Jacob argued. "Not to mention it was your hand that tried to throw me face-first into the Through and nearly succeeded."

"I know that in your eyes, and the eyes of all your Nephilim brothers at Havenhid, I'm not as intimidating a presence as Gothamel and Damiel here. The brawn gifted me resides with impressive measure in the confines of my head rather than the musculature of my arms. That said, trust me when I tell you if, indeed, it was my true desire to see you plunge into the dark waters of the Through, or run you through with my sword, you would not be here this night to question me."

It was hard for Jacob to argue further the angel's words. True Thaniel was not the physical specimen of might that Damiel, Gotham or even Zophiel were, but neither was he anything remotely close to weak or delicate. Jacob came to know this firsthand and could still recall the power of strength coursing through Thaniel's body from when he came to tangle with the angel inside the Forest.

"You have to remember, while I may have succeeded in delivering Gothamel from his cursed existence, the second key part of my scheme remained undetermined; and that was ensuring the Sword of Destiny found its way into your hands," Thaniel said to Jacob.

"Gothamel had delivered to me a sword that looked very much like the Sword of Destiny, and in taking his life it had proven itself to hold a power absent all other swords. Yet I remained fully unconvinced that the sword in my possession was indeed the one created by the spearhead sought all over the world for centuries. I also knew Gothamel well enough to know he never would have allowed his last breath to pass his lips without first ensuring the Sword he had so valiantly guarded reached the hands of the one for which it was destined."

Thaniel stood before the boy staring back at him with cold expressionless eyes and placed a firm yet comforting hand on both his shoulders.

"When I grabbed hold of you and dragged you in the threatening manner in which I did to the Through, I knew my gut feeling concerning the Sword would reveal itself one way or the other, and sure enough, to my surprise and even greater elation, you proved me to be right when you revealed the true sword hidden within the confines of your coat, and with it your one bargaining chip," said Thaniel. "Everything that came after—my perceived attack upon you—was nothing more than a show for Lilith in hopes that she would remain blind to the real pelt of wool I had pulled over her eyes. You must believe that. Don't you know by now I could never harm a single hair on your head?"

Then looking to the other Nephilim he said, "On any one of your heads."

Jacob said nothing in response for some time, wanting desperately to hold onto the hate he had fermented inside him for the traitorous murderer he had come to believe Thaniel to be. But the artless sincerity that emanated from the angel's face, like some inner glow, caused the frigid shell that had come to encompass Jacob's eyes to slowly beginning to melt.

"He's telling you the truth," Zophiel spoke up to reassure the boy. "He sought me out shortly before what took place at Broken Earth and, after swearing me to secrecy, he confided in me his elaborate and painfully selfless plan. The one sticking point to his plan he struggled to resolve was the idea that any one of you would be left believing he was the image of the monster he would be forced to paint of himself in order for his plan to succeed. The thought of you hating him and looking upon him as you have tonight was simply too unbearable, and so he instructed me with the task of revealing the truth to you."

"Now you know why the last word I uttered to you has stayed with you as it has," said Thaniel. "I'm only grateful the fates allowed me to be present here this night so that I be given the chance to tell you myself."

Jacob struggled to keep the runoff of his thawing hate from spilling down his cheeks, but he didn't deny his arms the desperate need they suddenly had to reach out wrap themselves around Thaniel in a tight, almost suffocating hug. Soon Max, Ethan, Leos and Kairo joined in, forming a big group bear hug around Thaniel, and for the first time since uttering his final word before being dragged down into the depths of the Through by a frenzy of clawing hands the angel beamed with gratitude.

"Boy, can you imagine the looks on everyone's faces back at Havenhid when they see we've returned with not only Gotham, but Thaniel as well, and tell them the truth about what really happened?" Kairo said excitedly, once everyone had gotten their fill of hugs.

"Wait a second; let's not get ahead of ourselves here," Thaniel was quick to pump the brakes. "I never said anything about going with you to Havenhid."

"What are talking about? Of course you are," Jacob begged to differ. "Havenhid's your home."

"And perhaps one day it will be again," said Thaniel, "but for the time being I need to remain where recent events have placed me."

"I don't understand. Why would you willingly choose the company of the Underneath over those who love you?"

"It's not a matter of choosing one over the other. I've decided to join forces with Zophiel and his band of moles."

"But—"

"We've all a path placed beneath our feet," Thaniel continued calmly. "Until now, mine was to fill the heads of impressionable Fledglings with the needed knowledge to combat the Dark forces and navigate your way through a world where danger lurks at every corner. Yet paths are known to veer unexpectedly, and just as you have been pointed in one direction, so, too, have I been pointed in another."

Thaniel could see his usual words of wisdom did little to lend comfort to the boy as they had so many times in the past, and so he did the next best thing and gave the top of Jacob's head an affectionate pet.

"Who knows," the angel said with a warm smile, "maybe this new path I find myself upon will eventually lead me to a road of salvation, just as it did Gothamel."

Jacob's eyes instantly lit up. "You really think so?"

"I would think by now you of all people would hold tight to the adage 'anything's possible.'"

And with those words Thaniel finally managed to succeed in drawing a spark of optimism that forced the corners of Jacob's mouth to curl into a faint smile, but a smile nonetheless.

Again they hugged, until they were interrupted by a timid voice coming from somewhere behind them stammering for attention.

"Um…excuse me…Mr. Thaniel?"

It was Ty with his hand half-raised as if he were sitting in a classroom back home.

"Just Thaniel," replied the angel.

"Okay, Thaniel," Ty repeated. "I'm a bit new to all this and not really schooled on what is appropriate or not in these kinds of situations…but I was just wondering if I might be able to ask you a question regarding something which you may or may not be particularly touchy about?"

Jacob closed his eyes both in prayer that his best friend wasn't about to launch a conversation sparked by one of his many absurd hypothesis regarding life, and in preparation that his prayer would go unanswered.

"What is it you wish you know?" said Thaniel.

Please, please, please… Jacob pleaded his silence mantra to whomever might be listening.

"I was just wondering," said Ty. "Is Hell…or the Underneath…or whatever it's actually called…is it really as bad as it's been made out to be? Because…and don't take this the wrong way…"

Jacob's eyes squeezed all the more tighter.

"But for someone who's been sent, you know…" Ty continued while turning his right thumb into a gesture of an unfortunate object plummeting to the unknown depths complete with sound effects, "you don't look half bad."

"Why I thank you for that interesting compliment," Thaniel replied cordially. "But to answer your question: No, the Underneath is not quite as bad as you likely imagine it to be."

Ty responded with a deep sigh of relief only for his throat to immediately contract with a renewed stoppage of dread when Thaniel was quick to add to his answer three halting words: "It's much worse!"

"Did you say worse?" Ethan, his eyes enlarged at the prospect, squeaked like a mouse. "How much worse?"

Thaniel suddenly found himself before a captive audience all sharing the same bugged-eyed look reflecting a mix of fear and timid curiosity. The Underneath had always been an unspoken topic that held great intrigue and even greater wariness amongst the Nephilim, and one the Guides consciously avoided so as to not needlessly seed the sleep of their young pupils with traumatic nightmares. Thaniel was never one to subscribe to such cosseting believing, instead, that knowledge of all things was as powerful as a sword and protective as a shield; particularly knowledge that held within its folds a component of terror. As he stared into the faces waiting breathlessly for his reveal, however, he couldn't stomach the idea of staining their thoughts with visions of what he had personally come to know, and so he simply said, "Do your penance, and pray you retain your footing well north of ever having to discover for yourself the answer to that question."

CHAPTER TWENTY

T he hour eventually came calling for the group to say their goodbyes and retrace its steps through the cemetery to the other side of the isle where they had first arrived. As they climbed into their gondolas and made their way back across the dark waters of the lagoon they soon realized it would be some time, if ever, before the island would leave them, even as it receded from sight into the inky darkness.

This would prove particularly true for Hunter.

For some time, he sat on the ledge of the window inside the hotel room he shared with Jacob, Wray and Ty and stared down at the view of the Grand Canal whose waters reflected the surrounding lights of the city like stars in the sky. A light rain which began just as the group returned from their excursion across the lagoon continued to fall, and as Hunter watched the raindrops gently pelting the window streak their way like tears across his glum reflection captured in the glass, he heard his father's voice in his ear.

"What's this? A look of bereavement from a son who only a few short hours ago likely would have beamed at the sight of my portrait affixed to one of the burial markers just beyond these cemetery walls," he recalled Zophiel saying to him as the two prepared to say goodbye to one another while standing on the platform near the waiting boats.

"I've been harboring such incredibly hateful feelings for you for so long," Hunter admitted with some reluctance. "I'm not sure even confession would help me to rectify it."

"You don't need confession; what you needed was the opportunity presented to you this night to learn the truth," Zophiel replied with a smile of understanding. "But if it offers your heart any buoyancy, I forgive you your completely predictable transgression of the condition better known as 'human.' It's a trait I believe you inherited from your mother."

Hunter managed half a smile. "I wish I could stay here with you."

I know you do, and it gladdens my heart to hear you say it after being apart for so long," said Zophiel. "But take comfort in the fact that this isn't goodbye; I am your father, and I will always be watching over you, of that you can be assured."

The angel's parting words were suddenly drowned out by the emergence of another voice barking Hunter's name.

"Yo...are you listening to me?"

Hunter turned his head away from the window to find it was Jacob who was sprawled out on his stomach across a large bed waiting for some kind of response and realized he had momentarily checked out the conversation the two had been having.

"Sorry," Hunter apologized, "I must have zoned out."

"I'll say you did."

Jacob then noticed Hunter, as indiscreetly as he could, wipe away a tear from his eye.

"You okay?"

"Couldn't be better," answered Hunter even as he looked back to the window to conceal from Jacob the sadness wetting his eyes.

"It's been quite a night, hasn't it?" Jacob said, trying to fill the awkward silence that suddenly settled itself over the room. "I can imagine it's been pretty overwhelming seeing your father again."

"You could say that. I only wish..." Hunter said before pausing, as if silently debating finishing out lout his thought. "I only wish my mother were here to have seen the two of us coming together again. I know it broke her heart when I left home."

"Don't worry, she's here," said Jacob.

"How would you know?" Hunter replied in a most-disbelieving grumble.

"Believe me, I know!"

Hunter, however, hardly seemed reassured by Jacob's affirmation.

"I wanted to ask my father tonight, you know, about my mother," said Hunter. "After all, if he's an angel, you would think he would know firsthand where she is, and how she is."

"I know what you're going though; I felt the same way after my own mother passed away, and for a long time I didn't think I would get out from under the weight of sadness I felt crushing me. But trust me I did," said Jacob.

"I know, I know...keep you face to the sunshine, tomorrow will be a brighter day and all those other aphorisms made courtesy of Hallmark cards."

Jacob remained quiet for a moment or two as he quietly debated whether to let the next words perched on the edge of his tongue be heard when finally he said, "Look…there's something I haven't shared with anyone before now, not even my best friends who I trust implicitly."

Hunter looked away from the rainy view framed by the window and his glum expression dissipated slightly to give way to a glimmer of intrigue.

"What is it?" he asked.

Jacob then went on to recount the strange if not uplifting encounter he had with Glory Dey, the reality TV psychic phenomenon and self-proclaimed humbug. Hunter listened intently with an unmistakable look of pessimism that slowly eroded itself away the more Jacob spoke about the otherworldly visit he experienced when he took hold of the medium's hands and suddenly found himself face to face with his deceased mother. It was the last words Isabeth Parrish left with her son, however, that seemed to cause an overwhelming burst of serenity to bloom within Hunter; when Jacob inquired with great desperation for his mother to describe the place she now resided, and she replied with an answer as blissful sounding as the look on her face: "Paradise."

"I don't know if that brings you any comfort to hear; I know it did me," said Jacob when he had finished his retelling. "I'm pretty confident your mother is in that same paradise."

"It is comforting to hear, and I thank you for sharing it with me," Hunter replied while doing his best to keep his tweaked emotions in check. "Why didn't you tell any of this to your friends?"

"I don't know," Jacob said finally with a shrug. "It just seemed at the time to be a personal matter; you know, a private thing between a mother and son I wished to keep to myself."

"I can understand that. I'd probably feel the same way," said Hunter. He then suddenly perked up in a noticeable way. "Do you think if I were ever to pay a visit to this Glory Dey that I would be able to have a similar visit from my mother?"

"After the experience I had, I'd say anything's possible," answered Jacob who was just happy to see the gloom start to fall away from his new-found friend. "On a brighter note, I'm just glad to see that you and your father got a chance to work things out. That must at least bring you some happiness, especially considering how you didn't even want to see him when he first arrived here.

"You know, it really does make me happy. I still can't believe the whole thing about him being a Fallen was all a big hoax," Hunter mumbled half to Jacob and half in conversation with himself. "Don't get me wrong; it was hard for me to believe in the first place that he could ever be one of them…you know, a Fallen. I know my father, and it just seemed like such an impossibility to me. Then again, I guess all Nephilim think their father wears the brighter halo, huh?"

The smile on Hunter's face suddenly widened. "Who would have ever thought that after all this time I'd set out into the world doing exactly what he's been doing since before I was born?"

The question drew a frown from Jacob. "What are you saying? That you're some kind of secret cloak-and-dagger spy like your father?"

Hunter suddenly looked as if he had momentarily forgotten that Jacob existed on the other end of the conversation.

"No, of course not. Spy! Don't be ridiculous," he laughed off awkwardly the notion of such a preposterous idea. "I just meant I've been living the past few years of my life as a renegade of sorts which isn't too far of a leap from what my father's been involved in, wouldn't you agree?"

Naturally, he dared not reveal the memories he consciously guarded of his run-ins with the hideous Pethens long before the masquerade ball, much less speak about them. At least for the time being, if ever.

"Did you notice anything strange about Damiel tonight?" Jacob asked suddenly from out of the blue.

Hunter thought for a moment before answering with a slow shake of his head. "Not really aside from his complete displeasure of being forced to parade around like he was a member of the Arabian version of the Blue Man Group."

"I'm talking about later after the ball. Didn't you find him to be unusually quiet on the boat ride back from the island?" asked Jacob.

"To be fair, I don't think any of us spoke more than two words. That was some pretty heavy-duty stuff Thaniel dumped in everybody's lap," suggested Hunter.

Maybe, Jacob conceded silently, though he was far from convinced that was the reason. Thaniel's confession had moved Damiel to near tears, and the image that continued to surface in Jacob's memory was of the angel seated in the gondola and closed off from everyone with an unmistakable ember of ire and unrest smoldering deep within his faraway gaze. It was a look Jacob first took notice of while aboard the flight to Venice. Damiel explained then he had found himself suddenly haunted by the ghosts involved in the death of his son. Were those same ghosts still haunting him, Jacob wondered, or was it something far more sinister at play?

~ ~ ~

There suddenly was heard ringing out from the damp night, a distant chiming of bells tolling the late hour.

"Well, I don't know about you, but I'm beat and ready to turn in," Jacob announced as he got to his feet.

His hand disappeared inside an opening of his costume he was eager to shed, just beneath his left arm to the mid part of his back, and quickly reemerged holding his sword which he carried concealed in his hidden wings. Hunter's eyes immediately glued themselves with an enlarged look of awe to the sight of the weapon whose legend was known far and wide but, to many, was still thought to be nothing more than a legend.

"Is that it; the actual Sword of Destiny?" he asked.

"The one and only," Jacob replied somewhat dishearteningly, as he looked over the magnificent-looking weapon in his grasp, only to be reminded of how he had so far fallen short of living up to the role as the owner to such an instrument of unimagined power.

The sword was deceptive in appearance, with the light reflecting off the blade in bursts of brilliance in the same way a cluster of diamonds dazzle admiring eyes with their sparkle. But anyone who knew anything about the sword looked immediately past the flash and glister to the dull and aged spearhead forged between blade and grip, as that was where the soul of the sword resided, along with its legendary power.

"How exactly does that work anyhow?" asked Hunter.

At first, Jacob thought he was referring to the sword itself, but Hunter clarified his question with a gesture mimicking the way Jacob retrieved the sword like some kind of a performing magician from the confines of his folded wings.

Jacob proceeded to show Hunter by first removing the top portion of his costume. Hunter immediately moved in for a closer look when Jacob stretched out his left wing for him to examine and his eyes narrowed studiously on a thin patch of skin hidden amongst the feathers on the underside which formed a discreet pocket, much like the distinguishing pouch found on female kangaroos. Then to demonstrate the ease and convenience of this marvel of nature, Jacob slid his sword into the perfectly sized sheath which appeared to grip the weapon and hold it securely in place with a gentle flexing of muscle in the wing.

"No different than a holster worn by a gunslinger, really," said Jacob.

"That's pretty sweet!" declared Hunter who was clearly impressed by the demonstration.

He quickly let out a yelp when the finger he was using to gently examine the pocket grazed the edge of one of the large surrounding feathers which caused a minor yet stinging slice to the skin.

"Sorry about that!" Jacob apologized with a wincing look. "I should have warned you these feathers aren't quite the same as a bird's."

"You can say that again," Hunter mumbled in return while sucking on his bleeding finger. "Who needs a sword when you've got wings like that?"

Hunter fell back onto his bed and went about quietly nursing his finger, while Jacob unsheathed his sword and leaned it carefully against the wall next to the side of the bed where he slept.

"How do you get them, exactly?" Hunter asked as Jacob proceeded to change out of the rest of his costume and into a much more comfortable choice of gray sweat bottoms and a white t-shirt.

"Get what?"

"Your wings."

"I wish I could tell ya."

"What're you saying…you've already forgotten?"

"No, I just mean I really wish I could tell you," said Jacob. "You see, we've all been made to swear an oath not to reveal what happens at Broken Earth to other Nephilim who have yet to pay a visit there."

"That definitely works to calm the nerves," said Hunter who was not at all pleased to hear such a reply.

"Trust me, you'll understand once you get there. You definitely need a clear head space when you step foot on Broken Earth, so the less you know the less chance you risk of really psyching yourself out."

Despite his good intentions to put Hunter's mind at ease, what little Jacob said about the cryptic Broken Earth, the more unsettled Hunter became.

"Can you least answer me this: does it hurt at all?" Hunter inquired.

"Not at all. In fact, it feels pretty phenomenal," Jacob said much to Hunter's relief; that is, until Jacob made a slight amendment to his answer.

"At least, it does if everything goes the way you hope it does."

"And if it doesn't…go the way you hope?" Hunter was quick to press.

Jacob could only offer a sympathetic smile and reply with a, "I wish I could tell you."

Hunter let out a groan and slammed his balled-up fists against the mattress.

"But look on the bright side," Jacob was quick to try to quell Hunter's growing frustration, "Max, Leos, Kairo and Ethan all managed to get their wings with little trouble. So did most of the other Shrikes."

"And what about you?" Hunter asked after Jacob's noticeable omission of his own name.

"I'm not really a good gauge when talking about getting wings," said Jacob.

"Why's that?"

"In a nutshell, I didn't do too well the first few times I tried. Actually, I didn't get my wings until long after everyone else did, and there's more than a few times when I thought I might never get them."

"But why? What happened?" asked Hunter. "I mean, you are the Light Bearer, aren't you?"

"The struggle I had with my wings was caused by other issues long before I knew about the whole Light Bearer thing."

"Like what?"

"Well—like not knowing who my father really was played with my mind. Then again, so did learning who my father was when I finally did. There was also a long period where I had some difficulty in accepting this whole Nephilim existence, and when you harbor any doubts or don't fully embrace who you are, it's a recipe for failure when one is attempting the impossible like flying. That's why I say it's so important to keep a clear head when it's finally your time to head up to Broken Earth," said Jacob. "Personally, I don't think you'll have any trouble, in that regard. You've known all your life where you come from and, luckily, tonight you were reunited with your father who cleared up a huge misconception about who you, and he, really are."

Hunter felt a bit of ease work its way through his body with that little reminder.

"Plus," Jacob continued with his pep talk, "you'll likely receive an extra shot of confidence once you visit the Crescent Scar and learn what your Grace is? It was definitely a courage booster for everyone else when they found out."

"What's this Grace thing?" Hunter asked with a completely blank face.

"You're not being serious, are you?" Jacob replied with a half chuckle. "Surely, your father told you about Graces at some time growing up."

Hunter's expression went instantly flat as if someone had let all the air out. "Surely, you haven't forgotten how my father lied to me about being the son of a Fallen. I think it's safe to assume this would be the first time I've heard anything about Graces, and probably anything else that has to do with Eden."

Jacob felt his face go flush over his momentary lapse, and taking a seat on the bed, he proceeded to give Hunter a cursory lesson on the secret and untold powers the sons of angels inherit from their fathers upon birth. And with each reveal Jacob made of the individual Graces, the more riveted Hunter became until his eyes glazed over with wonder and curiosity at the possibilities of the special abilities which might have been lurking inside himself unbeknownst to him all this time. Once Jacob had finished, Hunter sounded his approval in the exact same manner he did when he was given a gander at the sheath nature formed on the inside of Jacob's wing by issuing an enthusiastic yet measured "Sweet!"

"Anything else you're curious about?" Jacob asked.

Hunter thought for a moment before answering.

"Actually, there is one other thing," he said. "Is it true what they say about that special sword of yours; that it has the power to destroy any and all things, living and otherwise?"

"That's how I understand it," Jacob answered while giving his sword a defeated glance. "I couldn't really tell you from experience. You see, it only came to be mine not so long ago and, well…let's just say I'm still in the beginning stages of training with it."

Hunter's gaze shifted to the wall beside Jacob's bed and he instantly grew stony-faced at the sight of the mysterious sword.

"I want you to know, Jacob, I'm not quick to trust people, but in the short time we've come to know each other I've come to feel I can confide in you," Hunter said turning back to Jacob.

"Thanks, I feel the same about you," Jacob replied in return.

"Tonight, you trusted enough to share with me that story about your mother paying you a visit through a medium, and now I'd like to return the favor."

Jacob's curiosity was instantly aroused when Hunter motioned him in an almost impatient way to have a seat beside him on the bed.

"It's been eating at me for a while now, but I think I know why that attack happened on my family's house, and it has nothing to do with my father or anyone uncovering the fact that he's a mole," Hunter said in a quiet yet intensely laced voice.

"What did it have to do with?" Jacob asked with bated breath.

"It had to do with me," Hunter answered in an even quieter and reluctant whisper. "I think I'm the one who's responsible my mother's death."

The unexpected revelation left Jacob visibly shocked, but before he could he could question what would make Hunter blurt out such an assertion, both boys suddenly became acutely aware that they were no longer the only ones in the room.

~ ~ ~

They both turned their heads at the exact same time and looked across the room where they found much to their surprise, Gotham, standing quietly.

"I didn't mean to interrupt," the angel apologized. "I figured you'd be asleep by now, but I was passing by and heard voices."

Jacob shot Hunter a questioning glance and Hunter in return answered with a subtle shaking of his head.

"That's all right. I was just giving Hunter here a little insight on what to expect when he finally visits Havenhid," Jacob said before quickly adding. "Don't worry…I didn't reveal too much…just a little here and there."

"Well…so long as the here and there is kept to a minimum. A large measure of the potency of Eden's power, after all, are the secrets and mysteries she keeps hidden behind her gates," Gotham said as he settled his penetrating gaze on Hunter.

"I'm starting to understand that more and more," Hunter agreed.

"Then can I take it by your late-night chin wagging you've made the decision to join this travel party on its return to Havenhid?"

"I discussed it with my father tonight during the walk from the church back to the boats, and, well—" Hunter said while shooting Jacob a look that barely veiled the excitement bubbling inside himself, "wild horses couldn't keep me from tagging along, if that's all right with you, sir."

"That would be more than all right," Gotham remarked agreeably. "I'm certain you will make quite an impressive addition to Eden's brood."

To hear such words coming from an angel of Gotham's stature made Hunter sit up noticeably straighter and beam with pride.

"You can be sure I'll make every effort," he said.

"Of that I'm certain," said Gotham. "Now, then, if you wouldn't mind, there's something of a personal nature I wish to speak about with Jacob here."

"Sure thing…just pretend I'm not even here," Hunter replied as he shifted his attention to the cut to his finger.

"That would be a much easier task if, in fact, you were indeed not here," said Gotham. Hunter's face turned an immediate beet red.

"Oh, I get it…you want to have a chat *alone* alone. I should probably go and find a Band-Aid for this anyway," he noted with a chuckle before saying to Jacob, "We can finish our conversation later."

He got up from the bed and was about to disappear into the bathroom but not before looking over his shoulder to the angel one last time and saying, "Thanks again huh, Gotham?"

At first, Gotham wasn't sure what he had done to earn the young man's acknowledgment.

"It's really set my mind at ease knowing there was still opportunity for me to get my wings," Hunter explained. "Not sure what I would do if I couldn't fulfill my destiny of being what I was born to be."

A faint smile appeared on Gotham's face.

"I've a feeling there's much more to that young man than meets the eye," the angel said once Hunter had disappeared into the bathroom. "And I suspect we will all come to appreciate the seat we've added for him at our table."

The angel then settled his sights on Ty and Wray who were sprawled out on top the neighboring bed while still dressed in their costumes and dead asleep.

"I can only imagine how exhausting a night like tonight has been for the two of them," said Gotham.

"They were passed out before their heads even hit the pillow," said Jacob.

"It's not always a great recipe when angels—and to a greater extent Nephilim—allow their existence to overlap with those of civilians," Gotham remarked quietly as he continued to watch the two sleeping teens who were oblivious to his looming presence. "I've always been a staunch believer that, perhaps, we might better serve to protect both worlds by supporting the belief embraced by many civilians: that we indeed are myths of the imagination."

"Well, all I can say is thank goodness you're a minority on that stance otherwise I and most of my Nephilim brothers probably wouldn't be here right now," Jacob wise-cracked.

"You are hearing my words but you are not understanding them," said Gotham. "The civilian world can be accommodating—welcoming, even—to angels when it wants to be, but it is quite the opposite for civilians wishing to experience ours."

"But they're my friends," said Jacob.

"Don't misunderstand me. They are a fine pair, and I'll even admit I've found them to be engaging company in the short time I've come to know them. But I've also watched you, particularly tonight, struggle to straddle these two separate worlds while facing down the Darkness and I think even you will concede, if not out loud, that it puts one's self in an extremely precarious situation…even a Light Bearer."

Jacob declined to argue Gotham's observation, nor could he dismiss it outright, either out loud or otherwise. Instead, he reacted how he usually did whenever Gotham made a valid point he wish he could ignore and brush away like a piece of lint clinging to his shirt but couldn't: he let loose a sigh of disgruntlement.

"It's not really worth discussing now," he said. "They'll be leaving for home tomorrow."

"So they will. I'm just worried if they'll be taking a piece of you back with them,"

Gotham said with a stilling seriousness.

He then took a seat on the edge of the bed beside Jacob, and as he did a glint of silver instantly caught his eye.

"Your friends, however, are not the reason I came to speak with you," he muttered quietly as the image of the Sword of Destiny leaning against the wall beside the bed seared itself into the golden reflection of the angel's intense gaze, "but rather the sword I passed into your care as I took my final breath at Broken Earth."

"What about it?"

Gotham paused for a moment, clenching his jaw, before answering, "I wish it returned to me."

~ ~ ~

The request caught Jacob completely by surprise.

"Sure—sure thing…it is your sword, after all," Jacob, his face reddening somewhat from embarrassment, said. "I feel kind of ridiculous now…I probably should have thought to return it where I got it after the whole mess with Thaniel was settled in the Silent Forest. I guess I just assumed you meant for me to keep it…you know, because of the whole Light Bearer thing. Which just goes to prove that old saying about when you assume things."

Jacob forced forth an awkward chuckle, but the angel could see his request had unintentionally stung the boy, and he offered a sympathetic smile in kind.

"It's probably just as well you take it back," said Jacob. "Damiel's been trying to train me in how to use it and, well, frankly…I'm not all that confident I was meant to handle something so powerful."

"Perhaps I should have prefaced my request with an explanation for why I am seeking its return," said Gotham.

Jacob attempted to tell the angel there was no need for any explanation, but the angel insisted.

"Before the Sword of Destiny became what you now see before you, it was known as the Spear of Destiny—an aged relic once belonging to a long-dead Roman soldier, and sought the world over by an endless hoard inveigled by the legend of untold power consecrated upon the lance by the divine blood it once spilled," Gotham began. "History would watch claim to the Spear pass through many hands—some good, some not so good. It was when the Spear fell into possession of the not so good—evil, in fact—that I came to find it, and the moment I swindled it from the cruel and wretched fingers gripping it, the darkness that had briefly covered the earth began to part.

"Thereafter, for nearly a quarter century, I secreted the Spear out of sight and out of mind from the rest of the world, but always under my close watch and guard. Then came the unforeseen, yet no less blessed news that my son possessed inside himself the Seventh Grace, and I understood immediately that it was not I who had managed to liberate the Spear from the Darkness' brief possession of it, but the fates which had delivered it into my safekeeping. And so I retrieved it from where I had hidden it away all those years, and guided by some unknown voice of instruction, I turned the Spear of Destiny into the sword destined for the hand of the one who would be called Light Bearer. That hand would turn out to be my son, David, and never had I a prouder moment when I placed the newly forged Sword of Destiny into his hand during his Blessing."

Jacob expected to see the angel's eyes grow misty at the mention of his son as was usual whenever the subject had been brought up in the past, but to his surprise there was no look of sadness, only undiminished pride.

"After tonight, we no longer are burdened to look upon the tragedy of what would come to be with immense sadness or shame, but rather with humility for the sacrifice and deep love shown by both a son and a brother," said Gotham. He then trained his gaze all the more intently on Jacob. "I can now embrace your destiny, Light Bearer, without the shadow of an untruth clouding my vision. And so I ask for the return of the Sword of Destiny so that I might be allowed the opportunity to pass it along properly into your hands; not in a desperate final act while on all fours in a pool of my own blood, but in the proud manner in which I placed it in my son's care during his Blessing."

The angel's words reached straight inside Jacob's chest and took hold of his heart until he thought for sure he would start blubbering like a baby, but he managed, somehow to keep the waterworks in check.

"I don't know what to say," Jacob croaked forth. "But I've already had my Blessing."

"Yes…I know. Unfortunately, I was unable to attend those festivities," said Gotham. "But there's nothing to say we can't have another one."

With his insides swelling with pride, Jacob reached for his sword, but he hesitated as he was about to hand it over to Gotham's waiting hands. It wasn't that he was having second thoughts about parting with the sword he had been so possessive in guarding since removing it from the hidden space at the foot of the crypt where Gotham's son was interred. What caused him to pause was the memory that instantly flashed before his eyes of the angel Betreyel who attempted to take possession of the sword during a struggle inside the Silent Forest and was promptly reduced to a smoldering pile of ash.

"What do I do?" the boy asked.

"You just need to hand it to me of your own accord," Gotham replied with an encouraging smile.

And so Jacob slowly placed the sword into Gotham's hands, as freely and willingly as he could muster until he looked like someone preparing to blow out the candles on a birthday cake. Only when he released the sword and saw that Gotham remained intact and not consumed by some internal combustion of fire, did Jacob release the breath he was holding.

Then, unable to contain himself, he threw his arms around the angel in a tight embrace.

"I'm so glad you're back!"

CHAPTER TWENTY-ONE

"I wish you wouldn't cry," Jacob pleaded. Wray sniffled in reply as the two stood at a quiet shaded spot just above the banks of the Grand Canal watching the traffic of boats make its way along the choppy highway of turquoise water glistening beneath the bright afternoon sun. A short distance away, Ty could be seen standing at the end of a short and narrow, curved wooden dock protruding from the canal bank where he was loading his and Wray's bags aboard a waiting water taxi reserved to take the two to the airport for their flight home. Yet even the amusing sight of Ty, with one foot on the ledge of the boat bobbing upon the water, and the other planted on the pier nearly losing his balance while loading the bags aboard the burled-wood water taxi, and taking an embarrassing bath in the canal wasn't enough to crack the glum expression on Jacob's face.

"Would it make you feel any better if I let you haul off and give my face a good slap?" Jacob asked half-jokingly. "Or maybe, at least, let you dump a milkshake over my head?"

Wray chuckled, even as she continued to blubber, and gave Jacob a loving push.

"I was hoping you'd somehow forget that by now," she said with a pout.

"Forget it? How can I possibly forget it when I can still feel it?" Jacob said, feigning a lingering soreness as he rubbed his left cheek and succeeded to squeeze another giggle from Wray.

Their moment of levity didn't last long and, when it had evaporated, Jacob looked at Wray with a pained longing, and she him.

"Heterochromia," she said in a murmur after a long moment of staring deep into his eyes.

"I'm sorry…heterowhat?" The sound of Jacob's voice nudged Wray from the trance she had momentary slipped into.

"I uh…I just said heterochromia," Wray repeated with a shy-like laugh. "Just something I had learned in biology class that for some strange reason popped into my head."

"And what exactly is heterochromia?"

"It's the name of the condition that causes someone to have two different colored eyes."

"You mean, kinda like mine," said Jacob whose one blue eye and one green eye fixed themselves firmly on Wray's warm stare.

"That and certain breed of dogs…like Australian Shepherds."

"So…what you're saying is I look like a dog, is that it?"

Unbeknownst to him, Jacob tilted his head like a curious pooch attempting to understand the words coming out of its master's mouth, which only brightened Wray's smile all the more.

"Have you see an Aussie pup? They are soooo cute," she cooed. "You might also be interested in know that less than one percent of the world's population is known to have heterochromia. *AND* among the notable people in history who are known to have had two colored eyes was Alexander the Great. So what do you think about that?"

Jacob's eyebrows rose up on his forehead and he pursed his lips while chewing on that impressive tidbit.

"So basically you're saying I rank somewhere up there between a Macedonian king who once conquered much of the free world, and a cute pup."

"I'm just complimenting your pretty eyes," Wray offered matter-of-factly. And when she smiled her smile that Jacob found so pleasing to behold, he couldn't keep himself from leaning his body closer to Wray's and pressing his forehead gently against her's.

"You know I'd take you with us if it was at all possible," he told her with quiet words. "Heck, I'd even take Ty along."

Wray's smile wilted instantly. "Don't press your luck. You might just push the powers that be upstairs to revoke those wings of yours."

"That reminds me," Jacob said suddenly. "There's something I wanted to give to you before you left."

"What is it?" she asked curiously as he bent down and began to quickly rummage through his backpack resting on the ground between his feet.

When he finally straightened back up, he handed her a book with a cover made of soft brown leather that was noticeably aged and well-traveled.

"What's this?" Wray, looking somewhat stumped, asked.

"It's my journal," answered Jacob.

"I can see that," said Wray who recognized the diary the instant she set eyes on it. "I meant, why are you giving it to me?"

"I just figured after everything you've seen and experienced on this trip that there were likely still a lot of questions swirling about inside your head; probably the same questions I had when I was first discovering all this," explained Jacob. "I'm sure reading this would go a long way in answering those questions."

"I—I can't read this. This is filled with all your personal thoughts and feelings," Wray protested.

"It's okay, really…I want you to. Besides, it's not as if you haven't read some of it already."

Wray grew slightly insulted at the accusation, true as it might have been. "In my defense, I didn't realize it was a diary when I picked it up."

"Journal," Jacob corrected her.

"Excuse me?"

"It's a journal."

"What difference does it make?"

"It makes plenty of difference. Diaries are for girls. Guys on the other hand write in journals. This is a journal."

"My point is," Wray continued with an annoyed roll of her eyes, "had I known this was your *journal*, I never would have opened it in the first place."

Jacob's eyebrows curled upward at the bridge of his nose in response as he leveled an "who are you trying to kid?" look of amused skepticism at Wray.

"Think what you'd like, but I wouldn't!" she argued steadfastly while turning her nose upward with pious defiance.

"Look…Wray…it's not that I'm giving you permission to read my journal; it's that I want you to," Jacob said and slowly bringing Wray's nose back down to earth. "I started writing in it the day I left Cain's Corner. It holds every secret and every thought I've ever had since then. I want you to read it because I want you to know everything there is to know about me that I can possibly share with you. I want you to know me as well as I know myself."

Clearly caught off guard by his words, Wray was speechless for a moment or two.

"Alright then…I shall," she finally replied in as composed a manner as she could, even as she fought the overwhelming desire to throw her arms around him in gratitude for filling her heart in a way she'd never before experienced.

"Wait a minute," she said suddenly. "If I have your journal, how will you continue to write."

Jacob opened his mouth to answer but he found his tongue too twisted to explain, and so he said instead, "It's a little too complicated to explain, but you'll see for yourself I've found a way to manage."

~ ~ ~

They were suddenly interrupted by the sound of Ty's voice calling for them, and when they turned, they saw their friend running up the walk from the pier towards them.

"The driver of the water taxi said we've got to leave now if we want to make it to the airport in time in catch our flight," Ty huffed out of breath when he finally reached them. "At least that's what I think he said; the English was a bit on the side of an Italian Godzilla movie."

Jacob turned back to Wray whose eyes were growing misty once more.

"Now you know why I left Cain's Corner without saying goodbye," he said. "Both times."

Wray couldn't bring herself to say anything in return, and so, instead, she flung her arms around him and hugged him for dear life.

"I'll miss you," said Jacob.

"Don't forget me," Wray whispered in his ear in return.

Ty, meanwhile, who stood idly by looked as if he had unwittingly stepped in a pile of doggy doo while taking a stroll through a park as he was forced to witness the impassioned display.

"Oh god!" he groaned in disgust. "For the love of all things mushy."

Eventually, they parted, and while Wray wiped away the tears from her eyes as inconspicuously as she could, Jacob turned to Ty.

"So…" said Ty, his face instantly darkening when he realized the moment to say goodbye to his friend was suddenly upon him.

"So…" Jacob echoed with equal gloom.

"Well, this was certainly a trip you won't find in any travel brochure," Ty said with a forced bit of awkward jollity. "Angels to the right of me, demons to the left…you'd think I'd be anxious to click my heels together three times and get home."

"Don't worry," Jacob said in return, "before you know it I'll be back in Cain's Corner and you'll be testing my last nerve over lunch at Rabble-Rousers with one of your concocted yet, surprisingly, not drug-induced theories regarding hobbits, superheroes or something or other."

Ty's face suddenly brightened.

"Funny thing you bringing that up," he said. "I've actually been noodling something in regards to Captain Avenger and—"

He abruptly stopped himself, even before the expression on Jacob's face grew weary at the prospect of suffering through such a dissertation, and in flash he rushed forward and landed a smothering bear hug on Jacob.

"Don't forget your best friend," Ty pleaded as his arms squeezed tighter.

Jacob smiled and gladly returned the gesture. "Don't forget yours."

There came a loud tooting of a horn, and looking toward the pier, they saw it was from the driver of the water taxi signaling impatiently that it was time to depart. Jacob gave Wray another hug along with a parting kiss and watched sadly as his two friends hurried their way to the waiting boat and climbed aboard.

"Am I ever going to see them again?" Jacob asked the presence he had felt lurking behind him for some time as he continued waving while watching the boat grow smaller and smaller in the distance.

"Why wouldn't you? They are your friends," came the reply.

Once the water taxi had disappeared from sight down the canal, Jacob turned around and found Gotham sitting on a bench beneath the cool shade of a tree.

"It just feels more and more like eventually we're going to be forced to choose between two lives: either to live as a civilian, or as a Nephilim," said Jacob. "I'm not sure I could choose between either."

Gotham remained quiet for a moment, mulling the boy's words that were obviously weighing on him.

"You speak of a dilemma more oft to plague Angels than Nephilim," he said. "Ours is a bloodline which extends to all four corners of the world with multitude generations of Nephilim yet, believe it or not, there remain many of my brothers who have found it less complicated—easier, if you will—to remain on one side of the gate and not blur the lines that separate their world and this where the Dark things roam freely."

"So, you're saying Nephilim are able to live just as normal of a life as a regular civilian?' asked Jacob.

"Many are doing just that as we speak, albeit under more guarded conditions than your average civilian," answered Gotham.

"But before you go out and begin the task of picking out your china pattern there is one thing you need to take to heart, and take to heart fully," the angel was quick to add. "You are of neither normal or average Nephilim stock, and neither are the circumstances for how you came to be here."

Hearing that, Jacob took a deep deflating breath and grumbled, "I figured as much."

~ ~ ~

They blended with the other tourists, Jacob and Gotham did, as they casually strolled the walkway made of paving stone running alongside the canal on their way back to their hotel. The strong, fishy stench coming off the murky canal water was interrupted intermittently by the more welcoming aromas of veal sautéed in tangy white wine and mushrooms, sweet desserts and freshly brewed cappuccinos wafting from the numerous restaurants looking to attract hungry passersby like pollen to a honeybee.

"Is that the reason you and my grandmother never stayed together…because you wanted something easier and less complicated?" Jacob asked Gotham out of the blue after a long stretch of silence as they passed a street merchant trying to peddle her wares to tourists seeking souvenirs.

"To an extent," answered Gotham. "Though it wasn't so much my own ease I was particularly concerned about than her own."

"Do you care to elaborate on that?" Jacob prodded when Gotham didn't seem to care to volunteer anything further at first.

"You may find it hard to believe, but I find Ava—your grandmother, that is…to be as beautiful today as the day when I first met her," said the angel.

"Um…I don't want this to come out wrong, because I love my grandmother and think she's beautiful as well," Jacob interrupted. "But she's a woman in her nineties. How can you say she's as beautiful now as she was when she was, say, in her twenties?"

"Thank you for proving my point," Gotham replied. "Your grandmother was a stunning woman in her day. Yet, quite unfortunately, someone like her who possesses the gift of mortal beauty can never accept their reflection captured within an immortal gaze; especially when the specter of age creeps ever closer. Much as I loved her, I couldn't give her the one thing that would bring her happiness: to grow old with someone who could wear the passing of years shared together in the same manner as she rather than be forced the indignity that comes from the eventual surrendering of oneself to a rocking chair while being forced to look upon her love's face untouched by time."

"So, that's it? That's the reason the two of you parted...vanity?" Jacob balked.

Gotham didn't answer one way or the other at first. In fact, he wished to drop the entire conversation, but he felt the intensity of Jacob's gaze would not soon leave him without further discussing the matter.

"It also doesn't help when a couple loses a child as we did, and the tremendous weight of guilt it brings...especially in the manner in which we did," he said.

Jacob's stare softened as he understood instantly, though not completely. "You felt she blamed you for what happened," Jacob quietly assumed.

"I blamed me! Do you not see? And that was more than sufficient for the both of us," Gotham grumbled with an edge of tension. "Every time I looked into her eyes I saw reflected back at me the deep-seated pain I had caused her. And what's worse, I found myself to be too cowardly to own up to the truth of what had actually brought about our son's demise."

"Then it actually was as much about your own ease as it was hers that she ended up marrying Silas Parrish. Maybe even more."

Gotham's temple began to pulsate as he clenched tight his jaw before quietly admitting, "Yes...I guess you would be right."

Jacob suddenly stopped dead in his tracks.

"What is it?" Gotham asked with alarm.

"I just realized...I told my grandmother about what happened to you at Broken Earth. She was almost in shock over the news," said Jacob. "Now here you are alive and well, and she has no idea."

Gotham placed a hand on the boy's shoulder in an attempt to calm him down.

"It's all right...I've already been to see her. Shortly after you and your traveling caravan left on your trek, in fact."

Jacob became visibly relieved.

"Of course, I'm not all that assured the sight of me alive and breathing was a welcoming one to her," Gotham noted.

"Why would you say something like that?" Jacob asked, looking at the angel as though he were one twist short of a slinky, as Max would say.

"She told me you told her the truth about what actually happened to David; the same truth Thaniel touched upon last night."

Jacob nodded nervously. Had he, he wondered, spoken out of turn? "Anahel showed me the missing pages from David's journal. He found them in a book in the Library. It explained David's plan to free you from your Fallen status…like you are now. Anahel thought it would give her closure to know."

"It's okay. I'm not upset with you. I'm glad she knows," Gotham assured the boy. "I just wish that I could have been the one to tell her. Though I'm doubtful it would have done little to change the monstrous vision she now sees when she sets her gaze upon me."

"W-w-wait…I don't understand," said Jacob. "The journal pages clearly explain David's plan to make you think he turned traitor so you would—"

Gotham stopped walking, and when he turned to face the boy he was wearing an expression upon his face that Jacob didn't quite expect: an expression of peace and, strangely enough, humility.

"Hear me when I tell you, it doesn't matter what David's plan was or that of his wishes, or whether he was traitor or simply acting a part. The only thing of relevance, of which not a single scenario can be molded any differently, is that I acted to take my own son's life," said Gotham. "Whether or not David purposefully placed himself upon the altar as a willing sacrifice does not shift the tide to this marked and inescapable fact.

"It is through the grace of my father that I have been reunited with my boy, and through such grace I have finally forgiven myself and been granted the peace which before now my anger and self-hatred had denied me," the angel continued with his thoughtful words. "Perhaps one day your grandmother will bestow upon me a gift of equal forgiveness. And if that day never comes I will, too, accept that, hard as it will be. Either way I will not refuse her, nor attempt to speed her through, her rightful period of mourning as a mother over an unthinkable truth which I selfishly denied her: I killed our only child."

There was not a word in what the angel said that Jacob could bring himself to argue against, and so he kept his mouth closed and clenched his jaw tight for good measure.

~ ~ ~

Without saying anything further on the subject, they continued on their way, passing several small shops, including a quaint little dress boutique with a couple of headless mannequins posed outside the entrance displaying some of the wares inside, and a costume store whose window offered a spectacle of Venetian masks peering out at the passersby.

When they came to the steps of a small arch bridge allowing passage across a narrow canal, Jacob broke the silence by asking Gotham, "Why do you think he did it?"

"I thought Thaniel explained it perfectly clear last night at the church. If not, I would have assumed you to have read the journal pages Anahel gave you," answered Gotham.

"I wasn't talking about David; I actually meant Thaniel," Jacob clarified. "I was kept awake part of the night thinking about the lengths he went to in order for you to be redeemed. I mean, I know you are brothers and all that, but still...it's an awfully huge sacrifice to make for even a brother."

For a moment, Gotham looked as if Jacob had not been alone in mulling about the same curiosities in his head.

"Thaniel and I have always been extremely close. He looked up to me as a luminary in many regards, and I came to adopt the role of protective overseer where he was concerned," said the angel. "What drove him to willingly give up his place in the Light so that I might be returned to it is not something that has been made known to me, aside from one brother's selfless love for another. That said, if I were to conjecture a reason, I would say it stemmed, at least partly, from a sense of gratitude he still carries with him from when I saved his own life."

"You saved his life?" Jacob, his curiosity perking up, asked. "How? When?"

"It was in the early days, before Havenhid even existed. The Great War had long been fought, but there still remained stragglers of that unfortunate rebellion who continued to infest my father's house looking for ways to spread their disease before they were found out and cast out of Heaven like the vermin they were. And so it happened, two such malefic parasites set their sights on Thaniel," Gotham began to explain. And like all of the angels' stories, when he was prone to share them, Jacob listened with undivided attention.

"Thaniel was in the midst of designing what would become the beating heart of Havenhid: The Library. It was his labor of love and he became all-consumed in every minute detail of what would become this vault of knowledge where Nephilim from all over the world would come and fill their heads. And it was likely the reason he was blinded to the menace stalking him and waiting for the right moment to pounce. You see, the Darkness was observant enough to learn that the immense gift of knowledge endowed to Thaniel could wield as much power as a sword, if not more, and so they plotted to relieve Thaniel of his gift. They waited until Thaniel was alone in Eden breathing life into the Library, and while he was working with the trees to position their boughs and entwine their branches just so to create the colossus we now know it to be, two angels who had not yet earned the mark of the Fallen accosted him.

"Powerful a fighter as Thaniel is, he could not hold his own against his two attackers. In quick measure they overpowered him, and while one subdued him the other drew a sharpened dagger that he intended to use to cut the coveted knowledge from the confines of Thaniel's skull. They surely would have succeeded in their ghastly bid had it not been for the quick action of a thrush watching from its perch in a nearby tree who raced to the highest point of the sky of which it could climb, and caught my attention with its frantic screeching. The bird led me to the disturbing scene threatening to blacken Eden's serene surroundings like some raging wildfire and, in short order, the two foolish assailants learned first-hand the fervor of Heaven's wrath. Thaniel, meanwhile, went on to complete his Library."

Jacob listened intently and his eyes grew larger with every detail as he continued walking. "They actually attempted to cut out the knowledge from inside his head?" he asked aloud, unable to get past such a cringey and gory imagining. More importantly, he now understood without question the depths of Thaniel's gratitude toward Gotham after being spared from such a dissection that made undergoing a lobotomy seem like a trip to Club Med.

~ ~ ~

Shortly thereafter, they reached the hotel, and when they went upstairs to Jacob's room they found Hunter anxiously awaiting their return, along with Max, Leos, Kairo and Ethan. Beautiful as Venice was, there was an unmistakable eagerness to depart for their next far more beautiful destination: Eden. A quick look around, however, revealed one member of their travel party was missing.

"Anyone know where Damiel is?" Gotham inquired, only to be answered by a half dozen faces with blank expressions.

"Last I saw him was last night," said Max.

"Same here," Leos and Hunter said in unison.

"Maybe he's out looking for Jacob," offered Ethan.

"Why would he be out looking for me?" asked Jacob.

Ethan shrugged. "I don't know…maybe he came by here earlier, saw you were gone and thought you had reneged on the deal the two of you made to return back to Havenhid," Ethan joked with a light-hearted chortle that was instantly silenced by the unamused look Jacob returned his way.

Gotham rested his inquisitive-filled gaze on Jacob. "What deal is this that he's talking about?" he asked.

"It's nothing," Jacob replied at first, while attempting to make Ethan shrink a little more from the glare of annoyance he kept fixed on him before turning to the angel.

"The truth is…I left Havenhid a few weeks backs. In fact, I left Eden altogether."

"Left Eden? For what reason?" asked Gotham.

"It just got a bit much for me…especially when Creed's father barged in on the celebration following my Blessing and threatened to basically put me on trial in order to discredit the idea of me being the Light Bearer."

Gotham's face softened. "Yes, I've heard about his move to convene the Iudicium Tribunal," he said with a sigh of perturbation. "Quite an unfortunate and underhanded attempt on his part to delegitimatize what has already been proven true. Then again, I would expect nothing less from Sandel."

"Damiel found me in Cain's Corner and tried to talk me into coming back," Jacob continued with his explanation. "That's when we made our deal. I told him I would go back to Havenhid with him if he first helped me to try and locate Zophiel so I could finally put to rest what had happened in the Silent Forest."

"I see. Well, I'm glad to hear you had a change of heart. You cannot allow someone like Sandel to succeed in his aim to squelch that which has made itself known as truth."

It was then Gotham took notice of the fact that Jacob was absentmindedly rubbing between the thumb and forefinger of his right hand, an object that was attached to a silver chain which hung around his neck, which he was oft to do. And when he looked closer he discovered, much to his surprise, that the object was the vial-shaped pendant that had long hung from his own neck until the day he succumbed to the perilous fall awaiting him at Broken Earth.

"Well, how about that? There's something I wasn't sure I would ever see again," he said.

At first, Jacob didn't know to what Gotham was referring, until he saw the angel's glowing eyes were fixed on the pendant whose soothing warmth emanating from the Begend fire contained inside often drew the caressing of his fingers.

"Oh…I can't believe I forgot I had this. Anahel gave it to me during your, uh…well, your funeral," said Jacob. "I suppose you'll also be wanting this back, too, huh?"

"When I was named one of the Messengers of the End Days, that divine ornament was placed in my care to be used at the unknown future hour of my calling. With my place in Heaven once more restored, so, too, have I reassumed my position as Messenger of the Judgement contained within that vial. So, yes, it is quite vital that it finds its way back around my neck," said Gotham. "And I thank you for your thoughtful safeguarding of it during this period when it was briefly lost to me."

"No problem," said Jacob.

As he removed the pendant from around his neck, Jacob came close to telling Gotham about the incident in Las Vegas where instinct drove him to unleash the Begend light trapped inside to ward off the threatening, snarling pack of Infector-possessed dogs and equally nasty swarm of turned birds that were poised to attack him and his friends, but he thought better of it. Some things, he thought, are better left unmentioned.

"Here you go," he said as he handed the necklace over to Gotham.

The angel thanked the boy, and as he inspected the pendant, a faint but noticeable glow of white light that was the Begend emanated through the smooth but extremely dense black rock from which the vial was shaped.

"I'm curious. What exactly did you mean by 'too'?" asked Gotham. The question drew a blank stare from Jacob.

"When I made mention the pendant, your reply was 'I suppose you'll also be wanting this back, too,'" said Gotham.

"Oh, that," said Jacob, finally understanding. "I just meant, you know, first you asked me to return the sword, and now your pendant. That's all. I didn't mean anything snarky by it."

Now it was Gotham who was left with a blank look upon his face.

"Sword…of which sword are you speaking?" he inquired in a cool and quiet tone.

"Funny!" replied Jacob. "You know exactly which sword."

"I wouldn't have asked if, indeed, I knew. Which makes me all the more afraid to press for an answer."

"The Sword of Destiny…remember…last night…when you showed up late and asked that I give it back to you until it could be presented to me in a more proper way rather than how I came to have it."

It wasn't a common sight to see blood drain from an angel's face, but when it did happen, it was a noticeable and unsettling sight. And so it was that Gotham's face became like that of a refrigerated corpse when Jacob attempted to jog a memory inside his head that did not exist.

"Personally, I thought it was an Indian-giving move to take back the sword," Hunter interjected. "But then, when you explained your reasoning why, I actually thought it was a cool gesture on your part."

"You observed me here, in this room last night, asking Jacob for the sword?" Gotham asked Hunter with a chilling seriousness.

"Well, yeah…but don't get the wrong idea; it wasn't like I was eavesdropping or anything like that. You asked for a moment alone to talk to Jacob and I went into the bathroom to brush my teeth. But trust me, it's pretty much impossible to not hear what's going on in here through these paper-thin walls."

Gotham then looked once again to Jacob and asked him, "You no longer have the Sword of Destiny in your possession?"

"Is this like a trick question or something? How can I if I gave it back to you?"

Gotham began to frantically pace the floor, and the longer he did the more uneasy Jacob and the other boys became.

"What is it? What's the matter?" Jacob asked finally.

"I never visited this room last night. In fact, I wasn't even anywhere inside this hotel," Gotham replied before looking to Hunter. "I went to the neighborhood where you and your family used to live at Damiel's suggestion. He thought I should see the spot where your house used to stand but no longer exists as it once did."

Gotham resumed his pacing as Jacob looked on with a growing horror creeping over his face.

"What are you saying?" Jacob asked with growing alarm.

"I'm saying you've been swindled," answered the angel. "I'm saying someone came here with the intent to deceive you into believing they were me, and obviously they were successful."

"But who-who would do that?"

"You kidding me? With all the cast of shady characters we've crossed paths with on this trip, you could take your pick," said Max. "But if you ask me, it was that creepy Miseri who's behind this."

"It could also be someone we're not likely to suspect?" suggested Kairo.

"Such as?" asked Leos.

Kairo hesitated a moment, glancing over in Hunter's direction before answering. "No offense or anything Hunter, but what if it was Zophiel?"

"You're joking, aren't you?" Hunter replied in shock.

"Kairo may have a point," Leos jumped in to co-sign on his friend's behalf. "All this time Zophiel has been rumored to have become a Fallen. He even had Hunter believing all this time that he was the son of a traitor. Now, out of the blue, we find him here in Venice—or rather he's the one who finds us—and confesses that all this time he has been serving as a spy on behalf of Heaven. Smells a bit fishy, if you ask me."

"So does your sense of reason," an offended Hunter shot back. "For starters, have you forgotten the Fallen scar on his forehead was phony and something he could remove at will? Or did you find that impossible feat to be fishy as well."

"If you ask me," Ethan offered, even though no one had, "I think it's someone we're even less likelier to suspect than Zophiel."

"If you even suggest one of us inside this room, I may be forced to give you the wedgie of a lifetime," Max threatened with calm assurance.

"I'm not talking about one of us, but rather Thaniel."

"Thaniel!" the room as a whole answered with disbelief.

"Why not? We've already witnessed what he's capable of, and why? Because of his obsessive twisted desire to possess the Sword of Destiny," argued Ethan.

"Were you not present at the church last night? Did you not hear his confession that everything he did was a carefully well-thought-out scheme to make Gotham and Heaven good again?" asked Leos.

"And you just assumed everything he said was on the up and up?" said Ethan. "How do we know this isn't an elaborate second attempt by him to get his hands on the sword? Do you know of a better way for a wolf to get close to a flock of sheep than disguising itself as a sheep?"

No one would ever admit outright that Ethan had made a valid point, but it was clear by the silence that followed that the young Nephilim had managed to offer up a person of interest worth chewing on.

"What do you think, Gotham?" Jacob looked to the angel for his take on the various theories that had been bandied around.

Gotham, however, didn't appear to have been paying much, if any, attention to the back-and-forth discussions. Instead, he continued to stare off into space toward the ceiling as though he were sorting through his own conspiracies swirling about in the ether.

"Samael!" he finally muttered as his eyes grew large with alarm.

Before anyone could question what he meant, he rushed toward a large window on the far side of the room that opened on its own as he approached. There then came a loud shredding of fabric and the loose button-down shirt he was wearing instantly disintegrated into bits of cotton and flyaway threads as his wings burst into view from his back and carried him skyward when he made the leap through the open window.

"Where's he going?" cried Leos.

"He said, 'Samael,' " said Max. "I'll bet he's going to the Infernal Desert."

They all quickly prepared to follow after Gotham, but Hunter beat the boys to the window and blocked their way.

"What are you doing?" asked Jacob.

"No way you're leaving me here," said Hunter.

"What do you suggest...or have you forgotten you need wings to make this trip?" Leos replied.

"One of you could allow me to hitch a ride...or in your case maybe two," Hunter suggested.

All five boys gave Hunter an incredulous look.

"You're kidding us right?" asked Max. "You want us to carry you there? Do you have any idea how long a trip it is to the Infernal Desert, never mind carrying someone as big as you are?"

"I don't weigh all that much," Hunter argued. "Besides, you can each take turns."

No one seemed eager to take part in such a proposal.

"You can count me out," Leos made adamantly clear.

"Me, too," echoed Kairo. "Besides, my wings are still sore from helping to schlep Ty from Las Vegas to your loft."

Hunter wasn't budging.

"Look, we can do this the easy way," he said, "or we can do this the hard way."

"What would be the hard way?" asked Max.

The answer came when Hunter sat himself on the ledge of the open window, offered a coy smile and a simple wave goodbye before falling backwards and surrendering his body to the long waiting drop that sent his body careening toward the street below.

The Nephilim screamed in horror as their eyes bulged from their sockets, and in a flash their own wings tore through their shirts as they leapt one by one out the window in a desperate chase after Hunter.

CHAPTER TWENTY-TWO

GONE

Dawn was just beginning to creep its way across the vast rugged wasteland that was the Infernal Desert when Gotham dropped from the sky at a barren spot he had not visited in more than half a century.

Even in the soft pink light of the approaching sun whose presence brought with it an insufferable heat which could already be felt in the rapid warming of the air, it was clear to see at first glance why this desert within a desert (which most of humankind had no idea existed) was the cruelest place on earth. There existed not one sign of life; neither did a scrub of vegetation or the faintest rustle of wind, and even critters who were known to thrive in harsh desert environments—snakes, lizards, scorpions and even certain insects—were nowhere to be seen. All that existed was thirsty, rocky, mountainous terrain stretching as far as the eye could see.

The last time Gotham cast his shadow upon the ground of this hellish pocket was just after the death of his son when he sought revenge on the one he deemed responsible for his loss: the execrable Samael. For three excruciating days and nights, the two engaged in a savage fight fed by their feral hatred for one another until, finally, it ended when Gotham, in a masterful maneuver, ensnared Samael with the Herrinsu vine he had secretly brought with him. Once tightly bound, an enraged Samael realized his fate had been forever sealed, for the only thing that could ever free him from the unbreakable Herrinsu vine was the Sword of Destiny. And so, thereafter, his screams of rage and desperation and anguish brought, finally, the first stirrings of life to the Infernal Desert; and the desert, in return, became an inescapable prison without bars for this most worthy captive.

What greeted Gotham all these years later, however, immediately darkened his face with the gravest of looks. The sunbaked earth crunched loudly beneath his feet as he stepped hurriedly to the dry dusty spot where he had left Samael to his rotting; only there was no Samael to be found. All that remained was the strand of the Herrinsu vine that had once tightly fettered him laying useless on the ground like a dead snake. Gotham reached down and picked up the vine to examine it more closely, and sure enough he found it to have been cleanly severed in two.

He stood mulling who could have been so emboldened to oversee such an escape and, more importantly, what Samael's regained freedom would mean to the world at large, particularly for one certain boy who had the unfortunate distinction of being his son. It was then he was met by some unexpected company arriving in the same manner as he had: from the sky, but much more raucously. Glancing over his shoulder and upwards, the angel caught sight of Leos and Kairo, their wings flapping furiously as they descended the blue stretch above them at an uncomfortably fast speed. They each had a hold of one of Hunter's arms, and Hunter, whose eyes were growing wider with each passing second, as were his urgent cries to slow down, looked like a rag doll kicking desperately its legs as he dangled helplessly between the two struggling to come in for a soft landing. Unable to hold on to the flailing body in their grasps any longer, Kairo and Leos let go of their cargo a few feet shy of touchdown sending Hunter tumbling and somersaulting across the rough, abrasive ground until he skidded to a stop face down on the desert floor.

"Remind me the next time I fly with either of you to make sure I strap on a parachute pack beforehand," Hunter said, when the dust cleared and he got to his feet, only to create another dust cloud when he gave his mop of hair a needed shaking.

"You try carrying a hundred-and-ninety-pound salami for a couple thousand miles and we'll talk," Leos grumbled in return.

"I only weigh a hundred and seventy."

"Yeah, well, it felt like two hundred and ninety."

Arriving in a much more graceful and quiet manner, Jacob and Max touched ground soon after, followed by Ethan. They gave the stark desolation surrounding them which they had only heard about in passing a quick survey, and the desert, in return, made its introduction to them with a breath of hot air better acquainted to a furnace. The air was noticeably dry; so dry one could feel the water instantly beginning to evaporate from the skin and being wrung from the throat like a sponge.

"Crikey, Gotham sure knows how to deal out his punishments, doesn't he?" Max asked, as he wiped away the beads of sweat that were already beginning to form on his forehead.

Jacob, meanwhile, rushed to Gotham's side, and when he did the angel showed him the severed vine.

"He's gone?" asked Jacob.

"Like a foul wind," came the angel's quiet reply. "Just as I suspected."

Jacob felt a shiver of fear move through him, but it was nothing like the overwhelming sense of humiliation he felt.

"I'm really kicking tail and taking names as Light Bearer, aren't I?" he mumbled shamefully. "How could I have been so stupid to hand over the Sword of Destiny like I did to an imposter? The reason he gave me alone should have been enough to raise my suspicions."

"Chalk this up to a lesson learned. The ability to change one's appearance on a whim is a potent power to possess as it is difficult, if not impossible, to detect such a manipulated charade. And now you know why outside the gift of healing it is the most desired amongst the Graces," said Gotham. "What I do find to be curious, however, is the reason my fake doppelgänger gave in convincing you to give up the sword because, interestingly enough, as luck would have it, I just so happened to be mulling such a consideration last night when we were making our way across the lagoon to the island where we came to meet Thaniel."

"Really?" For a fleeting moment Jacob's mood lifted at hearing the phony reason used to dupe him wasn't completely bogus and that Gotham had actually thought enough of him to be worthy of such regard; but only for a moment. "But who would have attempted to do such a thing?"

"I'm telling you it was Thaniel," Ethan stepped forward to repeat the conspiracy theory he had earlier put forth to everyone at the hotel.

"You're crazy! Why would he meet us in the dead of night inside a church located in a cemetery and lay out the confession he did to all of us just to turn around and steal the Sword of Destiny?" argued Kairo. "Zophiel, on the other hand, I believe is our prime suspect."

"You're both wrong; I've already told you it's Miseri," Max jumped into the fray. "We all saw him stand before a room full of powerful people and basically reveal his intention to raise an army and take control of the Underneath. What better way to ensure success than to gain possession of the sword?"

The boys started squabbling over one another as they each argued their case when a voice both familiar and unexpected made itself heard and declared, "You are all mistaken!"

There came an abrupt silence and all eyes looked in the direction of the voice, and sitting a distance away on a rock was a figure distorted by the intense heat that was already beginning to rise off the desert floor in the form of a sheet of vapor.

"And I can assure you it was not nearly as sinister as your bickering is attempting to make it out to be," came the voice once more. The group watched with increasing vigilance as the figure stood and slowly made its way toward them, and when finally it stepped past the wavy, heat-rippled curtain of heat and they were able to see who it was, they released a collected gasp of shock when they saw the stranger was Damiel.

And clutched tight in the embrace of his right hand was the Sword of Destiny.

~ ~ ~

"Damiel…"

Surprisingly, anger was slow-coming to Gotham who found himself to be more in the grips of astonishment at the sight of the angel than anything else. "Am I to conclude from the sight of you that it is by your guile we find ourselves in the middle of this insufferable desert?"

"If you wish to argue the methods which brought me here at this precise time then by all means proceed," said Damiel. "But I have done nothing that would cause me to keep a heedful eye on the heavens for any wayward strike of lightning aimed in my direction."

"Whether or not your transgression is deemed Fallen-worthy or not is of no consequence to me," said Gotham whose face sagged all the more with disappointment at Damiel's perceived lack of ruefulness. "What I wish to know is the why…why would you do this?"

"I would rather keep my reasons to myself, if you wouldn't mind."

"Oh, but I do mind…greatly, in fact," said Gotham. "If not me, I think, at the very least, you owe your young pupils here whose trust you undoubtedly torched some reasonable explanation for your chicanery."

The mention of the Nephilim who stood idly by seemed to draw a pang of conscience from Damiel, especially in light of Gotham's harsh charge concerning the boys' dashed confidence.

"Fair enough…though I'm afraid they'll only come to know further disappointment should they await an apology to accompany my explanation," said Damiel.

And so in the presence of the harsh and unforgivable heat of the morning sun as it continued its upward ascent while whitewashing everything in its path, including the very blue sky from which it hung, Damiel began the telling of how he came to hold the Sword of Destiny in his hand without being reduced to a pile of incinerated ashes; only it didn't begin in the hotel room where he pulled his simple but effective hoax on an unsuspecting Jacob, but the night of their arrival in Las Vegas that by now seemed more than a memory ago.

"I had warned Jacob of the peril we would be enticing by embarking on this hunt for Zophiel, but it seemed a risk he and the others were willing to take," he said.

"What are you saying? That this is all somehow my fault?" Jacob asked with defensive tone.

"To the contrary. Here I was so ripe with worry about the abundant dangers young Nephilim like yourselves are oftentimes too naive to safeguard themselves against when left to roam this gateless world and yet, ironically, it was I whose foot would step upon a waiting snare.

"You'll remember I confided in you while on the plane to Venice about visiting that den of iniquity in Las Vegas, and the unexpected run-in I had with the truth while inside that feculent sewer regarding the murder of my son and a dozen other Nephilim on Akdamar Island," Damiel reminded Jacob. "By sheer force of will, I managed to walk away with the blade of my sword as unstained as it was upon my arrival, or most certainly I would be keeping company with Thaniel and the rest of our Fallen brothers this very moment sure as I'm standing here. Having to walk away from Miseriel was an altogether different test to my resolve"

"Miseriel? What has Miseriel to do with this?" asked Gotham.

"Damiel found out it was Miseriel who actually killed his son," Jacob attempted to explain as quietly as possible.

A look of mournful clarity came to rest itself upon Gotham. "So you know."

The response drew a surprised reaction from Damiel.

"You knew of this?" he asked.

Gotham's silence was all the answer Damiel needed.

"And you didn't see fit to enlighten me with this crucial bit of information?" he prodded.

"I learned of Miseriel's involvement long after the fact; after the death of my own son, in fact, while I was wandering the world trying to outrun the shadow of sorrow that was determined to stalk me," Gotham explained.

"I saw no need to inflict upon you a new wound when finally you looked to be in state of healing; that is why I kept my lips sealed. And I would say to you now, as both your brother and your friend, do not let this revelation, unsettling as it may be, serve to be your downfall. You must let it go, or surely be consumed by it."

"Let it go? That is a pearl of wisdom coming from you, Gothamel," Damiel chortled. "Even if I had the willingness to 'let it go' as you so counsel, I came to the realization last night at the masquerade ball that I would be squandering the burying of any hatchet were I to choose such a path in anything less than Miseriel's head, and I attest to you now I would have, had he not proven himself a coward and vanished in a flight of birds."

"I understand the anger you find yourself wrestling with now," said Gotham. "But what does your newly sparked hatred for Miseriel have to do with what is happening at this very moment?"

"You still don't get it, do you?" seethed Damiel, his eyes alight to reveal his ire like twin vats bubbling with molten gold.

He began to pace about furiously, and as he did he began a fevered rant:

"Witnessing Miseriel at the masquerade ball proudly preening about in that ridiculous cape and macabre mask as if he were some newly crowned Omen of Death and we were all attendants at his coronation was one thing. It's what came later, when Zophiel revealed to us his band of exiles in that serene cemetery under the veil of darkness and secrecy and explained to us the nature of the ball and, most specifically, those who were in attendance that a desperation I had never before experienced took hold me.

"And from that desperation I came up with the only ruse I could think of that would allow my spirit to remain intact."

"By ruse, I'm assuming you mean tricking Jacob into giving you his sword," said Hunter.

"Callous as it may sound, whatever act of deception I employed in order to gain possession of the Sword of Destiny was nothing more than a means to an end, and in no means meant to be malicious or dishonest."

"Dishonest? That's a good one, that is," Max tittered. "I'll have to remember that the next time I give Ethan here a wet willy."

He then proceeded to take hold of Ethan in a playful headlock and take aim at his friend's exposed ear with his finger (minus the spit) as he was inclined to do whenever the mood for some benign torment struck him.

"Remember...it's just a means to an end in expressing my love for a friend," Max teasingly taunted Ethan who began giggling incessantly.

"Then, by all means let me turn the other ear," Ethan joked in return.

Damiel, however, was not one to delight in shows of mockery, especially if he happened to be the target of the ridicule. And so, while looking on at the lighthearted tussle that continued play out in front of him, his gaze narrowed on the two boys and his eyes flashed with an inner brightness. Instantly, both Max and Ethan let out a yelp of pain as an electric spark—like that generated when one rubs his feet briskly against a carpeted floor, only much more intense and painful—simultaneously jolted the end of Max's finger and Ethan's ear.

"Now then, if you're quite through with your juvenile demonstrations, I'd like to continue on before this sun has the opportunity to make jerky of all our hides," said Damiel.

Max obediently fell back in line while sucking on his scorched finger as did Ethan whose only aid of comfort was to gently massage his burning ear.

~ ~ ~

A faint whistling of wind kicking up swirls of dust as it blew across the harsh desert terrain was the only sound to be heard when quiet finally returned to the group.

"Night had already settled in when I descended into this desolate pit," said Damiel when he finally spoke, "and I was immediately taken by the fact that the cruelness which resided here knew no rest. The day may have reigned over the land with an intolerable and unforgiving heat, but the dark, when it came, brought with it a biting cold with the power to splinter the bones of any poor unfortunate soul who found himself marooned here after the sun had finished the task of stripping away from them the flesh. And that is just what I found right over yonder: a poor unfortunate soul languishing in the merciless chill after being released from the searing torture of the sun.

" 'Who's there?' he called out when he heard my footsteps.

"I didn't answer at first and he struggled in his bindings to get a glimpse of whose presence he suddenly and most certainly unexpectedly found himself in.

" 'Ah…it's you,' he spat as though he had just been offered a tall glass of brine when he finally managed to catch a glimpse of me. 'Come to see if your captive was still alive and kicking, have you, or in hopes of finding an expired carcass?'

"I realized I was still donning my disguise and had given him the impression, as with everyone else, that I was Gothamel, and so I shed his skin in favor of my own.

" 'Damiel…' he uttered my name with complete surprise when he saw it was I who was standing before him, but the surprise was fleeting.

"My own, however, was not as I was instantly struck by the imprint the years of captivity had left on Samael. Had I not known it was him, I'm doubtful I would have recognized him by face; his skin was blackened and horribly scarred from the constant exposure to the merciless sun, and the pent-up rage roiling inside him from the indignity suffered through his imprisonment had morphed his once beautiful face into something quite beastly.

" 'You'll forgive my appearance,' Samael apologized while astutely taking note of my shrinking reaction as I laid eyes on him for the first time in a very long while, even as I tried to mask my astonishment at the sight of him. 'It's so rare one gets visitors this far southward of nightmares where conditions are far too inhospitable for even the common scorpion.'

"The good or bad that he once was, this was not the Samael I remembered. It was more than seeing him trussed up and disfigured on the ground; a mere emaciated shadow of his former self. There was a surrendering taking place at my feet, as if his very spirit was slowly being ground into the dirt by the oppressive surroundings, and I found myself torn between feeling immense pity for him and an overwhelming sense of leeriness one might feel for a caged animal I don't ever recall feeling before in his presence.

" 'Really now, Samael…even I would have thought you to have more smarts than trifling with another angel's offspring, much less Gothamel's.' My half-joking comment was met first by a disturbing grumble, as if Samael's entire insides were twisting about in such a way as to become his outsides.

" 'If you've come to impress upon me the virtues of en*light*enment like some door-to-door bible pusher then trust me when I say you can save your breath,' his voice resonated with contempt at the very mention of the word 'light.'

" 'I wouldn't be so quick to slam the door in my face,' I advised him. 'Salvation has a propensity to manifest itself in many forms, not that I would assume you to be well-versed on such things any more than I would expect to find a pig on a farm with an innate dislike for wallowing in mud.'

"He glared at me with a growing annoyance. 'The sound of blisters forming on my skin from the merciless sun is more enjoyable than this,' he growled at me.

'Fair enough…I'll come straight to the point as to why I've graced you with my presence,' I said to him. 'I wish to discuss the possibility of you performing a favor of sorts for me.'

" 'A favor? For you?" he said, nearly teetering over into hysterics at the mere idea before sinking back into the dark glumness with which I found him. 'What possible favor could you hope to receive from me? And even more importantly, why?'

"It was a fair enough question, as anyone looking at Samael could see he was in no position of granting even himself the simplest of favors of scratching away an annoying and tormenting itch.

" 'You might be quite surprised the effortlessness of the favor I've come to request from you,' I assured him. 'As for the why, well, let it not go ignored by you the sentiment which states, "One good deed begets another." '

"Now I had his attention, if not quite undivided.

" 'But before we get too far ahead of ourselves, there's something I must know from you,' I continued. 'If that stubborn vine which has held you prisoner to this place with its unyielding hold were to somehow lose its grip, what would you do with your newfound freedom?'

"It was a question that I could see visibly grab hold of him even more tightly than the Herrinsu vine in which he was ensnared, but the glimmer of light brought to his eyes by the mere mention of his freedom was quickly dimmed by a smothering of inner darkness.

" 'You are nothing if not sadistic, Damiel, for even dangling such a hopeless idea in front of me,' he growled hatefully. 'For even the great Angel of the Sword would find defeat against this cursed vine.'

" 'I would greatly think twice about harboring such convictions,' I answered in return. And to argue my point, I brought into view the Sword of Destiny and with a hard thrust I embedded it into the ground within reach of Samael had his arms not been bound. The whites of his eyes shone like twin white diamonds captured inside a black lump of coal as he sat transfixed on the one and only thing that held the power to grant him freedom from the hellish prison to which Gothamel had sentenced him.

" 'And so I ask you again, Samael: What would you do with your freedom if, indeed, freedom were to find you once again?' I posed the question to him before quickly adding, 'And if I were you I would think carefully on how you answer.'

"I then turned and walked away leaving Samael to ponder his response as he stared at the sword with both disbelief and quiet longing.

" 'What favor is it that you wish from me?' he asked before I had taken my third step. "And so I proceeded to tell him about Miseriel. I told him about the Masquerade Ball and the guests who were in attendance, and more specifically, I told him about Miseriel's blind ambition to step into Samael's shoes and warm the seat he had left to turn cold. And when Samael sniggered at such an idea and denounced my claims as nothing more than unproven hearsay and rumormongering, I revealed to him the vast army that was quietly being assembled which would, in the very near future, accompany Miseriel unimpeded to his coronation. If there's one thing one who is drenched in power fears most, it is losing it, and Samael's dismissive snickering came to an abrupt halt when he saw not the faintest glimmer of deceit or bluff in my eyes.

" 'What is it you desire me to do so much so that you would set me loose out into the world from which I've been chained?' he asked with a curiosity he by himself couldn't seem to satiate.

" 'I simply want you to do what you do best and dash his dreams by placing your foot upon Miseriel's wring-worthy neck,' I answered pointedly.

" 'What possible reason could you have to care one bit about the goings-on in the Underneath? Samael asked, as he searched my face for any wayward telling with his conniving eyes, and hard as I tried to keep the iron mask I wore in place, he spied something.

" 'There's more, isn't there? Returning Miseriel to his rightful place beneath my heel is only part of the courtesy you request from me, isn't it?' he asked, knowing already before he even asked the question that my trade for the sword's services would require a far greater bounty.

" 'I want you to produce the promised war Miseriel is hoping to dodge by deposing you,' I answered in a straight forward manner, perhaps too straight forward judging from the look on Samael's face.

" 'You want war. And why would an angel campaign for such a thing as war?' he asked with understandable curiosity. An unheard voice must have whispered to him the answer he was seeking for there suddenly came creeping over his blackened, sun-blistered face the first sign of a smile I had yet to witness him muster.

" 'Of course…I think I understand now. I see no sign of the Herrinsu vine entwined around your limbs, but you're just as bound as I am now, isn't that the case?' he asked me. 'You have the sword to free me from my bindings and, strangely enough, I have the only sword that can free you.'

"I said nothing in return, except to ask him, 'What say you…do we have a deal?'

"I had expected some hemming and hawing from Samael; I got the opposite.

" 'If those are the terms of my release, I shall gladly deliver,' he said without hesitation.

"I had every reason not to put trust in his word, and yet, I reached for the Sword of Destiny. Samael's eyes widened with anticipation and he held out with untethered desperation his tightly bound hands for me to free, but before I even aimed the blade of the sword in his direction I leveled my eyes upon him and issued him a stern and certain warning: 'Attempt to default on our bargain and I promise you I'll return you to these chains just as easily as I freed you. I think you'll agree I'm the one angel who can see through such a threat.'

" 'Why should I even entertain the idea of dishonoring our agreement,' he replied with an unnerving twinkle in his eye. 'After these long years of banishment you've given me an outlet for my pent-up frustrations…so to speak.'

"I'd be lying if I said I didn't give what I was about to do one last lingering of reconsideration, but my mind was settled and I moved forward with the sword.

"The edge of the blade barely grazed the Herrinsu vine for the tightly wound coils to be severed, and in that instant, in a moment of escape so swift, it was as if Samael vanished into thin air.

"All that remained was the rope of vine lying limp and useless upon the dusty ground."

~ ~ ~

"War!" Gotham proclaimed with disbelief following a ruminative moment once Damiel had finally finished giving his account of what had occurred. "Are you to stand here and tell me you actually bartered Samael's freedom in exchange for an act of war?"

"I freed Samael so that the earth can once more turn unblocked on its axis," said Damiel. "You have always been an adherent of the divine plan set in motion by our father, whether it be dictated through nature's due course or the curated whispers of sacred writings. Or have you suddenly grown perfectly content continuing on with this standstill that Miseriel has shrewdly schemed to ferment in perpetuity?"

"Don't attempt to hand me that nonsense, Damiel. This has nothing to do with righting the divine course and everything to do with one thing, and one thing only: revenge!"

The word brought a slant to Damiel's mouth, like a scale teetering between the weight of mirth and offense. "You dare speak to me of revenge?" the angel exhaled under his breath. "Perhaps you would like to remind all of us present how it is Samael came to be abandoned, if not forgotten, here in this god-forsaken wasteland?"

"You cannot compare what occurred between myself and Samuel and what has taken place here," said Gotham.

"You're absolutely right," Damiel agreed. "Revenge may have been in my heart when I loosed the vine ensnaring Samael, but at least my act of revenge was not selfish and self- serving as was yours."

Gotham's jaw tightened noticeably. "Selfish?"

"We both had sons, and we both came to know the pain of their loss through the manipulative and baleful ways of the Darkness," explained Damiel. "You sought out your revenge as any father would, but by satiating it you denied me mine which I had been patiently awaiting in an oh so painful way. I will admit when I cut Samael's binds it was so that I might finally breathe freely again, but also to set in motion the coming of justice which you inadvertently also stole from our father. And from all humanity who have had had to live and suffer in the Darkness' shadow far longer than they needed."

Much as Gotham may have wanted to argue Damiel's words, he knew he couldn't.

"And when you freed Samael, did you also think about the six boys standing in front of you now and what this so-called war you so enthusiastically champion will mean for them, not to mention the countless other Nephilim scattered across the world?" he asked.

"I did," Damiel replied as his face darkened. "And I am at rest with knowing we have trained them to more than sufficiently and effectively stand up in the face of what we knew would one day come.

"It is," he added, "the reason they were brought into existence…including our own."

"You're a traitor!" Max, who had been doing his level best to keep his tongue pinned down between his teeth in order to prevent such an outburst, suddenly spat out. It was a sentiment unfortunately held by all present, but to hear it spoken out loud with each syllable dripping with vile was cringing.

"Did I say something that was untrue?" Max asked in a defensive tone when all eyes came to rest on him. "If this doesn't make him a traitor, then what?"

The answer to his inquiry came from Damiel.

"I am a collector of debts…and I will not allow Miseriel to skirt the payment I am owed from him," said the angel in a cool and measured tone yet simmered with a contentious hatred that had been slowly fermenting over the years. "If that makes me a traitor in your eyes…then, so be it."

Try as he managed to prevent his stony facade from cracking, Damiel was unable to keep his heart in one piece as he looked into the face of each Nephilim and saw only disdain and disappointment reflected back at him instead of the adoration and regard he had come to know from this particular group of boys that he himself had come to cherish.

"I made it a point to remain here in this desolate spot knowing your eventual arrival would be short in coming and I could explain to you my reasoning for what I've done. It was the least I owed you," said Damiel. "Now I think it best if we were to part company."

Before he could disappear into the sky, Jacob, who had remained noticeably quiet throughout Damiel's confession, called out to him.

"I believe there's something of mine you still have," the boy said while glowering at the angel, "and I'd like to have it back, if you don't mind."

Damiel was instantly reminded of the Sword of Destiny in his possession and he approached the boy with it. But before handing it back he took a moment to look it over as he held it up into the light of the blazing sun.

"Curious thing: rarely has this sword, and before it the spear from whence it became, been passed on courtesy of free will."

The angel's eyes became captive to the dazzling reflection of myriad lights bouncing off the mirror skin that gave shape to the sword's blade. For a moment, Damiel came to acquire a look known to occupy the faces of the rare privileged few throughout history who held the power of the spear in their hands. Briefly, it appeared as if Damiel had succumbed to the enslavement such adoration was known to cause. Yet unlike so many who could never find it within their strength to part with the spear once it was in their possession, except through death, Damiel was able to take leave of the sword's tugging nature and he, indeed, placed it back in Jacob's hands without struggle by his own free will.

"For what it's worth, it was never my intent, nor my wish, to unsettle the trust you placed in me," Damiel said to the boy.

Then, with the flapping of the wings that unfolded themselves from behind his back, he was gone.

~ ~ ~

For some time, it was as if the power of speech had somehow been stolen from everyone. Standing in the center of the lonely, forsaken desert, they each stared at the coiled remnants of the cut vine left discarded on the ground and silently confronted a swirling of thoughts about what Samael's release would mean to them, and the world at large.

No one appeared more unsettled about what had been learned than Gotham. "We should be going," he announced quietly when finally he spoke.

"Where to, now?" inquired Leos.

"Back to Eden, of course. I'll need to inform Anahel and the others of what's taken place here."

"You don't actually think Samael's going to follow through with his end of the bargain he made with Damiel and start a war, do you?" asked Ethan.

"Keeping his word is a trait Samael has shown himself to lack. I can only hope the same is true now," answered Gotham. "But whether or not he holds up his end of the promise he made is only partly what causes me concern."

"What does that mean?" asked Max.

"It means a call to war by the Underneath is not the only pressing matter confronting us." Jacob's throat immediately tightened when the grave look fixed upon Gotham's face came to rest on him. "Let it not be lost on us that Samael is very much aware that he has a son somewhere out in the world, and I'm certain he has been informed, much to his displeasure, that the boy he sired has taken up with the enemy.

"Now that Samael is free, I'm almost certain if there's any war to had it will first be waged to gain possession of young Jacob here."

"He'd be wasting his time. I'll never go willingly with him!" Jacob said with unwavering defiance.

"That's why it's vital we get back to Havenhid," said Gotham. "Eden's the only place where you'll be assured protection."

"But I can't go back to Eden…not just yet," said Jacob.

"What do you mean you can't back?" asked Gotham. "Did you not just hear—"

"I know what you said. But what about Wray? And Ty?"

"What about them?"

"They're on their way back to Cain's Corner right now as we speak. How do I know they'll be okay once they get home? I mean, they were seen with all of us while we were in Venice…at the masquerade ball and at the cemetery, not to mention when we were nearly attacked by Infector-possessed dogs and birds?" said Jacob much to Gotham's chagrin. "Then there's my grandmother. If Samael's first mission is to find me like you said, then I'm sure the first place he's going to look is my home."

The mention of Jacob's grandmother Ava brought a softening to Gotham's resistant demeanor.

"I'll tell you what…you return with me to Eden and I'll send the fiercest angel I know to keep watch over your grandmother. I'll send a small army if it better suits you," offered Gotham.

"What about Wray and Ty?"

"Them, too."

When Jacob still appeared hesitant to accept the offer, Gotham said assuringly, "I can promise you they will all be much safer in their hands than your best intentions."

With some reluctance, Jacob finally conceded, and with a heaving sigh, Gotham once again was about to lead the young party out of the sweltering doldrums of the Infernal Desert when the sound of Hunter's voice kept them in their place.

"I may know of a way to end all of this."

A quick glance around found him still staring at the discarded Herrinsu vine in a quite engrossed state.

"End? End what?" asked Jacob.

Hunter pointed to the severed vine and answered simply, "This!"

He then slow-walked over to the group, but when Kairo and Leos approached him for the taxing task of carrying him for the duration of the log flight ahead of them, Hunter waved them off.

"What if I were to tell you I have the key to cast the Darkness into a pit from which it could never surface again: The Infectors, the Furies even the newly freed Samael?" Hunter posed the question to the growing look of confused gazed fixed on him. "What if I were tell you we can end this war before the first shot is ever fired?"

"The heat must already be causing your brain to broil. You're speaking in riddles," said Max.

"Before we go, there's something I haven't told you…or rather, something I've kept from you," said Hunter.

"So…out with it!" Gotham prodded with what patience he had been left.

"It has to do partly with my family's house and the reason I now believe it was destroyed," explained Hunter with some reticence. "I think, however, it would be better if I showed you. And, in order to show you, we need to make a quick detour back to my place."

"You're pulling our leg, right?" both Kairo and Leos groaned in unison.

"Absolutely not!" Gotham stated emphatically. "Out of the question."

"Look…I wouldn't even suggest such a thing except, well, I've been giving it a lot of thought just now, and seeing as how Samael's back on the prowl and all this talk about a possible war…" Hunter paused for a moment and bit down unsurely on his bottom lip as if he suddenly was considering retracting whatever it was he was having a hard time attempting to say.

"Trust me. If, in fact, Jacob here is in the kind of danger you think he might be, please, just trust me," he pleaded while looking Gotham dead center in his eyes. "You'll want to see this.'

This.

The word, and more specifically the way in which it left Hunter's mouth, made Gotham's eyes narrow with curiosity. Whatever 'This' was, it seemed to be the cause of an overwhelming sense of angst bubbling just beneath the young man's exterior. The question looming over Gotham was whether it was worthy of risking a detour off the beaten track to find out exactly what 'This' was.

CHAPTER TWENTY-THREE

When the traveling company eventually reached the destination of their impromptu detour made all the more arduous for a disgruntled Leos and Kairo struggling to carry their weighted passenger while trying to keep up with the swift and taxing pace set forth by Gotham, they immediately discovered they were not the only ones to have recently paid the loft Hunter called home a visit.

Whoever the unknown visitor may have been, however, it was more than obvious they were likely not the sort of guest Hunter would have invited inside.

For starters, the door leading inside the loft was in complete shambles and left dangling from the door frame by a single hinge, despite the arsenal of deadbolts and heavy-duty locks.

"Well...on the plus side, it looks as though your anti-intruder system was in working order," Ethan commented buoyantly as he and the others heedfully poked their heads through the open doorway and discovered that Hunter's makeshift, jury-rigged defense system had been triggered, leaving a debris field of refrigerators, stoves, engine blocks and other heavy and crushing objects scattered across the floor.

Glancing upward and finding only a cargo net holding a dozen or so sacks of cement and a massive tire made for a tractor still hanging menacingly overhead from the rafters, Gotham issued a word of caution to be mindful of their steps before leading the way inside. As he stepped his way around one of the rusted-out refrigerators, he paused suddenly when he noticed the side of the hulking appliance was smeared with a black substance. It was cold and gooey to the touch, and when he ran his forefinger across the gunk and brought it to his nose, he grimaced at the smell that made its way into his nostrils.

"What is it?" asked Jacob.

"Blood," Gotham answered matter-of-factly, while taking note of the numerous drops made of the same black matter splattered on the floor and forming a trail leading further inside the loft. "Whatever was here received a nasty welcome from your deterrents."

"Uh…don't you mean whoever?" Ethan asked hopefully.

"Unfortunately, not in this case."

Wading further inside the loft they made an even more staggering discovery: the entire place looked as if a tornado had somehow swept its way inside through one of the windows and unleashed its full destructive power upon every inch of the already rustic space and left behind barely anything recognizable when it finally dissipated. Whatever furnishings there were had been overturned and tossed about, and in several cases completely demolished and turned into rubble, and vast sections of wall were marred with large holes as though they had taken on cannon fire.

"Now this brings a whole new meaning to the word 'ransacked,' " Max said when he managed to find his tongue inside his gaping mouth.

"Who could have done this?" asked Kairo.

If anyone had an idea, Hunter didn't wait around to find out as he suddenly launched into a full sprint across the loft, leaping over the wreckage that stood in his path, until he reached the area that used to be his bedroom. There he fell to his knees and urgently felt his way through the litter covering the floor until he located the loosened floorboards that served as the lid to his secret hiding place. Desperately, he pulled them up and only when he was given a look inside the hidden recess did he exhale the breath trapped inside his chest and appear to relax.

"They didn't find them," he sighed with relief.

"Didn't find what?" Jacob asked, as he and the rest of the group gathered closely around Hunter with necks craned in an effort to see what hidden treasure he had secreted away beneath the floor.

"I'll admit…I find myself more than a little curious about the answer to that question myself," Gotham himself remarked, as he slowly lowered himself into a squatting position facing Hunter and eyed with some intrigue a mound of white he spied inside the secret compartment.

"So what is it already?" Leos impatiently asked the question that was at the forefront of everyone's minds.

"Whatever it is, it must be something pretty valuable for someone to turn this place upside down and inside out like they did," said Kairo.

"It looks…it looks like a pile of sugar," Ethan hedged a guess while his face scrunched itself up with bafflement when Gotham reached down into the dark hole and took a small pinch of the white granules with his fingers.

"Not sugar," said Hunter. "It's—"

"Salt," Gotham cut in with the answer as he studied closely the sampling he took from the pile he held in the palm of his hand.

"Hold on a tick," said Max who didn't seem all that pleased with the revelation. "Here I am half buggered and so hungry I could eat a horse and chase the rider, and you're telling me we came all this way for some salt?"

Ignoring Max, Gotham's prying gaze shifted from his palm to Hunter. "This has long been nature's greatest purifier," he spoke directly to the young man. "It's also quite effective at not only warding off evil entities but ensuring that certain possessions one wishes to keep out of such hands remain hidden…almost like an invisibility cloak. But why do I suspect you already are well aware of all of this?"

Hunter didn't answer one way or the other and, instead, took a steadying breath and dug the fingers of his two hands into the mound of salt and pulled out a sack that was buried out of sight beneath the mound. After giving it a good yet careful shaking and sending bits of salt flying every which way in the process, he got to his feet and directed Max and Leos' attention to a large kitchen table that, like most everything else in the loft, had been toppled over by whatever destructive force had blown its way and instructed them to set it back on its legs again. Once the table was hurriedly put back in its place, Hunter set the mysterious sack down in the center of the beat-up wooden surface and a deathly quiet settled itself upon the room as everyone waited with a gnawing anticipation for the big reveal.

"So, what are you waiting on?" Leos asked as the seconds ticked by.

"Nothing, I guess," answered Hunter who looked like someone who had been given the unpleasant task of opening the body bag holding a fresh corpse in need of identification inside a police morgue.

But open the bag he did, and from it he pulled out the peculiar object he had gone to great lengths to thieve some time ago and, in the process, nearly lose his life on the platform of a London tube station. The sight of It, when he placed it on the table beneath the halo of light shining down from a low-hanging light fixture, made the other boys lean in simultaneously with mouths agape, as if the object were a magnet with a pulling power aimed specifically at flesh and bone. And, indeed, it proved itself to be such a lodestone judging by the way the boys were drawn almost hypnotically to the sight of the black shapeless shape in a constant state of morphing that they spied housed inside the glass womb which glowed an iridescent green.

"Isn't this the thing you were accused of trying to steal from that weird-looking giant with the silver mask at the masquerade ball?" Ethan asked when he managed to pry his eyes from the mesmerizing object.

"Not exactly," Hunter answered with a subtle evasiveness.

The younger Nephilim weren't the only ones to find themselves transfixed by the strange- looking canister; Gotham had leaned in within a nose's length of the object and was studiously examining it, and when the angel's gaze shifted away from the eerie bust of a most wicked-looking creature affixed to the top of the container and settled itself on Hunter, the young man felt his pulse tick up a couple notches.

"I don't know which question I wish to hear an answer to first: How did you come to possess this object, or why?" said Gotham.

~ ~ ~

The loft became quiet as church as Hunter stood before Gotham and his engrossed group of friends and began the telling of how the entrancing whatsit on the table had come into his possession. His story began a short time after he left home for parts unknown and unfamiliar to him rather than live with a father who, at the time, he believed to be a Fallen. And like most young children who run away from home before they are ready to face the harsh realities of the world, he quickly found himself roaming the streets with empty pockets and an even emptier stomach.

It was during a desperate search to quiet his growing hunger late one night that he came to meet a man who would end up changing the trajectory of his life.

"I was scrounging through the garbage behind this market that I earlier discovered had a tendency to throw out perfectly good produce way before its time, and came upon not only a whole buffet's worth of fruits and vegetables, including nearly pristine watermelons, bananas, strawberries, but a host of pies, Danish and dinner rolls," Hunter recalled without a hint of shame of being forced to dumpster dive in order to feed himself.

"Scrounging through the garbage? Ugh…that's so incredibly gross!" Ethan muttered to himself as he listened with a twinge of disgust pinching his face.

"As I was stuffing my face with the first sizable meal I'd been lucky enough to gorge myself on in a good day or two, I heard a loud scream. At least I thought it was a scream; it happened to be pouring rain that night, and at first I wondered if maybe what I heard was a howl coming from the wind accompanying the storm," continued Hunter. "But then more screams came, only much louder, and there was no mistaking them this time. I followed the screams which continued to come in frightful bursts, and they led me to a nearby house. All the windows were dark except one on the second floor, and I was curious enough to scale a nearby trellis entangled with vines in order to steal a peek inside."

"What did you see?" Kairo, who like the other boys was transfixed on Hunter, asked with an edge of impatience.

"Nothing unusual, at first," answered Hunter. "There was a man in the center of a large bedroom dimly lit by numerous candles, and he was standing at the foot of a bed holding a sack in his left hand. I could hear him reciting what I first thought to be a chant of some kind, but the patter of the rain wouldn't allow me to quite make out what it was; that is until I saw the woman on the bed. She was thrashing about as though she had been strapped to a bed of nails, yet the howling that came from inside her were more rage than pain. And it seemed like with every chant coming from the man's mouth, the more her body would contort in ways that were completely unnatural and grimacing to witness, and her incessant enraged caterwauling became so that the window I was peering through suddenly shattered and sent an explosion of glass to rain down on me.

"It was while I was plucking the few sharp shards that had embedded themselves in my shin and shaking the rest from my hair that I noticed the man reach into his sack and retrieve something from inside. What it was I couldn't see as his back was turned to me, but it instantly silenced the woman's wailing when he held it out in front of him for her to see. Her body ceased its writhing, and she lay there on the bed panting like some rabid dog with her eyes fixed firmly on whatever it was the man had revealed to her as if she had been placed in an instantaneous trance. The man resumed his strange chanting and with a forceful voice he called out for a demon and demanded it show itself. That's when I saw it: a movement of black sliding across the bed from beneath where the woman was lying and over the edge of the mattress toward the floor. It was almost as if the woman's shadow had managed to detach itself from her person and move about of its own free will. Only there was nothing womanly or feminine about this shape, or even human for that matter. In fact it looked to be something quite inhuman."

"What was it?" all five boys listening asked in unison.

"An Infector," answered Hunter. "I had never seen one before that night, but my father had schooled me about them enough when I was growing up that I knew immediately it couldn't be anything else than one of those evil creatures when it finally revealed itself in all of its grotesque hideousness."

"It sounds to me as though you were witnessing an exorcism," said Gotham.

"That's what I assumed as well, but it wasn't…not exactly."

Hunter's remark caused one of the angel's eyebrows to arch itself with piqued curiosity as he continued listening to the story.

"The sight of the Infector was so shocking I barely took notice of the tickling sensation moving across my hand. And how I wish I hadn't because when I finally went to flick whatever it was away, I discovered the tickling was caused not by beads of water from the rain, or maybe an insect, but a spider crawling along my arm—not some harmless everyday small garden variety spider, but a large, gray hairy kind."

Just the thought of the arachnid made Hunter pause a moment and shudder severely at the phantom legs he suddenly felt creeping their way at several points on his body and causing the other boys to chuckle in the process as they watched.

"If there's one thing I can't stand it's spiders; even more so than Infectors," Hunter confessed, albeit with a small sense of embarrassment. "So you can imagine my horror when once I shook away the one on my arm, I discovered I was surrounded by hundreds, if not thousands more. They were crawling up the side of the house to the ledge where I was crouched as well as making their way down from the rooftop above. The swarm of spiders was so large it made the Infector look like a cuddly Raggedy Ann doll in my eyes, and even though they paid no attention to me as they scurried past, as though I weren't there and instead made their way inside the bedroom through the shattered opening in the window, I was ready to turn tail and retreat down the trellis I had earlier climbed, and I would have, too, if it wasn't for what happened next."

"What? What happened?" pressed Jacob.

Hunter described the terrifying sight of the Infector looming over the man who had summoned it to show itself like a gigantic nightmare come to life. And yet the man showed not a hint of fear or dread while staring straight into the red glow of the menacing eyes leering back at him. Nor did he flinch the slightest bit when the phantom-like figure wrapped in its black vaporous shroud swept in even closer like some slow-crawling fog until it looked to Hunter as if the Infector might just consume its taunter as easily as a python feeding upon a small rodent.

" 'Your time is finished here dark specter of Hell!' I heard the man tell the Infector without so much as a trace of worry over the destructive end it appeared he was all but certain to meet, and his disregard of such fear only made the Infector bellow with rage," continued Hunter. "But just when I expected the inescapable to happen, a figure dressed all in black stepped out from the opposite side of the room where he had hidden himself from sight. He looked to be only a few years older than what I am now, and he held in his left hand a bow which was already nocked with an arrow. In a focused flash, he shot his bow and sent his arrow sailing toward the Infector's back at which it was aimed. Just as quickly and precisely, the Infector, without so much as a glance over its shoulder, reached behind and snatched the arrow from its charted course before it struck its intended target. The bowman instantly went to grab for another arrow but the Infector was far quicker and grabbed hold of his assailant by the throat, wrapping his long spindly gray fingers around his neck, and lifted him effortlessly off the ground until they were eye to eye with one another. Then the Infector raised his other hand still holding the arrow which he clutched like it were a large knife, and I braced myself as it looked as if he had every cruel intention of plunging it right into the center of the bowman's chest. I could tell by the panicked look in the bowman's face he had the same sinking feeling I did, and we both shut our eyes when the Infector drew back his hand. But instead of skewering the bowman with the arrow, the shrouded demon embedded it firmly into the wall. Then he took the bowman and hung him on the end of that arrow by the back of the shirt as though he were a winter coat.

"Both the bowman and I breathed a sigh of relief, but had either one of us knew what would come next we would have both agreed having the arrow run through the chest would have been a much more welcoming end."

"This isn't going to end well, is it?" Ethan surmised aloud.

"The Infector shifted away from the bowman and the huge gray spiders instantly moved in. They swarmed the bowman by the hundreds as he hung helpless and growing more and more terrified as they quickly wrapped him from sight in an unbreakable cocoon of silk like any fly who had the misfortune of getting tangled in a web. His screams were short-lived, and to this day I could only hope whatever unpleasantness he suffered was equally short-lived." Hunter again paused for a brief breather and he took note of the fact that anyone who had earlier found his arachnophobia condition somewhat amusing no longer did so after hearing such a grisly account.

"Paralyzed as I was by what I had just witnessed, I had enough sense at hand to realize there were still two other people in the room and I couldn't allow them to suffer the same fate, or worse, as the unfortunate bowman had," continued Hunter. "I looked first for the woman on the bed from whom the Infector had been lured out of, but to my surprise, she was no longer there. I gave the room a quick search and found that she had discreetly slipped inside a nearby closet, and placing a finger to her lips, she motioned for me to keep quiet as she carefully slid the door closed. Relieved that she was at least hidden away and out of any immediate danger, I snuck my way over to the other side of the window where the man was standing, and I instantly saw how it was he managed to appear so brave and unnerved with a terrifying Infector looming over him: he was completely blind. My unexpected presence startled him at first, but once I let him know I was there to help him he became cooperative. I, on the other hand, became less sure how exactly I was going to lead a blind man down a twenty-foot trellis, but seeing how it was our only avenue of escape, I knew I had no other option except to leave him there at the mercy of the Infector and its army of spiders, and there was no way I could do such a thing.

"The man quickly tucked away whatever it was that had mesmerized both the woman and then the Infector back into his raggedy sack, before he allowed me to take hold of his arm to help guide him. But before I even managed to assist him in climbing through the window frame and onto the ledge, the Infector's attention was suddenly torn away from the enjoyment of watching the spiders and their squirming prey by my unexpected intervention. It's eyes blazed with anger at the sight of me aiding in the man's escape, and with a simple gesture of his hand he sent the large brass bed hurtling across the room toward us. I barely managed to shove the startled man back inside the room and onto the floor so he was clear of being hit by the incoming projectile; I on the other hand didn't fare as well and was hit full force by the bed as it smashed its way through the window, creating an even larger opening in the side of the house. My breath was squeezed from my chest as I was knocked off my feet and sent tumbling head over heels across the short slope of roof leading to a fairly dangerous drop to the ground below. How I managed to grab hold of the rain gutter at the very last second to stop my fall I have no idea, but with a burst of stars exploding in bright white lights from being knocked senseless clouding my vision, I found myself dangling from the edge of the roof, and beneath my flailing feet was the remains of the bed lying in a crumpled heap on the ground below where it had come to a crashing rest.

"As I struggled to pull myself back up onto the roof, I felt something grab hold of me by the nape of the neck."

"The Infector," Kairo hedged a guess.

"It was hovering over me like some macabre wraith, and as it lifted me upward to get a better look at me, the threat of the long harrowing fall to the ground beneath me was no longer the most frightening thing in my sights," said Hunter. "Somehow I found the courage to look the unearthly monster square in the face, and what a face it was; as unsightly a creature as I would hope to ever have to lay eyes on again. 'And just who might you be?' the fiendish entity asked me in a voice that sent an icy chill straight down my spine. But before I could answer, it stretched its unpleasant face closer to mine and gave me a suspicious sniff, then another, and suddenly the black empty eye sockets that held nothing but two red glowing embers of hatred burned themselves into me even more so, as if they had spied something unusual concealed by my flesh and bones, and it asked, 'Or maybe the better question I should be asking is *what* might you be?' The rain was still falling and I was soaked to the skin, yet I could feel the beads of sweat begin forming across my forehead, especially when the Infector punctuated his question with a hissing '*Neppphhhliiiim.*' I knew then I was a goner and I cried out; not from fear, but the feel of the Infector's razor-sharp claws digging their way into my back.

"There was, however, an even louder cry which drowned out mine and the Infector's, and we both turned and saw it was coming from the blind man. He was standing at the gaping hole made by the airborne bed and trying to get the Infector's attention by shaking the sack he continued to carry guardedly in the same way someone looks to entice a dog with a squeak toy. 'I thought you were interested in this,' the man taunted the Infector, and the Infector became incensed. 'Give it to me!' it growled in reply. 'I'll trade you mine for yours,' the blind man bartered, which only seemed to anger the Infector even more. But after a few grumbles of rage the Infector begrudgingly tossed me aside. Luckily, I came to land on the roof, though barely, and the Infector rushed to where the man stood to collect his trade, only instead of handing over the sack as he promised, the man threw it as hard as he could into the storm. And for someone who was blind, it was a darn good throw, as the sack landed in the gutter of a nearby street. I thought the Infector would end the man right then and there as it twisted in rage over being tricked in such a deliberate manner. Instead, it let out a howl of alarm at the sight of the thrown sack and whatever mysterious object it held inside being swept up by the stream of rainwater rushing down the gutter and carried to the open mouth of a storm drain just a few short feet away."

~ ~ ~

"Oh, man, what an ace move," Leos remarked, after Hunter took a quick breather to grab a bottle of water he managed to scavenge from the kitchen area which was as turned upside down as the rest of the loft.

"So, then what happened?"

"The Infector raced off in a desperate attempt to take possession of the sack before it disappeared down into the dark underground hole. Only it was too late, and in a huff of fury the Infector ripped its way through the sidewalk as easily as if it was tearing a piece of paper in two and disappeared down into the sewer. That's when the blind man and I were safely able to finally make our getaway," Hunter said, before taking another swig from his bottle of water.

"That's some story," said Max who found most accounts of someone escaping a face-to-face with an Infector in one piece to be well-earned bragging rights. "But what does any of this have to do with this weird doohickey?" he asked, motioning to the object on the table that remained just as foreign in nature as it had when Hunter brought it out from under the floor.

"I'm getting to it," Hunter replied.

And again he continued with his story that was not yet finished.

"The blind man led us back to his place which was a loft inside an abandoned building much like this place, only smaller, and a bit more rundown," said Hunter. "Once he got a fire started, set out some towels to dry us off from the rain and put a kettle of tea on the stove to help warm our chilled bones, he finally introduced himself to me as Ben…Ben Graybark. And he thanked me for coming to his rescue that night. I returned the introduction and went to shake the hand he held out for me, and as I did, I felt a twinge of sharp pain I'd been feeling on and off just past my right shoulder from where the Infector had dug its claws into my back. Ben, surprisingly, immediately honed in on my discomfort. 'You best take off your shirt so I can take a look at your injuries,' he instructed without any hint of irony to his obvious handicap. I declined at first for the obvious reason, but he was persistent to say the least. I was hesitant to comply, but only when I looked deep into his eyes and was certain they were as dead as they appeared, did I remove my wet shirt. It was the first time I had ever broken one of the four primary rules my father had drummed into me since I was a little kid and exposed my back to anyone as I took a seat on the floor in front of Ben, and

I found it to be quiet unnerving. Sightless as Ben may have been, I had an inexplicable feeling he somehow was still able to see more than most men with two good eyes, something I sensed in strong order when I felt him tense up noticeably as he began tending to my wounds with a cotton- ball dabbed in alcohol just above the spot where my right wing would one day be protruded from my back.

"If he suspected anything, he didn't say a word. He asked me what a young boy like me was doing roaming around the streets on such a disagreeable night. I told him the truth: that I was a runaway, figuring quite confidently that I could be well on my way before the proper authorities were summoned if he chose to pick up the phone and report me. But he didn't report me and instead lent a guess, and rightly so, that I was probably waiting for an explanation from him about what had transpired earlier that night. That's when he revealed to me that he was a Silencer."

"A Silencer?" Kairo echoed with a stumped look.

"Of course...a Silencer," Gotham was heard to mutter. "Then it wasn't an exorcism you witnessed, but an Ekballo."

"Ek-what?" asked Jacob.

"Ekballo," repeated Gotham. "It's an obscure and unorthodox practice that has its roots in the more conventional exorcisms known today, only far more...aggressive."

"Aggressive? In what way?" asked Jacob.

"When an Ekballo is performed, a Silencer doesn't just excise a demon from a possessed host as is done during an exorcism; he attempts to draw them out into the open, in their physical state where they can be exterminated in order to prevent them from infecting anyone else."

"That explains the fitting name: Silencer," Leos muttered.

"Frankly, I'm a bit surprised to hear there are still practicing Silencers in this day and age, as it was commonly believed the practice had all but gone extinct long ago," said Gotham.

"Yeah, well, no offense to this Ben person," Max remarked to Hunter, "but I'm much more surprised how someone who is blind could manage to last five seconds in a room with an Infector, much less be one of these Silencers."

"Believe me, the same thought was weighing on me, that is until Ben showed me how just because someone might be blind doesn't mean they don't have the ability to see," replied Hunter.

"What is that, some kind of riddle or something?" Leos questioned suspiciously.

"No, it's not a riddle; in fact, the way Ben explained it to me it made perfect sense. You see, every living thing radiates some form of energy in the same way that the sun puts out light and warmth. Humans—you, me— believe it or not, emit light, only it's in such small quantities the naked eye can't detect it. The same thing is true with Infectors; they don't emit light, but anyone who has been in their presence, which includes everybody in this room, knows firsthand the intense coldness that surrounds them."

"At the risk of pegging myself as some kind of nerd," Ethan, who had been listening rather intently, started to interrupt somewhat reluctantly.

"If it makes you feel any better we had you pegged long before now," Leos, unable to allow such an opening to be ignored without a good-natured poke in return, chimed in.

Ethan, expecting such a jab, responded with a nettled sigh before continuing on with his thought: "I just wanted to point out that coldness isn't, in fact, a form of energy like heat given off by the sun, or even light that humans supposedly emit; it's just temperature."

"That's not exactly true…at least when it comes to Infectors and other entities created by the Darkness," corrected Hunter. "See, the Darkness itself is a living and powerful mass of energy just like the light, and the numbing frigidness it radiates is really no different than the heat radiated by the sun, only infinitely more powerful."

Much as he tried to explain it, Hunter could see by the look on his friend's faces that they weren't fully grasping the concept.

"Don't worry…if you're like me you kinda have to see it to really get it," said Hunter.

"And how do you do that: see it, that is?" Jacob asked inquisitively.

"With this," Hunter said, gesturing to the table where the object whose identity still remained clouded in mystery rested.

"It's how Ben finally managed to make me understand what he was talking about. He pulled it out from a pocket on the inside of his coat and I instantly recognized it as the thing the Infector was so desperate to gain a hold of. I was also surprised to find that he still had it, seeing how the last I recalled, he had thrown the sack that both the Infector and I believed held the object inside out into the street where it was swept into the sewer. 'Infectors are vicious and menacing creatures, but trust me when I tell you they are not the sharpest shears in the shed,' Ben, who was visibly tickled by the success of his ruse, told me.

"That I can vouch for," Gotham remarked in agreement.

"So tell us what Ben showed you already," Ethan pressed impatiently.

"First, he tossed me a scarf and instructed me to blindfold myself with it, which I did. Then he placed the object into my hands," continued Hunter. "I immediately felt this intense and very uncomfortable chill enter my hands and flow like lightning to every limb of my body; so intense, in fact, that I not only nearly dropped it, but wanted to hurl it as far away from me as possible. But Ben kept me from doing such a thing by holding my hands in his and keeping them enclosed around this thing. Then he told me to focus my senses—not just my eyes, with which I couldn't see anything but blackness due to the scarf covering them, but all my senses—on the sensation I was feeling emanating from the object in my hand. I did what he told me and at first I experienced nothing. But then, after a while, something strange happened. I gradually began to make out through the darkness filling the inside of my eyelids an even darker shape. It was much like the weird ink blot-looking thing you can see inside the object in a constant state of metamorphosis, but the more it changed its shape, the more frightening it became, and the more frightening it became the more I could feel the bitter cold aura of its unpleasant energy surround me and attempt to penetrate its way through my flesh until even Ben couldn't keep me from pulling the scarf from my eyes and tossing the evil thingamajig far from me.

"When I had managed to catch my breath and shake the shivers off of me, I asked Ben what that horrible object was and he told me he wasn't exactly sure; only that it contained what he called a piece of Hell. He also said there were more like it in existence. Then I asked him how it was he came to have it, but he was reluctant to tell me except to simply say he had stolen it..." Hunter's lips suddenly squeezed together tightly as if to stop his tongue from wagging any further, but they just as quickly loosened themselves once more and he added, though quite faintly, "from someone he called The Walking Serpent."

"The Walking Serpent? Sounds like the kind of bizarre creature you'd expect to see in a B horror flick," said Jacob.

"Only there's nothing make believe about what Hunter was told," uttered Gotham, which caused all the boys' heads to swivel around and look his way with intrigue.

"Are you saying there's actual walking serpents that exist?" asked Leos.

"All in good time, my boy. First, I wish to know how this canister came to be in your possession," Gotham inquired as the piercing focus of his eyes settled themselves all the more intently upon Hunter.

~ ~ ~

"It wasn't until sometime after Ben asked me to be his Toxotai," Hunter answered the angel's question.

"Toxotai?" queried Max.

"This Ben character actually suggested you serve as his Toxotai?" questioned Gotham who looked visibly surprised by Hunter's statement.

"What exactly is a Toxotai?" asked Jacob.

"Why the stunned look? You don't think I'm capable enough to be a Toxotai?" Hunter ignored Jacob and, instead, answered Gotham back in a rather abrupt manner.

"It wasn't a matter of capabilities that caught me off guard," Gotham replied.

"Would someone please explain what a Toxotai is already?" Kairo all but shouted in frustration.

"Originally, Toxotais were a small group of highly trained archers that comprised ancient Greece's military force. In an Ekballo, they are the assassin lying in wait to strike down an Infector, or other foul creature of the Underneath lured into sight by using an arrow whose tip has been laced with a specially blessed amalgam of water and oil," answer Gotham. "What I was questioning was merely why a skilled Silencer would be recruiting a complete stranger he had just met to be his Toxotai. Blind or not, he had to realize you were a mere boy at the time and that the only bow you've ever likely handled were the ones you untied from Christmas and birthday presents."

Hunter appeared to settle down once the angel explained his reaction.

· "After Ben showed me how it was he managed to be blind and still see things like Infectors, I noticed his eyes fixed on me in that strange way I observed earlier, where they seemed to be fixed on something other than darkness. I asked him if anything was the matter. He didn't answer me right at first, but then he said something that caught me off guard; he mentioned again how the energy contained inside humans revealed itself as a faint and nearly undetectable radiance of light, but when he looked at me he saw what appeared to him to be a swarm of unusually bright fireflies decorating a dark summer night," said Hunter. "Naturally, I assumed he was somehow able to detect the angel blood running through my veins in the same way he was able to see the cold evil of things coursing with the Darkness, and I suddenly became self-conscious of the fact that my upper body, particularly my back, was still exposed, and quickly wriggled back into my shirt still damp from the rain in hopes of dousing whatever light he was seeing.

"He must have sensed my discomfort and said to me, 'I don't expect you to reveal anything to me about yourself that you don't wish to, but it's obvious, even to this blind man sitting before you, that you are someone special. Then he told me, 'I have always been a God-fearing man, one who believes he was put on this earth for a specific purpose. And I now, at this moment, see clear as day the gift I was given with my blindness in order to recognize the specific tools he would eventually hand me that would be needed to see forth his mandate.' That's when he proposed that I become his Toxotai, and while I was completely taken aback by the offer, I reflected back on what he had said to me, particularly about believing he was put on this earth for a specific purpose, and I accepted. After all, the whole reason I had left home and set out on my own was to prove myself to be someone worthy of the name Nephilim and not some shamed son of a Fallen. How better to do that than to be an exterminator of Infectors?"

Hunter then proceeded to tell the small captive audience gathered around him how he spent the next several weeks of intense training to become a fleet-footed archer, and only when he proved himself to be skilled enough to hit the bullseye of a target depicting a crudely drawn caricature of a hideous Infector dead center each and every time he let an arrow fly from his bow with unbroken speed, did he move from paper marks posted on a bale of hay to the real deal, and his first Ekballo.

He recalled standing poised and ready in the darkest recesses of a room with beads of sweat dotting his brow, even as his shivering breath from the intense cold gripping him revealed itself in ghostly wisps. Gripping his bow tightly in one hand and nocked arrow in the other, he watched anxiously as Ben performed his calling and attempted to lure into sight the very malevolent thing that was causing an otherwise mild and unassuming-looking middle-aged man bound to a wooden chair, to thresh and flail about wildly while wailing unspeakable things in a voice than was anything but human, and he waited for his cue. Suddenly, and for a brief moment all too soon, a shadowy figure detached itself from the drained man, just like Hunter had unintentionally observed peeking through the window of the house he had been drawn to by screams that fateful rainy night, and the black shape rose up to take the form of a frightful Infector. Hunter took a bracing breath, tightened his grip on his bow and waited for the sign from Ben. When it came, he abandoned the darkness which cloaked his presence and advanced on the unsuspecting Infector with three purposeful strides before taking aim. Before he could fire, however, the menacing phantom, suddenly aware of the ambush set upon it, turned and became enraged at the sight of Hunter, and Hunter, in return, shrank slightly at the sight of the demon's ghastly face molded from venom and vice. It came at Hunter with swift speed, but Hunter's arrow, when it finally was released from the cradle of its bow, was faster, and it struck the Infector in the very center of its black-filled chest. There came a deafening howl as the specter was instantly engulfed in a breath of flames ignited by the arrow tip laced with its holy elixir, and in a flash the Infector was wholly incinerated.

"It was the most empowering and satisfying feeling I'd ever felt annihilating that Infector," recalled Hunter who looked quite gratified while revisiting the memory.

"So then you weren't quite being honest with us when you said you had never been trained in weaponry, were you?" asked Max.

"I believe I stated I'd never used a sword before, which is the truth," answered Hunter. "A bow and arrow, on the other hand, I'm quite proficient in using. And I was being completely honest when I said I preferred doing my fighting with my fists, as well as my brain."

After demonstrating his skills in fisticuffs at the masquerade ball in Venice with impressive effect, no one in the room dared argued with him.

"So how long did you act as this Toxotai?" Jacob asked, shifting the discussion back to the topic at hand.

"Ben and I eventually ended up taking down at least a dozen more Infectors over the course of the next six or seven months, and I never experienced a moment of hesitation like I did that first time," Hunter replied.

He suddenly grew quiet as a cloud of gloom appeared out of nowhere and positioned itself directly above him. "That is, not until that last unfortunate Ekbello we were called upon to perform."

~ ~ ~

Everyone was anxious to find out what had dampened Hunter's mood, but no one was so eager as to ask him knowing the odds were good that what would be told next likely wouldn't be all that uplifting, and so they quietly waited and watched in silence as he circled once and then twice around the table.

"A young girl believed to be under the sway of an Infector was in a terrible state and was doing all sorts of horrible things to herself, and we were called to perform an Ekballo on her," Hunter eventually went on. "We were summoned to a big stately big house late one night, but when we arrived we found no one there to greet us. The two of us walked inside and Ben called out to whoever lived there to alert them of our arrival, but we received no reply. I told Ben to stay put while I ventured upstairs to seek out who it was who had hired us, but as I went from room to room, I found the upstairs as vacant as downstairs, and equally as dark. Not only did I not find anybody at home, including any sign of young girl, but I noticed none of the rooms were furnished. And when I tried to turn on the lights, I found there to be no power. My first thought was that we had somehow made a mistake and come to the wrong house. Then I heard Ben scream.

"I readied my bow while I raced to the staircase and peered over the banister overlooking the large foyer where I had left Ben, and to my horror I discovered he was in the grips of the very thing we had been called to the house to eradicate."

"An Infector?" asked Kairo.

Hunter nodded. "It's gnarled, clawed fingers were wrapped around Ben's throat visibly squeezing the air from him as his legs flailed about in a desperate search for the floor which he was left dangling above. This Infector, however, was not just any Infector, but the same Infector Ben had head-faked months earlier and sent down into the sewer on a wild goose chase. And it was clear that black smoky shroud had no intention of being gulled into being made to look like a schmuck this time around."

"What did you do?" asked Ethan whose wide eyes were fixed on Hunter as though he were being read a spooky bedtime story right before lights out.

"I had been trained to respond one way, and one way only, whenever an Infector entered my sights, and that was with my bow. Only this time I completely froze."

"How come?" asked Leos.

How come?

Had they not been listening to him? Hunter wondered to himself. Did it not leave an impression lasting more than a minute or two when he shared with them how an Infector meets its end when it's struck by a laced arrow? He suddenly seemed to part company with the others in the room by way of his faraway gaze which gradually became more distant, and began to drift backwards in time to the night in question when he stood at the railing of that second-story landing with his arrow trained on the unsuspecting black-shrouded shape of evil who loomed like some infernal plague come to life over his hapless friend and mentor, captured in the menacing clutches of its clawed fingers. And while Hunter had neither lied nor flagrantly stretched the truth in any manner when he spoke of having never demonstrated a moment's pause when taking aim at an Infector and sending it impenitently back to the perdition from which it had been created, he would quickly discover this time to be quite a different story.

His mettle, which had never before abandoned him, suddenly began to melt like the wax of a burning candle when, out of the blue, a vivid and overpowering image of the first Infector he ever speared came rushing to the very forefront of his thoughts and caused him to become like a deer caught in the unexpected glare of headlights lighting the way of a car speeding down a dark road. And nothing short of looking into the eyes of Medusa herself could have caused Hunter to become a motionless statue of stone than the moment Ben turned his head and looked directly his way with a gleam of recognition, as though he had spotted a familiar swarm of bright fireflies congregating at the rail, and proceeded to give the signal he always did once he had lured an Infector into plain view for Hunter to take his shot.

Hunter, however, remained incapacitated and, despite his impulse to do otherwise, he found himself unable—no, unwilling—to send his nocked arrow straight into the resurrected memory of that first Infector (and all the ones that followed) which continued to ignite before his very eyes like a tinderbox into an all-consuming ball of flames. For he knew if he attempted to put down the Infector he would essentially be aiming the same arrow straight at Ben.

"DO IT!" Ben's voice suddenly rang out in a clamorous and jolting boom almost as though it took on the shape of a phantom hand that reached out and struck Hunter across the face in an effort to knock the boy free from whatever trance had taken hold of him. And when Hunter's gaze met Ben's he was overrun by a tugging anguish when he realized his friend understood only too well what his fate would be with the decisive release of the arrow in which he demanded, and embraced it.

"Do it!" Ben mouthed pleadingly to the boy once again.

Hearing this, the Infector followed Ben's blind gaze to the stairway landing, and when it spotted Hunter standing there with his bow and arrow in hand, its black shrouded face lit up with rage. It pitched forth a deafening shriek and in a last desperate attempt made a grab for the sack Ben was clutching in plain sight which held the item coveted by the Infector. As Ben struggled mightily to keep the gnarled hand from taking possession of the bag, Hunter impelled himself to refocus the point of his arrow on the unsightly creature before him. Then he closed his eyes and whispered prayerfully, "Forgive me."

The arrow, when finally sent on its way, sliced the air with a swift reckoning guiding its aim and caught the Infector squarely on its left side just beneath its overly-long outstretched arm. Even with his eyes closed, it was impossible for Hunter to blot out the roar of the conflagration that instantly erupted from the point of impalement, or the far worse agonizing screams that came from both the Infector and, more horrifically, Ben, as both were wholly engulfed in the unforgiving lick of flames.

Once the roar of the inferno gasped its last breath, a loud weighty *CLUNK!* punctuated the instant resettling of quiet that followed.

Only then did Hunter force open his eyes and, with great apprehension, glance down at the spot in the foyer where last he saw Ben in the clutches of the hulking Infector, but both had vanished from sight and all that remained was a faint haze of smoke hanging like a delicate veil in the air. He then quickly noticed something on the floor of the foyer: the mysterious spherical object Ben had so carefully guarded. While the fire had completely and fully incinerated the Infector, Ben, and even the sack in which the object had been concealed, it left not so much as a blackened smudge of soot on the eerie artifact whose mysterious innards cast a sickly green radiance against the shadowy surroundings of the dark house. And from within that green glow there could be heard a faint congregation of whispers. They seemed to be calling out for Hunter, beckoning him to descend the stairs and retrieve the thing he gazed down upon with so much intrigue and, yes, uneasiness. And retrieve it he was about to, when something else caught his eye: a nebulous shape of black whose shadow slithered its way across the foyer floor toward the object.

Hunter grabbed for another arrow and readied his bow while his keen eyes remained locked on the unexpected creeping visitant, and he quickly deduced, much to his relief, that it wasn't another Infector lurking about the premises.

Neither, however, was it human.

That much was certain when Hunter finally managed to catch a glimpse of the figure as it entered the foyer. Whoever, or rather whatever it was, stood at a great height and, despite wearing what appeared to be a long dark coat with its collar turned up obscuring the face, appeared to be impossibly, nay, unnaturally thin. So rangy was the figure, in fact, that the description "thin as a rail" would imply something far more portly than the faceless presence Hunter eyed with a mixture of intrigue and repugnance. But watch he did, first with idle curiosity and then alarm, as the sticklike shape slunk rather than stepped its way across the foyer floor to where the object that survived the burst of flames which had consumed both the Infector and Ben had come to rest, and took custody of the abandoned relic. And as it knelt there upon the cold floor clutching its newfound possession in a hand as pallid and macilent as a week's-old corpse, the jade-tinted luster radiating from within the mystifying object managed to illuminate the unexpected countenance shielded behind the turned-up collar of the coat donned by the obscure figure.

That, Hunter recalled with a hint of the willies surfacing in the faraway stare still fixed in his eyes as he continued to tell his story, was the first time he ever caught a glimpse of a Walking Serpent.

~ ~ ~

"When you say Walking Serpent, you don't really mean a walking serpent, do you?" Leos posed the question that sprang to the forefront of ever one of the boys' minds.

"I mean exactly what you would envision from just hearing the name," answered Hunter. "Walking down the street you probably wouldn't take much notice if you ever crossed paths with one; they have a way of blending in with regular people despite their freakishly tall and slender stature. But catch a glimpse behind the collar or the hat they usually position low on their forehead to obscure their identity, and you'd understand instantly why they are referred to as Walking Serpents. It's like looking straight into the face of a cobra—a very large cobra. Hideous things they are, you can trust me on that, with their thin, evil-grinning mouths and overly large hooded black eyes that have an ease of slicing their way right through you as effortlessly as the swords you have tucked away in your wings; which I would guess is why they tend to only venture out under the cloak of night."

"Pethens."

The strange remark uttered by Gotham suddenly caused the collective gazes of the young boys who were huddled together and listening intently to Hunter, as well as that of Hunter himself, to shift their focus onto the angel.

"These so-called Walking Serpents, as you deem them…they're called Pethens," Gotham explained in repeating the peculiar name. "Though believe me when I tell you they are far more deadly than any cobra you might come across slithering on its belly."

"As you all witnessed front and center at the masquerade ball," Hunter reminded everyone.

"And never will you find them at their most lethal than when it comes to this most dark and sinister vessel," the angel commented ominously as he leaned in over the table to take another close and guarded look at the puzzling container which cast its green-glowing luminance upon the dubious look etched in his face.

But what was it about the harmless-looking weird whatsit that made it so dangerous, each of the boys found themselves wondering to themselves as their curiosity was stirred even more? And why did it attract these snake-faced creatures called Pethens?

CHAPTER TWENTY-FOUR

THE SCOURGES

"It's called a Scucca Urn," said Gotham when finally he answered the question that was at the forefront of each of the boy's minds concerning the strang e object on the table.

"Scucca," Ethan echoed under his breath as the strange name tickled a giggle from him.

"Also known as a Demon or Devil Urn," Gotham was quick to elucidate, and immediately the chuckling ceased.

"Accounts of their existence had long been rumored for as long as I can recall, but this is the first time I dare say I've ever caught a glimpse of one, never mind up close," Gotham muttered softly while leaning in to give the queer little object a closer study with his scrutinizing gaze.

"I'm guessing it's fair to say something called a Demon Urn isn't like a box of Cracker Jack with a cheap, harmless prize hidden inside, am I right?" Leos speculated aloud with unease, and from the timid expression shared amongst his friends he wasn't the only one asking himself that very question.

"Shortly after the Great Flood God unleashed from the heavens to wash clean the grime of wickedness and offense with which humankind had dirtied the pristine earth he had created, he was so overcome with grief for what he had been forced to do that he did something quite unexpected to all those who witnessed it," said Gotham.

"Oh, I know! It's got to be the promise he made afterward to never do anything like that again in the shape of a rainbow," Ethan answered enthusiastically.

His reply, however, was met with a chorus of groans and more than a few eye rolls.

"I really have to ask the question: Is there an Ewok working the controls inside your head?" Max asked facetiously.

"As I was about to say: he requested a conclave with the Dragon himself," continued Gotham. "Despite handing down to Moses the ten divine governing rules in a last-ditch effort to guide man's feet along the path of righteousness, he knew the Dragon so hated him that it was only a matter of time before those who had been banished to the netherworld that smolders with brimstone and anguish would once again feed on the souls of his most precious creation. And so it was during this face to face that God put forth a rather unexpected proposal: Neither he nor the Dragon would, from that day forward, place any influence or sway in whichever direction mankind's soul chose to take him for a period of five thousand years, and should man at the end of such time show himself of his own inclination, the preference of embracing the Darkness over the Light, then God agreed to go back on the promise he made after the Flood to never destroy life in such a way again and put an end to all humankind once and for all."

The revelation drew a stunned response from the angel's young captive audience, including Hunter who had obviously never before heard the telling of such a story.

"Naturally, such a proposal proved quite enticing to the Dragon," said Gotham. "The prospect of mankind's eradication was appealing on its own, but to have it come at the hands of its own creator was something the Dragon couldn't deny himself the perverse pleasure of beholding twice in one lifetime; particularly when such an action would call upon God to humble himself before all who he had previously cast his judgment upon through the simple act of breaking his own sacred word. And so, the Dragon agreed to the pact; but as we have all come to know, his own word is as binding as a severed rope, and he proved it so when he returned to his lair deep beneath the ground like all worms and began doing what it is he does best: scheming. And in that scheming he hatched a diabolical plan in which the powers of Darkness would be wielded as they always had: to guide man to his fated end, and the Dragon, for the first time in his deceitful existence, could prove without hint of falsehood that he had in fact stayed true to his word."

"True to his word?" Jacob cried with offense at even the idea. "But you just said he planned to go on using his powers to tempt and manipulate people even though he swore not to.

"That I did," answered Gotham, causing a taxing look of confusion to settle itself upon the young boy.

"How is that even possible, even for the Dragon…unless he—" Jacob's perplexity suddenly gave way to a glimmer of clarity. "Unless he allowed someone else to wield that power for him."

And as soon as spoke those words, the filament from some inner lightbulb instantly sparked with light. "That's it, isn't it? The Dragon entrusted his powers with someone else to get around the deal he made with God. It's the only thing that would make sense."

Then the light in Jacob's eyes grew all the more brighter, and focused.

"But it wasn't just anyone. It was Samael, wasn't it?" he inquired, though it was obvious he had already realized the answer. "That's how he ended up becoming so powerful: The Dragon placed control of the Darkness into his hands."

"You are well-served by your insightfulness, Jacob," Gotham noted with a half-smile which failed to wipe away completely his underlying quiet and dour expression brought to the surface by the boy's theory, before quickly adding, "but you still have much to learn about that which lurks beneath your feet."

The loft grew noticeably quiet and the sound of Gotham's footsteps upon the floor as he began to slowly pace were like the pendulum of a clock ticking off the passing seconds.

"Like the one divine Light, the power that gave life to the Darkness was born from the breath of its creator," the angel continued finally. "But an impious force, it is—beholden but to one master, yet seditious by its very nature when its insatiable hunger to abrade all within its reach in the same way fine grains of sand gnaw away at the landscape is fed by the hand of another. The Dragon, in all of his cunningness, failed to take this into account when he hatched his dubious plan, and overlooked any surety when the time came for Samael to relinquish this most caustic and corroding power he'd be handed.

"Samael, however, proved to be far more artful."

Without explaining any further his ominous remarks, the angel glanced at the rest of the group gathered around the table and inquired, "Anyone here familiar with what a canopic jar is?"

There was a moment of quiet at first as the boys traded blank looks with one another until Kairo piped up with a clearing of his throat.

"Weren't they used by the ancient Egyptians during the whole mummification process they did when someone died?" the boy answered.

"Quite right, Kairo," Gotham commended the boy. "There were four canopic jars used during each mummification ritual, inside of which would be placed certain organs the Egyptians believed would be needed by the deceased in order to be reborn in the afterlife. Each jar was decorated with a head carving depicting the four sons of Horus, whom the Egyptians worshiped as the god of the sky, and it was the job of each of these four deities to guard these organs. Imsety, depicted by a human head, protected the liver; Hapy, with the baboon head, protected the lungs; Qebehsenuef, with the falcon head, protected the intestines; and Duamutef, with the jackal head, protected the stomach.

"This Scucca Urn," Gotham said, gesturing to the object of note, "serves a role much like a canonic jar."

"Strange they didn't have one of these canopic jars thingies for the brain," Ethan pondered aloud, while staring transfixed at the mesmerizing object on the table. "Not to say the lungs and liver and all that aren't important or anything, but you'd think even in ancient Egyptian times the mummy makers would recognize how vital the brain is to the human body. I mean, it's like the hard drive operating the entire system, know what I mean?"

When he looked to his companions for reaction, however, he found his straying musings on the matter was met with disinterest and even a touch of familiar annoyance.

"That Ewok sure is really working overtime tonight," Max grumbled under his breath while shooting Ethan a cease-and-desist look.

"Let's try and stay focused on figuring out one thing at a time, okay?" Kairo suggested diplomatically while giving Ethan's shoulder an attention-directing kneading.

Gotham's quieting glare left the squabbling boys when Hunter posed a question his way: "Are you saying this urn thing is like one of those Egyptian mummy jars? That it's holding a heart or a liver or some kind of body part of a demon inside?"

Gotham stood silent for a moment or two as though quietly debating how, or perhaps if to answer the question.

"When Ben told you a piece of the Underneath resides inside this inimical vessel, he spoke quite accurately," the angel said when, again, he spoke. "And, yet, not accurately enough."

~ ~ ~

"Each of you, save for the exception of one, has come to know the untold divine force you came to inherit from your fathers called a Grace; or in some of your cases—Graces. These Graces, as you came to learn at the Crescent Scar, are the manifestations of the Seven Virtues. What you have likely not come to fully realize of yet is that the Darkness is an opposing reflection of the Light, and the devilry that burrowed its way into the lair known as the Underneath did so with seven tentacles endowed with its own inherent powers, though they were anything but divine," Gotham continued in his explanation that everyone listening strived hard to keep up in their following.

"What are you saying; that the Darkness has its own set of Graces?" Max wondered aloud.

"Don't be a dill! Gotham just said the Darkness is an opposing reflection of the Light, which means opposite. It wouldn't have Graces," Ethan chimed in, and appearing quite content to be, for a change, the one who got to deliver a verbal nose-slapping, not to mention use one of Max's native pet insults against him in the process.

"What would be the opposite of Graces?" Kairo posed the question which everyone was already visibly mulling about in their own heads.

"Sins," Jacob muttered after a moment of quiet pondering. "The Graces stem from the Seven Virtues. It's only logical the Darkness' version of Graces would come from the Seven Deadly Sins."

"Nicely deduced, Jacob. Only we dare not refer to them as Graces, but instead as Scourges," noted Gotham. "That is what they are called, and that, as I hope none of you are privy to witness firsthand, is what they are."

Jacob pondered the angel's words for a moment as he turned his attention back to the canister on the table which was becoming in everyone's eyes, more and more mysterious with each passing minute of the clock, before asking, "Were these urns part of Samael's plan to hold onto the power the Dragon had handed him?"

A sliver of a smile appeared to subtly curl Gotham's mouth, as the boy was slowly unscrambling the coded message placed on the table.

"Once the Dragon had entrusted control of the Darkness into Samael's hands, Samael moved to ensure in his hands such power would stay, even when the final grain of sand marking the end of the five-thousand-year truce agreed upon between God and the Dragon had slipped its way through the hourglass," began Gotham. "His plan was quite ingenious if not wholly foolproof. In short order, Samael encased each of the Seven Scourges inside seven Scucca Urns, which he then placed in the protective custody of seven Shadow Keepers, or as they are better known: the Pethens. These vicious and deadly creatures who were brought into being solely for this furtive task, were then sent into hiding to the darkest lairs of the known world with the precious urns in their tightly guarded clutches.

"And it would seem these Shadow Keepers have, until this one misstep, been quite successful in the task given them," Gotham added, while motioning to the urn on the table upon which all eyes were suddenly drawn now that they understood what it was they were looking at, and how it came to be.

"That's not quite entirely true," said Hunter.

To everyone's surprise, Hunter returned to the sack he had unearthed from the secret niche beneath the floorboards, and from it pulled out not one, but two more Scucca Urns and placed them on the table next to the first.

"How many of these things do you have squirreled away?" asked Leos.

"That's it; just the three," answered Hunter.

"You stole these? From Pethens?" Jacob inquired incredulously.

"That's right. The first I recovered from that spindly, snake-like figure who had snatched it from the ashes that were once Ben and the Infector in whose menacing clutches he had met his tragic and selfless end, and who then tried to escape with it like a vampire trying to outrun the rising sun," recounted Hunter. "The other two I managed to track down through the help of some writings I found amongst Ben's belongings. Apparently, he had been on the hunt for the same two long before he met me."

"Don't take this the wrong way," Ethan began diplomatically after a quiet pause, "but how exactly did you manage it? Steal them, I mean. Last we saw, one of those Pethens had you by the throat and dangling you in the air like a piñata he was just about to rip apart."

"If it's all the same to you, it's a long and tangled story I'd rather not rehash at this late hour. The important thing, as you can plainly see, is I managed to get them," answered Hunter. "Besides, I'm afraid you'll think I'm a tad screwy if I told you."

"No offense, mate, but after what I saw tonight, anyone who willingly goes looking to mess around with a Pethen already has a few kangaroos loose in the top paddock, if you want my opinion," said Max.

"Believe it or not, I'd be inclined to agree with you, especially when I think back to that first Pethen I attempted to swipe back one of these blasted urns," Hunter confessed with a weak smile that lacked the usual self-confidence of which the young man seemed to have a ready supply.

"I had hoped to avoid having to admit it out loud, but truth of the matter is I nearly saw my end that night. Probably would have, too, if I weren't so full of hate and rage over what had happened to Ben," said Hunter. "That and…"

"That and what?" Leos urged anxiously when Hunter hesitated from speaking further and all but bit down on his tongue.

Hunter shot a worried glance to the others positioned around him before uttering uneasily: "I know this going to sound whacked…but I made myself disappear."

The other Nephilim exchanged confused glances with one another at the disclosure.

"Disappear? What do you mean disappear?" Kairo inquired on behalf of everyone.

"I mean disappear, as in I was in one place one moment, and in the next I wasn't," replied Hunter before taking a breath to calm his increasingly agitated state.

"Like I said, I was on the receiving end of a brutal pummeling by this Pethen, Shadow Keeper, whatever it is you call him," Hunter continued in as measured a tone as he could. "When he saw I had followed him to take back the urn he had swiped from Ben's ashes, he exploded in a ball of fury I still get the shakes over whenever I think back on it. That's when he set out to try and destroy me, and he likely would have if what happened next hadn't."

"But what was it that happened?" Max pressed impatiently.

"This thing was tossing me around like a rag doll and slamming me into walls so hard I could hear my bones crack," continued Hunter. "At one point, I found myself lying on the floor while somehow still clinging tight to that urn, and as I gasped in pain while trying to get to my feet, I saw that merciless creature coming at me again. I knew my strength wouldn't hold out against another brutal assault at the hands of this monster and, strange as it may sound, I suddenly found myself thinking about Stone Soup."

"Stone Soup?" echoed Leos.

"It's this small hole-in-the-wall restaurant. Clarence,—he's the old man who owns the place—he used to feed me and let me crash on a cot he had in a storage room when life on the streets got particularly harsh and unpleasant. All I had to do in exchange was wash a few dishes for him, and as I lay there in a crumpled heap on the floor, all I could think was how I would trade anything to be up to my elbows in soap suds sponging off a mountain of dishes, and then enjoying a nice warm slice of Clarence's apple pie and glass of milk to wash away the taste of blood in my mouth. Then before I knew it—POOF! The sight of the Pethen as he reached down to take hold of me again vanished, and to my shock, I suddenly found myself standing in the middle of the kitchen at Stone Soup. I'm not talking about my imagination getting the best of me, mind you; I mean I was physically in one place one second, and the next I was somewhere entirely different."

Hunter let go a deep breath, as if he himself found it hard to believe the very incident he had just finish recounting.

"At first I thought I had suffered some kind of damage to my head from the beating I got from the Pethen, but it wasn't the case," he then continued. "It took some time on my part to try and repeat what had happened, and one day I was finally successful. I realized then that I wasn't going crazy; that I could really do this…this…whatever it is I suddenly found myself able to do. And, well, to make a long story short, it's the thing that helped me take possession of the other two urns and live to tell about it."

The loft became quiet for a moment or two before Jacob exclaimed quite enthusiastically: "Well, don't you see? That's your Grace!"

"My Grace?" Hunter repeated looking somewhat gobsmacked.

"It's called Drifting. I have the same Grace. It allows you to move not only from place to place in a blink of an eye, but present to past," explained Kairo.

"And now that I think back on it, I'm willing to lay bets from that story you told me about how you were able to sic sharks on those dolphin poachers, you might actually have two Graces: Drifting and Whispering," said Jacob.

"Drifting and Whispering," Hunter repeated the names of the two Graces to himself, and as he did, a smile slowly unfolded itself from the intense expression he had been carrying with his for some time. "Well, what do you know about that!"

~ ~ ~

The moment of levity was short-lived when Gotham, who had been quietly listening to conversation take place, made his voice heard.

"Now that you've explained the manner in which these urns came into possession," the angel remarked to Hunter, "I'm quite eager to learn the why. For what reason would a Nephilim risk his very life in stealing these repositories of evil?"

"To destroy them," Hunter answered without hesitation, which by the angel's expression was not expected.

"That was Ben's sole purpose in attempting to hunt these things down in the first place. He believed that if you were able to seize all seven urns and destroy them, and the thing they hold inside, then you would in essence destroy the heart of the Darkness," explained Hunter. "Only problem is, there doesn't seem to be a way to destroy them."

"What do mean there doesn't seem to be a way to destroy them? Looks like it wouldn't take more than a swing of a hammer to smash them to smithereens," observed Max.

"By all means, be my guest," Hunter offered while tossing onto the table besides the deceptive-looking containers a mangled piece of metal he picked up from the debris-covered floor, which anyone would have a hard time recognizing as being a hammer at one time.

"I've tried just about every method you can think of with every tool known to man to smash, chop, shatter, burn, and basically annihilate these things. I even managed to get my hands on a gun, and lined the urns up for target practice, but as you can see I wasn't successful in defacing any of them with even the tiniest scratch," said Hunter.

After surveying the debris field of instruments Hunter had attempted to use in his futile if not all-consuming mission that now lay strewn in various broken and decommissioned states across the floor, the boys settled their sights on the three urns with renewed wonderment.

"I don't know if whether or not that's amazing, or scary," Kairo noted quietly.

"Definitely the latter," Ethan whispered even quieter still.

"Ben had the same luck as I did; it's why he eventually became a Silencer. He figured if he couldn't destroy the urns then he would at least use them to destroy the evil things they helped create one by one, and being in possession of an urn made him one of the most feared Silencers ever," said Hunter before turning his attention to Jacob. "Like him, I finally became resigned to the fact that these urns are simply indestructible; that is until I realized the power vested in the sword you carry. That's what I was attempting to talk to you about last night in Venice, before Gotham—or who we thought was Gotham—interrupted us."

"What are you saying? That you want to use my sword to try and destroy these urns?" asked Jacob.

"It is the Sword of Destiny. As I understand the legend, it is the one weapon with the power to slay all. One would assume it would have no problem in completely pulverizing them."

"I'm most certain now's not the time to be entertaining such…means," Gotham, who remained somewhat unsettled since Hunter's possession of the taken Scucca Urns was revealed, suggested as diplomatically and measured as possible.

"You're kidding me, right?" Hunter replied a tad agitated at the angel's advice. "I would think you out of everyone would be champing at the bit for such an opportunity. I mean, who's to say we'll have another chance like this?"

"Chances are like four-leaf clovers: they are few and far between. If you had any regard for those you may have the good fortune to possess—not to mention a single working brain cell—you might think twice before contemplating using the Sword of Destiny, or any sword for that matter, to run through an object of which you haven't the foggiest notion what it may unleash when breached," Gotham chastised sternly.

Whatever reply Hunter may have considered, he thought twice about making it heard and instead kept silent.

"Don't take this as any kind of criticism or judgment," Leos eventually chimed in after the awkward silence that followed, "but I have to say from the looks of all the busted-up tools scattered across the floor, you seem pretty fixated—obsessed even—at wanting to destroy these urns."

The observation appeared to catch Hunter off guard.

"Maybe I am," he said with a slight crook of a smile, after silently pondering Leos' assertion. "In the beginning, my attempts to try and destroy these things was really nothing more than to see through what had been Ben's goal that eventually took the shape of a nagging challenge when I quickly discovered I couldn't accomplish the deed any more than he could. Our little excursion to Venice, however, changed all that when I visited my home, or what used to be my home, and learned what had happened there."

A visible grimness suddenly appeared to sweep over him. "My mother was the single most kindest soul I've ever come to know, and they killed her. But the worst part is they killed her because of something I did!"

His new-found friends quickly jumped in to assuage him from voicing such self-loathing thoughts, but Hunter wanted to hear none of it and quickly waved them quiet.

"If working my way through every single last tool man has ever created in hopes of finding the one that drives a shiv into the heart of the Darkness makes me obsessed, then so be it," he said in a tone laced with hate. "There's a Pethen out there responsible for taking my mother's life, and if these Scucca Urns are the key to their existence—or better yet nonexistence—then you better well know I have every intention of adding to the collection I already have in my possession."

He then quickly turned away, but not before shedding the first few tears of the sorrow he was adamant to keep hidden. And while the other Nephilim were quick to form a cocoon of support around Hunter, Gotham looked on quietly from a distance, a reflection of compassion alight in his face. He could not help but feel torn over which he had more sympathy for: the young man's grief, or his anger; for the angel knew intimately they were two thorns with the ability to inflect a festering wound.

~ ~ ~

With the mystery of the Scucca Urns unraveled and explained, along with the malignant dark matter called Scourges that were interred in each, Hunter gathered up his pilfered loot and returned them to the hidden confines of the sack in which they were kept. Then he, along with Max, Kairo, Leos and Ethan, took advantage of the late hour to rest themselves from what had been a long and taxing day journeying to and back from the Infernal Desert.

Despite being just as exhausted as his friends, Jacob found himself, instead, wandering about the dusty and cobwebbed remains of the deserted paper mill downstairs from where Hunter's loft resided. The rustling of a few stray decaying remnants of paper once produced in bulk at the mill could be heard as a mild evening breeze pushed them about across the ground as Jacob stood in an open doorway staring out at the passing lights of a steady stream of traffic humming its way along a neighboring stretch of highway beneath the moonless night sky. So much had happened in such a short span of time that his brain remained unable to focus itself on any one specific thing. When finally it managed, he was interrupted by a familiar presence he felt making a slow approach toward him from behind.

"Do you think what he told us was true?" he made audible the very thought he could hear being whispered inside his head.

"You'll have to be a bit more specific in your question, as there's been much that's been expounded upon over the course of the past two nights," Gotham's voice was heard to answer as the angel stepped his way closer toward the boy.

"What Hunter said regarding the Scucca Urns," Jacob clarified. "Do you think it's actually possible to put an end to the Darkness just by destroying them?"

"That's a query I'm not sure I'm qualified to answer with much authority," Gotham replied with a heavy sigh, as though he had been left pondering the same thing as the boy. "All I know about the Scucca Urns and how they came to be are from the wisps of rumor one happens to catch from the abundant whisperings of their legend. Had we been privy of Hunter's secret cache earlier in our travels we could have tapped a much more reliable source of information when we had the brief chance."

"You're talking about Thaniel?"

"Do you know of anyone else who would likely have been able to enlighten us more on such matters than we are now?"

As the angel stood chatting beside Jacob while sharing in the peaceful urban view and the soothing breeze that moved like fingers through his hair, he felt a pensiveness in the pause of silence that followed and gave the boy a searching glance out of the corner of his eye.

"Something more is weighing on you, isn't it?" Gotham, his eyes narrowing, inquired. "Is the idea that you may hold the one existing key to the urns' destruction that daunting a prospect?"

Jacob didn't answer, at first.

"When you explained to us earlier about what the Scourges were—you know, how they were the Darkness' version of the Graces, only instead of originating from the seven Virtues they derive from the seven Deadly Sins— was that based on rumor as well?" he finally asked.

"Hardly! In fact, I would argue it to be an irrefutable verity," Gotham said emphatically in reply. "What has been the source of tittle-tattle comes from the whispers surrounding Samael's cunning sleight of hand to hold in perpetuity the powers of the Darkness, as no one residing north of the Underneath was there to witness it."

Jacob cocked his head and gave the angel a curious look. "Tittle-tattle?"

"Yes," Gotham replied with a slow and suspicious drawl. "It's a word used to mean gossip, is it not?"

"I'm not sure; I wasn't alive in seventeen forty-three to know what the jargon of the day was," answered Jacob who had often chided the angel for his odd hoary word choices that had a habit of tweaking the ear in the same manner as a particularly bad note plucked from the strings of a Stradivarius.

"Perhaps, it would suit your stellar proficiency in linguistics if I relegated my communication to simple sign language, or better yet, cave drawings," noted Gotham, who could face down the maligning things of the world without blinking an eye and yet find himself unable to sidestep getting his feathers ruffled, even slightly, from such ribbing.

Jacob was quick to apologize for interrupting, but only when he managed to erase completely from sight the lingering traces of amusement seen in the twitching grin his lips struggled to wipe clear, did Gotham continue.

"As I was saying," he began again, "The Scourges are every bit as real as the hellfire and brimstone of which it feeds. And now, after looking upon three of the vessels long-rumored to hold the unholy spring of these seven afflictions this night for the first time, it would appear the means of Samael's scheme to hold reign over the powers of the Darkness is no longer a product of...*tittle-tattle*."

This time, the angel's intentional use of the archaic word he had moments earlier been good-naturedly derided for went ignored by Jacob, who suddenly looked quite glum.

"Do you think that could be the reason why the Blackstone couldn't read my Graces?" the boy asked almost fearfully.

"I'm not sure I know what you're asking," said Gotham.

Since the day it was discovered Jacob possessed the Seventh Grace—the one divine power unobtainable to all other Nephilim which also revealed him to be the Light Bearer—it was believed the mystery as to why the Blackstone had failed in its ability to uncloak the elusive gift at the Crescent Scar had been solved. Now, Jacob wasn't so certain.

"Isn't it obvious? I'm the son of a Fallen; and not just any Fallen but the one whose name you just mentioned," Jacob tried to explain, yet failing to bring any visible clarity to Gotham. "If what you said is true about how the order of the Darkness works, then wouldn't I have had these Scourges passed onto me, and not Graces like everyone has assumed?"

A twinkle of light finally found Gotham's eye.

"Ah, now I believe I'm beginning to understand what it is that troubles you," he said with a gentle smile. "You think just because Samael's blood runs through your veins so, too, does the lifeblood that waters the Underneath. Rest easy in knowing no such curse exists. The scion of angels, whether Fallen or not, who are brought into this world, each inherit an untold Grace, or Graces, as pure and untainted as the innocent child who comes to receive it. Like an angel who comes to carry the shameful mark of the Fallen, it takes a willful betrayal and rejection of the Light to befoul the divine gift of a Grace. When a

Nephilim turns his back to the Light, the Grace he holds instantly tarnishes and corrodes until it becomes something quite…impure."

"A Scourge," Jacob spoke the name out loud though he hated even uttering the word.

"A Scourge," repeated Gotham. "So you see, you have nothing to worry about."

The assurance from Gotham, as well as the loving tousling of his hair he received, was just what the boy needed at that exact moment.

"Oh, by the way, I received a text from Wray before you came out here," Jacob said abruptly shifting topics. "She noticed a strange man lurking around outside her house when she was trying to rest from her trip home, and sent me a photo she took of him."

Jacob's fingers quickly gave his phone a couple taps before holding up the illuminated screen for the angel to see.

"That would be Yairel," Gotham said after glancing at the photo of a hulking figure with long hair positioned as inconspicuously as possible on the roof of a neighboring house, keeping watch like a guard in a prison tower. "I told you I would send a few of my brothers to watch over your friend. There should be two more just like Yairel standing guard over your grandmother along with your other friend; the exasperating one."

"You mean Ty," Jacob said with a chuckle.

"Yes, how could I forget?" Gotham uttered while looking quite pained by the reminder. "Well, now, if your worries have been settled enough, I think you should try and get some rest. We'll be leaving in only a few hours and we've a long journey ahead of us."

The angel turned to make his way toward the stairs leading to Hunter's loft when he realized Jacob wasn't following.

"Jacob?"

"I hate to admit it, but I'm feeling a bit fearful," Jacob confessed quietly.

"What's there to be fearful of? I told you I have sent three of the most formidable angels to stand watch over your grandmother and friends. Trust me when I tell you they are quite safe," the angel attempted to assure the boy.

Jacob shook his head. "It's not about that, but this," he said, as he pulled from his pocket the now worn and rumpled envelope left on the ledge of his bedroom window weeks earlier by some avian messenger.

"The summons ordering you to appear before the Iudicium Tribunal. What of it?" Gotham asked after taking note of the Caelestian scrawl on the front of the envelope. "Certainly, this hasn't left you in a cold sweat."

"No, not exactly," Jacob dithered at first. "It's not that I'm afraid to show up for the hearing because that would mean I'm afraid of Sandel and I'm not, not in the least bit."

"Then, what?"

"I'm not sure I know how to explain it, but I've just been having a bad feeling about whenever I think about it. Like something dreadful is going to happen if I were to show up there."

Gotham reached out and gave the boy a comforting kneading to the back of his neck.

"Nothing dreadful is going to happen," he assured Jacob with a smile. "How can it when we're all going to be standing right there alongside you: Your friends, Anahel, myself and, from what I've heard, even Eksel himself."

Jacob, however, heard not a word after Gotham uttered "Nothing dreadful is going happen," when something quite to the contrary, in fact, did. It was a familiar feeling of dread that had visited him on more than one occasion. It took hold of him like a phantom hand grabbing the front of his shirt, and, in an instant, his face went colorless when the world appeared to vanish before his dazed eyes and the only sound to greet his ears was the muffled nothingness one hears when submerged in water.

"What is it, Jacob?" an alarmed Gotham asked, but Jacob heard not word coming from his mouth; neither did his eyes, which were slowly rolling upward into his skull, pay any mind to the image of the angel trying to gather hold of him and keep him from collapsing to the ground. All Jacob felt was a sudden stab of pain to his rib cage on his right side, and he sent forth a piercing howl.

~ ~ ~

"Jacob…"

Gotham's voice eventually managed to pierce the noiseless realm that had momentarily encapsulated the boy before he was released from its grip as he collapsed upon the floor onto all fours. The pain remained, deep-set and searing, and when Jacob grabbed at his side, his hand was greeted with a warm and sticky ooze, and an even more horrific sight when he looked to see what it was.

Blood.

His blood!

Panicked, he fought the confines of the t-shirt he was wearing with his wings until there was heard a swift shredding of cotton as his left pinion ripped itself free and allowed Jacob to take in hand that which he knew was his invisible assailant: The Sword of Destiny. The blade of the weapon flashed a radiant light as Jacob held it before him, and his gaze became terror- filled when he peered into the mirror-like steel and saw the hair-raising image of a hideous Fury reflected back at him.

In a flash, he was up on his feet still staring with horror at the hideous black creature that appeared to be have been created from a tar pit of unspeakable nightmares captured in the blade of his sword.

"It's a Fury!" Jacob alerted Gotham, while completely oblivious to the cloud of vapor his breath left in the air that was suddenly bitterly cold.

"That it is," Gotham replied with an unusual blasé tone that caused Jacob to look his way and see the angel's attention was not fixed on the sword, but a particular area of the paper mill. Precisely, the angel's gaze held captive an identical image of a Fury reflected in the blade of the sword that was no mirror image, but a real-life nightmare in the flesh.

The lights then began to flicker.

Once.

Twice.

On the third dimming they were completely snuffed out like the candles on a birthday cake following the making of a wish, and all that was left was the nighttime which had somehow transformed itself into something quite menacing, particularly when the Fury's hissing voice emerged from it.

"You have something which is not yours to possess."

At first Jacob was grateful for his Nephilim eyes which cut through the darkness like a pair of fog lights, that is, until he spied the Fury emerge from the shadows within which it had been cloaked and crept slowly toward Jacob.

"I haven't the foggiest notion what you're talking about," Jacob struggled to reply in as fearless a manner as he could manage.

"Where you have seen success as a thief, you fail as a liar," the creature grumbled. "The Pethen who was here earlier failed to find what it was looking for and left me here to wait for your return. Now tell me, WHERE ARE THE SCUCCA URNS?"

"I can honestly tell you I did not steal these urns you're accusing me of stealing," Jacob said with a nervous chuckle, all while gripping tighter his sword. "I think you might have me confused with someone else."

The flippant response enraged the Fury who opened wide his grotesque mouth with its two massive upturned tusks and released a deafening screech that caused several windows to shatter in bursts of glass.

"Feel free to step in anytime," Jacob implored Gotham with a growing uneasiness.

The angel, however, much to Jacob's utter surprise, took several steps back while leveling upon the boy a look that all but stated aloud his sword would remain in its sheath.

"If you don't have the urns, then I have no use for you," the Fury announced with its white empty eyes attempting to sear their way into Jacob before adding with a beastly hiss, "Neeeppphiliiiim!"

With lightning speed, the Fury charged at Jacob and made a swipe at him with its razor-sharp claws and, while the move caught him off guard, Jacob's reflexes proved to be swifter as he maneuvered his body just out of reach of being dealt a most unpleasant shredding. When Jacob returned to his battle stance, there was no sign of the Fury to be found; only the *PAT-PAT-PAT* coming from a pair of unseen feet as they scurried seemingly in every direction at once along with the occasional blur of the dark figure they carried.

Then, suddenly, there was silence, and for a brief moment Jacob was able to breathe a sigh of relief in the hope that the Nephilim-hating Fury had retreated from the building. It was a blessing, however, that was short-lived when Jacob became aware of something wet on his shoulder and looked to find a thick strand of black ooze drooling its way from somewhere above where he stood. An unpleasant chill made its way down his spine as his eyes turned slowly and cautiously upward with great reluctance to see the source of the drizzling drool. To his horror, but not surprise, he was met by the unsightly sight of the Fury poised on the rafters above like a deformed panther preparing to strike, and no sooner had Jacob locked his sights on the white-eyed demon than the Fury did just that. It lurched at Jacob, it claws out and screaming its unbearable caterwaul, but it was the creature's tail and the scorpion-like pincher that came at Jacob with a rabid urgency like a giant pair of dangerously sharp shears slicing at the air in a desperate bid to amputate at the wrist each of the boy's hands that were gripping tightly the Sword of Destiny. Jacob managed to retaliate by dealing a powerful blow to the Fury with one of his wings, but not before the Fury was able to deliver a painful gash beneath Jacob's right eye with its wicked tail before the foul creature was sent airborne across the plant.

Ignoring the blood trickling down his cheek, Jacob swung around to face the black beast he knew was coming for him again, and he took hold of the sword clutched tight in his hands like he never before had. For the first time, it seemed as if the sword he long-felt had held command over him had suddenly surrendered itself to his sway. And something extraordinary then occurred: an unspeakable surge of power entered Jacob's body through his hands gripping the sword, and it was not the overwhelming experience it had been in the past, but one of empowerment. In that moment, it was as if the Sword of Destiny had attained supremacy over all things as the very layer of dirt and debris that covered the ground slowly levitated several inches upward and objects all around the plant began to stir and bend in its direction as if the sword had become a powerful magnet from whose forceful pull they could not resist or escape.

The Fury unfurled its leathery, dragon-like wings, and with a howl of rage sailed across the wide expanse of the plant with great speed and ferocity to destroy once and for all the very thing which fed its insatiable hate. In spite of the frightful vision barreling toward him through the surrounding darkness of the night, Jacob closed his eyes, took a calming breath and attempted to spy through his eyelids the energy of evil Hunter's blind friend and mentor, Ben, had sworn was visible in the most darkest of situations. Sure enough, he caught sight of the swarm of fireflies coming fast at him, and just as it descended upon him, he swung his sword, and the glowing swarm was instantly scattered then extinguished in a burst of soot and an anguished cry.

The lights immediately returned, the cold dissipated, and not a sign existed of the Fury.

~ ~ ~

"Appreciate the help," Jacob remarked sourly to Gotham once the ashen remains of the deceased Fury had cleared. "So were you just going to stand there and watch my demise?"

"Don't be so theatrical," Gotham replied with an indifferent smile. "The only risk of your demising was your resistance to taking ownership of your sword, and that was something I could not allow to lapse one day further. Tonight you showed you have finally become one with the Sword of Destiny, and might I add, you demonstrated it quite impressively."

The compliment made Jacob instantly release his grudge against the angel at being forced to put his life on the line against the vicious Fury.

"It was pretty impressive, wasn't it?" he attempted to pat himself on the back.

As he smiled, he was instantly reminded by the sting of pain from the fingernail-sized laceration to his upper cheek by the Fury's tail that he still had a lot to learn. Yet it was the sudden reminder of another source of pain that drew his attention downward to the right side of his torso just below his chest where earlier the sight of blood had marked the presence of a mysterious and inexplicable wound. Only now, as he stood examining himself, he saw the blood that stained the front of his t-shirt had vanished, and both the wound and the pain which accompanied it were no more.

"It's known as stigmata: a malady, if you so wish to refer to it as such, where the appearance of wounds suffered by the Son of God at his crucifixion spontaneously appear on a person's body," Gotham offered in an attempt to defuse the look of confusion suddenly upon Jacob. "The soul of the sword you carry was first born in the Roman spear which pierced the side of Christ in his final breaths, and it's from the blood that stained its blade that it came to carry the power it now holds."

"I've had a few similar episodes in the past where something seems to take hold of me and draws me to look into the blade of the sword where I'm shown visions of things that are either happening or going to happen. But this is the first time I've actually experienced this—what did you call it? Stigmata? What would be the point of such a thing?" Jacob said as he tried to make sense of everything he was trying to understand from Gotham's words.

"The stigmata serves as sign—a warning, if you will, when the life of the one into whose hand it was destined to be placed is in peril," explained Gotham. "It also serves as further proof that you, indeed, are the Light Bearer whose coming was foretold; proof that will be presented posthaste to Sandel and his tribunal for all to see."

There suddenly was heard the thundering sound of feet, and both Jacob and Gotham turned to see Hunter and the other boys charging their way down the steps from the loft where they had been sleeping soundly.

"What's happened? What was with all the racket?" they all began asking all at once.

"It's no big deal. Just a little run-in with a Fury," Jacob announced, drawing an even louder chattering of questions.

After Jacob offered everyone an abbreviated recount of what had transpired while they were snoozing away, Max stepped forward and took a hold of his chin.

"Cripes, looks like that Fury really spit the dummy with you," he commented as he turned Jacob's head slightly in order to get a better look at the nasty cut that mirrored his own scar from a similar run-in he had with a Fury before arriving at Havenhid. "Keep this up and I'll most definitely take the lead as the best looking one in the group."

They both shared a chuckle before Gotham stepped forward to offer his assistance in returning Jacob's face to its blemish-free, pre-Fury encounter state. But just as the angel placed his hand upon the tender wound, Jacob stopped him.

Actually, I think I'll keep it. You know, sort of like a badge of honor," he said, shooting a knowing wink to Max who returned the gesture in kind.

"As you wish," Gotham acquiesced before turning his attention to the group as a whole. "Now that you are all awake I think it best if we take our leave of this place. Where there is one Fury, there is bound to be others, not to mention several Pethens who are obviously closing in on your scent like a pack of bloodhounds," he said to Hunter.

As the Nephilim hurried back upstairs to gather their belongings and prepare for the long trip to Havenhid, Jacob took a moment to look over the sword still gripped in his hand. He then returned it to its rightful place inside his wing, and for the first time it no longer felt like the uncomfortable weight forced upon him to lug through life; it now felt every bit a part of him, just as the very wings attached to his back. And while a nagging sense of uncertainty remained with him, the prospect of returning to Havenhid no longer seemed as daunting as it had previously been.

"So now what?" he asked Gotham with readying breath once the two were alone again.

The angel placed a hand on the boy's shoulder, and with a gleam of assurance alight in his golden eyes, he replied: "You faced down one fear tonight; now it's time to face another."

Thank-you for reading
The Beloved Exiles (Book III)
*Please add a review and share
your thoughts with others.*

Book reviews are extremely helpful for authors, and I thank you for taking the time to support me and my work. Don't forget to share your review and encourage others to read and follow my other books in the Series:

Tales of the Nephilim Brotherhood

Current Books in the Series:

Book I
The Crossing Point

Book II
The Seventh Grace

Book III
The Beloved Exiles

And coming soon:

Book IV
The Quietus Hour

www.ingramcontent.com/pod-product-compliance
Lightning Source LLC
Chambersburg PA
CBHW060241030726
47493CB00024B/1442